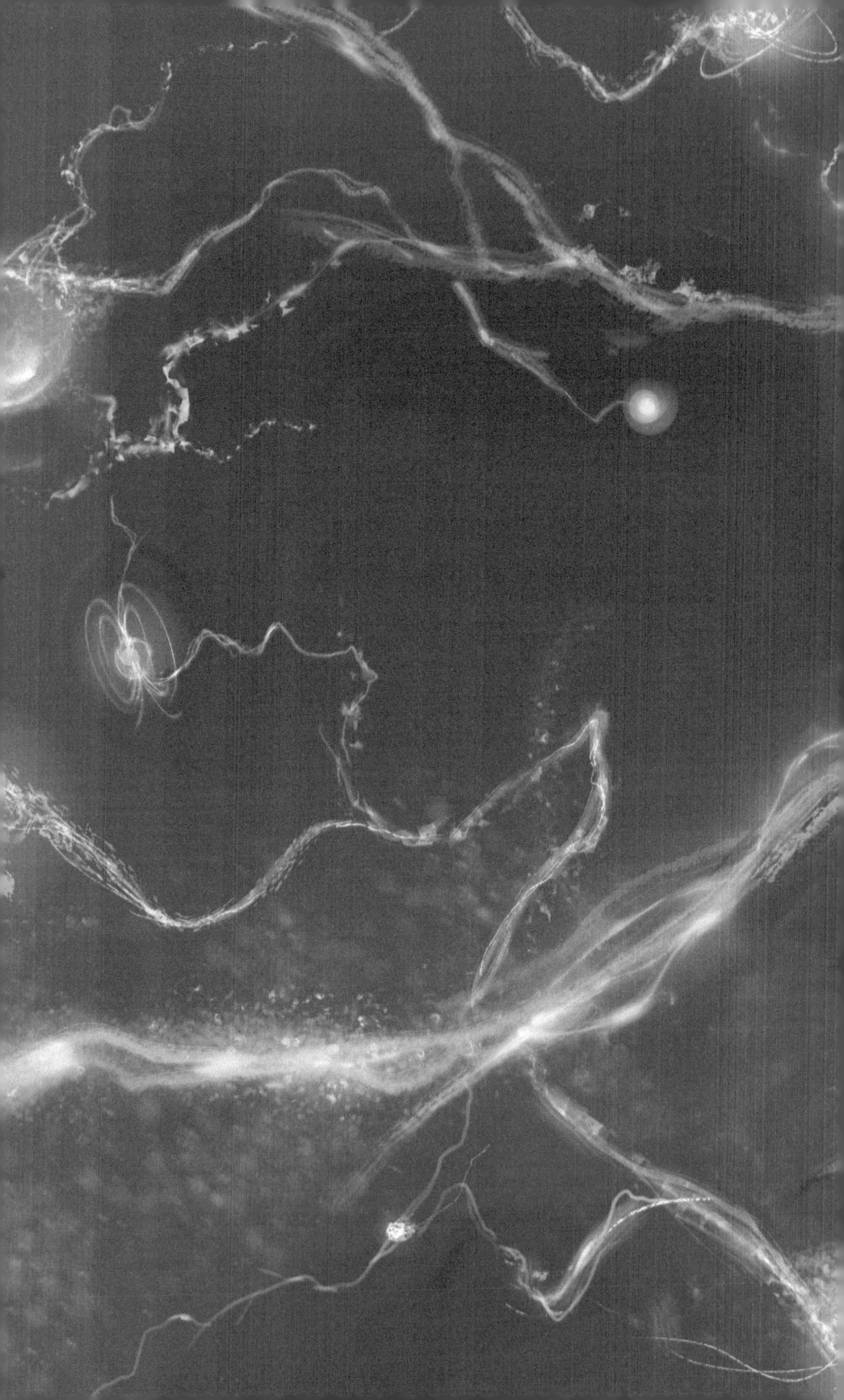

GHOST OF THE TRUTHSEEKER

STRUNGBOUND

GHOST OF THE TRUTHSEEKER

BOOK 2

A CULTIVATION LITRPG

STRUNGBOUND

Timeless
Wind

First published by Timeless Wind Publishing LLC 2023

First edition

Editing by Silas Sontag and Lorne Ryburn.

Cover art by Macarious. Typography designed by Sarah Anderson.

RECAP

Alistair Tan is a normal college student when the alien cultivator Atavius Meloi lands on Earth, killing over a billion people. As a result of his actions, the Final Frontier Empire decides the best rectification for his wrongdoing is to initiate them into their Empire. This separates Alistair from his girlfriend and friends and forces him to survive on his own.

The Empire instantiates the Pathfinder AI on Earth, a helpful program designed to enhance cultivation. As Earth is integrated, everyone receives their first quest—kill a sapient. Meanwhile, monsters rise out of the ground and humanity receives a second quest to defeat them. Alistair must defeat an invading wave of orcs in his subregion. He finds a compatriot in Alexandra Lykaios, another loner who had to fend for herself after her previous partners were killed by the Iceman, George Moulin. They team up and defeat the head boss of the orcs, clearing the monster wave of their subregion and completing the second quest.

Along the way, they pick up Donna and Tamia, a mother and daughter who nearly died at the beginning of the initiation, and save Oliver Cambry, a teenage necromancer who was falsely accused of murder by a nefarious local politician.

After finishing off the Orc Prince, they meet the other powers in the region after being recruited by John Desmond, the Flamesmith. The New Boston Alliance is a group of the strongest new cultivators in the area, led by

Sofia Mostafa, an ice-cold and all-business individual who wields an invisible sword. They first work together defeating ogres in a nearby area. Then they meet with Anthony Ricci, the tyrant ruler of the Ricci Empire. His territory is a violent and lawless region where only the strong survive.

While the two groups seem to be coming to an agreement, the third quest suddenly starts. A select group of the most powerful initiates on Earth are selected to join the universe-wide tournament, Felons vs. Fellows. This series of trials is populated by the most powerful recently initiated cultivators below the soulcore stage of development across the Final Frontier Empire. Alistair and a group of lesser nobles led by Kevan Macadeen of the Disputed Shard collaborate to defeat a powerful felon, succeeding in the first stage.

Afterwards, Kevan befriends Alistair, explaining details about the Final Frontier Empire that Alistair was ignorant about since he came from a nearly Mana-less and Dao-less world before the initiation. Unfortunately, Alistair obtained negative Karma in the fight against the felon, so his resulting bad luck ends with him beaten up in jail. He fortuitously survives and makes it to the next stage, where he must team up with his sister Evangeline, Anthony, Alexandra, and two English brothers, Bartholomew and Alfred Wood, that he knows from the Soulnet, a connective spiritual plane that can tie together realities.

They squabble amongst themselves but eventually work together, fighting through the trial and making it to the end, where they battle Carmen Romero, ranked #3 in the world, and her team, which includes Sofia Mostafa.

During a brief period of rest, Alistair is visited for the first time by his sponsor, the Lazarene Minister representing the Clear Water Sect. The elderly man's projection informs Alistair that in return for 50 years of service to the Clear Water Sect in the future, the sect will provide Alistair with limited resources and important information. He notes that the sect is less powerful than most other sponsors.

The next round is a tournament-style bracket where Alistair, Anthony, and Carmen fight both the felons and initiates. During this period, Alistair reaches level 30 and undergoes a Heavenly tribulation to form a soulcore. During his tribulation, he travels to a faraway plane of existence where he picks up Dev'rox, the ghost of an imp from hell. Dev'rox is an irritable and sarcastic devil on the shoulder, but he means well, and they team up.

One of Alistair's opponents is the A-class felon Nenna Spindoller. Before their fight, Nenna appears to Alistair with another cultivator named Red. She explains herself to Alistair, noting that she steals from the rich to give to the poor and that she belongs to an organization named the Cabal. She gives him a black marble containing a miniature lightning storm and tells him that he'll be able to find the Cabal when he's ready.

In the final round of the tournament, the top eight newly initiated cultivators fight against each other, with only one winner to rule them all. It is a close battle, the final three coming down to Anthony, Alistair, and Xanathar, a robotic humanoid who seeks revenge against the Final Frontier Empire for slaughtering his technologically based people.

Alistair recognizes that Anthony, who has shown a propensity for evil, would become too powerful if he were to win, so he intentionally stops Anthony and lets Xanathar win. This invokes Anthony's wrath, and Anthony promises to kill Alistair and everyone he cares about when they return to Earth.

This comes to fruition when back home, Anthony declares war on the Northeast Freehold, formerly known as the New Boston Alliance, attacking Sofia's territory with abandon. The war feeds into the fourth Quest, [Territorial Dominance], where empires vie to gain subregions.

Sofia and Alistair hold no grudges over their temporary animosity during the Felons vs. Fellows, and work together to fight Anthony's numerical advantage. Anthony can somehow employ extremely expensive weapons and summons, which he uses against the Northeast Freehold to terrifying success, bombing their most important centers.

In the end, Anthony and Alistair agree to a one-on-one fight, winner-takes-all. After the toughest battle of Alistair's life that forces him to use every single trick he knows, he comes out victorious, defeating Anthony and seizing the man's empire as his own. However, because of the negative Karma he had to take on to win the duel, Sofia dies in an explosion set off by Anthony's remaining bombs.

After Alistair wakes up, he learns of this from the Woods, who have come from Europe to help. They begin the rebuilding process for the Northeast Freehold, and Alistair begins a new day, ready for anything that comes his way.

"The Pact should never have been made. They are abominations under Heaven's gaze, a remnant of a bygone era of libertine sciolists. I would end the acquiescence and deliver the heads of the Princes of Hell."

– A CANDIDATE FOR THE JADE THRONE

"Did this idiot just say that? Is he stupid? I say to you, my worthy friends, that this proves how stupid he is. You don't have to choose me—just promise me you won't pick him."

– ANOTHER CANDIDATE FOR THE JADE THRONE

1 NEW START

ALFRED HADN'T FELT this stressed since, well, the last time he'd encountered the Americans.

When he first met Alistair almost two months ago, he hadn't expected much of the lad. Good for his subregion, but not someone who could one day become #2 in the global rankings. Honestly, nothing stuck out about him. In terms of height, looks, and physique, he was all above average, but not by too much. He seemed smart, but not excessively so. Alistair's rise was a mystery Alfred was still trying to unravel.

Whatever the cause of his success, Alfred had to treat him as a true partner, and truth be told, Alistair wasn't the junior in that arrangement. That was why after he saw Alistair's broken body sprawled across the ground in the aftermath of the explosion, he'd had the tiniest desire to snuff him out then and there to seize all of the man's possessions for himself. Besides his conscience advising against it, Alfred felt a greater concern. The Satharvon representative had warned his family that FX-14752 had an unusual amount of Fate. In the future, Earth would need a protector, and Alfred knew he wasn't cut out for the task.

"Father sent a message," Bartholomew said, tapping Alfred's shoulder and extracting him from his reverie. "We are to assess the strength of the Northeast Freehold. Depending on your analysis, we have permission to engage."

Always the black sheep, Alfred thought. A simple message had to be relayed through his brother. Before the initiation, Alfred was always used as the bad example at family gatherings, the spoiled rich kid who only liked to party. Bartholomew and his sister, Imogen, were the gold standard. Bartholomew, the dutiful son, and Imogen, the daddy's girl. Father wouldn't even let her leave England, as far as he knew. Alfred's Class, Spymaster, made him useful to the family, but Father never let him forget his true place.

"Tell him we can't make a move. They're too powerful," Alfred replied. "Alistair will surely be a superb partner for the future."

Bartholomew nodded and left the tent. Alfred worried for him often these days. Always the strong and silent type, he covered up his feelings. Others might have thought they didn't exist, but Alfred knew they did. His biggest worry was the physical and possibly mental changes the Supersoldier faced from his Species evolution. Bartholomew's formerly brown skin now had a gray and metallic tint to it, and Alfred felt he was becoming even more reticent than before.

He kneaded his temples, tension shooting down his body like a burning fire. The flap to his tent opened again. Alfred called out, "Carmen, if it's not urgent, don't bother me!"

"Uh, sir, it's James, not Carmen. You told me to alert you if any of the Northeast Freehold became active."

Right, Alfred thought, smacking his face. The stress was getting to him. Of course it wasn't Carmen; she wouldn't have been so tactful.

"What's your report?" Alfred asked.

"Alistair has gone missing," the scout said. "Sometime within the last hour and a half."

"Damn it," Alfred muttered under his breath. He didn't want there to be any confusion over what had happened. "I'll get on that myself."

Ever since he reached level 30 and upgraded his species, he could go a couple days without sleep and suffer no adverse effects. The downside was he was now busy 24/7, with barely any time for respite. The biological effects on his brain attenuated some of the stress and anxiety, but not all of it. Alfred wanted some real sleep, but first he had to hunt.

As a Spymaster, he had an arsenal of tricks up his sleeve. His bugs could survey a one-hundred-meter radius, relaying all sensory information in the region. It was surprising how little people cared about elementary stealth practices, now that everyone had aura signatures. They only focused on hiding the signs of their aura and Mana, forgetting the basic physical clues they left behind. A broken twig here, a footprint there—combined with a unique scent and some excellent deductions, Alfred could track a man over ten kilometers.

It seemed like he wouldn't need his skills since the moment he left his tent, he found himself face-to-face with Alistair.

The sunrise in the distance cast golden light behind Alistair, making him look like a god out of myth with an auric halo that bloomed wide. The other tents felt so far away, distant as the horizon. Alistair towered over his surroundings, his cold brown eyes meeting Alfred's like icy daggers.

Alfred couldn't help but feel intimidated by his presence. Alistair was probably five levels higher, but it felt more like thirty. There was something about him that exuded strength and authority.

"Morning," Alfred said, trying to break the tension.

"We'll forever be in your debt for what you did," Alistair replied, gesturing to the cityscape. "You were the ones who intercepted the enemies we missed coming out of the tunnel."

"That may be true, but don't worry. It was a favor for a friend." Alfred smiled. "You would have survived anyway—you're from sturdier stock than most. Though, if you had waited another five minutes, you might not have needed to fight Anthony alone."

Alfred had intended the remark to be a harmless jab, but a darkness enveloped Alistair's face. For all of his talents, Alfred found that his companion tended to wear his emotions plainly. It was something he hadn't mentioned to the man. Alfred couldn't give away all his cards, after all.

"Sofia, was she the only one who didn't make it? It's my fault—how could I be so dumb? If I was just a little bit stronger, I wouldn't have needed to go into negative Karma and she would probably still be alive. Or like you said, if I waited five minutes instead of trying to be the hero. I fell right into Anthony's plan."

"Don't be too hard on yourself," Alfred chastised, putting his hand on Alistair's shoulder. It was funny how he was being the big brother in this scenario. "You might have stopped him from killing a few dozen people by acting sooner. I'm sure *they* aren't disappointed in you."

"You know, I was holding out hope that Bartholomew was wrong some-how," Alistair said, regaining his composure.

"She was the closest to the blast. Sofia might have saved you all by diverting part of the explosion; it's hard to tell exactly what happened. Of course, across the city, tens of thousands perished. A true tragedy. I assume you killed Anthony and we won't be seeing that war criminal again?"

Alistair concentrated on something in his line of sight for a few seconds, and then procured a blue screen. Alfred read the pop-up, which listed Alistair as the owner of over 400 subregions, including 310 former Ricci Empire territories.

"Killed him in a one-on-one duel and now I have all of his stuff," Alistair said. "Still have to return the subregions he forced me to take from my allies, though."

Mid-sentence, Alfred noticed him dart his eyes up and to the right and wince—something he jotted down in his mental notes not to forget.

"Where is she buried?" Alistair asked.

"I can show you. Shall we talk while we walk?" Alfred asked.

Alistair nodded. "That sounds good."

Alfred guided him through empty streets to a small cemetery next to a church. The golden hour light struck the steeple, casting deep shadows that danced around the graves. He showed Alistair where they'd buried Sofia, a simple grave marked with a headstone bearing her name.

"What's your next step?" Alfred asked, after giving Alistair some silence.

"I'm not sure," he answered. He dropped to a knee and procured what Alfred could have sworn was a pie, placing it over her grave. "I have to find my family and friends, but I can't just leave all of my responsibilities behind for a wild goose chase. If I falter, thousands of people die."

"I can be of help there," Alfred said. "The Wood informational network is the best in the world. We'll be glad to assist our partners."

"Thank you," Alistair said. "I don't know how I can repay you for all that you've done."

"If I ever need a favor, I won't be shy." He meant that too. If he bestowed favors on anyone else, he wouldn't have known if they'd ever be repaid, but he was certain that Alistair wouldn't forget any kind deeds. "In the meantime, you can prevent us from getting killed by one of those mutated beasts that have been popping up."

"What?"

———

Alistair got the rundown from Alfred on everything he had missed in his frantic past few days of either fighting or being passed out.

Two things had happened, or three, depending on the perspective. First, all across the globe, there were rampant reports of local animals transforming into powerful beasts. Alistair had heard reports much earlier, but back then the animals were just a few times stronger than their pre-initiation counterparts. Now, there were credible claims that a pack of rainbow wolves as tall as men had torn apart the #19 ranker in Brazil. Nature was changing and changing fast. In another month's time, many feared they would be even more powerful than the humans, sparking massive hunts across the globe. Some succeeded, but most failed, undertaken by inexperienced and weak go-getters. The powerful factions all seemed to be calm and even-handed about the matter, though this early on, it was difficult to tell what the common course of action would be.

Second, precisely at the start of the fourth Quest, [Territorial Domination], thirteen individuals from the top 100 had disappeared. Nothing tied them together, except that they were psychopathic murderers, or at least that was what the rumors said. No one knew what had happened to them. The most obvious answer was that they all died, but considering they were all in different locations spread across the globe, it didn't make any sense. Alistair specifically noted that George Moulin, the former #10, was one of the missing.

The third thing was the monsters. Alistair already knew about how the surviving monsters continued to grow in strength and numbers, but they were becoming a problem for the surviving settlements. Alfred's brother had stomped out some closest to the Northeast Freehold, but like the beasts, their potential seemed to go up with humanity.

There was still an issue Alistair had yet to solve—where Anthony had received his money from. The most obvious answer was his unknown sponsor, but Alistair couldn't imagine why the sponsor would spend such exorbitant amounts on a potential liability like Anthony. From what he understood, while the sums spent on Earth were nothing for the great powers of the Final Frontier Empire, the Pathfinder AI implemented a limit on spending.

Alistair returned to the center of the city with Alfred. They had set up a conglomeration of tents near where the city hall once stood. Someone had cleared the debris from the explosion, and workers were using a combination of Skills and their bodies to rebuild. Alistair spotted hundreds of laborers attending to other buildings that used to be museums, corporate buildings, or residential abodes, exchanging brick and wood for materials Alistair didn't recognize. One was a fused black stone that sucked in light, the other a variegated marble that came in a plethora of colors.

"It's standard work, really," Alfred explained. "The danger of wild beasts and monsters—and even other people—is the death of agrarian society, don't you think? Everyone seeks the safety of power and numbers. This will be your shining city on a hill. You need it to serve the part. Protective walls, cultivation-enhanced agriculture and irrigation, improved apartments, schooling, and more. Old society disappeared, but the people remain. The bankers and insurers haven't forgotten their trades."

"Thanks for the, uh, advice," Alistair replied, not really sure what to say. "Are you paying for all of this renovation?"

"Just to get you started," Alfred said, handing Alistair an informational missive in the form of a sealed letter. "Here are some schematics and logistical data."

"It seems you have some practice with all of this," Alistair remarked.

"Do you know anything about the Wood family?"

Alistair shook his head.

"I suspected not. My father tries to stay out of the tabloids. Let's just say the Woods have a *global* influence. My father in particular has quite a wealth of experience in growing empires."

"I feel like I'm growing in debt to you by the second," Alistair said. "Let me repay you for all of this—I'm actually quite wealthy now."

And he could feel that even now. Every second, his wallet added more and more drachma and credits from the taxes on his growing empire.

"Nonsense—to you paying, of course, not the rich part. You're a proper moneyed chap now. It's a gift. If there's one lesson I can impart on you, it's knowing when a gift's a gift and a gift's not a gift, since you'll be receiving many of those in the future."

"And your gift is just a gift, nothing more?" Alistair asked.

"Quick study, aren't you?" Alfred tapped his earpiece. "I shouldn't keep you waiting anymore for your reunion."

"Reunion?"

"I think there's someone you'd like to meet," Alfred told him. He pointed at a tent a few meters away. "Why don't you go check?"

2 THE DREAMS OF THE FATHER

ALISTAIR'S KNEES almost buckled under his own weight with every step he took towards the tent. It was the same size as all the others, four meters by four meters, yet it felt larger than life. Alfred hadn't told him exactly who was in the tent, but Alistair had a good idea.

He finally made it to the entrance, taking a deep breath. There was one aura signature in the tent he remembered, and another he didn't, but somehow it felt similar. He ducked down and walked inside.

Evangeline sat in the center of the tent with her eyes closed. She surrounded herself with a circle of treasures that emanated spiritual energy. But that wasn't what Alistair focused on. In the corner of the canvas, his father was engrossed in a book, his fingers sliding across the pages.

"Dad?"

His father's eyes shot up, but his gaze didn't meet Alistair's face. "Alistair?"

Alistair ran over to his dad to hug him with open arms, but he stopped just short when his dad flinched away from him.

"It's me, Baba," Alistair said.

"You've changed a lot."

"Have I?" Alistair asked, knowing the answer was yes. He had packed on an extra twenty pounds of muscle on his frame and even grown a couple inches, though he felt his father was referring to something more substantial.

"When did you lose your accent in Chinese? You've finally caught up to your sister," his dad said, giving him a suspicious glance.

"It's the soul translator," Alistair explained. "To me, you're speaking English."

"Ah, yes, I had forgotten about that," his dad said, though Alistair wondered if he actually had forgotten. "Your sister tells me you've done well for yourself."

Well is an understatement, Alistair thought, though he didn't say it out loud.

"I'm number two on the world rankings," Alistair said, with a bit of bluster in his voice. "All this land belongs to me."

"They told me that. Good job." After a moment, he added, "About time you lived up to your potential. Angie, your brother is here."

His dad tapped his sister on the shoulder, but Alistair noticed that she had already opened her eyes.

"Alistair!" she exclaimed, smothering him with a boisterous hug. She brought him in close and whispered into his ear. "Don't worry, I wouldn't have let them do anything."

"Thanks, sis," Alistair said. "What were you just doing?"

"It's part of my cultivation," Evangeline explained. "As a Spiritualist, I'm tapping into the primeval spiritual energies of the world. These conduits emit natural aura that allows me to feel the pulse of the Earth."

"I can feel them with my ghost cultivation as well." Alistair closed his eyes, taking in each individual presence. "But it's like something isn't right."

"That's to be expected. A tethered soul and an untethered one are quite similar, but the little differences are everything." Evangeline said, turning to her father. "But please, don't let me get in the way, Baba."

His dad stroked his chin like he always did. "You know, I can tell the difference in speech between you two. If you're looking for it, it's as subtle as a crane standing in a flock of chicken."

"Thanks, Dad," Alistair said. "You always know just what to say."

"I'm only trying to further your education," his dad said. "You know, I always have your best interests in mind." He beckoned him closer. "Come here and let me pretend to see my only son."

"Pretend to see?" Alistair asked as he walked forward, turning towards Evangeline.

"He lost his eyesight early on," Evangeline explained.

"You never told me that," Alistair protested.

"It's fine, Alistair," his dad said. "What I lost in vision, I've gained in true sight. I can see the future now."

Even with his father sitting on a stool with legs longer than his own, Alistair towered over the man. Sheng Tan was shorter than his son by a good margin even before the initiation. Yet, when he placed his hand on his son's shoulder, Alistair fell to his knees.

"I'm proud of my son," the Tan patriarch announced. "You've done very well. Your mother would be proud if she was here."

Swelling happiness met a pang of sadness as he felt the absence of their mother.

"Have you heard from her?" he asked.

"Nothing," Evangeline said. "We don't even know where she got transported to in the initial stages."

"I can't see her," his dad added. "But I've seen you, Alistair. Beware the gold fingers that choke your neck."

"Father isn't even sure what all his premonitions mean, despite his pretensions," Evangeline chided. "Don't worry too much."

"Considering I had a series of cryptic dreams last night, I'm not sure what I should be worried about first. What do you think, Dad?"

"Dreams are powerful," his father said. "I asked out your mother because of a dream. Listen to them."

"Evangeline? What do you think?"

"If you spend all your time worrying about what could be, you'll lose sight of what's happening now," she said.

"That sounds suspiciously like generic advice from a Disney movie, sis," Alistair teased.

"Really? Because I had no idea," Evangeline said. "Seriously, you'll be fine."

"Thanks for the vote of confidence," Alistair answered, rubbing his ear as he felt a sharp buzz. He'd noticed a small metal bug fly into the tent with his sharp senses, judging it to be harmless after he realized it was from Alfred.

"There is a matter that requires your attention," said Alfred's voice, sounding like it came through a vocoder. *"Prisoners from the former Ricci Empire. We have more than a few, though not all share the same level of culpability. I wanted you to have a short break before we moved on to more serious topics."*

"Sorry, I have some work to do. Looks like a full reunion will have to wait until later," Alistair said, scratching his neck in embarrassment that he already had to go.

"*Aiya*, no time for your father and sister now? Shame on you," his dad chided, rapping his knuckles on Alistair's shoulder. "We understand, right Angie? Your little brother is important now, so he has to leave us all alone."

Alistair groaned internally. His father loved joking around and pretending to have an opinion before changing his mind on a dime—or vice versa. It was somewhat endearing, though it often got on his nerves.

"I'll be with you, Baba," Evangeline reassured him, while giving Alistair a look that said, *Don't worry, it'll be fine.*

Alistair said his goodbyes once more and exited the tent, finding Alfred standing right outside with a smile.

"Were you listening to us the entire time?" Alistair asked. "If you were just going to stand outside the tent, why pretend to walk away?"

"Alistair, my friend, never ask questions you don't really want answers to," Alfred said with a grin.

"But I really do want an—"

"Anywho," Alfred interrupted, "we've captured almost a hundred of the Ricci Empire's fighters. We released the ones who were obviously brainwashed, but with others, it's hard to tell."

"Great," Alistair muttered under his breath. "Alright, take me to them."

———

Alfred guided Alistair down a few blocks to the corrections center. He was starting to worry that Alfred knew Alistair's city better than himself, but that was an issue for another time. The main problem was that he had no idea what he was going to do with the prisoners.

"A bit stuffed, isn't it?" Alfred remarked. "Jenny, everyone's behaving nicely?"

"Yes, sir," the blonde lady at the desk replied. Dozens of people lined the floors, some sitting, some lying down, and some standing. The hallway leading to the cells was also filled with people of all ages, colors, and sexes. Their unifying characteristic was the glass muzzles worn over their faces.

"What are those?" Alistair asked, gesturing to the mouthpieces.

"The System Store has inhibitor muzzles," Alfred explained. "They're cheaper than you might expect. It takes a while to take into effect and it's capped at level 30 in terms of guaranteed restriction, so it's not like you can use them as a weapon."

Alfred took out a handheld buzzer and pressed the red button at the top. Alistair felt a wave of tingling energy overtake him and noticed the slightest visible shimmer expand in an outward diffusion. While it did nothing to him, whenever it passed through a prisoner, they immediately jumped up to attention.

"Listen up!" Alfred announced. "This man is in charge of your fate. Every word he speaks is gospel to you. Don't look to me for redemption. Alistair will be much nicer than I would ever be."

Alistair coughed pointedly and pulled in Alfred for a whisper. "Alfred, what do you expect me to do here? I didn't even see what happened—how am I supposed to make a fair judgment?"

He didn't want to say the quiet part out loud. Up to this point, he had still never killed a helpless opponent. Luke Star was already dying and had tried to kill him and his friends, and he knew from a trusted friend that Marcus had killed dozens of innocent people. In this situation, he might have to serve as judge, jury, and executioner.

"Don't you have your [Eyes of Truth] Skill that can detect lies?" Alfred questioned.

"Yes," Alistair said hesitantly. "But my Karma is still low, and I don't want to make a habit of relying on it."

Alfred tilted his head and thought for a moment. "Good point."

He pressed the buzzer once again, and five individuals stood up and walked toward the duo, seemingly against their will.

"These five were spotted by several witnesses murdering people in cold blood and leading Anthony's troops, many of which we're holding here. As far as our tests can tell, they weren't affected by Anthony's mental manipulation. You have that item in your possession, do you not?"

Alistair fumbled around in the inventory of his mind's eye, manifesting a silver lute. With the addition of Anthony's inventory, he was about to hit the limit for the number of items he could dematerialize.

"It's called the **Chord of Desire**. I think it was Anthony's reward from the Felons vs. Fellows tournament."

Alfred looked like he was seeing the most beautiful woman in the world, the way he eyed the instrument. "Have you tried using it?"

"What? Of course not. I'm not in the business of mind-controlling anyone."

"Yes, but if you used it on a consenting test subject, you could—"

Alfred was cut off by one of the prisoners thrashing about, desperately trying to speak through his gag. He wasn't one of the five murderers that Alfred had pointed out, who remained silent, staring into empty space with dead eyes.

"Yes?" Alfred asked, snatching the inhibitor muzzle. It appeared to be made of the same material as the handcuffs Alistair remembered seeing on Faxor.

"That's what Anthony used on us!" the prisoner shouted, to the head nods of many of the others. "You gotta believe me, we had no idea what was happening!"

"Pipe down, you're hurting my ears. Alistair, would you mind using the **Chord** on me?"

"Excuse me?"

"I want to test how strong the effect is," Alfred explained. "Just do it."

Alistair eyed the lute with doubt. "Alright, here goes nothing."

He instinctively strung a few of the strings on the lute, turning his attention toward Alfred. While he consciously didn't know what he was doing, somehow it felt right. Each note came into place in a series of harmonious arpeggios.

"Do you feel anything?" Alistair asked. "I think it's working."

"Order me to do something," Alfred said, his eyes closed in concentration.

"Slap yourself in the face."

"Seriously?" Alfred asked, though he didn't move. "Try it with more force this time."

"Slap yourself in the face?"

Alfred opened his eyes and turned his palm toward his face. For a second, Alistair thought he was actually going to do it, but then he started giggling. "You believed me there. I got you good, Alistair."

"I can't fathom how that's a good punchline, but okay, it doesn't work," Alistair said. "Did you feel anything at all?"

"I do confess I felt a small desire to slap myself in the face upon your request, though I easily thwarted it. That confirms the diminishing returns. If I'm level 30…"

Alistair was already ahead of Alfred's thoughts, pointing the **Chord of Desire** to the guy who had shouted earlier. A quick [Eyes of Truth] scan revealed him to be Dimitry Ivanov, a level 16 Tutor. Alistair's Intelligence was easily triple that of Dimitry, so his target would never know the wiser.

"Pick your nose," Alistair ordered over a series of notes.

Dimitry immediately picked his nose without missing a beat. Right away, Alfred sent a swarm of his bugs out of the billowing sleeve of his cultivator's robes. Alistair finally got a good look at the tiny things. Each was smaller than a typical house fly, and they were black with a microscopic antenna that flashed red. Without his improved vision, and if Alistair didn't specifically focus on looking for them, he would have dismissed them as normal insects.

"I can track the energies emitted by the **Chord**," Alfred explained. "Each person gives off a unique aura, as you already know. My bugs can categorize them by color, timbre, temperature, viscosity, and more. The specific signature of the **Chord of Desire** is hard to miss. Can you see it?"

Alistair concentrated his vision, searching for the trace amounts of Mana that his instrument produced. He thought back to his time hiding underground during the second round of Felons vs. Fellows. On the insights he'd gained into Karma and its influence on the threads of Fate that connected everything in existence. The nature of the Dao and its seeming opposition to Karma. Was Mana a third horse in the race, or something else entirely? When he squinted his eyes and circled his internal Mana through his soul-core, he felt like he could almost see the traces of Mana that people left behind.

"Alistair? You there, mate? Don't tell me you actually *can* see it—I was just jesting. How damn good are your senses?"

"Didn't work," Alistair said. "What do your bugs say?"

Alfred tapped his earpiece. After a few seconds, the swarm returned to his robes. "Everyone except the five I already mentioned—plus five more—had extreme levels of the **Chord's** Mana in their system. Well, actually, one of the other five did have extreme levels of Mana, but she's level 30, so she should have resisted it."

"Release the ones who were legitimately under Anthony's spell," Alistair ordered.

"Your wish is my command." Alfred took a step before stopping mid-air.

"On second thought, I realize now that someone's going to have to remove them all manually. What about the others?"

Alistair felt the fearful glances from the condemned. They were wondering if they were going to die then and there. The terror was palpable, leaking out of their auras like oil in water.

"Let's keep them here for now, until I can find some people to make a proper legal system."

"A prudent decision," Alfred remarked. "Do you want me to get my people on freeing the rest of them?"

"You've already done so much, so let me handle that," Alistair replied, scratching his head.

As they walked out of the corrections center, Alistair realized that something felt off—like in those dementia tests, where an item broke the laws of common sense. There was something missing that Alistair couldn't figure out.

"Dev'rox?" Alistair whispered. "Are you okay?"

Alistair felt a bit guilty that he'd forgotten about his imp's absence until now. The wise-cracking, arrogant little demon could be annoying, but he had helped Alistair numerous times. Alistair would be dead thrice-over if not for Dev'rox's Mana pool and strategic tips.

"Finally, he speaks," he heard a voice say inside his head, though it sounded faint and weak. "I was beginning to think I had been forgotten."

"Never," Alistair promised. "I was just busy."

"I don't blame you. Honestly, I needed the alone time myself. It can be annoying being inside your head and hearing your every thought. I used up a lot of Mana saving your ass and materializing to kill Anthony."

"And I am in your debt."

"And you'll repay that debt exactly like you promised, by killing Kyraxadon—don't forget," Dev'rox said, wagging a metaphorical tail.

"I haven't forgotten."

Alistair opened up his status screen for the first time in what felt like years. He had been procrastinating doing so for a while.

Name: Alistair Tan
Species: Spectral Superhuman I (Partially Evolved)
Class: Magical Pugilist (Uncommon)
Subclass (HIDDEN): Arbiter of Justice (Legendary)

Level: 35

Health: 438/438 (.660 per min)
Mana: 779/779 (1.298 per min)
Stamina: 261/261 (1.038 per min)
Upgrade Points: 76
Balance: 1,360,981 Gold Drachma
Karma (Unlocked): +30 (.016 per min)
Full Stat Bonuses: +41% to All Attributes, +15% Mana

Strength: 78
Agility: 213
Constitution: 85
Endurance: 78
Intelligence: 221
Wisdom: 135
Charisma: 176

Items: Zanibar's Purification Ring, Thrice-Blessed Fate-Diviner, Ghostgrass Wraps, Cloak of the Divined, Lesser Cloak of Shadows, Sun's End Vanquishment Sword, Chord of Desire, Teleportation Circle x4 (stored)

Badges: "Premium Initiate", "Good Samaritan", "Deliverance of Justice", "Mythical Cultivator", "Precocious Killer", "Jack of All Trades"

Talents: System Tree – Two leaves, Pugilism Branch (II), Chaos Assassin – Void Watching Branch (II), Justice Quest Branch (II), Elemental Fighter – Summoning of Spirit (III), Body Tree – Heart Branch (I)

Skills: [Mana Strike], [Eyes of Truth], [Dash], [Fighter's Instinct], [Hand of Karma], [Void Beckoning], [Ghost Whispers], [Spectral Summoning], [Carmela's Happy Pies], [Phase Shift]

Quests: [Territorial Dominance]

Achievements: Discovery (I), Dueling (III), Conquest (I), Dao Node – Dao of the Ghost (I)

He was about to look into the options for his Upgrade Points when a beam of light shot down right in front of him from the clouds. Out of the bright light stepped out an eight-foot tall muscled god of a man with a flowing blond mane, dressed in a revealing toga.

The godly being warped reality as he stepped foot on the ground, each footprint glowing with golden light. The air shimmered around him like the hottest summer day, and Alistair could hardly bear to look at him due to his blinding halo.

"Do I speak to Alistair Tan, possessor of the territories that once belonged to Anthony Ricci?" said the lion god.

Alistair felt the words reverberate through his flesh. Even if he wanted to ignore the question or lie to this entity of untold power, his mouth would never obey.

"I am," he choked out.

In an instant, the mountain of a man shrank down to just over five feet tall, his toga replaced by a western business suit. His figure changed from that of a chiseled, square-faced specimen to that of a portly, middle-aged man.

"In the name of the 15th franchised branch of the Bank of the Mai Atal and the Pathfinder AI Lending Unit—with assistance from the loan's co-signer, the Portolon Clan—you are being served a debt of 15.65 million Gold drachma and 97,120 Land Store credits."

3 MASSIVE DEBTS

"WHAT?" Alistair exclaimed. "That can't be right."

Alfred was just as shocked by the sudden appearance of the descending creditor, looking toward Alistair for an explanation. He shrugged, completely blindsided by the lion-man. However, based on his mention of the Ricci Empire, Alistair guessed his arrival wasn't a fortuitous one.

"As Anthony Ricci's successor to his lands and titles, his debt falls upon you to pay, and the same goes for Sofia Mostafa," the suited man said. "I, Farsa Strongbite, am the Pathfinder-appointed representative in charge of your financial situation. This is a highly unusual circumstance due to the excessive amount owed."

Alistair let the details sink in. How unfair was it that just because he happened to inherit Anthony's land, he got saddled with his debt, too? That should've been the fault of the Bank of Mai Atal and the Pathfinder AI's lending unit, not his. But he didn't want to piss off the ridiculously powerful figure before him.

"I don't understand. How is this legal? I can at least somewhat get it for Sofia, since I was her ally and she would have passed the Northeast Order Freehold to me as a successor, but Anthony was my enemy. Is this how things work in the multiverse?"

Farsa snorted. "Laws? The Laws of Heaven barely shine upon the fron- tier. Here, the law is what Emperor Laketor decrees. And until your planet starts rearing Visionaries, the emperor's justice shall remain blind. The frontier looks on the involved and the core with jealousy for their perceived arrogance, yet this place is the most lawless of all."

The lion-man opened up a blue status screen, scrolling through it with a sharp fingernail. "However, I am under the impression this is no true thievery. I am no expert on the indigenous practices of this planet, but through a cursory glance there is a concept of corporate debt, yes? You can think of it as the price of acquisition. You've acquired Anthony's company, and as a result, you are responsible for all of his outstanding loans. And it is wise to think of your freehold as a company, I can assure you of that. Unfortunately, you won't be able to file for bankruptcy."

Alistair found Farsa's wielding of American business jargon to be funny —it was like he downloaded all the information, but without the natural experience. The rest of his statement was less humorous.

Despite how much he hated the idea, it did make sense to him. If you inherited a company from someone, or bought it in a sale, it was true that you were responsible for its previous debts. Alistair had been thinking about freeholds more like kingdoms or empires, but that was misguided. They were all only allowed to exist at the consent and behest of the Finale Frontier Empire.

And the only rule that he had seen of that Empire was the will of the mighty, the law of the jungle. They had destroyed hundreds of millions of families, thrust countless people into near-death scenarios just to breed stronger soldiers. Even if it felt petty for a powerful clan to impede the progress of a nobody Prime Initiate, it made perfect sense. But he still thought one thing didn't.

"Correct me if I'm wrong, but don't those organizations deal in the Orichalcum and Ambrosia drachma amounts?" Alistair asked. "Why would mere millions of Gold drachma matter?" Even if they were petty, were they really that petty? It would be equivalent to him threatening someone over a penny.

Farsa's eyes brightened up at Alistair's words. "Wonderful. I'm glad to hear that at least some of the youth are paying attention to economic affairs. As you might know, the denominations of money all across the multiverse go from Gold to Platinum to Palladium to Orichalcum to Ambrosia to Forged to Double-Forged to Thrice-Forged—each new drachma denomination increasing in worth by a hundred thousand multiple, and then a million from Ambrosia to Forged, ten million from Forged to Double-Forged, and then a hundred million from Double-Forged to Thrice-Forged. You are correct, the sum of your total debt in Gold drachma is equivalent to 0.00000001565 Orichalcum drachma. A drop in the ocean."

Farsa continued his speech, lost in the wonders of drachma. He or Alfred could have completely ignored him and he wouldn't have had a clue.

"However, you must understand something. This is not the amount they pay. The higher one rises toward the eternal truths, the more causality bends around their will. The laws of the multiverse and the Heavens look harshly on, say, Exalted or Visionary cultivators that interfere with mortal affairs. You may have experienced this yourself with the multiversal censorship. Certain topics are best avoided with Foundation and Adept cultivators, though the shrewd always find loopholes."

Alistair thought back to how Dev'rox couldn't tell him about Anthony's shadow clones, or how the demon had a limited causal impact on reality due to his lack of a physical body. Hearing about the laws of the multiverse piqued Alistair's interest. He wondered if they were laws as in the laws of physics, baked into the multiverse since its presumed inception, or whether they were more like the laws of humans. If they were more like the latter, what entities could even dream of passing laws that could affect every single being in the entire multiverse?

"In order to send the 15.65 million Gold drachma owed down to FX-14752, both creditors' expenses were many, *many* orders of magnitude higher. On the order of tens of thousands of Palladium drachma. Now, you might rightly wonder, does this principle work in reverse? Is your debt converted back into thousands of Palladium drachma that the bank can then keep?"

Alistair realized that Farsa was looking at him for an answer. "I would think not."

"And why is that?"

Am I being quizzed like in high school? Alistair thought.

Dev'rox gave a mental chuckle. "No help on this one, partner."

"That's just the way it is?" Alistair wondered. "I mean, I understand the rationale for why the laws of nature would interfere with powerful people giving exorbitant amounts to lower realm cultivators, but that doesn't mean that the multiverse would then have to convert lower denominations back into higher ones. Too easily exploited, and too expensive. With no good reason, it doesn't exist."

It was a shot in the dark, but Alistair had to come up with something. To his surprise, Farsa looked happy with the answer.

"Acceptable," he said. "Which leads to the question you asked before— why do they even care about the debt, since it's so inconsequential to them? Of course, Visionary cultivators still walk the mortal path. They have desires and grudges. Losing thousands of Palladium drachma is never a good thing, and they have an easy target."

An easy target, Alistair thought. There was something missing, however.

"What about my sponsor?" he asked. "The Clear Water Sect are really going to let this Portolon Clan get away with this nonsense?"

They had been such a non-presence in his life after the visit from the Lazarene Minister that he had nearly forgotten about them. The old man had popped up into his chambers during Felons vs. Fellows and given him some advice and gifts, but he couldn't help but feel others had more support.

He felt the golden ring and chain around his neck, the one thing that they had left him with. Alistair had no way to tell if it was working, since it was impossible to know what choices he would have made without his **Thrice-Blessed Fate-Diviner**.

"This Portolon Clan, as you put it, is one of the five most powerful Progenitor Clans of the empire, and close to the royal family themselves. The main branch doesn't deal with the affairs of initiates, but I can assure you the influence of a lesser branch of the Portolon Clan exceeds that of the Clear Water Sect many-fold."

"It's really like that, huh," Alistair said. "There's nothing I can do?"

"Shine brighter than a blazing star," Farsa said. "After the one year waiting period for new Premium Tier Beginner worlds, you will be allowed to join the Clear Water Sect. If your potential is high enough, this debt will be but a drop in the water of the grand cosmos. You will find there to be more rule of law at that point. Do you have any more questions?"

"Two more," Alistair said. "One, why don't they use an intermediary for transferring money? Surely there are some rich Foundation or Adept cultivators that would love to curry the favor of the Bank of the Mai Atal who have a much more favorable conversion. And the other is—why are they spending tens of thousands of Palladium drachma on us in the first place?

They probably have a net worth counted in Ambrosia drachma, but it's not completely insignificant."

"The eyes of the multiverse are not so easily thwarted by cheap tricks. It would be obvious what they would be trying to achieve through using an intermediary," Farsa said.

"That makes sense," Alistair conceded. "What about the other thing?"

"Prime Initiates from newly discovered star systems like your own have unique potential for growth compared to those who have been born under the Pathfinder AI system. Even the Fell Emperor knows not why, and if the Sublimed Machine does, they are not forthcoming. The average growth of a Prime Initiate is far worse than those from the Imperial Heartlands, even on Premium Tier worlds like your own. But the incidence of those with extreme potential, dare I say, peak potential, is higher from worlds close to the eternal Chaos surrounding the multiverse. Peak for the frontier anyway. Not since before the existence of the Final Frontier Empire over 150 million years ago has anyone from this corner of the cosmos achieved Ascendant, and that woman came from a planet near Chaos. By over 150 million years ago, I mean that we do not even have proper records attesting to anything about this woman, besides her existence. This was billions of years ago, before the royal line of Laketor was even a seedling. Of course, that does not mean you will come within a light-year of her. Since there are numerically far more cultivators in the Heartlands than Prime Initiates, in the end, a vast majority of those at the peak are still Heartlanders."

Alistair kind of understood what was going on. It had to do with a cultivator's inflated sense of pride, where saving face was as natural as walking. The Prime Initiates had great potential, but they were also backwater savages. And there weren't that many of them, so they weren't *that* important, yet they were also important enough to invest money in. Not a ton of money, but enough to be annoyed when it went missing. And they were meaningless enough that powerful clans could bend the rules, but meaningful enough that they cared if their chosen initiate died. It was all a confusing mess of culture, protocol, and laws that Alistair didn't want to disentangle.

Farsa looked enraptured by his own explanation and once finished, seemed a bit embarrassed that he'd rambled on for so long. "Excuse me. Now, let us discuss the timeline and details of your repayment plan."

He opened his suit jacket, taking out a clipboard with a piece of paper.

Alistair wondered if his attire was standard for the Final Frontier Empire, or whether he had gathered the clothing and business materials from Earth culture to appear more approachable to Alistair.

By tapping the clipboard with his finger, an illusion of what looked like a slip of paper appeared in the air. With the wave of a hand, Farsa directed the floating slip toward Alistair, who caught it in his palm. To his surprise, the ethereal-looking paper was blank.

"Your payment will take place over the course of six Earth months, split into payments of 2.6 million Gold drachma and 16,186.7 Land Credits each," Farsa explained. "That's six Earth months starting from exactly… now. Just think of transferring the funds into this card, and it should work. One day and also one hour before the designated time, the card will become hot and glow red. You can always send the money early; the monthly payments are bare minimums for time and amount."

Alistair turned the slip over. It looked like an ordinary eight-by-four-centimeter blank business card, though the material was cool and sleek to the touch, not bending even under Alistair's powerful grip.

"Don't worry, you can't lose it no matter what. I soulbound it to you, so if you lose it, it will come back to you eventually. Any questions?"

Alistair toyed with the card, attempting to flex it between his fingers. "And if I wanted to take out a loan of my own or discuss financial matters, can I contact you?"

Farsa chuckled, a hint of his lion's ferocity bleeding into his tone. "I would suggest against that for now, young cultivator. In normal circumstances, the mere act of summoning me to this backwater planet would bankrupt you thousands of times over. The only reason I'm here in person is that you're a Prime Initiate noted for his potential. You have a mountain's share of drachma and credits to pay for one of your status. With your reputation from the Felons vs. Fellows, many eyes will be watching."

"My time is up," Farsa said, looking to the skies. He dropped his gaze down past Alistair, making eye contact with Alfred instead. "Young one, I sense one day we shall be great allies or fierce rivals. Continue down your path without compromise."

The same beam of light that had brought the lion-man down erupted from the clouds. Farsa Strongbite disappeared in the brilliance, Alistair catching a glance of his true, glorious leonine form before he vanished entirely. He briefly wondered where Farsa ranked among all the powerful beings Alistair had encountered. With his position as a mere level 35 Foundation realm cultivator, he had no way to tell apart those multiple times stronger than himself. Alistair placed him up there with the Lazarene Minister, Nenna Spindoller, Kyraxadon, the conservators of the Felons vs. Fellows, and Sylas, the Herald of the Pathfinder AI.

"Looks like you've gotten better news than me," Alistair said to his friend. "How the hell am I going to pay off this debt?"

"I think you'll manage," Alfred replied. "You always seem to find a way. Like a hyperintelligent cockroach. I'm more concerned about this celestial deity telling me I might be his rival one day."

"Celestial deity? I'm pretty sure Farsa would be a Visionary at the best."

"At the best? You do realize Visionary is a full three realms ahead of us? Besides the Emperor, the highest realm in all of the Final Frontier Empire is Visionary."

Alistair looked up at the sky, breathing in the ambient Mana that stretched from the ground to the clouds. "Do you remember the saying, 'Born too late to explore the Earth, but born too early to explore the stars?' Obviously, that's thrown out the window now, but we've been given an opportunity that no one else in the history of humanity has received. We can never forget those who died because of it, but if you look at it objectively, what we are in right now is the natural state of the multiverse. We have to survive and make sure that Earth isn't left behind for some tyrant to conquer."

Alistair's Dao Inspiration had a more universal twist, but he didn't need to bother Alfred with lofty ambitions that he would only dismiss as foolish.

"Well, that's one way to put it. You really do plan on trying to make it to the top. Did your sponsor not explain how things work?" It was a rhetorical question, since he continued without letting Alistair speak. "We exist on the very fringes of civilization. The strongest cultivator in the Final Frontier Empire would be less than a speck of dust to the core polities. We can't even imagine what kind of power they have. You heard the lion-man, the last cultivator from this universe to achieve Ascendant was over 150 million years ago."

Alistair shrugged. "Guess I just have to get lucky then."

"You sound just like my father," Alfred responded. "If you don't set your dreams high, you'll never achieve them, he says."

"Smart man."

"Now you're just trying to antagonize me on purpose. Have I told you about the esteemed Lucius Wood? If not, you're in for a treat."

As they walked through the city, Alistair felt more at ease than he had been for a while. Alfred was a natural with banter and had a dry sense of humor that Alistair found common ground with. It was good to talk to a guy his own age. Oliver felt more like a little brother, and John was more of an older brother or father figure, and Alexandra—well, she was a girl, so it was different. They weren't together, but still.

After they arrived back to where Alfred had set up shop, Alistair came face-to-face with Carmen Romero, now ranked #3 in the world after Anthony's passing and one spot below him. While there was some tension between them, he greeted her and shook her hand. They had an understanding that the events of Felons vs. Fellows were unavoidable due to their high placement. They had no reason to be enemies in the real world, at least not at the present moment. However, the looming [Territorial Dominance] Quest was always present at the back of Alistair's mind.

Except for Evangeline, his dad, and a few other Americans that were stranded in Europe, the rest of Carmen and Alfred's group left to travel through the **Teleportation Circle** they had come from.

It turned out that they had contacted a small independent region wedged between the Northeast Freehold and the Ricci Empire. As the Wood family was most likely the richest organization in the world, the bribe for access to the small territory's **Teleportation Circle** meant nothing to them.

Alistair made sure to note the exact region the circle was located in and re-checked the ones in the vicinity of his capital to make sure they hadn't left a secret backdoor tunnel. He trusted Alfred and Bartholomew, but one could never be too careful.

Alistair got a headcount of all the most powerful people in the Northeast Freehold, which he now controlled after Sofia's untimely demise. He gathered them inside of one of the buildings that Alfred's people had constructed, a fortress of fused black stone called "valyrik." It could be purchased from the Land Store at an exorbitant price, boasting the highest defensive capabilities of any available substance.

It was time to discuss the future of the Northeast Order Freehold.

4 REBUILDING AND REGROWING

ALISTAIR HAD GATHERED ALL of the most important people in the Northeast Freehold, with the exception of Dr. Mehta, who was out in the field treating people. Besides those he knew and remembered as being in the New Boston Alliance's inner circle, there were a couple new figures who had risen to prominence.

One Alistair had already met. Robert Oakland was one of the first people he'd encountered during the initiation, along with his partner Jules Verdant. They had worked for the state senator Jackson Morley, but Alistair didn't hold it against them. It turned out that the politician had done nothing overtly evil before trying to execute Oliver, and he also had Karmic abilities that made everyone trust him more. Robert conveyed to Alistair that Jules had died a while ago, killed by George Moulin, the Iceman and former ally of Alexandra.

The other newcomers were Linda Sartor, a local architect who had gotten to level 30 helping build barricades, and Felix Mujinga, a transplant from Kinshasa who could craft weapons. Sofia had offered Felix passage home to Africa once transcontinental teleportation was available, but he'd decided to stay in the Northeast Freehold, claiming that was where he needed to be.

Alistair looked at the familiar faces as well—the Flamesmith John Desmond, his field partner Lily Baruch, the Moneylender Lauren Yoon, and the stoic Archer Blaise Blanchett. He owed an invaluable debt to Blaise in particular for keeping Donna and Tamia safe during the war.

"I know you are all incredibly busy people, so I thought I'd take this moment to gather us all here in one place before we run off to the next crisis," Alistair said, trying to bring some levity to the room.

He gestured outside. "First of all, I want to thank you for all that you've done for these people. While many of you have received substantial rewards over the course of your service, you've still risked life and limb many times."

Alistair transferred back the shares he owed, putting him down from 105 to 83 owned shares of the Northeast Freehold. He considered distributing the Ricci Empire subregions as well but decided against it. He needed all the money he could get for his debts. 2.6 million drachma and 16.2k Land Credits per month was a tall task, considering he only had 1.35 million drachma at the moment.

"Lauren, how much money do you have now?" he asked.

The haughty woman looked hesitant to answer, but she realized she had no other option. "30 million now that I've reached level 30, with a one million limit per person."

"And does that include your personal money? How does it work with your passive absorption?"

"[Cash Flow] absorbs 40% of all drachma earned to my personal wallet, which doesn't have a limit," Lauren said. "Storing money for others is a different skill altogether, [Transitive Banking]. Almost all of that 30 million is money stored for other people and not my own."

"Still, you must have made a fortune after Sofia died, since no one has been checking up on you," Alistair said, intimating at a potential embezzlement.

"Uh, I'm not sure about that," she replied nervously.

"As some of you might be aware, I possess a truth-discerning Skill called [Eyes of Truth]," Alistair said. "The cost to use it is somewhat annoying, so I don't want to have to do that right now, but rest assured, if I feel the need, I will," He didn't reveal that he had become so practiced at reading threads of Fate that he could make educated guesses about who was telling the truth or not. "Do you want to tell the truth?"

"Fine, take a look at my wallet if that's what you want," Lauren said, showing him her screen. She had over five million drachma in her personal collection. "One million of those are mine. You can use your **[Eyes of Truth]** —I'm not lying."

Alistair didn't feel any aberrations in her threads of Fate, and unless she was an amazing fibber, he thought she was telling the truth.

"Linda, you've been overseeing the rebuilding, correct?" Alistair asked.

"I wouldn't go as far as that, but I've helped out," the level 30 Architect said humbly.

"Whatever the case is, that's your job now. I'm appointing you as the head of infrastructure for the Northeast Freehold. Lauren, transfer the two million to her, and then the rest to me."

"Alistair—sir, I mean, I'm not sure I'm qualif—"

Alistair cut her off by closing his fist. It wasn't his intention to be rude, but he had so many things to do and there were only so many hours in a day. "I can't be bothered with false modesty right now. If you can find someone more qualified and capable to handle the reconstruction and reinforcement of this city, please do. All I care about right now is protecting everyone and giving them enough food and water. Lauren, transfer it now, and be glad I'm not renegotiating the 1.5% personal take of earnings Sofia gave you."

Linda nodded her head in acceptance, accepting the drachma from Lauren. Alistair received exactly two million himself, making his new total 3.36 million Gold drachma.

"Next on the docket, education," Alistair said, firing his words as fast as he could. "I would like to encourage a complete education, but I think martial skills come first. We need to train people on how to unlock Skills, fight properly, and create a coherent build. I'll purchase one each of the Warrior and Mage training missives from the System Store for a total of a million drachma, and we'll need experienced teachers who can help the average folk."

Alistair speculated on who should assume a teaching position. If he asked his strongest fighters, it would weaken his frontline army, but they would produce higher quality recruits. He put his worries aside. All they needed for the next week was something provisional.

"Blaise, I want you to set that up and be the first teacher. I'll compensate you with extra resources, and while you're at it, see if there's anyone qualified who has a knack for mentoring." He handed the Archer the two books that represented the Warrior and Mage missives, taking them out of the small storage space the Pathfinder AI allocated for extraneous items.

Blaise nodded, taking the books. Alistair would be sure to give the man generous compensation, since he owed him for the excellent job he'd done protecting the refugees.

"Related to that is weapons. Felix, I've heard you've done good work for us?"

"Yes, uh—excuse me, but what should I call you?" Felix asked.

Alistair was taken aback for a moment, thinking the answer was obvious. His name was Alistair, after all, and that's what everyone called him. But he thought about how he was now officially the leader of around five million people. The term the Pathfinder used was "majority owner," but that didn't exactly roll off the tongue.

"My name is fine, or sir, if you want," he replied.

"I've made over a thousand weapons for the Northeast Freehold, sir," Felix said with a big smile. "All of them of Rare rarity."

"Rare rarity?" Alistair asked, unaware of the term in reference to items.

"Ah yes, apologies. Such things are only available to those who have completed the 'unveil hidden statistical variables' leaf of the System Tree. Items follow the same pattern as Badges and Classes—Common, Uncommon, Rare, Legendary, Mythical, Heraldic, Divine, and then Sublime. Skills follow the planetary ranking system—Beginner, Basic, Journeyman, Expert, Master, Grandmaster, Exemplar, and Heavenly. From what I understand, it doesn't necessarily refer to the strength of the item. A Tier 8 Beginner Skill might be stronger than a Tier 1 Journeyman Skill."

Alistair checked his Talent Tree, seeing a 0/10 for the next upgrade, which would finish off the leaf. Since he had 76 Upgrade Points to spare, he used up 10 of them. A small wave of energy rushed over him, and when he opened his Skills and items, they had new qualifiers next to them.

The knowledge that washed over him said he could open up an abbreviated version of his Badge list so he wouldn't be inundated with text.

Skills:

[Eyes of Truth] (Tier 3 Journeyman Skill): Upgradeable (23/25).

[Mana Strike] (Tier 2 Journeyman Skill): Upgradeable (45/50).

[Dash] (Tier 2 Beginner Skill): Upgradeable (10/50).

[Fighter's Instinct] (Tier 3 Beginner Passive Skill): Upgradeable (13/100).

[Hand of Karma] (Tier 2 Expert Skill): Upgradeable (5/60).

[Void Beckoning] (Tier 2 Journeyman Skill): Upgradeable (1/50).

[Ghost Whispers] (Tier 1 Journeyman Passive Skill): Upgradeable (24/25).

[Spectral Summoning] (Tier 1 Expert Passive Skill): Upgradeable (29/30).

[Carmela's Happy Pies] (Tier 1 Journeyman Skill): Upgradeable (0/30).

[Phase Shift] (Tier 1 Expert Skill): Upgradeable (17/30).

It looked like Alistair had a mix of Beginner, Journeyman, and Expert Skills. The rarity of the Skill was somewhat correlated with how many Upgrade Points it would require at each level, but not entirely, since his Tier 3 Journeyman Skill [Eyes of Truth] only required 25 to bring it to Tier 4. Perhaps because it was an evolution of [Inspect], possibly the most used Skill in the multiverse, it upgraded more rapidly.

Items: Zanibar's Purification Ring (Rare), Thrice-Blessed Fate-Diviner (Rare), Ghostgrass Wraps (Rare), Cloak of the Divined (Rare), Lesser Cloak of Shadows (Rare), Sun's End Vanquishment Sword (Legendary), Chord of Desire (Rare), Teleportation Circle x4 (Legendary-stored), Regional Map (Common)

For his items, all of them were Rare except the **Regional Map**, **Teleportation Circles** and **Sun's End Vanquishment Sword**. It made sense the circles were so strong since they came from the Pathfinder itself. He felt a pang of guilt at seeing how he owned four of them. Three came from Sofia, who gave them to him on Anthony's orders. If he hadn't angered Anthony, he wouldn't have attacked so suddenly and killed so many people.

Alistair didn't regret the decision in the grand scheme of things, as he truly believed Anthony would have done far more damage to society if he was allowed the grand prize of tutelage from a Visionary cultivator and the "One Above Many" Badge, but he also regretted not being able to stop him more effectively. Even with cultivation, life was fragile, and Alistair would do his best to protect all of it.

Curiously, he noted his pills weren't included on the list of items. Maybe they weren't important enough.

Alistair snapped out of his thoughts, remembering he was still in the meeting and talking to Felix.

"What level are you?" Alistair asked, choosing not to use [Eyes of Truth] on the man out of respect. From what he understood, cultivator customs were slowly trickling down to Earth, and many now viewed it as a sign of an imminent duel if you inspected them.

"29, and I'm on the verge of forming my soulcore to reach level 30," Felix replied. "I don't feel like my Dao is strong enough, so I haven't attempted it or the tribulation yet. Once I get to level 30, my weapons should be even stronger. I just need more raw materials, either from the monsters and beasts we hunt, or from the System Store."

"You'll get that," Alistair promised. "Here's half a million drachma. I'm sure you'll create even better weapons for us."

An intriguing idea popped into his head, prompting Alistair to take out the **Sun's End Vanquishment Sword**. The 1.5-meter-long katana radiated a powerful aura, the familiar void represented by the black half, and destruction represented by the clear half. When Alistair paid close attention to the sword, he realized the imperfection of its construction, despite being labeled as a Legendary item. Void and destruction were elements that when in perfect balance joined in a sublime fusion that embodied Chaos itself—but in the katana, they were haphazardly combined in a mere replica of true Chaos. The ratios were all off, not that Alistair was an expert at crafting weapons, but he could just tell.

Everyone else in the room flinched at the katana's intimidating aura.

"I don't have much use for this, as it doesn't suit my path," Alistair said. "Until we find a suitable user, you can study this. Perhaps you'll find insights in its construction." Just as Alistair gained levels and insights into the Dao through combat and meditation, a forger-type Class would get similar benefits through analyzing and building weapons and constructs.

"Thank you, sir," Felix replied, gently accepting the sword. The way he touched the hilt, it was like he thought the blade would instantly kill him.

There were other smaller issues in the Northeast Freehold, but Alistair didn't have time to deal with them for the moment. The final item on his docket was the food situation, and then he would let someone else manage other day-to-day problems.

"Who is in charge of the food and water supply?" Alistair asked.

"That was Katie's job." John looked down as he answered. Alistair would never forget the way her body aged into a skeleton right in front of his eyes.

"I see," Alistair said. "Did she have any assistants or helpers with that?"

"There was her boyfriend, James Foster," Lily offered. "I think his Class was Harvester or something like that. He was the one who actually did most of the farming, while she handled the logistics."

"I want you to find him ASAP and tell him he's in charge now. Don't take no for an answer unless he can provide someone just as competent as him. People's lives are at stake here. If he protests too much without providing a suitable replacement, bring him to me."

Alistair understood that he would still be grieving, but others would start grieving soon if they didn't have access to crops and clean water. Some food came from the monster and beast hunts, but there wasn't enough meat to feed everyone.

"Alright, I think we're just about done, then. We'll meet at 7:00 PM on this day each week, so every Friday, at the Northeast Freehold HQ. If you can't make it in person, we'll try to relay information via the Soulnet. For now, we'll hold it in this makeshift fortress, but I assume we'll be getting something more permanent soon," he announced, looking at Linda. "Any questions?"

No one had any, so he turned to John. The large man was a steadfast ally and always dependable. "John, I want you to be in charge of day-to-day operations. Just keep things running smoothly since I won't always be around. This job won't be the easiest, and you'll basically always have to be inside the Northeast Freehold."

"It's not like I have anywhere else to be." John laughed. "I've barely left the city in the first place. Just give me some vacation days every now and then, alright?"

"Will do." Alistair smiled. "Oh yeah, that reminds me. Take this."

Alistair handed the Flamesmith a piece of paper, though it wasn't an ordinary note. He'd bought a **Digital Note** item from the System Store for a couple thousand drachma. The **Digital Note** looked like a large index card, but it could hold terabytes of textual information, and a person borrowing it could send it back to the owner at a speed many times faster than light. Because it wasn't made for combat or cultivation, it didn't count toward his item limit. Which reminded Alistair—he needed to look into ways to get around that.

Despite the gigantic amount of storage space, all Alistair had on it was the list of those in the corrections center who were to remain imprisoned and those who were supposed to be freed. It didn't matter that much; he'd use it for more important things later.

With that, the meeting came to a close. The others streamed out of the makeshift conference room, leaving Alistair alone. Well, not entirely alone.

"A bit of a lazy leader, aren't you, Alistair?" Dev'rox asked, appearing over his shoulder. "I guess you just want the fun parts."

"My skillset is more suited to defending our territory and continuously gaining resources than being a governor," Alistair said, defending himself, though he knew in his heart of hearts that Dev'rox was somewhat correct about him wanting the fun parts. He didn't let it bother him, though. No matter how hard you trained, the difference between someone who enjoyed their work and someone who hated it was as clear as night and day.

Alistair stretched his legs. He had a lot of things to review now that he finally had a tiny amount of spare time.

First, there was the nagging issue of his left arm. It would probably heal on its own in a month or so, but that was a long time. Testing out different punches and movements, he estimated it to be under 50% capacity, though by appearance it looked like he'd only lost a bit of muscle. The main damage was internal, and Alistair counted himself lucky he hadn't lost the arm altogether. The amount of energy he was able to channel through it using the recently deceased was far too much for his body to handle.

Alistair tackled this problem with something he had been wanting to try anyway—**[Carmela's Happy Pies]**. The description of the Skill read:

[Carmela's Happy Pies] (Tier 1 Journeyman Skill): *Cook delicious pies, no setup necessary, just matter! Aids with cultivation and general nourishment.* Upgradeable (0/30).

The general nourishment part was what Alistair was after. He activated the Skill, unsure of what was going to happen.

He felt a sudden wave of knowledge pass over him, almost causing him to buckle over. In his new eyes, that tile on the ground and a piece of the nearby table were perfect ingredients, and he tore them off with ease. He put them together on the table, closed his eyes and patted them down. By some arcane miracle, when he opened his eyes again, he saw a freshly-made apple pie.

"Now that's an interesting Skill," Dev'rox remarked. "I wish I could taste that."

Alistair hadn't had food since he was back on Faxor. He didn't need it now that he passively absorbed ambient Mana, but it didn't mean he didn't miss the delectable flavors. He wolfed down the large pie in under a minute.

The pie was the most mouthwatering, succulent dish he had ever eaten. As it went down his gullet, he immediately felt the effects on his cultivation. He could draw from ambient Mana even easier, letting it flow through his meridians into his soulcore. Besides the effect on cultivation, he just felt generally happier. It wasn't like he was depressed before, but now he felt a vibrancy that he hadn't in a long time. He was alive, truly alive. Right away, he could feel the connective tissue and muscle of his damaged arm start to mend faster. If it would have taken a month to get to 100% before, now it would only take two weeks.

He was so distracted that he almost missed his level up.

Level up! *You are now level 36.* +3 Agility, +3 Intelligence, +3 Charisma, +3 free Attribute points, +23 Upgrade Points.

The additional 23 Upgrade Points put him at an insane 89 points, and the new stats brought his Agility, Intelligence, and Charisma up to 217, 226, and 180 respectively. He decided to allocate the free Attribute points to Agility, wanting to bring it back up to his number one stat.

He still had so many things on his to-do list, but before he even allocated his Upgrade Points, it was time to do something he'd been unintentionally putting off—exploring the Dao Organizational Map.

5 DAO ORGANIZATIONAL MAP

ALISTAIR HAD UNLOCKED the Map a few days ago, but he hadn't had the time to go through it yet. It wasn't exactly an item, though it wasn't exactly a part of his status screen either. Instead, it felt like a part of him that was always there but that he hadn't noticed before.

Opening the Map drew him into an inner world unlike anything he had ever seen. He existed in a void of darkness, illuminated by spheres of light. The spheres were of every color of the rainbow and more, colors whose existence Alistair couldn't comprehend. They varied in size and shape as well, some as small as his fist, while the biggest were several times the size of a house. Some were perfectly defined and round, while others were wispy balls of gas. They were all connected in an impossibly complex network, forming a beautiful web of existence.

Alistair was in awe of it all, passing by the intangible spheres as he walked around. He could feel the emanation of the Dao from each and every one of them—a powerful resonance that spoke to the eternal truths of the world. If he focused on one for too long, it would try to infect his mind with its truth. In one instance, he gazed upon a fiery green sphere, getting lost in its promise of bountiful growth and nurturing. He eventually caught himself and gathered his own Dao energy to counter it.

That one must be something like the Dao of Nature, Alistair thought. It was one of the larger spheres, with a radius of perhaps ten meters. He couldn't believe how tempting it was, but he had his own path to follow.

The more he explored the web of nodes, the more he grew astonished. There were just so many spheres, each representing a different aspect of the entire Dao. As he continued walking, he found himself drawn to the center of the void.

With orbs floating in every direction, Alistair wasn't sure how he knew where the center was. However, once he laid eyes on it, he felt certain beyond a doubt.

Alistair gazed at the three largest spheres in the entire void. It felt like all the others were orbiting them, whereas they revolved around an invisible central point.

One of the spheres looked like a yin-yang symbol, except instead of white and black it was royal purple and golden yellow, both parts swirling together in harmony. Its surface was smooth and unblemished, perfectly defined and radiating a balanced duality.

The second sphere was a star of crimson brilliance. And by star, Alistair really meant *star*. The sphere looked like a miniature version of a red giant.

The final central sphere was the brightest, a mass of pure white light with a gigantic halo. It was the least defined of them all, the barrier between the star's body and illumination having no clear divide.

Just standing in their presence awed Alistair, and these apparitions were only a fraction of a fraction of an iota of their true power. As he soaked in their presence, he tried identifying them. To his surprise, when he focused on figuring out their names, a small window popped up.

The swirling yin-yang sphere was the Samsara Node, the window read. That made sense. The Dharmic concept of the cycle of rebirth that only ended when one reached enlightenment.

The crimson star was the Karma Node. That explained why Alistair found it so familiar. The color and timbre of Karmic energy was identical to that of the star, albeit at a much smaller scale. It intrigued Alistair that Karma had its own place on the Dao Organizational Map, considering the marked difference he noted in Dao energy and Karmic energy. The two were clearly different things, yet for some reason, this sphere was amongst the others.

Finally, Alistair analyzed the white light. The window said it represented the Dao of Virtue. The idea of virtue was not that far off that of justice, and Alistair felt similar ideas coming off of the sphere. Yet there were also clear differences. His Dao of Justice was about action, righting wrongs, and effecting change. Whereas the Dao of Virtue was more inward, focusing on having a pure heart and mind, and setting an unimpeachable example.

He didn't want to stay near them for too long, as he already felt the Dao of Virtue seeping into his heart. It had an easier time infecting him because of its similarity to the Dao of Justice. He didn't think he had perfected his Dao Path by any means, but it was a bad idea to let in the influence of an outside Dao, especially one that was kin to his own, espoused by the three largest spheres.

If he stayed for too long, he might even get a new Dao Inspiration, and the Lazarene Minister had already told him that maintaining three was tough. A fourth would be nearly impossible to progress with.

As such, Alistair turned around, fleeing the powerful presence of Samsara, Karma, and Virtue. His information screen informed him the reason they held a central position on the Map—they were the Supreme Daos. He read the system's description.

Three Daos become one will—the will of Heaven itself. The Supreme Daos of Samsara, Karma, and Virtue stand at the center of the Organizational Map. These Dao Nodes are an inexact representation of the true Supreme Dao, which cannot be truly replicated outside of Heaven's domain. That they are called the Supreme Daos does not necessarily mean that following their path will make you stronger than your peers, but the Supreme Daos do have certain advantages. All three concepts—Samsara, Karma, and Virtue—have made their indelible mark on the multiverse. There is now the cycle of reincarnation, decided by Karma, which is earned through virtuosity. Heaven's righteous path welcomes all comers.

There was something deep in him that recoiled at the message, but he couldn't figure out why. He was a Karmic cultivator himself, and honestly, it was an important part of his kit. Whatever the stirring was, he suspected his Dao of Justice might be the cause, because he felt a connection to a sphere—or Dao Node, as the description said—around a hundred meters away from the Dao of Virtue. There was a line connecting the two Nodes, an interesting battle between the white of Virtue and the gold of what Alistair had to assume was Justice.

While he jogged toward the Justice Node, he realized that there was another trio of Nodes rotating above the Supreme Daos. However, unlike every other Node, they were grayed out. The Dao energy they gave off was so faint that Alistair couldn't even recognize them. They were chained as well, bound to the impossibly high ceiling of the void. Alistair made a mental note to investigate what they were later. Right now, he had his own Dao to worry about.

As Alistair drew closer to the Justice Node, he realized that the battle between the white and gold lines was less clear than he'd initially thought. It was less of a battle and more of a choreographed performance, with elements of hostility. They pushed and pulled and tugged on each other, but in the end, they had a strong connection.

The Justice Node was not as large as the Supreme Daos, but it was similar in size to the Nature Node he had seen before, and slightly smaller than the Nodes he presumed were those of Life, Death, Space, and Time. It shone with a beautiful golden light, and it was more spherical than the Virtue Node, possessing only a small halo. It almost felt like a subtle insult, as if the Justice Node was calling the Virtue Node overly vain for its unparalleled brilliance.

Now, this is the Node I need, Alistair thought as he put his hand up to the light. It felt stern but soothing, firm but merciful. Justice was unending vigilance. It was the executioner's sword but also alms for the downtrodden. It called everyone equally under its banner without discrimination. It was permanent in its quest, yet it was also a Dao of change and dynamism. If there was injustice anywhere, it sought to make it right.

Something deep inside him stirred, urging him to go even further. Now that he was close to the surface of the Justice Node, he could feel the righteous heat burning against his skin. It felt like the full fury of an avenging god, testing his mettle. Did he have the mental fortitude to bear the burden of an endless quest for justice, no matter the consequences?

Alistair knew he did. He gritted his teeth and stepped *inside* the glowing sphere. His vision was swamped with golden light that seared his eyeballs from the inside out, yet he kept pushing forward. Every cell in his body screamed with pain, even more than he'd experienced while taking the Tier 2 Health pill.

Doubt spread through Alistair's mind. He had imagined talent, resources, and luck as quintessential factors in one's advancement through the realms. But willpower was another missing piece. Only one in a thousand cultivators in the Final Frontier Empire made it to Adept, and then perhaps one in ten thousand of those Adepts made it to Profound. If combining simple ingredients was enough, there would be more Adepts and Profounds. The eternal conflict of the multiverse constantly tested one's mental fortitude through both physical and psychological pain. He would have to overcome trial after trial for thousands or even millions of years, if he understood a cultivator's lifespan properly.

Can I do that? The golden light slowed his movement to a near stop. He was almost at the center of the Justice Node, needing just one more step, but it would be the hardest one by far. Alistair was no longer overcome by physical pain, but he still couldn't do it.

Alistair imagined all the people he cared about. The ones that stuck out most in his mind were the ones he couldn't save, at least not yet, like his mother and girlfriend and his friends. What was all his power good for? The demon Kyraxadon tried to tell him that his desire for power was really what motivated him, that his quest for justice was a facade. But that didn't feel right to Alistair. Sure, he enjoyed being able to shatter trees with his bare hands or freeze lakes with a touch. But he would trade that all away in an instant if he could stop the endless violence.

The old world wasn't much better. There was poverty, greed, and warfare aplenty. But nothing ever felt world-shattering, like the system could truly change. Perhaps through technological advancement, but that wasn't a sure thing, though the existence of the Pathfinder AI and the Sublimed Machine suggested it was a potential path. He wasn't really sure how strong the Sublimed Machine was, but they sounded pretty powerful if they could make the Pathfinder AI, which despite its immense power was considered a "hunk of junk."

In any case, once the initiation happened, things changed. For the most part, they got worse. Billions died, over 85% by most people's guesses. The quality of life for those not at the top dropped a significant amount. Yet it also offered people a sliver of hope, however unlikely. The message was simple and the results were clear: rise to the top and become a god. If an acolyte like Atavius Meloi can destroy your world with ease, what can *you* do if you achieve even greater power?

Yes, Alistair thought. *There is a path.* His Dao Path was like a tiny golden thread amidst a sea of misshapen yarn. Even if he didn't know it, he had been waiting for this his whole life. A greater destiny beyond this Earth. In one last Herculean effort, he heaved his body into the center of the Justice Node and saw all.

Not truly *all*, since the Justice Node around him was merely the limit that a Foundation realm could handle, but to Alistair, it was everything. Everything encompassing a Foundation Dao of Justice coursed through his system, but even that was far too much for his level 36 brain. He only got small snippets of wisdom, but they still gave insight. Alistair saw his eternal paradise for all, Heaven on Earth. That phrase resonated within him to such a degree he felt he might explode, forcing him to run out of the Justice Node before he hurt his cultivation by trying to absorb too many truths.

After Alistair spent a few moments calming down, he realized he had a new notification.

Achievement Unlocked: Dao Node (I) (Dao of Justice) — *Heaven on Earth added to Dao Elements.* Reward: +20 Strength, +20 Constitution, +20 Endurance, +20 Wisdom, +15 max Karma (45 cap), +10% to Strength, Endurance, and Wisdom.

He couldn't be happier with the results, the gains shoring up all his weakest stats. Even his currently weakest Attribute, Constitution, was at 111. His Endurance was all the way up to 113, letting him almost feel the life force flowing through his veins. The boost in that stat would make his weakened left arm recover even faster. Instead of the two weeks he'd predicted with **[Carmela's Happy Pies]**, it would only be a week and a few days.

Since Alistair already had his Ghost Dao Node, he only had one more Node to complete—the Dao of the Fist. Just like his Dao of Justice, it was very close to forming the Node. For a cultivator who was even moderately far away from their insight to forming a Dao Node, the presence of the spheres wouldn't help that much. But for Alistair, whose Dao of the Fist and Dao of Justice had been only slightly behind his Ghost Node, it made all the difference.

Of course, he still tried going to the Dao of the Ghost. The Ghost Node was similar in size to the Justice Node, looking like a giant wispy ball of auric mist. It was by far the least spherical and least defined Node Alistair had seen, glowing a blue so faint it was almost white. He tried the same procedure that he used on the Justice Node, walking inside of it. However, with the Ghost Node, it was almost trivial to enter. Perhaps it was just the ghostly nature of the Node itself, but Alistair thought it was more likely that he had already grasped all the insights the limited sphere could provide at his level. If it was so easy to progress in the Dao just by looking at spheres, everyone would be Truthseekers.

The Dao of the Fist was a different story. Alistair noted that it was around equidistant from both the Dao of Justice and the Dao of the Ghost, who were both around equidistant from each other as well, forming an almost equilateral triangle. It wasn't perfectly symmetrical, the Dao of the Fist being smaller than that of Justice or the Ghost—but the center of his triangle roughly corresponded to the center of the Organizational Map, and the orbiting Supreme Daos and the locked spheres above them. He wasn't trying to create such a perfect trinity, but it was nice to see that his Daos didn't have much overlap.

The Dao of the Fist was a raging star, looking most similar to the Dao of Karma. However, it was far angrier than the relatively calm red giant, bubbling with solar flares and ugly spots. Its hue was a reddish-salmon, tilting towards coral, not the color Alistair would most associate with violence or fisticuffs, but he remembered these were only visual representations for human eyes.

Alistair breathed in the fires of the Fist Node. It didn't draw him in like the Justice Node, having a more intimidating presence.

The Fist could never be tamed. It was conflict in its purest form, the physical representation of true combat. It was called the Dao of the Fist, but that was just a surface level understanding of its nature. Beings without arms or legs could access the combat Dao without a problem. Just like the Dao of Justice, it was a greedy monster that wanted to consume everything in its own glory.

He embraced the mercurial Node, entering it just like the last.

There were innumerable similar truths to the Fist. The Dao of the Sword, with its silvery sharpness; and the Dao of the Spear, with its piercing aura, were close by. But Alistair admired the Dao of the Fist the most. He was extremely biased, no doubt, but he felt like he could justify himself.

The Fist walked the middle of the Daos of War. It wasn't the largest sphere or the smallest, sitting near the median in size. Alistair still wasn't sure if the mass or volume of a sphere correlated to its strength, but based on the text describing the Supreme Daos, it likely had less to do with strength, and more to do with conceptual importance and simplicity.

The Dao of the Fist was warmer than that of the Sword. The Sword looked down on its brother's brutality and lack of sophistication. The Sword was elegant and clean. Yet the Fist was also more civilized and artful than barbaric Daos like Warfury or Conquest.

Most of all, the Dao of the Fist was an evangelist. It wanted to test its cultivators, to help them grow stronger. It was the Dao that resonated the most with Alistair's own competitive spirit; when he saw a strong cultivator, he wanted to see how he stacked up. He didn't want to let anyone beat him. Alistair could lose once, or twice, or even a million times, but he would have the last laugh one day. And it would probably take more than a million attempts against someone like Red, the prodigy whom Alistair had tested himself against while speaking with Nenna Spindoller during Felons vs. Fellows. And even Red almost certainly couldn't hold a candle to the true multiversal elites.

Instead of the Justice Node's fiery pain, the Fist Node toyed with him like an old sparring partner. He felt the stellar energy contort and fight against him, his own attacks coming at him left and right. Moves that he used in the past. Punches and kicks and elbows and knees and headbutts that followed his pattern of movement, his understanding of martial arts, to a tee.

Alistair let the trance overcome him, the same trance he had relied on many times to win in the past. If the Justice Node had tried to test his tenacity and willpower, the Fist Node was trying to see how deep he could go, how much could he subsume his ego into his pugilism.

And at last, when Alistair found himself past planes of consciousness, he landed at the same mystic point he'd found in the duel against Anthony. Before him stood the kiss of death, floating between an infinite army of knives and a calm sea below. Though he had no true thoughts, a deep urge in the recesses of his mind promised that he was almost there. He just needed to go a little deeper.

When Alistair broke through to that new deepest point, a wave of under-standing rushed over him, similar to his Heaven on Earth insight. He had a name for the place he visited, and names had power. The three-pronged vision was called "Kai'tazake Mutra," which translated to "the poetic home of the reaper of lost souls." Alistair had no clue what that meant beyond a vague understanding that he was supposed to be channeling the concept of a psychopomp—a spiritual guide ferrying souls to the afterlife—from mythology.

Just the name and vague insight were enough for him to form the Dao Node. Alistair was expecting just one notification to appear, but two did instead.

Achievement Unlocked: Dao Node (I) (Dao of the Fist) — *Kai'tazake Mutra added to Dao Elements.* Reward: +35 Strength, +50 Agility, +20% to Agility.

Skill Upgraded: [Fighter's Instinct] (Tier 4 Beginner Passive Skill): *Become preternaturally aware of bodily threats. Scales with Agility.* Upgradeable (1 / 150).

Badge Acquired: "World Leader" (Untiered Temporary Legendary Badge): *Achieve the highest overall Attribute points on your homeworld.* +30 to Attribute of your choice, All Attributes +20%.

A wide grin spread across Alistair's face as he looked at the "World Leader" Badge. His Fist Node's extra stats must have put him over the edge to give him the highest overall Attribute points in the world.

He couldn't help his smile. Seeing the "World Leader" Badge was one amongst many confirmations of his strength, but combined with his #2 ranking on the leaderboards, it felt the most real.

Alistair chose Agility for the +30 of his choice, reasoning that mathematically speaking, amplifying his strengths would do him better than shoring up his weaknesses. Because he was out of Badge slots, he removed "Precocious Killer." It had served him well, but "World Leader" gave more stats to every category except Endurance, and even that would change after he got the base number higher.

A thought passed through Alistair's head. How did he even get the Badge? Wandering Hobo was thought to be a few levels ahead of the pack. Alistair assumed the cultivator must have had some Dao Nodes of his own to keep up, since he knew Anthony had at least one. Perhaps he didn't have a stat-focused build, but it was still a little hard to believe.

At least his "Deliverance of Justice" Badge was putting in work. Checking the Badge, he saw that he had gotten 48/52 procs, missing another 2 with his new level. Alistair predicted he would get those points in short order after venturing out into the wild.

Seeing as he had upgraded all three of his Daos into Dao Nodes, Alistair didn't have much more reason to stay in the Dao Organizational Map. He had gleaned all the insights he could from the limited representations, and other Nodes could potentially sway his path. After a quick jog just to see how many spheres there were (there were more than he could feasibly count), he imagined leaving the inner world of the Map. In an instant, he returned to the real world.

"Oh my, you've gotten much stronger," Dev'rox pointed out. "I fear you're going to let it get to your head."

"You're right, I am stronger," Alistair said. His Strength was the biggest comparative difference, going from 78 at level 35 to now 171 at level 36, with help from the two new Dao Nodes and "World Leader" Badge. The table below him was supposed to be magically anchored to the ground, but Alistair found it trivial to break it from its tethering with his newfound strength. "I'm *much* stronger."

Alistair hadn't noticed much muscle growth since the start, but evidently it was still there, just at a slower pace. With his discrete jump, he'd gained at least fifteen pounds of muscle. At least, what fifteen pounds of muscle looked like on a normal human. His Constitution made every cell in his body significantly heavier.

Before, he had a lithe, lightweight boxer or swimmer's body, but now he was approaching fitness model territory.

Despite the added bulk, he didn't feel any slower or less agile. Quite the opposite, in fact. His Agility almost doubled, and Alistair could feel it in every muscle and nerve in his body. His control over his movements was near perfect, accompanying a feeling of nigh infinite speed.

With his giant jump in power, Alistair knew that he would progress slower for the upcoming levels, but it didn't matter. Since the world leaderboards didn't only account for pure combat strength in the rankings, Alistair was confident that he was the most powerful human on Earth in a one-on-

one fight, especially if he'd stolen the "World Leader" Badge from Wandering Hobo.

He was ready to take a break from cultivation, but Dev'rox had another plan in mind. The imp whipped his tail up, shooting himself off Alistair's shoulder and onto the table he had just picked up. "Looks like you're finally ready, brat. Do you want to learn about Mana affinities?"

6 MANA AFFINITIES

"Is that even a question? Of course I do," Alistair said. Dev'rox almost never gave him direct information, beyond small clarifications of things he already knew. "What's a Mana affinity?"

"Hmph. What's the best way to explain this..." Dev'rox thought aloud. In the end, he flicked his tail and shared a small portion of his space-attuned Mana. "You can feel this, right?"

"Yes." Alistair breathed in the bountiful Mana, cycling it through the twelve major meridians and into his soulcore. The other 349 would come later once he reached level 60 and could start opening them. "It's your Mana. Refreshing as always, if you have to know."

"I try my best. But don't pay attention to the energizing part for a second. I might be dead, but the quality of my Mana is still at a near-Profound level, even if I can't produce even a hundredth of what I could when I was alive. What I want you to see—no, *feel*—is the timbre and color of it."

"It's space-attuned Mana," Alistair responded. "So it's clear, with a hint of black. It's sparse as far as Mana goes, yet it also feels like it connects everything."

"Those are surface level observations," Dev'rox chastised. "What *is* it? At its fundamental core, what is my Mana made of?"

"Isn't all Mana the same?" Alistair questioned. "You've just made your

Mana closer to your Dao over time, so it's slowly molded to your will and become more effective at carrying the Dao of Space."

"Right and wrong. Molding implies changing the Mana itself from a pure form to a spatial form over time, does it not?"

Alistair nodded his head. That was how he interpreted it, how he felt when sensing his own Mana reserves within his soulcore.

"That is a false perception. The process of attunement is somewhat of a misnomer. What's actually happening is that the concentration of spatial Mana is slowly overtaking the concentration of pure Mana, through the more frequent production of spatial Mana particles."

"What?" Alistair exclaimed. That was a revelation to him. He had assumed that Mana was a gradient, but Dev'rox was telling him it was discrete? "So all Mana types just exist as Platonic ideals, a hundred percent pure in their simplest form?"

"Mana *affinities*," Dev'rox corrected. "But you could say that, yes. Of course, each individual soulcore produces a slightly different variant. No one person's fire Mana will be exactly the same as another person's fire Mana. Just as the aura of a cultivator is unique, so is their individual Mana. It has to be that way, since the aura of a cultivator represents the total of their Mana reserves and the purification of their body. But despite these individual differences, no one would ever confuse one affinity with another.

"The primary affinities of Mana are pure, sun, moon, liquid, fire, earth, air, chrome, life, death, space, and time. The individual Dao that represents each of these affinities is known as an Elemental Dao. The Elemental Daos, as you might expect, are the elements that create the multiverse. No one knows exactly why those twelve are the primary twelve, but that's just how it is."

"But there are way more Mana affinities than that. What about blood and ice..." Alistair trailed off. "Ah, so those must be, what, secondary affinities?"

"You've figured it out, congratulations." Dev'rox smiled, showing his fangs. "Yes, each combination of primary affinities creates a brand-new secondary affinity. For instance, blood Mana is the pairing of liquid and moon. However, opposites can never be combined. That means pairs like time and space, fire and liquid, and sun and moon don't exist."

Dev'rox continued. "Possessing a soulcore that can produce primary affinities is more commonplace than one that can produce secondary affinities, though both vary quite a lot in rarity. For instance, time is less common than lightning or magma."

Alistair immediately recalled Anthony's Skills. The deceased cultivator couldn't use any Skill without imbuing a small part of his Dao, which suggested he relied on his Dao since his Mana didn't have a high concentration of time particles. Perhaps if he had survived, he would've eventually had as pure a concentration as Dev'rox.

"There's one thing I'm missing," Alistair said. "I don't have any affinities myself. My **[Mana Strike]** takes pure Mana, and **[Phase Shift]** can turn pure Mana into any... wait a second, you just said that attunement is the concentration of particles changing. That doesn't make any sense with **[Phase Shift]**. If that were the case, where are all the different affinities coming from?"

"I didn't say it was impossible for Mana affinity to change. For a fast-acting Skill like **[Mana Strike]**, meridian filters can change the pure Mana to a different affinity temporarily, though this never captures the true essence of that affinity. Pure Mana always wants to return to pure Mana in the end. Soulcores are unique in that along with the Heart of All Creation, they are the only objects in the multiverse that create new Mana. Your original point does ring true, however. The pure Mana path is not without merit, but it is often harder than others. Instances of objects and regions that generate pure Mana are seldom in the multiverse. Now that you have Dao Nodes, the traditional next step is to associate affinities with each of your Dao that will carry their essence most effectively. With something like the Dao of Fire, the choice is almost mandatory, but you have a more interesting case."

Alistair contemplated his three Dao Nodes. None were Elemental, so he had no easy choices. "How do I associate affinities?"

"You must restrict yourself to using only one or two affinities with one Dao. I suppose you could use one affinity across multiple Dao Nodes if you wanted, but I don't see that working in your case. The more you produce a specific affinity with a specific Dao, the more your soulcore will specialize and lock in your understanding of the Dao with that mana affinity, making you more powerful. Listen here brat, having unified affinities and Dao is of the utmost importance. Up until this point, it was fine that you were using all different types, but if you continue to do that through the rest of this realm and into Adept, your foundations will be irrevocably in disrepair.

Imagine trying to associate six different affinities with one Dao. It would be disastrous."

"I think I understand now," Alistair said. "So two is okay?"

He wanted to test out a few different affinities for the Fist, but he had three good candidates for Justice and the Ghost. For Justice, he thought lightning fit perfectly, especially as his own replication of the Heavenly tribulation. For the Ghost, he had two candidates that weighed equally in his mind. Blood Mana seemed like it would work beautifully, with the innate association it had to the vital essence of a human and the practice he already had combining it with [Ghost Whispers]. But he also thought ice was another good choice, being associated with permanence, death, and apparitions from the beyond. Furthermore, blood and ice complemented each other. Blood was the passionate, vengeful aspect of a ghost, while ice was the dead, lingering aspect.

"As long as it fits," Dev'rox answered. "What did you have in mind?"

"I was thinking blood and ice for the Dao of the Ghost, lightning for Justice, and, uh, maybe fire for the Fist?"

"Lightning is a mix of chrome and fire and is fine with ice, but as a primary affinity, fire is hard to use with ice. Not impossible, but hard. You still have some time. Why don't you try your choices in combat and see what works?"

"That sounds like a great idea," Alistair said. "I've been inactive for too long."

He'd spent the past four days in a coma before waking up to non-stop meetings on the fifth. *Damn, those pies are really working,* Alistair thought. He had been mentally exhausted from fighting nonstop since Felons vs. Fellows and the war with Anthony, but now he was revving to go again.

"I think you're a battle-crazed, hairless ape," Dev'rox said. "But conflict is guaranteed on your Dao Path, I suppose. It *can* be entertaining from time to time. What are you thinking of trying first?"

———

Alistair left Boston, but not before first setting up his taxes, something he had not been looking forward to in the old world. But it definitely felt better being the one collecting the taxes rather than the one paying them.

As the majority shareholder of the Northeast Freehold, Alistair could set the taxation level for his various subregions. The default for direct ownership was 1% of one's total earnings each month, capped at 50,000 drachma from an individual person, and 0.25% from all non-directly owned territories in the Northeast Freehold. However, a month was counted from when that person joined the Northeast Freehold, so in practice he received a constant, low-level stream of money. The cap was fixed, but he could change the percentage, from all the way down to 0% to as high as 5%. Alistair wanted to reduce the taxes, but he couldn't afford to with the debt hanging over his head. So he kept them the same, at least for now.

The annoying part was that the system currently capped him at one million drachma a month. Surely, the average income generated was more than 100 Gold drachma, but he was blocked out of most of it. There were three ways to increase his personal collection cap: adding more subregions to his empire, waiting for the natural increases, or investing Upgrade Points into it. He really didn't want to use the third option. His 89 points were precious tools for cultivation, not greed. In the end he capitulated, spending 50 of his points to increase the cap to two million a month. Now, he would only be responsible for 600k drachma and would successfully repay his debt.

With his remaining 39 Upgrade Points, he spent 26 toward increasing his Badge slots, reasoning that he no longer had any bad Badges to replace. Now that he had only good Badges that he planned to keep for a long time, he needed an extra Badge slot urgently, or they would vanish after 24 hours.

Next, he turned to the Land Store. It worked differently, measuring the power and advancement of all individuals within the subregion, including improvements they made to the land, like fortresses or technological inventions. The Land Store credit generation didn't have a cap like Alistair's taxes, but it worked at a much slower rate. He had a debt of just over 16k credits a month for six months, and his current rate of generation was only 4k a month. Anthony must have taken a terrible loan to afford all the shadow demons and artillery bombs he'd employed.

What he needed to do to increase his Land Store generation was simple. Besides building and improving the land, which he was already doing, he just needed *more* of it. For Anthony, that meant conquest, but Alistair wanted to take a more diplomatic approach.

Prior to leaving, he did one last check-up to make sure that everything was running smoothly in his capital. Checking his notifications, he saw that his note had returned from John. The Flamesmith had completed the prisoner task and was searching for Anthony's Hall of Math contact. Under John's guidance, the Northeast Freehold could operate without Alistair.

As Alistair left one of the stores with a special item, he observed the streets. It was remarkable how quickly people moved on and rebuilt. The city was abuzz with energy, families buying food from the stores and construction workers placing down bricks of valyrik. Alistair would protect the Northeast Freehold to the last breath.

Hopefully, it won't come to that, Alistair thought. *I am ranked #2, after all.*

Moving on to happier thoughts, Alistair exited the city and ran down the interstate as fast as his legs would take him. Each step he took left cracks in the concrete from the sheer force of his feet. It couldn't be helped, now that his top speed was 400 kilometers per hour, nearly as fast as his previous [Dash] speed. That reminded Alistair—what was his new [Dash] speed? It scaled with his Agility, so it should be much faster.

He activated the Skill, feeling the rush of pure Mana contract the muscles in his legs beyond their normal capacity. The world in front of him became a blur for half a second, faster than even his absurd reaction time could keep up with. It was over in a blink, and Alistair found himself a hundred meters ahead of where he started.

Doing some quick calculations in his head, bolstered by his increased Intelligence, he found his speed with [Dash] increased to approximately 750 kilometers per hour. With just a few more improvements to his speed, he would surpass the sound barrier, though he wondered if it would be the same now that the Dao stood at the center of the universe instead of the laws of physics. The strongest cultivators clearly exceeded the speed of light, so it was possible that breaking the sound barrier wouldn't have the same effect for a Foundation or Adept cultivator as it had on a fighter jet.

As Alistair ran down the road, he couldn't help but notice how empty it was. In the old world, no matter what time of day, the highway was always full of cars. After oil production collapsed in the initiation, cars only lasted for as much fuel as you had or could find. Over a month later, barely anyone had working cars, and if you did, you didn't want to use it. Cars were perfect targets for monster hordes since they could only hold a limited amount of people and didn't fight back. It was safer to travel in large groups of ten or more.

Instead of going south to rendezvous with the Ricci Empire's remnants,

Alistair headed north. It would give Alistair peace of mind to eliminate any and all threats he encountered. Along the way, he could also invite unaffiliated towns into the Northeast Freehold.

Speaking of which, every few hours he felt a new subregion join. John had sent emissaries out into the wider world to recruit the leaders of ten-plus subregion freeholds, but the main bulk of joiners came from independent subregions neighboring the Northeast Freehold. Any nearby subregion saw the power of his empire, and almost all wanted to join for protection and resources. His unblemished reputation was putting in serious work in pumping up recruitment.

Alistair slowed down to a pace he could keep up indefinitely, around 250 kilometers per hour. The first item on the docket was eradicating the serpent horde deep in the Appalachian Mountains. According to the report Bartholomew left, they weren't from a monster wave, despite their monstrous appearance. Instead, they were mutated wild snakes that had grown until they were hundreds of times the size of their original species.

That didn't mean that monster hordes weren't a problem. Their sources indicated there were eight of them in the United States. There were other Pathfinder AI-created creatures from quelled monster waves scattered across America, but only eight had ascended to another level of power.

The serpent horde had destroyed hundreds of towns surrounding the Appalachian Trail in New Hampshire. Since it was the closest major threat to the Northeast Freehold, Alistair thought he would tackle it first. Along the way, he could pick up recruits and deal with criminals, all the while resting his left arm. If there was someone or something powerful enough to force him to use it, he would be very surprised.

After an hour of running, Alistair arrived at one of the larger towns in the region. He wasn't sure what its old name was, but after the initiation, everyone called it Port Locasta, after its ruler, Caren Locasta. Port Locasta was several dozen kilometers east of the former Ricci Empire, and south of the Maine Brothers Kingdom, a freehold formed by two brothers that controlled the most territory in the northeast US after Alistair. Port Locasta had around twenty subregions and was a local hub for trade between the Maine Brothers, the Ricci Empire, and the former New Boston Alliance.

The main town of Port Locasta was surrounded by ten-meter-high palisades that radiated protective energy. Not as impressive as the defenses he was building, but still enough for the residents to feel safe. Based on the size and curvature of the wall, Alistair estimated the city proper to have at least a hundred thousand people, which was a fair amount for a post-initiation city. New Boston had close to a million, and it was one of the largest in all of America.

As far as Alistair could see, there was only one entrance into the town, a thick metal gate guarded by two men. They radiated strong auras that he estimated were just below the soulcore stage.

But what he felt far more than any aura was the anguish of the people desperately trying to enter the town. The sun had just set, darkness starting to take hold, yet there was still a long line of travelers at the gate begging to be let in. He saw family after family turned away, only for the next to be let in without hassle. At first, he wasn't sure what criteria they were using, but as he moved up the line, it became obvious. Unless you were a strong combatant, had a decent sum of money or a useful Class, you were turned away.

Before he entered the line, Alistair made sure to suppress his aura as much as possible. He wasn't an expert at it, but his experience with the Dao of the Ghost had familiarized him with the sensation of nothingness. He slowed the beat of his soulcore until it only produced the Mana appropriate for a level 15, which was around average for those waiting in line. On top of his aura suppression, he put on the item he'd picked up at the special store, a disguise that changed the features of his face. Alistair didn't know how famous he was, but it was possible that people would notice him. He joined the back of the line, which stretched out for at least a hundred meters.

The family in front of him looked ragged, like they had been on the run for months and not bathed at all. They were so skinny that Alistair felt ashamed of how muscular he had become. Just a drop of his life force would be enough to heal their vitality thrice over.

"It's okay," he heard the mother say to her young son. "Everything will be fine."

The line kept moving at a fast pace—the guards turned away ninety percent of the refugees. When Alistair was halfway through the line, he wondered if any of the rejected individuals would get rowdy, but after the left guard flared his aura at an angry refugee, that behavior stopped right away. He wanted to intervene and let everyone in, but he knew he had no right to do anything.

Port Locasta had a finite number of resources and territory and an already large population. They couldn't afford to take in a ton of people and continue to feed and shelter everyone. It just sucked that some were welcomed because they were wealthy or powerful, while everyone else was screwed. Alistair made a mental note to extend an offer to Caren Locasta to join the Northeast Freehold, and to set up a better system for refugees to come to the Northeast Freehold from anywhere in the country. Perhaps they could ask Caren to have a **Teleportation Circle** ready?

Because Alistair was lost in thought, he didn't realize that he had moved up to the front of the line. A loud slap broke him out of his daydreaming.

"Get your hands off me, boy!" the guard roared, smacking the small child several feet back, the boy's teeth flying everywhere.

The guard moved to kick the fallen boy, but instead he found his wrist wrapped in an impossibly tight grip.

I wish I could pretend I didn't see anything, Alistair thought to himself, though deep down he knew that wasn't true. That fact about him aside, he was in trouble. He didn't imagine a guard who had gotten used to bossing thousands of people around would take his move very well.

"What the fuck?" the guard exclaimed, struggling to break free. Alistair let go right away, hoping that the guard would think his abnormal strength was a fluke. "What do you think you're doing, peasant?"

7 PORT LOCASTA

PEASANT? Alistair thought. Are we really already at that stage?

Alistair let all his pride fall to the wayside and put on the most obsequious act in his life.

"I'm sorry, sir, it was not my intent to touch you," Alistair pleaded. "Please forgive me and the boy for our actions." At the same time he used **[Eyes of Truth]** on the man, trusting there was no way his high Intelligence would allow him to be caught.

Name: Matthew Langford
Species: Superhuman I (Partially Evolved)
Level: 29
Class: Warrior [Primary Attributes: Strength and Constitution]

The guard eyed him suspiciously. He probably would have already acted if he wasn't still questioning why a level 15 man could have grabbed him so fast. Alistair guessed the guard had already inspected him, finding no information because of the vast gap in their Intelligence. He already had a convenient lie to explain the missing information if Langford asked.

"The reason I stepped in was because I have a Prophet Class," Alistair fibbed. "I felt a confluence of Fate. The boy has an unusually weak constitution, and another blow would have killed him. I knew you wouldn't want the blood of a young child on your hands, so I interfered. If my explanation is insufficient, I understand and will seek shelter elsewhere."

Langford looked incredulous at the idea he could have killed the boy, which was admittedly something Alistair just made up, but it sounded believable since the boy was so frail.

The man was about to say something, and through the threads of Fate Alistair saw there was a chance he would attack. It was good for all their sakes that future didn't come true—instead his partner pulled him aside and told him something. After a few seconds of hushed conversation, Langford turned back to him.

"Why is your Class unavailable? You can't be more than level 15. I know my Intelligence isn't the highest, but there's no way it could be multiple times lower than yours."

"Ah, apologies, sir. My Class restricts others from seeing any information about me," Alistair said, hoping that his excuse would work.

"I'm going to need some proof of what you claim." Langford manifested a single Gold drachma from his pocket. He tossed it in the air and caught it, then flipped it onto his other arm. "Heads or tails? If you're a Prophet, you should be able to answer that, no?"

Alistair honestly didn't know too much about the details of the Class he was impersonating, just that they could see into the future. So he didn't know if being able to predict near-term actions was an ability the Class possessed—all he knew was that Prophets were coveted for their more long-term Fate prognostication.

Unfortunately for Alistair, he didn't react in time to use [Eyes of Truth], and his natural Karmic vision was tied to his [Fighter's Instinct], so it was much less effective at seeing the future of non-combat related events. However, Alistair's dynamic visual acuity was good enough that he caught what side the coin landed on without using a single Skill.

"Tails," he answered confidently.

The guard repeated the test five more times to make sure Alistair didn't just happen to get lucky in the first instance. After he was satisfied with Alistair's performance, he tapped on the gate, causing it to disappear instantly. Langford and his companion stared at the other refugees, daring them to try breaking in while the gate was up.

"Since it's late, the registry will be closed, but bright and early tomorrow, you better notify your presence to the authorities. I'll be calling you in to the

Locasta Elite, and if I don't see you on the lists by noon the next day, it's your head on a spike. What's your name, Prophet?"

Alistair panicked, unable to think of a fake name. "Alistair Danger."

"Danger?" Langford questioned, raising an eyebrow.

"Alistair Dangierre," he repeated, this time saying "Danger" with a pseudo-French accent. "It's French."

Langford still looked suspicious, but he didn't make any moves, keeping the gate open for Alistair. Instead of entering, Alistair turned back to look at the family who had just been turned away. The mother had her son in her arms, nursing him while he cried, while the father looked down in impotent rage, knowing that he could do nothing but watch.

Alistair wanted to pay for their passage, but he knew doing so would cause a massive incident. Everyone else would swarm him and ask for money after seeing his generosity. It would be hard to turn them all down, or at least not be forced to reveal himself and tell them they could have lodging in the Northeast Freehold. So, he did nothing. He promised to himself that he would help them as soon as he could.

With a heavy heart, he walked into Port Locasta. The town bustled with energy even at night, the streets filled with people. He understood why they were turning people down. Usually, extra hands would have offset the cost of food and water, but the town was basically full. Alistair spotted new construction in the distance, but it wasn't enough, since everywhere he went was uncomfortably crowded.

Most of the buildings looked like medieval inns, except the signs were neon, creating a weird atmosphere that melded the modern and ancient. It looked like many people were keen to forget about their problems based on the number of bars and clubs he passed by.

That did make him consider the morality of having those kinds of establishments when there were people starving on the outside. Couldn't they turn them into shelters for people? It seemed unfair that there were people who had the privilege of going to a bar while others died in the wilderness.

Alistair walked by most of them without paying too much attention, but there was one bar that piqued his interest. He had been exploring the town for around fifteen minutes when he found it, a small tavern called The Boar Head. It was less crowded than the other establishments, but what interested Alistair were the strong auras he felt inside. One level 30, for sure, and then a bunch that had to be in the high 20s.

The Boar Head had a Wild West style saloon door and was open to all. Yet despite it not being as crowded as the other establishments, hardly anyone entered. Were the customers of The Boar Head limited to Port Locasta elites only?

Alistair started walking across the street, intent on seeing what the fuss was about, when he felt a hand on his shoulder.

"I wouldn't do that if I were you," a female voice warned him. "You must be new here."

Alistair turned around, seeing the top of the head of a young woman. *Oh yeah*, he thought. *I'm at least four inches taller now, so I'm not used to looking down so much.* The girl who stopped him looked to be around his age, standing just under five feet tall with dyed pink hair. Alistair thought most would find her pretty, but she wasn't his type. Her entire outfit was pink, not just her hair, including a pink sweatshirt and sweatpants, along with a pink winter hat.

"Yes, I just got here today," Alistair answered.

"That explains it. I saw you gunning for it, but there's a reason The Boar Head is half-full when every other bar and inn is practically overflowing. It's for Locasta Elite only," she said matter-of-factly.

"Oh, I see," Alistair said. "But they wouldn't kill me or anything?"

"What do you think we are, lawless savages? Of course they wouldn't kill you, but Jared is known for being rough on people who interrupt his peace. It's just a bad idea to stick your nose where you don't belong. Those guys exist in an entirely different universe to us." She looked at him more closely. "What's your name?"

"Alistair Dangierre," he replied, saying his pseudonym with confidence this time.

"Alistair," she repeated. "That's a cool name. I'm Melody Waters. Why don't you come party with me and my friends?"

———

Alistair debated with himself whether he should go several times over. He wasn't in a rush to clear the serpent horde. They were nocturnal and had a pattern of emerging once a week, so he had four more days until anyone was in danger. He had planned to gather information on Port Locasta and the serpent horde, along with the Maine Brothers and anything else that might come up. He would then finish off the serpent horde tomorrow, returning home right after that.

He wasn't in a time crunch, so taking a couple hours off wasn't an issue. The only problem would be if his heart and soul felt wrong. Technically, every second that he wasn't out in the field, an innocent person was dying. That was a fact. He could save even more lives if he spent his every waking moment running through forests and towns hunting for people to rescue. But that was no way to live. Alistair had a strong will, but even he couldn't keep that up for long. It wasn't human. Everyone needed breaks and relaxation. Paradoxically, *not* having periods of rest might harm his long-term potential.

Alistair would make sure his time with Melody and her friends was productive, however. His control of ambient Mana was growing, so even though the amount of Mana required to level up increased, the time it took to level up plateaued because he could absorb more Mana into his soulcore. He would spend the entire night absorbing Mana, cycling it through his meridians. Over time, he had also grown more efficient in his cycling, finding the best patterns to break down the tough meridian walls. The more his meridians expanded, the more Mana he could use for his Skills, increasing their effectiveness. For the time being, his ambient Mana absorption leveled him up faster than killing monsters.

On top of his Mana absorption, he also could use Melody and her friends for information. Her aura was that of around a level 15, so about average for the general population. But he wanted to know more about what it was like for the average Joe, especially one that was outside of his protection.

"What's with the long face?" Melody asked, as they made it to The Walking Tree club.

"Aren't we supposed to meet your friends?" Alistair asked. Apparently, The Walking Tree was one of the best spots in the town, offering special cultivator drugs along with psychedelic Mana lighting. It was remarkable how not even two months into the initiation, someone had set up a facility like that. Alistair admired how strong the human need to party was.

"They're inside, silly," Melody said. "C'mon, let's go."

The Walking Tree was carved on the inside of a two-hundred-meter-tall giant oak tree that was as thick as a normal building. Alistair had received reports that some flora and fauna had undergone extreme mutation, just like the monster hordes, and he guessed this tree was one example.

Two large rectangular windows offered a small glimpse of the revelry taking place inside. They were tinted, but Alistair still saw strobing lights and smoke. The music was so loud that it already vibrated his eardrums. Nothing bothered him more than loud noises, but at least now any damage wouldn't be permanent.

Groups of people conglomerated all around the trunk, nearly climbing over each other to get in. Alistair didn't see any security, so there must have been some other way they let people in. As far as he could tell, there wasn't even an entrance.

"How do you even get in?" Alistair wondered aloud.

"They let you in sometimes, if there's space, or if you're a VIP," Melody explained. "But we have reservations."

She went up to a bare spot on the trunk and tapped it three times. After a second, a human-sized door appeared, growing from the bottom. Melody walked right in, though Alistair had to duck his head. Behind him, dozens of people ran to get in through her entrance before it closed. In the end, only four strangers managed to outrace the temporary doorway.

As soon as they went inside, the music started blasting Alistair's ears. Even with his Constitution, it still was kind of annoying. On the dance floor, people were going crazy like there was no tomorrow. Strobing Mana lights filled the room, washing everyone in mystic light. It was beautiful to look at, the way everyone's skin changed from orange to pink to red in quick succession. A mist blanketed the space as well, light but omnipresent, suffusing everything in the vicinity. Alistair sensed a strange psychedelic property to the mist, similar to the juices of the Herax Turtle he had once journeyed inside.

Not wanting to take any chances, Alistair lightly flared his aura, forming a protective layer around his skin. He hoped Melody would be too busy to notice. Strangely, he saw the mist bounce off her too, though it wasn't an aura that protected her, as far as he could see. Perhaps it was something to do with her Class. He could probably get away with using [Eyes of Truth] on her, but it was improper manners and he couldn't get away with it on higher leveled cultivators. He wanted to treat everyone with respect, not just those with power.

Melody grabbed his hand. "Let's go dance!"

Alistair followed her lead, snaking through crowds of people. Clubbing wasn't really his thing, though he'd gone before and had some fun. Melody clearly was having a ton of fun, going wild like the others. Funnily enough, Alistair had become an expert dancer without even realizing it due to his top-tier Agility and knowledge of martial arts. After gathering up some courage, he tried some moves that wowed the crowd.

This isn't so bad, Alistair thought to himself. *Maybe I should have gone out more before the initiation.* Or maybe not, he amended, since his Agility had been nothing like this. If you knew you were good at something, it was hard to feel out of place, since you always had your skills to fall back on.

"Where did that come from?" Melody asked, laughing. "You struck me as more of the quiet type."

"Really?" Alistair tried laying on the charm. While the system didn't confirm that Charisma worked at increasing charm, he thought it had some impact. Or maybe that was a byproduct of accumulating positive Karma. "I bet I could surprise you. Why do you think I'm here in Port Locasta?"

"I don't know," Melody shouted over the music. "Your clothes are in bad shape, so I assume you were looking for shelter and a safer region."

Alistair had forgotten that his robe and Anthony's combined to form a black tattered cloak, making him look quite poor.

"I'm going to go after the serpent hordes," Alistair claimed. "I heard they killed a bunch of people."

"You?" Melody asked incredulously. "You know how powerful they are, right? They're level 30-plus giant snakes with a leader that's reached Beast Lord territory."

"Beast Lord?" Alistair asked.

"You haven't heard of that? A Beast Lord is one of the stages of evolution for beasts, similar to how we have realms of advancement in cultivation," Melody explained. "They become almost identical past the Visionary realm equivalent, but beasts start in a very different place from humans. The Beast Lord is basically the stage when they gain sentience."

"They all grow sentient at level 30?" Alistair asked, though he thought to himself that she really meant sapient. "That's crazy. Isn't that a really low barrier? On other planets they're just full of intelligent beasts?"

"I think it depends on how strong the initial species is, but I'm no expert."

"It must suck," Alistair remarked.

"Huh?"

"Well, if the leader of the serpent horde recently became a Beast Lord, I assume that means the others aren't. Imagine how lonely they are, just waiting for another one of their kind to talk to."

"I didn't think about it like that," Melody said, wearing her confusion clear on her face. "Don't tell me you're feeling sorry for them, though. They killed thousands of people."

"I know they have to be eradicated, especially if their leader is knowingly harming humans," Alistair said. "But there's nuance in everything. You can be firm in your actions, yet have compassion nonetheless."

"What are you, some kind of monk?" Melody asked. A shade of mischief entered her eyes as she looked down at his arm. "I thought monks weren't supposed to... you know."

"Know what?"

Melody made a jerking motion and pointed to his left arm. "Though it must have been hard to have done it so much that instead of your arm growing, it shrunk."

Alistair grew bright red as he realized what Melody was implying. Besides embarrassment, he was surprised that she could even see that it was smaller, since his cloak covered much of his arm. "That's not what happened."

"It's called a joke. Lighten up a bit, Alistair," Melody said. "Hey, it's my friend! Jason!"

Alistair turned his head, looking in the direction Melody waved. He expected it to be hard to find Melody's friend in the crowd of people, but to his surprise, the mass of people had parted. Walking through the divide was the tallest man Alistair had ever seen, a giant standing over seven feet tall and muscled like a disproportionate comic book character. He was shirtless, wore golden dragonscale shorts, and carried a two-meter-long axe on his back.

"Melody!" he exclaimed, so loud that his voice temporarily overpowered the music. "I missed you! Who is this?"

8 CAREN LOCASTA

As soon as Alistair saw Jason the giant, the gears started turning in his head. The powerful aura of the large man breached the soulcore stage, so he was at least level 30. Why would a mere level 15 be friends with such a powerful being?

Alistair took a step back and re-evaluated everything that had happened. He knew he wasn't in any danger since his [Fighter's Instinct] was completely inert and his understanding of Fate read nothing, but that didn't mean Melody hadn't misled him.

There were a couple of strange occurrences that meant little by themselves, but when put together told a different story. Melody entered the Walking Tree with just a touch of her hand and could resist the psychedelic mist with an unknown method; she knew a lot about Beast Lords and was attentive enough to notice that his partially covered left arm was 20% smaller than his right; and she just happened be at the very right place to stop him from going to the bar that the Locasta Elite frequented.

Jason picked up Melody and twirled her around, their over two-foot height difference making it look like a father picking up his toddler. She laughed with delight as he threw her in the air. Alistair wasn't sure if the crowd recognized them and this was a regular occurrence, or they were just giving them a large berth because of the man's physique and obvious power.

"Who are you really?" he asked Melody as soon as Jason put her down. "Why bring me here?"

"Couldn't I ask the same for you? Why are you in a disguise, Alistair Dangierre? And the reason I brought you here is the reason I gave you before. To have fun, duh."

No one said anything for a couple of awkward seconds. Alistair considered his options, but Melody was the one who acted first.

"Fine. I'm one of the Locasta Elite, alright?" Melody admitted. "I got the message from Langford about a Prophet coming in, so I tailed you. I noticed you were using a disguise, and when I looked very carefully at your aura, it seemed too perfect for that of a level 15. So I decided to stop you and take you out on a little adventure." She sternly crossed her arms. "Now your turn."

Alistair sighed internally. His disguise had been seen through as soon as he entered Port Locasta. It wasn't like he'd spent more than a thousand drachma on the mask, but he still hoped it would be at least somewhat effective. If he wanted actual anonymity, he would have to employ something more impressive.

In terms of revealing information to Melody, he wasn't sure what to say. In the end, he decided to go with the truth. His infiltration had failed, but it would serve as a teaching lesson for the next time.

"I'm Alistair Tan," he said. "The majority shareholder of the Northeast Order Freehold and #2 ranked person in the world."

Alistair undid his restraints, letting his Mana flow freely. The surrounding air warped slightly as his relatively pure Mana, compressed inside of him, escaped out. He didn't find it anything special, but those around him disagreed. Melody and even Jason jumped back a little, and the once-jovial partygoers started to flee the building.

"Alistair Tan, as in *that* Alistair, oh my god—" Melody started saying.

Jason looked at him with a new, competitive glance, holding out his buff arm for a handshake. "Well met, Alistair. Shall we shake hands?"

Alistair obliged the giant, since he also wanted to see how his Strength compared. The man clearly had a Strength-based Class and perhaps some special Talent or other unknown factor.

Both parties started out with a relatively weak grip, though still strong enough to crush the hands of any ordinary person. As Jason put more and more of his Strength into the grip, Alistair did the same. Melody, who had recovered from her temporary shock, looked at them like they were childish idiots. Alistair eventually found himself outmatched, and right before he reached his limit, he backed down.

"You're stronger than me," Alistair admitted, a mischievous idea popping into his head.

He [Dashed] behind Jason, using the flicker aspect and a drop of his Ghost Node. He could see all three of his Nodes clearly now as balls of Dao energy within his soulcore.

On the other side, he reached up and tapped Jason's massive shoulders. "Good job."

Jason started turning around when he felt the tap, but by the time the giant had swiveled, Alistair was already back to where he was before. Melody had unleashed her true aura too, which burgeoned to just under the soulcore level. He guessed she was at level 28 or 29, similar to the Langford guard. Eventually, almost everyone on the planet would pass the soulcore stage, since the usual bottleneck for civilians was level 60. But if she didn't have the talent for it, it could take many years.

"I'm sorry for the deception," Alistair said. "I didn't want to create a commotion. And I sort of just wanted to practice being incognito, too. In truth, I just came here for temporary lodging and information on the serpent horde. I'm not trying to invade you guys or anything."

"You know, no one was talking about invasion," Melody said. "You're making yourself sound worse. Let's go see Caren. He's going to want to hear about this."

"That sounds good. I don't want there to be any friction between us," Alistair said.

Jason gave a hearty laugh, a powerful bellow that sounded as deep as the ocean. "Nothing is certain except death, yet I think we shall get along fine."

———

Alistair absorbed enough Mana and reached level 37 along the way to Caren's citadel. He still had a couple more in him before his progression flat-lined. He put the two of the free points into Constitution and one into Endurance—his two worst stats—bringing them 114 and 113 respectively.

He contemplated his current arsenal as he sought for ways to improve his foundations and remove as many blind spots as possible. However, at the moment, he felt like his kit was pretty broken. There wasn't much he could do except continue leveling up and locking in his affinities; his path was currently clear.

Others might have stronger individual Classes, Skills, or Dao, but his combination was almost unstoppable. His stats were crazy high thanks to his Subclass and triple Dao Nodes, especially his Agility. Add his flicker [Dash] that made him invisible and allowed him to go in the opposite direction he was facing, and he was completely unpredictable. Plus, he could use the Dao of the Ghost to pass through solid objects. He had his Karmic vision and Fate-reading, which allowed him two seconds of muddy precognition, along with [Hand of Karma], that could temporarily give spells of bad luck and deactivate meridians. And even without any Skills, he had his hand-to-hand combat, bolstered by his Kai'tazake Mutra trance. All of that, and he hadn't even mentioned Dev'rox or his extra spatially-attuned Mana reserves.

Everything in his arsenal synergized together, except one thing: his [Void Beckoning]. It was a decent selection at the time, but now he couldn't infuse it with any of his Dao Nodes, making it much weaker. It worked against physical objects, but Alistair didn't have a weakness to physical attacks in the first place. If anything, physical resistance was one of his strengths. He'd needed it for a long-range option in the past, but now he had [Phase Shift], which he had used for long-distance attacks on numerous occasions. With the next step of choosing affinities, he would fully rectify the problem.

Cultivators had three options to gain Skills under the Pathfinder's guidance. One was to upgrade an old Skill into a new Skill, either on its own or by combining it with another. The second was to create it from scratch entirely, usually by incorporating an untrodden aspect of your Class or Dao. The final way was to receive it, either via a leaf of a Talent Tree or a Quest reward, or through purchasing it. Unlike with Badges, Skills had no limit to their number, though after a certain point, like items, they would start losing their effectiveness if you had too many for your current self to handle. The limit in Foundation was fifteen, giving Alistair five more Skills before reaching the soft cap. At his level, the fall-off for both items and Skills was extremely steep, giving ample incentive to stay under the restriction.

Perhaps with [Phase Shift], he could develop techniques that utilized blood, ice, and lightning. Since [Phase Shift] was borne out of convenience, he expected the separate Skills to be even more powerful.

Speaking of Skills, or things like them, Alistair still had to research *nue*, or killing intent, and the ten'gatsu, the masking of attacks using Dao energy, Mana, and *nue*. He had a feeling that there was more to *nue* than just using one's killing intent to freeze an enemy. But he also didn't want to spread himself too thin. He had expanded his arsenal a lot already, and maybe *nue* could wait.

"We're here," he heard Melody say, interrupting his thoughts.

Alistair was impressed by the crystal palace, which looked like it was made of diamonds. He wondered if Caren got it as a Quest reward, since he hadn't seen the material in the System Store or Land Store. The diamond bricks contained even more of a protective presence than valyrik, the highest quality substance he could buy in bulk.

The citadel stood over thirty meters high in the center of the town, a spire making up a third of that height and reaching up to the high heavens. A moat made of red water surrounded the building, emanating a spooky aura that reminded Alistair of his own ghostly presence. While the moat would defend against lesser beings, it was short enough that anyone with decent stats could simply jump over it, making him wonder what it was there for.

He wouldn't get to know, at least not yet, since when Melody walked up to it, a bridge made of the same diamond material formed out of nowhere. Instead of going down to the sapphire crystal door that Alistair presumed was the main entrance, it went up all the way to a bulge at the top of the spire. It looked like they were being fast-tracked to Caren's personal residence.

"Oh," Melody remarked. "He doesn't do that for just anyone. We'd best hurry, he needs to get to bed soon."

Alistair was curious about that remark, since he knew Caren had to be at least level 30. At that point, you barely needed any sleep to survive, no more than four hours a night.

The three of them scurried up the bridge, which now looked more like a staircase than a tilted strip of land. Horizontal steps emerged so they wouldn't fall, but the climb was still steeper than 45 degrees.

It would have only taken Alistair a little over two seconds to reach the top, but he slowed down to allow Jason and Melody to keep up. Jason was as slow as his burly body indicated, but Melody fared just as badly. Not a Strength or Agility-based cultivator then, Alistair thought. Based on her keen perception, he guessed she was in the Intelligence or Wisdom category.

Alistair looked down at the ground as they approached the apex. He had never been a big fan of heights—just seeing the perspective of someone rock climbing made his palms sweaty. That fear was muted now, and he wondered if he would survive if he jumped off.

The staircase led into an open window at the top of the spire. There was a large room fit for a princess at the top of the castle, fancifully decorated with all manner of crystals. The path narrowed at the window, forcing them to go single file. Melody went first, followed by Jason, and finally Alistair.

"You can come in," a soft voice said from inside the room.

As they entered the room, it became apparent it was less of a bedchamber and more of a library. There were books strewn about everywhere—on the floor, floating in the air, and in massive bookcases.

A slight, brown-haired man waved his hands, orchestrating the motion of the books around him. He would glance at something for a second, then wave his hands and send it away to be replaced by a new book. Despite his tan skin, there was something about him that suggested he hadn't seen the light of day in years.

Alistair sensed that the man's aura was the strongest of anyone he had met in Port Locasta, exceeding Jason's, yet it wasn't anywhere close to his own. While he didn't expect any hostility, if it came down to a fight, Alistair could crush all three of them without even needing to use his injured left arm.

"So you're the Alistair I've heard so much about," said the man who he presumed was Caren. "Slayer of Anthony Ricci and 3rd place in Felons vs. Fellows." Caren waved his arms and an ornate wooden chair flew from the other side of his bed to directly behind Alistair. "Please, sit."

Alistair obliged, finding the seat far comfier than its hard appearance. Jason and Melody bowed their heads to Caren but remained standing.

Caren conjured his own chair, of much worse build quality than Alistair's. He wondered if Caren was trying to show his deference and proper manners by giving him a better seat. No matter what happened, Alistair expected a better relationship with this neighbor than Anthony.

"How do you know about that?" Alistair asked. He didn't realize his escapades were public knowledge. He had disguised himself as an extra precaution, but he didn't actually expect to be recognized.

"Word travels fast. Not as fast without the internet, but still fast. I have my own methods of divination that give me an edge, but the various information brokers that have set up shop across the world are slowly catching up. I saw you on Faxor as well. Because my team failed in the second round, I broke my token to escape. But a day after it ended, they informed all participants from Earth who made it to the final round. That means you, Anthony, and Carmen are globally renowned. Well, I suppose just you and Carmen now."

"You're some kind of... book cultivator?" Alistair asked, realizing that each book surrounding Caren contained a tiny piece of the Dao.

"Indeed," Caren confirmed. "The reason Port Locasta avoided conquest from Anthony was because I sold him valuable information at a discount. I must thank you for removing that scourge from the world." He paused. "What brings you to my town, Alistair? You didn't have to sneak in. We would have welcomed you with open arms."

"You should mention that to your guard, Langford," Alistair retorted with a snort. "He seems to be fine with slapping young kids so hard they lose teeth."

Caren paled at hearing that. "I'll... talk with him. I posted rougher guards than before because the old ones had overgenerous hearts, letting in more than we could handle. Port Locasta doesn't control much farmland, and we don't have many strong cultivators. If I accept any more people, our current denizens will starve to death."

Alistair nodded. He thought as much, and had a solution for that, but that could wait for a moment.

Caren continued. "I must say, I'm surprised to hear that you were at one of our entertainment establishments. I thought you would be heading straight back to fight more monsters. That's the impression I received from hearing of your escapades."

"My plan was to spend only a few hours here in the first place," Alistair said, defending himself. "My cultivation hasn't slowed down at all since I'm always passively absorbing Mana. After that, I was going to head straight to killing the serpent horde. Also, why do you even have so many clubs if you actually care about people starving? Couldn't you turn them into places for sheltering people and growing food?"

"You're more balanced than I realized," Caren said. "And I ask you not to pass judgment before you know the full story. We *are* using those places as residences, many sleep inside of them after a strict curfew at 1 AM. Since most people only need six hours to sleep now, it's not a big deal. Those lights you saw in The Walking Tree are different types of special fruits we're growing."

"Oh, that's my bad," Alistair conceded. "So back to the topic at hand. I assume you want the serpent horde gone as well?"

"I do," Caren said. "I was planning to contact you about this before you even showed up. Those snakes have killed more people in these lands than the monster waves. I shall even give you a reward if you manage to succeed."

"A reward?" Alistair asked.

"I think so. If you successfully clear the serpents, I'll join your freehold."

"What?" Melody exclaimed. "Are you serious?"

"I've explained to you, dear, we cannot hold on for much longer. The monsters and beasts grow at a faster pace than our elites, and we're hemorrhaging food. I suspect this to be the machinations of the Final Frontier Empire, adjusting the strength of our foes so that we remain on the brink of survival, unless we join a greater power. They want all the power consolidated into the hands of a few."

Alistair sensed that needing to defeat the serpent horde before they joined was all but a formality—the Northeast Freehold already had all the leverage. Even if he straight-up refused to eradicate the beasts, they didn't have many options. The Maine Brothers were just over twice as large as Port Locasta and were probably facing similar problems. Caren knew this as well, and based on his previous statements, he also knew Alistair's personality. Caren was confident Alistair wouldn't betray or scam them in any way. It was true, of course, but Alistair was starting to grow concerned that others could abuse his image as a goody two-shoes.

"I accept your terms," Alistair said. "I was going to kill the horde anyway, but thanks for the extra incentive. If you want, I can send a message through the Soulnet asking for provisions for you guys."

The Soulnet had developed to the point where there were people who made decent amounts of drachma acting as couriers. All you had to do was tell them where your message needed to go and they would send it. It was important to find one with a good reputation, however, since it was easy to get scammed.

"I would appreciate that," Caren said. "We'll venture out before the crack of dawn. In the meantime, I must enter into slumber. Tomorrow, I shall come with you, along with the Locasta Elite, and we'll vanquish those serpents."

9 THE SERPENT HORDE

Since they would set out hunting the serpents at 5 AM, Alistair took a cue from Caren and spent the next six hours sleeping. He learned from Melody that Port Locasta's ruler needed ten hours of shut-eye per night because of his prodigious brainpower. His mind was so active during his waking hours that it needed more time to cool off.

Melody set Alistair up in one of their finest guest lodgings, a colonial-style house that most would have called a mansion in the old world. Alistair entered and immediately plopped into bed. He needed almost no sleep to survive, three hours being more than enough for him to feel more rested than eight hours did before he started cultivating. However, that didn't mean more sleep was useless—if he had infinite time, he still would have chosen a full night's sleep. Since he was still recovering from his injuries, the slumber would be even more effective.

Before he tucked in for the night, he activated **[Carmela's Happy Pies]** again. His body could feel that the previous one had worn off, so he grabbed his nightstand and converted it into a magical apple pie with his new Skill. It felt weird using the Skill, since he temporarily gained the knowledge of how to turn wood and paint into food—knowledge that would then disappear again after the Skill completed. He chowed down on the pie as soon as it was ready, basking in the current of healing energy.

"Are you fully recovered, Dev'rox?" Alistair asked as he wolfed on his dessert.

"Just about," Dev'rox replied. "I almost spent myself helping you, so it's impressive I'm healing so fast. I think it has to do with your progress."

"Huh? How does me progressing faster help you? So if I become Visionary, will you also break through to Visionary? "

"Brat, I don't know everything about ghost cultivation," Dev'rox said. "But from the little I *do* know, ghosts are more tied to the cultivator than vice versa. If I get soulkilled, your cultivation will barely be hampered, whereas if you progress, I'll gain the trickle-down benefits."

"You're not going to die," Alistair promised. He mused on what Dev'rox told him further. "It seems like ghost cultivation is broken, then. That's what Nenna Spindoller said, too. I can borrow the power of beings far beyond myself, and even if stuff happens to them, I'm fine. How is that fair?"

"All paths to the peak have their strengths and weaknesses. The Dao is the Dao," Dev'rox said, as if reciting a sutra. "Nenna meant in comparison to the standard path; the path that gets you to Adept and not much further. Everyone at the peak has advantages. Ghost cultivation is rare, but spatial cultivation is just as uncommon. I suppose Karmic cultivation is also on that level too, but I don't want to feed your ego. Time cultivation and emotional cultivation are even more rare than any I've mentioned. Ghost cultivation won't enhance your body, mind, or soul, but lets you borrow power. It comes at the cost of slowing down your own cultivation if you use it too much. And if you become reliant on the path of another, it will seep into your path, causing irrevocable ruin to your foundations. It's often known as a quick ticket to power that produces middling scions."

Alistair considered the mention of his body, mind, and soul. The only venture he'd made into the Pathfinder AI's trees for those three qualities was the Metabolism leaf of the Heart Branch, which let him replace bodily functions, such as breathing, with Mana. From what he understood, the body was governed by the physical stats of Strength, Agility, Constitution, and Endurance; the mind was governed by Intelligence and Wisdom (and possibly *nue*, but he hadn't figured that out entirely); and the soul was governed by Intelligence, Wisdom, and the Dao.

Because of his incredible all-around stats, he felt like he didn't need any of the special benefits to his body, mind, or soul. Even if he didn't put any Upgrade Points into those Talent Trees, his trifecta of the self would still grow. But he had a feeling that the types of cultivation Dev'rox mentioned offered unique guides or benefits that stats alone couldn't reach.

"How does a type of cultivation distinguish itself enough to get a name?" he asked as he tucked himself into bed and closed his eyes. "If I just started meddling with my soulcore, could I create Alistair cultivation?"

"I'm not entirely sure. It might be that the Heavens themselves conse-crated certain aspects of cultivation. What I am sure of is that if you wanted 'meddling with your soulcore' to be anything comparable to ghost or blood cultivation, you'd need to reach the peak of the multiverse by practicing that method."

"Okay, thanks for the advice, Dev'rox," Alistair said, starting to nod off. "You know, you never talk about yourself."

"What is there to talk about?" Dev'rox said, barely louder than a whisper. "We are allies of convenience. Humans are the prized creation of Heaven while demons are the scourge of existence. You shall complete the compact binding us together, and I shall disappear down to the depths of the Asura Hell, never to see you again. In all likelihood, I will never reach Visionary and my soul will eventually wither away from the ravages of time, and you will never fly beyond Adept or Profound, and die after less than a hundred thousand years of life."

"No," Alistair said.

"No?"

"You'll reach Visionary... I'll make it to the peak of the multiverse... promise."

———

What a fool, Dev'rox thought. The boy had potential. He'd seen it with his own eyes—powerful Fate beyond that of an ordinary Foundation realm—even without Karmic sight or Fate-divination, he could feel that. But poten-tial wasn't enough to make it to the insurmountable peak that Dev'rox hadn't even seen a sliver of. In the frontier, Visionary was the most one could realistically aspire to, and the chance of making it there was one in every hundred trillion. They simply lacked the qualifications, the heritage and Dao history. Alistair was still far from the trajectory of those era-defining geniuses who escaped the frontier.

Yet...why did Dev'rox feel a spark of hope, a hope that he thought had died out thousands of years ago?

"I believe you," Dev'rox said, half a truth and half a lie. He continued with a sigh. "Demons aren't like you humans. We don't have mothers or fathers. Like the divine progeny, we manifest from concentrations of spiritual energy. Each brood is assigned a spawnlord to raise it. Mine was Zalarik the Wise, an Abyssal Ruler of the..."

Dev'rox noticed that the human was sound asleep. It was good for the boy, but deep down, he hated it whenever Alistair slept. It meant Dev'rox would be alone again.

———

Alistair woke up feeling beyond refreshed, from both his good night of sleep and his pies. He moved his left arm around, satisfied with his level of recovery. The fact that it had only been five days since his arm was a burnt stick was crazy.

The first light of dawn still hid behind the horizon, so he knew he had woken up in time. Alistair was surprised when Caren himself showed up to the guest house a few minutes later, ringing the doorbell to announce his arrival.

"You've made all your necessary preparations?" Caren asked.

"Yep, I'm all good," Alistair replied. Everything he needed for combat he kept on his person at all times. You never knew when a fight was going down.

"Perfect. I've decided to keep the team small, so as to not get in your way. We'll be acting primarily as support."

Caren clapped his hands, and thousands of pages of paper flew out of his billowing robes. There was no way that he could actually fit that much paper on his person, so he was either creating the pages out of thin air or had a dimensional storage Skill, like Oliver. The pages had glowing blue runes on them, and they conglomerated into a small canoe capable of seating around ten people.

"This thing is safe?" Alistair questioned, poking the paper.

"It's how I got here," Caren said, looking a little surprised that Alistair was concerned about the safety of his vehicle. "I picked you up first. We have to collect the rest of the Elite and then we'll be off. I thought it would be better to fly together in this than to run separately. Not everyone is the most physically gifted."

"Very well," Alistair said, trying to regain his dignity. "Along the way, I'd also appreciate it if you gave me any intel you have."

———

Caren guided his paper boat to the houses of the Locasta Elite. Alistair expected them to be palatial like Caren's crystal palace, but to his surprise, they were around the same size as normal suburban houses. The first stop was at a larger house that four elites shared as roommates. They picked up Melody and Jason before moving on to a nearby house inhabited by a treeman.

When Alistair said treeman, he really meant it. If he didn't know any better, he would have assumed the newcomer was a treant monster sent by the Pathfinder AI and not a human. His skin had become gnarled bark, his hair turned into leaves, and even his gait had become sturdy and tree-like.

"This is Bark-Al," Caren said, introducing the two of them. Bark-Al offered up his barky hand, which Alistair accepted. "The second strongest in Port Locasta after me."

"If you didn't counter me, I'd win," Bark-Al grumbled. "Your very Class necessitates the slaughter of my people."

Alistair wasn't sure who was correct in the squabble, but Bark-Al did have an aura comparable to that of Caren and was certainly in the soulcore stage. There was something unique about Bark-Al's aura compared to anyone he had met before, however. The only person that felt similar was perhaps Kaesa Lansfeld, the murderous Warrior he had defeated in the ocean during the final round of Felons vs. Fellows. Her orange aura had been palpably warlike.

After Bark-Al hopped on board, they took off for the clouds, gaining altitude until they floated around a kilometer in the air. Caren ruffled through some floating papers, calculating the correct path. After a few seconds, they started accelerating until they reached a speed of around a hundred kilometers an hour. Slower than Alistair's most conservative jogging speed, but probably faster than anyone with an Agility less than 100. If it was one of your dump stats, you might not have 100 Agility even at Alistair's level.

He'd only reached 100 in all Attributes with the assistance of an overpowered Badge.

Before Alistair could even say anything, Bark-Al spoke in a deep voice that sounded like an ancient tree.

"You wish to know how I came to be—am I correct?" he asked, looking at Alistair.

"If it's not too personal, I would," Alistair answered honestly.

"It is of no consequence," Bark-Al said. "I was once an old man who tended to trees. My family died during the initiation, and all I had left were my beautiful trees. The arboreal path led me to a new life and a new purpose. My body, mind, and soul are unified by the almighty tree. Once an elder tree, I have been reborn as a sapling. As my Class continues to progress, I will one day leave this inefficient form and become a thousand-mile-tall Immortal Oak."

Alistair had never before met someone so dedicated to their path. Even he wasn't so inveterate in his path of the Fist, or the Ghost, or even Justice. That was another potential area he could shore up, though he doubted that one could just *choose* to gain dedication. It had to come naturally, or else it wouldn't offer any real insight to the Dao.

"Don't let his harmless appearance fool you," Melody said. "What level do you think he is?"

"31?" Alistair guessed.

"Wrong," she said, shaking her head. "He's level 23, yet he's already formed two Dao Nodes."

"What?" Alistair exclaimed. "That's possible?"

"I scarcely believed it myself," Caren said, "but a tree moves as a tree wills. He levels up at a far slower pace than us, yet his insights are as deep as the foundation of a mighty oak."

"You have no qualifications to speak of oak trees, paper man," Bark-Al spat.

Alistair honestly couldn't tell if Bark-Al and Caren had real enmity because of their rival Classes or if they were good friends playing around. Most likely a combination of both.

Their destination was only fifty kilometers away, so they weren't in the air for long. Looking at his companions, he couldn't help but feel like the Locastans were a strange bunch. There was Caren, the eccentric paper mage;

Jason, the overly formal giant; and Bark-Al, a weird human-tree hybrid. Melody seemed like the only normal one.

Caren explained their specialties so they could formulate a game plan. To Alistair's surprise, Jason Evandikis used to be a normal-sized human before the initiation. He underwent a special Quest soon after and received Cthonic ancestry as a reward. Apparently, ancestry was an inherited trait passed down from generation to generation that offered special bonuses to cultivation. It differed from bloodlines in that ancestries came from changes in DNA (or whatever equivalent the myriad of species of the multiverse possessed), while bloodlines originated from alterations in the Dao blueprint and soul.

Melody had a perception-related Class, as Alistair expected. She could make realistic illusions by weaving light and shadows, with a minor Fate-divination component unrelated to Karma. Bark-Al was a tree and did tree things, and Caren had a Class called Chronicler which allowed him to control paper and process knowledge tens of times faster than a normal human.

Their plan was to have Jason be the distraction, supported by Bark-Al who had healing capabilities, while Alistair went to town slaughtering everything. Caren would work point, since he could open a mental link with someone as long as they were touching a piece of his paper.

"Take this," Caren said, handing Alistair a nondescript blue post-it note. "Put it under your tongue and it will dissolve into you temporarily. I promise it's harmless."

Alistair took the note, staring at it for a minute. He didn't completely trust the Port Locastans, but neither his now Tier 4 **[Fighter's Instinct]** or Karmic vision sensed anything wrong. If Caren could sneak something by his Dao-improved danger sense and keep the threads of Fate from turning black, Alistair deserved it. He did exactly as Caren instructed, feeling a weird sensation as it dissolved into his tongue.

"*Do you hear me?*" Caren asked, beaming the message straight into his mind. "*I can't hook you up to the other lines yet, so if you need to send a message to any of the others, you'll have to talk through me.*"

"*Got it,*" Alistair thought back. It felt different from the mental pathways he used to communicate with Dev'rox, so he didn't think they would interfere with each other.

"We're approaching the serpent horde now," Caren announced out loud. "Look over there."

Caren pointed to the largest mountain in the distance, around two kilometers away. While Alistair was no geology expert, he was pretty sure that no mountains looked like this one before the initiation. The peak had clearly grown in size, standing over three times the height and width of the other mountains. Instead of snow capping its top, a luminescent green slime dripped down from a glowing sphere.

"Woah," Alistair exclaimed. "They've completely changed the landscape."

"It's a profaning of Mother Nature," Bark-Al said with scorn. "All living things close to their nest cannot survive. They must go on longer and longer hunts to feed as their brood grows and their viable hunting grounds recede further and further."

"If we were to go by sky, they'd shoot us down with that venom you see coming from the orb," Caren explained. "We think it's like their god. Before their weekly hunt, they all come out and slither around it. I'll set us down once we get a kilometer out and we'll walk the rest of the way by foot."

Caren piloted the paper canoe another kilometer, landing inside the dead zone. Everywhere Alistair looked, it was like an incarnation of death had ravaged the land. The grass was dead, the trees were dead, the animals were dead. Everything was black and gray, with trails of green slime all over the place.

"Don't step in the green stuff," Melody warned. "It's still potent even after a few days. It's strong enough to melt a man with 80 Constitution to the bone."

Alistair gulped. 114 was not that much higher than 80.

They all suppressed their auras as much as they could without dying, carefully walking toward the mountain through the slaughtered forest. Caren clothed them all in heat-absorbing paper to help them blend into the surroundings, while Melody covered their footsteps in sonar illusions. The snakes should still have been sleeping from their previous feast, but it didn't hurt to be careful.

The trek was long and arduous, but uneventful. They made it to the base of the mountain unopposed, as Caren had planned. The exciting part would start once they entered the peak. The serpent horde had grown large and powerful enough to hollow out part of the mountain and create a nest inside, housing potentially thousands of uplifted snakes.

Using his paper satellites, Caren had already located an entrance near the foot of the mountain, a smaller passageway that was human-sized and used by their adolescents. The tunnel was carved into the side of the mountain near a cliff face. Even though one of the main entrances was blocked by trees and hundreds of meters above them, they could still see it because of its massive scale.

Alistair could feel a sinister presence from deep within the tunnel that chilled him to the bone. An atavistic fear rose in his body, which he had to consciously suppress. That was news to Alistair, who hadn't felt true fear facing an enemy since he'd collapsed upon seeing Kyraxadon. Just what had happened to those snakes?

He looked at his companions, who didn't seem like they felt anything amiss. Perhaps their senses weren't as finely tuned as his.

Regardless, it was too late to turn back. If he was Fated to die here, so be it. Running away would do nothing—if he only faced enemies he was certain to defeat, he would never progress.

It was time to enter the den of the beast.

10 KING OF THE SERPENTS

"I'M SPEAKING *to everyone at once,"* Caren transmitted. *"Communicate only via thought with me. These snakes don't have the best hearing, but they still react to loud noises. Their primary means of sensing should be through detecting heat and vibrations."*

The darkness enveloped them as they trekked deeper inside the tunnel. Alistair thought the air would grow colder further in, but it became hotter and hotter instead.

"Melody tells me to tell you to relax a bit," Caren communicated. *"She's correct. We've charted these beasts quite carefully over the past two weeks. Other intelligence gatherers and I have sent probes into their den multiple times. Remember what I said before. There are around five hundred of them, but most are only level 30. We could fight thousands at that level and be fine. Their king is a level 52 Beast Lord, but you shouldn't have much of an issue."*

"I know," Alistair thought back. *"However, you never want to underestimate your enemies."*

From force of habit, he removed the cosmetic seal on his **Ghostgrass Wraps**, letting the blue-white wrappings swirl around his hands. It didn't serve any true purpose since they would appear anyway the moment he channeled Mana into his hands, but he enjoyed doing it as a battle routine.

"Dev'rox, what do you think?" Alistair mentally asked.

"If the man speaks truly, there is nothing to fear," Dev'rox said. "Of course, he could be leading you into a trap perfectly designed to kill you."

Alistair snorted mentally. "Their Karma would be suffering and I would see that. Leading a man who offered to help without desire for payment to his doom would be a Karmic sin of the highest grade."

Dev'rox had no answer to that, returning to silence within him. In the near pitch-black darkness, they navigated via Caren's paper scouts and Bark-Al's nature senses. Alistair was less blind than the average cultivator with his special sensory powers, but it was still unnerving. When the battle actually started, Melody would create a light source, but he still felt like they could get ambushed at any time.

The adolescent serpent tunnel snaked and curved so many times that Alistair often thought they were going in circles. Adding to the danger were puddles of green venom. Alistair was happy that his [Fighter's Instinct] subtly alerted him to the incoming threats before Caren alerted the group.

After around thirty minutes of walking, the heat had become so unbearable that Caren had to give Melody a special ice heirloom from his storage, a tiara that produced constant streams of snow. He also put an extra layer of paper on top of it to shield the cold from setting off any alarms. This was all within expectations—Caren already knew that it would get super hot within the belly of the beast, and had prepared accordingly.

"*Twenty feet ahead,*" he suddenly announced. "*We've arrived at the first basin.*"

Caren had explained that there were three main basins that the snakes lived in. The first was where most of the snakes slept, a gigantic cavern full of nooks and crannies they could burrow into. The second was the nursery for the young, more guarded than the first. Finally, there was the abode of the king, protected by the strongest serpents.

It was time to enact the plan.

Phase one began with Melody activating her Skill, [Empyrean Light]. It was her most offensive Skill, creating a ball of pure light infused with Dao energy. Normally, she would use it like a giant controllable fireball, although it could only cause a light burn at her stage of advancement. Caren directed her to let it hover fifty meters in the air, acting as a light source for all of them.

Alistair shuddered as Melody's light revealed what was inside the first basin. Hundreds of vipers filled every visible crevice, the largest beasts being dozens of meters long and thicker than the length of a person. Even the smallest ones were ten times the normal size of a pit viper, the species these snakes seemed to have mutated from. Besides the size difference, they were also all covered in green venom, like they had emerged from a green amniotic sac. From what Alistair understood, their entire bodies constantly produced an acid-like substance based on their venom that could melt organic matter like butter.

The moment [Empyrean Light] activated, it was as if the room came to life. Hundreds of snakes exited their slumber, not yet done digesting their previous feast. A feast that included hundreds of humans, Alistair was keen to remember.

It was unfortunate the ball of light woke up all the serpents, ending any possibility of a sneak attack, but these were their natural conditions. Caren and Bark-Al had done a good job of combining their sensory powers, but humans still relied on sight the most.

Jason activated his ancestral Skill, starting phase two of the plan. He started growing, or maybe a better description was he stopped shrinking. The reward from his Quest permanently changed his anatomy, his current size—while large for a human—being a restriction placed on him so that he didn't walk around destroying everything underfoot.

His Cthonic ancestry coursed through every cell in his body, darkening his skin to an earthy brown and growing his already large muscles to comical proportions. The process of undoing his restrictions took less than a second, transforming Jason from a seven-foot-tall muscular man to a fifteen-foot-tall golem. He radiated Strength that might have exceeded Alexandra's, though he didn't have her speed or versatility. Using [Call of the Earth] rooted him to the ground, which explained why despite the ridiculous Strength and Constitution he had in that form, he was outside of the top 1000 rankings.

In this case, Jason didn't need to move. The snakes would come for him. His two fellow Port Locastans worked to buff him to the maximum. Caren wrapped runic paper all around his body, creating parchment platemail armor. Jason picked up Bark-Al as the tree-man clasped his hands together, transforming his body into a three-meter wooden sword. Even sword Bark-Al looked somewhat stubby in Jason's enormous hands. Alistair only hoped that Bark-Al would be safe, but it looked like they had practiced this maneuver before. The gnarled bark was extremely tough to break.

Melody didn't do anything to buff Jason on the surface, just hiding behind him with Caren while keeping the **[Empyrean Light]** active. But Alistair noticed some little gestures she made as soon as the vipers struck.

It was a scene of biblical proportions, a nightmare from another reality. The snakes, furious that their sacred home had been profaned by human outsiders, struck with a fury. Hundreds charged from every corner, flying down the ridges and up the ravines to attack the giant at the center of it all. They came with such violent fury that Alistair scarcely believed them to be beasts. Could non-thinking snakes carry such malice?

Jason roared with the fury of the abyss, swinging Sword Bark-Al with enough force to shatter a small building. Everywhere the wooden weapon touched, snakes found themselves in two pieces. Blood spattered everywhere, joining the green acid pools on the barren ground. No matter how many he killed, more took their place.

That was where phase three came in. The snakes were completely distracted by the giant golem, leaving Alistair free to do as he wished. For the moment, anyway.

Alistair cracked his neck and stretched his hands. Technically, he hadn't been in a fight for five days, the longest period since the beginning of the initiation, though he'd been in a coma for four of those five days. Despite not fighting and only gaining two levels, his power had nearly doubled from forming two Dao Nodes and gaining the "World Leader" Badge. It was time to see what he could do.

He unleashed the restrictions on his aura, temporarily outshining Jason's magnificence. While Jason's aura was loud and powerful, Alistair's was sleek and quiet. Like a ghost of the night, it would kill you before you even realized what had happened. The overwhelming presence of his aura would manifest for a fleeting moment, passing away as soon the target died.

Of course, all the lesser snakes knew that at least two powerful presences were invading their sanctuary. They rushed at Alistair as soon as he revealed himself.

Name: N/A
Species: Mutated Pit Viper (1st stage)
Class: N/A
Level: 32

Alistair tried using **[Eyes of Truth]** on one, not expecting anything interesting. They were lower level than him and wouldn't pose any problems.

With a rush of energy, Alistair charged at top speed through a literal wave of enemy vipers, activating **[Mana Strike]** and **[Phase Shift]** at the same time. He kept his **[Mana Strike]** at a 20 Mana strength, choosing to experiment with affinities. While he was quite certain of his affinity choices for the Dao of the Ghost and the Dao of Justice, the Dao of the Fist had a bunch of options.

The first was the simple primordial fire. Alistair felt the flames within his hand coalesce as he used a drop of Dao energy from his Fist Node. Ever since forming his Nodes, he no longer felt Dao energy come from an unspecified place inside him—now he had three beautiful balls of Dao energy within his soulcore, just like the trifecta Supreme Daos, all equal in volume and power.

With his fist of fire, Alistair carved his mark into scores of snakes, burning them en masse. He used only his recovered right hand, his punches so powerful they blew holes through the serpents.

Alistair became one with fire, a burning conflagration that never ceased —the flames of war itself. None of the snakes were fast enough to keep up with him. The only tactic they could try was swarming him from every direction, some even flying off the stalactites growing from the ceiling, but it was futile. Alistair would just carve a path with his fire fist, roasting the snakes alive.

He spent around 100 Mana keeping his **[Mana Strike]** active, but he wasn't worried, since his total Mana reserves were 898 and he regenerated 1.61 per minute now. Still, just to be safe, he deactivated his fire-attuned Skill.

This is fun, Alistair thought, but he wasn't sure it fit with his path. Fire was wild and uncontrollable, full of infinite passion. He'd lost himself in the Kai'tazake Mutra, but that was not the wild throes of unfettered warfare; it was the purest expression of the dance of the fist. Plus, he could already tell that combining flames with ice would be tricky.

With his **[Mana Strike]** gone, Alistair switched to his bare hands. One straight punch with his full power easily shattered the skull of a titanic, thirty-five-meter-long viper. And Strength wasn't even his strong suit. As one snake reared its fangs from behind and another spat venom from a stalactite above, Alistair easily sidestepped them both, upkicking a human-sized snake so hard it got impaled on the rock formation above.

Alistair didn't need his left hand. He didn't even need his right hand. He fought with only kicks, slamming his foot and shin into snake bodies like a pinball machine. No kick went unused—roundhouse kicks, axe kicks, Brazilian kicks, sidekicks, front kicks, even crazy 720-degree spinning kicks.

The problem was that the wave of snakes seemed almost endless. Every time he smashed one, another one took its place.

As he carved into the backline of snakes, Jason and others still stood strong near the entrance of the basin. Melody kept her light active while also firing arrows of white Mana into the head of a snake every few seconds. Alistair wasn't sure what they exactly did—the arrows didn't seem to damage the snakes physically, but any snake struck with one stopped attacking Jason and instead moved around aimlessly.

While Bark-Al was still in sword form, Caren made his move. The Chronicler fired hundreds of paper bombs from out of his billowing sleeves. A single one wasn't enough to hurt one of the giant snakes, but twenty staggered them. And Caren's supply of paper was never-ending.

Alistair invoked his Ghost Node and his **Lesser Cloak of Shadows** to hide in one of the rocky crevices a snake once called its home. He remembered what Caren said about the potency of the acid the snakes created. So far, everyone had done an excellent job of avoiding the acidic venom. Caren flew in the air behind Jason, and Melody literally hid in his shadow. Alistair was too fast to hit, but he was still wary of slipping and falling in a puddle.

He let the pit vipers forget about his existence for a while, so they turned their eyes back toward the golem. Then, once they had all but forgotten about the other foe, he came back with a fury, killing dozens in quick succession before disappearing again. It took this happening twice for the dumb snakes to realize something was going on.

Alistair ditched fire-attuned Mana and went for something different—sun affinity. He wasn't sure how the twelve affinity system worked exactly, but he knew that sun was one of the primary affinities. He activated [**Mana Strike**] and [**Phase Shift**] yet again, the wild flame replaced by the focused sun. His hand looked like a piece of glowing metal, radiating orange energy and concentrated heat.

"They're retreating," Caren announced in his mind. *"I'd estimate we've eliminated more than half of their number."*

It was an impressive display of destruction, considering they had only been fighting for twenty minutes. But Alistair wasn't done yet, using his newly formed [Mana Strike] on some of the remaining snakes who didn't get the retreat orders. With the sun-attuned Mana, he could pierce their skin easier than with fire, but it didn't have the same area-of-effect destructive capabilities. It also still felt wrong.

One snake after another fell to his radiant fist when suddenly—Alistair's heart nearly skipped a beat. Something was stirring. His [Fighter's Instinct] blazed alarms all throughout his body. This enemy, this being, it was unstoppable. There was nothing he could do but lay down his arms and surrender —*wait what?*

Alistair steeled his mind with the help of Dev'rox, who seemed completely unaffected by whatever had just happened. Now that he could think lucidly, Alistair realized the uneasy feeling he'd sensed earlier outside the mountain and the wave of terror that passed over him now were both *nue*—killing intent. Anthony had used the ten'gatsu technique on him, combining the Dao, Mana and *nue*, while this was just a pure, unadulterated wave of killing intent. He remembered the missive on Wisdom, that it protected against psychic and spiritual attacks. It felt like his Intelligence also had some effect on abating the strength of the *nue* wave as well. While he wasn't sure what *nue* precisely was, it definitely affected him on at least the mental level. Alistair was never more grateful for his new stats than now.

Alistair ran back to check on his companions. Melody and Caren looked recovered, but Jason and Bark-Al, who had transformed back into his more human form, were both catatonic. They clearly lacked the Wisdom and Intelligence to weather the killing intent.

Then, the lights went out. Melody's [Empyrean Light] disappeared in an instant. The only luminescence left were two glowing, intelligent red eyes.

11 SKILL EVOLUTION

ALISTAIR'S MIND worked in overdrive as soon as he sensed the presence of the Beast Lord. He recovered from the initial wave of killing intent the serpent gave off and jumped into action. The first thing they needed was light. Alistair imbued his fist with the lightning of Justice, punching the ground with all his might. He'd picked up how to use electricity to alter potentials from Luke Star the Lightning God. After a short period of gathering potential, the golden lightning screamed down from the ceiling, imbued with a small amount of energy from his Justice Node. Its sole mission was to obliterate all evil in the area.

Because he was new to using lightning like that, his long-ranged lightning from above was both inaccurate and weak, often missing its mark. But Alistair had known that would happen from the start, intending to use it for illumination and not damage. After the bolt touched the floor, the light it provided didn't fade away, the effect lingering due to imbuing his Dao energy into the attack. The light of Justice wouldn't fade so easily.

At the same time he started making the lightning, he got a message from Caren. *"Jason and Bark-Al are out for the count. He hit us with some kind of psychic attack. Are you okay?"*

"Yeah, I wasn't that affected. I'll stop it from attacking you."

Barely a second passed from the moment Alistair felt the wave of *nue* until the lightning struck the ground, and there was not one more moment to spare. The basin was perhaps two hundred meters from end to end, but the Beast Lord was fast. Not as fast as Alistair, but it was terrifying how such an enormous creature possessed so much Agility.

Alistair finally got a good look at the red-eyed beast. It was easily the second largest creature he'd ever seen, after the Herax Turtle. Its full length was that of a football field, with a diameter of four meters at the thickest point of its body, and jaws large enough to swallow an elephant whole. Wherever it slithered, the ground sizzled and corroded from the sheer toxicity of its protective coating, leaving pools of acid behind. What stood out most beyond its immense size was its large red eyes. Instead of normal snake eyes, it had pools of infernal fire. Glowing red and black lines extended from its eyes all the way down its spine.

Activating **[Dash]**, Alistair charged headfirst at the Beast Lord. It had ignored him and headed straight for Jason. He was almost a little disappointed that the serpent king didn't perceive him as the greater threat.

This time, he used a new affinity for **[Mana Strike]**. Fire and Sun both lacked the *oomph* he was looking for. Clearing his mind, he let **[Phase Shift]** choose the appropriate affinity. It didn't make sense, but since when was the way of the fist about overthinking every step?

Ever since he'd formed his Fist Node and added the concept of Kai'tazake Mutra to his Dao Elements, Alistair had felt how easy it would be to slip into the trance. But now, instead of fully submerging himself into the ocean of tranquility, he could take half-steps, letting him retain his consciousness.

With an echoing boom, Alistair struck his fist into the serpent's hide. It was a fajin—a term from Chinese martial arts best describing a punch that projected explosive force and caused internal damage far beyond expectations.

Force, Alistair thought. His instincts told him he'd just used the force affinity, a combination of the primary affinities sun and earth.

The Beast Lord tumbled over several times, knocked off its collision course with Alistair's new companions.

"Deliverance of Justice": +2 free Attribute points.

Alistair's glee at his technique was sobered by the realization that two out of the four Port Locastans would have died without his intervention.

Putting the two points in Constitution to protect his body a tiny percentage more, he used **[Eyes of Truth]** on the serpent.

Name: Sessen Esshei
Species: Mutated Pit Viper (Beast Lord)
Class: N/A
Level: 55
Title: King of the Serpents

"Ssstay out of this, junior brother," the snake hissed, and somehow Alistair understood it.

Did this snake named Sessen Esshei just call me junior brother?

The colossal beast didn't even seem harmed by Alistair's fajin, rushing straight back at his prey. Caren blanketed his three elites in cocoons of paper, even Melody, who was still awake and protested the whole way. He waved his hand and sent all three of them flying back through the adolescent snake tunnel and out of the basin.

"It's safer this way," Caren explained. *"It's just you and me now."*

Even if Caren had a way to avoid the charging snake, Alistair wasn't about to leave it up to chance. Using **[Dash]** once again, he combined it with another force-attuned fajin. This time, he put Dao energy into his strike, creating a shimmering coral-colored outline around his fist that expanded as he landed his punch. Something about his fajin didn't obey the laws of physics, as there was no way he should have been capable of launching such a large creature any distance at all.

Unfortunately, Sessen Esshei didn't seem fazed by the blow, even though Alistair could still see the giant imprint of a fist on his hide.

"Junnnior brotherrr, do not interfere again, thissss isss your ffffinal warning," Esshei hissed.

"I'm not your junior brother," Alistair shouted back, standing between the snake and Caren. "Why do you keep saying that?"

"Is that not the blood of the demon within you?" the Beast Lord questioned. *"You would slay the kin of your brethren, marked one? Saturn would be disappointed."*

"Is he talking about you, Dev'rox?" Alistair asked. "What does 'blood of the demon' mean?"

"Oh shit," Dev'rox said. "Oh shit, oh shit, oh shit."

"Dev'rox? Talk to me here."

"Those spawnlord-less Final Frontier bastards! They've really done it, haven't they?"

Alistair stalled for time as the snake swayed back and forth, looking at him with piercing red eyes. "Uh, you call me junior brother? It's obvious I'm more powerful than you. I'm Saturn's favorite."

"They've made Devil Kings." Dev'rox spoke quietly. "Hmm. Looks like I can mention this out loud, at least. It's the violation of the ancient Pact. While both parties still breathe, the blood of a demon replaces the blood of a human. Untold power at an untold price."

"But this is a snake?" Alistair asked rapid-fire.

"Anyone can benefit from the curse of demon blood. I believe this one to be subordinate to a true Devil King, possibly the one it calls Saturn."

Caren told him that the snake didn't have the red eyes or lines going down its spine before, which indicated to Alistair that the snake had grown more powerful from the demon blood since the last time they'd seen it.

"Your puny powerrr could never compare to mmmmine! I am a Beast Lord, Supreme King of all Serpents. No human can sssssstand against me and live."

Esshei made his move, having had enough of Alistair's sophistry. Gathering Mana within his maw, the Beast Lord spewed a torrential wave of venom at Alistair and Caren. The paper mage grew origami wings and easily avoided it, but Alistair didn't have that option. He would have [Dashed] away, but the terrain contained too many divots and spikes. Despite flicker making it appear like teleportation, [Dash] was still conceptually a movement Skill.

It's time, Alistair thought. He used his 13 remaining Upgrade Points to raise [Phase Shift] from Tier 1 to Tier 2. But when he tried to use [Mana Strike], it had disappeared.

Alistair had no time to think, activating [Dash] while facing the incoming emerald wave, which was just meters away. He only prayed that infusing a bit of the Dao of the Ghost into his body would be enough. He had never tried to pass through multiple things in a row before.

It was a close call. Thanks to his Dao Node, Alistair [Dashed] the full 100 meters in half a second, passing through the various spikes and holes without issue. The wave crashed down where Alistair had stood, corroding the ground and settling into the crevices in the basin. Anything below the previous ground level of the basin was filled with the Beast Lord's substance. The only parts above the acid were any rocks over two meters in height. There were quite a few of them, but now Esshei had the terrain advantage. Alistair would have to jump from rock to rock, avoiding the acidic venom that could melt him, bones and all, while Esshei could slither as he pleased.

A notification window popped up in Alistair's peripheral vision.

Skill Evolution:

Accept (A/B):

A:
[Phase Shift], [Mana Strike], and [Void Beckoning] lost.

[Lightning of Justice], [Blood Hand], [Force Fist], and [Frozen Claw] gained.

[Lightning of Justice] (Tier 1 Expert Skill): *Strike the Earthly ground and bring down the Lightning of Justice from afar.* Mana Cost: 40. Upgradeable (0/100).

[Blood Hand] (Tier 1 Expert Skill): *Blessed be a sliver of the Eternal Blood. Drawing blood with this Skill will give the user a minuscule portion of the target's memories and abilities.* Mana Cost: 40. Upgradeable (0/100).

[Force Fist] (Tier 1 Expert Skill): *Force Fist.* Mana Cost: 40. Upgradeable (0/100).

[Frozen Claw] (Tier 1 Expert Skill): *Surround your hand or foot in a layer of piercing ice. Attacks the soul, scaling with Wisdom. Spreads encompassing ice as a function of Mana.* Mana Cost: 40. Upgradeable (0/100).

Achievement Earned: Pathfinder (Arcana I) — *Synthesize your own Skill(s).* Reward: +40 Upgrade Points, +25 Upgrade Points (only toward a Skill), +500,000 Gold drachma.

B:

[Phase Shift] becomes Tier 2. 75% efficiency becomes 80% efficiency.

Alistair would have to talk with the developer that designed the system so that it locked him out of his current Skills until he accepted or rejected the Skill Evolution notice. Maybe that was one of the things Kevan had meant when he called the Pathfinder AI "a hunk of junk." It only slightly tempered his annoyance when he realized that the Pathfinder AI's creator was probably a Divine or Truthseeker realm cultivator.

The choice would have been harder if not for the achievement. An extra 500k drachma and 40 Upgrade Points were no joke, not to mention another 25 for a Skill. He didn't want to give up the versatility of **[Phase Shift]** just yet, but he would still have four different affinities. "Synthesizing his own Skill" was a bit of an exaggeration, but Alistair had no time to think beyond choosing A as Esshei charged him once again.

This time, Caren swooped in from above. With his origami wings he was nearly as speedy as the snake, shooting paper spears from the "feathers" of his appendages. The spears took Esshei off his course, though the giant snake managed to dodge most of them despite his enormous body. The ones that hit pierced only the outer layer of his skin, not even drawing blood. Whatever this snake was made of, he was tough.

Alistair refused to let himself use Dev'rox's Mana or Karma. He couldn't always rely on them. A pang of guilt set in as he remembered that if he had been stronger, he wouldn't have had to use all that Karma against Anthony, and Sofia would have lived.

Shaking that feeling off, Alistair jumped from rock to rock in the sea of acid. Esshei was still distracted by Caren, hissing and spitting venom at the flying cultivator. The balls of venom weren't too fast, unlike the snake itself, so Caren wasn't in any real danger.

The Beast Lord detected Alistair's movement, swinging its head back faster than should've been possible. Alistair feinted a **[Dash]**, hoping the intelligent beast would bite. It didn't, and Alistair didn't know if that said more about Esshei or Anthony. Nevertheless, he continued forward, jumping over a lash of its gigantic tail. Thousands of tons of snake flesh whipped past at almost the speed of sound, nearly slicing off Alistair's head in one clean blow if not for his **[Fighter's Instinct]**. He dodged down, which was the only choice that let him live, as Esshei whipped his tail back on the rebound. If he had jumped up, he would have gotten caught in the back. As it was, Alistair jumped over the tail, directly onto Esshei's head.

Alistair was dying to try out his new Skills. The first thing he used was [Force Fist], the Skill with the most useless description. He activated it without using any of his Dao energy, just the 40 required Mana. Immediately, he felt the power of his blow increase to around 50% higher than that of a 40 Mana [Mana Strike]. The more efficient Skill halved the activation time to an eighth of a second, surrounding his Ghostgrass Wraps with a semi-transparent outline of a fist. The apparition was tinged salmon pink, larger and more defined than his Dao and force-attuned [Mana Strike].

A resounding shockwave emanated from the point of contact, blowing Alistair back several meters and forcing him to catch his balance mid-air and grab onto a stalactite. Esshei zoomed down into the acid pool of his own creation, splashing the liquid so high it dissolved some of the nearby rock formations. Alistair realized that his attack was a natural fajin without even using the knowledge of the Kai'tazake Mutra; it projected force far beyond its actual destructive capabilities.

Esshei didn't stay submerged for long. Caren fired more spears into the green liquid, but they dissolved before going too deep. The only thing that seemed to resist the acidic venom were the rocks on the ground, which gave Alistair an idea.

"I'm at 10% of my paper stores left. If I run out, my [Storied Wings] will fall off and I'll die. Will you be able to finish the beast off without my help?" Caren asked.

"Yes, you can leave. But if you stay, you'll be able to get some of the kill Mana," Alistair thought back.

"I think I value my life more than a level," Caren responded. "It's a shame you never got to see my ultimate Skill since I had to use so many resources protecting the others."

"One day," Alistair replied, but Caren was already off. Now came the dance Alistair knew best: one-on-one combat. He could deal with groups of mobs, but others close to his level could do it better. Fighting an enemy alone was the true test of mettle, in Alistair's opinion.

"Forgetting about me?" Dev'rox asked.

Not entirely alone.

Emerging from the pool, Esshei roared with all its might, so loud and primal that it awakened Alistair's most atavistic instincts to flee. A wave of pure *nue* assaulted his mind from all corners, infusing more anxiety and doubt into him than he'd ever experienced before.

Is this it? Alistair thought. *Am I going to die?*

"Brat, gain your composure!" Dev'rox shouted. "You've defeated an opponent stronger than this beast."

Alistair felt his senses return to him. It worried him that he could get overwhelmed so easily. That needed to be fixed, but his main problem was that Esshei had grown even larger.

The black and red lines down its spine glowed with demonic light. Alistair could almost feel the fell blood coursing through the snake's system, granting it power beyond that of a level 55 Beast Lord. A spectral green exoskeleton formed around Esshei, its combined size making the viper nearly three times as thick. It was like the Beast Lord was piloting an enormous energy mecha.

Alistair just smiled. It was time to have his first real fight since Anthony.

12 SESSEN ESSHEI

"You think it's still weaker than Anthony?" Alistair asked, darting backward from spike to spike. Despite the snake's new spectral armor somehow speeding it up, Esshei still wasn't as fast as him.

"Beast Lords aren't like normal humans," Dev'rox explained. "Their stats are higher, but at the cost of versatility, so it's hard to compare."

Esshei roared again, obviously displeased with Alistair's evasive tactics. He was ready this time and reacted right away, dipping into the Kai'tazake Mutra trance. He didn't have any direct counter to *nue*, but he figured that if it was a mental attack, having his mind deep within a flow state would help.

Alistair tried to minimize the time he spent in the trance as much as possible, but when he came to, the snake was almost upon him. *At least I avoided the nue*, Alistair thought.

Standing his ground, Alistair whipped his torso and legs with all his might, unleashing a [Force Fist] kick using his entire body as a whip. At least that assuaged his concern that just because the name of the skill was "Force Fist," it didn't mean he couldn't use his feet. He also pumped a healthy amount of his Fist Node into the blow.

The salmon-colored halo around his foot resonated with his Dao energy, becoming more solid, more *real*. His kick struck with the enhanced weight of true martiality, projecting through the energy armor like a pendulum. That was the difference between adding more Mana to an attack versus adding

Dao energy. More Mana would make the attack more physically powerful—Dao energy could do that as well, but it more importantly added a conceptual layer to the blow that altered the fabric of reality. Alistair's kick pierced the armor, traveling straight into the beast itself.

This time, Alistair was sure he hurt the serpent. He found that he could no longer pour extra Mana into his attack like he could with [Phase Shift]. But thanks to the formation of his Nodes his Dao energy reserves had doubled, so he wouldn't have to be as stingy with Dao energy as before, offsetting the Mana concerns.

Esshei skidded across the battlefield, his armor protecting him from any stray rocks, not that they could pierce his skin. Alistair readied himself for the snake to come slithering back, but after the Beast Lord's momentum halted, it coiled up menacingly.

Alistair didn't understand what was going on until he felt the pain. Looking down at the leg he'd used for the [Force Fist], he saw acid melting through his boots and skin. The pain was unbearable, dropping him to a knee. He had suffered far worse injuries before, but nothing that hurt so much.

"*You fooooool, I let you kick me. Feeeel the burnsss of my acid, which exceeed the firesss of hell!*"

Dev'rox scoffed at that. Alistair forced himself back up and shouted back at the snake, "Don't you ever shut up?" Esshei sounded like the arrogant villain in a B-movie. Where did a sapient snake learn to talk like that?

After a second, the acid stopped actively sizzling, having melted what it could. Alistair's muscles and a small hint of his shin bone were visible. It hurt like hell, but his combat prowess wouldn't suffer much. He was surprised the snake had bypassed his [Fighter's Instinct], but if he had to guess, he was so preoccupied with imbuing Dao energy that he'd distracted himself.

He was confident he could eventually whittle down Esshei, but the main problem was just how tough the beast was. The snake had to have a Constitution exceeding Alistair's own Agility. *Beast Lord stats are just too unfair*, he thought. His [Force Fist] had pierced through a handful of scales and perhaps caused minor internal bleeding, though he couldn't be certain. It was time to change up tactics.

Alistair started running for the giant cavern that Esshei had emerged from. After he made it within a hundred meters of the cavern, he activated

[Dash], knowing that he would reach solid ground. If the information Caren provided was correct, the second basin contained the young and any surviving snakes who'd retreated from the first basin.

The wave of fury that erupted from his opponent nearly stopped Alistair right in his tracks, something he had not thought possible while using [Dash]. Fortunately, he was too far away from the beast for it to have any major effect.

"How dare youuuuu!" Esshei roared.

Alistair didn't bother looking back and used [Dash] again, putting his Mana at 646, or 72% of his total capacity. The second basin was just as dark as the first, so Alistair activated [Lightning of Justice]. Touching the ground like he did before, an imposing bolt of golden lightning came down from above, illuminating the entire cavern. The second basin was more organized than the first, consisting of a depressed area containing a mass of smaller snakes and ridges full of all manner of human items, such as books, jewelry, and even cars.

The snake came crashing through the halls of the mountain, not bothering to avoid causing destruction. From the cracked armor near Esshei's head, it looked like the Beast Lord's bulldozing act did more damage than his [Force Fist].

Esshei calmed its rage, at least outwardly, as soon as he entered the second basin. Despite the young snakes lacking the sapience of their Beast Lord leader, Alistair felt like they were more intelligent than their smaller, pre-mutation counterparts. He could feel their fear like a scent in the air, and their respect and admiration for their king.

"Not to fret, little ones. It will all be over soon," Esshei hummed to a different tune than the one it had used before. *"Your king is here."*

"You've killed hundreds of families," Alistair retorted. "Yet you sit here trying to protect your kin as if every human you killed didn't matter?"

"The Dao willsss as the Dao willsss," Esshei said. *"Humans are the dominant species of this planet. Life begets death and death begets life in the cycle of Samsara. In order for you to grow, you need the ceaseless slaughter of beasts and monsters. With the blood of a demon, I was given a chance to contest that. You think I don't know my chance of victory against all of humanity is slim? But I guarantee you would do the same. That is why I shall never lose against the likes of you."*

"Enough."

Alistair didn't want to contemplate philosophy at the moment. He called down another **[Lightning of Justice]**, punching the ground as fast as he could. The bolt of electricity he created seemed more muted than before, not even cracking the snake's armor despite being reinforced with Dao energy. Alistair couldn't believe it. He should have known better than to let the snake's words get to him.

Esshei coiled its hundred-meter-long body tight around a single point. The spectral armor smashed and ground against itself, forming green sparks like two metals colliding. Alistair was astounded at how compact the snake could make itself, compressing its body to the size of a small house. At the final point of compression, Alistair felt an inkling of the Dao coming from Esshei. An image of a black hole popped into his head, its infinite tidal forces represented by the constriction of an anaconda. It was a congruous Dao, even if he didn't want to admit it.

Once Esshei stopped moving, the armor came off, floating into the air like a ghost. Alistair could feel the snake's material body losing its spiritual energy, all of it being transferred to the suit of armor. Even the Beast Lord's physical blood joined it, carrying all of his life force with it. A mysterious black orb with a single patch of green flew out of the center point of the snake's coil, joining the armor at its core, while the blood formed a network of veins and arteries. **[Fighter's Instinct]** told him it wasn't a good idea to attack, even if it looked like the Beast Lord was inert. The armor shifted forms, transforming from that of a snake into what looked like a mecha. It looked familiar, with giant shoulder pads and a horned helmet, but Alistair couldn't place the exact origin of the design.

After completing the transformation, the new energy mecha charged at Alistair, forming a sword in its right hand and a shield in its left. It was even faster than Esshei's snake form, approaching Alistair in speed.

Alistair used **[Dash]** to dodge, stepping sideways but moving backwards toward the tunnel that presumably led to the third basin, the den of the king. He put a hand up, asking for a temporary truce.

"Wait. We shouldn't fight here. One missed swing of that sword and you could kill all your, uh, kids. And even if we don't hit them directly, the impact of our blows might destroy all of your caverns. Let's go outside and finish this."

"*Humanssss are full of liesss. If I go outside, your friendsss will attack, no?*" The words came from the core at the center of the spectral mecha, not Esshei's body. *Wait, is that black thing his soulcore?*

"I swear that no harm will come to you from anyone else," Alistair said.

The green mecha considered his words for a few seconds.

"I accept these termsss. Go into my den," Esshei said.

Alistair carefully walked into the third basin, which had the largest connecting tunnel by far. Even Esshei's armored form could pass through the all-encompassing darkness with ease. The only light was the dim luminescence of the phantom armor and the disappearing **[Lighting of Justice]** afterglow.

For some reason, Alistair simply knew that Esshei wasn't trying to trick him, either. Of course, he had **[Fighter's Instinct]** and his Karmic sight if anything went wrong, but something about the beast's pride made Alistair think it wouldn't try any underhanded tactics.

"I'm going to create some lightning in the center so I can see, okay?"

Alistair didn't hear any objections, so he lit up the area with another **[Lightning of Justice]**. The king's den was actually smaller than the first and second basins. It was barebones and lacked the ostentatiousness Alistair expected. As far as he could see, the only thing inside the cavern was a twenty-meter-tall throne carved out of stone. With his better than 20/20 vision, he could make out what looked like a glass terrarium on one arm of the throne.

"Behind my throne, there isss another exit," the snake hissed.

"Where's your body?" Alistair asked, noticing that only the armor came with him.

"If thisss form is destroyed, I die assss well. My soulcore powerssss this armor. Do you not feeeeel it with your aura sssense?"

Esshei was right; now that he was closer to the black core, he could feel its spiritual presence. Unlike his sister, he didn't have a natural sense for embodied souls, but because it had left Esshei's body, his **[Ghost Whispers]** could comprehend it better.

"Lead the way," Alistair said.

He followed the disembodied soulcore through another large tunnel, leading directly to the opposite side of the mountain from which they'd entered. Dead things lay silent in the morning light, the rising sun peeking out from behind the clouds. It was the dawn of a new day.

A fitting place to end their battle.

Alistair jumped back twice, creating a hundred-meter gap between him and the giant suit of armor. He had been toying around with his food for too long. The martial arts of the {Assassin Fist} were about killing your opponent as quickly and efficiently as possible. The same mantra he'd recited in his fight against Anthony appeared in his mind. *Fluid, then still. Soft, then hard. The Kiss of Death.* There was no self, there was only the Fist. Submerging himself in the ocean of tranquility, he struck.

A mighty blade arced down from above, cleaving the earth in two, yet Alistair was not there. He [Dashed] to the side, ending the Skill prematurely with his increased reaction time, and then [Dashed] again forward. With flicker making him invisible between [Dashes], Esshei couldn't predict where he would turn up. Even if he had a Fate-divining power, Alistair's **Cloak of the Divined** protected him.

Alistair went for the legs first. He aimed a [Force Fist] to the left ankle with a third of his Fist Node's pool of energy, and then another [Force Fist] to the right ankle. With that much Dao energy, the outline of his fist was almost solid, cracking open the armor with a deafening blast. A true fajin of the highest order, its impact splattered the blood that pumped within the suit's interior.

[Fighter's Instinct] harmonized with the Mutra trance like never before. The silent and sharp anxiety it gave him moved his body instantaneously, avoiding the dark red blood before it splashed over him. Wherever the liquid touched, the ground disappeared into smoke, an even more potent acid than before.

With both of its ankles destroyed, Esshei's spectral mecha lost most of its mobility, but that didn't make it any less deadly. After destroying the second ankle, he skidded a few dozen meters across the ground. And just in time, as quicker than Alistair expected—even in the Mutra—Esshei stabbed himself in the chest with his massive sword.

Sensing danger, Alistair attempted to [Dash] away and gain some distance from his opponent, but he found himself unable to use his Skill. He felt an irresistible pull from Esshei's soulcore, like the image of the black hole he'd seen before.

Then came the sky of arrows.

Not arrows like that from a bow, but Alistair didn't know how else to describe them. Bolts of energy flew out of the construct faster than the eye could see. It didn't seem like the snake could aim them, other than letting them spew from the front of his armor. The green arrows blotted out

Alistair's entire vision, expanding like a cone of angry locusts, each imbued with a tiny piece of the Dao.

Without thinking, Alistair activated [Frozen Claw]. From the midpoint of his forearm to the tips of his fingers, a thin layer of reflective ice formed, chilling the surrounding air to near-freezing temperatures. Just like the name suggested, a small spike appeared on each of his fingertips.

As he'd planned before, Alistair channeled his Ghost Node into [Frozen Claw], focusing on the eternal chill of the ghost. Far past the end of stars and even black holes, there would only be the cold—and ghosts. A somewhat clumsy image, but it worked fine for now. Alistair casually swiped his claw down.

It was as if time came to a stop. The moment Alistair's frozen fingertip touched an arrow, it halted. A magical hoarfrost appeared, instantly stealing the arrow's momentum and forming a lattice that jumped from arrow to arrow. In a harmonious pattern of ice and frost, the initial arrows affected by [Frozen Claw] spread the icy disease to their brethren, cascading until it reached Esshei himself.

Alistair felt 108 points of Mana leave him instead of the listed 40. It seemed that unlike [Force Fist], whose Mana cost could not change, [Frozen Claw] had an initial cost and then a variable cost depending on how much it froze.

Punching and kicking through his own ice like a madman, Alistair broke through to his giant enemy, though he wasn't as large anymore. Esshei had poured the substance of his own armor into the flood of arrows, and his new form was only ten meters tall and much slimmer.

The Kiss of Death, Alistair repeated in his head, and he saw his path to victory. He let himself get pulled in by Esshei's gravitational Dao. It was weak enough to resist if countered it with his own, but that wasn't how an assassin operated. Death was delivered at any cost.

Alistair activated [Blood Hand], congealing a viscous mass of glowing, blood-attuned Mana around his fist. He ran forward with reckless abandon, not bothering to dodge when Esshei sent another volley of arrows from his body. With [Blood Hand], he whacked away the arrows aiming for his vital points. He found blood-attuned Mana worse than pure Mana at protecting his hand, but it was still tough enough that he got away with only a few scratches. That didn't apply to the rest of his body.

Even with his Agility, there were only so many arrows he could swat away, leaving many to strike his stomach and left arm. It wasn't worth using the Dao of the Ghost to counter his opponent's Dao, since Esshei's Dao imbued within the arrows grounded the attacks in reality, countering the Ghost Node's intangibility effect. His 116 Constitution allowed him to walk away without fist-sized holes in his body, but he still received hundreds upon hundreds of major and minor cuts.

By the time he reached Esshei, the armor had shrunk down to a pedestrian five meters and was barely thicker than an average person. Alistair was far too deep within the Mutra to feel his wounds, easily sidestepping another sword swing and getting within grabbing range of Esshei's broken ankle.

With his **[Blood Hand]**, Alistair imbued half of his Ghost Node's reserve, using the Skill as a medium for the spiritual history of the Ghost. Just as ice represented the eternal, silent ghost, blood represented the vengeful emotions and tethering to the longing flesh. He had decided his Dao was one of duality, and blood and ice were its best receptacles.

The moment he touched the beast's blood, it was over. Alistair overpowered Esshei's spirituality with ease. The Beast Lord's nascent gravitational Dao was no match for Alistair's triple Dao Nodes, though he only used the Ghost Node to fuel the attack. His overpowering spiritual power flooded into the circulatory structure of the suit of armor, destroying the constructed meridians and even reaching the black soulcore itself.

Like a second sense, Alistair could feel the life force draining out of the snake's blood. It wasn't as clear as his aura sense or Karmic sight, but after using the gigantic blood-attuned **[Mana Strike]** against Anthony and now with his **[Blood Hand]**, it had become apparent. A trickle of energy entered his own life force, which he could now feel was not concentrated in the soulcore and meridians like Mana, but present in each and every cell like a spark of verdant vitality. *How many senses is that now? Aura, Karma, danger, and now life force? If I'm ever ambushed by someone at my level again, I deserve it.*

Just as the Skill description indicated, a tiny memory from the dying snake passed to Alistair. But instead of just being a small fragmented memory or nigh-useless piece of procedural memory, Alistair entered a full-on vision, becoming the snake within a vivid, lucid dream.

———

Sessen Esshei was a pet. A beloved pet, but still a pet. He didn't remember his mother's warmth—all he knew was the girl. At the time, he'd lacked the intelligence to understand, but the girl's name was Shay.

This tiny girl would be his caretaker. Her parents had foolishly purchased a pit viper without realizing they were venomous. Not the most traditional of parents, they somehow let her keep the snake after hearing Shay's cries that her new pet was already a part of the family. So long as they never touched, it would be safe.

Six-year-old Shay, in all her wisdom, couldn't come up with a proper name for her pet and named him Shay's Snake. Every day when she came home from school, Shay would tell Shay's Snake all of her problems. What she ate for lunch, how her teachers were so mean, what she did with her friends—he heard all of it. Elementary schoolers are not known for their reticence.

Even though Shay was little, she knew that her pet couldn't understand what she was saying. But she still opened up to him, anyway. It was her routine, and it made her happy.

As all children must, she grew up. Now that she was older, her friends teased her that she named her snake "Shay's Snake," but she didn't mind. Besides, none of them had a venomous snake as a pet, so they could screw off.

Shay never stopped telling him about her day. Her problems weren't just who didn't play nice at tag anymore—life wasn't that easy. Shay's Snake had to sit through countless hours of boy trouble. Did he like her? Did she like him? Did he like her best friend? Homework, tests, college—the life of a teenager carried a ton of stress. Every weekend, they would watch a movie together. Usually a shitty one, though he never minded. He was a snake, after all. He was there for it all, her dependable ear that only ever listened.

There were good times and there were bad times, but Shay and her pet snake made it through them all. Her parents were surprised that Shay's Snake lived for so long. If they had done their research, they would've known pit vipers could live for decades. Still, when Shay graduated college, her beloved snake was nearing the end of his life.

She was back home after graduation when the initiation happened. His primitive brain didn't understand true emotion, yet in every way a snake could be happy, he was thrilled at seeing his owner's return. But something wasn't right. Everyone spoke in hushed, fearful tones. The sky turned orange and, in the distance, smoke blossomed.

Shay was always a resourceful girl. She and her family survived the early days of the initiation, defeating many of the monsters that sprung up in their town. But they weren't prepared for the threat coming from their own home.

Something *changed* inside of Shay's Snake. His body grew before his mind did, and so did his ravenous hunger. An affliction burned within his body, with only one solution—consume. Consume every living thing in sight.

Shay didn't stand a chance. Not against her childhood friend. Not against the one whom she had shared her deepest secrets with and the one that had seen all her tears. For a fraction of a second, she hesitated, and that was enough.

For the first time in her life, Shay met her snake, skin to scale. A fleeting moment of happiness forever sealed away. Shay's Snake was reborn as King of the Serpents, Sessen Esshei—language of the Basilisk for the Snake of Shay.

His body grew and grew as he feasted on the flesh of human, beast, and monster alike. That was until his mind grew to accompany his burgeoning body. A madness overcame him. A madness of grief and anger and disgust. How could he have killed her? How? The universe gave no answers. Only Quests and level-ups. Only the Heavens and the Earth, and the Grand Dao. The multiverse had no law except the law of the jungle. As a snake, Esshei understood. He would build his own Fate.

And so he did. He gathered the serpents of the area, ruling and protecting them from the outside world, for he knew the harsh reality.

It was all fine before the Devil King. As a proud Beast Lord, Sessen Esshei feared nothing. Nothing except the creature that froze him with just his presence. Every cell in his body screamed the same thing—run and hide. He was nothing. Nothing next to this man, this man that demanded complete obeisance from all lesser beings.

"What a peculiar creature," the man named Saturn said. "Why do you mourn for such a weak human? Your ferocity might have even scared me if you bared your fangs like a true beast. I can help you with that."

Sessen Esshei knew what was coming. Saturn was right. He was no true Beast Lord. But he fought anyway. For his pride, for his memories, and for his brood. There was no contest between the two of them. Saturn did as he promised.

"Accept my blood freely," he whispered. "Or I shall slaughter your so-called kin."

With no other choice but to acquiesce, Esshei lapped up the pure black liquid that looked and smelled like no blood of a man. That was when the second madness began. It wasn't like the first, born from his incipient mind and body. No, this was the madness that came from the turning of the heart and poisoning of the mind. Even his soulcore found no respite, turning black like the mysterious man's blood.

"George will love this!" Laughter echoed in the halls of the mountain king. "Absolutely love it. Oh wait, he won't care at all. Fuck that arrogant prick. Just because he's the strongest he thinks he can boss us around and act all 'strong, silent type.' Oh wait, he can. Fuck."

It looked like he was not the only one to succumb to madness. Well, not entirely succumbed. With more willpower than he had ever conjured, Esshei clung on to the last piece of his soul that made him human. Human wasn't the right term, but he didn't know what other word made sense. To Esshei, to be human was transcendent. Humans could cry and laugh and love. He had killed so many of them and seen their pain. They weren't Fated—just like himself.

Even now, as his mind grew dimmer and the world grew distant, Esshei lamented upon seeing his latest prey. *How unfair the world is*, he thought. *Born into this world to die, when there are those born into this world to live.*

———

Alistair returned to his senses with a gasp of air. It wasn't like he'd just seen Esshei's memory. He had been Esshei, at least for a brief moment. He didn't know what to make of the snake's memories. It was all... too sad. How could anyone think there was cosmic justice when such cruelties existed? He could feel his Dao of Justice cry out with the force of a thousand suns.

There was also the matter of the presumed Devil King, Saturn. That he mentioned a man named George only made Alistair more convinced that George Moulin and the other twelve missing people had become Devil Kings.

But Alistair put that on hold for the moment as he gazed upon the dying snake. Perhaps it was wrong to call Esshei a snake in his current form. The armor dwindled down to the size of a human, his soulcore cracking with white light. Nearly all his remaining blood had been purified and absorbed into Alistair's **[Blood Hand]**, entering his system like a warm apple pie.

His life force felt demonstrably stronger, like it had grown from a hearty sapling into an immortal oak. Alistair guessed it had to do with Esshei willingly offering his blood, and that he couldn't expect such benefits from a typical usage of the Skill. He also absorbed a hint of Esshei's powerful *nue* capability, but just a hint. **[Blood Hand]** couldn't handle such a complex concept at its current tier, even if Esshei offered it willingly.

Alistair knelt by his fallen foe, recognizing he posed no threat.

"He shall soon pay the ultimate price," Dev'rox said solemnly. "The one who takes demon blood as their own cannot enter the cycle of Samsara."

"Even against his consent?" Alistair asked. "That doesn't seem fair."

"The price is the price. Even out here in the frontier, they shouldn't be messing with forces beyond their understanding."

Esshei refused to die through sheer willpower—even Alistair felt the tug of the beyond on the snake's soul. The cracks grew larger and larger until his life force had faded to a single dot, yet he still held on. Alistair had never seen anyone resist death like the serpent king.

"Spare the younglings." In his death throes, Esshei no longer seemed like a monstrous beast, but a scared pit viper who longed for his family. *"Do this last thing, I beg of you."*

"Would you do the same for me?" Alistair wondered aloud. "Do you regret killing all those people?"

His heart toward his enemy had softened after he saw the serpent's memories, but he knew that if he had met the families of those who'd suffered and died, his whole stance would have changed. Justice, vengeance, sentiment—Alistair didn't have some cosmic guidebook that told him what true justice meant.

"I was born into this world against my will and I shall leave this world against my will," Esshei croaked from a disembodied voice. *"Infinite scores of Fateless beings live and die without any hope, without any future, without any providence. What is the purpose of a meaningless life? I have seen hope, and though my thread may have run dry, my existence is greater than that of one who shall never escape Samsara. One blessed by the Heavens such as yourself could never understand. Your Fate burns as bright as the living sun."*

"I'm not blessed by the Heavens," Alistair said. He remembered Kyraxadon invoking a prayer to a higher realm. Whatever his Subclass meant—which was the only thing Alistair could think was suspect enough that a level 29 needed Heaven's attention—someone up high didn't approve, though they weren't watching closely yet.

"And you're wrong. And even if you're not, I'll climb to the peak and shatter it with my own hands. I don't think there's such a thing as a meaningless life. Hope springs eternal—we all come from the same source and return to the source. We can all be nothing together or rise above." Alistair quoted the Dao De Jing, though he felt more like a hopeless acolyte than a wise master.

Alistair felt Esshei's life force dwindle to nothing. His soul glowed with a hallowed white light. In his fervor to deny the snake his last philosophizing, Alistair almost forgot to give him peace before his end. "I won't lay a hand on your younglings. My foundations will crumble and shatter before I break my word."

He could feel an indelible promise etch itself within his immortal soul. It felt so real and immutable that he wondered if even a Truthseeker could break it.

"Thank you."

Sessen Esshei—Mutated Pit Viper, Beast Lord, King of the Serpents, and once beloved pet—passed on, his soulcore crumbling into nothingness as his ethereal spirit departed.

"Eternal Buddha, may you grant mercy and let this soul enter Samsara." Dev'rox dipped his head. "May King Yama's gates below open up."

Alistair cocked his head to his imp partner. "You're praying?"

"To die a true death, a souldeath, is a terrible thing. Now that his soul has separated from his body, his destination is unknowable to mortal eyes."

Level up! *You are now level 38.* +3 Agility, +3 Intelligence, +3 Charisma, +3 free Attribute points, +23 Upgrade Points.

Alistair ignored his level-up notification for now, confirming what Dev'rox said to be true—after Esshei's pure soul left its body, it disappeared into the ground, sinking too far for his ghost senses to reach. That was customary for all souls entering the afterlife, Dev'rox told him, and didn't mean he was going to hell. In all probability, as Dev'rox said, his soul would be annihilated, but they would never truly know what happened.

His thoughts wandered to Esshei's last words about Fate. It brought to mind his own mundane life and destiny. Hadn't he been searching for cultivation his entire life? Something to bring him out of his boring existence? Was that why he never truly hated the initiation, even if it killed so many people? It granted him a life beyond the ordinary, a chance to be truly special.

But he shook those thoughts off. No, he remembered better now. The world could always change, even without the Pathfinder AI and the power of cultivation. Even before the initiation, he had been a dreamer, a person with endless greed toward improvement. Now he just had the power to actually do something.

Alistair checked his stats. He had 250 Health and 286 Mana, along with 150 Stamina. Most of the Dao energy of his Justice Node remained, along with a third of his Fist Node and half of his Ghost Node. It was all unacceptably low. He hadn't used any Karma or Mana from Dev'rox, and he hadn't used his left arm at all, but he should have been able to handle Esshei without using so many resources. Part of the problem was the Kai'tazake Mutra. He had inadvertently sacrificed his Health for the kill because that's what the Mutra felt was best.

Popping a Tier 2 Health and Tier 2 Mana pill into his mouth, Alistair sighed. He had a healthy stockpile of Health and Mana pills for emergencies, and since his meridians had fully recovered from the last one he had imbibed, it would be safe. In fact, because the damage he received was far less than before, the healing process didn't sear his insides as much. If he needed to take another one for a medium-sized injury, it wouldn't cause any permanent harm.

He had promised not to harm the serpent younglings, but that meant he also had to do something with them. There had to be someone with a Beast Tamer Class in the Northeast Freehold, right? He imagined a future where his people harnessed the power of a thousand Essheis in battle.

"I'm too greedy, Dev'rox," Alistair smiled.

"What?"

"Nothing." He bent down and observed some of the remains of Esshei's blackened demonic blood. For a hefty 100,000 drachma, he purchased a small glass vial from the System Store that promised protection against any acid. To his surprise, it actually succeeded in holding the temperamental liquid when he dipped it in a puddle of the blood. "Things can't ever be easy, can they? Thirteen Devil Kings…"

"*Alistair, are you alright? My telepathy just registered you in range,*" he heard Caren say from inside his head.

"*Yes, I'm fine. I've dealt with the Beast Lord. We have some things to discuss. I'll meet you back at the entrance we used to get into the mountain. Oh, and we need to connect our Teleportation Circles in the Soulnet. Just saying so I don't forget.*"

Alistair was ready to go home, but he wasn't looking forward to the talking-to he was going to get from Alexandra. He hadn't said he would leave so soon—he had just done it to have some alone time. Now that they were all reunited, he was going to be seeing a lot more of his friends—friends that he had shed blood with. Ties like those were forged from unbreakable steel. He missed fighting side-by-side with Alexandra, and Oliver too. He didn't know anyone more reliable than Ms. Lykaios when it came to bashing in monster heads with a giant sword. Not that he knew many others like that.

He smiled as he ran with the wind on his shoulder. Life was harsh, as it always was, but life was good.

13 HOME SWEET HOME

ALISTAIR'S first order of business was to allocate his free Attribute points. He put 1 into Constitution and 2 into Endurance, bringing both up to 118. Keeping his stats relatively close to one another was important to him, since he guessed there was a version of the "Jack of All Trades" Badge below level 60. Being an all-rounder had worked out for him many times. If his Wisdom wasn't nearly 200, he probably would have died against Esshei and his waves of *nue*.

Thinking about the King of the Serpents still made him uneasy. He could still feel his inner turmoil when he considered the idea of Fate. It wasn't clear what Esshei meant by his Fate burning bright—Alistair saw nothing different about himself. Perhaps it was a figure of speech, but he didn't think so. The concept of certain people being born with grander Fates than others didn't sit right with him. Did his mother and his friends have a lesser destiny than himself? After seeing his father, he hadn't stopped thinking about his mom.

Luckily, Port Locasta had a person with the Beast Tamer Class who was eager to master her abilities. Bark-Al stayed behind to protect her from the adult snakes that might attack, promising his presence was calming to Mother Nature's children.

When they arrived back at Port Locasta, Caren officially transferred ownership of the freehold to the Northeast Order, adding 24 subregions.

There was someone else to greet them there as well—the Maine Brothers. The two were said to be identical twins, but due to their signature black masks no one was entirely certain. They wore the exact same clothing and had the same height and build, so the rumor made sense. After hearing about Alistair's visit, they also wanted to join. The Canadian border had tons of strong beasts and monsters that were getting difficult for them to push back. Alistair accepted them with open arms. It helped that they were known for being benevolent and competent in their rule.

Adding up all the new subregions, the Northeast Freehold had increased to 550, with new ones being added everyday along their southern border. To the west, Pennsylvania had been taken over by Final Frontier Empire cultivators, though the state remained cordoned off. No one could exit or enter, the region blocked by an impenetrable black wall. The wall wouldn't go down until a year had passed since the initiation, standard for Premium Tier worlds. At that point, Alistair would go off to join the Clear Water Sect. It was something he didn't like to think about since it was so far away.

Finishing up his business in Port Locasta, he linked one of his spare Teleportation Circles to their headquarters. Connecting every necessary location was a bit of a math problem, if you wanted to do it as efficiently as possible. Not that he had to worry since he was so rich, but he still had to pay off Anthony's debt and he didn't want to waste money. He had already reached the minimum debt payment, his wallet ballooning up to 2.89 million drachma.

With his 25 Skill-specific Upgrade Points, Alistair upgraded his [Ghost Whispers] and [Spectral Summoning] to Tier 2, since they were already so close. The range and potency of his [Ghost Whispers] increased, along with Dev'rox's total power. He could handle around 20% more of Dev'rox's Mana with the new Tier 2 Skill.

By the time Alistair returned to New Boston, the sun had reached its zenith. Just over a day had passed since he woke up, and he'd accomplished so much. Those [Carmela's Happy Pies] were wondrous.

As soon as word got back that he was at their valyrik-crafted HQ, Alexandra showed up.

"The first thing that happens after I see you again is you disappear?" she chided him.

"I was on a mission," Alistair protested. "It was only like half a day."

"Uh huh. And that mission included partying with a pretty pink-haired girl?"

"How could you possibly know that?"

"Did you not see the Soulnet changes?" Alexandra asked. "There were rumors that someone in Asia got a major side Quest to build an infrastructure upgrade. Required a special technology-based Class or something. If that is why the Soulnet changed, they probably got a huge reward."

"So it's like a message board now? Or Facebook?"

"Kind of? You have to pay to use it, so it's a bit more serious. Giving actual information gives you points you can use to spread your messages further. There were enough people who pitched in because of missing friends and family members that we have a permanent beacon that covers the entire globe."

"That's amazing!" Alistair exclaimed. "Now that we have **Teleportation Circles** connecting continents, anyone who wants to come can make it."

"Yeah. My dad sent me a message actually," Alexandra mentioned, looking down. "Surprise, surprise, he owns 100 subregions in Greece. He told me I should come over there since he's not going to visit, after he heard that I'm safe."

Alistair knew their relationship was strained, but that Alexandra's own father wasn't willing to visit her when she could have died many times over since the initiation? That just seemed cold.

"Anyway, how did your mission go? I heard you defeated the Beast Lord. Damn, your Intelligence is so much higher than mine I can't even see your level."

Alistair got a warning that someone was trying to use an investigation Skill on him.

He grinned. "I'm level 38 now."

"Damn you. I'm only 35. You're going to leave me in the dust if I don't do something. How many Dao Nodes do you have?"

"Three. Ghost, Justice, and Fist."

"Three? Fuck you. Wait, what? They're actually called that specifically?" Alexandra asked.

"I'm positive." Alistair opened his Achievements page publicly. "Yep, here you go."

"I have one—the Barbaric Rage Node. My Nature's Attendant Dao Inspiration is close to forming a Node, though."

Dev'rox popped up on his shoulder. "Both approaches are acceptable. Some choose a small aspect of the Dao to start with and build it up over time, others start large and go small. Or you can start small and stay small, or start big and stay big."

Alexandra jumped back. "What the hell is that?"

"What the hell is correct, Miss. Since you are one of my partner's closest allies, I thought it prudent to introduce myself," Dev'rox said formally. "I am Dev'rox, a Profound realm imp from the Asura Hell, and contracted ghost of Sir Alistair." He bowed his tiny heart-shaped head before Alexandra.

After she recovered from her initial shock, Alexandra knelt down and observed the crimson imp.

"Don't let his initial charm fool you; he's quite annoying," Alistair grumbled.

"Oh, this is your ghost buddy? Alistair, he's so cute!" Alexandra tried pinching Dev'rox's cheeks, but her fingers passed through Dev'rox's form.

"I am not cute. I am handsome," Dev'rox corrected, his forked tail curling.

Someone outside the room awkwardly knocked on the door, tapping it once so lightly Alistair wouldn't have heard it without his impressive hearing. It was followed by two more knocks in quick succession, as if to cover up the first. Alistair felt a familiar aura of death emanating from behind the door.

"Come in, Oliver!" he shouted.

The teenager physically looked almost the same, yet Alistair felt a certain stability in his aura that he'd never noticed before. Even his power felt only slightly below Alexandra's. It looked like Oliver had done some maturing while Alistair was gone.

"It's good to see you when we're not under imminent threat," Alistair said. "I just got back."

"Knowing you, you want to jump right back into action, right?" Oliver asked, grinning. "Are we gonna go mash some monster heads?"

"You know me well," Alistair admitted. "I found this."

He took the vial of Esshei's black blood out from the pocket of his hybrid cloak. It didn't assimilate into him like his other items, though he didn't know why. Alistair had to spend 0.5 Mana a minute to maintain the blue lid that held the blood inside the glass vial.

"What's that?" Alexandra questioned, her eyes widening. The blood seemed to pulse at her presence, which worried Alistair.

"I may not look it now, but I got pretty beat up in the fight against the Beast Lord," Alistair explained. "To be fair, I held myself back for training purposes, but the Beast Lord was stronger than anyone realized because of this stuff. It's the blood from a demon, though not one like Dev'rox."

"Lo, the ancestral sorrow and divide, betwixt two nations on either side." Dev'rox recited the verse without a hint of humor. "It's a short poem about the split between the spiritual and physical demons. Everyone back home gets taught it."

"Uh, got it. Dev'rox, can you explain more to them?"

"Brat, are you trying to get me to break the Law of the Heavens?" Dev'rox looked them up and then down, pausing as he tested something. "Actually, nevermind. It seems fine to talk about since the Final Frontier Empire was the one that opened the bottle first. Because I'm closer to the topic, I should be able to tell your friends."

Alistair assumed Dev'rox was referring to how he couldn't explain Anthony's shadow clones. They must not have been demon-related, despite what he initially thought.

"Put simply, if you ingest any amount of demon blood three things happen—you'll go mad, you'll gain a bunch of power, and you won't be able to enter the cycle of Samsara. If you die, you're done for good. While I can't explain further, all you need to know is that living things and the infernal shouldn't fraternize. The effects of madness and power both increase the more demon blood you consume. If you take enough to replace your entire body's supply, you become a Devil King. They gain power on a conceptual level—through the Dao."

"So if I were to drink that vial, even though it's no more than a few cups, all that shit would happen to me?" Alexandra asked.

"Yes. Though the power increase and madness wouldn't be nearly as much as for a true Devil King."

"Why don't people use it as weapon?" Oliver stroked his chin. "Like if you had a gun shooting blood bullets. You'd make them go mad. And then, once you killed them, they would never be a problem again."

"You'd be giving them a significant boost in power. In general, a normal death is a good antidote to your enemies, even without the guarantee of souldeath. Perhaps the higher realm cultivators' spirits can persist after their body dies as a vengeful soul, capable of affecting causality enough to be a threat, but we're far too weak to worry about that," Dev'rox said.

Alistair put the vial back in his pocket after he saw Alexandra staring at it longingly. "Alexandra? You there? You worried me for a second."

"Yeah, sorry," Alexandra apologized. "You have to admit, it sounds enticing, if you can contain the madness."

"Are you serious? You don't want to mess with that."

"Do you plan on dying, ever?" Alexandra said matter-of-factly. "'Cause I don't. And if you don't plan on dying, the only downside is going crazy. My Class has twenty different methods of reducing that kind of thing."

"And every genuine orthodox faction won't accept you, and depending on how zealous they are, might even kill you," Dev'rox added. "Though this universe seems to be nonchalant about those sorts of affairs."

"You don't know if that would work," Alistair countered. "Can we wait on making life-altering decisions for a bit? Even with Dev'rox's information, we're still woefully uneducated about cultivation. I mean, we've only been going at this for a month and a half."

"It wasn't like I was going to snatch it from you and drink it in your face," Alexandra said defensively. "Fine. Okay, I agree."

"Oh, I almost forgot to mention. Those Devil Kings—they're almost certainly the thirteen missing people from the leaderboards. In the memories I stole from Esshei, a guy named Saturn mentioned George as their leader," Alistair said, dropping a bombshell.

A cold expression came over Alexandra's face. "Fuck. That's not good. George is completely mental. If he increased his power many times over…"

"Not good," Alistair finished. "We'll find him, I promise. In the meantime, we need to get stronger."

———

Alistair had a few things to do before he went out again. First, he deposited 2.5 million of his 2.86 million drachma with Lauren. He had to boot out some people who stored their money, but this was really important. He could make it up to them later. If he could keep compounding his money for the rest of the month, he would be rich even after paying off his debt.

Next, he gave the **Chord of Desire** to John. The item would be dangerous in the wrong hands, but Alistair wasn't ready to write it off completely. If there was an opportunity to use it later, he would regret having destroyed or sold it.

Eating another one of [Carmela's Happy Pies], this time comprised of some floorboards, Alistair meditated. While he doubted that he could substantially improve his connection to the Dao, that wasn't his purpose for secluding himself.

His office in the new HQ was basically his bedroom. He had a bed installed in the small room, along with some of his old stuff from his college house. It was nice to look at sometimes and be nostalgic about his old life. Alistair didn't want to forget his roots entirely, no matter how far he had progressed. His book collection had been growing since he was a kid and was worth a fair amount.

As Alistair closed his eyes, he focused inward. His vision went black, of course. But then, he took away his hearing. It was a combination of the mental and physical, forcing his body not to register any sounds, while also letting his mind go, to embrace its inner nothingness. Taste and smell vanished next. It wasn't like they were sensing much at the moment, but even the delicious aftertaste of the pie went away. Finally, there was touch— the hardest to diminish. He did it piece by piece, slowly letting the sensations of his body fade away, until there was nothing left.

That was when he opened his other senses. Karmic sight was not true vision, after all, but he could still sense the threads of Fate connecting every living being. His basic Skill allowed him to see things in black and gold, but when he focused on not forcing it, his vision opened into the colors of the rainbow. Things did not just exist in black and white—or black and gold, but on an infinite spectrum.

He tried reaching out with his aura sense after testing out his Karmic sight for a while. Whereas he saw Fate as a colored web, aura was like a gaseous haze that peaked and troughed. When he concentrated, he could feel everyone inside of the building, and some people outside as well. Aura was just as colorful as Fate, if not more so. Everyone appeared as bubbles of energy, each with their own flavor.

But the only reason he cycled through all of them was to access his sense of life force. It had emerged right as he received [Blood Hand]—and he needed it to understand *nue*. He imagined his blood circulating through his body, giving him nourishment. But his blood was not entirely his own.

There was a tiny amount, an almost invisible amount, of foreign blood within him. Alistair urged it to the forefront of his mind.

Eureka struck after what felt like hours of focus. Alistair had a tentative hypothesis of what *nue* was. If the Dao aligned with the soul, and Mana aligned with the body, then *nue* aligned with the mind, in a perfect trinity. It didn't explain why Mana and Dao energy saw far more usage than *nue*, at least to Alistair's knowledge, but it was a start. If he envisioned his mind in the same way he did his soulcore, he could extend it beyond himself with something he decided to call "psychic energy." Compared to the tsunami of psychic energy Esshei produced, his was like a ripple against a paper sailboat. But a skyscraper didn't appear out of nowhere. He would build a foundation, step-by-step.

When he opened his eyes, he was shocked to see that almost a full day had passed. Alistair could finally understand the concept of a cultivator secluding themselves in meditation for decades at a time.

The next two weeks passed in a blur. Alistair, Alexandra, and Oliver all went out hunting monsters and beasts that threatened their territory. Blaise, Robert, Lily, and his sister all came along at certain points, though John stayed back as he had promised. Alistair hung out with his family when he had the time, and he even ate real food for the first time since they provided it on Faxor. Cultivators at his level could survive on Mana absorption, but that didn't mean he missed cheeseburgers and xiaolongbao, or soup dumplings.

Speaking of Mana absorption, his level progression had slowed to a halt despite slaying thousands of monsters and continuing to absorb Mana. It took him a fortnight to go from level 38 to 40—though he did fill up his "Deliverance of Justice" with ten more procs after he saved Lily twice and then a bunch of strangers fleeing a drake. Using 28 of his 109 Upgrade Points, he upgraded the Badge to Tier 3, which was now capped at three lives saved per level instead of two. Tier 4 of "Deliverance of Justice" cost an insane 500 Upgrade Points, so he expected that to be a commensurate improvement, maybe something like retroactively doubling all previous his procs. As things stood, he couldn't afford to sit on his Upgrade Points for 10+ levels, so he added the remaining 81 points to his Badge slots.

Through both active and passive recruitment, the Northeast Order Freehold had added over a hundred subregions, to bring their total to 697. They completely shored up every subregion north of Long Island and were making inroads into New Jersey. No one power had dominated the region so there were a bunch of local conglomerates vying for domination, leading to human-on-human conflict. They had sent envoys, but some of them were attacked without provocation.

Alistair had confidence that they would eventually gather all the territory, which left him most concerned about their closest major neighbor: the US Government. It made sense that the former nation was one of the strongest powers in the new world—they had trained armed forces and weapons galore, along with a lot of rich people. They didn't have any one person with extreme power, but they were far richer than he was, with over 1000 subregions in their possession.

Alistair meditated in one of his purchased cultivation chambers, trying to ignore the brewing political conflicts while he attempted to reach level 41 and dig deeper into his Dao.

Someone knocked on his chamber furiously, breaking Alistair out of his trance and forcing him to open the door. Two urgent messages, the courier said, and Alistair felt both relieved and like the world weighed down on his shoulders.

They had discovered Devil King activity near their borders, and his friends and girlfriend had arrived in New Boston.

14 BELATED REUNION

"ALISTAIR!" The soft and beautiful voice of a woman he thought he might never see again flitted lightly through his ears.

Am I dreaming?

Katelyn jumping onto him and kissing him disabused that notion. Alistair grew red with embarrassment at the public display—he wasn't one to engage in PDA, but he didn't blame her. Another familiar face felt... good. He would have preferred if it wasn't in front of dozens of people on the first floor of their HQ, though.

He spotted his old roommates Tommy and Nathan a couple meters away, acting like jesters at the public kiss. Not that it wasn't expected from them.

After what felt like an eternity, she let go of her hug and jumped down. "You've grown taller!"

Alistair smiled. "Shallow, that's the first thing you notice about me."

"I didn't mean it like that," she said, playfully punching him in the shoulder. "There's something different about you."

Alistair could already feel that. There was an incomprehensible gap between the two of them. Katelyn's aura and life force felt like a drop in the ocean compared to his. So tiny and small, like the wind could blow out her fire if she wasn't careful. He estimated her to be less than level 20.

"Looks like you're a big shot now," Tommy said. "I never thought I'd see you again. You know, seeing your name on the leaderboard was the only thing that kept me going. I thought, if Alistair can do it, I can survive. Not that I got nearly as far as you."

Tommy and Nathan both had similar auras—stronger than Katelyn's, but not by a lot. But that didn't matter. A weight on his back that he didn't even realize was there had evaporated. Katelyn, Tommy, and Nathan—they were all fine.

"What the hell is this? Let me in!" a man shouted at the entrance to the building, a series of glass doors.

"Sir, you're not authorized to come in here," one of the guards stated.

"I was the one who saved the most recent batch of people!" he shouted. "I'm here for my reward!"

Alistair held up a hand and indicated for the guard to let him in. He was a nondescript-looking man with black hair and a scar going down his cheek, wearing modern designer clothing. Alistair wouldn't have thought anything of the interloper, but he noticed Katelyn's expression change to disgust upon seeing him.

"Thank you, my lord," the man said obsequiously. "I, Corey Castro, managed to survive in the wilderness of the Dinaric Alps, protecting and shepherding these people for the past two months."

"Fuck off," Nathan spat. "You didn't save us from anything. You let dozens of people die. The only reason you were the leader is because you got lucky finding a Rare item."

"Talking back to me now?" Corey raised an eyebrow. "That's fresh. I apologize for his actions, Lord Alistair."

"You don't have to call me 'lord,'" Alistair said, shaking his head. But he was more curious about his girlfriend's reaction. "You have a problem with this guy?"

"He's been creeping on me since the day we met. He said if I slept with him, he'd give me all sorts of special privileges."

"That's n-not true!" Corey stammered. "I mean, my eyes might have wandered from time to time, but you can't blame a man! We were out there in the wilderness for so long, it's only natural. I never touched her!"

"Is that last part true?" Alistair asked Katelyn. She nodded her head. "Okay."

Alistair went up to Corey and punched him in the stomach, throwing his weight into an uppercut. He purposefully modulated his strength to Corey's level 25, not trying to kill the man.

That felt better than it should have. He was glad that Corey hadn't done anything further. Primarily for his girlfriend's sake, but also because he might have done something rash that would crack his Dao Heart.

"Get Mr. Castro situated in his quarters. We need to properly reward him for his good deeds," Alistair said, motioning to the guards.

The sleazy man was still coughing from the punch, but he mustered up the strength to bluster as the guards carried him away. "Wait! I'm sorry! I promise I didn't mean anything by it! I would never have done anything if I realized she was your woman!"

"Good riddance to that creep," Tommy whistled. "He was pretty strong, though. Or at least, I thought he was strong until I saw you. You're in a whole 'nother dimension."

"We need to catch up," Alistair said, changing the topic. "Let's go to my room."

Alistair had the time of his life sharing stories with his friends. Apparently, the three of them had landed somewhere in rural Croatia. The closest they came to death, Katelyn said, were in those first few hours when the monsters struck. In their case, it was a hive of giant hornets. They only survived because they found a house to shelter inside.

It took a couple hours, but they met up with some other survivors. Despite everyone being Croatian, they were still able to understand them through the soul translation. Corey was the only other American, and had tried to ingratiate himself to their group, though it failed when he kept hitting on Katelyn despite her rebuttals.

Unfortunately for them, Corey found an item in the first week that allowed him to level up faster than everyone else. He quickly took control of the group and made their life a living hell. They only stayed with him because the alternatives were worse.

Surviving on the fringes and never causing too much trouble, they gathered with some other North Americans and slowly tried to find their way home. It took the generosity of a woman in the top 100 of the leaderboards for them to find passage to a transcontinental **Teleportation Circle**. That was when they saw the Northeast Freehold's message in the Soulnet.

As Alistair sat and listened to their story, he couldn't help but think about how different their experiences were. It felt like they were passive observers in their story, their arrival in his territory being a series of lucky incidents and goodwill from those more powerful. In contrast, he'd been the orchestrator of his own destiny, for the most part. He had luck and allies on his side, but if he hadn't seized every opportunity by the reins, nothing would have happened. It made Alistair wonder if all his providence was just him getting the luck of the draw, or if it was actually his talent and hard work.

He laughed and smiled with them, but he knew it would never be the same. There would always be an inseparable wall between them now that he had started down the path of a cultivator aiming for the peak.

"So then I had this crazy battle against Anthony Ricci. You might have heard about it. I was like 'pow pow' and punched him a lot, but he was tough. He hated me so much it fueled him. And then he made these shadow clones, and then after I destroyed the shadow clones he somehow brought them back with his Dao technique."

Alistair relayed his whole war with Anthony to his friends and girl-friend. They had been talking for several hours by that point, and he was getting a bit antsy. There was still the other news he had to deal with, and he couldn't gain levels simply by sitting around anymore. His soulcore had reached the peak density of Mana that it could obtain from atmospheric absorption. He would need to keep killing monsters if he wanted to level up at a rate faster than once every month or so.

"Holy shit, you've been through a lot," Tommy said. "So you saved two strangers' lives in the first hour, then you kill the leader of the monster wave in your subregion, then you get transported to a different planet where you have to fight alien criminals? You've probably had more unique experiences in the past two months than most people have in a lifetime."

"I guess so; I never really thought of it like that," Alistair said. "I'm sure you guys must have been through a lot, too."

Nathan and Tommy gave each other a glance.

"Hey, I know you're a busy man. We don't want to hold you up too long. I mean, you're kind of in charge of our safety now, so I would rather not die because we talked for too long, you know what I mean? Tommy, you ready?" Nathan ruffled through his hair awkwardly.

"I couldn't just *not* see you guys. But yeah, I should be taking care of my responsibilities." Alistair didn't want to make things more troublesome than they had to be, but Nathan was right.

"Good to see you, man. For real."

Tommy hugged Alistair, with Nathan joining in. Katelyn watched from the side with a smile on her face. There was an unspoken understanding between his two friends that they would give the couple some time alone.

After the two of them left, it left Katelyn and Alistair alone on his bed. A pregnant pause passed between them before anyone spoke. Alistair started to say something, but Katelyn cut him off.

"I know things are different."

She spoke bluntly, without melodramatic sentiment. "It's been two months—not that much time, but I can tell you've changed. There's something different about you that I can't put into words."

"I never cheated on you," Alistair choked out after a pause, not sure what else to say.

"I never thought you would," Katelyn said. "Not that I would blame someone else. You probably wrote us off as dead. But you're a bit of a romantic guy, aren't you, Alistair?"

Alistair could feel his heart constricting. "I didn't write you off as dead, either."

"I had a feeling you wouldn't."

Katelyn looked enchanting under the piercing morning light. There was no sound but the gentle susurrus of her silky black hair in the draft. Alistair's heart pounded as all his feelings came flooding into his system. She'd lost her clear-rimmed glasses, making her eyes look smaller. He looked into her alluring dark brown eyes that were almost as black as the night sky, eyes that he'd found himself lost in thousands of times.

He drew her in and their lips joined together. It was a tender kiss that lasted just as long as it needed to. Katelyn draped her arms over his neck, pulling him down. Alistair went at first, but he stopped halfway.

The kiss ended abruptly. "It's fine," she said.

"Kat, it's not like that," Alistair protested.

"You need time alone. Come to me when you're ready," Katelyn told him.

And that was that. Katelyn left, leaving Alistair in solitude.

I've screwed that up big time, he thought to himself. *Fuck me. Relationship of three years and I've thrown it down the drain. What would my mother say?*

Alistair couldn't stop himself from feeling that pain. He'd harbored hope that miraculously his mom would return with his friends, but that obviously wasn't the case.

He told himself that he didn't even know why he'd stopped the kiss. His body clearly wanted more. Deep down, he knew the answer, but he didn't even want to think it. So, he moved on to the side Quest he'd received.

[Vanquishing the Devil Kings]: *The world of man faces a threat from the beyond. Thirteen men and women, transformed by demon blood, seek to burn the world to ash and reform it in their own unholy image. Stop them before they can complete their mission. For each one you slay, gain a bonus reward.*

Task: Kill 0/12 Devil Kings. Reward: 200 Upgrade Points, one Journeyman Foundation Skill, Appropriate Dao Fruit. (Bonus Reward: 40 Upgrade Points). Time Limit: N/A. Penalty: None.

Alistair greedily stared at the rewards. Killing all twelve Devil Kings would give him 680 Upgrade Points, a Journeyman Foundation realm Skill, and a Dao Fruit. He had asked Dev'rox what a Dao Fruit was. Apparently, the fruit part was a bit of a misnomer—it was an exceedingly rare treasure that originated from the planetary cores of worlds ranked Journeyman or higher. A Beginner world like Earth didn't have that luxury. Consuming an appropriate insight Dao Fruit and meditating was a commonplace method for breakthroughs in the Dao, which made them worth a ridiculous amount of drachma.

He did notice that for some reason instead of thirteen Devil Kings to kill, there were only twelve. Was it a glitch? Kevan said that the Pathfinder AI was buggy, but he hadn't seen anything too weird other than his Subclass. He would've thought if someone else already killed a Devil King, it would say "1/13" rather than "0/12."

"Ah, to be young again," Dev'rox sighed.

"Please don't tell me you were eavesdropping on my conversation."

"I can't *not* eavesdrop, Alistair, I thought you knew that."

"I did know that, I just did my best to suppress the memory." Alistair grew red as he re-remembered the implications of Dev'rox always being around.

"Are you thinking of going for [Vanquishing the Devil Kings]?" Dev'rox asked with a raised eyebrow. It wasn't really a raised eyebrow, since he didn't have any, but the motion was the same.

"Well, considering Alexandra and Oliver also got the Quest, I have a feeling that anyone who is involved with the Devil Kings, or maybe just those powerful enough, has received it. And I *really* want those juicy rewards. Better start now, right?"

"It's okay to take breaks sometimes, Alistair. Even Sakaleon the Hundred Eyes rested a day with a beautiful princess on his journey to the Heavens."

"I get that, but stopping my momentum isn't what I need right now."

Alistair took out the vial of demon blood. He kept it on his person, just in case anyone was tempted to try it. There was a science department he built that kept a tiny droplet for research purposes, but that was it. Gripping it tightly, he opened the door to his room. It was time to hunt some Devil Kings.

15 CHASING THE DEVIL KING

IT WAS remarkable how fast the city was progressing. They did have superpowered laborers, but even Alistair didn't expect this level in just under three weeks. Linda, the level 30 Architect, had underestimated herself —while they didn't have any skyscraper-level buildings, they now had enough housing to fit everyone. Alistair was also happy he could pay everyone who had helped a fair wage.

The city looked something like a cross between a medieval European and East Asian city. Linda's Class allowed her to purchase architectural blue-prints that sped up and perfected construction to a superhuman level. A towering wall surrounded the outskirts, visible to Alistair even from a kilo-meter away. They were improving their battlements and protective measures as well. Any intruder would be subjected to a barrage of magical arrows and lava raining down on them.

Tommy and Nathan had already gone to work, saying it was the least they could do. Katelyn had an Agility-related Class that focused on her running speed to the detriment of other abilities, so she helped out as a courier. After their debacle in his bedroom, he wasn't sure what was happening between them. They definitely hadn't broken up, or at least that's what Alistair thought. It was just... weird. He would talk to her later and really sort things out.

In the meantime, Alistair wasn't trying to manage his land—he was trying to leave it. He unfortunately wouldn't get to leave through the front gates, since the fastest method was taking the **Teleportation Circle.** Alistair cast a wistful glance back as he headed off to adventure.

"You ready?" he asked Alexandra and Oliver, who were accompanying him.

"Yep, I got everything," Oliver replied.

Alexandra flipped her dagger. "Me too."

"Okay, let's go." Alistair stepped onto the mirrored disk that could transport them halfway across the world. However, they were just using it to go a few states south. On the prompt menu, he tapped a location a few kilometers below their southernmost territory.

Blue light enveloped them. After just over a second, it vanished, leaving them in what looked like a classroom.

In the corner of the new room, a man reading a book fell off his chair, scrambling on the ground in surprise. "Ex-c-cuse me, can you identify yourselves?"

"Alistair, from the Northeast Order Freehold," Alistair announced. "I've spoken to your boss before."

The man grew pale as he realized who he was speaking to. "Y-yes, of course! I apologize for the condition this place is in. We've been under constant attack these last few nights."

That piqued Alistair's interest. "Under attack? What do you mean by that?" The briefing he had received stated there were reports of red-eyed and black-blooded creatures, but nothing of a coordinated attack. That was a problem with the current information situation—anyone could read a larger organization's messages, but the smaller groups lacked the capital to respond on the Soulnet.

"Why didn't you flee?" Alexandra asked.

"Excuse me, miss, if I overstep, but you don't understand this town. Most of us have lived here for more generations than I have fingers. We survived the apocalypse and we're not gonna leave now." The man winced a little and rubbed the back of his head. "Though things are getting tougher now, I must admit. Every night, the legions of hell knock on our doors."

"We're here to help," Alistair said. "Why don't you show us around?"

The man, whose name was Beau, gave them a tour of the town. He was one of the stronger residents, being just around level 25. The most powerful person and leader of their town was an old lady named Gertrude who was close to forming her soulcore. She had previously spoken to Alistair via the Soulnet, where she'd described the overall situation of the area.

Alistair had wondered what would happen when an already old person started progressing. Each species upgrade would increase one's lifespan, but it did so by adding more life force to a youthful body. If an old body received life force, it was unclear what would happen. Gertrude looked younger than her 79 years, but not considerably so. In contrast to her physical appearance, she moved with a grace and power nearly identical to a young person at her level.

"I lost my grandson and daughter-in-law defending this town," Gertrude said with longing in her voice. Alistair's group observed the defenses, which consisted mostly of shoddily constructed palisades and some makeshift weapons, along with the cheapest options from the System Store. "We're at our wits' end."

"Have you seen our offer?" Alistair didn't feel any need to cushion his words. He had broadcasted the same terms to everyone bordering their freehold, terms that he thought were more than fair. They were getting stretched thin, finding it harder to recruit enough people to protect their current territory. But even the freehold's sparse resources were better than the alternative. There were hundreds of stories of towns being wiped out to the last person.

"I've talked it over with the leaders of some neighboring towns. After hearing stories of your decency, we've decided to accept." Gertrude offered him a handshake. "I hope I'm not making a mistake."

"I promise, you aren't." With that, the number of subregions in the Northeast Freehold bumped up to 740. He had to delegate almost every task these days—his main responsibility was protecting everyone from the powerful threats, and that meant getting stronger. And *that* meant fighting monsters nonstop.

Gertrude and Beau, who was one of her ten living grandchildren, brought the trio to a shed on the outskirts of town. Despite the lack of pomp and circumstance, the shack was one of the most guarded parts of their subregion. Three level 25 guards were stationed outside, and the area was riddled with booby traps.

With all of his senses, Alistair could easily detect the hidden staircase, but Alexandra and Oliver were shocked when, at the wave of a hand, a portion of the paneled floor opened up into a dungeon-esque trapdoor.

Gertrude motioned for them to follow her down into the darkness. She held up her hand and conjured a blue flame, which separated and flew onto torches on the walls. The eerie blue light added to the creepiness of the whole affair.

"These are our two discoveries."

There were two metal cells built into the stone walls. Alistair could feel a dampening effect from the bars which weakened the two prisoners. On the left, a large white dog fiendishly clawed and bit at its cage. Alistair thought it was a mutated animal, but there was something about it that made him classify it as closer to a monster than a beast. On the right, a human man acted just as wild as the monster to his side, pounding on the bars like a madman. Both had glowing red eyes and lines of red and black covering their skin, just like Esshei.

Right away, both of them reacted to his presence. Alistair wasn't sure, but he had a strong sense that they wanted the vial of demon blood in his pocket.

"Jesus, they've never acted like that before," Beau said, as he noticed their raging increase upon seeing Alistair. "Vinny, run some more Mana into their cells."

Alistair flared his aura to its maximum level, letting his powerful soul-core warp the Mana around him. Despite their greed, the dog and human cowered back in their cells. They were mindless beasts, but even the lowest animal knew the law of the jungle. "I don't think they'll cause any trouble."

"Thank you," Beau said, though his face drained slightly from seeing Alistair's display of power.

"That's them all right." Alistair fiddled with the vial. "The changes are exactly the same as the Appalachian serpents. Looks like the information was correct."

Alistair activated [Eyes of Truth] on the two prisoners. The monster dog was level 33 and the human was level 27, though both exhibited an aura that he estimated to be around 50% stronger than their level indicated, around the same multiplier as Esshei. Digging into his stolen memories, something he tried to avoid due to their emotional gravity, he gathered that not even a third of Esshei's blood had been replaced. If under a third was enough for a 50% increase, Alistair didn't want to know how strong Devil Kings like George and Saturn were.

"They almost feel dead to me," Oliver observed. He opened his hand and a wispy black energy flew toward the duo. "Their aura is like that of a living person, but their life force has something wrong with it."

Alistair realized that Oliver might have an even better life force sense than himself, considering his Class. When he tried feeling the prisoner's auras, he did notice an unnatural pulsing sensation. Whereas normal living things had a continuous ebb and flow of their vital aura, the dog and the human had an artificial pulse to their life force that made it feel like something was controlling them.

"I think we're good here," Alistair said. "Can you tell us where to find them?"

————

Alistair felt like the forest disapproved of his presence. No matter what he did, his danger sense tickled with the permanent sense that something just was *not* right. It was like the sense of dread from a delirious fever dream, muted and brought into his waking mind.

Gertrude had told them that no matter what they did as they ventured south, they wouldn't find any demon-blooded enemies during the daytime. That all changed at night, when waves upon waves of ferocious rocs and mutated deer would assault their town. One time, Beau and his brother tried following them back into the forest as the sun started to rise, but it was like they disappeared into the morning shadows.

Alistair hoped that their level 35+ trio would do better. Between his incredible extra senses, Oliver's necromantic capabilities, and Alexandra's nature attunement, he planned to catch the creatures off guard in a diurnal attack.

Oliver opened up his screeching cracks in reality, which had, incidentally, lost their screeching noise. His new storage skill was called **[Otherworld Gate]** and gave him more dexterous control over the shape and location of his portals, along with a greater volume of storage.

Out of the dozens of cracks Oliver created, his legion of zombies stepped out. With his Talent Tree upgrade, he could see through the senses of his zombies, which now numbered just over a hundred. Kalgur and the other Bloodsun orcs were still his primary combatants, as they grew stronger with him, but he'd also added some of their recent foes to his collection, including the soulcore-less and shrunken corpse of Esshei. Even the condensed form of the former Serpent King was twenty meters long. Oliver wanted them to ride the beast, but Alistair convinced him there was no point, since they all had practically unlimited stamina, at least at a walking pace.

Alistair felt uncomfortable looking at his former enemy. Still, he didn't regret saying yes when Oliver asked for the body. Esshei's soul had passed on, so this hunk of flesh was just an empty vessel. The body of a Beast Lord was still valuable, and if it saved Oliver's life one day, he would be glad to have given it to him. Though, since it lacked a Beast Core—which only formed at level 75—it wasn't as lucrative a corpse as it could have been.

"Shit, this forest is creepy as fuck," Alexandra said softly, always the articulate lady. "I feel like there's something that's gonna shank me from behind any second."

Alistair had to agree. The maps indicated that the forest had been far smaller before the initiation, and even just a month ago. They had been walking for several hours now, with no end in sight. It seemed to get only thicker as they went, the deciduous trees growing so tight and tall that Oliver had to clear their path with his zombies and Alistair had to punch away branches just to see.

"I feel like we're going in circles." Oliver let his eyes turn black, which meant he was seeing through his zombies. Alistair couldn't help but feel a chill run down his spine. Looking into those black pits was like looking into death itself. "I'll place my zombies in intervals of maybe a hundred feet in a line. Then, if we walk forward and find them, I'll be able to tell."

"How could we have gone in circles?" Alexandra questioned. "We've been walking in a straight line."

"They say it's remarkably difficult to walk in a straight line without an aid," Oliver pointed out. "So we probably wouldn't know if we were walking in circles."

"Okay, but I think I would know if we were *literally* walking in circles. I'm not talking about just going slightly off course."

"Did you really think I meant that we started walking in circles just because we're not walking exactly straight? Of course I mean there's something else going on too."

"Alright guys, let's just test Oliver's theory," Alistair interjected. "There's no reason to fight amongst ourselves."

Oliver positioned most of his zombies in a straight line in front of them. Not all of them, though. As always, Oliver kept his three most trusted zombies—Prince Kalgur and the orc's former generals, the Gyzorr Brothers —by his side.

However, because the forest was so thick, they couldn't even see the first zombie that was supposed to be thirty meters away. Oliver promised he could still sense his zombies from kilometers away, so there was nothing to worry about. Using his zombies as a line, they walked forward, following Oliver's lead.

After passing by the first two zombies in the line, Oliver stopped. "Holy shit, we *are* going in circles. The one in front of me is James 2.0. But the one that was supposed to be next is James 3.0. What the hell is going on?"

Alistair narrowed his eyes at the confirmation. After the incident with the Herax Turtle, he'd purposefully tried to master every form of perception he could. If your opponent couldn't surprise you, their chance of victory went down significantly. So when he activated [Eyes of Truth], he was happy to see that his efforts were not in vain.

Whatever magic was affecting their normal senses, it couldn't bypass his [Eyes of Truth]. The melancholic loss of Karma almost felt nostalgic at this point, as his eyes started glowing crimson red with Karmic energy. Now that he had seen the red star of the Karma Node, he understood the solar color his Skills emanated. The mark of fiery Karma connected to the threads of Fate like parasites to cattle.

Normally, the threads of Fate would tie everything together in one universal web, but Alistair instead saw that they all pointed in one direction. Not waiting for his friends just in case it was urgent, he rushed toward the source—the hollow of a nearby tree. Both his danger sense and his Karmic sight told him it was safe, so he just stuck his hand in and pushed.

The scene that followed reminded Alistair of the warping of reality that occurred right at the start of the initiation. As he pushed the inside of the tree, the air around him distorted like a canvas being removed from its frame. It was as if he was pulling the image of the forest out of the world. After a few seconds, he'd torn off the fake picture, and his eyes feasted upon the hidden truth.

They were in a forest, but it wasn't nearly as dense or dark as the illusion. Next to the tree he had touched was a small paved path leading up a wide, grassy barrow. The vegetation was yellow and sickly, like the life had been drained out of it. There were scores of headstones and tombs littered over the hill, adding to the eerie atmosphere. Despite it being daytime, the sky was dark and the stars shone above—all part of the ambiance high-lighting the mansion at the top of the hill.

The black and red palace loomed over its surroundings, a gigantic home as large as some of the biggest mansions on Earth. The main foundations and walls of the classic château were black, with certain flame emblems and spires colored a bold red. In other words, an exact color match for the glowing lines on all the demon-blooded creatures he had seen. There was no mistaking that a Devil King called this mansion home.

"I think we found our mark," Alistair said.

"You think?" Alexandra fiddled with her two daggers. She had decided to dual-wield, holding the **Tang Clan Dirk** in her left hand and a new, whitesteel knife in her right. "Let's go kill some devils. Not including our buddy Dev'rox."

16 CHATEAU OF THE DEVIL KING

"I'M NOT A DEVIL," Dev'rox grumbled to Alistair, "I'm an imp."

Alistair was more focused on the mysterious château. It looked like something that belonged in a fantasy novel, not the real world, making him suspect it was another illusion. But [Eyes of Truth] didn't see anything wrong. The unnatural night sky could have been a Skill, but as long as they weren't under any illusions, Alistair was satisfied.

Like a haunted graveyard, strands of mist floated around the headstones and between the rotted trees. The air felt both heavy and sparse, like a humid city smog.

"Guys... there are actual bodies in those graves," Oliver said, stopping mid-stride. "I think they died recently."

Alexandra looked at Alistair. "I suppose we're going to have to go gravedigging?"

Alistair sighed. He didn't want to disturb the dead, but if it gave them clues as to what was going on, it would be invaluable. "Let's be respectful, at least."

Oliver kept a free slot in his arsenal just in case, so he was able to [Zombify] one of the bodies without destroying the grave like Alexandra probably would have done. Alistair was impressed with how versatile his Skill was, as he could get it to work within a few seconds.

The new zombie broke free from the dirt with a decomposed hand, pulling itself out of its grave with unusual strength. Alistair had gotten used to Oliver's other zombies after seeing them time after time, but it always felt weird to see their birth.

"If only I could see their memories," Oliver complained. "My build manual says that I'll have to wait till after level 100 for that."

"Can't believe you have a build manual," Alexandra grumbled.

Alistair was a bit jealous, too; build manuals were exceedingly rare, and no one was quite sure how to get one. Oliver said that he obtained his after forming a Dao Node. It was like a more explicit version of his Fate-divining necklace, showing possible synergies and paths which combined different Talents and Skills suited to the individual.

"Look there." Alistair pointed at some tiny holes in the corpse's neck. "Don't those look like needle marks to you? And there are some faded lines on the skin, which could be like the other effects we've seen from demon blood."

"That does seem likely," Oliver said.

Oliver fiddled around with the body for a few minutes, but they didn't find any other clues. All the buried bodies had the same needle holes in their neck and faded lines.

"Why do I have the feeling that this is some kind of trap?" Alexandra sighed. "Let's get this over with."

The three of them hiked up the hill, following the stone path set before them. The further they climbed the thicker the fog became, eventually reaching the point where they could barely see five meters in front of them. The mansion loomed in the distance, only visible since its height exceeded the reach of the fog.

By the time they reached the steps to the front door, Oliver was breathing heavily. His body wasn't as tough as Alistair's or Alexandra's. There was something in the fog or atmosphere that was bearing down on them.

"I'm okay, don't worry," Oliver said, panting between words.

"It's the ambient Mana," Alistair exclaimed. "I didn't realize it at first, but that's why we feel like we're walking through molasses."

"Holy shit, you're right." Alexandra held out a hand. "It's so thick that it doesn't even seem like Mana."

"Try cycling your Mana. It should protect you against some of the effects," Alistair advised.

He started doing the same himself, despite the pressure only being a slight malaise for him. His soulcore stirred like a beating heart, pumping his internal Mana throughout his meridians and clogging his magical pores against the thickened atmosphere. While his movements were still physically slower, the oppressive feeling disappeared.

Oliver and Alexandra copied him. They both cycled their Mana in their own way, which Alistair found intriguing—was there a correct or objectively superior way to cycle Mana? He did notice that Oliver's Mana reeked of the final oblivion, the inexorable feeling of death. His own Mana hadn't even come close to attuning to lightning, blood, ice, or force. He relied on his Skills to convert it, making the Mana less effective. It was a reminder that others still surpassed him in certain areas, and that he shouldn't grow complacent.

With his lower physical stats, Oliver still didn't move as smoothly as him or Alexandra, but at least he no longer felt like he was dying. The oppressive feeling persisted with Alistair's companions, suggesting that their weaker auras meant they couldn't block out all the ambient Mana.

Alistair knocked on the ten-meter-tall arched doors, not expecting a response. The clang of his knuckles on the knotted wood reverberated in a more profound way than he expected, shaking the very foundation of the château.

Then, with a creaking that sounded like it came from the depths of hell, the doors opened into interminable darkness. Dank, cold air washed over the trio, full of silent screams. Alistair's danger sense went haywire, similar to when he entered the serpent's den but magnified to the extreme. Because of the overall danger that permeated everything, unless there was an imminent threat to his life, he doubted [Fighter's Instinct] would be as effective.

They all looked at each other. The beast's maw was inviting them in. It was the most obvious trap ever, yet this was their opportunity. If they left now for reinforcements, who knew if the mansion would even be there when they came back? Alistair took the first step inside, closely followed by Alexandra and Oliver.

The moment all three of them crossed the line of no return, a large screen popped up, visible to all.

Dungeon Prompt:

Dungeons are a limited instance found on newly initiated worlds

after a certain amount of infamy is reached within a specific physical area. Each dungeon must have the potential to lead to further growth through conflict. A dungeon's strength is always relative to the strength of those that enter, up to a certain point.

Limitations: Max 4 challengers, Level 60 and under, No Adept realm items or above.

You have entered the Kestrel, moving castle of the ninth Devil King, Saturn Alius. These unholy grounds have been the site of experimentation, death, and torture. Both the living and the dead cry out for vengeance, the wrath of both man and nature unrelenting.

Task:
1) Save (5) prisoners from Saturn's control
2) Slay the Devil King.

Reward:
1) +30 Upgrade Points and "Devil May Cry" Badge
2) +2 levels and additional Talent Tree added, "Blood of the Devil."

Time Limit: Indefinite.

Accept (Y/N)?

Alistair almost licked his lips at the rewards. The 30 Upgrade Points and 2 levels were fine, but a new Badge was just what he was waiting for. An additional Talent Tree sounded interesting as well, and considering that was the big reward for slaying Saturn, he expected it to be good. Of course he had to save the prisoners—they were most important. But the rewards... they were nice.

"Ugh, these rewards are way too tempting," Alexandra muttered. "What's this 'Rage of the Devil' thing?"

"'Rage of the Devil?'" Alistair asked.

"Yeah, it's the second reward. You don't have it?"

"No, I have 'Blood of the Devil.' What about you, Oliver?"

"I have 'Death of the Devil,'" Oliver responded.

"Tailor-made rewards—how nice," Alistair said. "We don't have much of a choice, do we? He has five prisoners, and it said they've been torturing people here."

"I think you just want the rewards," Alexandra teased. "Just kidding, just kidding."

Alistair shook his head. "Very funny."

Hitting accept, the prompt disappeared and was replaced by a red carpet floating on a sea of darkness. Orbs of burning rose-colored fire flickered into existence just above their heads, illuminating the carpet which extended forward for the length of a football field. Even if the mansion was large, Alistair had to imagine some magical mischief was at play with the spatial dimensions.

At the end of the carpet were three doors. The first and leftmost looked like one of Oliver's portals. The outline of the doorway was blue and warped the surrounding air, with the actual rectangular entrance being a pure white. It looked so clean that it almost seemed painted on, an unreal gateway to a different dimension.

The center door was an ornate brass piece that looked like it belonged in a medieval fantasy movie. There were thousands of carvings engraved in the metal, consisting of what appeared like Chinese characters and scenes of humans fighting against monsters.

Finally, the last door was blood red and pulsing with a disturbing life force. Alistair would have sworn it was alive if it wasn't just a dripping, goopy door. The handle to open it was a piece of bone that looked like the femur of a human.

As they drew closer, the sensations the three doors gave off amplified. The white door felt purifying and empty, an embodiment of mental order. The fancy brass door gave off imperial gravitas and worldly power, humming in Alistair's heart like a general preparing for war, while the melting door of blood was the vampiric temptation of eternal life, a Greek gift that would only lead to ruin.

No new prompt appeared when they reached the doors, leaving them to figure things out. Alistair walked up to the white emptiness and stuck the tip of his finger through it, but nothing happened.

"That was stupid. What if it cut off your finger or something?" Alexandra chided.

Alistair huffed. "I was pretty confident it wouldn't. It doesn't seem dangerous at all, actually."

They poured over all three of the doors for at least thirty minutes. Alistair rotated through all of his senses, trying to glean anything about what was inside them without actually stepping through. Nothing worked; even his Karmic sight couldn't make heads or tails of what lay beyond.

Oliver opened a portal in front of each door, having stored his zombies away earlier since the carpet was narrow. "How about I try sending a zombie through each one of them?"

Alistair and Alexandra agreed, having no other ideas. Oliver sent one of his new zombies, a dog-sized crystal spider, through the white door. Alistair felt goosebumps form on his forearms when he saw the zombie. He had a particular dislike of arachnids, especially gigantic ones.

The spider passed through the portal with ease, but Oliver shook his head. "The moment it crossed over, I lost all connection to it."

"Damn it," Alexandra cursed. "What are we gonna do?"

Alistair tapped his foot on the carpet. "I think we're just going to have to make a choice."

"He's right," Oliver said. "This is going nowhere. Did you notice that we can't access any information from the outside? We don't want to waste any more time."

Alistair tried checking his freehold information and leaderboard. Oliver was correct—those screens came up empty, like something was blocking them. Alistair didn't like the idea that the Dungeon was preventing him from seeing what was happening in his own subregions, only furthering his desire to complete it as quickly as possible.

"Which one should we choose?" Alistair asked. The rightmost door gave off creepy energy, but at the same time, the center door was almost too inviting. The more neutral left door appealed to him, but that also made it suspicious.

"I say the bloody door," Alexandra said at the same time as Oliver blurted out, "The middle one."

Alistair chuckled. "I was going to say the white void. That doesn't really get us anywhere."

Oliver patted Alistair on the back. "Since you're kind of the boss, I'll cast my vote for that one too."

Alexandra gave Oliver a suspicious glance. "Since when did you get so buddy-buddy with Alistair?"

"I can't be nice now cause I'm the Necromancer guy? Talk about stereotypes." Oliver shook his head.

"I actually think we should follow Alexandra's lead," Alistair said, interrupting the argument. "If it's the most dangerous one, then we'll probably get more rewards. If it goes against its appearance and is the least dangerous one, well, that's good too."

"And if it's the middle dangerous one?" Oliver questioned.

"Then it will be the perfect mix of both options."

"Doesn't that apply to every door?" Alexandra asked.

Alistair put on an exaggerated face of betrayal. "You were the one who suggested it in the first place, weren't you?"

He walked up to the door of blood, putting his hand on the cold bone handle. With just a tiny bit of force, the door opened, revealing a desolate island in an endless ocean of crimson liquid. The moment he opened it, the other doors vanished. "Who wants to go in first?"

———

If Alistair had a nickel for every time he'd had to run on a liquid, he would have three nickels. Not a lot, but it was weird that it had happened three times. Now that he had perfected the art, he helped Alexandra and Oliver get started. The speed required to run on water was surprisingly low at just over a hundred kilometers an hour, so even Oliver could easily do it. The harder part was maintaining your balance, but after a few minutes of practice, they got it down.

"There's no way this is in the mansion, right?" Oliver asked as they dashed across the ocean. As far as they could tell, the red liquid wasn't actually blood, it just looked like it and had a similar viscosity. At least, they hoped it wasn't blood.

Alistair tried using [Eyes of Truth] to see if they were in an illusion, but he found his vision blocked by an invisible barrier. It might have been the Pathfinder AI itself intervening to make the trial fair, since the barrier felt far stronger than anything even a Devil King should've been capable of.

A faint splashing sound brought him out of his focus. "Do you guys hear that?" he asked, turning his head. On the far horizon, he could make out a dark figure even through the mostly opaque blood. If it was that large...

"I don't see anything," Alexandra said, and Oliver shook his head too. Alistair forgot that their vision wasn't as good as his, so he wasn't going to wait for them to realize. He picked up Oliver and carried him in his arms like a baby.

"What the hell?" Oliver exclaimed.

"There's something gaining on us!" he shouted over his furious acceleration. Since Oliver had the lowest speed, Alistair wanted to make sure he wouldn't fall behind.

Alexandra rushed to keep up, but she was slower than him by a significant amount. Alistair looked back again and saw that the underwater threat was only a hundred meters away. If he was alone, he could outpace it, but he couldn't carry both Alexandra and Oliver at the same time. It wasn't a matter of strength, but the size of his body. If only he was a true behemoth like Jason from Port Locasta.

Alistair realized that no matter what they did, it would catch up to them. He motioned for Alexandra to turn around—at the same time, he threw Oliver dozens of meters in the opposite direction to keep him safe. The beast finally emerged from the ocean, its head cresting above the surface. It was easily the size of a blue whale and looked like an enormous, carapaced dolphin. Alistair could not help but imagine the leviathan beast as an ancient warrior steeped in blood, cherry-colored drops sliding down its pale red shell.

The aura the beast gave off was similar to that of the serpent Beast Lord, yet it felt less refined and more animalistic. If Sessen Esshei's aura was like the imposing glare of a lion hunting its prey, this dolphin-crab's aura was that of an elephant in musth. Both were powerful, yet the latter was undirected aggression, lacking an intent.

Name: N/A
Species: Elegian (Leviathan)
Class: N/A
Level: 51

Alistair's scan revealed the level and species of the beast, and not much else. He rushed toward it with Alexandra, intending to meet it head-on—or at least that's the impression he wanted to give. When he was close enough to see the pupils of the elegian's eyes, it opened its mouth wide and roared, sending out a wave of *nue*.

Do all beasts naturally produce nue *in their roars?* Alistair wondered as he braced himself. It was weaker than Esshei's, only slightly disrupting his mind. He imagined it might have done more damage if he hadn't already experienced a stronger wave of *nue* and adapted to it. Alexandra wasn't so lucky, falling into the ocean from both the physical and mental shockwave.

Alistair [Dashed] forward, bringing himself within a meter of the beast's maw. He fired an uppercut with his entire body, activating [Force Fist] and using a portion of his Fist Node. His spectral punch met the inside of the leviathan's mouth, crushing serrated teeth and launching the hundred-ton beast into the air. Alistair couldn't help but love the propulsive aspect of the Dao of the Fist even if it didn't add much damage.

In the depths below, Alistair felt an explosion of aura at a level exceeding even his own. Alexandra came bursting out in a crimson aura befitting the ocean, since it came from her own evaporating blood. She looked like an avatar of wrath, her dagger emitting purple gasses that even Alistair didn't want to get close to. Instead of how Alistair would infuse discrete amounts of Dao energy into individual attacks, Alexandra seemed to continuously burn her Barbaric Rage Node. It altered her features, making her look older and more beautiful, shaping her into a serene goddess of war. It wasn't how Alistair would interpret Barbaric Rage, but everyone had their own understanding of the Dao.

Alexandra chased after the tumbling leviathan, slashing her whitesteel dagger and dirk in an x-shape that released two lines of green energy. The lines grew as they zoomed across the ocean of blood, cutting deep lines into the red water and striking the underside of the falling beast.

Instead of leaving an x-shaped cut, her Skill vibrated and rotated with life-attuned Mana, grinding against the dolphin-crab's flesh. The beast crashed into the sea as its underside was infused with foreign life Mana which attacked at a cellular level. This was Alexandra's ultimate Skill, [Partition Vitae], a Skill that Alistair thought had a cooler name than any of his own.

"Hey!" Oliver shouted. "I found land!"

Alistair turned his head to see Oliver beckoning to them while standing on three of his zombies. Alistair looked back at the thrashing whale. With how powerful its aura was, he doubted that **[Partition Vitae]** and **[Force Fist]** had killed it. Killing the leviathan might give him a level up, but... Alistair shook his head. It wasn't worth the resources they would have to put in.

Alexandra had already stopped **[Barbarian's Fury]** and was running toward Oliver like a madwoman. Alistair joined her, not looking back at the elegian leviathan they had left behind. Oliver had devised an ingenious movement system using his zombies, having them throw him dozens of meters at a time, and then absorbing them back into the portal before he got out of range so he could keep the chain going.

Alistair spotted the land Oliver was talking about, a large cave mouth sticking out above the liquid surface. The angry beast behind them was catching up, even with their head start. Adjusting his pace, Alistair caught up to Alexandra. Seeing Oliver's throwing technique gave him an idea. "Sorry, Alexandra!"

Alistair grabbed her by the waist and pulled from his Fist Node as he threw her into the air with all his might. She was heavier than she looked because of her high Constitution, but Alistair could lift pickup trucks with his bare hands at this point. With the additional propulsion of the Dao of the Fist, Alexandra rocketed forward. At the same time, Alistair activated **[Dash]** twice in quick succession.

By the time Alexandra landed, Alistair was there to catch her like a knight in shining armor awaiting his princess. He carried her down the entrance of the cave, side-by-side with Oliver. Just as they got a few meters in, a wave came crashing down into the cave, soaking their already stained robes again. They were safe after that, since the leviathan was too large and too sea-bound to enter the rocky alcove.

The cave entrance jutted out over the ocean, but the tunnel itself quickly turned down diagonally, going far past their line of sight. Alistair put Alexandra down, who looked embarrassed that he'd picked her up and thrown her. Oliver didn't pay them any attention, instead having his orc zombies dry him off in a royal fashion.

Alexandra complained about the fight while she got Oliver to give her the same treatment. "Damn, I wish we could have finished that thing."

"Me too, but we can't afford to waste any time," Alistair replied.

Oliver took out a blue lamp to light the way as they walked further into the cavern. Alistair made sure to test his **[Eyes of Truth]** to verify that they weren't walking into the orifice of some giant beast, not wanting a repeat of the Herax Turtle situation. The sides of the cave had the texture of porous rock, but he wanted to be sure.

After a few minutes of exploring, the tunnel led into an underground hot spring around the size of a stadium. There were hundreds of smaller bubbling pools all around, surrounded by crystal formations that reached as tall as five meters. Streams of attuned Mana so thick that they looked like ribbons swam through the air. Alistair felt like the truths expressed within the hot springs might have been even greater than the cultivation chamber on Faxor.

But what piqued Alistair's attention even more than the mysterious energy were the two people bathing in the center of the hot springs. One man and one woman—both brimming with absurdly powerful auras that rivaled his own. The moment they arrived, the man opened his eyes and stared directly at him.

The gaze of a predator stalking its prey.

17 THE PHARAOH OF LOST SANDS

THE MAN STARING Alistair down was tall and skinny, standing at least six inches taller than himself but without a hint of muscle mass. He wore what looked to be the garb of an ancient pharaoh, though without the traditional pschent crown. With his golden tan skin and an aura that felt like the sands of time, Alistair imagined he could have stepped out of Memphis in the 25th century BC.

While the man radiated a focused killing intent, a more sinister aura came from the woman. She was almost two feet shorter than the man and looked more cute than deadly, with a bob haircut and pale rosy cheeks, but that didn't fool him. Alistair knew it very well by this point—the profane power of a Devil King. He could tell right away she was the real deal, and not merely one of the experiments. The feeling of strength he sensed from her rivaled if not exceeded his own.

Right before his eyes, the pharaonic man crumbled into sand. Only a slight cry from his [Fighter's Instinct] alerted him to a danger behind him. Alistair turned around just in time to see a man forming from the dust on the ground, kicking him to the side by instinct alone.

"That's a poor way to greet someone," Alistair said.

The man blasted into the rocky sides of the hot spring, ricocheting about ten meters away into a steaming pool. He nonchalantly got up and dusted off his outfit. "Who are you?"

Alistair activated his [Eyes of Truth], the polite convention of not using inspect Skills vanishing now that they were in combat.

Name: Hidden
Species: Spectral Superhuman I (Partially Evolved) / Pharaonic Bloodline (Stage Unknown)
Class: Hidden (Lacking Intelligence)
Level: 42

Name: Whimsy
Species: Elemental Superhuman I (Partially Evolved) / Devil King (Stage 1)
Class: Watertide Charmer (Rare)
Level: 39

"Didn't you already check?" Alistair asked.

The nameless man darted back to his previous position, joining up with the woman. She had walked forward at a leisurely place before sitting down on the ground in apparent meditation. "Get up, Whimsy," he said.

"I don't want to." The woman stuck her tongue out.

He sighed and looked back at Alistair and his friends. Alexandra took out her two daggers and Oliver opened up a dozen [Otherworld Gates] from which his hundred zombies processed. A tense silence passed between the two sides, only broken by the man's next words.

"You're a candidate for the conversion?" he asked.

"Yeah, I don't know what that means," Alistair replied. "You're going to need to be more specific than that."

He shook his head and made a beckoning gesture with his hand. "I can sense demon blood on your person. Give it to me."

"Why should I do that? And why are you with a Devil King?" Alistair countered.

"Give it to me."

"No?"

"Whimsy, you deal with the woman and the boy. I'll handle this one." His clothing spontaneously combusted, leaving a hairless and sculpted bronze torso, devoid of any body fat and muscle. "Have you not figured out my identity, number two? After meditating in these waters, I have transcended even further beyond you."

"We still don't have to fight," Alistair said. "How about we talk things out?"

Out of the corner of his eye, he spotted Alexandra lunging at the Devil King, who'd started waving her arms and controlling the nearly boiling water surrounding her. Oliver kept back but circled his troops around her.

"I don't want to, though?"

A new window popped up, this time red instead of the typical blue.

Limited Challenge Instance:

Wandering Hobo challenges you to a total contest. The Heritage Springs were part of a reward for a completed task, and he is willing to share them with you if you survive his onslaught.

Reward: Non-aggression from Wandering Hobo's party for a one-week period. Penalty: -2 levels and -50 Upgrade Points.

Accept (Y/N)?

Alistair looked at the window in confusion. You could actually lose levels and Upgrade Points as a penalty? The reward wasn't even good— why couldn't Wandering Hobo just choose not to attack him? It wasn't like he'd even done anything to him in the first place. Still, if he was going to be aggressive and continue attacking their party, they wouldn't be able to complete the Dungeon at all. Speaking of which, they were also competitors for the Dungeon. Or at least, he thought they were, since he assumed Wandering Hobo was also part of the Dungeon Quest. Considering all those factors, he couldn't just back down. Especially now that he had stolen Wandering Hobo's "World Leader" Badge, he knew that his death would be a significant boon to the man. It was time to see who the real #1 was.

He hit accept and let himself fall into the Kai'tazake Mutra, but only to the level of the ocean of tranquility, retaining most of his mental faculties. He had practiced separating the Mutra into three stages of depth, focusing on its three distinct images which each had their own meaning. The ocean of tranquility calmed his nerves and honed his reaction time like an ultra instinct boost, but didn't give him any deadlier moves or martial knowledge.

At the same time, he activated [Dash], bringing him down to 822 Mana. As he turned invisible, he saw Whimsy jump over him in a gush of water and face down his friends, but he ignored that. They could handle themselves.

Adding a drop of the Ghost Node, he attempted to pass through his opponent, but found himself stopped right at the edge of Wandering Hobo's skin. Alistair tried hopping backward, but his foot got wrapped in a shackle of sand. His danger sense blazed near the small of his back, causing him to throw a punch as he twisted his body to the side.

His punch pushed Wandering Hobo back several meters, though his feet remained grounded like an oak's roots. A spike of condensed sand jutted out behind Alistair, narrowly missing his backside.

Alistair stared at his opponent, not making a move as he studied him. Despite being in the trance, his moves still felt sluggish. Fighting in an area with higher ambient Mana made his movement feel closer to what it was at level 30—overall slower and less coordinated than at level 40.

It also meant that they would both do less damage with their attacks. Alistair was the one typically on the offensive and looking to end the fight quickly. He would have to figure out Wandering Hobo's special traits, similar to how he had the advantage of his Subclass, triple Dao Nodes, and Dev'rox.

Striking the ground with alacrity, Alistair cast [Lightning of Justice] down from the ceiling, its golden light being a warm reminder of home for him. When Wandering Hobo didn't react at all, his hopes fell. He didn't even make any blocking or evasive maneuver at all, straight up tanking the lightning to seemingly no effect.

Alistair wondered if the man had a monstrously high Constitution or some protective item. He ran forward and casually dodged more sand spires that shot out of the ground, [Fighter's Instinct] alerting him to their presence just a moment before they hit him.

Dev'rox's voice appeared in his head. "It feels more like a bloodline ability to me. A powerful one, at that."

Right as he got into range, Wandering Hobo crumbled into sand. Alistair bent backward to avoid another spike right where his opponent's body used to be, turning around to see where he teleported to. The moment Alistair's eyes locked into his new location, he used **[Dash]** to catch up.

They played this game of cat and mouse for a while, Alistair being the chaser while Wandering Hobo fled. Each time Alistair caught up, the number one ranked man would unleash a torrent of spikes. He dodged most of them, but occasionally one would glance off him, opening up a minor cut.

Alistair got tired of playing catch-up and asked Dev'rox for a boost. As Wandering Hobo disintegrated, Alistair was already turning around. In his peripheral vision, he caught a glimpse of a reforming body, using **[Dash]** plus Dev'rox's spatially-attuned Mana to bridge the gap faster than normal. He caught Wandering Hobo by surprise, smashing in his face with a **[Force Fist]** and then following up with another **[Force Fist]** body hook infused with Dao energy. The shimmering salmon outline of his fist blasted Wandering Hobo into the wall of the hot spring, echoing loudly from the sound of the impact.

Wait, what?

Alistair wasn't expecting his attack to work *that* well. After all, Wandering Hobo had just face tanked a **[Lightning of Justice]** like it was a prickle of static electricity. He cautiously made his way over to Wandering Hobo's apparently dead body. After getting within five meters, he cautiously put one foot after another.

He was dead. Like, *actually* dead. Alistair felt no life force, no aura, not even any threads of Fate—an impossible feat for a living creature. Somehow, despite Wandering Hobo's immense power, he had died to a two-punch combo. That didn't seem right at all.

A buzzing sound alerted him to a threat behind him just before his danger sense did. Alistair **[Dashed]** to the side, avoiding a stream of locusts at his previous location. There were so many insects that they formed an almost solid stream of darkness, devouring the rocks and ambient Mana.

Right behind him, Wandering Hobo was alive in the flesh. There was no sign of any injury he had sustained earlier, either. Alistair couldn't come up with any logical explanation other than that he had risen from the dead. He tried very hard to detect an illusion and found nothing.

The locusts swarmed around the man, forming a living shield. Alistair could feel an ancient and powerful Dao inside those insects, like he was in the presence of a godly pharaoh. At the same time, the rocks around Wandering Hobo's feet disintegrated into sand, joining the locusts that orbited him. Each grit and grain carried the curse of decay, sparkling in the atmospheric light of the Mana.

Wandering Hobo lifted his palms in benediction, sending twisted arms of bug and sand at Alistair. The particles vibrated in tandem, causing all the rocks and pools in the nearby region to start humming. There was already the obstruction of the higher ambient Mana, but now Alistair felt like he was in the middle of a foreign Dao. Everything around him receded into the primeval lost sands, turning the real into the unreal.

When he tried activating [Dash], the Skill slipped away from him, nearly causing him to be swallowed up by the swarm. He used all of his speed to run away from the lost sands, but they chased after him. Jumping over a hot spring, he noticed Alexandra engaging Whimsy in combat. His partner looked like she was a spiritual fire, an embodiment of rage, bringing her weapons down with such force the water around her splashed out of their pools. Whimsy just laughed, manipulating the surrounding water into rotating spheres that defended against all attacks. Right as he passed into their half of the makeshift arena, an explosion of boiling water almost caught him straight in the face.

"Stay in your lane!" Whimsy shouted over her own laughter.

The sudden burst of water avoided his danger sense since he was so focused on the threat behind him, forcing him to jump back. His slow reaction let the spiral of sand and locusts catch up to him, striking him in the back.

Alistair felt like his body was being torn apart by the forces of nature. Dev'rox gathered his Mana and tried to alleviate the damage by making Alistair's body more intangible, but it only worked so much. It was as if his spirit itself and the pathways in his body were being attacked by the decaying Dao and Mana. He twisted his body as the force of the blast rocketed him sideways into the ground, bouncing him against the rocky terrain into the near-boiling water of a hot spring.

Alistair found himself at 401 Health, or just a little under 2/3 of his total. But it wasn't just his Health that was affected, as his injury was more than a flesh wound. His back dripped with blood as the locusts and sand tore at his skin, but everywhere they attacked, he couldn't cycle Mana through the affected areas anymore.

Wandering Hobo was already revving up another attack, but Alistair wasn't paying attention. Instead, he slipped into the second stage of the

Kai'tazake Mutra, surpassing the ocean of tranquility and forming the sky of infinite knives. Each knife represented a move in his endless panoply of techniques, all under the purview of the Zenaitsu Morogoni—Alistair still wasn't sure if that name was a school, person or martial art. All he knew was that it gave him knowledge beyond his own.

He drifted into Karmic sight, studying Wandering Hobo with such intensity it was like he was trying to bore a hole in the man's soul. Alistair [Dashed] forward, seeing potential futures as afterimages of varying opaqueness. His newfound focus allowed him to suppress the oppressive Dao field. The more likely futures appeared almost as solid as the real Wandering Hobo, distinguished only by their illusory threads of Fate.

Like before, when Alistair used [Dash], Wandering Hobo had already started crumbling away, along with his sandstorm and locusts. But Alistair had already predicted where his opponent was teleporting. Instead of appearing where Wandering Hobo was, he had already set his direction to where the man was going, flickering in front of him with a prepared [Frozen Claw].

With his fanged fingers, Alistair swiped at his opponent's protective swarm. Using the Ghost Node, he froze each grain of sand and insect in a cascading web of hoarfrost. The freezing virus spread rapidly, first as frost and then as a second, crystallizing layer of eternal ice. The last ghost of all living things threatened to end the man's existence outright. Just as the ice was catching up to him, Wandering Hobo killed himself.

Alistair didn't see how at first, but as the cultivator's body crumpled to the ground along with the atmosphere of his Dao, he noticed the man had taken a decaying hand and plunged it into his own heart. Once again, at a first glance, he couldn't see anything unusual about the body. It was just a corpse. But when he activated [Eyes of Truth], his eyes glowing crimson and reducing his Karma to 42, he saw a tiny hint of what was happening.

The body before him was a soulless husk. Or more accurately, it felt to his Karmic vision that it never had a soul in the first place, lacking any potential for the threads of Fate. It was as if a soulless homunculus had been substituted for Wandering Hobo, suffering his death for him as his true soul escaped into a new form.

As Wandering Hobo's new body incarnated into the world, its threads of Fate appeared ex nihilo, alerting Alistair to the new threat. He jumped forward and activated [Force Fist] on his foot, destroying the ground beneath him in a mighty stomp. His opponent's new body formed inside the ground as particles of sand.

However, Alistair didn't realize that the ground beneath them was not a simple underwater ocean floor, but a relatively thin firmament above a gaseous ocean of colorful mists. They fell through the gasses together, wrestling each other along the way. It seemed like they both had trouble activating their movement Skills in the thickest part of the mists.

Alistair kept using his Karmic sight in combination with the Mutra, easily besting Wandering Hobo in close-quarters combat. Every movement the man made, Alistair countered before it even happened. He punched his opponent's face, elbowed his side, and kneed him in the stomach for what felt like minutes as they kept falling. The infinite sky of knives gave him so many options, but the choices never felt paralyzing. His moves were impeccable, embodying the mantra of fluid, then still and soft, then hard.

In such close quarters, both of them avoided using Skills, though after beating up Wandering Hobo enough that the man's reactions slowed, Alistair felt the opportunity to finish him off with a [Blood Hand]. With his congealed bloody fist, Alistair grabbed him by the throat, slowly applying pressure as he absorbed his life force.

Surprisingly, Wandering Hobo seemed to accept his fate, not even attempting to escape Alistair's hold. Not sensing any trap, Alistair continued to squeeze and absorb until his enemy's body crumbled into sand, just like the two previous times.

Because it was an unwilling sacrifice, Alistair didn't gain as much as he had from Esshei, but he still felt a small increase in his life force suffuse his cells and a small memory pass into him.

It was dim and far less lucid than Esshei's memory, but Alistair got the message all the same. He saw himself in Wandering Hobo's body during the initial period of the initiation. He was exploring an Egyptian pyramid and as a result had to fight mummies as his subregion's monster wave. After using his ingenuity as an ex-military archaeologist, he had defeated the final boss and reached a previously undiscovered royal chamber—the tomb of Thutmose II.

Similar to how Saturn's château had gathered infamy, a historical location like the lost tomb of a pharaoh could also hold conceptual meaning. Whoever Wandering Hobo was before, he was reborn with a Pharaonic Bloodline—the Sovereignty of Osiris. At the cost of his Health becoming a tenth of what it was supposed to be, he would have fourteen lives. Fourteen lives that would regenerate every week.

Alistair felt some anxiety build up. He would have to kill him fourteen times? He had already used up 30% of his Mana for only three deaths. Having to conserve that much Mana, Dao energy, and Stamina would completely change his tactics.

As Wandering Hobo's body finished turning to dust, they finally reached the bottom. But instead hitting a floor, Alistair's movement naturally slowed as the ambient Mana grew thicker and thicker, until it was so dense Alistair could float on it. He wanted to absorb it all and meditate, but he would have to finish his fight with Wandering Hobo first.

If Alistair could find him.

18 FIRST DEEPENING

ALISTAIR GAZED up in wonder at the vast array of gasses. It was like every color of the rainbow combined, and he was swimming through it. The density of the Mana blocked out most of his senses. Even threads of Fate were barely visible through the clouds.

He waited in anticipation for Wandering Hobo to attack, but nothing happened. Diving through the environment like a swimmer on an alien world, Alistair looked for his opponent for several minutes, but came up empty. Worry rose in his chest as he realized he couldn't tell up from down. How would he get out of the weird subterranean mists even if he did defeat Wandering Hobo?

After another ten minutes of frantically stumbling around, Alistair centered himself and calmed down. Sitting cross-legged, he started absorbing the dense Mana. It was far more concentrated than what he was used to, and it dribbled into his system like molasses. It was perhaps the case that the ambient Mana of Earth was slowly growing more concentrated as people leveled up, but this Mana would be considered at the upper end of the Foundation realm.

"Do you know what this is?" he asked Dev'rox.

"It looks like a facsimile Dao Heart," Dev'rox said. "Though a crude one, I might add."

"I feel like we've had this discussion a million times where you say some term that I don't know, and then you have to clarify it," Alistair said, rolling his eyes.

"Hush, it's not my fault you're an uneducated savage. As I mentioned before, there exists the Heart of All Creation at the center of the Physical Plane, the source of all Mana. In each individual universe, there exists a Dao Heart, which is the source of the Mana within that universe."

"Mana?" Alistair asked. "Not Dao?"

"The Dao comes from no source. But as you might have noticed, the Dao Heart expresses a myriad of truths. A facsimile Dao Heart is taken from a tiny piece of the true Dao Heart at the center of a universe."

Alistair listened to Dev'rox and felt beyond the Mana in search of truths —a hint of the Dao. As the Mana churned through his system, he first focused on capturing the Mana types that he was aiming for, like lightning and blood, rather than trying to access the power for his own gain.

This place reminded him of the Dao Nodes in the Organizational Map, but there were certain differences. The strength of the Dao was stronger in the gasses, but much more diluted because there were so many. He had to sort them out in his head to focus on the ones that felt fruitful to him.

Eventually, he gravitated toward a small tremor that felt like the Dao of the Ghost. As he mentally moved toward the sensation, it grew in his mind until it overcame all the other pieces of the Dao. No longer did he feel fire or life, just the infinite hollow land of the Ghost.

Alistair felt like the truth in this sliver of the ghostly Dao was more in line with the part that was expressed in ice-attuned Mana. The eternal ghost that would exist beyond the heat death of the universe. He let his mind recede into the darkness, all thoughts vanishing. There was nothing but a spiritual winter that was both everywhere and nowhere.

For an aeon, his consciousness absorbed these immortal truths. Time lost all meaning in his cold, dark center. All his previous attempts to capture this nothingness were failures stemming from a lack of imagination. The human mind was not meant to understand eternity. But slowly, as best as his mortal intellect could, he began to comprehend. Not entirely, of course, as that was impossible for his level, but just a small piece.

The moment of infinite time faded, and a notification popped up.

Achievement: Dao Node (I) (Dao of the Ghost) — First Deepening. *Gains "Permanent Haunt" division.* Reward: +50 Intelligence, +30 Wisdom, +30 Charisma, +10% Mana.

With the new bonuses, his max Mana pool went up to 1,279, which was timely since his Skills had increased in Mana cost, along with the Ghost Node's reserves nearly doubling. He also noticed that his max Karma went up to 60—Alistair assumed that it came from his Charisma increasing, but he didn't know the exact conversion rate. While he wanted to investigate what the "Permanent Haunt" division meant in regard to the Dao of the Ghost, Alistair felt a powerful presence behind him.

"Finally," a voice said from the mists. "I've been waiting for almost a day."

Alistair felt a sense of alarm overwhelm him when he heard that. *A day?* If that were the case, the fight between his friends against the Devil King might have already finished. He gulped, not wanting to think about the worst-case scenario. That couldn't be the case, no matter what. There was no point fretting anymore about it, in any case. Either they were fine, or they weren't. Right now, finishing his current fight as quickly as possible was paramount. He could deal with the ramifications of a day's worth of cultivating the Dao passing in a blink of an eye later.

The mists within a ten-meter radius around him vanished, leaving just a sunset colored aether. Wandering Hobo crossed his arms and let forth a field of his Dao energy, a shimmering, slightly beige dominion that reminded Alistair of the authority of an Egyptian pharaoh. Alistair felt the depths of its strength and understood that even though his opponent seemingly only had one Dao Node and he had three, that one Dao Node had a deeper truth than his.

"You've been waiting just so I can grow stronger?" Alistair raised an eyebrow, not making a move.

"It would have been rude to interrupt," he said. "I didn't want to kill you without a fight."

"That's a bit arrogant, don't you think?"

Out of nowhere, Alistair bolted at Wandering Hobo, punching him in the face. Bone cracked under his fist as the man went flying into the mists. Alistair chased after him, the condensed Mana receding into the distance with the Dao field his opponent produced. Another hit—an uppercut to the gut—sent the cultivator flying up through the clouds, Alistair following right after. He returned to the second stage of the Kai'tazake Mutra with ease, delivering blow after blow.

Wandering Hobo raised a hand, summoning sand from his palm, but Alistair caught it with a [Frozen Claw]. His ice-blue talons sliced through the particles, freezing them in place as he imbued his Skill with the Dao of the Ghost, specifically trying the "Permanent Haunt" division. It wasn't like an element that he added—such as Heaven on Earth for the Justice Node, or Deathblow for his Fist Node—but more like a quasi-Skill he could employ with the Dao. He intuitively understood that instead of turning himself intangible like he was used to doing, it turned the objects he touched with his [Frozen Claw] intangible, though it wasn't *actually* permanent like the name suggested.

Alistair flew through the incorporeal mass of frozen sand, which looked like a ghostly ice crystal surrounding a mass of grain, piercing Wandering Hobo's stomach. Immediately, hoarfrost spread from the wound, enveloping his body in its icy demise. Alistair briefly activated [Eyes of Truth], draining 4 Karma to peer into the hidden nature of the world.

As he expected, his vision revealed nothing. [Eyes of Truth] went beyond normal Karmic sight, allowing him to see deep emotions and desires, but the dying body of his enemy held no special characteristics. Alistair didn't understand. His [Eyes of Truth] hadn't failed him yet. Why had the man let him beat him up and sacrifice his fourth life?

The crystalline ice completed its total imprisonment, subsuming the previous layer of hoarfrost around the lifeless corpse. However, as Wandering Hobo was reborn into a new body, Alistair felt something wrong with his own.

Alistair looked down at his fists. There were two black hieroglyphics burning into the skin of his hands, along with further marks growing on his chest and stomach. Panicking, he tried pulsing Mana, then Dao energy, and even Karma to stop them from spreading, but nothing happened.

Wandering Hobo just stood there and watched in his new body, while Alistair slowly realized that the markings weren't *doing* anything to him, at least not yet. So, he focused back on Wandering Hobo, running toward him with a renewed frenzy. He shifted his vision into Karmic sight once more, but this time something had changed. As he envisioned the potential future of punching his opponent in the face with a [Force Fist], he saw himself fly back with a dent in his cheek in exactly the same place he struck.

Seeing this future, Alistair jumped back, uncertain of what he should do. He looked to Dev'rox for advice, who shrugged uncertainly. "It could be a Formulaic Skill you triggered the requirements for."

"What's the matter? Why aren't you attacking?" Wandering Hobo asked, smirking.

It's like he's not even trying to be subtle about it, Alistair thought. It made him want to smash his face in, but he was too unsettled by the afterimage he'd seen. Tiptoeing closer to Wandering Hobo, he knew he had to try something, so he sprinted forward, jabbing the man in the face with 50% of his normal power.

At exactly the same time his fist connected, the brand on the back of the hand burned red, and a gray silhouette struck Alistair in the face. The fist of the mysterious entity landed at the same spot as his own attack, disappearing after Alistair's own fist lost contact. Alistair stumbled over himself and somersaulted backward, reorienting after drifting five meters.

Rubbing his cheek, he noticed right away that the amount of damage he took was much less than the amount he gave out. But his minor punch hadn't affected Wandering Hobo that much, who arrested his momentum by flapping his arms like a bird, swimming toward Alistair in a spiral as he gathered sand around him.

Alistair was uncertain of how to proceed. He was fairly sure that Wandering Hobo had a higher Constitution, though it also seemed like the reflection transferred about 50% of the damage. Activating [Frozen Claw], Alistair touched a finger to the incoming spiral, wanting to test a hypothesis.

Assisted by an infusion of Dao energy, ice spread from the sand onto his opponent, encasing him in a solid ice crystal. At the same time, a gray ice consumed Alistair, starting from the head down, just like the Wandering Hobo. As Alistair expected, the part of the Skill created by Mana had the same effect, but it was unable to fully replicate his Dao energy.

Breaking free of the replica ice, Alistair twisted his body and shattered the pharaoh's ice crystal with a [Force Fist] imbued with a hefty amount of Dao energy. The air warped around the salmon-colored spectral knuckles, disintegrating the ice and blasting Wandering Hobo dozens of meters to the left. Of course, that also meant Alistair got hit with a giant gray fist himself, but it was much weaker than his punch.

It still hurt and sent him flying, breaking several ribs and dropping his Health to 512. The shock of the attack jettisoned him out of the Mutra, though Wandering Hobo received the worse end of the stick. Alistair spotted him in the distance, floating in the aether. His side was bloodied and battered, though not to the extent he expected. Around his waist where Alistair directed his attack, a shimmering golden band floundered, drooping off his waist and losing its shine. Some kind of protective item or Skill, Alistair assumed as he rushed at Wandering Hobo, intending to finish the job.

A tingle from **[Fighter's Instinct]** warned him of something from below, so he dipped into his Karmic sight and used his arms to maneuver out of the way.

A blast of scorching sand passed by his shoulder, searing his skin. Burning Karma like a madman, Alistair identified Wandering Hobo's newest trick—forming sand out of the ambient Mana and firing it like a geyser of water. The manipulation of ambient Mana in that manner, which saved a ton of personal Mana, was something outside of Alistair's purview, but clearly not for the number one ranker.

Wandering Hobo deactivated his Dao field, disappearing into the mists and leaving Alistair to deal with the bursts of sandy Mana. Now that the Dao field was gone, Alistair could use **[Dash]** again, but that didn't help very much when he couldn't see more than three meters ahead. Only because of his **[Fighter's Instinct]** and Karmic sight did Alistair have the capacity to react against attacks. The only problem was he was losing Karma at an expeditious rate.

A beam of radiant sand blasted him in the leg faster than the previous attacks, causing Alistair to stumble. He managed to dodge another burst of black and purple flaming sand, ducking at the last second before it seared his brain. The mysterious Mana affinity made him see nightmarish figures that only disappeared after he re-entered the Mutra. Diving directly into the third stage, he saw the familiar red lips representing death. Singular in his purpose, Alistair felt a strong intuition to **[Dash]** to his left.

The mists retreated as Alistair conjured a **[Blood Hand]**. In this deepest state of the Mutra, he lacked all thought. There was only action, effortless action—the wuwei of Daoism. Every move was in harmony with a greater schema that was emergent and unknown to his consciousness, yet existed nonetheless.

Wandering Hobo seemed surprised that Alistair detected his location, hastily scurrying backward. Alistair caught up and grabbed him by the arm. They traded blows for a few seconds, but his opponent was outmatched in that field. After some basic hand-to-hand, Alistair elbowed him in the jaw with his left arm in such a way that the shadowy retribution knocked him into Wandering Hobo's chest. Using their momentum, Alistair punched him in the solar plexus with his [Blood Hand].

The congealed crimson blood cut into Wandering Hobo's chest, releasing spurts of his own blood. As the ranker's blood assimilated into Alistair, his own blood went in the opposite direction, attacking the man's spiritual network and life force like a parasitic organism. Alistair infused his attack with the vengeful aspect of his Ghost Node, conjuring the anger of the unjustly killed souls he had encountered.

Due to Wandering Hobo's Formulaic Skill, a copy of his attack entered his chest. However, in his trance, Alistair instinctively selected [Blood Hand], which attacked the life force and meridians of its target. With Esshei's freely taken essence—and that of all the monsters and beasts he had used the Skill on in the past two weeks—Alistair's life force was as solid as a thunderous oak. The weakened shadow [Blood Hand] damaged him to some extent, but not nearly as much as his adversary.

Still, his Health dropped by a fifth and he—ironically—coughed up blood. Wandering Hobo died a fifth death, decaying into dust as soon as his life force left his body. Alistair darted his head in every direction, trying to detect where Wandering Hobo would spawn next. He knew he couldn't sustain his Karmic sight for much longer. He'd already dropped down to 27 Karma and wanted to save some for an emergency.

To his surprise, the first sign of his opponent came from below. Faster than he could react, a wave of Dao energy passed by him, erasing all the mist within a ten-meter radius. But this wave didn't harm him; it was a sanctifying explosion that wasn't intended as an attack but more like a landscaping tool. The reality around Alistair changed from sunset mists in a gaseous chasm—to a desert of sand and wind.

There was nothing but the desert. Alistair's mind didn't accede to this idea, but his soul felt certain this marble of reality was what the entire world was. A ten-meter radius sphere of the lost sands. The primal sun beat down on him while waves of sand ate his skin. The quicksand at his feet dragged him down while swarms of locusts gnawed away at his Mana.

When he tried to move or cast any Skill, he felt an oppressive weight on him. Everything in this new domain was a part of Wandering Hobo's Dao. Each grain of sand and locust and ray of sunlight was both real and not real, just as the Dao was greater than existence and less than existence.

Now that he was inside it, he had a name for the powerful Dao Node, a name that he was certain the man expressed to him on purpose—the Dao of Lost Sands.

19 PROTO-DOMAIN

BATTERED by the harsh desert sands, Alistair felt his Health decreasing at around one per second. More than just the physical bombardment, the mental strain of the foreign Dao impressing upon his soul gave him brain fog. Alistair felt lost, like a man trapped in a sewer in complete darkness, never to find his way.

"Concentrate, Alistair," Dev'rox grumbled, feeling the effects of the Dao field as well. He had an immaterial body, so he suffered more from the effects, but his soul was still stronger than Alistair's. "You must resist with your own Dao."

Alistair imagined drawing from all three of his Dao Nodes, letting the pools of energy suffuse his body and defend against the foreign Dao. The mental effects of the desert sands immediately abated, but the physical battering of his body didn't stop.

"Do you know what this is?" Alistair asked as he activated [Frozen Claw], trying to use the ice to pull himself out of the quicksand.

"A proto-Domain, I suspect," Dev'rox said. "An inner dimension created out of one's own Dao. As the predecessor to a true Domain, it is not fully instantiated within the physical boundary of the soulcore. It operates more like a highly condensed and contained Dao field."

Alistair could feel the motes of sand tear into the very being of his two cloaks. His items could regenerate from normal attacks, even Dao-infused ones, but for some reason he could tell right away that the proto-Domain was destroying the very core of his **Cloak of the Divined** and **Lesser Cloak of Shadows.**

He considered storing them away so he wouldn't lose them forever, but his life being in jeopardy was a higher concern, so he would take any protection he could get, however slim.

Using his chilled fingertips, Alistair spread frost to all the surrounding sand and locusts, halting them in mid-air with the added power of the Dao of the Ghost. The drain on the Ghost Node was substantially higher compared to outside of Wandering Hobo's proto-Domain, so unless he wanted to expend all his Dao energy, he needed to act quickly.

The sandstorm blocked most of his vision, but he could still sense Wandering Hobo's aura. He wondered why Wandering Hobo didn't attack him while he was vulnerable, instead choosing to stay hidden in the sand.

Alistair struggled to his feet. The frozen sand served as stepping stones for him, helping him walk toward his target. The pale blue color of his ice tinged the air around him as he poured more and more Mana into keeping **[Frozen Claw]** active. Unlike his previous **[Mana Strike]** Skill, it didn't make the attack stronger, but allowed him to keep it up for longer.

A stray lash of sand procured a drop of blood over his eyebrow, falling into his eye. His Health had dropped to 225, his Mana was down to 742, and his Dao energy was falling by the second. But he stayed focused on his prize. Every step was a gargantuan effort that felt like wading through lava. The pain of the foreign Dao entering his skin in every minor crack in his shield burned in agony. The more cuts opened up in his spiritual circulation, the more pain he felt. He knew his Skills would be less effective with all the cuts in his meridian network, compelling him to move faster.

After what felt like a lifetime, Alistair approached Wandering Hobo. He was seated on the ground, cross-legged and eyes shut. Alistair considered throwing down a **[Lightning of Justice]**, but he remembered how it did absolutely no damage before, so he saved the Mana. Instead, he kept walking closer, until he was within striking distance. Wandering Hobo opened his eyes, springing to life. As Alistair had anticipated but secretly hoped would not be the case, the man was just as agile inside the proto-Domain as outside of it.

Alistair threw a straight punch, which Wandering Hobo surprisingly managed to dodge. Even while using his own Dao energy as a shield, the

Mutra felt inaccessible to him. The environment leveled the playing field between the two of them. They exchanged a series of blows—Alistair took a haymaker to the jaw while Wandering Hobo got elbowed in the ribcage and punched in the solar plexus.

Seeing his Health and Mana still decreasing, Alistair knew he had to make a drastic move. Surely this entire apparatus was draining an insane amount of Dao energy, but he couldn't rely on Wandering Hobo running dry. Despite him only having one Node, Alistair sensed that the cultivator had more Dao energy than himself.

It was time to try something he had never done before. Alistair mustered up as much energy as possible and sprinted for his opponent, who was taken off guard by the sudden burst of speed. His intention wasn't to put an end to Wandering Hobo, but it wouldn't hurt to kill two birds with one stone.

As Wandering Hobo turned his back to run away, Alistair prepared a [Force Fist]. Into the Skill he poured more Dao energy than he had ever used in a single strike. He could *feel* the Dao energy as a powerful torrent of spiritual energy within his soulcore, paradoxically occupying the same seat as his Mana. The Dao energy exploded out from his Fist Node, the stellar coral-colored energy that had to be dominated and tamed like a wild beast. The spectral outline of his fist grew as large as a beach ball, glowing brighter than ever before. The air sizzled and warped around the outline as he punched through reality. The Fist was martial force incarnate, unable to be stopped by anything in its path, even this false Domain.

The world of Lost Sands cracked at the seams, shattering into a million pieces as Alistair launched his punch. He felt Wandering Hobo splatter against his Skill and instantly die as the world collapsed. It was possible that killing Wandering Hobo would be sufficient to end the proto-Domain, but Alistair wasn't confident enough to waste time with that, so he went with the all-in approach.

Sunset colored mists replaced the sand and harsh sun. Alistair immediately felt a hollow pain throughout the right side of his body where he had channeled his Fist Node. It wasn't as bad as when he'd overloaded his arm from the blood-attuned [Mana Strike], but he knew something was wrong. Visibly, the arm was fine, but the spiritual network "inside" of it was severely damaged. It was like a part of his flesh that wasn't a part of him, something that lacked a metaphysical identity. He wouldn't be able to channel Mana or Dao through it for the rest of the fight, though Alistair wasn't even focusing on that; he just hoped the damage wasn't permanent.

With that attack, he had just killed Wandering Hobo a sixth time. Alistair cursed under his breath. Not even halfway through his fourteen lives, yet his own resources were dwindling. He had 198 Health and 755 Mana, and his Fist Node was completely gone. His Ghost Node had just half of its energy left, while the Justice Node had three-fourths.

"It's just a matter of whittling you down now," a voice called out behind him.

Alistair's danger sense alerted him to the threat before a spiked column of condensed sand shot out of the mist. Each muscle in his body moved exactly the way he wanted, contorting his head just a few centimeters to the right to avoid the spike. There was nothing like feeling the freedom of his own body, Alistair thought. Now that he was out of the proto-Domain, he felt as light as a feather with the reflexes of a cat.

He knew the man's words to be true. Wandering Hobo just had to make sure he didn't die eight more times while Alistair only had 198 Health. But that didn't stop Alistair. He knew he wouldn't die here. Not yet, not stuck on his homeworld when he had barely tasted the wonders of the grand multiverse. He dove straight into the deepest stage of the Kai'tazake Mutra. It lacked a certain depth because he had nothing left in his Fist Node, but it still gave him some advantages.

With a [Dash], Alistair flew at Wandering Hobo. He let his instincts take over, not letting a single thought distract him. Karma flooded his eyes as he connected to the threads of Fate.

All action flowed without hesitation. Waves of dust and decay poured out of Wandering Hobo, but Alistair countered with [Frozen Claw]. He used "Permanent Haunt" to freeze the waves before they arrived, combining the Ghost Node with the icy Skill once more. Alistair passed through the intangible particles with ease, [Dashing] once more after clearing the wave.

With his Karmic sight, he predicted where Wandering Hobo would reform after crumbling into dust, arriving a moment after the man and crushing his throat with a [Blood Hand]. Alistair felt the life force flow into him like a trickle of water down a parched throat. The essence flowed into this right arm, partially healing some of his spiritual wounds. The purifying power of life force strengthened his cells at the DNA level, though he wasn't sure what the tangible effects of that were, since his stats didn't increase.

Maybe it increased his lifespan, if he ever got too old for his realm, something he didn't plan on doing.

Over the course of the next hour, the two of them played cat and mouse in the mists. Alistair tried to use as little energy as possible in his attacks, but Wandering Hobo was too crafty to injure without at least using Mana. Alistair pushed himself as much as he could, but he realized after a while that his Stamina was vanishing at a faster rate than it was replenishing. He had never been in a fight where his Stamina had run out before, but if nothing changed soon, that would be the result.

Alistair felt sweat dripping down over his face, stinging as it soaked into the micro-wounds over his eyebrow. Using Dev'rox's Mana, he willed himself upwards and grabbed Wandering Hobo by the leg. He activated [Blood Hand] with the same hand, crushing the bones and muscle in a vise grip. The life force and memories flowed into him with ease, further healing the spiritual wound in his right arm. Despite having a tenth of his Health, each incarnation of Wandering Hobo possessed the same life force, so by this point Alistair had absorbed the equivalent of three eminently talented level 42 cultivators.

He took a moment to catch his breath, panting like he hadn't done since before the initiation. How foolish of him to think cultivation had ended his days of gasping for air like after a cross-country race. Even his Mutra had vanished, the mental strain exceeding what his mind could handle. His Health had dropped into the double digits, as had his Karma. A flash of fear passed through his mind, not for himself but for all of his responsibilities. The thought of his mother was the one centralizing focus. He wouldn't get a solid night of sleep until he saved her, and that meant he had to live.

Wandering Hobo re-formed above Alistair, lording above him with a solemnity he hated. It wasn't like the sheer arrogance of Red, but a restrained curiosity that came from supreme confidence.

"Why are you still struggling? I've got five lives left and I can tell you're on your last legs," Wandering Hobo said.

"I can't... give up," Alistair huffed between ragged breaths.

"You were keen on talking before. Why haven't you asked me to back off?"

Alistair grew confused. "You were the one who attacked me, though?"

"Yes, but as the Limited Challenge Instance said, it was to test you. Did you notice that there was a penalty for failing? Obviously, if you were dead, you couldn't receive a penalty. Other than being dead."

"So you're telling me that you would have just stopped attacking me if I asked nicely?" Alistair asked.

"No, I wouldn't have done anything of that sort. I'm just asking you why you didn't ask me," Wandering Hobo said.

Alistair considered what to say next. The man was correct that the penalty existing indicated that his life wasn't in danger to some extent, which he hadn't thought about before. "You think about things in a weird way," he ended up saying.

"No, I think *you* think about things in a weird way. It would be normal for one to question why one vastly more powerful than oneself is attacking," Wandering Hobo said without a hint of irony. "In any case, you have passed my test with flying colors. No one has forced me to use nine or more of my lives since the beginning of the initiation. I think it might not be prudent to go on, considering your condition."

Alistair scoffed at the man's condescension, but he would be kidding himself if he wasn't relieved. He felt the Limited Challenge Instance disappear. Considering the system seemed unbreachable for cultivators of their level (except his Subclass, for some reason), he, Alexandra and Oliver would be safe for the next week. Reminded of his team, he began to ask Wandering Hobo, who just nodded. "They're alive and well, don't worry. Not a match for my partner, though."

"Even if you weren't going to actually kill me, I still don't get the point of all this," Alistair complained.

"Really? It's quite obvious to me. This facsimile Dao Heart is likely one of the greatest founts of inspiration on this planet. Through the fist, the mind is made more erudite—this is a self-evident truth. We taught each other much during the battle, no?"

Another status screen flickered into existence.

Achievement Upgraded: Dueling (IV) — *The beauty of a duel cannot be expressed in words. Trading blows is akin to the exchange of thoughts and philosophies. Inspiration from war, the eternal cycle of life and death, has always been the center of all insight.* Reward: Elemental Fighter Tree -> Communion of Spirit Branch -> Dead Warrior Whispers Leaf ->

Ancient Warrior Leaf **OR** Insight Vision about creating a proto-Domain.

Alistair read through the Ancient Warrior Leaf, which increased affinity toward ancient ghosts, especially ones that he had an emotional connection to. The more primal and historic the ghost was, the more power he could extract. Dev'rox wasn't historical or primal, but Alistair did have an emotional connection to him, and he was pretty damn old.

By his count, choosing that option would double Dev'rox's accessible Mana pool and increase the potency of the truths of Space contained within his power. But the other option was also extremely tempting, considering the singular power of Wandering Hobo's proto-Domain.

He turned to Dev'rox for advice. "I advise the first choice," he replied immediately.

Alistair gave him a dubious look.

"I know what you're thinking, it's not because I want more power personally," Dev'rox pleaded. "Never mind, I shouldn't lie—of course it's at least partially because of that, but I speak the truth when I say it would be more beneficial for you as well. A proto-Domain is a neat trick, but no matter how much of a prodigy you are, you can't form a real Domain until you're level 100 and confirm yourself as an Adept. And a real Domain makes a proto-Domain look like a bad joke."

"But surely it's still better to get a proto-Domain early?"

Dev'rox shook his tail. "Don't overestimate your own skill. You're talented, but at least in the Dao, this Wandering Hobo fellow utterly outclasses you. With your current progress, I would expect you need at least three Insight Visions to create a proto-Domain. Remember, he just has a single Dao node to incorporate. With your three Nodes, it will be at least three times as difficult."

"That makes sense," Alistair said, picking the first option. He could feel the difference in Dev'rox's power right away. Before, he would have pegged his imp's Mana pool at around 200, but it now increased to 400.

Wandering Hobo stood silent during Alistair's mental conversation, only speaking after Alistair had closed the window. It pissed him off to know that Wandering Hobo was correct in his assessment. While he wasn't on the verge of another deepening in any of his Dao Nodes, he had made a ton of progress. Likely weeks' worth of progress under normal conditions.

"Shall we return to the surface?"

Alistair still didn't know what to make of the man. It was just plain weird to go from actively trying to murder each other to being allies, but he supposed it wasn't anything he hadn't done before. But he placed more importance on completing the Dungeon, and Wandering Hobo would be an invaluable ally in that regard.

"I'm going to go along with you, but one day I'll pay you back, I swear."

"I look forward to the wonderful gift you'll give me for helping you get stronger."

20 A STUBBORN DOOR

THROUGH SOME UNKNOWN connection to his Devil King partner, Wandering Hobo could find the way out. They had truly fallen a long way, though after getting out of the dense area they could swim in, the path was clear. With his [Dash] unable to move him through the air, Alistair wished he had a skywalking Skill. Instead, Wandering Hobo levitated the duo on a compacted cloud of sand. Alistair stared at the sand with a healthy dose of suspicion. He had learned first-hand that sand was not to be trifled with.

The base of the hot spring connected to the gasses below with currents of condensed moisture. Each cloudy stream led to one of the pools. It was impossible to miss the cracked hole where they had fallen through over a day ago. Wandering Hobo lifted them up through the opening and back into the hot spring.

"How did you come by the vial you keep?" Wandering Hobo asked as they ascended.

Alistair conjured up the vial from his robe, giving it a brief glance. "This thing? There was a nest of mutated snakes near my subregion. I ended up defeating the leader, who turned out to have been some sort of semi-Devil King? As I understand, unless all of your blood is replaced, you don't get the full benefits."

"Whimsy calls them 'Devil Princes.'"

Alistair stepped out onto the rocky terrain once more. "So, how did you meet her?"

"I first saw her when we fought in the Grand Canyon for seven days and seven nights. After defeating her, I gave her the gift of reason again, and she's been helping me hunt down the remaining Devil Kings ever since."

That explains the 0/12, Alistair thought. It must have considered Whimsy separate enough from the other Devil Kings to not include her for the purposes of the side Quest.

"But don't get too hopeful. The method I used cannot be replicated on the others. As far as I know, Whimsy has certain abilities that make her unique, even amongst the Devil Kings."

The aforementioned Whimsy floated on a bed of water at the center of the hot spring. Alexandra and Oliver were sparring in one of the pools. Alistair assumed they were practicing close-quarters combat, since Oliver wielded a silver sword he only used in dire situations. Alexandra was teaching him at the same time as they battled, being sure not to overpower the less physically invested cultivator with brute strength. He could tell that they were both more powerful than when he'd left, perhaps having deepened Dao Nodes.

Whimsy sprung to life from her pedestal. "Finally! I was beginning to think you'd lost, Pharaoh. I cleaned up these weaklings right after you fell."

"This one is strong," Pharaoh said. Alistair assumed it was his name or title. "You know my style. I fight as the march of time."

She gave a brief look of amusement at the phrase, and then continued, "It will bite you in the ass one day, I promise you. A killer move is important," Whimsy lectured. "So, are they joining us?"

"Joining you?" Alexandra butted in, having stopped her sparring session with Oliver.

The Devil King rolled her eyes. "Yes—why the hell would we follow a weaker group? That makes no sense."

"Whimsy, please behave." Pharaoh sighed. "Did you explain to them what is going on here?"

Whimsy nodded. Pharaoh turned to Alistair. "How much do you know about Devil Kings?"

Alistair opened up his side Quest and showed Pharaoh. "I know that George Moulin is one of them. And a guy named Saturn. He was the one that turned the snake king."

"Ah, good. So you know our greatest enemy. I'll give you a quick rundown of everything Whimsy and I know." The man looked at his companion and nodded. "Tell him what happened on that day."

The short woman sighed and began her story. "I used to be #43 on the leaderboard before the fourth Quest. Right as it started, I found myself in a dark chamber with twelve other rankers. There was this shadowy figure sitting at the head of a glass table who invited us to sit down."

"Of course, with most of the people involved being generally evil, many of them decided to attack the guy. He put them in their place quickly. Then he explained to all of us what the deal was. At the start of the initiation, the Pathfinder AI selected certain individuals using an algorithm to 'start the chaos,' so to speak. Did you ever wonder why there was such extreme violence at the beginning of the initiation? Humans aren't as chaotic or evil as some post-apocalyptic stories would have you believe. No, all of that fighting had a sneaky cause: the system messed with the brains of 1% of the population, according to the shadow dude. Wars are much easier to start than stop. Once one person starts attacking, everyone else gets on edge and you reach the state we had just hours into the initiation.

"He told us that we were all part of that 1%. Not that *I* ever murdered anyone. I was one of the few people that controlled those impulses. I didn't really notice a difference in my personality, to be honest, until after the fact when I looked back and thought, 'Hmm, maybe I was a little more violent.' As compensation for meddling with our heads, he told us that since we were the thirteen strongest members of that 1%, he could give us a gift. As you guessed, that gift was demon blood. He told us all the consequences, like permanent death and complete madness, but do you think that the other people cared about minor inconveniences like that? These people were already mad. Tripling your power is nothing to scoff at. I was the only one who hesitated. At that point, I was fearing for my life if I didn't accept, so I ended up taking it too. He hooked us up to a stone table and bled us out— not a fun experience, FYI, and then he pumped in this viscous, black gunk. It was by far the most painful thing I've ever experienced. I could feel the blood changing my Dao and giving me strength with every second. That ambition and lust for power were the only things that kept me alive."

Whimsy shook her head, shuddering at the memory. "After that was done, he gave us all ranks based on his estimation of our power. Not everyone got the same increase in power from becoming a Devil King, since compatibility matters. For instance, Long Junkai who was #6 on the leader-board—the highest of all the Devil Kings—only ended up being #2 of the Devil Kings. #1, as you already know, is George Moulin. He was the only one not to receive a new name too, for whatever reason. He was the third highest of our group before the transformation, but ended up being our leader. George is stronger than Dragonus—that's Junkai's new name—by a good bit, too. I'm #8 of the Devil Kings, so not the strongest of the pack, but not the weakest either. The shadow guy left George in charge and gave us a Quest, similar to the Quest you and Pharaoh have but in reverse. We have to kill the top 10 on the leaderboard or possess over 50% of the planet's subre-gions. At that point, George will be named Global Mayor. I think becoming Global Mayor is the end questline for you normies too, but it might take a bit longer. The Devil King method would speed up the process—if George succeeds."

Alistair soaked in all the new information. "How far along are the Devil Kings with their Quest?"

"I can't be sure. The other twelve Devil Kings are bound to George's command, but after Pharaoh freed me around a week ago, I don't have any up-to-date information. At the time, I think they had around a thousand subregions. The plan was to gain strength and then take the world by storm before anyone could coordinate. Unfortunately for them, now that I escaped to tell the tale, that strategy won't be as effective anymore."

She scratched her chin in thought. "Is there anything I'm missing?"

"Jakk," Pharaoh said.

"Oh yeah, and we came in here with another guy named Jakk, who turned out to be a sleeper agent for the Devil Kings. Any other questions?"

"Hold on, let's go back to that point," Alistair said. "You guys came in here with someone else?"

"Jakk was my best friend, or so I thought," Pharaoh answered. "He was also an Egyptologist, and a colleague of mine. After we entered the Dungeon, he tried to kill Whimsy out of nowhere, and then he fled."

"Yeah, good thing you didn't forget to mention that. Anything else you're missing?" Alexandra asked sarcastically.

"I believe that's all," Pharaoh responded with full sincerity.

"How strong are you compared to George and Jakk?" Alistair wondered.

"I haven't met George, but from what Whimsy said, I should be much weaker than him," Pharaoh admitted. "Jakk, I don't know. He used to be just in the top 50, but when he revealed his true colors, his strength was several times what it was before. That is why this Dungeon is so important. They're growing stronger at a faster rate than we are, if left to their own devices. We need the rewards to keep pace."

"There's only a little over a week left for the fourth Quest," Whimsy said. "All bets are off after that. I wouldn't be surprised if there's an all-out war for the next one. It's only the natural conclusion."

Alistair subconsciously felt inside his pocket for the slip from the debt collector Farsa Strongbite. He had easily gathered over three million drachma, so the debt wouldn't be a problem. Next time he got back to HQ, he would withdraw his money from the Moneylender and pay off his debt. Alistair was pushing it with the deadline, trying to compound as much interest as possible before paying. Hopefully, they wouldn't be stuck in the Dungeon for that long.

"So, where do we go next?" Alistair asked.

Pharaoh pointed at an ivory door at the far end of the hot spring. "Before you arrived, we spent nearly a day trying to get through that door.

"A day?" Alistair asked. "We weren't in here that long before we got to you."

"That's interesting. Do you remember the date you entered the Dungeon? Perhaps in terms of the countdown to the end of Quest 4?"

Alistair gave him a sheepish grin. "I'm terrible with dates and all that." He turned to Alexandra and Oliver. "You guys know?"

Oliver looked up, trying to remember. "I think one week and four days? Yeah, I'm pretty sure that was it."

Pharaoh stroked his pointy chin with a crooked finger. "We entered at the same time. I wonder if the Pathfinder AI employed time dilation to make you fall behind. Perhaps we were being rewarded for a higher pedigree."

"Do you think that means there are others in the Dungeon besides us?" Alistair wondered.

"It's a possibility," Pharaoh conceded. "Regardless of if there are or aren't, we should try to finish this as quickly as we can."

They walked over to the foreboding blockade. It was shaped like a circle with a radius of around a meter and was fixed into the cavern itself. There were no handles or divots to grab onto, but there were a series of hieroglyphics and patterns engraved into the bone-like stone, so small that Alistair had to get up close and squint to make out the finer details. Besides the physical and artistic complexity, the door radiated a powerful aura, almost as if it were alive.

"Why hello there, young fellow!" a male voice burst out from the door. "You feel quite interesting!"

Alistair jumped back in surprise.

"Oh, yeah, and it talks."

"Young man, I recommend you separate yourselves from these two scoundrels as soon as you can! The same goes to you, young lady and the other gentleman. These fiends wish to pass through to the other side, which I must *not* allow." The door had a highly affected manner of speaking, sounding like an English drill sergeant reading slam poetry.

"Shut it, you stupid door!" Whimsy complained. "Just let us in! Why do you care so much?"

"Young lady, I have already explained to you. I am Saturn's guardian door. I exist everywhere my master wishes and nowhere. Since my master wished for a door here to lead to his inner sanctum, I shall protect it as long as I draw breath."

"You don't draw breath. You're a door," Whimsy pointed out, rolling her eyes.

"And there goes the miscreant again! Young man, if you silence this most insolent lady, I shall grant you a wish!" the door declared.

"What if my wish is to go inside?" Alistair asked.

"I think that is accept—wait just a moment, young man. I can see through your scheme! How dare you take advantage of me, a mere door! Do all young people these days have hearts full of evil?"

"So, I assume you've tried methods involving force?" Before Pharaoh could answer, Alistair punched the door right in its center.

He felt a small shockwave reverberate through his body upon impact, but other than that, nothing happened. Based on the feedback he got from the vibrations, he knew that his Constitution would limit the strength he could put into a blow. With how little give the ivory had, any punch he threw would reflect a decent portion of its kinetic energy. Given his Strength and Agility were much higher than his Constitution, if he went full power, he would shatter his arm, even if he was willing to try using a Skill (which he wasn't since he wasn't sure his spiritual network had fully healed from his previous fight). Besides, Pharaoh and Whimsy were bound to have already attempted the brute-force approach.

Pharaoh nodded his head. "The door appears to be crafted at an Adept level quality. Our attempts at breaking through haven't been successful in the slightest."

"Of course they've failed, evildoer! You will never get in!"

"We tried exploring this area outside of the cave, but there doesn't seem to be anything else out there," Pharaoh continued, ignoring the door's tirade. "At least not in a ten-kilometer radius. There's an impenetrable barrier beyond that point. So, we're stuck with this *thing*. The only reason we haven't packed up is because it gives us clues."

Alexandra raised an eyebrow. "Clues?"

Whimsy walked over to the door, rapping her knuckles against the surface a couple of times. "Hey, what's the password?"

"I will never—"

As if it had just encountered a shocking scene, the churlish voice suddenly stopped before taking on a more monotone and subdued intonation. "You have received three hints so far. Would you like for me to repeat them?"

"Yes, please," Whimsy said.

"Very well. Hint one: The first part of the password is a number that is the answer to the riddle of horses. Your task is to identify the three fastest horses out of twenty-five. You will race the horses against each other in groups of five as the race track only has five lanes. At a minimum, how many races are required to find the three fastest horses? The second hint is the answer to the physical puzzle contained on my surface. The third hint is the name of my master's favorite album. For more hints, please provide more information. Thank you."

Alistair gave Pharaoh a blank stare. "I can't say I was expecting that."

"It's a strange thing, that much is true," Pharaoh said. "In order to get a hint, you have to tell it a secret about yourself or someone close to you. Not a secret like, 'I shoplifted a sweater when I was nine,' but something about your abilities or where you've hidden your secret stash of items."

Pharaoh saw the realization dawn on Alistair's face and nodded. "I think you understand the implications. Saturn is telling us that in order to keep moving forward, we have to give up key strategic assets."

"Surely he can't expect us to do that, can he?" Alexandra asked. "If I was him, I'd set up this door and have it lead to nowhere to string along any nosy people. I mean, we don't even know if there's anything behind this thing. What if he just carved it into the wall?"

Whimsy shook her head. "It doesn't work like that. If the Pathfinder AI created this Dungeon instance, it has to be somewhat fair. It wouldn't let Saturn do something like that."

Pharaoh sat down on one of the damp stone rocks. "Our concern was more that we would give up vital information without ever solving the riddle. On that account, I regretfully admit we haven't been able to figure out even one of the clues."

"I know the first one," Alistair chimed in.

Pharaoh and Whimsy gave him an incredulous look. "You figured it out that fast?" the reformed Devil King asked.

"It's a classic coding interview question. It's actually not that hard once you get the idea behind it. First, you race all of them in groups of five. Then, you take all the winners and race them together. So now you know the fastest horse. Next—"

"You're sure you know the answer?" Whimsy interrupted.

"A hundred percent," Alistair replied.

"Well, thank goodness. Now I guess we have to figure out the other clues."

———

Over the next few hours, the unlikely allies worked together to solve the weird riddle Saturn had laid out in his door. It reminded Alistair of when he would do group projects back in school. Everyone would bicker and there would be a couple of slackers who would let one or two students do all the work.

In their case, the ones doing the lion's share of the work were Alistair and, surprisingly, the Devil King. Alistair had to admit he was still a little unnerved by the woman. She had the same eyes of raging fire as Esshei, but it was much more disturbing on a human than a snake. It was nearly impossible to tell when she was moving her eyes, making her look like she was always staring at you. Coupled with her potent and frightening aura, Alistair could feel his fight-or-flight response ready to activate.

The Devil King's aura was overwhelmingly powerful—yet hollow. Visually speaking, it was a miasma of black and gray goo and haze, slimy and dripping with decrepit and unsanctified energy. But despite the strength of the dark penumbra which pressed against Alistair's own aura, it was just that: a shadow. A borrowed power that felt illusory. Despite her seemingly normal personality, he understood that there was something deeply wrong with the woman. The thought made him sad more than anything else.

"Is Saturn a superfan of the group who made his favorite album?" Alistair asked.

"Yes, you could say that," the door responded. "That's the last extra hint I can give."

"Okay, I got it. It has to be *Animals* by Pink Floyd."

"No, I think it's *The Piper at the Gates of Dawn*. That's the more stuck-up pick," Whimsy retorted.

The two had been arguing for some time about the album hint. No one else had listened to enough music to be of use, so it was just them going back and forth. Through asking other questions to the door about Saturn, they were able to narrow it down to a Pink Floyd album, but they were still divided on which one it was.

"It's definitely possible, but based on the earlier clues, I think *Animals* makes more sense," Alistair said.

Alexandra tapped her foot on the ground. In order to get all the hints for the password, they'd had to give up a lot of personal information. There were seven hints in total and they had all given up secrets about their abilities to get each one. Alistair was hesitant to whisper to the door that Dev'rox allowed him to access spatially-attuned Mana as a last resort, but he convinced himself it was for the greater good.

"We get three attempts, so let's just try it already," Alexandra insisted. "We've already been going at this for nearly a day."

"Fine, fine," Alistair said. "7palefirepiperatthegatesofdawncall278three-pencesolomonswisdom?"

For a moment, the door was silent. The peace was broken by a low wailing noise that ground on the ears like nails on a chalkboard. Each intricate detail on the white slab shimmered and glowed with blue light. Alistair grabbed onto a stray stalagmite as the entire cavern started shaking. The door groaned and slowly receded toward the right as the surrounding rocks cracked from the pressure.

No one spoke in the aftermath of the sudden shaking. They could see where the door led to now, a long hallway that looked like part of a temple.

Pink fire burned in the sky, illuminating the path. However, Alistair was more concerned with the corpses.

On the sides of the path laid dead bodies, blood splattered across the ground. It had to be recent, since he could still feel remnant life force diffusing into the air.

"I'll go in first," Pharaoh volunteered, taking the lead.

No one argued with that. Having five extra lives was a solid defense against any ambush. The rest of the group followed behind him, stepping into the hallway. Alistair entered last, bringing up the rear. As soon as he crossed the threshold, the door closed behind them and disappeared, leaving them trapped. Alistair went back and kicked the spot where the ivory stone used to be, but to no avail. Looking closely at the walnut wall, there was no hint of the previous passageway in the slightest.

Seeing no other avenue but forward, they continued onward. Oliver knelt down and started fumbling with some of the corpses strewn about. Many of them had wounds that leaked a familiar black liquid, sizzling on the carpeted floor.

"Very recent," he said, standing up. "They were alive less than an hour ago."

The pale fire illuminated a winding path, culminating in what appeared to be a profane altar. It was a mockery of a religious space. A dark throne glowed with low purple light, attended by scores of robed sycophants and acolytes who chanted with a subharmonic resonance that vibrated every cell in Alistair's body.

At first, they took up a defensive stance upon seeing the prostrate worshipers, but they turned out to be an illusion. Alistair went up to one and stuck his arm through it, revealing their lack of essence. It didn't make it any less creepy.

Alistair might have been the first person to realize something was wrong, even before Pharaoh. Looking at the larger-than-life throne, he realized that something was off. There was a cloaked figure seated on it, but it lacked vitality. The Devil King aura was still there, so the others, except perhaps Oliver, didn't realize something was off just yet, but Alistair could tell right away that whoever sat on the throne was dead.

An update window appeared in front of him, confirming that he had finished the Dungeon and received the rewards. Considering he hadn't finished any of the requirements, he was surprised but happy, as the +2 levels, 30 Upgrade Points, the Badge and the Talent Tree were no joke.

Then he remembered Jakk, Pharaoh and Whimsy's former companion. Pharaoh had explained that the man had a Class that could produce fire, somewhat like John's Flamesmith, but in a more combative manner. Except for the outside chance of another person having entered the Dungeon besides the six they knew about, Jakk was the most likely explanation for the carnage before them. Alistair moved to get a closer look at—

With more intensity than ever before, his danger sense exploded.

21 SATURNALIA

THE DANGER SENSE appeared to Alistair as an eruption of white-hot lava coursing through his system. He instinctively moved forward rather than retreat, knowing that he had to protect the others. A wave of purple fire exploded from Saturn's presumed corpse, a conflagration infused with a Dao Node of burning and hatred and passion. Alistair **[Dashed]** to intercept it before any of the others reacted, activating **[Frozen Claw]**.

Channeling the Ghost Node through the Skill, he solidified the fire with a swipe of his hand. The raging fire instantly froze, resembling a photographic still. It retained the appearance of burning, but without movement, now possessing a blueish, crystalline sheen.

A cloaked figure darted out from behind the throne, just as a shimmering portal opened up beside it. It looked like one of Oliver's dimensional doors, but larger and with more distortion on its surface. Pharaoh and Whimsy reacted quickly, the former sending a sand spike at the fleeing person, while the latter threw a shuriken covered in water. Both were too late to stop the man from escaping through the portal, with the spike and shuriken fizzling out on the surface.

Alexandra moved to chase the fleeing man, but Pharaoh held out an arm to stop her. "The portal takes you back to where you entered. Going after him will only bring you back to where you were before."

"Damn it," she swore under her breath. "That was anticlimactic. No boss battle or anything. Not much of a dungeon, if you ask me."

A public status window popped up in front of everyone, flashing red.

Dungeon will collapse in 9:59. Please leave through the open portal or risk termination.

"Looks like it was listening," Oliver wryly remarked.

Alistair's mind went elsewhere. "What do you think happened to the prisoners?" he wondered aloud, remembering that one of the Dungeon objectives was to rescue five of Saturn's captives.

"If I know what Devil Kings are like, and I damn well should—since I was, or am one of them—after they rescued the prisoners to complete the Quest, they killed them," Whimsy said.

A pit formed in Alistair's stomach as he processed what he'd already suspected. His Dao of Justice burned with avenging fury as he imagined all the people across the globe wronged by the Devil Kings' madness. And yet, he tempered his anger, recognizing that even the Devil Kings were but pawns in a greater game.

"Should we meet up on the outside?" he asked.

"That sounds like a good idea," Pharaoh said. "We're on the West Coast. Formerly California. I'll send over a messenger with a **Teleportation Circle** so we can meet up. You're in the northeast, correct?"

"Yep, our main base of operations is in Boston," Alistair replied.

"Understood." Pharaoh nodded. He then turned to the charred throne where Saturn once sat, adorned with a crispy corpse. "I'd like to take the body for analysis, if that's alright with you."

Alistair hesitated for a second. Not that he thought Pharaoh had malicious intentions, but the truce they had was still tentative. He was under no illusion that they were die-hard compatriots. Perhaps letting Pharaoh and Whimsy take the body would come back to haunt them later, but what else could he do? It would be weirdly confrontational to just say, 'no, I'll be taking that, thank you.'

"Let me take a look now and then you can have it. I need to try something out," Alistair said, not saying more than he had to.

Pharaoh didn't look overly concerned, just nodding his head as he often did instead of giving a verbal response. Alistair glanced at Alexandra and Oliver, telling them it would just be a moment.

Alistair finally looked over his update window, checking out his unmerited rewards while he approached Saturn's body. When he thought about it, it didn't make sense to him why Jakk went through all the trouble to complete the components of the Quest for everyone else. Was he so arrogant to think his own reward was enough to offset the strength gained by five of his enemies? Or was completing the Quest necessary to get to Saturn? The way the Quest rewards were worded implied otherwise, but Alistair couldn't be sure. And most importantly, if Jakk had betrayed humanity, why had he decided to kill Saturn? Could there be discord among their ranks?

He spent all 76 of his Upgrade Points toward a new Badge slot. That still left him 17 short of the 200 required to get a new slot, which he needed to equip "Devil May Cry." Looking at the Badge, Alistair had realized that he needed it, despite not wanting to invest his Upgrade Points yet. He *wanted* a more general Badge, preferably a stat-booster, but considering he had eleven Devil Kings to fight, it felt necessary to take. Now he had a day to level up and get the requisite Upgrade Points to unlock the slot, or he would lose the Badge for good.

Badge Acquired: "Devil May Cry" (Tier 1 Legendary Badge): *All demonic and demonic-adjacent entities emit an obvious and pungent aura unable to be hidden by methods less than two realms above user. Holy Will: When fighting a demonic or demonic-adjacent entity, if on the verge of death, the user will gain a second wind of energy and willpower fueled by sacred fury.* Upgradeable (0/40). **Warning: You have exceeded the number of Badge slots you possess. Swap out Badges or buy another Badge slot.**

Despite not being fully equipped, the "Devil May Cry" Badge was already starting to take effect. Alistair always felt Dev'rox's presence because of **[Ghost Whispers]**, but now the imp appeared to him in a different way. It was like the difference between looking at an apple and tasting an apple. Both referenced the same object, but each offered a whole new perspective. If **[Ghost Whispers]** offered a muted, spiritual presence, "Devil May Cry" made Dev'rox smell like a void of darkness, an unfortunate aberration of reality.

"What's with the funny face?" Dev'rox snorted.

"Nothing," Alistair replied hastily. "I'm just going to have to get used to this new sense. What's that now, five? I don't know if my brain can handle much more."

"What do your fancy senses say about the Devil King?"

Alistair jumped up onto the throne, the seat towering above him in height. It seemed impractical to have such a large throne, but the Devil Kings seemed to have a flair for the theatrical, if Esshei and now this room were anything to go by.

The Serpent King's memories of Saturn still lingered in Alistair's head, though whatever remained of him now was completely unrecognizable, burnt to a black husk. Despite obviously being dead, Alistair could feel a colossal life force emanating from the corpse, though it was dwindling by the second. He saw an imperfect image, half in his mind's eye and half in reality, of a pulsing black heart, slowly expelling its last reserves of discolored blood. Saturn's soul had already been annihilated. Nothing was left of the Devil King but his earthly body.

Luckily for Alistair, the Dungeon reward bestowed the Blood of the Devil Talent Tree with its initial root, first leaf and underlying branches already instantiated. Reading the description, it too conveyed benefits specifically for dealing with demons. The Purification leaf allowed him to safely handle the corruptive effects of demon blood, which was especially relevant for a full Devil King like Saturn. With Esshei, he was able to target the parts of the Beast Lord's life force unaffected by the demon blood, an impossibility when dealing with Saturn.

Alistair activated [Blood Hand] with a grimace, gingerly touching the corpse. The crimson red aura of the Skill oscillated rapidly like a fluid on a subwoofer, spiking in every direction as he absorbed the dissipating life force. He felt the effects of the Blood of the Devil start to work, creating a sizzling halo around his [Blood Hand]. Black vapor billowed upwards, leaving a purple gradient across the crimson aura.

Alistair breathed in deeply as he accepted the bountiful amount of energy. It was so much greater than what he'd received from Esshei or any of the monsters and beasts he'd absorbed before. The force and vitality of the life force was so great it was hard to believe Saturn was even dead—it somehow rivaled Alistair's own vast life force, and he was quite alive.

For a moment, Alistair wondered if, with his new leaf, he could save the remaining Devil Kings instead of killing them. But that hope vanished as he realized that the purification process was inherently destructive. The Purification leaf wouldn't activate without him absorbing the energy. Once inside his system, it suffused into every cell, permeating and reinforcing his own life force. It wasn't as if he could just give it back, or at least, he didn't know of any method for that. He assumed that stronger cultivators could do more interesting manipulations with their life force.

Unfortunately, Alistair didn't feel that spark of inspiration from when he'd drained Esshei, or the primal instincts he'd obtained from the random riffraff. It looked like the Purification leaf worked a little too well, stripping Saturn's life force of any individuality. But it was still a *ton* of energy—Alistair felt like he was brimming with vital power. He still wasn't sure what he could use it for, but there was no way it could be bad, right? Hopefully, he wouldn't need to put it to the test, but Alistair imagined he had an increased resistance against disease and a longer lifespan.

Disease? Alistair thought. *Are there like cultivator plagues or something?*

His train of thought was cut off by Pharaoh, who pointed to his wrist to indicate time was running out. "Two minutes left."

"Sorry, I didn't realize how long I was standing there," Alistair said. He lifted the burnt body with gentle care. After feeling how strong Saturn was, lifting the defeated Devil King was something of a *memento mori* for him. How pitiful it was for the Final Frontier Empire to experiment on helpless humans, and how little value a life had in the eyes of rulers of the universe.

Whimsy opened a gourd of sparkling water, as in *literally* sparkling water, wrapping the body in streams of shimmering liquid. In an instant, it collapsed into a miniature version of itself and returned to the gourd. She capped it and put it back in her cloak, offering a handshake. "Good to meet you, Alistair. And goodbye to my two students."

Alexandra rolled her eyes in response, but Whimsy didn't seem to notice. Pharaoh didn't say another word and walked into the portal with his partner.

"Well, that was something," Alexandra remarked after they left.

"We have one minute before we all die. I'd appreciate it if we left before the last possible moment," Oliver stated.

"Let's go," Alistair said. They had a lot to talk about when they got back. He hadn't anticipated the rapid increase in complexity of their situation, with many moving parts acting in the shadows.

22 CALM BEFORE THE STORM

THE NEXT WEEK WAS UNEVENTFUL, much to Alistair's surprise. He was expecting more chaos after their excursion to Saturn's castle, but they couldn't find any signs of further Devil King activity. In Alistair's absence, John had expanded the Northeast Order's Freehold bureaucracy to almost frightening levels. He had hundreds of spies and informants across the country, reporting via the Soulnet.

It was a positive feedback loop, where they gained new and valuable information that scored higher in the Soulnet's inscrutable algorithm. The more value they accrued, the more they could extend their network, letting them gather more news and rumors, which they could then leverage and start the loop all over again. Of course, they were not alone in noticing this, but the Northeast Order was by far the strongest organization in its eponymous region.

They rapidly expanded their borders, ballooning to 1010 subregions the day before the fourth Quest's end. Alistair knew he could've gone even faster if he resorted to force, but he had already decided there would be no coercion in joining their freehold. It was better to be a shining city on a hill—a place where any person could feel safe despite their strength or lack thereof.

Crime was lower than he expected—everyone was too on edge to try anything funny. John appointed a man named Carter Delacroix, a former homicide detective, in charge of public safety. Despite not having modern technology like DNA sequencing or video cameras, there were many with the ability to sniff out crime thanks to their Classes.

Alistair retrieved his money from Lauren and paid off Anthony's debt with two million drachma to spare. The Land Store credit situation was more precarious, as they were harder to acquire than drachma. As they developed more land with academies, cultivation chambers and other cultivation-related buildings, he could increase his rate of production to 700 credits per day. For now, he barely exceeded the 16,186.7 requirement, though next month would be much easier.

As for his own progression, he spent the first day fighting the highest-level monsters he could find for seventeen hours straight to reach level 43 to avoid losing his "Devil May Cry" Badge. He came almost as close to dying as he did against Wandering Hobo, wading into hordes of thousands of slime colonies and direwolves. He was so desperate he almost swallowed a leveling pill, despite knowing that those who had taken Tier 2 leveling pills were already being harmed from their impurities. He had the purification ring, but he still didn't risk it, and it paid off in the end since he leveled up naturally. With his 23 Upgrade Points, he put 17 toward the Badge slot and kept the rest for later.

The week gave him enough time for his arm to heal naturally. [Carmela's Happy Pies] put in work, expediting the process. Alistair still had to be careful about channeling too much Dao energy in one location of his body.

"Do you ever take time off?" Alexandra said, breaking Alistair's meditation.

The cultivation chamber he was in wouldn't help his progress in the Dao at all—his Dao Nodes were far too advanced for anything they could afford at the moment, but he enjoyed the peace and quiet. He'd never been a big fan of the loud bustle of the city, and New Boston was growing livelier by the day. Based on the pricing market and progression of Builder-type Classes, people speculated they could build megastructures in a couple of months.

"Weren't you getting on me about 'partying at a club' a couple of weeks ago?" Alistair smiled and hopped up, seeing Alexandra at the entrance of the pitch-black chamber.

"You say that as if it didn't happen."

"It was for a *mission*, not that I expect you to understand that. And wait a minute, didn't Oliver say that you spent a day trying to beat a guy at arm-wrestling?"

Alexandra gave him an overexaggerated look of horror. "Oliver said that? That bastard. He's always liked you more than me. He left out a key detail—it wasn't the whole day, it was just a couple hours, and it served an important purpose since me winning was what convinced his group to join us."

Alistair walked out of the chamber, putting his hand up to block the sunlight. He had been in the chamber for almost a day, furthering his integration with Dev'rox and practicing his control over his life force and Dao energy, along with trying to produce *nue*. His killing intent was still unusable in combat, but now he could extend a mental tendril a meter from his brain. It was fun to play with, acting almost like an extra noodly limb.

"So, how are things with your girlfriend?" Alexandra inquired once they had exited onto the terrace overlooking the city.

"Ex-girlfriend," Alistair corrected. "We broke up, didn't I tell you?"

A moment of silence passed before Alexandra asked, "Why?"

Alistair sighed, not quite sure how to explain it. "I don't know, really. I think too much has happened. I've certainly changed more in these past two months than I have in my whole life. It would be like if your girlfriend woke up one day and she suddenly had a new personality. It's weird."

"You're saying you'd break up with someone because of that? What if they hit their head or something and that's what made them change? In sickness and health and all that?"

"It's different. First off, we weren't married," Alistair said. "I wouldn't abandon someone just because they got in an accident. Surely you can see how the initiation is… a unique situation."

"I'm messing with you, Alistair. Holy shit, you are dense sometimes. Don't you have a ridiculous amount of Charisma and Intelligence?" Alexandra laughed, punching him playfully in the shoulder.

"Through systematic experimentation across the world using randomized controlled trials, it was found with a $P < 0.01$ that the 'personality' based Attributes have no impact on—"

"Fuck you, I thought you were serious at first," Alexandra cursed. "You're better than I thought."

"What can I say—I do my best."

"Have you ever thought about what romance or marriage would even mean in this new world?" Alexandra asked after a pause.

"I guess I never thought about it that much, but now that you mention it, yeah, it's hard to imagine. Even if you're in a committed relationship, could that really last for a million years?"

"We could probably find out if we looked at some cultivator romance stories," Alexandra suggested. "But I kind of want to make a prediction? Before we look."

"Oh?"

"I bet there are some couples who do make it. Not as many who make it from marriage to deathbed on Earth, but they still exist."

"Didn't expect you to be much of a romantic, if I'm being honest," Alistair said.

"Just think about it. Yes, there's more time to grow apart and probably more beautiful people than we can even imagine. But there has to be more beauty as well. If the multiverse is as big as they say, then there are mountains and valleys hundreds of times more beautiful than the best on Earth. And maybe you could see one of those—what's it called when a star explodes again?"

"A supernova?" Alistair offered.

"Yeah, a supernova. Imagine being up-close and watching that. You can see this clip that's making the rounds on the Soulnet of this gigantic golden eyeball watching the birth of a star, sped up a hundred billion times. I want to see that. I want to explore the multiverse."

"I like the sound of that," Alistair said. He was so focused on justice and getting stronger that he had forgotten about those kinds of things. His wide-eyed childhood wonder stirred inside him. As a kid, he had always dreamed about exploring alien worlds, and now it was staring him in the face. The thirst for adventure and the limits of his imagination. There was no reason he couldn't synergize that with the path of Justice.

"Anyway, I should be going." Alexandra shifted in place. Alistair thought she was going to say more, but she held her tongue. "The fifth Quest is about to start soon. We better get ready."

"Almost forgot about that." Alistair checked and saw there were only twelve hours until [Territorial Dominance] ended. The freehold had 1011 subregions and counting—just 15.35% of the total subregions in the former United States territory, and a minuscule number compared to the 159,873 subregions over the entire globe. Still, he was #2 in the world—even if others had more subregions, he felt confident.

"Catch you later."

Alistair wasn't sure what he was going to do next, but his uncertainty was answered in the form of a holographic projection.

"Greetings, Alistair," it said. Alistair's first reaction was to jump back in surprise, but then he remembered the figure. The Lazarene Minister, appointed by the Clear Water Sect to look after him and guide him on the path of cultivation. Not without stipulations, of course, which made Alistair hesitant about the minister's sudden appearance.

Alistair bowed his head. "Greetings."

"You're much stronger than you were before," the projection said, stroking his ghostly beard. "Congratulations. You are exceeding all expectations."

"Thank you," Alistair said tentatively.

"You must be wondering why I'm here. Now that your planet is becoming more integrated, contact will be more common. From now on, I can visit you once per Quest, though I cannot offer any direct advice for any problem you face."

"How's that work?"

"The meeting is reliant on our discretion of proper timing," the Lazarene Minister said, though Alistair translated that as, "Whenever is convenient for us."

"Right now, I want to assess your progress and inform you of anything I can within the bounds of the Law. Come here."

Instead of waiting for Alistair to move, the blue projection zoomed toward him and placed his hand on Alistair's forehead. A pulse of energy passed through him from head to toe before rebounding up back into the Lazarene Minister. For a long moment, the man said nothing, just contemplating whatever information he'd received from the scan. Alistair held his breath, remembering how Kyraxadon had detected the presence of whatever gave him his Subclass. The giant demon had immediately tried bringing down Heaven's wrath on him. Either the scan didn't reveal his secret or the Lazarene Minister remained silent, since he continued on without mentioning it.

"I see, I see," he murmured. "Remarkable, remarkable. Your talent is prodigious. Already selecting an appropriate set of Mana affinities of blood, ice, force, and lightning to match your Dao Nodes of Ghost, Fist, and Justice. Further integration of ghost cultivation and Karmic cultivation. Yes, yes, it's all coming together. However, you're stretching yourself a little thin, if I might add. Versatility is good, but is there an overarching theme? It is fine if you do not wish to tell me, I understand. There are some things that one must keep private, even from one's master."

Alistair thought about what he was going for with his different powers. The Dao Nodes he possessed worked as a cycle; by taking on a quest of justice for departed souls, he borrowed their power for his own, channeling it through his fists both metaphorically and literally. Though he hadn't codified this idea explicitly before, he thought of the borrowed, eternal ghost as represented by ice, while the hungry, vengeful ghost was represented by blood. He stole with blood and borrowed with ice.

They were two halves of the same coin—contrasting, yet the same when viewed from a different lens. Stolen blood gave birth to new life, while borrowed souls gave birth to new spirit. The two halves of body and soul were made more whole, and more powerful together than either was apart in a synergistic symbiosis.

"How effective have you found your **Thrice-Blessed Fate-Diviner**?" the Lazarene Minister asked, pointing at the golden chain and ring Alistair always wore.

Alistair felt a little uncomfortable about the scan—it was like he was an animal at an auction, but he set those concerns aside. He had thought about trying to go solo, but from what he'd read, it meant almost certain death. Things worked the way they did for a reason. Plus, if the Lazarene Minister was going to sell him out like Kyraxadon, there wasn't much he could do about it. There wasn't an easy escape like he had with Dev'rox. Luckily, the Minister seemed unaware of anything suspicious, not noticing his Subclass.

"I think it's good," Alistair replied truthfully. "I don't know for sure because I can't imagine what the counterfactual me who didn't receive the necklace would have done. There are certain feelings I get sometimes that maybe are coming from it, but like I said, I don't know for sure."

"That's fine. It's supposed to be subtle. What about **Zanibar's Purification Ring**?"

Alistair looked down at the silver ring. He had barely given a thought to the item his sister had given him. "It saved my ass once. But I'm not sure if pills are really worth the downsides."

"You haven't seen what pills from a master alchemist can do, young one. But you shall, one day." The Minister sat down cross-legged. "On your general cultivation path, I can only commend you for what you've achieved, considering your conditions. I recommend trying to find a suitable bloodline or ancestry of quality pedigree. You'll be competing against those who have spent millions of years refining their clan's lineage."

"Lineage?"

"It refers to the class of cultivation wisdom regarding both bloodlines and ancestry. Anything that is pertinent to what you would directly pass on to your children just by nature of their birth."

"I'll keep that in mind," Alistair said.

"I saw your life force has more than tripled since the last time we met. You're stealing it from others, I gather?"

Alistair huffed. "I haven't attacked anyone without a good reason."

"I'm not passing any judgment. You must be wondering what the purpose of all of this energy is then? The simple answer is that life force refines the body's representation of itself. I suspect that you won't be able to understand what that means, so I shall disclose my understanding of the Akashic Records."

Alistair could hear the profundity of those last two words despite not having an ounce of Mana or Dao behind them. There was something about it, something deep and ancient that chilled him to the soul. He'd heard of the concept of the "Akashic records" from the old Earth. It was some kind of occult belief about a universal compendium of all information that was and ever will be.

"Even from our section of the stars, we've heard of the Akashic Records. The Hall of Mathematics, which stands near the top of the multiversal hierarchy, won't let us forget. The monkey archivists control the Akashic Records, but even they know not the creator. The very concept of the Akashic Records is so transcendent as a Dao archetype that many uninitiated have heard of them. Based on your reaction, I understand this to be the case for FX-14752 as well.

"The Records serve many purposes," the Lazarene Minister continued, "but the relevant aspect here is the representation of the body. The idea of the body is not merely blood and flesh, it is the Physical Plane made immanent through the process of a mind and soul, enshrined in the Dao."

"I'm going to be honest; you're losing me here," Alistair said. All the words the old man was saying made sense in isolation, but when you put them together, it was a jumbled word salad that he barely understood.

"It is of no consequence. Your theoretical foundations will be shored up later. As I was saying, as a unique property of the Physical Plane, the body has its own representation of itself in the Akashic Records. When you add points to your Agility or Strength, your body improves, but not the body's representation of itself. Only a large change such as death or species evolution can change the body's representation of itself in the Akashic Records. You can imagine this as the body being a stubborn brat that doesn't want to change itself without outside intervention.

"A standard species evolution occurs through the process of body cultivation. This is even more essential to those with strong bloodlines and ancestries, where the heritage you are calling upon is far greater than your own measly body. Those with the strongest lineages therefore require extensive outside support, or they fall far behind. Or... they can expedite the process. Absorbing the life force of one's enemies is a standard. Your method is similar to that of the Shaded Ones, using blood as the medium. A tried-and-true method. Those who practice blood cultivation and 'feeding' can maintain their powerful lineage without stuffed coffers. But there's a reason the bloodsuckers are almost universally reviled."

"So absorbing all this life force will help me evolve my species faster?"

"Not just faster, but the results will be of a much higher quality. As the seat and anchor, a higher quality body increases everything *except* one's stats, at least at this level. This means superior integration with one's Dao, superior usage of Skills, superior control of *nue*, and more. You're around halfway to a species evolution as of now. Continue your bloody conquest and you shall reap the rewards."

Alistair wanted to roll his eyes at the Lazarene Minister calling his [Blood Hand] usage a "bloody conquest," but he resisted. "Thank you for your advice. Is there anything else? I don't want to waste more of your time than is necessary."

"Better than half my students in that regard," he grumbled in response. "Ah yes, the other topic I wanted to mention was regarding Charisma. The Clear Water Sect must express our disapproval with your Karmic cultivation outside of an appropriate Class and registration. That is why I must show you this slip, in order to show you the grave consequences of continuing to increase your Charisma."

The Lazarene Minister gave Alistair a knowing glance and showed him a jade slip. Alistair saw a chart appear in his mind.

15 Base Karma = 0-249 Charisma
30 Base Karma = 250-499 Charisma
60 Base Karma = 500-999 Charisma
120 Base Karma = 1000-1999 Charisma
240 Base Karma = 2000-3999 Charisma
480 Base Karma = 4000-7999 Charisma
960 Base Karma = 8000-15999 Charisma
...

That explained why hitting 250 Charisma had pushed him up to 60 total Karma. In order to double his Karma again, he needed to get all the way to 500 Charisma. Seeing the importance of Karma as his trump card, Alistair recalibrated his priorities for stats.

"We shall see each other again soon, Alistair. The last advice I give you is this: do not overstep yourself. You are meddling in many forms of cultivation, some of which are taboo. Growing in strength before growing in fame is always prudent. Good luck."

The holographic projection of the man vanished into thin air, leaving Alistair alone on his terrace overlooking the city below. It was time for the next Quest.

23 THE GAME OF LIFE

The Imperial Heartlands were mind-bogglingly large. Stretching for hundreds of millions of light-years around the universal Dao Heart, quadrillions of people called the lands home. A portion of each of the thirteen fiefs of the Final Frontier Empire comprised the Heartlands, though some held more than others.

The Portolon Clan were one of only four Progenitors to own a fief, their clan leader Xavian being a bona fide Prince of the Empire. Their wealth was unimaginable, stretching over millions of planets—they even had a direct voice in the Emperor's ear. Many whispered bold calumnies that Xavian was the true Emperor, claiming that Dragus Laketor had gone mad from excessive indulgence in the pleasures of the flesh.

Da Shai Eltor was one of the twenty greatest holdings of the Portolon Clan, a planet made of pure gold larger than the sun of Earth's solar system. Nearly eight trillion people called it home, and Da Shai, third wife of Seperati Portolon, owned all of it.

Da Shai came from a storied lineage herself, the Da Clan of Mai Atal. Not as high as the Portolon, but high enough that as her astounding talent became evident, she garnered quite the list of admirers. A peerless jade beauty who reached Visionary before her 5000th birthday—and with a rare dual ancestry-bloodline—would always be an object of desire.

She was lucky that her family had enough influence to annul Seperati's marriages with his first and second wives. Sharing a husband was not in her Dao Heart. Of course, this had caused friction between her family and some weak merchants and nobles, but her contributions had outshone any lost face.

Seperati had even been more handsome than she had expected of a 600,000-year-old Visionary cultivator. The ravages of time had not yet struck the golden-haired warrior of the Portolon, who in mortal terms looked no older than thirty-five.

He was twenty-third in the line of succession, part of a rich branch of the Portolons—though still a branch. Their family would never attain the status she desired unless their children turned out to be the geniuses of the next generation.

But the children could be a hassle. The children, and oh-so-many nieces and nephews and second cousins once removed, not to mention Seperati's own past children, grandchildren and great-grandchildren. His eldest line was in its 52nd generation, though they were barely Portolons at that point. Overall, it was an interminable list of names that Da Shai had to memorize.

"Mother! Fyordim is cheating!"

"No, I'm not, Auntie Da Shai! Guntei is the one cheating!"

Sighing, Da Shai used her Dao Focus of the Night's Kiss to force open a portal to the other side of the planet. At her level of mastery, despite her death-related Dao being unrelated to teleportation, she could force reality to bend to her will through sheer power like most Visionaries.

Her son Guntei and one of his infinite legion of cousins, Fyordim, were playing some children's game near one of the thousand-meter waterfalls.

"Guntei, you must play nice," she admonished her youngest. "You know better than to lie to me, isn't that right? Fyordim was just using the rules against you. That's not cheating."

"But it's not fair! Just because he has a Skill his father gave him, he wins? When can Father give me a Skill?"

Da Shai recoiled at how idiotic Fyordim's parents were. Those fools were leeches on her husband's generosity. Everyone with a brain knew it was foolish to interfere so early in a child's development with outside Skills. The early years of a child cultivator were supposed to be fun and enjoyable, to help them find their own Dao Path.

"Your father is busy fighting the enemies of the Empire, my sweet Guntei." *And that's where I'll be as well, once Yarik graduates. Good riddance to this golden world.*

Speaking of Yarik, Da Shai felt his presence close by. Teleporting once more to her second youngest son, she found herself in the hall of one of the greatest libraries in all of Faden Gohm. The ceiling was so high that it might as well have been shrouded by the clouds, millions of books floating on silver threads to millions of eagerly waiting readers. The Prime Eltor Library housed the most permanent residents on the entire planet, despite that not even being its primary purpose.

"Mother!" Yarik exclaimed, hugging Da Shai. Both of them had their aura cloaked to level 60 strength, so to the mortals in the library, the sight of Yarik calling Da Shai mother would have seemed very strange. With Yarik's wide shoulders and masculine facial features, he looked older than his mother, who was a slender and short woman that appeared no older than twenty years old.

"My son," Da Shai said, returning the hug. Yarik looked least like her of all her eight children, but that didn't bother her. The nasty rumors did, however.

"My ship leaves soon, mother," Yarik said, looking troubled. "I'm not sure I'm ready to visit Chaos."

Yarik was testing his mettle in order to become an Inner Disciple at the prestigious Divine Sword Sect. They didn't give any special privileges for being the son of the fourth most powerful member of the Portolon Clan. In order for Yarik to prove himself, they were taking him and the other Outer Disciples close to Chaos to test their dedication to the Dao.

"I'm sure you'll do fine, Yarik. You have your father's phoenix bloodline and my elven ancestry. You've consumed more rare elixirs and Beast Cores than all your brothers and sisters combined, and that's only a slight exaggeration. There is no possibility of failure," Da Shai said bluntly.

"Of course, Mother." Yarik was a good son who demonstrated all the virtues of filial piety, though he could be a hothead at times. That made it easy for Da Shai to sense that something was wrong.

"What is it?"

"It's my investment," Yarik groaned. "I spent my entire allowance sponsoring a human Prime Initiate from this planet FX-14752. And then he got himself killed by a stupid guy sponsored by the Clear Water Sect."

Clear Water Sect? Da Shai thought. They were once fierce rivals on par with the Divine Sword, but had fallen by the wayside over the past few thousand years.

The Portolon Clan didn't typically sponsor initiates, deeming it beneath their dignity. In addition, the lesser nobles and merchants didn't appreciate when a princely clan involved themselves in base matters, since clans could throw way more resources at their initiates. But Yarik wanted to do it as a pet project, and Da Shai hadn't had the will to say no to her beloved son.

She had heard from him and the Clan's scouting team about this "Anthony Ricci." Personally, she thought his character was unsuited for further investment, but Yarik loved his juvenile braggadocio. And even she couldn't deny the man's skill. Chronologist was a Rare Class for a reason, some saying it even deserved Legendary status. The only reason the Pathfinder AI relegated it to Rare was so that it wasn't outright barred to precocious youth.

"That is the risk in such ventures, Yarik. We cannot control all of Fate," Da Shai instructed.

"Yes, Mother, but it still makes us look bad! You haven't seen the initiate either," Yarik complained. "Farsa came and visited me after. He told me there's something special about him. He's a Karmic cultivator."

Da Shai considered her son's words carefully. Farsa Strongbite had been a valuable asset of the Da Clan for thousands of years, and she trusted his word implicitly. He was loyal but not obsequious. If Farsa had used a **Soul Splitter** and sent in the paperwork to visit a new world personally, the boy was something special.

Plus, Karmic cultivators were barely tolerated in civilized space—respected for their immense utility, but feared for the ruin they could bring on their enemies. The Final Frontier Empire kept a close eye on Karmic cultivators, forcing registration upon those who reached the Profound realm. The taboo of Karmic cultivators was stronger in some parts of the empire than others, with Da Shai's homeland of Mai Atal being one such place. A budding Karmic cultivator who was one of the strongest Prime Initiates of a cycle? Lots of eyes would be on that man.

Da Shai let her next words hang like a heavy coffin. "And what do you plan to do?"

Yarik stroked his impeccably sharp jaw. "I'll kill him."

"Yarik, you don't need to be giving your father any trouble. Killing a newly initiated Foundation realm cultivator is beneath you."

"I've already discussed this with Father," Yarik said. "I'll challenge him to a duel, at his level. There is no law against that, as long as it is truly fair in the eyes of the Law. Like that stupid tournament all the peasants enjoy. Since it'll be a fair fight, no one will complain. And if he refuses, he can say goodbye to his planet. I just have to let the other Prime Initiates flee first."

A duel? Destroying planets? Da Shai thought. She was spoiling her children far too much. Not that she cared about the peons, but letting her child exercise so much power in the frontier was a surefire path to an imbalanced adult. The sparse Dao near Chaos made an Adept realm like Yarik dozens of times stronger than in the Imperial Heartlands, and many got drunk on that kind of destructive power, only to be killed by an actual warrior once they returned to normal territory.

"No child of mine is destroying a planet of the Fateless," Da Shai said. "Did you see what happened when that Meloi bastard tried? You debase yourself to even suggest such a thing. Go on your mission and speak no more of this. I will talk to your father."

Only the relevant sponsors knew the location of the newly initiated world to prevent any outside manipulation. Seperati was too doting if he was willing to risk the family's reputation on a childish grudge. Her grandfather had complained about the decay of the empire's standards for millennia—perhaps the bullying of Foundation realms was the culmination of his complaints. She imagined what he would say if he were here. *"Oh, how the youth have fallen! In my days, we fought with honor and would never lay a finger on a lower realm!"*

Her grandfather was half-senile, however. Though she wasn't happy about it, Da Shai didn't want to fight her son over romantic ideals. Better he learn the lesson himself.

She had more important things to worry about, opening up the radiant imperial summons in front of her. Why in the name of the Celestial Dragon was the Fell Emperor calling a High Council? The Progenitor Clans, corporations, and other nobles had all been ordered to the Palatial Satellite on pain of death. It was the largest and most important meeting of the last ten million years, and no one knew why. There weren't even any rumors, at least not those with any credibility.

Da Shai clutched her jade medallion. Anything for the family.

———

No one knew exactly what the next Quest was going to be. Would it be like Felons vs. Fellows, where they got whisked off the face of the earth? To prepare for any eventuality, Alistair gathered with his closest allies in their HQ. Everyone had prepared for this very moment, arming themselves to the teeth with weapons and items.

"I'm telling you, it's probably going to be nothing, like [Territorial Dominance]," Alexandra complained. "We're going to look very stupid. Also, even if they do take us away, wouldn't it not matter if we're like physically next to each other or not?"

"I'm just covering every possibility," Alistair replied.

"Ten, nine, eight, seven," Oliver said while looking at the Quest timer.

Alexandra gave the Necromancer a pointed look. "Seriously?"

"Six, five, four, three, two, one, ze—"

As Oliver said the last number, the world turned black, the same thing that had happened before the third Quest. But instead of being transported to an alien planet, Alistair remained suspended in the void as an enormous status window appeared a few meters away.

Congratulations on placing 42nd in [Territorial Dominance]! As majority owner of the Northeast Order Freehold with 1,020 subregions, please choose your reward(s):
A) 150,000 Land Store credits and one Legendary rarity item
B) +1 level, +50 Upgrade Points, Mastery Scroll

Alistair didn't have to guess what a Mastery Scroll was—somehow he knew it was an aid that would help improve an aspect, like his pugilism or his Dao energy control. The system presented a clear dilemma, forcing him to choose between personal rewards that would benefit himself or options that would benefit the entire freehold. Of course, the distinction wasn't so fine since anything that helped him grow stronger allowed Alistair to better protect his territory, and anything that helped his freehold grow stronger increased his influence and power.

He ended up going with the first option, deciding to take a forward-looking approach. 150,000 Land Store credits seemed like a lot, even with the rapid price inflation, and it was enough to entirely pay off his debt. It was a gamble on his own strength, but he was confident in his chances against anyone but Pharaoh or the Devil Kings.

After he selected his choice, he felt a glowing sensation against his fingers. His **Ghostgrass Wraps** fell off, replaced by a pair of slick, blood-red gloves. The metallic surface gleamed under the soft light of the status window. He twiddled his fingers, finding his movement unimpeded by the gauntlets. Each fingertip converged to a sharp claw, just like his **[Blood Hand]**.

The notification told him that they were called the **Devilsbane Gauntlets** and were especially good at carrying blood-attuned Mana. In addition, the protection they offered his relatively dainty hands was much greater than his previous wraps, though he lost some ghost-related synergy. Unlike his previous wraps that turned invisible for cosmetic purposes when he didn't need to use them, these condensed into a pair of red bracelets that he could grow into gauntlets or shrink back to their jewelry form at will.

Alistair raked the gauntlets lightly over his 147 Constitution skin, drawing blood with ease. A smile blossomed on his face as he imagined the combos he could pull off with them. *Goodbye* **Ghostgrass Wraps**, *hello my new little friends.*

His newfound happiness at his Legendary rarity item was interrupted when a window appeared.

[The Game of Life]: *The majority shareholders of 100+ subregion freeholds and subordinates of 1,000+ subregion freeholds with over 50 personal subregions shall participate in the "Game of Life," a common pastime in the Final Frontier Empire. Instead of going head-to-head in physical conflict, participants will fight in a battle of intellect and cunning, for the cultivator is not just one of sound body but also of sound mind. The ideal of the sage warrior will be cultivated, with participants using their subregions as a currency to partake in a series of games and puzzles.*

Task: Place as high as possible in subregion ranking at the end of

**one month. Reward: To Be Determined. Time Limit: 729:59:58.
Penalty: Dependent on placing.**

A chart showing the people with the highest subregion counts accompanied the Quest screen. Unlike the general leaderboards, the subregion list used pseudonyms. Number one was named "Illustrious Kingpin," possessing a ridiculous 6,321 subregions. Everyone in the top ten had over two thousand subregions, which made Alistair feel bad about his measly one thousand. At least he had a cool name, his pseudonym being "Martial Avenger." He consoled himself with the knowledge that most had likely attacked surrounding freeholds, which he had refrained from doing. Still, it meant he would be at a disadvantage if they were using subregions as a currency.

After he finished reading the Quest description, the darkness faded and Alistair found himself inside an icy cavern. Chunks of rectangular ice blocks filled the walls and ceiling, the largest of which were twice as tall as a man. The dome-like chamber had a radius of perhaps a hundred meters, with the floor being so smooth and polished Alistair could see his reflection almost perfectly.

Besides the awe he felt from the grand natural beauty of the cavern and the intricate patterns of ice, Alistair was hit by the freezing cold. Even his exuberant life force and decent Constitution couldn't fully protect him from the chilling environment. He wrapped his new robes around himself tightly. Both the **Lesser Cloak of Shadows** and **Cloak of the Divined** had turned out to be unsalvageable after his fight with Pharaoh, so he'd purchased his new outfit, called **Mammothskin Raiment**, from the System Store for 40k drachma. Compared to his old cloaks, it wasn't anything special, but it offered decent protection against physical and magical attacks. That it was quite thick and wooly was a stroke of fortune.

At the center of everything stood a smaller dome, this one made of transparent glass. Inside, there were two stone pedestals on opposite sides, around five meters apart. Right as Alistair popped into existence, others followed suit, forming a ring around the central dome. Alistair counted eight people including himself, though he didn't recognize anyone. He suppressed his aura right away along with his life force, which he had practiced manipulating. While life force detection abilities weren't common, he didn't want to risk anything. Life force didn't extend from the body in the same way that aura did, so all he had to do was center the energies near his soulcore. In the long run, it wasn't healthy to deprive his extremities of their vitality, but it would be fine for a few days if it was required.

Alistair couldn't be a hundred percent confident, but his extra senses indicated that none of the other seven people were anywhere near his level. Useful in a fight, but based on the Quest description, there would be more than just brute force involved.

Before anyone had too much of a chance to react, a notification window appeared over the dome, accompanied by a voice inside his head.

That's never happened before.

Trial 1: The Commons of Peace and War

The eight participants will partake in a series of one-on-one games to determine winners and losers.

During each game, the two players will enter the game site and head to a pedestal. While playing the game, both players will have complete privacy from the other six participants, with the glass turning black, so there is no communication in or out of the game site.

The two players will have up to ten minutes to discuss before entering their selection on the pedestal—it is also acceptable for both players to enter their selection before the ten minutes is up, in which case the individual game will end and move on to the next two players.

The game is simple—each player has two options: peace or war. If both players select peace, each player receives three points. If both players select war, each player receives zero points. However, if one player selects peace and the other selects war, the one who selects peace will lose two points, and the player who selects war will gain ten points.

The notation (10,-2) means Player 1 receives 10 points and Player 2 receives -2 points.

War-War: (0,0)
War-Peace: (10,-2)
Peace-War: (-2,10)
Peace-Peace: (3,3)

Everyone will play each participant ten times, for a total of 280 games. After 140 games, there will be a six-hour intermission. Between games, there are three minutes of discussion time.

Besides earning points through the game, participants may also earn points by correctly guessing the outcome of the game. If you guess the exact configuration of the game (identifying what each player did individually), you earn one point.

Violence is strictly forbidden and transgressors will be severely punished. No combat abilities are allowed, even if not intended for violence. Only utility Skills are allowed, barring Inspect-related Skills. At the end of the 280 games, the participants with the two lowest scores will be eliminated and forfeit all their subregions to the winners, split proportionately to final placement.

The total number of subregions on the line for all non-losing participants will be a third of their current subregion count or up to three hundred subregions, whichever is greater. These collected subregions will be proportioned to the winners as following:

1st place: All of their subregions wagered + 25% of remaining pool
2nd place: All of their subregions wagered + 20% of remaining pool
3rd place: 20% of remaining pool
4th place: 15% of remaining pool
5th place: 12.5% of remaining pool
6th place: 7.5% of remaining pool

Pool: 1,924 subregions + (Max: 1,057, Min: 0), dependent on 7th and 8th place

Let The Commons of Peace and War begin!

24 THE COMMONS OF PEACE AND WAR

THE LARGE WINDOW above the dome vanished while numbers written in ethereal flames appeared over all eight of their heads. The individual directly to Alistair's left was assigned number one, and the rest were numbered in ascending order going counterclockwise, making Alistair number two. Considering he was very confident he was both the strongest and had the most subregions, it seemed the numbers were just random.

Alistair's fiery number two and the number one of the man next to him flew off of their heads and through the glass dome, hovering over the pedestals. An image above the dome declared Number One to be "Player One" for their game and Alistair to be "Player Two," with accompanying images for each of them.

Number one and number two will play the first game. You have three minutes to discuss and make your guesses. A private window will appear in front of all participants, where you can select what outcome you believe will happen. Please remember—no violence!

The voice faded out as quickly as it came, leaving the eight participants in awkward silence. Alistair looked toward his left, sizing up the man he would play in the first round. He was tall with braided hair and wore a military-style camo jacket. If his life force was anything to go by, he was one of the stronger cultivators in the room. Everyone else was about the same in that regard—it was unfortunate for his information gathering purposes that most people hadn't differentiated in terms of life force yet. That completely changed for aura; they all had the sense to cloak their leaky Mana, so Alistair couldn't measure them in that metric.

"You want me to find out?" Dev'rox asked, appearing on his shoulder.

"You can do that?" Alistair thought.

"Ever since you upgraded to the Ancient Warrior Leaf. My powers have doubled since the last time we met, and that includes for reconnaissance. I'm more *real* now."

"Okay, you have my permission," Alistair said. He focused on the others, who seemed reticent to speak.

"Looks like we're up first," Number One said loudly. In the absolute silence of the ice cavern, his voice sounded crisp and clear. "What do you think, Two?"

"It's the first round, so how about we both do peace?" Alistair replied. "And then everyone predicts peace-peace. Just to get a feel for things, you know."

Obviously, no one had a lot of time to analyze the intricacies of the game, Alistair included. But he knew what the game was, which not everyone was liable to know. The system called it Peace and War, but he knew it as the Prisoner's Dilemma. An infamous problem from game theory, where the best option was clearly for both sides to choose peace, but the natural equilibrium was to select war, since war strictly dominated peace as a strategy.

If a player always chose peace, they would get either -2 or 3 points. But if a player always selected war, they would either get 0 or 10 points. Therefore, war was always the superior option no matter what the opposing player did.

"I'm fine with that," Number One said. "But aren't we missing the obvious?"

"What do you mean?" Number Eight butted in, an older woman wearing a headscarf.

"There's one way six of us can win big," Number One explained. "I know I have exactly 256 subregions. I assume other people have somewhere in that range?"

Alistair's mind started racing, trying to figure out where Number One was going. He made sure to be the first to offer up his own—false—number. "I've got a bit over 300."

"Exactly," Number One continued, not missing a beat. "The bottom two players will have their subregions taken and put in the pool. That's fine. But my question is, how is the max extra pool 1,057, then? Since we have less than or around 300, me and Number Two already have all of our subregions in the pool. I think we all can guess based on your own number that those counts are about average. That means there's gotta be one huge whale with us right now."

"So what does that mean?" Number Five said, a shirtless warrior-type who was clearly a little slow on the intake.

"So what does that mean?" Number One parroted. "If we force that person to be last, then we can take all of their subregions. If we get the two wealthiest people in last place, we can get the pool up to 2,981. Most of us will get out of here better than we started. All we have to do is agree that whenever we play one of the two whales, we always select war, but when the rest of us play, we always select peace. No matter what they do, they'll be helpless."

Alistair immediately realized how dangerous Number One was. He clearly was quick on his feet. It wasn't a fair comparison since Alistair was the whale, so he wasn't trying to find ways to win against himself. Still, he couldn't have come up with such a strategy that fast. But there was one glaring problem.

"How the hell are we going to figure out who the two highest subregion owners are?" asked Number Seven, a handsome red-headed woman who looked tough as nails. "Even if I agreed with your strategy, that seems like the crux of the problem."

"I'll tell you when I figure it out," Number One said, but he was quickly cut off by Number Five.

"Oh, I get it now," the shirtless man said, "I know your type. Smooth talker, always in a strong man's ear. When push comes to shove, you're on the fence, waiting to be a parasite to the winner."

"I'm sorry for any prejudices you've come in here with, but I can assure you that I mean what I say. I'm no altruist like you *surely* are, and I never claimed to be. This strategy will lead the two whales to their graves. If I was the one with all the extra subregions, what incentive would I have to even mention this strategy? There's no guarantee someone else would have thought of it. "

Thirty seconds left before the game begins. Please lock in your predictions.

Alistair looked down at the menu. There were four rectangles on the window, each spaced around fifteen centimeters apart. The top left was the "both players choose peace" selection, which he pressed, while the top right was "player one peace, player two war." The bottom left was the inverse of that, and then the bottom right was "both players choose war".

He knew he was going to select peace, and there was no way Number One, who was trying to garner sympathy for his cause, would already go for war. It would be an aggressive move that would make him appear untrustworthy, and Alistair put that probability as quite low.

At first, he was a bit confused about what to do for the game, but as soon as the three minutes were up, his body shifted inside of the glass dome and to the pedestal with his number. Dev'rox returned inside of him before the period was up, just as the glass turned pure black, rendering them completely cut off from the outside world.

The ghostly imp whispered in his ear, "If I'm not one with you, I won't be able to enter the dome. I can give you what I've gathered so far."

As soon as the two of them were inside the dome, Number One started speaking.

"I know you're the whale. You can come clean."

Adrenaline rushed through Alistair's bloodstream as he panicked at the man's words. But he quickly centered himself by falling into the first stage of the Mutra trance, returning from the dive right away so as not to arouse suspicion.

"I'm not," Alistair said. "I can see what you're doing, though, and it won't work on me."

"And what is it you think I'm doing?"

"Don't patronize me. There's no way you know who's who yet. You were trying to gauge my reaction."

"That might be true," Number One admitted. "Can't blame a man for trying, can you? I was being a hundred percent genuine with my idea. It's just basic math, really. If you are the whale, I'm sorry, but if you aren't, then we can work together, can we not?"

"He's trying to corner you," Dev'rox said. "Imps are quite good at these sorts of manipulation games, believe it or not. I know his type."

Alistair had his Karmic sight on a low-energy mode the whole time they spoke. The rules said no violence, but they didn't say anything about applying cultivation abilities in other ways. In fact, Alistair was fairly certain that they *wanted* people to use unconventional means.

As far as the threads of Fate revealed, Number One appeared to be sincere in all of his statements, though his technique wasn't flawless. Lies that didn't involve severe injustice or lacked emotional meaning to the speaker were much harder to detect. He could have been more accurate if he used **[Eyes of Truth]**, but it was barred by the rules of the game.

"I would say in both cases that I have a lower subregion count and that I'd work with you, so you're not gaining information," Alistair said.

"I'm gaining the information that you're saying that instead of being cooperative and happy to have an ally," Number One replied without missing a beat. "Which might lead me to think that you're a cunning man who would have no problem with lying."

"Only if you think that I would be stupid enough not to say the same thing in both scenarios. I'm just protecting my range."

Number One chuckled. "Poker player, eh? This will be fun."

"On the topic of the actual game, we're both going to select peace, right?" Alistair asked.

"Of course. You'd think I'd be the first to defect from my own plan?" Number One gave Alistair an incredulous look.

"Just making sure," he responded. "You can never be too careful."

"Let's see how this works." Number One looked down at his pedestal. After a moment, the flaming number over his pedestal turned blue. "Hmm. Once you lock in your selection, the other person knows for certain. I wonder if being the first mover has an advantage or disadvantage? I digress, my apologies. Are we going to talk more or end it here?"

Alistair metaphorically turned to Dev'rox. "What do you think?"

"Number One has by far the best cloak. Even I can't tell how strong he is. In my opinion, he seems suspicious. There's a whiff of a psychic, if you ask me."

"A psychic? Shit!" Alistair thought, attempting a shoddy mental barrier.

His *nue* was still unpracticed, but he did his best at shielding his mind. Hopefully his relatively high Wisdom would pick up the slack.

Recognizing that he had left the silence hanging for too long, Alistair hurriedly selected peace for his own choice. Better be safe than let any of his thoughts leak to Number One.

As soon as he made his choice, Alistair instantly found himself back on the outside of the dome. The result of the game was front and center over the dome, showing his number and face along with his action alongside his opponent's choice. Both of them had selected peace, represented by a serene white symbol. Alistair hadn't ever seen the language before, but somehow he knew what it represented, as if he'd had the knowledge his entire life.

Next to the window for placing guesses, a scoreboard popped up, showing everyone's current score and the change from the last round.

1) **Holden** – 4 (+4)
2) **Mozi** – 4 (+4)
3) **Arjuna** – 1 (+1)
4) **Gilgamesh** – 1 (+1)
5) **Heracles** – 0 (+0)
6) **Medea** – 1 (+1)
7) **Scáthach** – 1 (+1)
8) **Bast** – 1 (+1)

His fiery two along with the number three of Arjuna to his right flew into the dome, though this time, he was Player One and his opponent was Player Two.

Alistair assumed that the Pathfinder AI had assigned the nicknames, which was interesting as they didn't seem completely random. As far as Alistair could tell, they fit along gender lines and also were more appropriate than random chance. The huge shirtless man got Heracles, and the red-headed warrior lady was named Scáthach. The Chinese philosopher Mozi felt like a crude pairing of his own justice-related baggage.

"Why don't you have a point?" Scáthach—formerly Number Seven—asked, turning to Heracles with suspicion in her eyes.

"What do you want from me, woman? I didn't trust long neck over there," he said, pointing at Holden. "I thought he'd do a trick. I was wrong, sue me."

Holden didn't seem to care. "It's fine. I'm not offended by it. If he wants to lose free points, by all means, he can do it."

"Welcome back, boys."

Alistair turned his head, finding the origin of perhaps the most seductive voice he had ever heard coming from a beautiful blond woman in a striking red dress.

"We were just talking about you," Medea continued, though the others in the room shrunk at her words. "Don't be shy everyone, it's not like we gossiped behind their backs."

"I'm glad to hear that," Holden answered back. "Gossip is the devil's telephone, they say."

Medea smiled. "Well, let's not go too far."

As they discussed the game, Alistair noticed that directly to his right Arjuna and Gilgamesh were having a private conversation. Since they were next to each other, it didn't arouse much suspicion. They were close enough that he should've easily made out what they were saying, but for some reason, he couldn't hear them.

"Can you eavesdrop on them for me?" Alistair asked Dev'rox.

"Why, I thought you'd never ask. Scáthach and Heracles are similar in strength, by the way. I'd put them on par with someone like Blaise. Perhaps level 35 or 36."

Alistair returned his attention to the discussion, where Bast was objecting to Holden's plan. "I know we didn't have time for you to fully explain everything, but how do you propose that we figure out who the whales are?"

"They'll reveal themselves to us eventually, I guarantee it," Holden explained calmly. "Even if you don't believe me, honestly, I haven't done anything to garner suspicion. I still recommend we all continue selecting peace, and I'm not advocating for anything but that until later on. We have plenty of time."

No one could give a rebuttal of Holden's idea. Alistair had a sinking feeling that he would take control of things if no one opposed him.

"What do we do if someone decides to get greedy?" Alistair asked. He knew what answer made sense, but he wanted it to be public knowledge. There were certainly others who had already formulated the idea, but no one could claim ignorance if everyone heard it said aloud.

"None of us will ever play peace against that person, of course," Medea said. "They gain an extra seven points in the short run, but in the long run, they lose."

Dev'rox flew back to Alistair. "Arjuna and Gilgamesh are pretty weak, I think. Their cloaks are shoddy and underneath, they're weaker than Heracles or Scáthach."

"What were they talking about?"

"That's the weird part. It was completely incomprehensible. Like a code language. Seeing one of those at this level would be weird, I suppose, but not impossible."

"A code language?" Alistair asked.

"As you know, most languages get automatically translated by the Pathfinder AI via a program installed onto the soulcore. It's a specific set of languages—millions and millions of them, but still finite. Species with enough power can get theirs removed, but most just create a code language specifically to avoid translation. It's not easy to make one, however."

"Hmm," Alistair murmured. His thoughts were quickly interrupted by Arjuna to his right, who now spoke in understandable words.

"Hey." Arjuna whispered from almost five meters away, yet Alistair heard what he said as if the man was inside of his skull. "We're up next. Awesome, right? Let's both pick peace and have an awesome time."

The countdown dropped to ten seconds and everyone hurried back to their private windows to input their guess. For his part, Alistair had stood still the entire time, and had already chosen peace-peace at the start of the intermediary period. Most of the others had naturally congregated closer together over time, except for him, Medea, and Holden. He made note of that.

As the timer hit zero, Alistair once again teleported inside the dome.

25 BETRAYAL OF THE PACT

ARJUNA MADE his choice the moment they arrived inside of the dome. Alistair still couldn't get over how the glass turned black and blocked out all light, yet somehow the light of their burning numbers was not only sufficient for sight, but created the same brightness as a normal room. The selection turned the number a blueish hue, casting deep craters into Arjuna's angular face. Maybe one day when he didn't have to spend every moment fighting for his life, he could have time to enjoy the wonders of cultivation. That his mother was still out there stung every day, the guilt building up like a stack of unfinished papers.

"Let's rock on, man," Arjuna said.

"Sorry, I thought we might use this time to talk," Alistair said, shifting into the same low output Karmic sight he had employed against Holden.

"Nah, I'm good. The more you talk, the more you balk."

"Weren't you talking to Gilgamesh?" Alistair knew there was a possibility he was playing his card early, but the upside was too high. He turned up his Karmic sight to the level where he would actually burn a full point if he kept it up for another half-minute.

The light changed behind Arjuna's eyes. It was subtle and almost impossible to see, but Alistair caught it. His Karmic sight made it unmistakable, as the threads of Fate shifted around the man's harmonious features. Dark, billowing emotion came forth but was restrained in under a fraction of a second.

"No? Why would you say that?" Arjuna said, but Alistair's eyes told him *yes, yes, yes.*

"No reason in particular. What were you talking about?"

For a second, Alistair thought Arjuna was going to spill the beans, or at least say some blatant falsehood that would be uncovered by his Karmic sight. The man opened his mouth but closed it soon after and simply refused to respond to Alistair.

Alistair even waved his hand in front of Arjuna's face, but it was as if the man was catatonic.

If only I had a way to record these conversations, he thought. The rules said no violence, but they mentioned nothing about sneaky recordings. Alas, his vast arsenal had no such techniques. Dev'rox investigated the glassy-eyed cultivator for a while, but found no irregularities, so Alistair ended up choosing peace well before the full ten minutes were up.

1) **Holden – 5 (+1)**
2) **Mozi – 8 (+4)**
3) **Arjuna – 5 (+4)**
4) **Gilgamesh – 2 (+1)**
5) **Heracles – 1 (+1)**
6) **Medea – 2 (+1)**
7) **Scáthach – 2 (+1)**
8) **Bast – 2 (+1)**

The scoreboard updated with the new round. This time, everyone selected peace-peace for their prediction. Their selection was the opposite of what they practiced, however, as Alistair and Gilgamesh came back to a full-fledged shouting match between Scáthach and Medea.

"What the fuck did you do?" Scáthach growled, unsheathing her sword from her scabbard.

"You don't want to do that." Medea smiled. "The one rule they were *quite* insistent about was no violence."

"What, this?" Scáthach said, twirling her gladius' blade. "This is how I express myself. Don't start getting scared on me."

"Wait, what happened?" Alistair asked.

"Scáthach says she saw Holden and Medea do… uh," Bast started.

Scáthach scowled. "They fucking kissed! Who even does that when we're in the middle of something so important? I bet they know each other from the outside and they're plotting together. It wouldn't surprise me if they're the two whales."

"Just because I'm attractive, you think I'm some kind of temptress?" Medea protested with indignation. "What is this, the 19th century? Have you no shame? You've been opposed to Holden from the start, with no good reason."

Before Scáthach could respond, Alistair stepped in to be a mediator. "Did anyone else see them kiss?"

No one came forward. Not Gilgamesh, Bast, or even the giant, Heracles, who had voiced concern with Holden earlier.

Alistair couldn't imagine how everyone except Scáthach could just miss something as blatant as a kiss on the lips, so he was inclined to think the redhead was making it up. The thing that gave him pause was just how *suspicious* Holden and Medea were. Scáthach appeared to be a more down-to-earth woman, perhaps reminding him of an older and gruffer Alexandra. Contrast that against a mysterious orator and a woman of singular pulchritude straight out of a period piece, and he didn't want to dismiss her claims out of hand.

But he couldn't let his TV-brain instincts run his higher faculties. "Scáthach, let's cool down here. Maybe you're misinterpreting what you saw."

The woman sheathed her sword on her back scabbard and scoffed. "I think I know what I saw. But if you want to ignore it, fine by me."

Gilgamesh spoke for the first time. "Arjuna, we're both choosing peace, right?"

"Of course, man. I'm chill with anything," Arjuna replied.

"Good. Have you figured how to find who has the most subregions yet, Holden?" Gilgamesh asked.

The tall, camo-laden man shook his head. "I'll tell you when I figure it out."

Scáthach rolled her eyes and Heracles didn't look happy at that either, but no one said anything. The countdown ticked away and Alistair got to see firsthand what happened when the players teleported. Their bodies *stretched* inside the dome in a millisecond, passing through the glass barrier, which darkened as they entered.

Alistair zoned out as the others started discussing. He considered all the facts and ideas presented so far. Holden had garnered the suspicion of at least two of the others, but the basis underlying what he was saying wasn't wrong. If they actually figured out that Alistair was the one with over a thousand subregions, it would make sense to collude against him.

Speaking of subregions, he checked his status window. His subregion count was up to 1,023, confirming that the real world was still operating in the background. Alistair wondered if the Pathfinder AI had selected a precise amount of people from each freehold to preserve the dynamics of the contesting groups back on Earth. Perhaps it also punished loners who chose incompetent subordinates that might lose subregions to enemies.

Just as the timer passed the nine-minute mark, the game suddenly ended. Projections of Arjuna and Gilgamesh's faces appeared over the dome, with the accompanying character for their selection. However, instead of both symbols saying peace, Gilgamesh had deviated from the plan and gone with war. The red character next to his face and name pulsed with a feeling that reminded Alistair of the Fist Node—a small slice of living war.

1) **Holden – 5 (+0)**
2) **Mozi – 8 (+0)**
3) **Arjuna – 3 (-2)**
4) **Gilgamesh – 12 (+10)**
5) **Heracles – 1 (+0)**
6) **Medea – 2 (+0)**
7) **Scáthach – 2 (+0)**
8) **Bast – 2 (+0)**

"What have you done?" Heracles growled. "What about our agreement?"

"My finger slipped, sorry," Gilgamesh said. "I actually meant to hit peace, I promise. Right, Arjuna?"

"Oh yeah, he's a cool dude." Arjuna gave him a big, toothy smile. "We had a nice conversation and all that. I think he's telling the truth about it being an accident. Live and let live, my friends."

"I don't buy that for a second," Scáthach said. "If it was an accident, you should have been more careful. Everyone in agreement to go to war on his ass?"

"Agreed," Heracles muttered.

"I concur. It can't be helped," Holden said.

The others came to a consensus on the matter, deciding to lock Gilgamesh out for the rest of the game. What Alistair tried to understand was why Gilgamesh chose to go with war, and why at this point? Was it a nuclear first strike to try to get ahead for the rest of the game? If the group never found their whale, the cooperation would have to break down at some point. There would have to be two losers in the end, and even if you didn't lose, you didn't want to end up at the bottom and get just 4.5% of the pooled subregions. Someone would have to break from the peace agreement at some point, so maybe Gilgamesh was trying to lock in his advantage.

But by getting ahead now, he would be hurting his prospects for the rest of the game. By being the first aggressor, he became an easy target for the entire group to attack unanimously and make one of the losers. Without Gilgamesh, there was no socially acceptable person to just deem the loser without recourse. If they tried, that person would resist and most people would feel sympathetic to their cruel plight. But Gilgamesh had essentially become the pariah on purpose. Was he just stupid? Or did he see something that Alistair didn't? Why was he talking to Arjuna, the man he screwed over? There was an aspect he was missing, but he couldn't see it.

Maybe Gilgamesh also had a bunch of subregions and was worried about Holden actually figuring out who the whale was. If that was the case, Alistair wondered if he should be scared of that as well.

Alistair could tell that the trust in the group was breaking at the seams. No one was talking, even though there was still time left. It looked like people were gathering into smaller groups, such as Holden and Medea, or Heracles, Scáthach, and Bast. Alistair sensed that they wanted him to join as well, but he resisted. He thought his best chance of winning was to play as the outsider.

The discussion period ended, Gilgamesh and Heracles going into the dome. Alistair predicted war-war, and five minutes later, they confirmed his guess. Everyone else had done the same, so they all gained one point.

After going through the adjacent pairs, the cycle went back to the start, matching #1 vs. #3 and so on. It was mostly uneventful, with no one deviating from the established peace-peace strategy. That was, until it was Holden and Gilgamesh's turn.

With help from Dev'rox, Alistair had snooped in on the conversations of every single player around the dome, while using his Karmic sight when he could. He was down to 30 Karma, a fair price for obtaining essential information on the truth of what his opponents were saying. Those last 30 points he would save for a pivotal moment.

The fact that he had heard what everyone said made the next result all the more shocking—after the full ten-minute countdown, two white doves of peace floated by Holden and Gilgamesh's names.

1) **Holden – 26 (+4)**
2) **Mozi – 19 (+0)**
3) **Arjuna – 20 (+0)**
4) **Gilgamesh – 26 (+3)**
5) **Heracles – 21 (+0)**
6) **Medea – 22 (+0)**
7) **Scáthach – 22 (+0)**
8) **Bast – 22 (+0)**

Alistair noted the +4 next to Holden's name. That meant he had not only convinced Gilgamesh to cooperate, but he also had predicted it in advance. *What's going on here?*

"The idea was for us to punish Gilgamesh, not to help him out," Scáthach growled the moment Holden returned. "It was your fucking idea, too. What the hell are you doing?"

Holden didn't betray any emotion, his countenance a completely blank mask. "I judged it was the best thing to do."

The gears clicked in Alistair's head. The surreptitious discussion between Arjuna and Gilgamesh, Holden's prior prediction and newfound cooperation with the betrayer—the math was so clear. How could he have been so dumb?

Now the only question was what he should do. His position was more precarious than he realized, especially with the background collusion. Holden's decision meant he probably didn't know Alistair's identity as the whale, but that didn't mean that he couldn't still figure it out. Sharing too much information might reveal enough for Holden to connect the dots. What he did know was that he needed to make some allies fast.

Alistair was up next, along with Heracles, so he was the perfect first recruit.

"Dev'rox, are you following what I'm thinking?" Alistair asked.

"Loud and clear," Dev'rox replied. "You want me to go haunt him?"

"Be cool about it. He's probably a bad actor, so if you scare him, you might get caught."

"Me? Get caught? I might be a ghost, but I'm still thousands of years older than you pipsqueaks. As if I could be caught—you're funny some-times, Alistair," Dev'rox said as he zoomed toward the warrior.

Alistair crossed his fingers and hoped to the high heavens that this would go according to plan.

———

Holden knew something was awry, but he couldn't put a finger on it. Up to this point, things were running exactly as he'd envisioned. When he realized that the fifth Quest would be a series of games, he had leaped for joy. With his deficiency of martial strength, he served as the advisor to a medium-sized freehold. His ability to ascertain truths that others couldn't made up for certain shortcomings, but apropos of that, he was suited better as a puppet master who manipulated events from the shadows.

When he realized that Gilgamesh and Arjuna were conspiring together, he realized it was the perfect opportunity to strike. Holden knew he would never get eliminated, but being number one was of the utmost priority. What a stroke of luck that Gilgamesh and Arjuna knew each other from the outside!

According to them, the system did something to everyone's appearances to hide their identities, even altering their aura. The only thing that let them figure out who they were was Arjuna's code language. No one could mistake that. But the stupidest part was their plan. They agreed to let Gilgamesh win against Arjuna every time, putting all their cards on him winning. Did those idiots not do the math? If the rest of the group punished him properly, both of them would lose.

That was why they needed a third member. Instead of being 2 against 6, now it was 3 and against 5, and much less obvious. Holden and Gilgamesh would trade winning and losing against each other, and grind free points from Arjuna. The sum winnings of games he played in the trio would be 14 per round, while the other five players could only make 12 per round, 3 for each game against the other four in the group. And that wasn't even counting the subterfuge they could pull with the guessing. Even if the others figured out his plan, they wouldn't be able to guess the outcome of the game with 100% certainty.

The plan would guarantee Holden and Gilgamesh the top 2 spots, and Arjuna one of the two bottom places. All that was left was putting Mozi in the bottom slot.

Holden had no strong evidence for Mozi being the whale, but he had learned to trust [Hypercalculative Induction]. When he popped the accusation to the others, nothing suspicious came up. Mozi probably thought he was a good actor, but nothing got past his discerning eyes. Every single possible variable factored into his calculations—microfluctuations in aura, the tiniest change in facial expression, a barely noticeable fidget or bead of sweat. Those imperceptible inductions gave a 71.5% chance of Mozi being the whale, which was good enough for him. He thanked the wisdom of the Pathfinder AI that his Skill didn't count as an Inspect-related one.

The moment before Heracles and Mozi entered the dome, he caught a change in expression on the large warrior. A look of confusion. Hundreds of thoughts raced through Holden's head as he walked through the chain of events, trying to figure out—

A saccharine odor permeated the surrounding air. "You look like you're thinking hard, handsome," Medea cooed.

Holden groaned internally. That was his other problem. Contrary to what Scáthach thought, Medea wasn't his partner-in-crime. In fact, she was the most dangerous person in the entire game for the simple fact that his [Hypercalculative Induction] broke down when trying to analyze her. She was a complete enigma, unlike every other person he had met so far post-initiation. Even Mozi, who he could tell was a big shot outside of the game, was an open book compared to her. Like her namesake, Medea was the prototypical femme fatale, the siren that led men to their deaths.

"What do you want?" Holden asked carefully. A wisp of cold energy passed by him, but he paid it no mind.

"Everything," she said, like that was an appropriate answer. "Can you give me everything?"

"I'll finish first in this Quest, if that's what you're asking."

"So bold and confident." Medea's blue eyes teased him with mysteries he could only dream of. "I can't wait to see."

"Why should I help you?" Holden asked. "If you're smart, you'd know I've already won. What's in it for me?"

"Have you?" she asked, her voice so persuasive that it even made Holden question reality. He made sure to double-check his aura barrier to see if she had used a Skill on him, but it confirmed that there were no breaches. "None of the others will select peace against you again. It looks like you're losing to me."

She walked away, swaying with unusual grace. *She's like a 1950s noir stereotype come to life,* Holden thought. *And it's working on me because of undetectable magic. Or because she's fucking hot. At least she doesn't seem to understand the plan.*

He couldn't let her talk to his two "partners" without supervision. Not that he trusted them—no, he didn't trust two buffoons who couldn't do basic math. Arjuna's communication Skill let him talk directly to Holden from across the floor of the cavern. Others could hear his words if they listened carefully, but they would only hear gibberish since Arjuna gave him temporary access to his code language.

The cold energy passed by him once more. Some small subsystem in the machinations of his brain whirred, calculating tail risks. But he ignored that. His preternatural induction had to be tempered, else it led to conspiratorial delusions.

"Stay away from Medea," he said. "She'll try and get in your head. She just tried to flirt with me."

"Affirmative," Gilgamesh responded.

Medea was talking to Bast, who hadn't yet taken a visible side. The older woman didn't seem swayed by her charms, however. Just as he was about to give out the next phase of instructions, the game ended, six minutes in.

Mozi had lost, selecting peace while his opponent selected war. Yet instead of a -2 next to his name, there was a -1, indicating that he had predicted the outcome.

1) Holden – 26 (+0)
2) Mozi – 18 (-1)
3) Arjuna – 20 (+0)

4) Gilgamesh – 26 (+0)
5) Heracles – 31 (+10)
6) Medea – 22 (+0)
7) Scáthach – 22 (+0)
8) Bast – 22 (+0)

Holden smiled. The possibility had always been there, and despite it throwing a wrench in his plan, he enjoyed the competition. It was time to have some fun.

26 GAMBLE RUN

SCÁTHACH DIDN'T UNDERSTAND what was going on. She trusted Heracles—they were both people of action, and Warrior-type Classes. They had a certain camaraderie that she didn't think he'd have betrayed, but here he was, choosing war against Mozi—

Wait... Scáthach thought. *Why did Mozi only lose one point?* The only answer was that he predicted it, and if he predicted it...

"Talk—now," she demanded.

Heracles grunted.

"What?" Scáthach managed, but he grabbed her arm and brought her aside.

"Mozi explained to me what's going on," he said. "Holden, Arjuna, and Gilgamesh are working together. They're going to let Arjuna lose on purpose in order to gain as many points as possible. They get more points per round than the rest of us do, as long as they keep trading peace and war. Did you notice that the net points gained in war versus peace is greater than that of peace versus peace?"

Scáthach glanced at the leaderboard. It was true, the net points gained from war-peace was 8 compared to just 6 for peace-peace.

"What does he want us to do?" Scáthach asked.

"We just have to do the same thing, minus the sacrificing of one person," Heracles said.

Scáthach wasn't a strategic genius, but even she could see the problem there. "Won't we fall behind them, then? I can't imagine Bast or Medea will just fall in line, either. The more people we add, the less we can be sure they won't betray us. What's our end goal, too? If this all ends up in a wash, it becomes the Wild West again, right? The only reason Holden, Arjuna, and Gilgamesh are cooperating is because they know that they'll win in the end."

"Trust me," Heracles said, though Scáthach didn't trust him farther than she could throw him. And since she could throw him a few meters, she trusted him a medium amount. "This guy is the real deal. We just gotta follow his plan. We'll lose if we do nothing anyway, so we have to try."

Scáthach gulped. She wasn't the trusting type. She had made that mistake at the start of the initiation and paid for it dearly. Since then, she'd operated alone, carving out a nice chunk of territory for herself. There wasn't a gambling bone in her body—she played by the book, with caution and planning. Now, she was putting her fate in the hands of someone else. She rubbed the hilt of her sword like a good luck charm. *Let's hope this works.*

———

"You think that was good enough?" Alistair asked Dev'rox as he returned from the game against Heracles.

"I believe so. But aren't you the one with eyes that pierce a man's soul?" Dev'rox retorted. "Why are you asking me?"

"You're thousands of years older than me. Excuse me if I thought you might have some sage wisdom." Alistair shook his head.

"I do have much wisdom, and you should listen to me more. Young people these days, no respect. When I was your age, my spawnlord..."

"Please, no more about your spawnlord, okay? I think I've heard enough 'spawnlord' anecdotes for a lifetime."

"I usually only tell you when you're going to sleep," Dev'rox began, shaking his tail, "but okay, if you insist, it's just that I think this concept of a 'parent' makes no sense—how could a parent possibly raise spawn without the knowledge of what other spawn are like and use that—"

"Dev'rox!" Alistair shouted out loud by accident. "Focus," he whispered in his thoughts, not trying to garner any more attention.

"Sorry," the imp said sheepishly.

Alistair surveyed the floor. Holden, Gilgamesh, and Arjuna had secluded themselves in a corner ten meters away from everyone else. Heracles and Scáthach were talking, which was good, since that was what he'd asked of the tall warrior. Medea was giving him a sultry look while Bast seemed confused as to why everyone was ignoring the obvious defection from the norm that Heracles had just committed.

"Listen up!" Alistair shouted, breaking the hushed conversations. "You're probably wondering what's going on."

Everyone turned their attention to him immediately, even the group of three conspirators.

"The reason Heracles went to war against me is that I asked him to. And I asked him to because those three are colluding," Alistair announced, pointing at Holden, Gilgamesh, and Arjuna. The latter two overacted shock to a comical extent, while Holden just smiled, like he knew everything in advance. "Arjuna and Gilgamesh know each other from the outside. They probably planned on Gilgamesh winning it all and then splitting the reward. Then Holden came along."

The only thing that bugged him was why did they make it so obvious? Holden didn't need to sequester himself with the two of them or predict his cooperation with Arjuna. In fact, he didn't need to cooperate with Gilgamesh at all. Maybe Gilgamesh was short-sighted and required his partner to already prove his loyalty, but that sounded dumb. Alistair perhaps could have figured it out anyway, but surely they could have worked to gain points secretly for longer?

"Holden's choice of peace against Gilgamesh was no accident. With only two people, their strategy wouldn't have worked, but with three people, it would be effective. Look at this." Alistair took out a glass wand that he had purchased before the Quest for these exact purposes, letting him draw in the air like a canvas. "Imagine that Holden and Gilgamesh trade equally between peace and war and Arjuna always loses. You'll see the expected value they obtain per round, not counting predictions for now, is 14. On the other hand, the five of us would get 12 per round. A guaranteed win for the two of them."

Alistair expected one of the other participants to be the first to speak, but Holden himself took point.

"Even if what you say is true, what are you going to do about it?" His words were careful to not admit fault, putting the onus back on Alistair instead of answering for any perceived wrongdoing.

"Good point," Alistair conceded. "That's why I propose the rest of us team up."

He drew some more numbers. "Following the same peace-peace convention, there's no way we can beat them. And even if we get four people, we'll still be making a bit less than them. But there's nothing else we can do."

Alistair motioned Scáthach and Heracles. "We're going to be making a team. Anyone's welcome to join."

For a long moment, there was silence. Alistair grew nervous that no one would take up his offer, but luckily Bast swooped in to save the day. "I'll join. I'm tired of these games. Let's just get this over with."

Alistair looked over at Holden. He had prepared a dozen lines of argumentation and potential counter-arguments if Holden intended to speak against his idea, but the man stayed silent. Alistair didn't like that his ever-present smirk didn't vanish—it felt like he was somehow playing into his hands, but there was nothing he could do about it.

The next round began, with Arjuna facing off against Medea. Therein lied one of the issues of their current set-up: what was going to happen to neutral parties like Medea? Perhaps if Bast had figured out how advantageous the position of being the swing vote was, she wouldn't have joined Alistair's team so readily. *That's why I didn't say anything.*

If they all choose mutual peace with Medea, she would easily win, gaining 21 points per round, not counting predictions. But if one of them chose war, Medea could easily join the other team, punishing them for their decision. And neither party could accept that outcome. Holden's team had the advantage on paper, but they would still be screwed if Medea went to Alistair instead. That meant a weird truce for the moment, where Medea was the clear winner. He wondered if she had been thinking that far ahead from the start.

They played through five cycles of the 28 rounds with no significant deviations from the standard. The last game was Alistair against Bast, with the older women choosing peace against Alistair's war, as planned. Medea kept racking up free points, taking a clear first, while Arjuna fell further and further behind.

1) **Holden – 212 (+1)**
2) **Mozi – 206 (+11)**
3) **Arjuna – 156 (+1)**
4) **Gilgamesh – 209 (+1)**
5) **Heracles – 206 (+1)**
6) **Medea – 232 (+1)**
7) **Scáthach – 209 (+1)**
8) **Bast – 207 (-1)**

Both parties were relatively close in points, but Alistair already calculated that if things continued along the same path, his team would surely lose. Something needed to change. The six-hour intermission was the perfect opportunity for that.

"You're sure this will work?" Alistair asked his imp companion.

"99%. Just do it," Dev'rox replied. "Have I ever misled you?"

Alistair didn't answer that, just stating, "Fine," and sitting down. He started meditating a few meters off to the side, where no one would talk to him without expressly intending it. Slipping into the Kai'tazake Mutra was as easy as walking at this point. Not bothering to work his way through the stages progressively, he dove in straight for the bottom. He swam through the ocean of tranquility, seeing the sea of knives and the kiss of death above him.

At the same time as he reached the deepest part of the trance, he opened up his Dao Nodes, letting his congealed Dao energy out of his soulcore. He still couldn't quite get over the weird quantum nature of the soulcore, where it possessed both Mana and Dao energy simultaneously.

Sure enough, just as Dev'rox predicted, he felt a tap on his shoulder. Perhaps he shouldn't have underestimated the imp, who had lived for thousands of times his lifespan.

Medea brought her lips to his ear. "You haven't been very talkative in our games."

"What's there to talk about?" Alistair asked. "We both know the outcome."

"I thought you would be trying to woo me more, old man. Everyone can see that without my help, you'll lose to Holden and Gilgamesh. You need me more than I need you."

"Do I?" Alistair grabbed her hand off his shoulder and stood up, staring directly into her eyes. "What if I have a secret plan that leads me to victory?"

Medea gingerly withdrew her hand. "Now that would be a sight to see. Sadly, it's quite unlikely." She let a small pulse of her Dao energy out, a sensual burst of what Alistair could only describe as raw passion. A Dao of a certain emotion, perhaps, but he couldn't name the exact one. It could have been anything from lust to ambition. "It's my turn for a question. You actually are the whale, aren't you? I have no idea how Holden figured that out."

Alistair had Dev'rox leave his body, using him to intercept any eavesdroppers, as long as their abilities leaked Mana or Dao energy. "That's classified information. Holden told you he thought I was the whale?"

"I'll take that as a yes. Holden told me that so I'd join up with him. I thought I'd shop the offer around. He needs me less than you do, so he can afford to offer me less. What will you give me?"

She batted her eyes, and Alistair could feel the pressure she exuded. *Dev'rox, are you sure about this?* Alistair thought. *It's such a weird thing to say. Is anyone listening?*

"Alistair, trust me. I've been manipulating the demonic nobility since I was five years old. And no one's listening, I guarantee."

"Everything," Alistair replied to Medea, staying as solemn and mysterious as possible, while internally cringing at his faux grandiosity.

Medea looked genuinely taken aback by his words, her eyes widening in surprise. That initial shock faded soon after, her confident exterior returning as soon as it left.

"You're more interesting than I would have imagined," Medea said carefully.

"You accept, then?" Alistair asked. "You'll join us?"

"First, let me ask you one thing. Have you noticed that it isn't just our names that are disguises? These forms we take are mere illusions. We can barely show any identifying features of our cultivation."

"Really?" Alistair scratched his chin and looked to Dev'rox, who nodded in confirmation. "The reflection I see in the ice looks like myself to me."

Medea gave him a mirthful glance. "When you look at me, what do you see?"

Alistair grew flustered as he tried to find an appropriate response. "A tall blond woman with a... full figure. You have a strong jawline and very pale blue eyes."

"Which is completely wrong. Well, not entirely, I am beautiful, but I'm of average height with black hair and red eyes, a side effect of some of my powers—when I'm not wearing contacts," she said, and Alistair found no easily detectable lies with his remaining 23 Karma.

"That's interesting," Alistair conceded. "But what's the relevance?"

"Let me tell you one thing. And I'm doing this because I like you. You'll never win versus Holden if you're putting your brains against his. He's like a real Sherlock Holmes. He can deduce what your favorite color is from the way you walk. But he has one weakness—me. For some reason, he can't figure me out," Medea explained. "The relevance of the disguises is that I'll never know your true identity. Unless you tell me. Which you're going to do, if you want me to join you."

Medea dropped the bomb like it was a flower petal. *Damn it,* he thought. Alistair knew that this was coming since the moment he sat down, yet he still felt weighed down by the pressure. He and Dev'rox had discussed this moment, yet for some reason it was still hard to put himself in such a vulnerable position.

No, Alistair thought. *That kind of thinking won't get me anywhere.* There were times to be risk-averse, and times to seize the opportunity. If he couldn't win here, how was he supposed to win later on, against stronger and smarter opponents?

"Keep your head cool," Dev'rox told him. "There's not much choice here. You have to give it to her."

"I'm Alistair Tan," he whispered as he lowered his head to her shoulder, careful to not let any prying ears hear. "#2 on the leaderboard. Northeast Order Freehold. You might have heard about me."

Alistair watched as shock slowly spread over Medea's face.

"You're not even joking, are you?" she finally asked.

"I'm not," Alistair confirmed. "Do with that what you will. But I hope to see you on our side next round. I have to go."

His heart was pounding, and he felt beads of sweat on his forehead, but he had accomplished his plan. He was under no illusions that Holden was going to take his moves lying down. But that was part of the game. There was only so much you could control, only so much your schemes were good for when the game began in earnest. Alistair cracked his knuckles. The intermission was almost up.

27 PLANS WITHIN PLANS WITHIN PLANS

"Greetings, Mozi," Holden said.

Each new round of 28 games began with the same pairing. Number One against Number Two—Holden versus Alistair. Each time, Alistair felt he was on the back foot. Now, he *knew* he was on the back foot. According to Medea, the braided man had an ability to supernaturally deduce information. He would have said something about it being unfair, but considering his own repository of overpowered abilities, including but not limited to ghost cultivation, Karmic cultivation, life force absorption, and a hidden Subclass, he had no right to complain.

To avoid any information leaks, Alistair employed the somewhat puerile but effective tactic of literally keeping his mouth shut. If Holden was really as good as Medea claimed, he would be able to glean information anyway, but it still would be less than if he tried to be clever.

"This is foolishness, and you know it. Why must you do this, Mozi? What did Medea tell you about me? Did she explain what I can do?" Holden asked. "She might have exaggerated, you know. She's in love with me, after all. I am the perfect man."

Alistair stayed quiet, despite Holden's relentless prodding. Dev'rox wagged his tail in Alistair's face, telling him, "Don't give in!" without words.

"I've studied much of the top one hundred on the leaderboard. There is a ton of variation in the amount of publicly available data. But I have narrowed your identity down to a few people. You can pretend to not be afraid, but I know you are. Your team will abandon you once I can prove it. With Arjuna occupying one of the losing slots, even a fool could see how advantageous it is to put you in the other losing position."

Holden unzipped his camo vest, revealing a series of gnarly scars on his chest. "Do you see these, Mozi? These aren't recent. No, they're from before the initiation. When I was eighteen, I was camping with my friends. In the dead of night, I heard rustling outside my tent. A monstrous grizzly bear was trying to get our food. Big bastard, nine feet tall at least. Do you know what I did when I saw it? I didn't back down. I took out my machete, and I fought that bear. I walked out with some scars, but the bear didn't walk at all. The pelt was lost in the initiation, but the memories, the memories still remain."

Why do I always attract the crazies? Alistair thought. He knew he shouldn't respond, but he did nonetheless. "There's no way that's true. Come on. You really expect me to believe you fought and killed a gigantic grizzly bear with a machete?"

"It's the truth, regardless of whether you believe it or not. I can tell that you were the sheltered type in the before. What many of us lived through every day of our lives, you only saw for the first time when Atavius Meloi came down from the stars. Am I wrong?"

"You just said you were camping with friends when this happened. So you were probably a West Coast Canadian or American, middle class or better, and in high school. The chance that you were fighting for your life every day seems pretty low to me, but what do I know?"

"Alistair!" Dev'rox admonished. "Why are you letting him get to you?"

Holden roared with a baritone laughter unbecoming of his slight frame. "My initial estimation of your intellect underwhelms. What do you know of the tides of life? In this ephemeral existence, the timeless truths of war are without end, in every moment and breath. If you claim to not have seen them before, you know nothing of the human condition."

"This conversation is over," Alistair said, re-picking the war option in his head over and over, to no avail. He was stuck in here until the ten minutes were up unless Holden ended his torture early.

"Let it be so."

Holden selected war, ending the game prematurely. Alistair couldn't help but feel suspicious. The last four times they had played each other, Holden had purposefully stalled the entire time, fishing for information. Whatever game the mysterious man was playing at, he was glad he wouldn't have to talk to him anymore. Alistair's own eyes were a dark brown, but Holden's were so dark they actually looked black, like a bottomless pit of inhumanity. Sure, it sounded like 80% of the things he said were nonsensical bluster, false bravado, and purposefully complicated with misused philosophy, but he couldn't help the creeping feeling that said, "maybe he's the real, evil deal."

As usual, there was little communication during the three minute discussion period, outside the coteries. Alistair still had Dev'rox monitor the other side, but he couldn't gain anything out of the conversations, since they all spoke in Arjuna's code language. Holden had caught on to it quickly, conversing just as fluently as Gilgamesh. Alistair's main concern was not on his opponent's end, but that one of his teammates would cross the icy curtain. So far, he hadn't intercepted any communication, but he couldn't see everything.

"You're sure about this?" Heracles asked. He conveniently had a Skill that allowed him to summon a barrier of impermeable honey. The wall of solid honey was completely seamless, allowing for no energy transfer in or out, but it was very weak. Not useful in the battlefield except under very niche conditions, but amazing for avoiding interlopers.

"We have to make the first concession," Alistair said. He had experience with that. Thinking back on it, he had been far too overzealous in starting his own cycle of players. Because of the order of games, when he started the war-war regime against Holden, Gilgamesh, and Arjuna, he had fewer games played than almost all of his partners.

Bast complained, raising her head in annoyance. "She could easily betray us after this game. I don't like this at all."

Scáthach raised an eyebrow at the older woman. "You do realize she's already winning by a fair margin? She doesn't need our points. Mozi, you said you trust her, right?"

Alistair tilted his head. "Eh, I wouldn't go as far to say I trust her. There's a possibility she's swindling both of our teams. But that's a low probability outcome."

"It's fine," Heracles said. "I'm no coward. I'll do it for the team."

A couple of seconds later, Heracles shifted inside the dome along with

Medea. This game wasn't the moment Alistair was nervous about. Nor was it the next one after that. After hearing about Holden's abilities from Medea, he had come up with an idea. An idea that was so crazy, there was no way even Holden could predict it. Dev'rox told him it could work, but he hadn't practiced it in so long, and he only had one shot.

―――――

1) **Holden** – 217 (+1)
2) **Mozi** – 212 (+1)
3) **Arjuna** – 158 (+0)
4) **Gilgamesh** – 223 (+0)
5) **Heracles** – 211 (+1)
6) **Medea** – 246 (-1)
7) **Scáthach** – 225 (+11)
8) **Bast** – 213 (+1)

Holden stared at the board. Scáthach had won her game against Medea, for a juicy 11 points. 11, not 10. That put her in second place with 225 points, behind Medea who had 246, and ahead of himself and Gilgamesh, with 217 and 223 respectively.

"What?" Gilgamesh exclaimed. "What's going on here, Holden?"

"It's fine. All within expectations," Holden said, which was true.

That woman, Holden thought. *She drives a hard bargain.* Her joining Mozi's side didn't matter to the greater plan. As long as she delivered the actionable information in time, it didn't matter. And he had contingencies for such a scenario as well.

Holden looked up to the rectangular blocks of ice above them. "Keep up your work."

"Got it, boss," Arjuna said. "You can count on me."

"I'm sure I can."

―――――

The following three rounds went as expected. They were now five against three, yet it was difficult for Alistair's team to catch up. Ending the eighth round, Holden still had a slight lead in points against everyone except Medea.

1) **Holden – 342 (+1)**
2) **Mozi – 338 (+1)**
3) **Arjuna – 223 (+1)**
4) **Gilgamesh – 336 (+1)**
5) **Heracles – 339 (+1)**
6) **Medea – 364 (+1)**
7) **Scáthach – 341 (+1)**
8) **Bast – 339 (+1)**

Alistair's group each made 16 points per round, whereas Holden's group was split between Holden, who earned 16 points per round, and Gilgamesh, who earned 12 points per round, since he took one more game for the team than Holden. They probably had an agreement that Holden would come out on top, which would happen if they split the last two rounds 50/50.

Little did Alistair know of the omnipresent eyes watching him and the almost 200 players participating in "The Game of Life." While the Pathfinder AI was in charge of the initiation, the Final Frontier Empire sent out arbiters for certain worlds deemed noteworthy of closer attention. FX-14752 was one such world, as the only planet initiated at the Premium Tier in the current three-month Prime Initiate cycle. Resources were being pumped into the planet at a terrifying pace.

The obscene spending shocked even the arbiters, two Profound realm cultivators. First of the two observers was a young-looking man with crystalline spectacles, the second an eight-foot-tall elf, elegant and slender. The elf practiced his prestidigitation skills with an impossibly complex assortment of silver blocks. His fingers danced around the mercurial object, which fit into the palm of his huge hand with ease. The different shapes and expressions looked stochastic, but on closer inspection, they pulsed with a regular pattern.

"Trouble is brewing," the elf, Kazian Bromas, said. Like all male elves, his voice was deeper than any human's, a croaking bass that resonated in the air without any Mana or Dao. "Have you heard of the edict?"

"The Crusade Against Usury?" Johannis, the human Annalist, responded. He was bred from birth to have a recall exceeding the most powerful computing automata the Final Frontier could buy. "A histrionic and grandiloquent imperial reaction. The Laketors know they cannot seriously intend to upend all of society on the cries of the *hoi polloi*."

Kazian sighed, though because of his physiology, it sounded more like the rumbling of an engine. How he had dealt with the arrogant apprentice Annalist for the past few months was a great mystery of the multiverse. "Your wisdom is surely unparalleled and your eloquence is surely unmatched," he said. "However, I believe you are wrong. My cousin's cousin tells me the purges and seizures have already begun."

Johannis stopped scrolling on his crystal glasses, raising them up to his forehead. "What?"

"A million Orichalcum drachma," Kazian said. "All the big ones were hit. Feiyn Goods, the Akata Corp, the Siar Ka Company, Corlyon, Kesslar-Xin."

"What about our position? We have a group of nobles, Progenitor Clans, sects, and corporations already at a fever pitch. Have they heard about it?"

Kazian internally chuckled at how fast Johannis's advanced vocabulary faded once something urgent came up, but he restrained himself. Technically, the bookworm was his supervisor. "They've heard of the edict, of course, but the seizures just happened. The imperials are trying to crack down on information leakage. I only know because my cousin's cousin is a Grand Imperator."

"By Tianlong's tail!" Johannis cursed. "What are the sects doing?"

"Most of them are biding their time, as far as I know," Kazian said. "To defy an imperial edict means death."

"An *enforced* imperial edict. What madness."

"We shall do our part and keep the peace and continue to host the Quests. No one will dare touch an Annalist and a Mindaugust unit," Kazian said confidently. "On a lighter note, how do you find this game I created?"

"It's interesting," Johannis said, his mind already having moved on from the previous discussion, as was wont of an Annalist with their massive memory banks. "This game looks interesting. It has the #2 on FX-14752."

The man pointed toward the numerous informational display bubbles on their ship. Kazian blasted a minuscule amount of Mana at one bubble, bringing it closer to them and blowing up its size several times.

"Alistair Tan," Kazian said, stroking his chin.

While his memory was not eidetic like his partner's, he remembered that person very clearly. Along with Pharaoh, the jewel of the Corlyon Company, he was the most valuable initiate on FX-14752. Alistair excelled in almost every category. Privacy shields prevented the arbiters from seeing exact details—those were only available to their sponsors, but it was obvious he had at least three Dao Nodes along with Karmic powers.

"He's smarter than I expected," Kazian said, uploading the history of the match into his brain. "Who do you think will win?"

Johannis did the same, catching up on the details. "In a battlefield, there is no doubt Alistair would vanquish all seven others without breaking a sweat. However, I fear he is outmatched in wits by this Holden."

"Pattern matching is not cunning," Kazian murmured. "Medea is the one winning at the moment."

"I can see that," Johannis retorted with some attitude. "Look here."

Johannis created a sub-bubble, rewinding the game back to the 7th round. "She swindles both Holden and Alistair for information. Baseline men and their hormonal thinking. Alistair tells her his identity to get her on his side, yet she betrays him anyway and tells Holden. How duplicitous."

Kazian took control of the sub-bubble, moving to the start of the 8th round, and played a conversation between Heracles and Scáthach.

"Do you think Mozi will betray us?" Scáthach asked.

Heracles, who had been focusing on polishing his broadsword, shot up to attention. "No? Why, what's the matter?"

"I don't know, it's just a feeling," she said. "He's talked to Medea a few times alone."

"So? She's part of our team now. And look at her, I don't—" Heracles cut himself off after catching a glimpse of Scáthach's glowering stare. "I mean to say, I don't see the problem with it."

"We only have two games left against every person now that the ninth round is beginning," Scáthach said. "If you look at our plan, we're the ones who are supposed to win against Mozi in the last round."

"I'm not following."

"Well, let's say we give Mozi the win in the previous round, right? But next is the last round. What if he decides that he doesn't want to give the win back? What incentive does he have then, in the moment of going up against us, to give us the win? Even if he doesn't actually get the points, if he makes us go to war too, we're losing out on 10 points."

"Damn, you're right. So what are we going to do?"

Johannis minimized the sub-bubble once more. "There are many schemes going on, it seems."

"Superior information is the key to victory. Know the enemy and know yourself, and you have no reason to fear a hundred battles," Kazian recited.

"What is that, a General Kashtiya quote?" Johannis asked.

Kazian shook his head. "No, it's from their world. Sun Tzu, an ancient philosopher."

"Hmph. Savages can have inklings of sagacity, I suppose." Johannis said.

Kazian switched to the real-time main bubble as something caught his eye. "Look, Johannis. The ninth round is about to start. Holden against Mozi."

Kazian finished his puzzle toy, aligning the set of metallic blocks so precisely that it looked like one solid piece. The nanometer-precise manufacturing made it so smooth, even his powerful vision couldn't spot any divots or edges. Kazian Bromas was a careful, methodical elf, with a melancholic temperament, yet even he felt excitement at seeing the end of the trial.

28 GHOSTS ALWAYS WIN

"WE MEET ONCE MORE," Holden said. "But this time, I think you'll want to talk."

Mozi—or should he say Alistair—remained silent. He was getting better at hiding his emotions, Holden estimated. In the first of their meetings, he'd worn his heart on his sleeve, but now he was a cold wall. Standard methods, like trying to analyze his aura and soulcore, failed outright on account of how well cloaked he kept himself. Holden had never seen such an impressive cloak, except on himself, of course. But their approaches were different. Holden had a dexterous and skilled touch, while Alistair seemed to use brute force.

Holden sat down on the icy ground, sighing. "I know your identity. I think everyone left on Earth has heard about you at this point, once the Soulnet opened up. I tried using it before, by the way—we're completely cut off. Your real name is Alistair Tan. You thought you could hide from me, but my eyes see all," Holden bluffed, not revealing that the source of his information was Medea.

"That's not true," Alistair insisted.

Holden tapped on the **Spatial Ring** he had on his right ring finger. The convenient bodily storage system the Pathfinder AI provided let him keep around ten Rare items, but his style necessitated more than that. As such, he'd spent nearly a half a million drachma on the tiny hexagonal ring around his finger. It had around the same amount of storage as his person, but it let him hold so many more goodies.

Out of the pocket dimension stored inside the ring, he pulled out a large glass marble. The surface was frosted, but there was a visible pink light at the center.

Holden started spinning the marble in the palm of his hand. "I never thought I'd use the **Annalist's Aid** for this purpose."

"What are you doing?" Alistair asked, but his words fell on deaf ears. Holden continued whirling the marble until a dazzling display of unknown symbols materialized in the air.

The symbols were in all the colors of the rainbow and were completely illegible to anyone who hadn't been trained to read them. It had taken even Holden a few days to get used to the absurdly complicated patterns. But once he had perfected its usage, it was an invaluable tool. He had read that Annalists were a type of humanoid subspecies created by the Sublimed Machine for archival purposes, though there were a surprising number of Annalist warriors. The **Annalist's Aid** was a child's toy, used by young Annalists who hadn't developed the brainpower for perfect recall, yet to Holden it was a priceless artifact.

One of its characteristics was that it could hold true memory. It recorded every sensation the individual had felt in perfect detail, down to the tiniest part of aura. The problem was that it had an extremely high Mana cost to use, even with his 555 Mana pool. That was the only reason he hadn't tried it before. He only had a few chances to confirm an identity, and there were dozens of potential people who could have been the whale. Some on the leaderboard were still obscure figures, having only their name and approximate territory known. But now that Medea had given him the bait, Holden was ready to go.

"Show me Alistair Tan!" Holden shouted unnecessarily for dramatic effect—just his thoughts were sufficient to control the device.

The sphere spun so fast the skin of his palm began to warm. It cycled through hundreds of different dream-like holograms in less than a second, settling on a memory in a dank cave. It was the closest memory of the #2 ranker than Holden could afford. A fight was brewing between Alistair and some unknown opponent who wielded blue fire. Most of the people fled for their safety, but one curious bystander stood about seven meters back, watching the fight.

After dodging the fiery man's attacks with ease, Alistair ended the fight with a single punch, a devastating icy blow that froze the man and everything else in the vicinity almost instantaneously. While in an immature state compared to today, there was no mistaking that the aura of the man in the memory was the same as the one before Holden.

Holden wanted to leap for joy, but he kept his cool. With the help of the memory, it was so obvious. While the wizened, long-bearded cultivator in front of him looked completely different from the youth in the hologram, his mannerisms were identical. Now, the only thing left was removing every out Alistair could possibly play to. For that, Holden turned to his [Hypercalculative Induction].

"That's you, isn't it?" Holden asked, displaying the memory on repeat right in front of Alistair's face. "Just admit it. Let's stop playing games."

"That's not proof," Alistair said hastily. "Our auras could be very similar. Or who even knows if that's a real memory? I have no reason to trust this thing."

"It's embarrassing to see you grovel like a worm when you have the power of a king," Holden retorted. "A man should never debase himself in such a manner. A king stands with his head held high, possessing not even a modicum of shame."

While they talked, Holden ran his Skill in overdrive, combing over uncertain threads and connections at lightning speed. The only unfortunate part of his Skill was that even he couldn't understand why he came to certain conclusions. The reification of the enormous amount of data that came through his brain's subsystem was impossible to justify with his normal mind. While he had been nigh certain of Mozi being the whale from round one onward, he'd needed to wait until now for proof, or he would miss his opportunity.

A thorough examination of all of Alistair's actions while inside the black dome led him to believe the current course of action was safe. His opponent was crafty—Holden had to give him credit for that, and at first he had worried that revealing his identity was somehow what Alistair wanted, however counterintuitive that sounded. But after an exceptionally intense analysis with [Hypercalculative Induction], Alistair seemed to be utterly effete to Holden's strategy.

"What do you want me to say? I'm Alistair, I'm the whale, you win? Is that what you want?" Alistair complained, his voice growing to a near shout. "What's wrong with you, man? Are you cracked in the head? You know, I've met a ton of messed up people since the initiation. There were all the psychopaths at the beginning, though apparently a bunch of those people got messed with by the Final Frontier Empire. Just another in the long list of unthinkable crimes. Anthony Ricci was way more of an asshole than you, for sure. But at least he had something you're completely lacking —authenticity. He knew he was an arrogant asshole and never pretended to be otherwise. You, on the other hand? What's with all these weird metaphors and patently made-up stories? Okay, I admit it. I'm the whale. I'm Alistair Tan? Are you happy now? Are you happy?"

Even Holden couldn't fully hold in his mirth, letting the edge of his lips curl in a grin. The final part of his plan had come to fruition. He activated the memory capture retriever on the **Annalist's Aid**, recording the last thirty seconds of conversation into the device. Alistair's own confession would do much to assuage the doubt of the others and confirm his identity.

"Thank you," Holden said. "It's been a pleasure."

Ever the careful plotter, Holden had to do one last check with his Skill. For some reason, his base, non-mathematical instincts hummed that there was something off. It was just the slightest buzz, no more than a drop of doubt, but that made him wary. But his analysis revealed nothing. No plots, no secrets. It was as if Alistair was a ghost, unable to change his fate.

Whatever, Holden thought. He had gotten this far trusting his Farsighter Class. Now was not the time to stop. He selected war, ready to win The Commons of Peace and War.

———

"Holy shit," Alistair cursed the moment the game ended. "I don't know how much longer I could have held on."

"You did swimmingly." Dev'rox gave him a toothy smile with his words of reassurance. Alistair chuckled; it was nice to have the approval of a grumpy, hard-to-please imp sometimes. The presence of an over hundred-thousand-year-old mentor certainly helped calm his nerves, which had manifested as him playing with his red bracelets. It was a good thing he couldn't activate them.

In the game against Holden, Alistair had laid everything on the line by drawing deeper into the Dao of the Ghost than ever before. He had tried the tactic once before in the war against Anthony, using his ethereal form to spy on his enemies without being detected. He used it this time for a different reason.

After hearing about Holden's powers from Medea, he had wracked his brains thinking of how to counter such a broken ability. It was like the man was tailor made for winning the fifth Quest.

But then he remembered what being a ghost meant. Ghosts had only weak tethers to the laws of causality, existing as mere shades of their original life. When Alistair turned himself into a living ghost, he lost his self-awareness and spark of consciousness. Everything he did while in that form was a consequence of the state of his mind and body at the point of transformation. And since he was disconnected from the chain of natural causality, Holden's Skill couldn't detect anything awry. If Holden had questioned him under normal circumstances, he surely would have given away his true intentions through minute changes in expression and cadence. His true intentions, of which Holden hadn't the slightest inkling, were hidden, as the tall man told the others what happened inside of the dome.

1) **Holden – 343 (+1)**
2) **Mozi – 339 (+1)**
3) **Arjuna – 224 (+1)**
4) **Gilgamesh – 337 (+1)**
5) **Heracles – 340 (+1)**
6) **Medea – 365 (+1)**
7) **Scáthach – 342 (+1)**
8) **Bast – 340 (+1)**

"I have something to announce," Holden shouted, his voice echoing multiple times in the cavern.

Just like from before the first game, he once again caught the group's attention with his innate presence. Even the members who distrusted him were at least interested to hear what Holden had to say.

"I'd like to apologize," Holden continued. "I'd like to apologize for not finding the person with the high subregion count earlier. I know a long time ago I said that I'd find out who that person was, and unfortunately my abilities weren't good enough for the longest time. However! I am confident that I have now found the whale."

"Who is it?" Bast asked vociferously.

"I think it's better if I show you." Holden took out his weird marble, which started spinning in his palm. Like before, it displayed a swirl of esoteric symbols before shifting into a three-dimensional projection showing the same memory he showed Ghost-Alistair. The differences this time were Holden made it dozens of times bigger, so the people in the hologram were actually larger than life, and that he juiced it up, so the Skills and Mana in the memory felt real, to a certain extent. When Johnny used his flames in the memory, the room got a little hotter as the Skill took on a semi-corporeal form.

"I don't understand," Heracles said. "What's the #2 in the world have to do with the whale?"

Some of the quicker individuals had already started to catch on, but to emphasize the point, Holden outstretched his arms to the Heavens. "Behold! The man we call Mozi is actually Alistair Tan. I hope I don't need to explain further. It's obvious to anyone who looks that their auras have the same unique signature. But, just in case, let me show you another, even more damning memory."

Holden changed the projection to his own memory, the one he'd created just a few minutes before in the dome. He replayed it for the world to see, showing Ghost-Alistair's angry tirade. Real-Alistair didn't even remember saying those words. *Is that really what I would have done if it was the true me in there?* he wondered.

Alistair didn't even try to avoid the torrent of prying eyes, who were double-checking what they had seen in front of their eyes and under their noses. He could have played a strategy of denying everything, but he doubted that would have worked against the preponderance of the evidence. Plus, as an Arbiter of Justice, he probably shouldn't be in the habit of lying.

"It's true," he said. "I am the whale."

He could feel the shock from the others right away. His words hit hard, but he knew that they weren't just thinking about his position as the whale, but also his status as #2. That number carried a lot of weight, whether he intended it or not.

"You're Alistair Tan?" Heracles asked incredulously, as if he couldn't match the older man that Alistair took the form of to the muscular (though not compared to him) barefisted fighter.

"That settles it for me. If you're the whale, then it's in everyone's best interest to make you lose. Count me out," Bast said a little too quickly, even physically moving over to Holden's side.

"We both know you've been flirting with that for some time, Bast," Alistair said, pointing toward the ceiling.

Bast scowled at Alistair's comment, though he was mostly trying to take control of the situation rather than say anything meaningful. He hadn't figured out that Bast was working with Holden until near the end of the 8th round. Before that point, Alistair had been relatively sure that there was no communication between Holden and anyone on his team besides Medea, since he had Dev'rox track them quite often. Except for Alistair, Holden's games against the rest of his team took less than ten seconds on average, making him believe it was almost impossible for them to communicate. Yet the answer had been right in front of him. Or more accurately, right above him.

Holden had Gilgamesh put signals on the ceiling of the cavern, over fifty meters above the floor. It was so high that Alistair had sensed nothing amiss, and yet it was there in plain sight. Holden had gambled on him not looking up, and that gamble had paid off.

"It's over," Holden said. "Now that it's four against four. With Arjuna on my side, you're bound to lose. I plead to Scáthach, Heracles, and Medea—please don't throw your game away. Come to the right side before it's too late."

"I wouldn't recommend that," Alistair said. At last, it was time for his machinations to pay off. "Look at your position. As it stands right now, we're behind in points. In fact, I have the least points on our team by one. Now that Bast has joined them, they'll pull further ahead in points. If you join them or not, I'll be in last place. But I think you're all missing one factor. *Me.*"

"Yes, I am the whale. I own 1,035 subregions. But you know what that makes me? Powerful. I'm the #2 ranked person on the leaderboard. I'm level 43, which I know for a fact is higher than any of you by a long shot. You probably know by now that I was in the top three of Felons vs. Fellows. I defeated Anthony Ricci, the former #2, in a duel to the death. I fought the #1 ranker to a standstill. Now, can you understand the magnitude of what I'm talking about?" Alistair forced authority into his voice, remembering how Kyraxadon moved him across space just through a word. His was not even a thousandth of that strength, but his words still carried more weight than the most resonant of voices. "If I lose today, the system isn't going to kill me. The penalty for failing this trial isn't death. It will be a huge setback, I won't lie, but I will come back. I still have all of my powers at my disposal. And you don't want to be on my bad side."

"You're bluffing," Bast responded. "You don't even know who we are."

"But I have my memories, don't I? You have Holden to thank for that, I had no idea the **Annalist's Aid** even existed. But now, all I have to do is to go to a person with an extensive collection of memories in their **Aid**, and then find anyone whose aura signature matches one of the people here who betrayed me. You think it's that difficult? There's likely around 200 people in [The Game of Life], based on the total number of subregions in the world. You're not hiding among a billion people, you're hiding among 200, from a very, very angry and dedicated loser."

Alistair followed up his threats before anyone had a chance to interrupt. "But it doesn't have to be this way. If you know anything about my abilities, you might know that I follow the Dao of Justice. I don't harm innocents, and I don't break my word. If you agree to help me by always selecting peace against me, I promise I'll reward you handsomely. How does 250,000 drachma, a Legendary rarity item, and a guaranteed position in my freehold sound?"

In the fifth round, Alistair had realized something. The Commons of Peace and War made no sense. Or at least, on face value, it made no sense. It was a game of wits, cunning, psychology, game theory, alliances, and betrayal—something that anyone had the potential to be great at. Perhaps there was some selection pressure toward the strongest cultivators being more intelligent, which made some amount of sense, but were they really necessarily the most analytical, the most book smart? Alistair had to imagine there were hordes of cultivators who used brute-force and reached the peak through martial might with relatively little thinking involved.

The game rewarded smarts, but far too much. That realization made Alistair consider the reason why they had anonymized everything. It was obviously to prevent the strong from outright threatening the weak, but that also meant it was a very effective strategy. He had been thinking about things too much like a scholar. What would Alexandra's first instinct have been, if put in the same place as him?

It was Dev'rox's proposal for him to leak his identity, but recognizing those facts gave Alistair the necessary edge to employ the strategy as effectively as possible. Medea "leaked" Alistair's name to Holden, who would be unable to use his Skills to see through the plot since he couldn't read Medea at all. There was one close call in round 6 where Holden got Alistair riled up, but he never veered into the subject. He wasn't sure how powerful Holden's Skill was, and whether it could glean information about his secret plot from even that interaction, but based on how it went in the first game of the ninth round, the man had no idea. With the Ghost Node, Alistair removed any suspicions and reservations Holden might have had about using his identity against him.

If Holden had thought without using his analytical Skill, he might have seen through Alistair's plot. At the end of the day, the conclusion he came to wasn't so obscure or complicated that Holden couldn't have seen it in advance. But he had leaned on his Skill as a crutch, abdicating rational reasoning for the impenetrable algorithms of his analytical Skill.

No one spoke for a few seconds, and Alistair started to sweat, catastrophizing about his situation.

It turned out to be for nothing when Gilgamesh spoke up. "I'm not taking my chances. I'm in."

"If he's in, I'm in," Arjuna said.

"What are you doing? This is all nonsense!" Holden shouted. "We can't be sure about what he said! There's no way that he would realistically be able to—"

"You're just about out of Mana, aren't you," Alistair said. "You've been draining your Mana the entire time running whatever Skill you have, plus you just coughed up another hefty chunk by amplifying those two memories. You lost for two reasons: your overconfidence in your ability, and because you underestimated Medea."

Holden didn't respond. Alistair guessed he was still in shock at losing. Ever since the initiation, he probably hadn't been blindsided a single time.

"Alright. Let's finish this one up."

29 TRIAL OVER

ALISTAIR WAS GENEROUS, but he also didn't want to give off the vibe that he was a harmless do-gooder. Cultivating an air of authority took a careful hand, and so even though he would never actually kill those who didn't join him, letting them think that he would was a necessary evil. He liked the idea of the rest of the world believing he was harsh but fair, so any leniency or mercy on his part would be even more valuable.

For those reasons, he told his allies to go to war against Bast. The one thing that he had to make clear was that betrayal was not an option. As for the rest of them, he let them decide how to sort the remaining placings. Alistair was actually intrigued as to how the rest of the games would play out. With his victory assured and Bast's and Arjuna's losses all but confirmed, the remaining five spots would be up for grabs.

The games were faster than before, with little discussion in the ten-minute break periods. Everyone was on edge, knowing that their placement could come down to one mistake.

Arjuna went peace on purpose against Gilgamesh to give him the victory, an unsurprising outcome that was predicted by all the participants. But Gilgamesh against Heracles was more interesting. Ostensibly, the two were on his team, but as he had given no instructions on intra-team game-play, anything was on the table. Alistair himself predicted them both to go war, as the payoff matrix this late in the game made it practically necessary without strong trust between them. Given the current situation, Alistair felt safe in his prediction, and he was proven correct when the scoreboard confirmed war-war. Sadly, Heracles himself had gotten it wrong, somehow believing that they would both select peace, along with Bast, who had Gilgamesh selecting war and Heracles choosing peace. Alistair felt a little touched by Heracles's naiveté.

The next interesting development came from Holden against Bast. To everyone's shock, the outcome was war-peace, in Holden's favor. The man himself was the only person in the group to correctly predict the outcome, the others going with either peace-peace or war-war. After the game was over, Holden just smiled, while Bast grew despondent after seeing she had been swindled. A classic case of the betrayer being betrayed. Alistair was only unhappy that Bast losing meant Holden was essentially guaranteed to not be one of the losers.

Holden's game against Arjuna directly followed, containing another surprising result— the outcome turned out peace-peace. Heracles and Scáthach immediately accosted Arjuna, asking why he had done such a thing, to which he just shrugged. "My bad guys, Holden said that he felt really bad about losing, so he just wanted to get three points. I told him as long as he didn't choose war, it would be okay, so that's that."

Alistair didn't understand why Holden would have chosen peace if he'd already got Arjuna to pick peace. Surely war would have been better? *There's no way Holden thought that Arjuna was operating on some next-level 4D chess,* Alistair thought. He internally chuckled at the thought of the carefree man sedulously calculating that he would only select peace if and only if his simulation of Holden also selected peace when Arjuna selected peace. Perhaps they all had underestimated Gilgamesh's unassuming friend. After all, he was named after the hero of the Mahabharata, one of the greatest epics in human history.

On a different note, Alistair realized that he had never explicitly told his followers to go to war with Holden like with Bast, so he corrected that right away. It was only fair the embargo against Bast should also apply to the leader of the plot against him.

The rest of the games went as expected. Alistair looked up at the score-board after the final game of the ninth round. He was an unassailable first, as expected, with Medea taking a commanding second. Despite the sanctions against Holden, he had managed to stay in third place. Arjuna and

Bast were looking to be the clear losers, while Gilgamesh, Heracles, and Scáthach were locked in a competitive struggle.

The final round was upon them. In some ways, it would be the most straightforward round yet—Holden and Bast would get zero points from everything except predictions. In other ways, it was the most complicated round. During the break after the final game of round nine, Medea, Bast, and Arjuna announced they would be selling choices. Medea could afford to lose once and keep her top two slot, while the two last places had nothing to lose. Alistair also let up on his requirement that his teammates had to choose peace against him upon seeing that Holden was dangerously close to second place. Giving the people he wanted to get ahead of Holden a -2 was not the smartest move.

Alistair wondered if Arjuna and Bast were serious about selling their selection choice. Arjuna was close friends with Gilgamesh and had every incentive to lie, while Bast wasn't that far out of the running. As he imagined, no one took their offers, at least right away. Arjuna gave ten points to Gilgamesh like he always did, landing the Mesopotamian hero ahead of the pack for the moment.

The first surprise was Holden against Bast. After the last round in which Holden betrayed Bast, Alistair was confident they wouldn't be able to come to an agreement. Yet, for some reason, that bastard always found a way to win. Once again, he strangely played peace knowing Bast played peace. Was he feeling bad about tricking her last time? Whatever the reason was, it increased his lead on fourth place. Those predictions added up, and Holden was by far number one overall in their accuracy.

The next relevant game came between Heracles and Medea. Alistair decided to step away from the scheming and watch the results for entertainment, though he still had Dev'rox monitoring the situation, just in case. Better safe than sorry.

They waited a full ten minutes for Heracles and Medea to finish their game. After it was over, Heracles's face was bright red and he looked pissed as hell, but victory was his, gaining a meaty ten points. Whatever Scáthach promised Medea, it wasn't good enough, as when they went up next, they traded war for zero points. For the first time in a while, Heracles pulled ahead of Scáthach.

Most of the next games were war-war. Gilgamesh tried to argue his case with Alistair in their game, saying that Alistair was already guaranteed a clear first, so if he rewarded Gilgamesh with the win, he would forgo some of his reward and help the Northeast Order gain territory. Alistair refused, not wanting to create more strife within the group.

That strife revealed itself when Heracles and Scáthach faced off a couple of games later. Everyone knew those two had been the closest of allies during the trial, yet now, when everything was on the line, they both chose war.

Alistair was hoping for some fireworks near the end, but the rest of the trial was uneventful. As scores solidified, the options for differing strategies declined. The war-war strategy was the Nash equilibrium for a reason. Two rational agents would end up on it just by realizing they could employ no better strategy. The trust, cooperation, and unequivocal punishment for warmongers had vanished, leaving everyone fending for themselves. Alistair found it somewhat melancholic, truth be told—the only exception was Gilgamesh and Arjuna. Despite not being on the same side as them originally, he found it somewhat comforting to see them work together so easily.

At the end, the scoreboard rearranged to show the final rank for each individual.

1) Mozi – 455
2) Medea – 452
3) Holden – 417
4) Gilgamesh – 411
5) Heracles – 411
6) Scáthach – 403
Not Placed: Bast – 388
Not Placed: Arjuna – 288

Payouts:
1st place: 1,141 subregions (Current Total: 1,839)
2nd place: 872 subregions
3rd place: 400 subregions
4/5th place: 206 subregions
4/5th place: 206 subregions
6th place: 103 subregions

Alistair profited mightily, gaining 802 subregions. He was practically salivating at the idea of the extra Land Credits, but he also wondered how exactly the distribution of the subregions was going to work. With perfect timing, a window from the Pathfinder AI popped up to explain.

Congratulations on completing the first of the three trials of [The Game of Life], The Commons of Peace and War! With 196 participants, only 147 move on to the next trial. Those who found themselves on the losing side will be returned to Earth shortly, where they can continue to vie for power.

For those moving on, due to the opportunity cost of lacking monsters and beasts to battle for level ups, there will be certain cultivation provisions for continuing participants as follows:

1st place: +2 levels, +50 Upgrade Points (not including those gained from leveling)
2nd place: +2 level, +25 Upgrade Points
3rd place: +1 level, +25 Upgrade Points
4/5th place: +1 level
4/5th place: +1 level
6th place: Nothing

All gained subregions will be proportioned in an appropriate manner, connected to the new owner's territory mass. This will be done in a fair manner so that all gains and losses are proportional to the monetary and cultivation value contained within each subregion.

For the integrity of the game and safety purposes, all participants in the first trial had their appearances and voices anonymized. The identities of participants shall not be revealed by the system itself, though any individual can choose on their own prerogative to reveal their pseudonym from The Commons of Peace and War.

This instance of the first trial took 45.7 hours. As the maximum time is 66.5 hours, not all games will finish at the same time. As we wait

for all games to finish, qualified participants will be sent to a temporary lobby in a physical demiplane. The edict prohibiting violence stands for the lobby, except in specially designated regions for dueling.

Just like that, the icy cavern disappeared, replaced by a tropical island. Or at least, that was the best word Alistair had for it. The physical demiplane the Pathfinder AI teleported him to had a sky of saturated purples and oranges and pinks that defied any conventional color, feeling almost like a surreal painting. Instead of directional lighting from the sun, it looked like the entire sky was alive with luminescent energy, blanketing the entire miniature world in light. There were no shadows of any kind, making it appear like an unfinished video game.

Hundred-meter-tall alien palm trees dotted the pale blue-and-gray sand, reaching up to the variegated sky. But the biggest attraction was the gigantic building at the center of the island. It wasn't as large as some of the truly world-shaking structures he'd seen on Faxor, but it was still larger than any building on Earth. A twisted mixture of glass and a matte white material, the geometric patterns swirled together into a massive structure that looked half-ugly and half-sublime.

Alistair marveled at the sheer opulence of what the Final Frontier Empire could muster for a mere *lobby* on a newly initiated world. To be fair, they were at the Premium Tier, which he gathered was uncommon at the furthest edges of the frontier, but it was still insane. A physical demiplane the size of the lobby island was possible for just one Visionary cultivator to make using a portion of their Domain. Alistair had met some Visionary cultivators—but only in forms with the heaviest of cloaks. It was hard to conceive of the power required to make a pocket dimension.

The first thing he did once he stopped staring was activate [**Carmela's Happy Pies**]. In his focus over the last trial, he had forgotten to even attempt to use it. Despite not being the real world, the Skill could still convert the sand into a delectable pie, which Alistair gobbled up with disturbing speed. He'd figured out that it took him longer to level up than others because of his Subclass, so the pies were useful in offsetting that extra cost. His brain, which was fried from the cutthroat trial, buzzed back to life.

After he finished his meal, he checked his Attributes. At level 45, he was about halfway to the level 60 meridian bottleneck. It felt weird saying that, as it had seemed so far away not too long ago. With his 6 free Attribute points, he allocated 2 to Endurance, 1 to Constitution, 1 to Strength, and 2 to Charisma, intent on getting that to 500 with more expediency now that he understood that it would double his base Karma. Alistair had a suspicion that 500 in every category would grant him a Badge in the same vein as "Jack of All Trades," as long as he got there before a certain level. If only he had won the Felons vs. Fellows tournament, then he could have gotten the "One Above Many" Badge.

Given that his Agility was so high yet he hadn't received any Badges for it, Alistair had a sense that going for his all-rounder approach meant he had to eschew stat-specific Badges, at least for now. It was sad, but even without that his Agility was still near the highest in the world.

As for his Karma, Alistair was happy that his max was now 60 points, but it lacked the multiplicative effectiveness he'd expected. 60 points of Karma didn't seem twice as good as 30 points—his speculation was that it took more Karma to influence higher-level beings who were more solidified in their Dao and standing in the Akashic Records. If that were the case, he predicted that his higher Karma would still be better for smaller things like gambling or having a fun, mundane day, which he wanted to test.

Dev'rox coughed conspicuously, interrupting his thoughts.

"Yes?" Alistair asked.

"Aren't you forgetting something important?" the imp teased.

"What? Oh, yes. Thank you for your help. Without your initial idea, I would never have come out on top," Alistair said, patting his imp on the head, who resisted the gesture. "As a token of my gratitude, why don't you tell me hundreds of stories of Zalarik the Wise, Abyssal Ruler of the Kingdom of Sheoth-Omatra, or how you and your brood-bond bravely dove into a hellfire lake before your fiftieth name day. It's not like I haven't heard those before."

"Bah. I'll tell you a new story then, if that's what you want."

Alistair chuckled. "I'd *love* that."

If he focused closely, Alistair thought he could see the outlines of others on the shores of the island, maybe two kilometers away. Given that the Pathfinder AI said that it would reveal their identities, Alistair wondered if it had held people in temporal stasis to spread out the newcomers from his trial. Or maybe it had placed them at distant spots all over the island. In any case, Alistair walked up to the building, taking his time to enjoy the sweet summer breeze.

He was joined at the steps by a few other people he didn't recognize, though one of them seemed to recognize him. "Alistair Tan of the Northeast Order Freehold? Is that you?"

The woman in front of him on the glassy steps up to the entrance turned around after hearing someone behind her. "It's nice to meet you. I'm Layla Younis."

"That's me. Nice to meet you, too," Alistair replied, shaking her hand. "How can I help you?"

"You're acquaintances with my boss's sons, Alfred and Bartholomew Wood, correct? Their father, Lucius Wood, wishes to speak to you. It's no secret that he is Illustrious Kingpin, the man in possession of the most subregions in the world. After the first trial, he has almost 7,500 subregions across the British Isles and continental Europe."

Lucius Wood, Alistair thought. He had seen the name creeping up the leaderboards for the past couple of weeks. While Bartholomew was the highest of the family at #5, Lucius had gotten to a respectable #69. From what he knew about the Woods, the patriarch controlled everything, meaning that as a unit, Lucius's power far exceeded his rank.

"I'd love to meet him," Alistair said. "Is he inside?"

"Yes. I can take you. He's been waiting for you in particular. He thinks that there's a massive opportunity for both of you to profit."

Based on how he'd seen Layla coming from the shore of the island, he assumed that she hadn't been inside the building yet. But for some reason, she seemed to know it like the back of her hand. The way she occasionally tapped her ear reminded Alistair of Alfred's Spymaster Class and his mechanical bugs. If all of the Wood conglomerate were connected via an information network, that was a huge advantage. Not that he felt like he was competing against them.

The inside of the twisting establishment was just as labyrinthine as the outside. It hurt Alistair's brain to see all the impossible angles and strange geometries, reminding him of an Escher painting. Despite all of that, somehow his instincts knew how everything connected and where to go so that he wouldn't fall through a dimensional hole.

Layla led him down a winding path across a floor of hexagons that curved upward. Alistair almost lost his pies, as he grew dizzy from the constant looping. Gravity somehow kept him rooted to the upside-down floor, but it still felt like he was hanging head first from a set of monkey bars.

"Why is it so weird in here?" Alistair wondered to Dev'rox as they passed through a forest of bioluminescent trees that looked half-living and half-machine.

"This plane is from the Domain of a Visionary realm cultivator," Dev'rox said. "The Domain is the inner world of the soul, molded from the Dao. Of course it will be strange. Only the most boring people have Domains that make sense."

"You never talked about your Domain before."

"I've told you before—I can't tell you everything before you get there yourself. It is the Law of the multiverse. Imagine I could give you all the secrets that brought me to the Profound realm. It would be unfair. I would wager even the elites of this universe aren't bold enough to spoil their youth to the extent they defy Heaven's edict."

After around ten minutes of walking through a path in the forest, Layla stopped as they reached a compound of rooms. From what Alistair could make out, each trunk had a carved opening, connecting to every other tree to form a massive network of interconnected spaces. Layla went up to the biggest tree and opened the hatch, revealing a simple, futuristic hotel room. "Mr. Wood should be in this room. Please come in."

Alistair hesitated for a moment, not wanting to get caught in a trap. But he released those fears and stepped inside. What did he have to fear, with the prohibition on violence and his keen senses?

He had no idea how little Lucius Wood needed the frivolities of cultivation to be dangerous.

30 PATRIARCH WOOD

THE ROOM inside of the tree felt like a splinter from a lucid dream. The walls and ceiling were comprised of aquamarine glass in byzantine patterns. A viscous liquid flowed through the small gaps in between the panels of glass, glowing and humming with low ultraviolet light. The mysterious liquid managed to find its way into every nook and cranny of the walls, despite the normal presence of gravity.

Around ten meters away, on the far side of the room, there was a window to the outside world. But it wasn't an outside that made any sense for the location of the room. There were massive skyscrapers and pagodas, similar to Faxor, but different in their rounded, softer architecture. Surely the physical demiplane wasn't large enough to host an entire city? When Alistair looked closer at the metropolis, he saw it had no verisimilitude or spirit. The former Domain captured a snapshot of a transient moment, one that could be either real or imagined.

A man sat on one of the floating discs near the center of the room, calmly sipping a cup of chamomile tea with an upturned pinkie. While Alistair was no fashion expert, the man's perfectly tailored Loro Piana suit screamed money. The Wood patriarch looked like a mix between Alfred and Bartholomew, with a buzz cut hiding his strangely golden hair. Without even trying to slip into his Karmic vision, Alistair could see the strands of

Fate buzzing around him with more intensity than anybody he had seen before besides himself.

"A pleasure to meet you, Alistair." Lucius Wood had a deep voice like Bartholomew but with the charm of his other son. "It's a shame I couldn't join my boys when they visited you. I would have been overjoyed to come, but I had pressing matters to attend to on the home front. Pardon my curiosity, but how did the first trial go?"

"I got first place. And you?" he asked, though he was sure of the answer.

"The same. An intriguing game, though more elementary than I would have expected. The key to victory was simple, at the end of the day. What do you think?" Lucius's eyes glinted with desire, a desire that Alistair knew as the hunger for something beyond this world.

"I kind of want to know your answer," Alistair said. "I feel like I got pretty lucky."

Lucius chuckled heartily. "You seem to be in the business of making your own luck. And may I respond to your question with another question? Between a wealthy man, a strong man, and a politician—who is the most powerful?"

Despite the utter lack of physical danger, Alistair felt like he was leaping into the maw of the beast headfirst. He ended up answering truthfully, because he thought lying would somehow be even worse.

"If this is an actual question, and not just sophistry, I think that before the initiation, the answer would be the wealthy man, and now it's probably the strong man. If there were people who could blow up cities with a fireball in the before, I don't think that it would have gone too well for the rich."

"That is where you are wrong. The answer now is that all three are the same. You cannot be rich without being powerful, and you cannot command sectors of the stars without wealth. You might then wonder if being the strongest is the only thing that matters, since you surely can leverage this to obtain the other two—but one lone cultivator cannot compare to the might of a thousand of the same realm. There will always be the wealthy and poor, even of Visionary cultivators.

"The only question is how to achieve this," Lucius went on. "For one such as yourself, becoming the strongest might be the most effective approach. From my own vantage point, I find the accumulation of wealth to be much easier. And that is the key to everything. Follow the money, and you shall know the truth. I know what people desire in their heart of hearts, and if I offer this to them, then they are mine forever. What is it that you want?"

"What are you going to do?" Dev'rox asked.

"You're going to get caught one day if you keep popping up out of nowhere," Alistair thought back viciously.

"Not likely, unless the other person is a Profound realm or has a special ability to see spirits. Get back to my question."

"He reminds me of a more well-adjusted version of Holden. Everything I say, he's going to use it against me in some way."

"Then just tell the truth. You can never go wrong telling the truth," Dev'rox replied, popping a grin. Telling the truth was something that *he* was supposed to advocate for, not a demon from the Asura Hell.

Alistair decided to listen to his ghostly companion, ending the awkward silence caused by his silent communication. "I want to be the strongest. I want to reach the true peak far beyond this universe, no matter how long it takes or how difficult it may be. This world is full of evil and misery and the only way to create true change is to be the one at the top."

"A lofty, but admirable goal," Lucius said. "I can see no need for enmity between us, young man. I would love to discuss philosophy with you more some other time, but we really must discuss the imminent threat against all of mankind."

"You mean the Devil Kings?"

Lucius nodded. "Indeed. While the competition between us humans for the title of Global Mayor can be intense, the Devil Kings cannot rest until they purge the leaderboard and own half the planet. They've shown no regard for human life or ethical standards of any kind. My own brother was killed in Greece by the fourth and third amongst their ranks. Oracle and Admiral, they called themselves. I didn't see what happened directly, but I have a shoddy memory from an **Annalist's Aid**."

Alistair grew jealous over hearing about that broken item once more. Sadly, it cost 3 million drachma and he simply couldn't afford to splurge his money on that while his freehold needed more infrastructure. *One day, one day,* Alistair promised himself.

"We need to work together to stop them, and completely root them out of society. Then, our *friendly struggles* can return." Lucius smiled warmly, but it didn't reach his eyes. Alistair knew that the "friendly struggles" that had been going on before the Devil Kings arrived were heavy on the "struggle" side.

"I can agree with that. What do you propose?" Alistair asked.

"A truce in this Quest, at least until we're the last two left. You've worked closely with my sons multiple times—they've seen you operate and trust your character. I do as well. You don't know me, but hopefully you can give me a chance to show that I am also trustworthy. For full disclosure, I have met with your peers, such as Pharaoh, Carmen Romero, and Brigid Mwangi. They were lovely people, but I'm only offering this to you, because I believe in you."

"What a vote of confidence," Dev'rox said. "He's practically in love."

"Shut up," Alistair admonished the imp. Speaking to Lucius, he replied, saying, "That sounds workable to me. Do you have any idea what's happening back on Earth?"

"Unfortunately, no. The seal on information from the outside world is perfect. As far as I know, the only aspect we can glean are the changing subregion count numbers. Clearly, there are still those back on Earth who were not selected. I can only pray that the Devil Kings are with us, for if they are running free without any of us"—Lucius shook his head in disgust—"we are all doomed."

"I don't think the Pathfinder AI is that unfair," Alistair said. "They want the fight to be relatively even. They're gluttons for combat, not necessarily needless slaughter."

As he said those last words, he was reminded of Atavius Meloi. At least he was punished, Alistair reasoned. It was better than nothing, though after learning more of the politics of the Empire, he knew the Meloi Clan wasn't one of the powerhouses by a long shot. He wondered what would happen if the spoiled cultivator descending upon them was an Akata adoptee or Kai Esoi young master. Would they just sweep it under the rug, like how it often happened back on Earth?

Lucius stroked his chin. "Hmm. I pray you are right. Putting that aside, as a token of my gratitude, I grant you a million drachma."

Alistair saw a notification alerting him that Lucius was attempting to send exactly one million Gold drachma. After taking a look over just to make sure there were no stipulations, he accepted the money.

"Some of your allies have probably made it here as well. I'm sure you're eager to meet them, so don't let me bother you any longer. One question before you leave—have you heard from a group calling themselves the 'United Polities'? They're a bunch of ex-US government officials that landed in northern Africa."

Alistair was taken aback upon hearing the words "US government." He hadn't thought about the old-world authorities in a long time. From what he knew, since no nukes, missiles or drones worked anymore, their entire power structure had collapsed. Their capital was almost as much of a mess as Anthony's.

"No, I haven't. Should I be concerned?" Alistair asked.

"Oh no, it's nothing. A word of advice: the most important thing you can do is hedge. A true winner can profit from any situation. That is how my father built our family wealth into a fortune, and how I made that wealth multiply tenfold. If you can remember one thing from this meeting, it is to always hedge yourself."

Lucius leaned back in his chair, almost as if he realized he'd been too aggressive in pushing that point. Alistair wondered if it was for sentimental reasons, but Lucius quickly returned to his normal suave self after a split second.

"As you leave, my assistant Layla will give you a phone. We call it a phone because it works like a phone, but it looks more like a crystal prism. It's a part of one of my Skills, so it's pre-linked to my person. The phone only works in one direction, so if you want to contact me, you can, but I can't talk to you until you call me first. It was nice to meet you, Mr. Tan."

"Likewise," Alistair said, shaking the man's hand. In his Karmic vision, their bright threads of Fate clashed together, making flashes of golden lightning and radiant sparkles. While he was still new to the machinations of Fate, if he had to put a name to it, it looked like a new thread between the two of them was being born.

It sounded like good news on the surface, but Alistair wondered if that was really the case. Of course, sworn brothers were tied by Fate... but so were sworn enemies. Despite the cordial first meeting, Alistair wasn't sure what his and Lucius's ending would be. Those tides of Fate would only be revealed with the progression of time.

———

After receiving the crystal phone from Layla, Alistair turned to his own matters. A notification prompted him to open up his status screen.

Achievement Earned: Land Baron (Conquest II) — *Freehold ownership of at least 3,000 subregions OR personal ownership of at least 1,000 subregions.* Reward: 50,000 Land Credits.

Name: Alistair Tan
Species: Spectral Superhuman I (Partially Evolved)
Class: Magical Pugilist (Uncommon)
Subclass (HIDDEN): Arbiter of Justice (Legendary)
Level: 45

Health: 751/751 (1.212 per min)
Mana: 1,339/1,339 (2.156 per min)
Stamina: 461/461 (1.797 per min)
Upgrade Points: 102
Balance: 3,170,551 Gold Drachma, 201,257 Land Store Credits
Karma (Unlocked): +16/60 (.026 per min)
Full Stat Bonuses: +61% to All Attributes, +10% to Strength, Endurance, Wisdom, +20% to Agility, +25% Mana

Strength: 178
Agility: 460
Constitution: 148
Endurance: 147
Intelligence: 364
Wisdom: 233
Charisma: 285

Items: Zanibar's Purification Ring, Thrice-Blessed Fate-Diviner, Devilsbane Gauntlets, Mammothskin Raiment, Crystal Caller, Fall of Fleet, Laser Gun (II), Teleportation Circle

Badges: "Premium Initiate", "Good Samaritan", "Deliverance of Justice", "Mythical Cultivator", "Jack of All Trades", "World Leader", "Devil May Cry"

Talents: System Tree – Three leaves, Pugilism Branch (II), Chaos Assassin – Void Watching Branch (II), Justice Quest Branch (II), Elemental Fighter – Summoning of Spirit (IV), Body Tree – Heart Branch (I), Blood of the Devil Tree Purification Leaf (I)

Skills: [Lightning of Justice], [Force Fist], [Blood Hand], [Frozen Claw], [Eyes of Truth], [Dash], [Fighter's Instinct], [Hand of Karma], [Ghost Whispers], [Spectral Summoning], [Carmela's Happy Pies]

Quests: [The Game of Life], [Vanquishing the Devil Kings]

Achievements: Discovery (I), Dueling (IV), Conquest (II), Dao Node – Dao of the Ghost (I) Dao Node – Dao of the Fist (I), Dao Node – Dao of Justice (I), Arcana (I)

His status screen was becoming incredibly fat, full of all his various powers and abilities. 201k Land Store credits would go a long way toward building his freehold and improving its defensive structures.

In his preparations for the Quest, understanding that they could be going far away from home, Alistair had used drachma to buy automatic energy fortifications for certain key locations. The Land Store had far better siege defenses and general territory improvement items, but he'd had zero credits at the time. With his newfound credit intake, he inched ever closer to his dream of making the Northeast Freehold an impregnable bastion of prosperity.

Alistair pondered what to do with his Upgrade Points. He was one point away from upgrading "Good Samaritan," one point away from upgrading [Eyes of Truth], and three points away from upgrading [Dash]. Since it would only take five points total, he decided to spend them, going against his usual policy of avoiding manually using Upgrade Points on Skills and Badges.

Badge Upgraded: "Good Samaritan [Altered]" (Tier 2 Rare Badge): *Put your life on the line for a complete stranger against all odds.* All Attributes +15, also when fighting enemies you deem as reprobate evildoers, gain +25% to your two highest Attributes. Upgradeable (0/100).

The new "Good Samaritan" gave him 8 more points to all Attributes and a 25% increase to his two highest ones when fighting evildoers, but it wasn't that big an increase. He was reminded of why he typically avoided using his Upgrade Points on Badges.

Skill Upgraded: [Dash] (Tier 3 Beginner Skill): *Run across long distances in a single step through enhancing your body with Mana. Flicker – (Disguise movement with invisibility).* Mana Cost: 35. Upgradeable (0/100).

Choice 1: Gain airwalking (when performing one step during [Dash], may step on air).

Choice 2: Gain trucking (when performing [Dash] targeting a location that is blocked by a physical obstruction, slam into it if you possess more Constitution).

Alistair weighed the upsides and downsides of both options, in the end going with airwalking. Ever since he'd seen Po Shaido stepping on the air like it was a staircase, he had wanted a similar ability. Knowing how the Pathfinder AI worked, that was probably why it gave the option in the first place, albeit a much weaker version. Trucking was interesting as well, but since his Constitution wasn't that high compared to his other stats, it wouldn't be effective against the opponents he really needed it for.

Moving on to **[Eyes of Karma]**, Alistair spent a point of Karma so that he could see what the Tier 3 added. Without a lie to see through or a thread of Fate to investigate, it didn't seem that much better, but there were small improvements in the clarity of the details.

With the rest of his Upgrade Points, Alistair had two main options—invest in the Talent Tree or Badge slots. The Talent Tree was perhaps the most neglected part of his cultivation, so he greatly wanted to improve on that front, but the Badge slots were tempting. It would take 300 Upgrade Points to get his eighth slot, which he might need relatively soon. On the other hand... the Blood of the Devil Tree's options were tantalizing.

After the underlying Purification leaf, there were three Branches. First was the Sanguine Empowerment Branch, which involved taking the blood essence of others and using it to improve the power of one's body. The second was the Internecine Demon Branch, which helped the user fight other demons with blood. Finally, there was the Arcana Daemones Branch, which revolved around magical abilities, specifically Formulaic Skills, like Carmen's replica Heavenly lightning.

Alistair was struck with choice overload as he examined the various leaves associated with each branch. He saw two options that interested him a couple of levels above the baseline. The Sanguine Empowerment Branch contained a leaf called the Letting of the Beast that gained him a permanent amount of Endurance after absorbing the blood of certain beasts.

What beasts he needed to absorb it didn't precisely say, only stating a requirement of sufficient infamy. The description for Saturn's castle, the *Kestrel*, said that it was a site that had gathered infamy, so Alistair assumed infamy was something along the lines of negative Karma, but with some distinctions he didn't yet understand.

The other leaf that interested him was the Inkbrush Bloodspot of the Arcana Daemones Branch. It synergized with his **[Blood Hand]** Skill, turning specific characters he painted into traps for his opponent. For example, one symbol would make the ground slippery, while another summoned a loud, one-directional noise that promised to momentarily stun almost any enemy.

While he wanted both, he only had enough for one, and the Inkbrush Bloodspot Leaf was a bit too complicated for him at the moment. He was still harmonizing his other Skills and abilities into a coherent unit, so adding a brainy Skill like that would be something he would only do once he streamlined his fighting approach. With that in mind, he spent 95 of his 97 Upgrade Points obtaining the Letting of the Beast Leaf and its prerequisites.

{Blood Scent} *User's sense of smell for blood improves by 10x, 50x for demons.* 15 Upgrade Points.

{Beast Shell} +5 Constitution, +3 Endurance. 30 Upgrade Points.

{Letting of the Beast} *When absorbing a significant amount of blood essence from a beast with sufficient infamy, permanently gain an amount of Endurance. If the beast is demonic in nature, double this gain.* 50 Upgrade Points.

It was a hefty sum, but Alistair felt it was worth it. He could contribute to the Badge slots with his next few levels. Now that he was in the Talent Tree screen, he looked at another one of his leaves, the Assassin Fist. Despite it being an upgradeable leaf and him using it all the time, it had stalled out at the second tier. What he needed was a deeper insight, an opponent to go head-to-head with his fists, over and over. Alistair felt so frustrated it even made him reminisce about his fight with Red.

Dev'rox appeared, hovering over his shoulder. "Have you thought about what the Lazarene Minister said?"

"Yeah. He's right. I need to integrate everything into a more complete whole. What do you think of this idea: what if I pair the portion of my Ghost Node that is associated with ice and eternity with my Justice Node? And then I pair the portion of my Ghost Node that is associated with revenge and blood with the Fist Node? Would something like that work? For the first one, I'd aim for the idea of a lost ghost who desires closure and justice for being wronged in their life. While for the second, I'd aim for the idea of an angry ghost who desires revenge and violence for the wrongs committed against them."

"I... like it," Dev'rox said. "It's fits almost too well."

"I know, right? Also, I have a 'special' power that goes along with each. My Subclass for the Justice Node, ghost cultivation plus blood absorption for the Ghost Node, and the Mutra for the Fist Node. Though I suppose I'm stretching the definition of special for the last one."

"So what am I, the bloody ghost that wants revenge or the icy ghost that wants closure?" Dev'rox smirked.

"You're both of them, but obviously we both know which one fits you more. I probably need another spirit to focus more on the ice-related side, then," Alistair thought aloud.

"Not so fast," Dev'rox warned. "And not because I'm afraid of being replaced—how dare you even insinuate it with that look on your face? I wasn't being entirely facetious when I told you that ghost cultivators are leeches or that it can harm your path. You have an exceptionally strong will, so I don't believe I've changed you in any way yet, but I'm just one being. If you take on another ghost, the chances of your Dao Path being corrupted go up exponentially. You're not ready for that yet. In addition, you're not going to find another ghost so easily. Look at this planet. What kind of dead people are you going to find? They'd all be weak mortals."

"You're right, you're right. Forget I mentioned it," Alistair said, continuing on to the next piece of his checklist. "How's my soulcore looking with Mana affinities now?"

Alistair still hadn't been able to figure out what exactly the properties of his soulcore meant. "Möbius strip torus, outside serrated, hyperflow variant, double-chambered" was a good amount of detail, but provided no concrete explanation. Alexandra had shown him her soulcore properties at one point, which were completely different: "Amorphous spheroid, pointillist, laminar flow, single-chambered."

Despite that, it had been easy to understand on an instinctual level. He could picture the strange, geometric object that was the seat of his soul inside of him, rotating slowly, growing and shrinking. Breathing in and absorbing the ambient Mana temporarily expanded the soulcore, just as breathing out and expunging excess Mana temporarily shrunk the soulcore, if he was at maximum Mana saturation. Through a series of breathing and cycling exercises he'd learned from a standard manual from the System Store, he practiced expanding his meridians, though at this point they were at the maximum they could be before the bottleneck of level 60. Build manuals like what Oliver had were likely to have specialized exercises, but Alistair knew that his unique situation made obtaining one of those nigh impossible.

"You're at about 50% saturation, but that's an average," Dev'rox instructed. "Your soulcore is much more attuned and capable of producing ice and blood affinity Mana than lightning or force."

"What can I say, **[Blood Hand]** and **[Frozen Claw]** are too awesome. The Ghost Node displaced the Justice Node as my primary Dao, too," he said, referencing his Dao Elements. He wasn't sure if that had any consequences, but it made sense, considering how much he was focusing on his ghost side at the moment.

"I'm sure you can find some injustice to quell and some monsters to punch soon." Dev'rox chortled. "I would say it's utterly impossible for the Final Frontier Empire not to have violence in the next trial, wouldn't you agree? These savages would rather sell their own mother into slavery than go without bloodshed for more than a day."

"You're right about that one," Alistair said. "Let's go find my friends."

31 BLOOD DRAGON

ALISTAIR HAD EXPECTED it to be difficult to find his comrades in the city-block sized lobby building, but it turned out to be relatively simple. Lucius had his people connected through their phones, but it wasn't like everyone else was done for. The weird thing about the shifting, surreal hotel was that it felt *alive*. Whenever he stepped, it was as if it knew where he wanted to go and guided him in the right direction.

He marveled at the miniature wonders of the multiverse as he traversed through melting hallways and open fields of grass. Alistair wondered just what kind of Domain the Visionary possessed to make this kind of diverse demiplane. At his jogging speed, which was just under a fifth of the speed of sound, he made it to his destination in under ten minutes, though a large portion of that was spent navigating uncertain terrain and having to back-track multiple times. Still, his instincts guided him, trusting in the judgment of the pocket reality.

The living building led him to a parched, amber desert, where the rays of a blazing red sun cast long shadows. Wherever he walked, the terrain warped, shrinking the distance between landmarks.

The desert biome looked hundreds of meters long, but at least three-fourths of that size was illusory. Strange cacti shacks dotted the landscape, basking ominously in the light of the crimson sun. Small people that came up to Alistair's knee flitted about between the shacks. They still moved at the speed of normal humans, so their legs were a blur of movement.

"There's something wrong with them," Alistair noted. "I can sense their auras and life forces, but they're missing something."

"You'd be correct," Dev'rox said. "I suspect they're homunculi."

"I met a homunculus before. His name was Drauku. He was like a guide to help newbies in the Soulnet. I didn't sense anything at the time, but I suppose I was a lot weaker when I met him. You know, what I thought was strange at the time was that he felt super old, but he didn't seem that strong. Maybe he had a cloak on?"

"It's possible, but it's more likely that he was reaching the end of his programming. Homunculi lack a proper soul. A cultivator has to mold their Dao into a pseudo-soul to implant in the body, but it can never reach the quality of a real soul. At least, not from an Exalted or Visionary realm. That energy eventually runs out, and then the homunculus dies. Without a break-through, the end of a homunculus *or* a true cultivator's life will be marred with infirmity."

Alistair remembered Drauku's warm smile and obvious loneliness—and his generosity. The Pallox Semper soul wine let him get only a small edge into the Dao, but back then, each tiny percent mattered when compared against the thousands of people on the leaderboard. Drauku was born into the world as a thinking being, knowing his mortal limitation from the moment of his birth. *Not unlike us Earthlings before the initiation*, Alistair thought. "So they're screwed from the start?"

"I can't say I know much more than that. Really, all of my knowledge about the Physical Plane comes from the Empire, and if they know more than that, they're not letting imps know. But likely, yes."

Alistair observed the tiny humanoids taking out tiny hammers to work on making tiny new cacti houses. All so full of life, yet completely devoid of meaning. Meaning that Alistair himself felt deprived of as well. He found himself unable to fully access his own Daos inside the demiplane. Without that connection, his own Nodes would dwindle in Dao energy until they emptied.

While most of the cacti houses were proportionate to the plane's denizens, he spotted a couple of structures more suitable for human-sized creatures. He sensed some foreign aura signatures in the first few that he perused until he got to one of the larger houses in the region. Alistair smiled as he felt a familiar red-green aura.

"How's everyone doing?" Alistair asked as he swung open the prickly door.

Like the treehouses of the cyborg forest, the interior of the cactus was more spacious than the exterior, which was no larger than a small shed. Based on his knowledge of the subregion counts of his various subordinates, there were six people that had the required fifty subregions—the Maine Brothers, Caren Locasta, Alexandra, John, and Oliver. However, only the first four of that list were present. John and Oliver were nowhere to be found.

"Good to see you again, Alistair," Caren said while Alexandra hugged him like a wild bear.

"N-nice t-to see y-you, too," Alistair choked out as Alexandra squeezed the air out of him. "I thought my Constitution would be high enough to avoid that. You know, I've really been allocating a lot to it recently."

"You're never going to outpace my Strength, buddy." She smirked. "You're a few hours late."

"I'm surprised I'm the last one. I didn't think my game was that long," Alistair replied. "When did you all get here?"

"I was first," Caren said. "Just five or so hours before you. The rest trickled in."

Alistair turned to the larger Maine Brother, a man by the name of Josiah Baxter. The two Maine Brothers—or more accurately, Maine Siblings—since the other half of the duo was Josiah's sister, Delilah. They were both from a rural area and had heavy accents that blended aspects of Southern and Boston dialects. He had only met them a few times, but they both were huge fans of his since he eliminated Anthony, who had sent some of his forces to harass, loot, and kill in their territory.

"How was your game?" Josiah asked.

"I won," Alistair said. "That reminds me, when I check my subregion count on my status screen, it looks like the number is frozen to not count your winnings. Unless everyone just came out break even? How did everyone do?"

"I won as well," Caren said, something Alistair had expected. If he *didn't* win with a Class called Chronicler that revolved around books and intellectualism, Alistair would've been disappointed.

"Fourth place for me, but I ended up gaining subregions since I think I had the least of anyone there," Alexandra said.

"Josiah got sixth place, while I got third," Delilah said.

Alistair took all of their information and manually calculated their subregion total. Discounting their original subregion counts so he wouldn't double their numbers by accident, he found the new total subregions for the Northeast Order Freehold to be 2,757. In other words, they had almost tripled their subregions just from Trial 1. If this was how things would go the rest of the way, Alistair was pumped, but he knew that the next two trials would be far more difficult.

Over the next twenty hours, Alistair meditated, absorbing the ambient Mana from the atmosphere. Compared to the stuff back on Earth, it had a cramped and artificial quality, but it would do. He focused on maximum efficiency, carefully breathing in the Mana through his pores, sucking it into his soulcore, and pumping it to every cell in his body.

Sadly, from what he gathered, the Pathfinder AI was indiscriminate in its Quest-related level ups. The automatic level up from the game reward obliterated his natural progress to level 44, not carrying over the excess Mana. He didn't have any qualms about it, since it would've taken him another five days to level up normally. It just meant that now he was at square one again, and it was becoming more annoying every time.

At his current pace, he expected it to take around a week to hit level 46, and there wasn't anything he could do to improve that rate, especially with Dev'rox and his Subclass slowing him down.

But then again, wasn't that also a boon? He was stronger than his level suggested, so that only gave him a higher ceiling of power. And maybe he could do something with his burgeoning life force, too.

Life force was less tangible than Mana. To someone like the treeman Bark-Al, it probably manifested as green, verdant energy, full of spring and life. To a Beast Ruler, the stage after Beast Lord, it might have been an invisible animus, a primal directive.

To Alistair, it was blood. Blood was the essence of life. Blood carried the desires and emotions of the living, and the cries of the dead. Overflowing, twisting, screaming—from the depths of Hell, blood fueled Alistair and suffused his body with the nutrients it needed to grow. Deep within his psyche, as he split his mind between cycling and breathing Mana and suffusing his blood essence, an image emerged.

Just as the Lazarene Minister had told him, a species evolution was the alteration of the body's image of itself on the Akashic Records. Alistair knew his puny, mortal mind was insufficient to comprehend the almighty and endless information stored within the Records, but surely there were desirable ideas, archetypes, or memes that he could latch onto that would fit his next evolution.

Alistair thought this was so important that he burned some of his Ghost Node's Dao energy, understanding he wouldn't get it back.

For a moment, he peered into an infinitesimal piece of a great Truth. He appeared before a symposium of light and darkness, creation and destruction, color and achromatism, all swirling together into one root, the eternal tome of knowledge called the Akashic Records.

He perceived the grand record as a harmonic tone, somehow possessing color as if he had synesthesia. The tone vacillated between tropical blue, royal purple and sunset orange, humming with power that went beyond the Dao. Just what were the Akashic Records?

Even in this mightily watered-down representation inside of his mind, Alistair could not bear to witness it for more than a few subjective seconds. He used all of his time trying to connect his blood essence to a suitable form for his next species. Burning the Ghost Node's energy, he went through dozens of ideas in less than a second. As the old man had said, his body's representation of itself was very stubborn, though just as his consciousness was about to break, he found his target.

The first time he'd absorbed blood essence had an irrevocable effect on his spiritual DNA. While his physical representation hadn't changed, this was not the case for his image in the Akashic Records. Sessen Esshei—The King of the Serpents, he called himself. As such, Alistair found himself gravitating toward the serpentine and reptilian, landing on the form of a blood dragon.

While blood dragons had struck fear into the hearts of many across the multiverse, they were hunted by their own brethren for sullying the majesty of dragonkind. *What majestic beast needed to absorb the blood of lesser beings to survive and grow stronger?* they asserted. The celestial and world dragons hunted them to extinction. The only blood dragons left were in memory—or, they were ghosts.

That was perfect for Alistair. He didn't follow the Dao of Blood, so a pure blood dragon species would be a stretch. But since they were all dead, the Akashic concept of a blood dragon shifted to something much more amenable to his Dao. Anger, revenge, and hatred boiled in his soul as he imprinted the idea of a blood dragon into the fiber of his being. It threatened to tear him apart—he only survived through sheer grit and willpower. An eye for an eye made the whole world blind. His sense of justice tempered the unbridled rage of the dragon, calming it within him.

And then it was over. If Alistair had stayed just one millisecond longer, his soul and mind would have cracked apart like a glass shattering.

"Holy shit, are you okay?" Alexandra exclaimed, rushing over to him.

Alistair didn't understand what was wrong at first until he looked down. His body was overheating, literally emitting a red smoke that reeked of bloody iron. He thought it looked somewhat like Alexandra's [Barbarian's Fury], except he was actually bleeding. Drops of coagulated blood dripped out of every pore in his body. Good thing he had stored his **Mammothskin Raiment** in his soulcore before entering his mental seclusion.

"Yeah, I'm fine," Alistair replied. "I... think."

Checking his status screen, his species hadn't updated, though he knew that would be the case as he hadn't gathered enough life force to evolve it yet. But in his Talent Tree, he saw that his Body Cultivation Tree had changed. In the Bloodline Branch, instead of a generic description, it now listed a new target to aim for.

{Bloodline Evolution} (Ghost) Blood Dragon [Peon] — *Draconic Physique, Emperor Will, Blood Affinity, Endless Mana, LOCKED, LOCKED, LOCKED, LOCKED.* (Upgradeable 258/500 – Only accepts blood essence).

Alistair was quite happy with the result, even if it only had him as a [Peon]. Dragons were one of the most powerful species in the universe, a fact known to even the Final Frontier Empire. A peon of a dragon species would have more standing than even a king of a rat-humanoid species. It sounded unfair, but that's just how it was.

Alistair had spent so much time meditating that he hadn't noticed that their time was almost up. The full 66.5 hours of maximum time had passed. It seemed unlikely that a game had actually lasted that long, so the Pathfinder AI had ostensibly given them more rest and preparation time.

That time had ended. Trial 2 was about to begin.

Trial 2: Capture the Beacon

Teams of eight will be formed from a basis of existing freehold groups. Groups with not enough participants will be matched with free participants to form appropriately sized teams.

In addition to the human participants, we will be introducing four additional teams: two teams of Beast Lords and/or Leviathans, one team of monsters, and one team of Devil Kings and their associates.

There will be two groups, Group A and Group B. Each group will consist of 11 teams, arranged so each group is relatively equal in strength. Each team in a group will play the other teams once. Then, using a proportional rating system, an additional four games will be played, matching up between groups, to compare both groups fairly. Each team will play 14 games by the end of the trial.

Hurting/killing your own teammates is strictly forbidden. If any participant does so on purpose, they will be instantly disqualified.

All games will be played at once on a massive battlefield with a wide variety of terrains, so it is possible to interfere with other teams' games, though you might find it more difficult to take advantage of this aspect than it seems.

Before the first game begins, each team will know which group they are in and who their teammates are. They will have 72 hours to construct their fort, using the given materials and their own abilities. Additional materials may be purchased using subregions as collateral.

Before each game, the team will decide where in their fort to hide the "beacon," the object of supreme importance in the game. If a team retrieves the opposing beacon and returns it to their fort safely, they win the game. If a team kills or incapacitates all members of the opposing team, they win the game. An immortality field will prevent all participants from dying and heal any injuries they may sustain for the next game. (Stats besides Health such as Mana and Dao energy will be replenished, but at a lesser rate.)

Each team's subregions will be pooled together and treated as one unit for the purpose of the game, and then reapportioned to the individuals at the end.

Win/Loss from stealing beacon: +/- 600 subregions
Win/Loss from eliminating enemy: +/- 400 subregions
Tie: +/- 0 subregions
These numbers are doubled for the four extra games after the group games.

The top two teams of each group will move on to the next trial, along with the next top 8 performing players on each of the remaining teams, for a total of 40 players moving on to trial 3.

The four bottom performing teams of each group will have all of their subregions confiscated and given equally to each of the top 5 teams. In addition, if a team drops to zero subregions or a would be negative amount of subregions, they are automatically deemed a bottom performer. All such teams will be considered losers, and are unable to regain subregions in subsequent rounds, as they have nothing to wager with. Even if five or more teams end up having zero subregions at the end, their subregions are still confiscated.

Let Capture the Beacon begin!

32 BASE BUILDING

NOT EVEN DEATH scared Dragonus as much as the man before him. As a Devil King, his death would be permanent, so it should have scared him more, but George Moulin was terror incarnate. Ironic, since that was what they were all supposed to be. George just did it better.

"You were demoted to number three?" the man asked, his voice soft and cold, just like his aura. You would never have guessed how powerful he was from his voice.

"Yes, sir," Dragonus said, his own voice barely louder than a whisper out of sheer fear. "I apologize for my incompetence. It will not happen again." His black dragon bloodline was livid at Dragonus for debasing himself, but his higher brain functions stopped him from making a fatal mistake.

Dragonus pressed his head onto the bloody floor of the lair of the Devil Kings. Their magnificent home was unseen and unheard, covered in impenetrable darkness. There was no light, yet they could all see perfectly with eyes that were pools of raging fire. Only George was allowed to speak to the shadowy man who had turned them into Devil Kings, and George told them that one day, their castle would be the capital of the new world.

"I do not care, Dragonus," George said. "Oracle will be fine as number two. If she has surpassed you in rank, it is because she is stronger. But that is of no consequence anyway. You will be the leader of our representatives in [The Game of Life], with Admiral as your second-in-command."

"But sir—"

George flared his aura, an icy cold that harbingered the end of all life, tinged with the unholy stamp of a Devil King. Dragonus pressed his head into the ground once more despite the raging fire within him.

"Do not protest. Do not disobey. Do not disappoint. The Pathfinder AI is limiting us in power, so as to be fair to the other teams. You will be the strongest among us on the team. It is yours to lead. Success or failure hinges on you. Do you understand?"

"I do," Dragonus said. "I will not fail."

"Good," George said. "Now tell me, why do we need to succeed, Dragonus?"

"Excuse me, sir?"

"I said what I said. Why do we need to succeed at all things?" George asked plainly.

Sweat dripped down his scaly forehead. What did George mean by that? He wracked his brain for the answer. "Because they're trying to keep us from winning?"

"Correct. We're lab rats for the Final Frontier Empire. Or perhaps..." George trailed off. "Whatever the case is, they don't want us to win. We're pawns in a greater game, meant to be the next stepping stone for the Prime Initiates, to show off their prowess to the various sects and clans and corporations."

"Are you saying—"

"Yes. Even if we manage to defeat every single one of the normal humans, they'll most likely kill us to cover up any traces of demon blood experimentation."

Dragonus's eyes widened in shock. "I'm confused, sir. If you think that we are all damned no matter what, why are we even doing this?"

The hint of a smile touched George's frigid lips. Having not been the healthiest looking man before becoming a Devil King, George now had a perpetual blue tint to his skin, in addition to his blue orbs of fire for eyes and frozen hair. "Dragonus, I do not view it like that at all. What more can we ask for, but a chance? Our backs against the wall, fighting against Fate and the providence of the chosen. I believe the greatest beauty comes from the greatest tragedy. We are in this together until the end, my friend. There is Fate, yes, but it is not set in stone. No matter how small the chance, I'll fight. That is what it means to be human, Dragonus. When all hope has fled and certain doom weighs down from the heavens, when mothers weep and children cry, when the world cracks at the seams, only then do you know your true nature. I ask you once and for all time, will you fight with me, Dragonus?"

An unmistakable pride swelled in Dragonus's heart of hearts. "I will, sir. I won't give up. You have my loyalty until the end."

"Good. I'll likely need it," George replied. "Start your preparations for the trial."

———

"Fate brings us together once again, Alistair," Holden, whose real name was apparently William St. James, said. It was going to take Alistair a while to view the scrawny, youthful William as the same person as the tall, camo-vested Holden.

"I'm surprised you're even telling me this," Alistair replied. "You could have just stayed hidden."

"Nonsense. You would have figured it out eventually and trusted me less as a result. I believe in complete transparency for our team—if we're going to win."

"I like the sound of complete transparency," another new addition to the team butted in.

Jesse Waterfall came from Australia, though after the initiation he'd landed in Central Asia in one of the regions most affected by Atavius's mass destruction. Alistair had encountered some of those areas, like the Midwest in America, and it wasn't pretty. Violence and barbarism were far more common. The initial blow to civilization had far more of an impact there than a place like where Alistair had started out.

Despite that, Jesse seemed to be a quite affable man. He was conventionally attractive, with sandy blond hair and a beach tan. And he happened to be the #7 in the world with the ability to teleport long distances at will. Not bad for an ally, all things considered. The best part was that he readily accepted Alistair's leadership. As a solo top ten ranker without any subordinates, he worried that Jesse would be more hesitant, but all signs pointed toward the man being a steadfast ally. Even when feeling the Karmic threads, Alistair sensed no deception.

The final member of their group was a woman named Fasha from

Malaysia. Based on her ranking at #612, she was the weakest member of the team, but from what Alistair gathered, she was a healer who focused more on politics than brute strength. In her community, she had gained a lot of respect and influence by offering her services to anyone, regardless of their financial status or cultivation power. Her small freehold community of just over one hundred subregions barely made the cutoff for the Quest, and Alistair was very grateful for that. Having two healers on a team of eight was most fortuitous.

"Alright everyone, gather round," Alistair announced. They had just a minute left before the build process started. The Pathfinder AI was reticent with the details of how it would work, so they had to be ready for any possibility. "I know it's weird how our team is five members of the Northeast Freehold and three strangers, but as long as we all have the same objectives, it will all work out fine."

"I'm hardly a stranger," William objected.

Alistair ignored him. "We're in this together. All of our subregions will be pooled as one unit, so we win or lose as a team. Top four is not just our target, it's our guarantee. We have the dream team right here. Me, Alexandra, and Jesse for combat. William and Caren for planning. Fasha as the healer. And the Maine Brothers as... general support. I don't want to be cocky, but I'm confident in us. Let's go out there and win. I want everyone to put your hands in the center and say 'team' on the count of three."

The other complied with his request to varying degrees of enthusiasm. The Maine Brothers were happy to accept, while Caren and William looked less than amused. Their first "team" call was tepid, to say the least.

"Come on, guys, what was that?" Alistair complained.

"It's a little cheesy, don't you think?" Alexandra giggled.

"Stop being a hater," Alistair said. "Everyone, let's do it again, and I'm serious this time. Here we go... one, two, three, TEAM!"

It still wasn't as loud as he would have liked, but it would do. Coincidentally, the timing was just right, as the temporary hall they were inside was replaced by a grassy plain. Behind them was a luscious forest, and next to that, a river.

Welcome to the base building portion of Capture the Beacon. All teams will be given 1,000,000 Yikayok Points that they can use to purchase building materials and other items for their base.

Additional Yikayok Points can be purchased using team subregions as collateral, at 500:1 rate (1 subregion gets you 500 Yikayok Points). Collected subregions will be returned to the owners if they make the top four, and otherwise will be split evenly among the top four teams. However, if a team's subregion count goes into the negatives from a loss, their collateral subregions will instantly be transferred to the winning team. The first game begins in exactly seventy-two hours. Good luck!

"The Final Frontier Empire really knows how to make an entertaining game," Dev'rox commented. "The trade-off between more of these Yikayok Points and losing subregions is quite interesting."

"I wonder how this applies to the monsters and beasts," Caren speculated. "Their territories cannot be as large as the biggest human lands—or Devil King, for that matter."

"They probably get a bonus for being monsters to even things out," Alexandra said. "These guys bend all the rules they want, just to have more bloodshed or bail out a noble."

Alistair opened up the Yikayok Point Store, a little number in the right-hand corner notifying him that he had 420,624 out of their one million total points. Looking at their subregion numbers, that number corresponded exactly with his personal percent of the team's total. Some teams would have trouble coordinating between different strategies, but he had a good feeling that their team would gel together.

Looking at the store, there were six different categories of items—building materials, siege weapons, defensive weapons, traps, protection methods, and miscellaneous. Selecting the building material page, he found fifteen different substances, each having a different price and profile, differing in effectiveness against magical attacks, physical integrity, durability, and more. The influx of information was overwhelming, especially knowing they had to build the base in three days.

Jesse lazily raised an arm. "How many subregions do you think we should wager, boss?"

"I don't know," Alistair answered truthfully. "If the effectiveness of the base scales linearly with the amount of Yikayok Points you spend, then it seems reasonable for us to go all in. Not to gas us up too much, but we have two people in the top ten, and everyone else is more than capable to play an important role in this game. As long as we win the first game or two, we'll be pretty safe."

"Safe if you expect us to get top four," Caren reminded him. "Otherwise, we'd be losing all of our collateral."

"We're getting top four," Alistair assured the bookish cultivator. "The other teams will vaguely know how powerful they are. And if they're smart, they'll know that we know that too. Between two evenly matched teams, a strong base will make all the difference."

"We don't know how effective—" Caren started speaking, but Holden (or William; Alistair had to get used to his real name) interrupted with a weird screeching noise.

"Aha!" he exclaimed.

The others stood in silence for a few seconds as William continued to stare at his Yikayok Point Store window without saying another word.

"—Oh, right. Sorry, while you were talking, I was calculating what the best combination of purchases would be," William said, ruffling through his overly pomaded hair.

Alexandra gave Alistair an incredulous glance, but he returned with a look that meant "just wait." He had tried to explain William's powers, but it was easier to see them in action.

"Well? Tell me the budget, don't dally now," William demanded, beckoning with both hands.

"I'm sorry, what?" Alexandra asked.

"I can't tell you what to buy unless you're telling me our budget. There are a lot of moving parts here."

"By my calculations, there are at least six teams we have to be worried about," Alistair said. "Lucius Wood's team, of course. I agreed to a truce with him, so he shouldn't be a concern. Of course, that's only as good as his word. Then there's Pharaoh's team. Wandering Hobo, for those unaware of his 'real' name. In a straight-up fight, I'd lose to him, so his team is bound to be strong. Carmen's team is another likely threat. And then the four unknown factors. The Devil King team—if they sent all their strongest members, we're honestly screwed, so let's hope the system did something about that. And then, if there are only two Beast Lord teams and one monster team, there's no way that they won't be strong."

"Meaning?" Fasha asked.

"If they're split up equally, there should be three other strong teams in each group. Meaning that we have a 3/10 chance of facing one in the first round."

Caren continued Alistair's logic. "If we have a 50-50 chance against any of the strong teams, just to put out a number, then our overall chance of being eliminated in the first round is approximately 15%, given that we spend all of our subregions."

"Sounds fine to me," Delilah said. "That's not a very big number."

"William," Alistair called out. "Can you calculate the difference in build effectiveness for 3,211,000 Yikayok Points versus 2,910,500 Points? That would leave us with exactly 601 subregions."

The scrawny genius stared intently at the window. A tense feeling filled the air as William didn't speak for almost thirty seconds. Alistair could literally see his aura fluctuating as he spent tons of Mana on his analysis Skill. *If this doesn't give us the best base ever, I'm kicking this guy off the team. He already has a reason to have a grudge against me*, Alistair thought to himself, only half facetiously.

"What happened to justice without mercy is cruel?" Dev'rox said. "Come on, give the guy a second chance. It was a zero-sum game; he did what he had to do."

"No, you're right. Ever since I had my future bloodline locked in as the blood dragon, I've been angrier. It's not like me to hold a grudge. What happened in the first trial is irrelevant now that we're allies."

"First off, you got that bloodline four hours ago," Dev'rox lectured him. "Second, you don't even have the bloodline until you actually evolve your species. And third, I was pretending to say what *you'd* say. You shouldn't trust that skinny brat at all. He's a schemer, I tell you. I know his kind well— as a schemer myself."

William finally spoke up. "I think it makes more sense to go with keeping 601 subregions in reserve. The 300k Yikayok Points difference shouldn't matter that much."

Alistair nodded. "Okay. Tell us what we have to do."

———

While Alistair was willing to trust William to a certain extent, he couldn't just accept William's schematics for their base without at least looking it over. The potential for William's betrayal was low, but not impossible. He and Caren scoured over William's idea, looking for any flaws or backdoors in his design. They couldn't find any. Caren's Chronicler Class gave him a near eidetic memory and let him process ten different streams of information without breaking a sweat. If there was anyone who could discover a mistake or trojan horse, it would be him.

The blueprint of their base was... interesting, but it made perfect sense given their abilities. The main structure revolved around a convoluted maze of reinforced stone passageways, layered in seemingly chaotic patterns. The reinforced stone was one of the medium-priced materials—not especially protective, but physically heavy and cheap enough that they could build a lot of it. And build a lot of it they did. They spent almost half of the entire Yikayok fund constructing the most complicated internals of a building Alistair had ever seen. Even the demiplane would have bowed down before the sheer intricacy of the design.

The reason for all the excess was twofold. First, with Caren's post-it note telepathy, they could coordinate from every position at once. With his [Paper Mind], he could identify all their positions from central command and notify them where they had to go next. Their enemies would be completely in the dark without someone like Caren in the chair. The second reason was the Heart-Render Engine. Not only were they making hard-to-navigate passageways, but Caren could move them at will with the Heart-Render Engine, which cost another 500,000 Yikayok Points. That left them with just over a million points for the rest of the build.

They got a long-ranged laser cannon for the back of the base, just in case any enemies decided to try to flank them, and a mirror on the roof. An enemy could be taken unaware by a carefully timed laser blast into the mirror, reflecting into them from above. There were some other hidden traps scattered across the base as well, to be used at Caren's discretion. The whole operation really relied on him rather than William, despite the latter dreaming up the idea in the first place.

William didn't even lay down a single brick of stone during the construction, so there was no way he could have set up any nasty betrayals. Caren was truly in charge of the Heart-Render Engine and communication, and there was no trick there. As long as Caren was loyal (which Alistair double-checked with his Karmic vision), William had no more leverage to betray him than the rest of his team.

After hiding their beacon in the agreed upon location, they were ready to start the first round with an hour to spare. With their extra time, Alistair and his teammates went over their plans, double and triple-checking them for mistakes. Alexandra, William, Jesse, and himself would be on offense, while Caren, Delilah, Josiah, and Fasha would play defense. At first glance, it seemed the offensive squad was far too strong compared to the defensive, but because Jesse could teleport to five saved locations at will, he was basically on both teams at once.

"Don't get too cocky, brat." Dev'rox smirked. "That Pharaoh fellow is going to smack you sideways again if you're not careful."

"I won't, I swear. I told him I'll pay him back one day though, so I kind of have to fight him—"

Alistair got cut off by the voice announcing the start of round one of Capture the Beacon.

Round One:
Battlefield – Mirror World
Opponent – Beast Team 1
You have six hours. Begin!

33 ROUND ONE: BEAST TEAM 1

THE MIRROR WORLD was exactly what the name indicated—a reality of infinite mirrors and fractal shapes. The moment after the system announcement, the team and the entire base were transported to the alien dimension.

Everywhere Alistair looked, he could see reflections of himself stretching onward to infinity. The ground, the sky, and everything in between were made of glassy crystals that both refracted and reflected an ambient, purplish light. At first, it seemed as if anywhere they walked was a solid surface, but that was just an optical illusion. As Alistair took several steps from his original location, he realized that reality bent around him, letting him walk in whichever direction he wanted.

"This is trippy," Josiah said, waving his arm through the shattered glass, which contorted around him.

Alistair agreed. The Mirror World was set up such that one could *choose* gravity's direction. If he wanted to walk on the "ceiling," all he needed to do was plant his foot upward and that would become the new floor. The only issue he foresaw was visibility. Something quite close could seem dozens of meters away, while something far away could appear as a reflection in a nearby mirror.

"Put one under your tongue," Caren said, conjuring some blue post-it notes out of his billowing robes and flying them over to the other seven members of the team. "It won't bite."

Alistair had taken the Chronicler's weird telepathic paper before, so he did it with no qualms. Some of the others hesitated for a moment before putting it in their mouths, but everyone complied in the end. The note dissolved without a hitch, leaving a tingly sensation.

"Hello, everyone," Caren thought.

Delilah jolted to attention, freaked out by the sudden voice. "Shit, you scared the hell out of me."

"Did I not explain before how this works?" Caren communicated with an amused grin. *"Think intentionally toward me and you will be able to transfer the thought directly."*

"Whoa, that's wicked cool," Josiah thought.

"I've set it so that you won't hear the messages of your group, whether it be offensive or defensive, to reduce clutter," Caren explained. *"If you want to do a cross-group chat, transfer the thought to me and I'll relay it."*

"Alright," Alistair said out loud for more dramatic emphasis. "Time to hunt some beasts."

Alistair, Alexandra, Jesse, and William split off from the base defense group. Their stone castle looked intimidating, especially with the mysterious gigantic mirror on top of the central tower. Despite being the size of a small manor, compared to the superficially endless environment, it felt quaint.

The next question was how they were going to approach the game.

"I would imagine the enemy base isn't too far away," William speculated. "The interaction between beacon stealing becomes less important the further away they are. There's more room for people to take their beacon back and it becomes harder to plan a heist. I can't imagine they would want us to miss out on that fun."

In a flash of red light and a loud crack, Jesse materialized a few meters away. Alexandra instinctively drew out her whitesteel dagger, **Withering Promise**, sheathing it back in its scabbard after she realized it was just Jesse.

"That's going to take some getting used to," Alexandra said wryly.

"Sorry, I can't control the effects," Jesse said. "It's what I get for having a massive range. I haven't found their base yet. Scouted everything within a kilometer radius. That's around six-tenths of a mile for you Americans."

"Wait," Alistair said, sniffing the air. "I think I smell something."

The others looked at him incredulously, which made sense, since none of them knew about his new {Blood Scent} leaf. His ten-times more powerful nose sifted through the air, hunting for the aroma he had picked up. The Mirror World was sterile except for the newcomers, Alistair realized, so it was easy to pick out foreign smells.

It was a dank and watery scent, reminding him of the ocean or moss. Alistair couldn't locate the direction exactly, but it felt like it was coming from the northeast.

"Try this direction." Alistair pointed toward the origin of the smell. "Try doubling your distance this time."

Jesse saluted him and disappeared in another flash of red light. It took less than a second for him to return. "Yep, that's them."

"How many?"

"Five, I think. But they're camping outside their base. I think they're goading us to come for them. Once we strike, they'll probably all come out and attack us, or maybe use their base as a weapon," Jesse said.

William offered his own thesis, narrowing his eyes as he scratched his ear. "Perhaps they want us to send all of our members at them, only to sneak someone into our base while we aren't looking."

"Relay the information back to Caren," Alistair told William. "I think we investigate how strong they are, to start."

Alistair pointed at the Australian top ten ranker. "Jesse, you and me. We'll strike them right now, when they least expect it. It'll give us an intimidation factor."

"You sure, boss? Some of them seemed pretty strong, I'm not gonna lie. Maybe stronger than me, but I was there for just a split second."

"I'm sure."

Alistair cracked his knuckles, letting the red metal bracelets around his wrists morph over his hands, forming the **Devilsbane Gauntlets**. It had been over three days since he had last fought, more than any one period since the initiation had begun. He uncloaked his aura, letting it run wild. Longing to be freed, it was now so powerful that it manifested around him as a mix of the colors of his Mana affinities—golden, red, light blue, and coral. It was nothing like a full Super Saiyan-style mantle of energy, but the very fact you could discern color at all was a testament to Alistair's strength. He allowed himself a small grin when he saw how shocked Jesse and William were by his power. Alexandra just rolled her eyes.

The colors and physical energy disappeared after a couple of seconds, burning through the pent-up condensation from wearing a cloak for so long, but the overall power remained. Having at least 150 in every Attribute would do that. That being said, Alistair didn't mind his lopsided Agility, especially for what he was about to do next.

"Two kilometers, you think? Umm…" Alistair calculated. "Teleport in 15 seconds."

Alistair crouched down into a sprinter's stance, remembering the first time he'd used [Dash]. It felt a lifetime ago, when he mustered all of his will and strength to rush General Krazz. Back then, he thought that was fast. Now, he was over a dozen times faster.

With a gargantuan first step, Alistair ran like the wind. He would never get over the way the air flowed against his skin, the sheer exhilaration of running faster than any car. After fourteen seconds, he prepared his movement Skill, ready to catch the Beast Team unprepared.

The landscape around him blurred faster than even his impressive dynamic visual acuity could follow. Still, his reactions were fast enough to recognize when [Dash] was about to end. As he sped through the last thirty meters, his danger sense alerted him to the presence of five enemies. Alistair used the airwalking aspect of [Dash] with his right foot, launching him nearly a meter above the ground as he decelerated into the thick of battle.

Time seemed to slow down around Alistair as he took in the situation. Three enemies behind, two in front. The closest one was the source of the foul scent he'd picked up earlier, a giant segmented animal that looked like a bear-sized tardigrade, while the one adjacent was a hairless white gorilla.

Alistair cocked back his right hand, gathering a [Force Fist] imbued with a portion of the Fist Node. The energy around his fist warped the air with its immense power. The water bear didn't stand a chance, taking a second stage Mutra-enhanced fajin to the underside. The explosive force of the uppercut sent the beast flying dozens of meters into the air, but Alistair had already pivoted to the gorilla.

The entire previous sequence took place in less than half a second, with the other beasts just reacting to their ally being catapulted into the sky. A red flash of light appeared a few meters behind the beasts, who had turned to face Alistair. Jesse caught their attention, leaving the white gorilla to the misfortune of being next in Alistair's warpath. It had the time to bare his fangs and raise his muscled arms, but Alistair was faster than that. Using

[Dash] and a drop of the Dao of the Ghost, he flickered past the gorilla, ending up behind it. The **Devilsbane Gauntlets** gleamed with primal crimson aura, bubbling like warm, living blood. There was no doubt the description of the item was accurate—Alistair could feel how much more powerful his [Blood Hand] Skill was as he plunged his claws into the gorilla's backside.

The ape looked like it had a high Constitution, but it was nothing compared to the combination of the sharp claws of his red gloves and the power of [Blood Hand]. He sent his spiritual power and life force into the beast like a deadly virus, destroying its body from the inside out until only a husk remained. The other three creatures didn't take the ambush lightly, attempting to attack him while he drained their ally. But Alistair was ready for that, using his underrated Strength to drag the half-ton gorilla backward, who acted as a shield against their long-ranged attacks.

A series of quills and sharpened feathers blasted into the dying beast. In fact, they hastened the process. Alistair absorbed the life force of the gorilla, incorporating the blood essence into his mighty pool of vital energy.

{Letting of the Beast}: +1 *Endurance.*

Anger brewed within him as Alistair received a flash of the gorilla's memories. As a Beast Lord, upon reaching level 30, it had gained sapience. Yet despite being relatively non-violent before, it was only after Gorilla Garreth gained intelligence that he started hunting humans for sport. It had nothing to do with his natural instincts, only pure cruelty.

Alistair kept a cool head and stared down the two that remained. To his right was a large porcupine that had grown multiple heads, while to his left was a normal sized black cat that blended into the shadows. Jesse handled the third beast, dueling a humanoid butterfly while slowly luring it away from the main battlefield with his teleportation abilities. Every time the insect struck with a gust of wind or glittering poison dust, the Aussie was nowhere to be found. From a safe distance, he launched oscillating balls of the same red energy that appeared when he teleported.

Alistair jumped back as the water bear's body crashed into the mirrors that formed the "ground," shattering them in all directions. He wanted a piece of its life force, but first he would have to deal with the cat and the porcupine. He activated [Eyes of Truth] on the two beasts.

Name: Shadoweater
Species: Mutated Bombay Cat (Beast Lord)
Class: N/A [Primary Attribute(s): Agility]
Level: 63
Title: Feline Ruler

Name: Echidnatus
Species: Mutated Porcupine (Beast Lord)
Class: N/A [Primary Attribute(s): Constitution]
Level: 62
Title: Mother of Rodents

Shadoweater lurched forward, becoming a flicker of darkness as it chan-neled what felt like a Dao of Shadow. Even Alistair's trained senses had trouble keeping track of it, the beast moving at speeds rivaling his own sans [Dash].

At the same time, Echidnatus raised its hind legs and unfurled its full coat of spines, firing baseball-bat-sized keratin missiles at Alistair. They spun so fast they whistled at a deafening volume, following him as he dodged Shadoweater's swipes.

The cat would emerge from the streak of shadow to swipe with a ghostly purple claw. Drawing to the third stage of the Kai'tazake Mutra, Alistair felt every attack coming as if from miles away, ducking and dodging each strike with ease. His Karmic powers fit seamlessly with his [Fighter's Instinct] and combat trance, turning him into a whirlwind of maximally efficient violence.

Activating his own claw Skill, Alistair grabbed one of the spinning quills out of the air, a testament to his absurd reaction time. Perhaps if he had pinched it with his bare hands, the rotational momentum would have skinned the flesh off his fingertips, but his Devilsbane Gauntlets were as solid as a diamond. [Frozen Claw] spread rapidly from the talons, zooming from quill to quill, freezing them all in a casing of crystal ice.

Shadoweater must have thought Alistair was distracted by using [Frozen Claw], as it struck the moment he turned his back. The black cat moved even faster than before, no more than a blur of darkness. A purple streak of deadly energy bloomed at the point of attack.

Even Alistair wasn't quick enough to dodge that at a short distance—if he had been unprepared. So deep into his trance, Alistair embodied movement without effort, transitioning his **[Frozen Claw]** into a **[Lightning of Justice]**. With his aura sense and Karmic vision, he predicted Shadoweater's location precisely. A smiting thunderbolt rained down from the sky, electrocuting the poor housecat with barely a smidgen of the Justice Node's reserves. Unlike Sessen Esshei, the Agility-based feline was unable to handle the power of the strike without serious damage, compounded by the extra power the Dao of Justice had against evildoers.

It wasn't dead, however, though Alistair cleared up that loose end with expedience. **[Dashing]** at the injured beast, he used nothing more than his pugilism to end the fight. Anything else would be a waste of Mana or Dao energy. Five clean blows with the hardened steel of his **Devilsbane Gauntlets** were enough.

To be efficient, Alistair grabbed Shadoweater's corpse and absorbed its life force with **[Blood Hand]**. At the same time, he turned around to deal with his two remaining opponents. The water bear had taken serious damage from the unexpected punch and the subsequent fall and shattered mirrors, while Echidnatus was unharmed though missing quite a few quills.

He had grown so much even compared to when he'd fought Sessen Esshei. The beasts before him were probably a tiny bit stronger than the Serpent King during his battle, but he had outpaced that level of power considerably.

Echidnatus continued firing more spiraling quills while Alistair kept dodging them. The injured mega-tardigrade tried expelling a weird green moss from its body, but Alistair leisurely jumped over it. The attack might have worked if it had been healthy, but the beast was profusely bleeding from its underside. Alistair hid behind the large creature's shadow, avoiding the Mother of Rodents. Before it could turn around, he spun and used all of his momentum for a jumping kick that spiked the tardigrade into the shattered ground.

Because Alistair overestimated the height of his jump, a quill grazed his left thigh. He ignored the wound for the moment, leaping up again in a double jump off the permeable Mirror World. Alistair imagined that from their perspective he must look like a bloodthirsty fighting demon, carrying the corpse of their fallen ally while he absorbed its life force. It wasn't the most "justice-y" image, but he couldn't always have good optics, could he?

Once he imagined that the air was the ground and the ground was the air, the world followed his command. He bounced off the makeshift platform and headed straight for the last enemy. The fallen quills around the area started vibrating in a possible Formulaic Skill, but Alistair had already expected the eventuality. Upgrading **[Eyes of Karma]** had a small but non-negligible impact on his muddy foresight, not increasing the duration, but making it just a little clearer.

As the quills congregated together, Alistair had already activated **[Dash]** again. The Mirror World complemented the Skill perfectly, since anything could become ground to push off of. He was already on top of the beast before the quills made it halfway to him.

With his free left hand, he unleashed another **[Force Fist]** fajin, utilizing the Dao of the Ghost to phase through the creature. Before the blow could send it flying backward, he was already behind it, facing the same direction. Alistair caught Echidnatus with his arm extended behind him in a seamless motion, expending more Mana to execute a **[Blood Hand]** on the beast at the same time as he finished digesting the shadow cat.

"Fuck man, you're one scary guy," Jesse swore out loud, foregoing the telepathy. "I'm glad we're on the same team. I just dealt with my guy, but I'm a bit beat up."

Alistair turned his head at the voice, seeing the blond man hunched over and panting for air. His skin had a weird radioactive tint, and he had massive cuts over his limbs and torso, but he was still alive.

"Oh, all of this? Don't worry, I can't even do this against good guys," Alistair said. "I'm just absorbing their life force now; it should be just a few minutes before I consolidate the energy."

Jesse chuckled. "Bad guys only, yeah. Just don't ever see me as a *bad* guy, and we're good."

Alistair wanted to protest that it wasn't like that and he actually had a strict Dao of Justice he followed, but he realized that it would be futile. The optics of absorbing his kills' blood like a vampire wasn't great, but it didn't affect the core of his beliefs. No one said Alistair's justice had to be sterile, like that of a pure law-and-order paladin.

"Did you find their base?" Alistair asked, switching back to Caren's telepathy.

"Yes, I did. It's another kilometer north. Looks like around a three-kilometer distance in between bases."

"Hmm," Alistair thought. *"We can handle the remaining three pretty easily, I would imagine. Relay back to base and ask Caren if he needs help, and if the answer*

is no, I want you to use your teleportation to scout out the other team's bases. See what they're like, how far away they are, and so on."

"Roger that," Jesse said, disappearing in his signature red flash.

The battle felt like it had taken a long time because of his slowed perception of time, but in reality, less than a minute and a half had passed. Alexandra and William arrived soon after Jesse left.

"You beat all of them, seriously? Couldn't leave any for us?" Alexandra asked, hand on her hip.

"They weren't that strong, okay?" Alistair defended himself. *"Their boss is probably in the base though, so we can handle that together."*

"[Hypercalculative Induction] indicates that there is a high probability their leader sent two agents to steal our beacon," William relayed, *"making their leader the likely remaining target. I also have a strong suspicion as to who the leader is."*

"Who?" Alexandra and Alistair asked at the same time.

"Analyzing the remains of your battle, these creatures are all mammals. It seems likely the Beast teams were split into mammals and perhaps reptiles or insects. The strongest mammalian beast that could comfortably fit inside a base is the Pride Lord, the thirty-foot long tiger-lion hybrid—or liger, for short—from a zoo in South Africa."

"That's just great." Alexandra fiddled with her daggers. *"If it's going to be three against one, there's no way we can lose, right?"*

They approached the Beast Team's base with caution. Only a small sliver of the six-hour time period had passed, so they could afford to take it slow. Using Jesse's scouted intel and Alistair's sense of smell, they found the base within a few minutes.

The Beast Team's building could hardly be called that. Instead of several tons of stone and machinery like their castle, Alistair observed a makeshift tent. It was big, perhaps the size of a large city circus, but seemingly without any protection.

"William, what's your read?" Alistair asked.

"Can you call down some lightning on it? For my calculations, of course."

Alistair double-checked his Mana, making sure it wasn't too low, which it wasn't at 953. He pressed his gloved hand against the mirrored ground, causing the skies to sunder and strike the tent with a bolt of cleansing lightning. For a split second, the golden lightning churned on the surface of the tent canopy, blocked by some warping shield. However, the shield was too weak, collapsing after just a few seconds. The bolt of lightning exploded in a flash of auric light.

"*I think… the beast is taunting us,*" William said. "*I doubt there are any more complicated defenses than that.*"

"*Let's move in,*" Alistair commanded. "*Stick together. Alexandra, you take point since you have the most Constitution. I'll have my Karmic vision ready to detect danger, don't worry. William, you focus on any traps.*"

As far as William had explained it, besides a couple of last resort items and a karate chop Skill, he had no offensive abilities. Alistair's own Karmic senses told him that there was a good chance that was false, though he didn't know how much William's Class could affect his Karmic abilities.

Just when they were about to begin their approach, a horrifying roar came from inside the tent, full of unadulterated killing intent. A wave of *nue* twice as strong as the Serpent King's washed over the three of them. Alistair hadn't practiced for the past few weeks for nothing, so the wave barely made him flinch.

Alexandra and William weren't so fortunate. Alexandra collapsed to her knees, while William just keeled over like a petrified statue.

"Fuck," Alistair muttered, seeing that William had actually just straight-up died, his life force blinking out. *Of all things, shouldn't he be able to predict his own death?* Alistair shook his head. At least nothing was permanent in this trial.

Feeling the growing threat with his danger sense, he hoisted Alexandra over his shoulder and retreated back.

"I'm good, I'm good," she told him. "*Just caught me off guard, that's all.*"

"*I told you to practice with* nue."

"*I have. Or I'd be dead, like William. We can't all be prodigies, Alistair,*" Alexandra retorted. "*Whoa, look at that thing.*"

Alistair turned his head to see the majestic beast stepping out of the tent. The Pride Lord looked like a standard liger, except much larger, with a spotted gray and gold coat. Its mane was the same red as Alistair's gauntlets —the hue of blood.

"You dare!" the liger roared with regal authority. "This is my kingdom. As absolute suzerain, you are not welcome in my dominion."

"*A lion has a bigger vocabulary than you,*" Alistair teased.

Alexandra gave him an exasperated look. "*I thought you'd be taking this more seriously. I know you can feel how powerful that beast is.*"

"Let's just say I'm confident."

Alistair clenched both of fists. It was time to go all out. No more holding back. In his right hand, he activated [Hand of Karma]. The Tier 2 Expert Skill looked almost like his [Blood Hand] from afar, though the color was slightly different and it warped the surrounding air like a heatwave. In his left hand he conjured [Frozen Claw], wrapping his gauntlet in a light-blue cloak of icy aura.

Alexandra's aura had grown as well. Her [Barbarian's Fury] produced a full-blown cloak of evaporating blood. She joked that they were vampire twins since he had a blood-based Skill as well. In one hand, she wielded her Tang Clan Dirk, which spewed out purple effluvium, and in the other she held Withering Promise, a whitesteel dagger heavier than a large refrigerator. Using [Empower Weapon II], she multiplied the size of the weapons dozen-fold.

"Dev'rox?" Alistair asked as he prepared to strike.

"Already ahead of you," the imp replied, giving Alistair a hefty chunk of his spatially-attuned Mana pool.

Alistair combined [Dash] with the Mana, compressing the space between him and the Pride Lord. Within less than a tenth of a second, he stood in front of the beast. Because of the immense spiritual pressure the liger exerted, Alistair could only get within a meter, but that was enough. For its size, it moved incredibly fast, lunging at him with an open maw. Its control over *nue* was impressive, releasing it in waves to catch him off guard, but with Dev'rox's help, it didn't affect him at all. The liger probably expected him to flinch at least a little from its lunge, but Alistair just pivoted into an uppercut with [Hand of Karma].

The absolute power of the beast made it difficult for him to cut off all the positive threads of Fate or disrupt its meridian network, but it was enough to discombobulate it for a second—just enough time for him to grab its snout with [Frozen Claw]. Alistair pumped a decent portion of the Ghost Node into his attack, so the hoarfrost and then ice zoomed across the entire length of its body in less than a second.

He knew that it wouldn't hold the beast for long, but just a fraction of a second was all he needed to set up for his partner. He jumped to the side, letting Alexandra take over. They had worked on their synergy to the point where, even before he froze the beast, she was already leaping through the air.

Using both of her enlarged weapons, she cast **[Partition Vitae]**. An enormous x-shaped blast of green energy flew toward the Pride Lord. The life-attuned Mana cracked the ice crystals and shredded into the beast's flesh at a cellular level.

But Alexandra didn't stop there, following it up with an **[Armageddon Slash]**, a Skill that temporarily quintupled the weight of her weapon. Using it on **Withering Promise** made the stiletto weigh over two tons, and Alexandra brought all that weight down on the liger.

Even Alistair's eardrums took a beating from the deafening impact. A shockwave knocked him back around a meter, though the main consequence of the two-ton strike was the complete destruction of the Mirror World's reality. The nearby mirrors and crystals broke in a cascading effect from the source.

As for Alexandra, Alistair saw her limping over the broken crystal. The force of the blow had broken her arm, bone protruding from the mangled limb. The only problem was... the liger wasn't dead. Alistair was amazed at the resilience of the beast. His life force sense indicated that it had lost about two-thirds of its Health, but that didn't mean it was out for the count.

A ball of void and fire mana congealed in front of its open jaws. Pure darkness mixed with the orange and red firestorm, forming a burning void. The Mana fused with the underlying Dao energy, though just like with Esshei, it felt much shallower than a comparable human's Dao.

Alistair pressed forward with **[Dash]**, scooping up Alexandra right as a beam of the burning void seared her former location out of existence. Had he been just a fraction of a second too late, the attack would've seared off her legs past her knee. She didn't protest at being carried this time. After he got her to safety far away from the battlefield, he turned back to the school bus-sized liger. Despite the injuries it had received from Alexandra's attacks, it stared him down defiantly. The Pride Lord was an apt name, it seemed.

"I have heard of you, human," the Pride Lord roared.

"You get news from the other beasts?" Alistair asked.

"We have a similar network to you, for all those who have gained the gift of reason," the liger said. "You are a great enemy to beastkind."

"Only when I have to be," Alistair retorted. "Leave us alone and we'll leave you alone. There's enough room on this planet for the both of us. I've only killed beasts that have attacked human settlements unprovoked."

"We both know that will not happen. We are in competition for the same resources—there can be only one outcome."

The Pride Lord gathered its incipient Dao energy and Mana, conjuring dozens of voidfire spheres. The Mirror World began to crack apart from the warping power of the Skill, melting like glass and further warping the already fraying seams of reality. Like a machine gun, it fired the spheres at Alistair in arcing beams of death. He knew that if any of them hit him directly, he would certainly die.

Alistair flowed as water, devoid of all conscious thought. His body moved as one with his deepest instincts as he dodged the beams. He sidestepped into a jump, followed it up with a midair [Dash], and then airwalked to change direction. Each time he narrowly avoided the all-consuming flames and darkness that exploded around him.

When he reached within ten meters of the liger, his danger sense exploded. He ignored it. Instead, he drew deep on his pool of Karma, burning ten points to activate a boosted [Eyes of Karma]. The pain of using his positive Karma stung, but it was worth seeing the web of Fate. Dev'rox pumped him with spatially-attuned Mana as he drew upon the Ghost Node.

With a mighty final roar, the injured Beast Lord gathered its remaining energy to a single point. Through a mechanism Alistair didn't understand, it seemed to congeal all the different types of cultivation essence. The density of the power absorbed the noise of the world.

Silence. Darkness. Fire. It simmered to one point and then exploded with the fury of a dying sun.

Alistair channeled the Dao of the Ghost through his entire body, along with Dev'rox's Mana. The explosion washed over him in an instant. If he hadn't foreseen the situation in advance, he would have been screwed. Not in the game as a whole, since their victory was practically guaranteed with the Beast Lord's self-destruction, but he really wanted to get the kill Mana.

"A shitty victory is still a victory," Dev'rox commented.

Alistair checked his Health. He had gone down all the way from nearly full to just 98 in one attack. It wasn't just his physical body that was a mess —his internal spiritual network was wrecked from the interaction the attack had on his incorporeal form. But he was still kicking.

Level up! *You are now level 46.* +3 Agility, +3 Intelligence, +3 Charisma, +3 free Attribute points, +23 Upgrade Points.

Alistair limped over to the Pride Lord's corpse. Amazingly, the body was perfectly intact, just without a hint of life or Dao. Whatever technique it had used, it cleared out all the things that made it a cultivator.

"Caren here. We're just about done dealing with two attackers. They were equipped with a ton of weapons, so it took us a while. How are things on your end?"

"Just beat their leader. We've got this one locked down now."

A few seconds later, a notification popped up on his status screen.

Round One Complete.

+400 subregions earned. Active Total: 1001 (3,821 stored)

After the six-hour period for round one is over, there will be another six-hour intermission period in the lobby. Teams that end their games before the allotted time period also stay in the lobby. Congratulations on your victory, and start preparing for the next round.

34 THE BIG EYE

A CURRENT OF cleansing energy sparked through Alistair's system, jolting him awake. The last thing he remembered was the Pathfinder AI notifying him of their victory followed by darkness. He took in his surroundings, though there wasn't much to go on. His body was submerged in a viscous black liquid, illuminated only by a glowing moss on the ceiling. He could barely see anything in the low light, though it looked like the liquid was in some kind of natural spring or pool.

Alistair carefully moved his arms and legs, making sure everything was intact. The Pride Lord's suicidal explosion had really done a number on him. If not for the black goo, which he assumed was a therapeutic treatment, he probably would have been injured for a few weeks.

He tried to remember the exact nature of the blast. It was like a more powerful version of the ten'gatsu technique Anthony had used, combining the three major cultivation essences, though Alistair suspected the self-destructive explosion had also used life force as a catalyst. Even with the Dao of the Ghost and Dev'rox's spatially-attuned Mana, it had seriously messed up his internal spiritual network.

Groaning, he climbed out of the pool. It had been only a few hours at most, Alistair figured. Surely they wouldn't have started the next round without him. He tried to use Caren's telepathy only to remember that it had a set time limit.

Alistair waded to the rocky shoreline and stepped out of the gunk. He was naked, but the moment he stepped out, white silk robes appeared around him and any leftover black goo vanished. There was a door carved into the rock a few meters ahead. Alistair opened it, revealing a long corridor made of pure white tiling.

An elderly man waited on the door's other side. "Young master, I hope you enjoyed your stay."

"Drauku?" Alistair asked incredulously. "What are you doing here?"

"I'm sorry, but I am unaware of this 'Drauku' you speak of. My name is Eavol, humble servant of the Pathfinder AI."

Alistair looked closer at Eavol, observing that there were slight differences between him and Drauku, the Akata Corporation homunculus. Drauku was shorter with grayer hair, while Eavol was more corpulent and had a slight limp.

"You're a homunculus," Alistair said. "Oh, sorry if that's rude. I mean no offense."

"None taken, young master. I am a homunculus. Nearly fifty thousand years old, if you can believe that. I've seen things you wouldn't believe. Weaponized black holes collapsing civilizations by the trillions. Expressions of the Dao that turned stars into flowers. War is a terrible thing," Eavol said, looking wistful in his remembrance of the past. "I digress, I digress. Let us get you back to your team. There is still an hour left before the next round."

"Thank you for your assistance. I feel brand new again. Do you mind if I use some of the tiling for my Skill?" Alistair asked. "It turns objects into pies. I'm famished."

"Go right ahead."

Alistair obliged, activating **[Carmela's Happy Pies]**. The white tiles turned into a delicious carrot pie, which he wolfed down like a maniac. They felt even more refreshing than usual, perhaps because of the unique composition of the hallway.

"Did everyone get sent here?" Alistair wondered.

"No, only a few such as yourself that suffered spiritual wounds or other deeper injuries. You were one of the worst cases. The Pathfinder AI, being the cheap system it is, would rather employ a less expensive method, such as using Abyssal Titan blood, than heal you directly. I pray it was satisfactory."

"Oh no, it was amazing," Alistair said. Except for his Dao energy and

Karma, he was completely healed, and even those were recovering faster than normal.

Alistair bowed to the homunculus when they reached the end of the corridor. Eavol looked embarrassed by the show of respect, shaking his head. "That is unnecessary, young master. I live to serve."

"I still appreciate it. Hey, maybe when I grow stronger, I can take you back out to see those things? Minus the trillions of people dying, hopefully."

Eavol let out a mirthful snort. "That would be something, young master. I look forward to seeing the cultivator you'll become."

———

The hallway led into a large soap bubble floating in an iridescent fluid field. There appeared to be other bubbles in the distance, but they were too far away to make out any of the figures inside them. The bubble he'd entered had all his teammates already present.

"I was beginning to worry you weren't coming back, boss," William said, hugging him.

Alexandra barely held in a laugh as Alistair's face contorted in an awkward smile. "Uh, thanks, good to see you too." The mental image he had of the mysterious Holden was hard to reconcile with the capricious young man before him.

"No contact allowed between the bubbles," Caren said. "At least, at a superficial glance. I may have some ideas to circumvent that."

"I have something for that already," Alistair said, taking out the **Crystal Caller.** "Lucius Wood gave this to me. Apparently it only goes one way, so I have to call him first before we can talk."

"You sure it's not bugged or anything?" Alexandra asked.

"I'm fairly certain." Alistair had tested it using **[Eyes of Truth]**, his aura sense, and enlisted Dev'rox to scan it. They'd all found nothing. "Do you guys think I should call him now?"

"With my abilities, more information is always better," William said. "I say yes."

No one had any objections, so Alistair poured a point of Mana into the crystal. The moment the Mana entered, the device started beeping and glowing. Alistair could feel a faint arrow of Mana shoot out rapidly, flying beyond the confines of their bubble.

A staticky voice faded in. "Alistair? Is that you?"

"Yeah, it's me. It's hard to hear you, though."

The other end was silent for a few seconds, and when the voice returned, it was clear. "My apologies. These lines have so much interference from these bubbles. I've altered the signal, so it should be acceptable now. How was your first round?"

"Good," Alistair said. "We won."

"Glad to hear it. Our intelligence suggested that the team you faced was one of the stronger ones in the group, so it was an impressive performance."

"How do you know what team we faced?"

"Oh, have you not seen?" Lucius asked. "There should be a window showing the current standings, in terms of how many subregions each team has won from the current round and the overall trial. They don't show you how many subregions each team has as a whole, however. I suppose that would ruin the fun."

Alistair navigated to the system window, verifying Lucius's information. Sure enough, there was a table displaying the eleven teams in Group A and eleven teams in Group B. The top half had the winners, some of whom had +600 and some of whom only had +400. One team in the middle was score-less because of the odd number of teams.

Each team was simply named after their captain, so their team was called Alistair Tan's Team, among other fan favorites like Wandering Hobo's Team, Brigid's Team, Carmen's Team, and Lucius's Team. The #1, #3, #4, humans were both in Group B, along with the Devil King squad—named Dragonus's Team—and the Monster Team, while Group A had Alistair, Lucius, and the two Beast Teams.

"Why don't we share some information, as allies," Lucius said. "How about descriptions of the bases we've seen so far? We can trade more than one, if you want."

Alistair beckoned Jesse to come over. "Okay, let's do it," he said. He whispered, asking for Jesse to tell him about the reconnaissance he'd performed while off exploring.

Lucius and Alistair shared the schema for two bases each. Alistair told the Englishman about the Pride Lord's base and one other that Jesse happened to see, while Lucius gave him the details about the other Beast Team's base and the next highest human team in Group A, which belonged the #8 ranker Marzhan. Alistair felt like he was the one getting the better deal out of the exchange, to be honest. If he was paranoid, he might have thought Lucius was trying to get Alistair indebted to him.

"Good dealings, my friend. We will talk more soon," Lucius said, cutting off the line.

"I do not like that man," William said immediately, tapping his ear. "I can't get a good read on him."

"That man is the richest person in the world with the most subregions," Caren said. "It would behoove us to stay in his good graces, at least for the moment. Even if it is a meretricious allyship, we benefit from diplomacy."

"He's been nothing but gracious so far, so I can't really do anything about it," Alistair admitted. His Dao Path of Justice was a huge boon in almost every way, but it could also be a limiting factor at times. It made it very difficult to turn down an offer of friendship, as long as it appeared to be genuine. "Anyway, can you give me a rundown on what happened?"

Caren explained to Alistair why they only gained 400 subregions in the previous round instead of 600. Apparently, they were going to keep one of the last attackers alive and retrieve the beacon, but the wolf-man self-destructed like the Pride Lord, though not as explosively. Alistair expected those sorts of things would keep happening. The beacon incentivized intelligent tactics over mere brute force by offering more points to theft than conquest, so it was obvious people would realize that in a situation where you were guaranteed a loss, it was better to go gently into that good night.

As for Jesse's investigation, he found the next closest base seven kilometers away from theirs, and then another stationed seven kilometers away from that one, both at seemingly random angles. From his limited sampling, opposing team bases were always two and a half kilometers apart.

For the next round, statistically speaking, they were likely to face a much weaker opponent. Alistair wanted them to delay their victory as much as possible in order to gather even more information and perhaps cut some deals. With the way subregion transfers worked, they could offer their assistance for extra subregions.

Everything went as planned and the next four rounds went swimmingly. They profited 2,400 subregions from stealing four beacons and an additional 800 from helping others steal beacons for their games. It turned out they weren't alone in that idea; at one point, they encountered Carmen's Team offering a similar deal to an opposing team. They agreed to a temporary truce, not wanting to get involved in a premature battle.

Slowly, Alistair could feel a shift in the temperature of the average players. Everyone had heard of the exploits of the top rankers but seeing it in person was different. Even those in the #20-50 range were completely outclassed. The dominant teams led by a top ranker completely steamrolled the others.

Sooner or later, the battle for Earth would reach a breaking point and people would have to take sides. The others weren't as magnanimous as Alistair with their mergers and acquisitions, that much was evident. If the weaker territories wanted to avoid slaughter and pillaging, they would have to find one of the preeminent freeholds and join them before it was too late.

Alistair hoped to capitalize on that with open arms and generous terms. He was already planting the seeds, but who knew when they would bloom?

The sixth round marked a stark shift. In lieu of the Mirror World, the setting for their battle was Volcanic Crag, a name befitting the land of brimstone and fire. Pools and streams of flowing, smoldering lava filled every nook and cranny, making a fifth of the terrain impassable. Volcanoes as large as some of the tallest mountains on Earth marked the landscape at odd intervals, an impossibility in terms of natural geography, but clearly this reality defied natural conventions. Smoke and noxious fumes filled the air, while an oppressive red sun made it feel even more like literal hell.

They kept the same offensive and defensive teams as they had for the previous rounds. Unlike the Mirror World, some of the settings allowed for enough visibility to see the opposing base. Volcanic Crag was one of those settings, as long as the cloud-scraping peaks didn't get in the way.

Alistair knew this moment was coming—it was a guaranteed eventuality due to the round-robin format. The base in the distance was enormous, easily twice the size of their own, constructed of variegated stone carved with magical glyphs and layers of palisade walls, all connected by sinuous and viridian vines. The central ivory tower had a rotating light that almost looked like a ravenous eye, looking down on its surroundings as if it was offended by their lack of erudition.

Alistair knew the base only from a description given to him over the **Crystal Caller**, but it was obvious upon seeing it. They were up against Lucius Wood.

35 ADMIRAL

"WHAT SHOULD WE DO?" Alexandra paced around, thumping her combat boots against the craggy terrain.

"Well, we agreed to a truce," Alistair said. "And we know his sons pretty well. So I guess we just chill for a couple hours? Check out the other groups?"

"I don't trust this fellow," Delilah said. "Rich people always have an angle. I bet he's gonna try something nasty. No offense, Alistair."

"None taken." Alistair felt his head hurt as he considered what to do. "We're not going to do anything that jeopardizes our partnership or gives Lucius a reason to distrust us. The Northeast Order Freehold's policy is always cooperation first, no matter what. But that doesn't mean that we have to let them into the henhouse. We can run counter-intelligence, you know, that sort of thing."

Caren raised an eyebrow. "Which I would assume falls upon me and my illogical friend?"

William would probably have replied to the quip, but he was busy tapping his ear while he ran some obtuse calculations. A hat covered his face as he lounged on a reclining chair.

"Not just you two, don't worry. Baxter twins, you've stayed off the radar pretty well, correct?" Alistair asked.

"I reckon that's the truth," Josiah said. "Though I can't guarantee it, we haven't shown our true powers to the public."

Josiah and Delilah were size manipulators, capable of growing larger than a house. It was similar to the ability of Jason Evandikis, the giant from Port Locasta. However, the twins had a more defensively minded transformation than Jason's Cthonic ancestry. They had shown off that ability multiple times, so if Lucius had done his due diligence, he would be aware.

However, they had never shown the complement of their gigantism: their ability to shrink down to sizes smaller than a grain of rice. It wasn't just their size that changed—the ability was a truly Heaven-sent genuine minimization of all their various signatures, including Mana, life force, and more. None of the security options in the Yikayok Point Store could detect them from a broad-spectrum analysis.

"I would guess he's going to ask for a meeting. Let's send our entire team," Alistair announced.

"Our whole team?" Fasha raised an eyebrow. "I don't understand."

"To show we have nothing to hide. I want to look them in the face and show them that we are serious and that we're real people."

Alexandra patted him on the shoulder. "Alistair, I know you're a good person and try to see the best in people, but come on, you think that if they were planning to betray us, they'd change their mind just because we all meet them face-to-face and open up our base to show how trusting we are?"

"No, it's not that insane," Caren said. "Studies in psychology indicate that people are less willing to betray those they meet in person compared to a faceless name over the internet. Even if Lucius runs a tight ship, any hesitation in his subordinates is a good thing."

"Exactly," Alistair said. "And if he decides to take our beacon, we're already so far ahead of the other teams. It won't matter much in the long run, since we just have to be in the top two of the group to move on, and it will just prove that Lucius and his crew are traitors who can't be trusted. That would be more beneficial to us than a mere 600 subregions. William, what do you think?"

William responded with a muffled voice. "I think it's fine. I don't want to invest too much of my Dao energy into it. The Dao of Induction is a fickle mistress."

"Good to note," Alistair said. "Jesse, you're exempt. We still need you scouting out the other teams, okay?"

"Sounds good to me, boss. Just making sure, after we finish this Quest, I get to keep all the subregions I earn? And you'll let me come on board your freehold with some serious pull? Like, as executive vice president, some shit like that."

"You'll have a seat on the council, like we discussed. I'm not going to screw you over, I swear it on the Dao." He took out the crystal phone. "Here goes nothing."

———

Jesse Waterfall was free. Totally, completely free. Free to go anywhere in the world. Free to see anything he wanted.

Yet he also knew that was a lie. Nothing was free. The Quests of the Final Frontier Empire were mandatory. The commands of those stronger than you were mandatory. Living was mandatory, if you didn't want to die.

That was why he liked his new boss. He called Alistair "boss," but that's not what it felt like. They had a connection, he could feel that mojo right away. Alistair wanted freedom as well, in his own way. As long as Jesse wasn't a straight-up evil person, Alistair didn't care what Jesse did. And that just made him want to do more good. It was some bloody reverse psychology trick, Jesse thought. Like he would be disappointed in Jesse if he didn't reach his full potential.

He'd scouted out most of the bases already. There were some real powerful folks, so he kept a safe distance. Though, in general, Jesse felt that they weren't that impressive compared to his team.

Each round, the configuration of the bases changed. Even William couldn't see any pattern in the arrangement, leading them to conclude it was random. That meant he had come across some bases several times, and others not at all. Conserving Mana and staying away from discerning eyes meant he could only cover so much of the field.

Jesse checked his jade slip. There were only three bases left he hadn't scouted. Looking up, the monstrosity before him was one of them. It was very large, in between the size of Lucius's and their own. But besides its impressive stature, there was something about it that made him uneasy. Like the feeling people experienced when a predator was stalking them in the wild, even if they couldn't see anything.

The enemy base was a mass of darkness that seemed to absorb light. Any volcanic activity disappeared before it touched the strange material. Jesse had no clue what was going on there, not remembering any material like that available for purchase. The idea that it was a Skill of one of the inhabitants made him shudder. Jesse wasn't necessarily the sharpest tool in the shed, but it was obvious who this base belonged to.

With the activation of his [Flatland] Skill, he squished himself down onto the ground like a pancake, turning two-dimensional. His [Scarlet Flash] was noisy and glaring, unsuitable for stealth operations. A pancake was much better.

No one else had figured out how his Class worked. It had so many disparate abilities, it didn't make sense unless you understood the underlying principle. Jesse still wasn't fully sure of it himself.

Gliding along the igneous rock, Jesse inched closer to the imposing base. Out of the corner of his eye, he spotted someone in the distance. He focused in with his [Eagle Eye]. *Wait a second*, Jesse thought to himself. *It can't be?*

Fearing the worst, Jesse picked up the pace, trying to confirm his suspicions. *Holy shit, holy shit, holy shit.* Jesse knew had discovered something huge. Not wanting to risk any more danger, he closed his eyes and activated [Scarlet Flash].

Nothing happened. He activated it again, but the Mana refused to flow out of his meridians. Two more times, but only fizzles came out. Panic started to set in. Not once in Jesse's entire existence after receiving the Writeship Class had he been unable to escape. Not once was he without freedom.

"That ability is convenient, Admiral."

Jesse snapped out of [Flatland], swiveling to face the sudden interlopers. The one who'd just spoken was a short Asian man with purple, scaly skin around his eyes and black horns. The other was older, perhaps in his 50s, with a vaguely Mediterranean appearance and a naval uniform. But there were two unmistakable features they both shared—their eyes of fire and the glowing red-and-black lines stretching back from those demonic orbs. The markers of a Devil King.

"No one exits my seas without permission," Admiral said. "And you, my little friend, do not have permission. Who are you and what are you doing here?"

"Did you not pay attention to Selene's report?" the draconic man said. "This is Jesse Waterfall, Alistair's errand boy."

"I don't concern myself with the opinions of ants. Do you think he saw our friend?" Admiral asked.

"Of course he did. If we kill him, he's going to talk..."

"Fine. Just come out and say it if you want me to use my Skill, you coward," Admiral said. With a lurching movement, the man pulled on the air, bringing Jesse into his grasp. "This will hurt."

Jesse's last thought before the pain suffused through his entire mind was one of regret. His loyalty was strong, but the torture was stronger.

"Apologies, Alistair. Father is unavailable at the moment," Alfred stated. "In the meantime, you are welcome in our base."

"Unavailable?" Alexandra questioned. "Where is he?"

"I can't get into the details," Alfred said. "He's simply... unavailable."

Alistair shook Alfred's hand. "It's fine. We don't mind, do we, guys? We still have to meet the rest of your team anyway, since we're going to be working together in the future."

Alfred introduced the rest of the squad to Alistair. Since Lucius's freehold, FavorWood Manor, possessed the most territory on the planet, they had over seven subordinates with an excess of 50 subregions. They had lost a few from the previous trial, but it still meant that there were a few trojan horses on other teams. Caren's prodigious archives had proved that the three new additions to Alistair's team weren't Lucius's stooges, but the presence of them on other teams was still a problem, especially since most didn't have the memory of the Chronicler.

Alfred brought them into the base, passing by several of the glyph-covered walls and into the main chambers. A giant eye bore down on them like a celestial judge, seated at the top of their highest tower. Even Alistair felt like his very soul was being scrutinized. Alfred said it was harmless, but he wasn't sure how much he believed his former ally.

The foyer of the base bore many similarities to an old European manor. There were countless balustrades and chandeliers, the space decorated with ornamented tables and glasses and Gauguin paintings. Alistair didn't even understand how they'd obtained all of it, since the store certainly didn't have any luxury housing items.

Waiting to greet them was Bartholomew, whom Alistair already knew.

The Supersoldier's skin and entire body looked to be made of metal, and his life force felt mutated beyond compare. In terms of his power, he had kept up and was ranked #5 in the world.

The last member of the family proper was their cousin Allegra, a Beast Tamer with a menagerie of some of the most powerful avian leviathans—which were failed Beast Lords that attained the strength of their brethren without their intelligence—in the world. She was just outside the top 30, a sign of the decreasing egalitarianism of the leaderboard. Once it had been populated with random people from all over the globe. But over time, as it always did in new systems, power coagulated and economies of scale led to the strongest freeholds having several members in the top 50.

They also had two item-laden members named Sword and Spear, who were clearly brought on as muscle. Their strength came from the obscene amount of wealth poured into their inventories, so Alistair hadn't seen them before in the top 100. The last two members of the team were Ginko, a white-haired man with a ridiculously bountiful life force, and a gorgeous woman named Phoebe. She had black hair and red eyes—Alistair stopped for a moment. Where had he heard that description before?

"Good to see you again, Alistair," the woman cooed, her voice as smooth as honey. "We made a good team, didn't we?"

"Medea?" Alistair asked, eyes wide in surprise.

"Out here, I'm Phoebe," she said. "How have you been? It looks like you've turned Holden into your little pet."

"I wouldn't put it like that," Alistair said. "William and I have a shared goal to win this trial. He's helping us out."

"Don't be so sure about that. I would keep a close eye on that man."

Alistair smirked. "Are you saying that because you really believe it or because you're trying to sow discord amongst my team?"

Phoebe changed the topic. "Touché. I—"

Her voice faded out as Caren communicated a telepathic message. *"Jesse just died."*

"What?" Alistair exclaimed, almost speaking out loud.

"His note is completely unresponsive," Caren explained. *"The communications stop working after a few kilometers, but if the user dies, the note comes back to me."*

"Thanks for the heads up," Alistair transmitted, standing up. "Excuse me, something's come up," he said to Phoebe.

Caren called the team over to a corner, laying out the same facts he told Alistair.

"*What the hell? How is that even possible?*" Alexandra asked. "*He can teleport anywhere.*"

"*If there's a big enough power gap, I think it's possible,*" Josiah said. "*I've seen something similar before. A top 100 ranker stopped a low-level guy from moving with just his Dao.*"

"*I've seen that before, too,*" Alistair said, recalling his first encounter with Anthony, "*but Jesse is powerful. It doesn't seem possible they could just cut him off like that. Maybe he got killed by a sudden attack? There are only a few targets powerful enough to do that. Maybe the Pride Lord or the leader of the other Beast team, Carmen, Pharaoh, the Devil Kings, possibly the leader of the monsters?*"

Caren interrupted with his own realization. "*Since he'll be alive next round, why don't we just ask him?*"

"*Ah. That does make some sense,*" Alistair said, embarrassed he didn't think of that sooner.

"Sorry to interrupt your silent circle," Alfred said, walking over to their team. "But I have some news for you. My father has arrived."

All the candles lighting the room flickered out of existence. The refreshing air current halted to a stop. Nothing moved. Reality itself buckled to one man's arrival. It was only when he opened the door to the base that things righted themselves.

When Alistair met Lucius before, he had been impressed. Even lounging in his hotel room, completely inert, he felt like a shooting star of charisma and magnetism. But it was night and day seeing him in action. He was slightly taller than both his sons and twice as imposing. Even after battling some of the most powerful creatures on the planet and proving his worth against the best Prime Initiates, Alistair felt that it would be a poor idea to cross this man.

"I apologize for my lateness," Lucius said. "I was attending to urgent matters. Alistair, you've taken an interest in gathering additional subregions as well, I see."

Before he could respond, Lucius continued. "Your method seems awfully pedestrian, my friend. Offering help to other teams in exchange for subregions is a fine idea, but you've just touched the surface. Let me show you."

Lucius opened his suit jacket and out fell five different beacons. "I sell them back to the teams at a ninety percent profit margin. There were a few resisters at first, but now they understand the way of things."

Alistair smiled warmly. "And you're not afraid of any backlash? What if those teams find a better option?"

Lucius took the thinly veiled threat in stride. "You think so little of me. I treat those loyal to me with the highest degree of generosity. More than can be said of you, if what I am told is correct."

"What is that you have been told, precisely?" Alistair asked.

"Oh, nothing that you have to be concerned about. We're amongst friends, remember? We're working together. On that note, I have some unfortunate news. I witnessed the Devil Kings kill your companion, Jesse Waterfall. While I was attending to the other teams, I noticed Jesse on Devil King land." Lucius shook his head.

"Damn it," Alistair cursed, trying to do his best acting job. "Well, that sucks. If you wanted to steal our beacon, you could be doing it right now."

Lucius laughed. "You're a funny man. I would never dream of that. Would you like some refreshments before you go?"

They stayed for a little while longer, fraternizing and sharing information. Alistair didn't know if it was his Karmic vision or just a deep, gut feeling, but he didn't trust Lucius. It was unfair, since the man hadn't done anything deserving of suspicion. From the intel he had gathered, FavorWood Manor generally operated without the egregious war crimes of some of the other freeholds, despite being the largest. As an Arbiter of Justice, he refused to attack first, but that didn't mean he couldn't take precautions.

At the start of the next round, Jesse appeared in their bubble, alive and well, but with no recollection of what had happened in the previous round. It wasn't from the death itself, as when William died he'd remembered everything. Any magical traces of what was done to Jesse were gone after the reformation of his body, so they really had nothing to go on except Lucius's alleged sighting of him in Devil King territory.

The next few rounds went without a hitch. None of the other teams in their group were powerful enough to contest them, and none of the teams in Group B wanted to mess with them either. He had seen Pharaoh and Whimsy in the ninth round since they were base neighbors, and Carmen in the tenth, but no fighting broke out between them. At last, they were in the tenth and final round before the extra four games.

The second and more powerful of the Beast Teams awaited.

36 REDWOOD FOREST

"SAME TEAMS?" Alexandra asked as they emerged into the last group round. A notification explained the round's battlefield.

Round Ten:
Battlefield – Redwood Forest
Opponent – Beast Team 2
You have six hours. Begin!

"Yeah, I don't see any reason to switch it up," Alistair said. "Any objections?"

No one said anything, so they started their preparations. Caren put on his paper wings and flew off to the central hub containing the Heart-Render Engine. The Baxter twins and Fasha joined him. Apparently, their job for the last few rounds was just lounging around in the stone lair at the center of the sinuous passages, having not been attacked since the first round.

William took out a futuristic bodysuit and suited up. It was black with gold lines, almost like the engravings on a motherboard, and radiated a sleek, technological aura. Based on the quality, Alistair knew it must have cost a pretty penny.

"That's some neat armor," Alistair remarked.

"Thank you," William said. "I paid a ridiculous amount for it, so it better be effective. They say the second Beast Team is the strongest in our group, you know."

"Because they beat Lucius? I thought it was obvious that they were sandbagging."

"That may be true," William mused. "Though I wonder. There are rumors that Emperor Vritra defeated two Devil Kings at the same time when they threatened his brood."

Dev'rox nudged his shoulder. *Man, it's annoying how corporeal that ghost is getting,* Alistair thought. Ever since he received the Ancient Warrior Leaf, he could only tell the imp was a ghost in direct sunlight.

"Fine," Alistair thought to Dev'rox, "I'll do it." He looked William right in the eye. "Are we good? I feel like we didn't talk about what happened in the last trial at all."

"What's there to talk about? You outwitted me, fair and square." William adjusted his bucket hat so the light of the morning sun reflected off the brim. "A forewarning to all who rely too much on their Skills and not their brains."

"Okay, I was just checking. I don't want there to be bad blood or anything. You're always welcome at the Northeast Freehold. Though I don't want to intrude on your current relationship. You work for someone else, correct?"

William took off his hat, smacking it against the side of his head as if swatting a fly. "They had to replicate the nature too?" He paused, scratching his ear awkwardly. "Sorry about that. Yes, I'm the second-in-command of a man named Gilbert Hornsby. I don't think you two would get along. Since we haven't seen him yet, I have to assume he's in the other group. I'm more than happy to ship my fortune with you lot instead of him. I always take the best offer."

"I suppose it's probably even harder to outsmart you out here in the wild," Alistair speculated. "In the previous trial, it was a controlled environment with a set of specific rules. The more variables you add, the more effective your Skill must be compared to us ignoramuses."

"There are tradeoffs too. It's not all sunshine and roses."

Alistair felt his curiosity overtake his better judgment. "So that story about you killing a grizzly. You just made that up to mess with me, right? I just had to ask, sorry."

"I reckon telling you would ruin the mystery. You're already cool enough to enchant a woman like Medea, so I need something unique of my own. Nice try, though. How about a trade? You tell me how you outsmarted my Skill, and I'll tell you the truth about the grizzly."

Alistair didn't say anything in response.

"I thought so," William said.

As they continued into the forest, the trees only got taller and taller. Their spawn point next to their base was a small clearing just large enough to host the stone castle, surrounded by fifty-meter-tall redwoods. After a couple minutes of walking, the gargantuan sequoias were approaching a hundred meters tall, rivaling the size of the largest on Earth. If Alistair spied further ahead, he could see that they grew even bigger deeper in the forest.

The sheer size of the trees was majestic beyond words. He had seen oceans of blood, a city that stretched across an entire planet, and a tome of infinite wisdom—but it didn't affect him like the forest. The layered canopy of leaves blotted out most of the sunlight, which snuck in through nooks and crannies.

"It's beautiful," Alexandra whispered out loud, forgoing the telepathy for a moment. "My Class is reacting to how strong the nature is. If I stayed here long enough, I think I'd have a Dao breakthrough."

"That would be great," Alistair said. "I really want you to catch up with me."

"Oh, shut up, you stuck-up brat," Alexandra playfully teased. "Before I met you, you were some bookworm college kid who wanted to play hero by punching orcs."

"Great word choice," Dev'rox said to him. "I call you brat all the time. Maybe she picked it up from me."

"Oh, I was a bookworm college kid? You were a Greek billionaire's daughter who did MMA because daddy's money was too boring," Alistair shot back.

Alexandra had her reply locked and loaded, but Alistair turned serious on a dime when his danger sense prickled. His Karma was full since he hadn't needed more than a few points per round, so he slipped into his Karmic vision.

Alistair called out to Jesse through the mental link, but the man was too far away. At least he knew he wasn't dead because Caren would have told them, but Jesse was the bedrock of their strategy. His mission was essential to their success and having no line of communication made Alistair uncomfortable.

"What are you sensing?" Alexandra asked, switching to their telepathic link.

"I don't know. I can't even tell where it's coming from and my Karmic vision isn't showing anything concrete. It's honestly not even helpful, it's just showing a general malaise of bad outcomes."

"That's just great," she communicated. *"Should we go further in?"*

Alistair looked at William, who shrugged. *"It's all the same."*

They slowly trekked deeper into the forest. Nothing changed, except the height of the trees and Alistair's burgeoning alarm from his danger sense. The trees were getting ridiculous in scale, standing over three hundred meters tall with trunks measuring over twenty meters in diameter. Their presence emanated a life force so strong it made Alistair's own feel as small as a mayfly.

"So going over the plan, if we encounter something too—" Alexandra began. She didn't get to finish the end of her sentence, as Alistair kicked her in the chest.

It was pure instinct on his part, Alistair following his **[Fighter's Instinct]** and Karmic vision before the enemy came into sight. Simultaneously, he slipped into the first stage of the Mutra as he jumped to the side. Out of the corner of his eye, he saw a speeding bolt of green fire obliterate the spot where Alexandra once stood, exploding in a mushroom cloud strong enough to melt the hyper-sized sequoias instantly.

Alistair kicked up as their attacker swooped down. The beast was agile enough to dodge his kick in midair, landing in between two trees with a gust of wind.

Alexandra recovered from Alistair's blow, entering **[Barbarian's Fury]** and unleashing her dual-wielding style. He had finally convinced her to whittle down the handles of the daggers so when she expanded them they wouldn't be too thick to handle.

The beast looming before them looked like a Komodo dragon on steroids, with a pair of enormous webbed wings that were almost larger than the beast. Alistair used **[Eyes of Truth]** to gain more information.

Name: N/A
Species: Mutated Komodo Dragon (Leviathan)

Class: N/A
Title: Vritra's Servant
Level: 67

"Me and William will take the other one," Alexandra transmitted. While he didn't see it, he could feel the other beast with his aura sense, a thirty-meter-long two-headed zombie alligator. Both of the leviathans were considerably stronger than his two companions. Alistair wasn't holding out much hope that they could defeat the zombie alligator on their own, so he had to clean up the Komodo dragon fast.

The Komodo dragon hissed and sent out a wave of *nue*, but that trick had lost its novelty a long time ago. Alistair had already reinforced his mental protection with his own psychic defenses. With his increased Wisdom, the energy washed over him like a cold bath.

Alistair held his hands out in open palms as he circled the reptilian beast. Even from ten meters away, he could feel its rancid breath. The fire within its belly shone through the skin, casting the surroundings in an emerald light. The foliage blocked so much sunlight it was almost as dark as night, leaving the internal fire as the only light source.

Every few seconds, the Komodo dragon would roar and whip its mighty tail around faster than Alistair expected of such a bulky creature. Even the redwoods weren't immune to the beast's incredible power, the whiplash taking out chunks of solid wood from the trees. Alistair found it easy enough to react to the tail itself, but the resulting shrapnel and wood splinters flew chaotically, one piece grazing his leg and opening a small wound.

Nervous sweat gathered on his palms as he continued to keep his distance from the dragon. The reptile seemed stronger than the mammalian beasts from the first round, except for the Pride Lord, but the regal lion lacked the *savagery* of his current foe. A lack of higher thought made for a ferocity than no human could match.

Burning positive Karma, Alistair noticed a buildup in the Komodo dragon's throat before it materialized as a glowing light. He dove sideways into a somersault, evading a stream of green fire that destroyed another swath of the forest. The dragon was relentless in its approach, blasting a small but continuous beam of destruction in a circle.

Alistair was forced to use **[Frozen Claw]** and expend a portion of the Ghost Node to freeze the fire before it consumed him whole. The conflagration parted around him like Moses and the Red Sea. While the rest of the plants and trees melted and burned, the surrounding fire turned into a sparkling crystal. He couldn't rest for a second, however, as his danger sense alerted him to the dragon's tail arcing down from above. Alistair refused to back down this time, gathering his composure. A rabid beast was more ferocious than its intelligent counterpart, but less dangerous.

Gathering his Dao energy into a [Force Fist], Alistair manifested the coral apparition around his hand and delivered an uppercut into the beast's tail. The ice crystals from the frozen fire shattered from the impact, creating a shockwave that would have knocked Alistair over if he hadn't already [Dashed] to follow up his attack. As the Komodo dragon went flying via the propulsive power of the fajin, Alistair airwalked up to its tail and grabbed on.

The beast let out a terrible scream that even the trees recoiled from. It flipped over from the impact, flying several meters into the air, but it swiftly recovered with surprising kinesthetic grace. The dragon flapped its overgrown wings, ascending into the air at rapid speeds.

Alistair dug the claws of his **Devilsbane Gauntlets** into its tail, holding on for dear life. It wasn't that he was afraid of falling; he had a high Constitution and **Fall of Fleet** boots that reduced fall damage and hid the sound of his steps. But if he let go, he would be a sitting duck to a fire blast since airwalking didn't work without a first step on solid ground.

"Can you do something?" Alistair asked Dev'rox as he dug his claws in deeper. The beast yelped in pain, a high-pitched scream that threatened to destroy his eardrums.

"You want me to stab this monstrous leviathan like I did with Anthony? That only worked because he was on death's doorstep, and this thing's skin is ten times as thick." Dev'rox laughed, a bit too casually given the situation.

Alistair wanted to climb up the tail to reach the head, but the beast kept flailing its tail so forcefully that he was doing his best just to hang on. The Komodo dragon kept flying up, to the point it had exceeded the height of even the three-hundred-meter-tall trees.

The sight was beautiful. Alistair was wrong about it being morning. It just looked like that because of the small amount of light filtering through the layers on layers of leaves and branches. It was actually midday, with the giant orange sun blistering the tops of the trees. Alistair wished he could have admired it more, catching a glimpse of even taller trees in the distance, but he was a little preoccupied at the moment. The beast used the tiniest bit of its reptilian brain, flexing its tail into full flexion and then let it spring free. One of Alistair's hands came loose as he slid down to the end of the tail.

"Dev'rox! Please!"

The imp sighed and flew to the front of the dragon. Alistair couldn't see what he did exactly, but he felt an outburst of Mana and a brief cry from the beast. Not waiting a second longer, Alistair rapaciously climbed the tail, moving like a cheetah now that it had stopped trying to shake him off. As he neared the head, it began to recover, but that was too late.

He activated [Hand of Karma] with his right hand and [Blood Hand] in his left. The two Skills had nearly identical colors, though the bloody Skill was slightly darker. They meshed together nicely as he plunged them both into the cervical spine of the beast.

[Hand of Karma] made first contact, cutting off threads of Fate and sealing meridians. The [Blood Hand] plunged in wrist deep, pumping his foreign spiritual presence into the beast's system. The Dao energy of his Ghost Node churned as he poured out its reservoir. Alistair channeled the anger of the ghost he was closest to—Dev'rox. The imp's acerbic temperament hid his deeper loathing, Alistair knew. He'd been overlooked, a mere messenger imp for the higher powers of the weakest Hell. *Why couldn't there be more?* he'd wondered as a youthful spawn. *Why did he have to die?*

Like the hardy creature it was, the mutated Komodo dragon refused to die easily. Its beastly life force far exceeded a human of the same strength, allowing it to resist the [Blood Hand]'s parasitic effects. He gained a point of Endurance from {Letting of the Beast}, but it wasn't dying just yet. However, that wasn't the end of the story.

The moment he plunged his Skills into the beast, it fell out of flight, careening toward the ground at a breakneck speed. Alistair wasn't concerned about that, and he prepared to jump off. That was until an explosion kicked him off first.

It came out of nowhere, blindsiding his danger sense and Karmic vision. The dragon let out a massive fireball into the sky, which promptly exploded like a vacuum bomb. The shockwave rattled his internals. The fire would have been a major problem too, if not for his insulating **Mammothskin Raiment.** But the main issue was the air. The thermobaric reaction sucked out all the oxygen. That wouldn't have been a problem because of his

Metabolism leaf, but the Dao energy contained within the blast countered it, causing him to choke.

If he had his wits about him, Alistair would have been embarrassed with the way he grasped his throat for air and flailed about beneath the plummeting Komodo dragon. They were still over four hundred meters in the air, but it only took nine seconds to fall.

He panicked for the first three, desperately trying to breathe. He calmed down after realizing that it would probably abate once he left the radius of the oxygen drainage. That took another two seconds. In the last four, he looked up at the dragon falling above him and thought, *Oh shit.* At the last moment before he hit the ground and the dragon crushed him, Alistair invoked the Ghost Node, pouring its energies through his system. He hoped to the high heavens it would be enough to bypass the twenty-ton beast landing on him.

There had been a couple of shockwaves during the fight, but this one was the loudest and most powerful of them all. A beast of the Komodo dragon's size had certain benefits, like an absurdly strong life force and a resilient body, but there were disadvantages as well. The bigger they were, the harder they fell.

It died instantly upon crashing into the ground. The fire inside its belly escaped, spreading through the undergrowth of the forest. The sight of the corpse was gruesome.

For a few moments after the crash, there was silence. Finally, a human groan pierced the sounds of burning cellulose. Alistair was alive.

Not without injury, as he saw once he borrowed Dev'rox's power to shift himself out from underneath the belly of the beast. He collapsed to the ground, feeling the impact in every cell in his body. The Ghost Node had saved him from the brunt of the impact, but he was still hurting. Dao-based attacks weren't as potent on gigantic beasts because of their immense vitality, which also meant his Dao-based evasion was less effective.

Alistair flopped onto his back, staring up at the thick canopy that blocked the sky. Dev'rox hopped over, conveniently without injury. "I'm touched that you made your attack stronger by thinking of me," the imp said.

"You're my friend," Alistair said through their mental link. "I haven't forgotten about my promise. Don't worry."

"You'd forget your own name before a promise, Alistair. That's what makes your naïveté bearable."

Alistair smiled, though he winced right after, as even the act of pulling his facial muscles was torture. *At least my mental communication is free of pain,* he thought. *Wait. Mental communication?*

He immediately tried contacting Alexandra and William. *"Guys?"*

A groan escaped his lips—to be expected as his injured body was swept up by a strong pair of arms. He looked up at his rescuer's face.

"Alexandra?"

She grinned. "I can't have you saving me all the time. Finally paid one back."

Alexandra carried him a few dozen meters away from the Komodo dragon's carcass. The zombie alligator she and William were fighting had found its deceased brethren. The undead beast had shed its rotting flesh and looked more like a skeleton burning with purple-and-black fire. It went crazy upon seeing the Komodo, bellowing and digging up the ground with its stubby legs.

"Your arm," Alistair thought, looking at Alexandra. Her left arm was burnt with a large bite wound.

"It's fine. I should use **[Healing Current]** on you first. William got lucky."

"Lucky?" William said. "I object. My grizzly bear pelt with this futuristic armor saved me."

Alistair gingerly moved his head to look at William as Alexandra pressed her hands against his body. Over top of his sleek armor, William wore a fur hide that culminated in a bear's head covering his own.

Alistair's suspicious look must have tipped William off.

"I lied about losing the pelt, yes, congratulations on figuring that out. Are we moving on to phase two of the plan?"

37 VRITRA'S FOLLY

ALISTAIR WOULD HAVE CARED MORE about William's lie if he wasn't half in pain and half intoxicated from Alexandra's **[Healing Current]**. Whatever she had done to upgrade **[Healing Touch]**, it felt amazing. It was like he was melting in his mother's delectable egg tarts, his favorite dish of her cooking. Even through the warmth of the medicinal Skill, Alistair felt a wince of pain at the thought of his absent mother.

"He needs some time to recover," Dev'rox said to Alexandra alone, making sure William couldn't hear. "Best get him to safety."

The alligator had stopped stomping on the ground near the Komodo dragon, turning back to the trio with a murderous rage.

"Let's get the fuck out of here." Alexandra roughly hoisted Alistair into a fireman's carry, beckoning William to follow.

As they fled, it became apparent that the alligator was faster than them despite its large frame. The only way they were able to escape was by darting around the massive tree trunks which the alligator couldn't avoid.

Alexandra pushed herself to the limit. She wasn't nearly as fast as Alistair, but she still outsped William. He tripped on a root trying to keep up, forcing her to grab him as well.

Dev'rox chuckled as he observed her with Alistair over her shoulders and William cradled in her arms. Her Strength was more than enough to carry them both—the only difficulty was the size of their bodies compared to hers. Alistair knew she was looking forward to deepening her Barbaric Rage so that she could leverage her Strength at a more conceptual level.

The alligator raged behind her, spewing purple fire in every direction, but it wasn't as powerful as the Komodo dragon's attack. It failed to destroy the trees, so it fell further and further behind. Alexandra let out a sigh of relief upon seeing the familiar mirror on top of their base. They were home.

Right as Alexandra made it to the gate, the alligator popped into view several dozen meters away. Locking its beady eyes on the fleeing humans, it charged with more fury than before, incensed that it had been denied its hunt.

Caren messaged them as the gate flew up. *"You're all good now."*

Reverberating like a huge gong, a laser beam reflected off the mirror and headed straight for the incoming beast. The deep, low hum of the bolt resonated in the air, shaking the surrounding trees. The alligator didn't know what hit it. The blast was too bright to make out any details, the impact of the beam leaving a crater and a smoking beast. Alexandra dropped William on the floor the moment the gate closed behind her before gingerly putting Alistair down.

"It's still alive," Caren relayed. *"Hard to believe anything of this level could be so hardy, but I believe it's severely injured."*

Alexandra got to work pouring her **[Healing Current]** into Alistair. She only had 239 maximum Mana, so the Skill was draining a sizable percentage of her total. On her person, she had a few of Alistair's purified Tier 2 Mana pills, which would last a few more hours before they expired.

With a crack and flash of scarlet light, Jesse teleported next to them. *"Good news everyone. The United Polities are more willing to talk than I thought. Oh shit, is Alistair okay?"*

Alistair gave a thumbs up from his prone position. *"Never better."*

"He'll be fine," Alexandra said as the room slowly shifted. The antechamber creaked and groaned as the Heart-Render Engine fired up, the seams of the passageway glowing with an orange light. The group moved slowly at first, then quickly accelerated, making it to the command room in under a minute.

Caren's paper arm—sticking out his chest—waved at them when they arrived. Fasha joined Alexandra in healing their leader right away. The mousy woman's healing ability worked on a different level than Alexandra's natural therapy, focusing on reversing the entropy and restoring the body to a previous point in time. Combining their Skills created a synergistic effect where they each covered the other's limitations.

The central chamber was small, just large enough to hold the eight of them without feeling cramped. At the center was the Heart-Render Engine, a gold and silver-colored reactor that constantly whirred and gave off excess heat. It was connected to the passageways by sprawling copper pipes inlaid in the stone walls. The only other objects in the circular chamber were a holographic map depicting the labyrinthine layout of their base and a pedestal with three stainless steel buttons.

Alistair sat up as the healing effects tapered off. He was up to around three-fourths of his total 803 Health. Despite the combined efforts of Alexandra and Fasha, his Health wouldn't go beyond his current threshold. There were certain things that only rest and natural recovery could do.

The collision had injured more than just his physical body; when he'd turned into a ghost and the life force-infused body of the Komodo dragon collapsed on him, it had damaged his spiritual pathways. He used **[Carmela's Happy Pies]** on some random bricks, much to the surprise of his teammates.

"Hewps me heal more. De're weally delishous," he said with a stuffed mouth. Realizing that he could just use Caren's telepathy instead, he asked Jesse, *"You're sure about the United Polities?"*

"Yeah, nah," Jesse said. "But I reckon they're fair dinkum about wanting a partnership."

The walls of their base lightly rattled. A loud boom echoed in the distance.

"And the beasts are here," William said.

Alistair had heard from Lucius about the second Beast Team. Vritra was a true monster, having reached level 75 and possessing an actual Dao Node, unlike the other Beast Lords Alistair had fought, including the Pride Lord. However, Vritra was the only actual Beast Lord on his team, the rest being various reptilian leviathans with no more intelligence than an actual lizard. You could only order lizards around to a certain point.

Caren raised his hand and conjured a video feed from outside the base. Alistair noticed a slight tremor coursing down Caren's arm. "Are you okay?" he asked.

"Oh me? I'm fine. This is nothing. I'm just tired and hungry. I need my beauty sleep. An unfortunate consequence of my heightened information processing."

"You want a pie?" Alistair offered. "They're good, I promise. They don't have magical effects for other people, but the flavor is the same."

"I appreciate you being considerate, but my palate is quite specific," Caren said as he turned to monitor the video feed. "Six leviathans are trying to breach our gates. What should we do?"

"Blast 'em to pieces!" Josiah exclaimed.

"That was a rhetorical question, dummy," his sister rejoined.

Caren pressed a button next to the Heart-Render Engine. Alistair felt a large amount of Mana gather behind him. Not even a tenth of a second later, the feed showed a laser beam even larger than the last one explode in the face of a twenty-meter-long king cobra. Caren was relentless, activating the laser cannon again and giving it even more energy to blast an overgrown salamander into the dirt.

"How much juice do we have left?" Alistair asked.

"One more," Caren said. "But I'll pour in my own Mana after that. We shouldn't run out any time soon."

The leviathans were astoundingly dumb. Alistair thought that after the first two were severely injured from the laser, they would try something other than slowly descending on their base. But they couldn't seem to put two and two together. They still seemed mad—based on how their cries could be heard even deep in the base—but not mad enough to all charge at once.

A single laser shot wasn't enough to kill them, but two would do it. Caren finished off the alligator and the cobra. He prepared another beam to end the salamander, but the laser bolt shot up into the sky instead of hitting the mirror and reflecting down. Something had destroyed the mirror.

The remaining four leviathans—the salamander, the turtle, the sauropod skeleton, and the horned lizard—all retreated. One being emerged. Nothing could compare to the size of his subjects, but their leader eclipsed them all in power with ease. Vritra, the Reptile Emperor, had arrived.

Vritra appeared humanoid, scaly and green-skinned, with a tail dragging behind him. His eyes were orange with a vertical slit as a pupil, and he wore plated gold and purple armor. And his life force—his life force was like nothing Alistair had ever felt before. If Alistair was a stalwart oak, Vritra was one of the giant redwoods that populated the forest.

"I do not appreciate your treatment of my kin," he said, his voice clear and resonant. "It is cowardice."

"I'm not sure how he broke the mirror," Caren said. "I'll be analyzing his abilities and relaying that information back to you."

"Uh, one thing," Jesse said sheepishly. "The United Polities want to meet *now*. As in, not after we finish the fight—but *now*, now. And I'm not good enough. They need to see you, Alistair."

"What?" Alistair asked as Vritra calmly walked toward the entrance gate. "Are you serious? What the hell are we supposed to do about the Beast Lord problem?"

"They said it's not their problem," Jesse said, "but no deal is on the table without a face-to-face meeting."

"They're fucking squeezing us," Alexandra muttered. "Waiting until we're up against the strongest team to pull this bullshit on us."

Caren pressed a different button on the pedestal that reformed the mirror, then pressed the first again. He fiddled his fingertips, which glowed with a spiderweb-like blue energy. Alistair assumed he was aiming the laser cannon, and based on the beam that obliterated the salamander in the distance, he was spot on. The newest blast had the most energy yet—Alistair could almost see the Mana exiting Caren's body at hundreds of points.

The salamander tried to evade the ray, but with the Chronicler's added Mana, it flew even faster than before. The resulting red explosion vaporized the poor beast to nothingness. Vritra responded with an ear-splitting cry that shook the foundations of their base and shattered the mirror once more. The three remaining leviathans cried out with their emperor, charging for the castle with renewed rage.

"Alistair, you have to make up your mind now," Caren said.

"Be honest, William, can you seven deal with Vritra?" Alistair asked.

"Probably not. But don't let that hold you up," William said, grinning.

Alistair closed his eyes, breathing in and out gently as he cycled ambient Mana. *Uneasy lies the head that wears a crown*, he thought, quoting Shakespeare's famous line. Sighing, he made up his mind. It was time to trust in his team. Well, most of his team. Drawing deep on the Ghost Node to etherealize himself was as effortless as getting out of bed for him. He just had to specify his intentions beforehand.

"William, good luck. The team will be relying on you," Alistair's ghost said, giving him an encouraging slap on the side of his face. "I believe in you all. I'll be back."

He slipped through the base's walls with ease. In his spiritual form, it would take a similarly strong spiritualist or ghost cultivator to notice him. Luckily, none of the beasts fit that requirement. Perhaps Vritra would have felt something, but the ghost slipped out the back, following Jesse's instructions on where to meet up.

———

"That's our deal," the woman said. "I think it's quite generous, all things considered."

Alistair raised his eyebrows in shock. He had met the United Polities at a lake around ten kilometers south of his base. The woman in charge was Sally Ryder, former Secretary of State and the highest-ranking surviving member of the United States government. He knew there were other officials, but Secretary Ryder's partners all looked like gruff military men, maybe spec ops.

"Are you serious?" Alistair asked. "You're basically annexing my freehold and turning me into a puppet."

"Alistair, that's a tendentious interpretation of the terms," Sally said. "I'd remind you that you are still a US citizen, and technically I'm the President of the United States, by chain of command. I could be ordering you, but I wanted to give you a chance to do the right thing."

"I have no idea what makes you think you have any leverage here," Alistair said, growing more irritated by the second. "Your freehold has just under 1,500 subregions. I'm #2 on the leaderboard. You don't even have any members in the top 100. Let's be real here."

"Busting out the braggadocio," Dev'rox snorted. "Every day, my dearest Alistair strays farther from the gods' light."

Alistair surreptitiously grabbed Dev'rox by the tail and threw him at the ground. The imp phased through the floor and floated back up to Alistair's shoulder. "Nice try."

Sally shook her head. "Richard Atwood would beg to disagree. Proud Navy SEAL—and the #6, as you know."

"He's on your side?" Alistair asked incredulously. Richard was Carmen's partner during the Dragon's Den Island round of Felons vs. Fellows.

"We've talked with him and Carmen," Sally said. "But as for what leverage I have, it's simple. Yes, it's true we aren't the strongest group. I never claimed to be the strongest. But we have eyes and ears everywhere. We have many friends. And I know that you claim to be a champion of justice. How wonderful. That's why I know you're not going to harm us; because we haven't harmed anyone else."

Shit, Alistair thought, *people are onto me*. It was an unfortunate strategic weakness of his—being too nice. He had reaped the benefits of a benevolent public figure many times in the past, but as Sally just proved, there were downsides as well. He had killed quite a few people, but almost always in direct combat fighting for his own life or that of another. "President" Ryder was testing his limits, and he didn't have a good answer.

"You're right. But I still don't need you. There are other people I can work with who won't demand ridiculous conditions. You've wasted my time." Alistair turned to walk away, but he could already see the threads of Fate twirl.

"Wait," Sally said. "You can think over our offer. But in the meantime, do you want to trade some info?"

Alistair smiled. "I think that sounds like a great idea."

———

Caren spat out a mouthful of blood, picking himself up from the trunk of one of the redwoods. His head still spun from the impact. Vritra had thrown him almost a kilometer from their battlefield.

"*I'm still alive*," he told all of his remaining teammates. *Barely*, he thought to himself. His Health was under a hundred and he was running low on Mana. He had almost a thousand maximum Mana, but he was constantly running [Paper Tongue] and [Paper Mind], on top of pumping a ton of energy into the laser blasts.

Fasha was dead. Vritra had targeted her first after realizing she was a healer. He'd used a Skill that let him cut invisible slashes with the swipe of a hand or tail, chopping off her head in one fell swoop.

Josiah and Delilah had snuck behind enemy lines in their miniature forms, growing to the height of the smaller sequoias in a surprise attack. They took out the horned lizard and the turtle while Vritra was distracted dealing with the combined efforts of Alexandra and Jesse.

It didn't last for long. The moment Vritra noticed the two giants, he sent a powerful slash that ended both the healer woman and severed Josiah's legs. She hadn't listened to his command to stay back, instead running outside to help the Maine Brothers.

The rest of the team retreated inside the base. Despite its inscrutable design, there *was* a purpose to the various contraptions and controllable passageways. Caren had each member take up specific positions and prepare for the Emperor of Reptiles. He and William communicated back and forth as they formulated a plan.

Vritra finished off Delilah and breached the entrance to the base. He held up his palm against the gate and sent out a ripple of controlled Mana that shattered it into pieces, striding in nonchalantly like he owned the place. Vritra didn't even bother to have his last leviathan join him, the fossilized dinosaur waiting outside like an obedient dog.

They used every trick in the book. A direct conflict meant death, so Caren employed every guerilla tactic from the past three thousand years.

Vritra was strong, but even he lacked the power to blow up their entire base, which mended itself as long as Caren pumped Mana into the Heart-Render Engine. He activated one of his most secret Skills, **[Resourceful]**, letting him convert Dao energy and *nue* into Mana so he could continue to power the reactor.

Caren would open a hole in the passageway the exact size of one of Jesse's explosive spheres, letting the man attack without fear of retaliation. They baited Vritra into all their traps, such as burning lakes of poison or spiked jaws that collapsed together.

The battle lasted over two hours, but Caren knew they wouldn't succeed. Somehow, Vritra had found the central chamber, defying his or William's predictions. The Beast Lord had grabbed Caren by the neck and thrown him upwards so hard he flew through several tons of stone. Only because of his last-second activation of **[Papyral Armor]** had he managed to survive.

A thought passed through Caren's head as he pulled himself to his feet. His deepest, darkest secret that he had told no one, not even Alistair. Luckily, a message came in from William before he had time to mull over the decision. *"He's here."*

Caren felt Alistair's presence before he saw his leader. Alistair always hid his strength, playing down his power level in front of others. But now, with his teammates in danger, he wasn't holding back anymore. The strength of his aura alone made Caren shudder. His life force was an all-encompassing mass of pulsating blood, his Dao an inviolable truth that refused to bend to anyone or anything.

Alistair moved so fast he disappeared, running into the base in a blur of motion. Not a second later, Vritra shot out of the entrance gate, the impression of a giant fist imprinted on his face. The Beast Lord ricocheted off the forest floor, kicking up dirt until he skidded into the trunk of a redwood.

They had whittled down Vritra to around a third of his total Health, but that didn't mean he was an easy target. In fact, that same injured Vritra had killed Jesse and Alexandra without issue once he'd discovered the trick behind the moving chambers.

"I've been looking forward to this!" Vritra cried out, his voice echoing for hundreds of meters. "None of these morsels have been appetizing enough for me!"

"What does he mean by that?" Alistair messaged Caren through [**Paper Tongue**].

"After he kills them, he, uh, eats their bodies," Caren forced out, trying to suppress the memory.

"And they're all dead?"

Caren could feel the anger bubbling from Alistair's mind. *"William is alive, but severely injured. The others are dead."*

"Thanks."

Caren was perhaps seventy meters away from the two powerhouses, but their radiant auras made them feel much closer. Alistair's aura shone auric and crimson, a fusion of bubbling blood and golden justice. Vritra's felt like the sharp edge of a primal hunter, ancient and deadly.

Their exchange didn't last long. Alistair made the first move, phasing through the reptile in a blur. He took advantage of Vritra's missing left arm, which he'd lost to a trap inside the base.

A backfist imbued with red Karmic energy knocked the Beast Lord over. Not to be denied his own attack, Vritra thrust his arm at Alistair, gathering his Mana and Dao energy in a spiral. Alistair took the blow to the backside, but continued forward anyway, following up with a swipe of his red gloves. Caren's pulse quickened at the sight of the coagulated blood aura. Alistair's talons opened up four gashes across Vritra's face and chest, all pulsating with foreign life force and Dao.

Vritra let out a Beast Lord's roar that nearly stopped Caren's heart. The entire forest seemed to shake from the animalistic furor. But it didn't freeze Alistair as it might have before.

From the skies above, Vritra called down a vast array of metal spikes that blotted out the sun. Caren took shelter underneath one of the trees, waiting for the torrential downpour to end. The spikes covered a circular area with a diameter of over a kilometer, unceasing in their barrage for almost fifteen seconds.

Caren opened his eyes after he heard the last spike thud into the ground. Unable to see over the person-sized nails, he activated **[Origami Wings]** with the last of his Mana. If Alistair had lost, he was done for anyway.

He found them at the center of the field of spikes. Alistair had five impaled through his back, bleeding profusely from his wounds. It was a testament to his Strength that he didn't keel over from the pressure of the titanium rods, each weighing hundreds of pounds. His left side had a nasty wound stretching from his trapezius down to his stomach, but Alistair wasn't the one who'd suffered the worst.

Alistair had torn Vritra in two. He stood in between the vertical halves of the Beast Lord's corpse, feasting on its dwindling life force. Caren wanted to throw up, not typically having the stomach for such violence. If it were anyone other than Alistair, Caren would have flown away and never looked back.

"It's not a pretty sight—I'm sorry. I have this ability that lets me absorb life force by taking their blood essence," Alistair said as Vritra's blood flowed upward into his gauntlets. "I acted too rashly. My temper should never get the best of me. It's just when you told me that…"

"Don't worry about it," Caren said. "I trust you. It's just a bit much for a literal paper pusher like me."

His deeper thoughts wanted to escape, but he reined them in again. The system had a new notice.

Round Ten Complete.

+400 subregions earned. Active Total: 6,256 (3,821 stored)

Congratulations on your victory. The current ten round group stage has been completed. The Pathfinder AI has decided to implement a different ruleset for the next stage of Trial 2.

38 CAPTURE THE BEACON - BATTLE ROYALE

Sharizak, Invisible Planetary Satellite over FX-14752 (Formerly Earth)

Hundreds of miles above the tallest mountains, an enormous satellite orbited the globe. Dozens of times larger than the International Space Station, it was a cylindrical construction comprised of materials costing upwards of hundreds of thousands of Orichalcum drachma.

Entitled Sharizak, it had been loaned by the Pathfinder AI to Mindaugust Kazian Bromas and Annalist Johannis LeoForte, for observational and magisterial purposes. Besides the satellite, they even got a full Pathfinder Herald to sweeten the deal. Premium Tier initiation truly had its perks.

It *should* have been a cushy job that would look great on both of their resumés. Kazian groaned internally. Why couldn't the Emperor have issued his edict just six months later?

"Tell me why I shouldn't rip you to pieces!" An eight-foot-tall man that looked chiseled from marble flexed both his physical and spiritual muscles —and the world obeyed. Miniscule cracks in space emanated from his body in jagged lines.

Just under two dozen representatives of the various factions that had taken roost on FX-14752 stood beside Kazian's table. Visionary cultivators of the Satharvon Clan, Corlyon Company, Clear Water Sect, Flaming Sword Sect, and more looked to him as an arbiter.

The giant man was Io, an elder of the Flaming Sword Sect. Even though the **Soul Splitter** let him project only a portion of his consciousness to Sharizak, Io commanded the Dao with more power than Kazian could muster with his entire being. The gap between Visionary and Profound was that of heaven and earth, Kazian understood.

His vituperative words were aimed at a slight woman, the sole representative of the Satharvon Clan, one of the Eighty-Eight Progenitors. Mishra Satharvon looked upon Io with disgust that only a Progenitor could muster. With the wave of a hand, she knitted the spatial tears back together with jade string.

"War dogs are still dogs. Dare raise your tongue to me once more in that manner and I shall punish you like a dog. I shall hunt you and your bloodline to the ends of the world and back again, and not even a bishopric of the Multiversal Church will be your haven."

Kazian thought that last part was a tad extreme, though he said nothing as the two continued to bicker. Verbal fights were breaking out amongst the cultivators, and he feared they would soon turn physical.

A platinum automaton turned toward Kazian and Johannis, who was quietly letting his partner take the lead. The SHA-909 was a machine of the Corlyon Company, a warrior-research golem shaped in the form of a wooden puppet. Kazian would've been a fool to underestimate it due to its status as an automaton—it was a bonafide Visionary realm in terms of power.

"For what reason did you call us here?" it asked. Even though it spoke only at a medium volume, the Corlyon Company was the most powerful organization fully invested in FX-14752. Everyone listened.

"Excellent question!" Kazian boomed. His deep voice sounded somewhat empty, as he wasn't as aligned with the Dao as the others. "As everyone is surely aware, the beneficent Fell Emperor Dragus Laketor of the Final Frontier Empire, thirteenth of his lineage, has recently issued an imperial edict calling for the 'Crusade Against Usury.' The situation in the Heartlands ripples out to the frontier, and there will be changes."

"Why are these capitalists still allowed on this satellite?" asked a Trexian noblewoman whose family was sponsoring several individuals near the bottom of the top 100. "Their properties are being seized in the Heartlands, yet we allow them to walk freely out here? And the sects too, for that matter. Any who harbors them is as bad as the merchants themselves."

"Lady Telurion, I must humbly remind you that the sanctions are quite precise in nature," Kazian said. "We are not justified in wantonly seizing assets from any corporation or sect. A Grand Imperator should be arriving in a few months to clarify the requirements. But there is a matter more germane to our situation that I called this meeting to address, unrelated to the usury affair."

"What is that?" SHA-909 asked. If automatons showed emotions, Kazian would have said it was relieved to change topics.

"The Pathfinder AI itself has authorized an increase of pace. For [The Game of Life] Trial 2, we will reduce the four planned rounds to a single melee between all the teams." Kazian honestly didn't understand the Pathfinder's reasoning, but he was in no position to judge. The buggy and heavily throttled version of the Pathfinder AI they received could gather its power into a being more powerful than Emperor Dragus, if it so desired.

The crowd murmured about the change, but in the grand scheme of things, it wasn't that consequential. Kazian took a deep breath as he prepared for the real shocker.

"Also in accordance with the increase of pace, Trial 3 will be removed, so [The Game of Life] will end with Capture the Beacon. There will also be a change to the final Quest. Instead of the previously planned [Collation of Skill], the *Pathfinder*"—Kazian emphasized the AI as much as possible—"has decreed [Armageddon] as the sixth Quest."

That was the straw that broke the camel's back.

"You fucking **DARE?**" Io shouted, loud enough to blast some of the empty chairs into the air. "Do you have any idea how much our sect has invested in this world?"

"This is outrageous!" Mishra exclaimed, not as loud as her former shouting partner but with just as much wrath.

The cacophony of indignant cries drowned out everything else. Kazian feared the situation was becoming dangerous. Sooner or later, someone would grow too angry and come to blows. The invocation spell to summon Sylas the Herald was on his lips when someone intervened.

"SILENCE!"

At once, the air inside the satellite grew still. No sound came out of any mouth, and all the representatives froze in their spots. There was only silence. Beginning with the Profound realm, Dao Commands weaved speech and fundamental truth together, but only a full-fledged Visionary could have done something like that.

The Perfect, Sect Leader of the Clear Water Sect, glided gracefully onto the fixed white center table. Kazian knew only vaguely about her, but he was struck by her beauty and poise. It was widely known that all Visionary cultivators had cleansed and purified their physical bodies countless times and imbued their material bodies with their Dao. To mortals, they were all impossibly beautiful and handsome, but there was something special about the Perfect that he wanted to ponder forever.

She was tall and elegant, standing nearly at the same height as Io. She wore a simple white gown that was almost the same color as her skin. Kazian would have said that her Dao Title, the Perfect, which she used as her name, was presumptuous. But seeing her in person relieved that idea right away. Kazian staggered mentally.

The Perfect is here? he thought. *In person?*

It was hard for Kazian to wrap his mind around. The Clear Water Sect weren't big shots by any stretch of the imagination, but for their matriarch to forgo a **Soul Splitter** projection and show up in person? It begged for an explanation.

The Perfect advised her fellow representatives. "If the Pathfinder AI wills it, what can we do but obey? Even Emperor Dragus must often heed its command. While I understand that it might be difficult to accept these changes, it is reality. We must adapt."

The Corlyon representative was the first to speak up following the Dao Command. "I concur with the Perfect."

"It's obvious that you two wouldn't care," said one of the noblewomen from a lesser house. "Pharaoh and Alistair are the two most promising candidates on this world. If [Armageddon] is instantiated, you stand to lose nothing."

While this was Kazian's first real mission after leaving the Mindaugust Academy on Faden Gohm Prime, even he'd been briefed on the various final Quests that the Pathfinder AI could spring on an initiated world. [Collation of Skill] was a participation trophy style event, to put it in FX-14752 terms. No deaths, just like the first two trials of the [The Game of Life]. After a certain point into the initiation process, sponsors much preferred non-lethal Quests.

[Armageddon] was the exact opposite. A full-blown apocalypse between all the factions of the planet, on top of natural disasters. It would forge the small minority of victors into killing machines at the expense of everyone else, which was why most sponsors opposed it so vigorously.

"Your concerns are duly noted, milady," Kazian said, bowing his head. "However, I fear the Perfect is correct. If I fail in my mission, the Pathfinder AI will appoint a new presider, or in a more displeasing circumstance, it might take over outright. The punitive fines would exceed your current investments."

Kazian could see that his words were making inroads on the representatives. However much they hated the idea of [Armageddon], the thought of the Pathfinder personally stepping in was worse. The Satharvon sponsor was the first to speak up following a round of heated discussion.

"Mindaugust, before you spoke of the alterations to the Quests, you mentioned changes rippling from the Heartlands to the frontier. What are those changes?"

Kazian groaned internally, reaching for his platinum puzzle toy. He didn't find it on his person, remembering that he'd left it in his bedchamber. "I think my partner, Johannis, will speak to that matter. Take it away, my dear friend."

———

Capture the Beacon Update:

Instead of an additional four rounds, Trial 2 will end with one battle royale between all teams with non-zero subregions. Your current active total subregions, minus 2,000 that will be added to the prize pool, will be tallied for free Yikayok Points you can use to improve your base for the final round. It is recommended to use all your Yikayok Points, as spending them will not reduce your subregion count.

The goal is to be the last team standing. Teams can lose by having all members eliminated or having their beacon stolen, like in previous rounds. There is no bonus for eliminating teams through either method. The immortality field still applies, so deaths will not be permanent.

The prize pool of subregions is comprised of all collateralized subregions plus an additional 2,000 per team. Current Count: 83,111.

These pooled subregions will be proportioned to the winners as follows, in addition to other benefits:

1st place: 35%, +4 levels, +100 Upgrade Points (not including those gained from leveling)
2nd place: 25%, +3 levels, +50 Upgrade Points
3rd place: 15% +2 levels, +50 Upgrade Points
4th place: 10%, 2 levels, +25 Upgrade Points
5/6th place: 5.0% (each) +1 level, +25 Upgrade Points
7/8th place: 2.5% (each) +1 level
9-16th place: Eliminated with collateral subregions added to the pool.

Trial 2 marks the end of the fifth Quest, [The Game of Life], and will be followed by the sixth Quest directly after its completion.

All subregions won by each team will be returned to the players in proportion to their original percentage of their team's total.

You have [2,128,000] Yikayok Points calculated from an active subregion count of 4,256. You have 24 hours to construct your base, after which the final round will immediately begin. Good luck!

Special Round:
Battlefield – Tropical Island
Opponent – All other teams
Time – 24 hours for construction, 24 hours for round

Instead of sending them back to the lobby for an intermission, the Pathfinder AI teleported them directly to the Tropical Island battlefield. Their stone castle, restored from the damage in the last round, was plopped down on a sandy beach right next to a deep blue ocean.

They could only see a few meters beyond the dimensions of their base, as a black dome blocked off everything else. It looked identical to the dome in Trial 1, except much larger. If it had the same properties, it meant no information could pass through, preventing collusion and attacks before the round started.

Of course, Alexandra wasn't satisfied without testing it herself, giving the dark material a heavy punch. "Just making sure," she said with a smile.

"They're moving things along quickly," Caren noted. "I wonder what's with the change."

"I don't suppose they'll just come out and say it," William said, "so does it matter?"

Fasha nodded. "As my mother says, 'the rice has become porridge.' We just have to keep moving forward."

Caren sighed, rotating one of his floating tomes in front of his face. "Sometimes, I feel like I'm the only one with intellectual curiosity around here."

Alistair allocated two of his free Attribute points to Charisma and one to Constitution. Killing Vritra had bumped him to level 47. It was exciting seeing his level shoot up so quickly. If they won this battle royale, he'd go up to 51 or even higher, depending on how the round went. It was a quantum leap past the level 43 he'd entered Quest 5 as.

The memory of ripping the Beast Lord apart replayed in his head on repeat. It wasn't that he regretted killing Vritra—it wasn't even a permanent death. Alistair really shouldn't have cared, but he did nonetheless. Revenge and justice were two separate concepts. His bloody ghost side embodied something akin to vengeance, but after locking his bloodline evolution on the Akashic Records, it verged on something darker. Absorbing the life force of a bunch of beasts and monsters didn't help, either.

Alistair wasn't worried in the least about going crazy and killing his allies, but adding such dark emotions to his Ghost Node wasn't good. It needed a counterbalance, or it would overwhelm his Dao Path. He could already feel the effects, as his Justice Node shrank by a tiny amount. Not more than 5% but still noticeable.

Ideas rushed through his head. Dev'rox had told him it was a bad idea to add another ghost, but what about improving another aspect of himself?

Perhaps it was time to try and upgrade {Assassin Fist}. He needed an insight to open a third-level leaf. The Kai'tazake Mutra had always calmed him and centered his emotions. If anything, it would be the perfect way to temper his new bloodline.

Alexandra nudged him. "You're supposed to say something."

Alistair snapped back to attention, realizing that everyone was looking at him. His brain caught up to his ears as he recalled the last few seconds of conversation about their plan for the battle royale.

Dev'rox complained in his ear. "Half of the ideas you claim are my ideas. You know, since I can't fight on my own, these sorts of games are my only entertainment. At least giving strategic advice isn't against the Law of the multiverse."

Alistair ignored him. "Here's what we're going to do..."

———

With their two million Yikayok point windfall, they added two more laser cannons and upgraded the first to be even faster and deadlier. They reinforced the mirror so that it wouldn't break so easily. The stone bricks were enchanted with glyphs like Lucius's base, and they added more booby traps and illusions to the passageways. The central hub also received a defensive upgrade.

But overall, they stuck to the general schematics of their old base. Caren requested an altar and some spikes and pipe conduits he said were necessary for one of his paper Skills, but that was the only major change.

Well, except for the location and protection of the beacon. At the last second, Alistair had Dev'rox surreptitiously alter the location of the beacon. You could never be too careful.

The day of construction went by in a flash. They had prepared as well as they could. Now it was time to see the fruits of their labor.

The final round started off with a blast.

39 AN UNEXPECTED REUNION

A<small>LISTAIR WONDERED</small> how the special round would play out. It was twenty-four hours, but there weren't any bonuses for eliminating the other teams. Why wouldn't teams just wait until the last second? He assumed the Pathfinder AI had something up its sleeve so the game wouldn't end in a tie, but Alistair wouldn't have to wait for that. Another team made the first move.

There were only sixteen teams in the battle royale compared to twenty-two in the group stage since six teams were eliminated for having no points. But that still left fifteen other teams to contend with. Most of them were weak, but the battlefield would be cluttered.

After the round began and the black dome disappeared, they could see their surroundings. The whole tropical island was flat and without vegetation, save for an enormous palm tree at the center. The tree was several kilometers tall, dwarfing even the tallest redwoods from the last round's forest, though it wasn't as thick.

The bases were arranged in a circle along the shore of the island, each around a kilometer from its neighbors. Doing some basic geometry, that meant each opposite base pair was around five kilometers apart, though it was impossible to see them with the palm tree in the way.

Nonetheless, the visibility was good enough that each team could make out every other base except the one directly opposite their own. Despite this limitation, Alistair's team quickly learned who owned the base opposite them. Only one group could so thoroughly brutalize its neighbor, the base across the island to Alistair's right: the Devil Kings.

The fort the Devil Kings attacked belonged to one of the weaker groups, so it couldn't put up as much of a fight, but the carnage was still ridiculous. The Devil Kings clearly didn't believe in half-measures. A massive tsunami erupted from the ocean, flooding the red castle. Not a second later, a missile of purple flame charged with more Mana than Alistair's laser cannon rocketed toward the base. It exploded in a cloud of steam and mist. When the plume cleared, nothing remained of the base but a broken foundation.

Ramesh's Team eliminated via loss of team members. Active Subregion Total: 637. New Prize Pool: 83,748.

Alistair remembered that name belonging to a man who had once been #8, though he had fallen into the low teens over time. His team was clearly one of those with the least subregions—but *still*, to eliminate them that easily? The Devil Kings were not afraid to show off their power and take initiative.

With his enhanced eyesight, he could just barely make out a figure standing on top of the rubble. As Alistair focused his vision, he realized that the man wasn't standing on the remains of the base but floating over it. He ascended even higher into the sky, raising his arms to shoulder height. Alistair could make out that he had black hair, but that wasn't his most discernible feature.

The man was flexing his aura muscles, and he was *much* stronger than Alistair. Alistair was almost five kilometers away from the Devil King, so he felt nothing at first. But gradually, like a frog slowly boiling alive, the aura became impossible to ignore.

Black flames erupted around the Devil King, so hot it warped the air in swirling patterns. It felt like a bottomless pit of eternal fire, marred by the profane energy of demon blood. There was no mistaking it—the conjurer of the black fire was none other than Dragonus, formerly known as Long Junkai and the original #1 at the very beginning of the initiation.

Alistair's heart almost seized up as a powerful presence awoke inside him and hungered for blood. He recognized it right away as his future bloodline. Despite not having evolved his species, it lingered inside his blood essence like a parasite. Dragonus's power, unsurprisingly, reflected that of a black dragon. His blood dragon ghost was responding to its unabashed challenge.

Dragons were solitary creatures. Put two of the same sex together and you were asking for conflict.

"Not now," Alistair said in a hushed tone. "I don't even have you yet."

No one responded to Dragonus's challenge. His black aura receded, and Alistair almost thought the man smirked. As the only one brave enough to take a stand, Dragonus looked down on their cowardice.

At this point in the trial, Alistair knew exactly what each base looked like and whom they belonged to. To the right of the demolished fort was Carmen's runic monstrosity. The base lacked actual walls, forgoing physical protection for magical wards. To the left of her base was another one of the smaller teams. Alistair knew that his former ally—Heracles, real name Samuel Simmons—was on the team. Alistair felt Dragonus turn his attention to their small base.

"Jesse, you ready?" Alistair asked.

"Boss, I don't know about this," Jesse said. "I know you have good intentions, but this just seems suicidal." He shook his head but still held out his arm for Alistair to grab onto.

Alistair grinned and took a hold of him. "We stick to the plan. Plus, I have a reputation to maintain."

Alistair braced himself for the dizzying experience of cutting through space-time. It was entirely different from his [Dash], despite the similarity in appearance when he used the flicker aspect. They were by his base in one instant, and then, in a flash of red light, they appeared by the central tree. Jesse wasted no time teleporting them forward once again.

In less than a second, Alistair found himself a body's length away from the simple dome fortress that Samuel's team called home. After sensing Dragonus's attention, they started climbing out the top to avoid the fate of Ramesh's team.

"Alistair?" Samuel asked. Alistair spotted him as the last man out of the hatch at the apex of the base. He looked nearly identical to his Heracles alias from Trial 1, with bulging muscles and a distinct lack of clothing, the only difference being his dark brown skin. "I can't believe you're here. I thought you were going to fuck us over."

"Never," Alistair promised. "A promise is a promise."

He nodded as a signal to both Dev'rox and Jesse, though the latter was unaware of the former. The imp flew toward the base while Jesse teleported over to the other members of the team and shuttled them away to safety.

In the meantime, Alistair felt a bead of sweat drip down his forehead as he stared down the Devil Kings. Dragonus slowly flew toward him, while the rest of the Devil Kings swarmed out from their haunting castle. The leader of the Devil Kings sprouted wings of black flame, matching the reptilian features on his face that made him look part-dragon. Even his eyes of fire that were typically red, were black.

Alistair could feel the arrogance dripping from their souls. Especially from Dragonus, who seemed to have a permanent smirk plastered on his face. The others weren't much better. There was one other close to Dragonus in strength, an older man wearing a naval uniform. His aura appeared as a blue, watery bloom that felt like the ocean. Alistair assumed he was the one that had summoned the tsunami.

They were arrogant... but they had the power to back it up. Alistair clenched his fists as they joined up with Dragonus at the front. He also identified a man with disheveled brown hair as Jakk, Pharaoh and Whimsy's former companion, based on his aura of purple fire that was identical to the explosion that had killed Saturn. The rest, while strong, felt more like Devil Princes than full-fledged Kings.

Alistair could feel everyone looking at him from their protected vantage points. Pharaoh, Carmen, Brigid, Lucius, the monsters and beasts—they were all interested in seeing the fireworks.

When the group of seven were within twenty meters of their target, they came to a stop. For a heavy moment, no one said anything. Seven against one, it seemed. No chance and no choice. Well, seven against two. Samuel had refused Jesse's offer of escape and stood side-by-side with Alistair.

"Are we going out like Rambo?" Samuel asked, clutching a huge flail in one hand and an oval shield in the other.

"Worst-case scenario," Alistair said. "I'd prefer not to."

"I hope you know what you're doing."

Me too, Alistair thought. He chuckled internally as he saw a notification that one of the Devil Kings was scanning him. He had stopped seeing those after his reputation grew to the point that no one believed it would ever be prudent to perform a scan. Returning it in kind with **[Eyes of Truth]**, Alistair found little actionable information.

Name: Dragonus
Species: Draconic Superhuman I (Partially Evolved) / Devil King
(Stage 1) / Black Dragon Bloodline (Stage Unknown)
Class: Hidden (Lacking Intelligence)
Level: 48
Title: Third Devil King

Name: Admiral
Species: Elemental Superhuman I (Partially Evolved) / Devil King
(Stage 1)
Class: Hidden (Lacking Intelligence)
Level: 47
Title: Fourth Devil King

Name: Jakk
Species: Elemental Superhuman I (Partially Evolved) / Devil King
(Stage 1)
Class: Mutated Pyromancer
Level: 44
Title: Ninth Devil King (Replacement)

Dragonus opened his mouth, his voice projecting across the entire island despite speaking at a normal volume.

"Defy us, and suffer painful death on the outside. Accept your fate, and you shall have a quick end." He spoke without a hint of humor over how ridiculous such an ultimatum sounded.

"What if I said no? How would that go? Would you—" Alistair activated [Dash] mid-sentence, targeting a woman named Naima on the periphery of the Devil King's posse who felt like the weakest among them. He gained a considerable amount of speed from "Good Samaritan," which added 25% to his Agility and Intelligence since he was fighting reprobate evildoers. His attack wasn't the most gallant of moves, but when facing demon-blooded psychopathic killers he didn't concern himself with optics.

Just before he closed the distance, he stopped. It was as if the rules of the universe conspired to prevent him from moving forward. His danger sense alerted him to a gigantic mass above him, and it took all his Strength to unroot himself from the mysterious force and jump backward, evading a huge metal sphere crashing down from above.

The older gentleman, whom **[Eyes of Truth]** identified as Admiral, wagged his finger at Alistair, as if he was admonishing him for even daring to try such a bold attack. The tall man named Gideon next to Naima pulled back his arm and the metal sphere retreated above and behind his body, where it floated menacingly.

Next, all hell broke loose.

Dragonus and Jakk struck together. The former breathed fire out of his mouth like a true dragon, while the latter just snapped his fingers and summoned flames with his hands. Their twin inferno of black and purple flame braided together in the air, warping reality with the combined power of two different Dao Nodes. One channeled wanton destruction while the other embodied burning torture.

At the same time, Alistair glimpsed Admiral grasp at the air out of the corner of his eye. Immediately, everything around him reflected an eternal Dao dead set on rooting him in place. He was already trapped in Admiral's Dao field.

Gideon thrust his metal sphere high into the air, far above the enormous spiral of Dao-infused fire, charting an arc straight at him. The other two Devil Princes probably attacked him as well, but with everything else going on, Alistair didn't notice.

If Dev'rox was there, he might have freed Alistair easily. But without his ghostly companion, he was forced to expend a portion of his Fist Node to resist the hold.

Alistair activated **[Frozen Claw]** and poured the Dao of the Ghost into it, employing the "Permanent Haunt" division to both etherealize the incoming fire attack and crystallize it. The former made the latter much more effective.

It was still a full-fledged attack from two Devil Kings. The fire had a mind of its own, surrounding Alistair as it tried to breach his icy defense. He also had to protect Samuel, who tried to help redirect the fire by spinning his flail.

Just have to wait it out a bit longer, Alistair said to himself. *Just a bit longer.*

He returned to the eternal calm of the Kai'tazake Mutra. No matter what stress was in his life or how difficult things became, his meditative trance conquered all. There was no time to waste. He plunged directly into the third stage. Time slowed to a halt as he looked inward, picturing the vision as clearly as if it were literally in front of him.

The ocean that calmed him and centered his fists and mind. The knives that represented an infinite arsenal of choices, a style of unlimited moves that flowed like water. The kiss of death, the finality that waited at the end of all things. But could he go deeper?

Returning to the real world, Alistair broke through the Admiral's movement restriction with ease. You could not stop the style of Zenaitsu Morogoni. It was uncontainable creation in martial form. For the first time, he used two of his Dao Nodes in the same Skill, activating [Frozen Claw] with both Fist and Ghost.

Alistair thrust sideways with his **Devilsbane Gauntlets**, using [Eyes of Truth] and [Fighter's Instinct] to identify the weakest point of the encircling blaze. He moved like a ghost, cleaving the flames in two and freezing them. His punch was so precise it carved a tunnel exactly his size through the flames, ice cascading through each weak point in the fire until [Frozen Claw] had spread like a ripple in water.

The metal sphere was a mere child's toy. It tried to intercept him as he turned, but the ice caught it in midair, covering it in hoarfrost and then an ice crystal. Gideon could likely free it, but it would take time. Time that he couldn't use to attack Samuel, who had wisely followed after Alistair intercepted the flames.

Alistair moved without thought, activating [Dash]. He aimed for the two Devil Kings on the outside of their formation. Without a doubt, one of the stronger Devil Kings could have lifted a finger to defend their brethren, but instead, they focused on taking out his companion. Admiral even forced them away from the main group with a twitch of a finger, leaving the two Devil Princes unprotected.

With 17 of his 25 Upgrade Points, Alistair finished off the requirement to upgrade [Blood Hand] to Tier 2 and activated it in the same stroke. The Skill was no more powerful, but Alistair could feel that it would let him absorb life force far better. Two swipes were all it took to immobilize his targets, striking at their femoral arteries.

The Purification leaf of the Blood of the Devil Tree let Alistair take in the demonic blood. His bloodline evolution was less than a hundred points of blood essence away. After tossing the bodies aside and evading a few more streams of fire from Jakk, he took in the situation.

Just as he had hoped, Samuel was not left out to dry. While Dragonus sat back and enjoyed the show, Jakk went wild, propelling himself forward with jets of purple flames from his palms and soles and charging at the muscular man. It would have worked if not for the red flash of light that stopped Jakk in his tracks.

Jesse had returned, and he came with backup.

Brigid Mwangi stopped Jakk with her enormous meat cleaver, the collision ringing as flesh met metal. The upstart Devil King was surprised by the sudden appearance of the Kenyan woman who stood at #4 on the leaderboard.

As Jakk scrambled to his feet, Brigid threw a glittering tomato in the air and smashed it with her cleaver right at the ground next to him. While he managed to coat himself in a protective casing of fire, the explosion of acidic tomato juice forced him back to the rest of his team.

Jesse wasn't done, coming back with another ally. Alexandra was in full combat mode, her red aura spiking uncontrollably. She looked like a warrior goddess, her long brown hair flowing around her as she dual-wielded her person-sized daggers.

Her eyes widened in shock. "Dad?"

40 TRUE DEPTHS

ALISTAIR SKIDDED AWAY, fending off enormous plant tendrils that sprouted from the ground and deflecting Gideon's metal sphere, which had broken free from its icy prison. He **[Dashed]** back from the Devil Kings and hurried toward his allies.

Jesse wasn't done with his airdrops, bringing over Pharaoh, Whimsy and several people from the United Polities, including Richard. But Alistair wasn't paying attention to that. He was focused on Alexandra, his closest friend and most important partner since the beginning of the initiation.

The boiling red aura of her **[Barbarian's Fury]** faded as she locked eyes with the man known only as Admiral. It was obvious once you pointed it out. His age. The Mediterranean complexion. A naval uniform and powers related to the ocean.

Admiral was Nikolaos Lykaios, the Greek shipping magnate—and Alexandra's father.

"Daughter," he said, his voice carrying across dozens of meters of separation. Dragonus patted his shoulder from behind, flying back to their base along with Naima, the plant manipulator. "It is good to see you again."

"What do you mean, 'it's good to see you?' You're a fucking Devil King. What the hell are you doing?"

Alistair had never seen Alexandra so mad. It was nothing like the times she'd played up her barbarian Class for fun. There was no extraneous rage or emotion, just cold anger. He could feel the pressure she was exerting on her weapons, her fists clenching with 600 points of Strength.

"I don't expect you to understand, Alex. I'm sorry," Admiral said. His words danced like fairies in Alistair's Karmic vision, feeling too good to be true despite sounding contrite.

"I'm sorry? *I'm sorry?* That's—"

Alexandra was cut off by the loud bang of a muzzle blast. Richard Atwood, Carmen's second-in-command, fired at Admiral with a heavily modified SEAL Recon Rifle. He carried the rifle like a pistol, with no need to carefully aim it due to this Sniper Class.

"Miss, they're just trying to get in your head," Richard said after firing his weapon, the smoke still wafting off the muzzle. "Devil Kings can't be reasoned with."

The blue bullet sucked all the light out of the world, striking Admiral three times at three different speeds. The first strike was impossible to see, at least at their level, traveling as fast as a normal sniper rifle bullet. Right before reaching his person, it ground to a halt, scraping against an invisible barrier. All of a sudden, the bullet disappeared, reforming where the rifle's muzzle used to be when Richard fired his gun. The second time, it flew a bit faster than Alistair's [Dash], but with far more weight than the first time around. The bullet streaked through the darkness of its own creation, slamming into Admiral. He slid back a few meters from the sheer force but still stood unharmed.

The other Devil Kings fled the scene, not even trying to help one of their own. Jakk taunted Pharaoh and Whimsy, pulling them away from the current battlefield, while Gideon and Brigid dueled off to the other side.

The final bullet strike was the slowest and the most powerful. After failing to penetrate the Devil King a second time, the bullet returned to its starting location and fired again, this time with a hefty impartment of the Dao. Alistair felt a hint of one of the greater Daos of War within the bullet, similar to how his Fist Node was a specific aspect of War. The Dao mixed with the blue stellar energy that carved light out of darkness, spinning together and adding power.

It moved with the same speed as Alistair's normal running, shimmering through the air. Admiral knew that even he couldn't take the attack head-on, lifting both of his arms above his head. From beneath the ground, ghost ships the size of frigates rose into the air. It was the first time that Alistair encountered someone else that employed ghost cultivation.

The spectral boats were shades of muted green, reminding him of lost shipwrecks. Whatever ghost Alexandra's father was channeling, it was powerful. Alistair thought the bullet felt decently strong, but the barricade of spectral energy stopped it right in its tracks. The spiral of physical metal, Dao energy, and Mana tried to penetrate the ships, but lost all momentum and clattered to the sand below.

Jesse's voice appeared in his head. *"I asked Carmen and Lucius, too. Carmen said that she doesn't trust us enough, even though I gave the same explanation to the others that we all have to band together to defeat the Devil Kings. And even if she did want to help, she said they're being attacked by the monsters. Lucius also told me he wants to help, but he's under attack from the Beast Teams too."*

Alistair spared a brief moment to look back at Lucius's base. The situation was mapped out as thus:

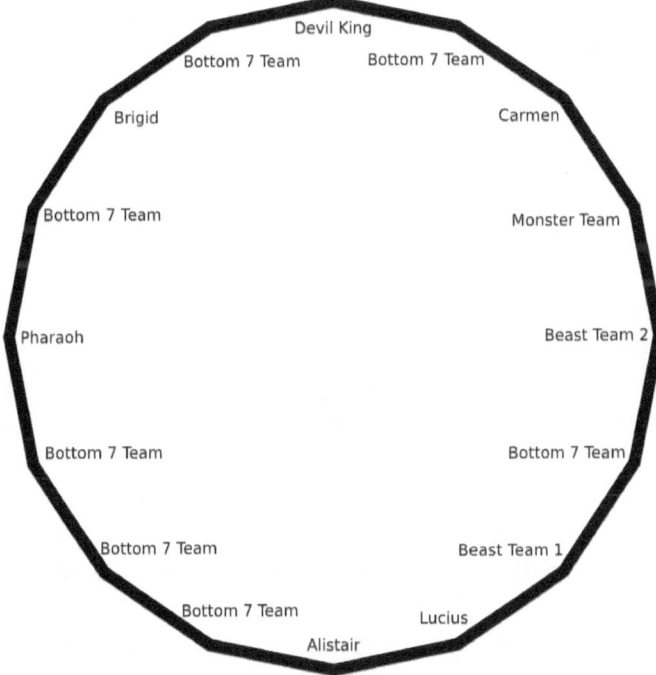

They were neighbors, with Lucius's base to Alistair's right. The big eye on top of Lucius's tower darted from target to target, surveying the entire battlefield. It locked in on a swarm of beasts. The reptiles and mammals had joined together, the Pride Lord and Vritra working in tandem to attack the richest human.

The Beast Lords were unsuccessful so far. Alistair had it on good authority that Lucius ended the tenth round with over 9,000 subregions, meaning he had an additional 3.6 million Yikayok Points after the 2,000 subregion fee. Combined with their initial construction, their current base was a nigh impregnable paragon of security. They'd also added energy shielding and multiple laser cannons manning each palisade and tower. None as powerful as the one Alistair had built at the back of his base, but combined they provided a ton of firepower.

Vritra stood at the front of the army of beasts and leviathans, shredding the incoming laser bolts with swipes of his claws that echoed with metallic sharpness. He roared multiple times, taunting the well-defended inhabitants of Lucius's base. No one dared show their face.

Carmen had her own issues with the Monster Team attacking her, but Alistair couldn't focus on that with the Devil King in front of him.

"You gonna be alright here, boss?" Jesse beamed into his mind. *"Should I get back to the mission?"*

"You're good. We're fine here," he messaged back.

"You think you can take all of us at once, Dad?" Alexandra taunted. "I knew you were arrogant before, but this is a bit much, no?"

Richard adjusted his military uniform, his reticle never leaving his target. It was four against one, but Alistair had never fought with Richard or Samuel before.

Admiral just stood there, content to wait for them to make the first move. After the ghost ships protected him from the Sniper's bullet, they dissipated into thin air. If they thought that would make him an easy target, they were mistaken.

Alistair and Alexandra moved in unison, as he picked her up by the ankle and threw her at her father as hard as he could. Right after, he followed up with a [Dash], overtaking her when she was halfway to their target.

It was a move they had practiced many times before, but Richard wasn't prepared for it. He fired a rubber bullet at the Devil King, which reached its target before Alistair and Alexandra. The bullet exploded and melted at the same time, a tan rubbery liquid spreading all over Admiral. The problem was—it blocked their attack. Alistair got his foot caught in the rubber, slowing his momentum, while Alexandra bounced off the elastic casing and into the sand.

Alistair adapted on the fly, activating [Frozen Claw] on the tan rubber. He pumped a healthy amount of the Ghost Node into the Skill, the hoarfrost rapidly coalescing into crystal. With two layers of sealing, Admiral was trapped, though Alistair felt a strong aura rise within the makeshift prison.

The Devil King would escape in less than a second. Luckily, Richard was already on top of it. The moment he saw Alistair using his icy Skill, he prepared his ultimate attack. Alexandra joined in as well, readying [Armageddon Slash] on both of her daggers.

Like before, Richard's bullet turned the world dark. This time, the projectile was a streak of red light. Nothing could stop the condensed energy, which cut a tiny hole through the ice and rubber—and through Admiral himself. Alistair was shocked at how effective the attack was. Surely it couldn't have been that easy to eliminate Alexandra's father, who was most likely close to Dragonus in power?

A second bullet came out of Richard's muzzle, or maybe it was the same one as before. The red ray retraced itself back into his sniper rifle. What came back out was not a bullet, but a humming, vermilion shooting star.

It was his slowest moving bullet yet, traveling at a leisurely jogging pace, but Alistair could feel it warp the air from the truths contained within. A Stellar Dao representing a supernova that brought certain doom, combined with a Dao of War that embodied the sniper.

"Hold him there as long as you can!" Richard shouted over the crackling of his own bullet.

Alistair nodded, pumping more of the Ghost Node into his [Frozen Claw]. His spiritual network groaned from the strain, unused to channeling so much Dao energy. He added a full-powered [Eyes of Truth] on top, burning positive Karma to discern the exact threads of Fate. He didn't know what, but something was building up inside the Admiral's prison.

While slow, it didn't take long for the meteoric bullet to reach the icy prison. Alistair employed "Permanent Haunt" on just the front of his crystal cage, letting the bullet pass through his Skill and cut into the rubber.

Alistair had the sense that Richard's Skill was messing with some fundamental aspect of reality. He had felt it truly pierce and kill Admiral, yet that thread of Fate had been reversed and somehow put in terms of the physical metric of the bullet. Causality would reorient itself to the previous thread where the projectile truly pierced Admiral's chest, if the second and slower bullet collided with the Devil King.

The threads of Fate unspooled before him as murky mirages, two paths that could occur with equal likelihood.

In the first, Admiral escaped with an explosion of Mana, summoning a ghost ship that captured them in its thrall. In the second, he slipped out of his prison stealthily, using a similar method to Alistair channeling the Ghost Node within himself. After that, he fired a cannonball out of his chest that would explode, killing Samuel and Richard.

Forced to choose between two options, Alistair decided to tackle the second. He jumped up and over the trapped Devil King, activating [**Hand of Karma**]. The Tier 2 Expert Skill warped the air with its crimson aura, cutting off Admiral's positive futures.

Right as the bullet was about to make contact, Alistair activated [**Lightning of Justice**], channeling the Justice Node. It was far stronger than normal. If anyone deserved justice, it was the victims of the Devil Kings. It still wasn't clear how much of their actions were truly done under their own volition, but even if it was just demon blood-induced madness, for the safety of everyone else, they had to be stopped.

All the attacks collided at once. Admiral shattered the rubber and ice with an explosion of aura, conjuring a ghost yacht around him that glimmered with twin Daos of Ghost and Ocean. Lightning billowed down from the sky, illuminating the sandy beach with golden light and weakening the yacht. Torrents of water flowed from the confines of his uniform, far more than it could ever contain naturally. The tidal wave knocked Alexandra off her feet and carried her back, along with Samuel, who had moved behind Alexandra with his flail in tow.

Alistair anticipated the wave, using [**Frozen Claw**] to create a surface for him to stand on. Richard detached two legs from his rifle's stand, staking them into the ground. As the wave of water crashed down, the legs exploded in length until Richard was literally hanging from his own rifle, five meters in the air.

But the flood was only one part of Admiral's Skill. Despite being weakened by [**Lightning of Justice**], the spectral yacht he summoned carried the Devil King into the air before plunging into the newly created ocean with an enormous splash. Alistair insulated himself with another [**Frozen Claw**], creating an air bubble encased with ice. He wasn't sure what happened to the others, since the second wave blocked his vision.

When everything cleared, he cracked open the top of his ice sphere and surveyed the situation. Admiral was at the bow of his green ghost ship, steering it with a look of frenzied madness on his face. His chest was bleeding from where Richard's bullet had hit, but Alistair wasn't counting on it doing much damage.

The water had expanded, engulfing everything in a hundred-meter radius. Despite being able to see beyond the reservoir, for some reason Alistair felt like the water was all there was in the world. A foreign Dao was trying its best to infect his system, whispering truths of Sea and Ghost. The Ghost part was different enough from his own to feel wrong.

Alistair knew what this was. A proto-Domain. Admiral's was larger than Pharaoh's but felt more diluted. He wasn't hemorrhaging Health by the second like he had in the Domain of Lost Sands, but the fact that it consisted of water was a huge inconvenience for the others.

The other problem was that while he was trapped in the proto-Domain, Dev'rox couldn't return. Alistair relied on his imp more than he liked to admit for advice and his space affinity Mana, and now his companion was trapped on the outside, completing the mission Alistair had given him.

He saw Alexandra in the distance, treading water. Richard had miraculously held on to his rifle stand despite the tremendous splash from when the ghost ship fell into the water.

Alistair used his leftover ice to jump-start a [Dash], airwalking over to Alexandra's position. He grabbed her as he ran, taking her by the waist and holding her above the water along his hip with his height advantage.

"Just start running along with me," Alistair told her. It was pretty easy to run on water if you were going fast enough.

Alistair had ceased his [Eyes of Truth] after Admiral attacked, but his low-level Karmic vision still worked in symbiosis with his [Fighter's Instinct] to alert him to danger. In this case, he felt something from the depths below.

It shouldn't have been possible. The flood couldn't possibly have created an ocean with dozens of meters of depth, but anything was possible in a proto-Domain. That didn't explain how Richard was able to anchor himself. Perhaps the legs of his rifle stand grew with the proto-Domain. Alistair didn't understand the rules behind it, and wished not for the first time that Dev'rox was with him.

However the rifle stand worked, Alistair knew that it wouldn't save Richard from whatever was below his feet. Alistair shouted at the Sniper. "Watch out below!"

Richard turned his attention downward, but he moved a second too late. From the unfathomable deep, a ghostly serpent emerged. The size of a blue whale, it was purple and partially translucent, and it hungered for its prey.

———

Carmen wiped sweat off her forehead. They had weathered the attack. She honestly had the worst position out of all the teams, sandwiched between the Devil Kings and the monsters. And then when Alistair pulled his little stunt and engaged the Devil Kings outright, her base got attacked by the original malefactors of humanity.

In some sense, it was tragic how the Pathfinder AI took genetic samples of various species in the empire and bred them into amoral, aggressive psychopaths for the sole purpose of having newly initiated worlds kill them for level ups. But she didn't give a fuck. Those monstrous bastards had killed her brother and mother at the start of the initiation.

Their leader was a brutish ten-foot-tall white orc, identical to the ones responsible for the death of her family. Each monster on the team was a different species, belonging to a separate monster wave. Carmen wouldn't have been surprised if the eight leaders were from the only eight monster waves left on Earth. At this point, there were very few that still existed. The remaining waves were those that had managed to monopolize their region completely, stomping out all competitors with an iron fist. They mostly survived in rural regions relatively untouched by man, where they grew in power at a far faster rate than humans.

Naturally, the monsters were completely uncoordinated, fighting with each other almost as much as they fought with Carmen's team. Only Zak'ryzz, the white orc king, kept them in line with his overwhelming power.

It didn't help that Richard had abandoned them because of the chain of command and the "oath he swore on the United States Constitution." That small-minded hick had too many ideas about honor and loyalty to be an effective number two.

With the monsters attacking them, they had the advantage. Carmen could rain down her [Cross of Lyrical], which had recently become twice as powerful with the First Deepening of her Dao of Magic. She had gone big with her Dao Node, choosing to encompass the entire purview of Magic rather than something specific, like her Thaumaturge Class suggested.

Carmen shot her titanic green crosses through magical rings that amplified their power, crashing them down on the monsters below. Her most trusted assistant, Anika, added her own magic powers, blasting orange slime that tried to burrow its way into any unsuspecting victims.

Their strategy was a resounding success. The monsters tried scaling their runic walls, but the various traps and abilities of her subordinates warded them off while she dealt with Zak'ryzz. They killed four of the monsters quickly with the combination of their abilities before the rest tried to retreat. Except the orc king. He tried to rally his troops, but they weren't listening, so he tried to escape too. Carmen wasn't going to let that happen.

The battle didn't last long. Carmen's Constitution was a pitiful 81. One hit by the orc's wooden staff would turn her into a splatter of blood. It was only a matter of whether Zak'ryzz could outlast her long enough to strike her.

Every cross, [Pillar of Binding], and cantrip damaged Zak'ryzz but didn't kill him. He deflected most of her attacks with his ebony staff, tanking the few that made it through with his tough skin. In retaliation, he chased her like a mad hound, unrelenting in his pursuit. Even when she activated [Flight] and tried to bombard him from above, he slammed his staff into the ground, calling upon the sky to ground her. Zak'ryzz had some kind of Dao that desired straightforward fights, forcing her to stay within a reasonable distance or else she felt a crushing force around her.

Carmen eventually created the pentagram she needed for her Formulaic Skill, [Replica Heavenly Lightning]. Spontaneous clouds parted and an empyrean bolt came down from the Heavens, frying Zak'ryzz to the soul. But Carmen didn't believe it would be enough. The sting of losing to Alistair was still bitter in her mouth.

She activated [Polymorph Swamp Beast] right after bringing down the lightning, charging at her opponent even as the bolt was still active. Her skin ruptured from the inside out, organic vines taking its place. While in the

Swamp Beast form, she channeled a simulated Dao Node—the Dao of Magic replaced by the Dao of Nature.

Her assumption that Zak'ryzz was too tough to go down to the lightning was correct. The orc met her gaze with savage eyes and attacked her with a new frenzy, splitting her head open with a heavy blow right as she polymorphed. If her usage of the Skill had been just a half second later, she would have died instantly. But as it was, her swamp form absorbed the damage.

It took a large chunk of her Health, but she continued forward, wrapping her tendrils around the white orc. "Now!" she called out.

Her entire team attacked at once while also activating their purchased weapons. At the last second, Carmen let go of the orc, compressing her massive swamp form down into a ball of highly dense organic matter.

She braced herself as a deluge of attacks rained down. The orc was fast enough to gather his energy and create a whirlwind with his staff, but there was just too much. Fire, slime, sand, and more overwhelmed his defenses from the front. From the back, Carmen undid her polymorph and charged an extra-large **[Cross of Lyrica]**.

Not even Zak'ryzz's sturdy constitution could handle everything at once. As the green cross caved in his chest, he tried one last attempt. A clone of the orc appeared next to Carmen, mauling her back with its sharp claws. Her assailant didn't live for long, and as the life force of the original faded so did the clone. At last, Zak'ryzz was dead, the last three monsters having secluded themselves in their base.

Anika jumped down from one of their glass towers. "Are you okay?"

"I'm fine," Carmen said as she flopped over on the ground. She popped a Tier 2 Health pill down the hatch. Following the Thaumaturge build manual she'd received as a prize from Felons vs. Fellows, she could purify Health and Mana pills to the point where she could take two in one sitting.

She looked over at the bases on the opposite side. There were three in a row belonging to teams with 0 subregions, having none left after the 2,000 subregion fee. The captains of those teams were all beneath #20 on the leaderboard, most of them having barely hung on in the previous ten rounds.

It was time to put them out of their misery.

Carmen popped a Tier 2 Mana pill as she took to the skies with **[Flight]**. She ignored the fighting going on below, rocketing toward the three opposite bases. Donning magical green armor, she flew inside the first base. It looked like an Eastern-style pagoda, stretching high into the sky but without much girth. She knocked open the gated doors with ease, preparing to blast everyone to smithereens—but there was no one there.

She frantically flew around the entire base, searching every nook and cranny of the pagoda. Nothing. Her aura sense was highly refined and even better than many fighters' danger sense, yet it felt nothing. Not a peep of Mana from any living person.

Frustrated, she flew over to the adjacent fortress, a simple stone castle composed of the lowest quality brown bricks. She needed just one [Cross of Lyrica] to blow open a hole and fly inside. Nothing, once again. She double-checked and triple-checked her aura sense. What the hell was going on?

The third base was empty, too. It defied all logic. She scoured it for several minutes, searching for the beacon, but she couldn't find it either. Carmen slammed her fist against the wall in anger. Whoever had done this was going to pay.

———

Caren used an origami finger to scratch his hair as he viewed the last of Jesse's arrivals. Caren was one of the people who had conceived of the plan, but even he was starting to grow antsy with the sheer number of participants under their protection.

"And that's all 48," Jesse relayed. "I should be going back to help Alistair now."

They had set this idea into motion several rounds ago. Their intelligence had identified nine teams who stood above the rest, those being Alistair, Lucius, Carmen, Brigid, Pharaoh, Beast Team 1, Beast Team 2, Monster Team, and the Devil King Team. That left seven teams who were, in unkind words, the losers of the trial. They weren't weak enough to be eliminated like the bottom six, but they all had less than 3,000 subregions, and most had 0 after the fee. Those were the teams they reached out to.

Lucius had mentioned the United Polities to Alistair before. At the time, they didn't understand why. But now it was obvious. Despite not commanding much physical power, the United Polities had an outsized amount of clout among the weaker freeholds.

It shouldn't have been so surprising. What you did and who you were in your previous life had an impact on your cultivation, affecting stats, Skills,

Classes, and even your Dao. Being the sole inheritor of the United States government, as Secretary Ryder was, came with certain conceptual bonuses that had allowed the United Polities to maintain a global network even before the Soulnet and its update came out. From what Caren understood, they weren't just the American government anymore, having incorporated elements of various countries like Brazil, China, India, and Germany.

Alistair had somehow convinced the weaker teams to work together. That was why his initial move was crucial. William had anticipated that the Devil Kings would attack the weakest teams first. Plans were just plans, and Alistair was the crux. By showing up alone and taking on all the Devil Kings by himself, he had demonstrated to the weaker teams, who had already heard about how well he treated his citizens, that he was the real deal.

Unfortunately for Caren, as the base's main protector, he was the one who had to deal with the logistics of housing 48 cultivators and hiding their beacons somewhere outside their base, so as not to trigger their automatic elimination. Josiah and Delilah were off completing Alistair's secret mission, which only he and Caren were privy to.

"You guys, come with me!" Fasha shouted. The Entropic Healer was a caring woman but knew when to be strict. "No dawdling. If you're over level 38, come with me. Under, you go with William."

Caren felt a cold hand on his shoulder. William St. James awaited him with a false smile. There was something about the gaunt cultivator that always seemed off, like there were a couple screws loose.

"Alfred would like to speak to you."

41 FATHER AND DAUGHTER

THE SERPENT SWALLOWED Richard in one fell swoop, leaping into the air and devouring him and his rifle whole. When it plunged back into the ocean, it simply disappeared upon contact with the water, creating no splash.

At the helm of the ship, Admiral gazed down from his perch on the proto-Domain. The pools of fire that had replaced his eyes were marked with unmistakable disdain and arrogance. To the Devil King, Alistair and his team were mere ants that had encroached upon his territory. To deal with them personally was an insult of the highest order.

Alistair knew that the ghost serpent that had swallowed Richard wasn't the only monstrosity lurking in the deeps. Through **[Ghost Whispers]**, he could feel dozens of spirits just as strong as the sea serpent. He tried hijacking Admiral's connection, but to no avail. Alistair was probably stronger in the Dao of the Ghost, but the Devil King had developed ties to his spirits, just like Alistair had to Dev'rox. They clearly had a different relationship and usage of the Dao of the Ghost, however—Alistair felt no intelligence or higher existence from the savage ghost creatures below.

"*I have an idea,*" Alistair thought to Alexandra through Caren's post-it note telepathy. "*Can you use* **[Armageddon Slash]** *on the water in front of us?*"

"*That's my last charge. It'll be on cooldown for a few hours. It's supposed to be my secret finisher, you know,*" she shot back.

Alistair kept his eyes on Admiral the entire time and focused the rest of his attention below the water. *"Trust me."*

Alexandra evidently did. Even as she was finishing her last sentence, she was already activating the Skill.

Veins bulged all over her arms and hands with the activation of **[Armageddon Slash]**. The Skill seemed similar to Anthony's Time abilities, inherently requiring Dao energy at their level. Mana was simply not powerful enough to alter reality the way the Skill required.

Despite the lack of visual change to **Withering Promise** and **Tang Clan Dirk**, he could feel their weight increase. The poison cloud surrounding her dagger coalesced and hugged the blade, making the metal look violet, while the gleam of the whitesteel knife felt more focused.

Alexandra reactivated **[Barbarian's Fury]** as well. The boiling red aura felt stronger than ever before, fueled by the depths of true anger. Just like how his Justice Node responded to severe injustice, her Skill fed off any actual rage, making both the emotion and the Skill increase in might.

She brought down her weapons with a mighty heave, utilizing all her absurd Strength. Alistair watched in awe as her muscle fibers contracted in unison. The force she generated was greater than even his strongest fajin, albeit much slower.

Alistair activated another **[Frozen Claw]**, giving Alexandra a surface to walk on so she could stop running. Upon reaching the edge, she finished the full arc of her swing, which took more than a second to complete given how heavy her daggers were.

Her Dao energy-infused attack met the proto-Domain's waters, churning up a large wave. But it was smaller than one might have expected. Instead, after crashing down a few meters, Alexandra struck sand. Alistair's theory had been confirmed.

He remembered when he'd fought Pharaoh in his proto-Domain, the way to escape was by countering it with one's own Dao. Alexandra proved this correct, unveiling the reality of the tropical island underneath the nascent ocean.

Alistair kept his **[Frozen Claw]** going, spreading the ice further by draining his prodigious Mana pool and his Ghost Node. In the wake of Alexandra's attack that had split the water in twain, he moved in with his ice to solidify it in place so it wouldn't fall back down on them. It took an additional 50 Mana to do so, bringing him down to 815, not to mention nearly a fifth of his Ghost Node. But it gave them a direct line of sight to Admiral's boat, which had beached itself on the underlying shore that Alexandra's attack uncovered.

Besides the difference in size and oppressiveness, another divergence between Admiral and Pharaoh's proto-Domain was how easily others could use their Dao energy within it. Alistair felt like he could access his nodes and the Mutra if he wanted to. Though it wasn't purely an advantage for the mysterious Egyptian cultivator, as Admiral's proto-Domain hadn't collapsed from the catastrophic damage they'd dealt to its center.

As Alexandra's slash met solid ground, the ghost creatures waiting for them in the deep vanished without a trace. Without the pseudo-physical water of the proto-Domain, they had no existence of their own. Alistair wondered what had happened to Richard, but he was more preoccupied with Alexandra, whose rage had not tempered from before.

Admiral shot a look of disgust at his own daughter. "Stupid girl. You are not worthy to be my heir. Your brain is mush, relying on this fool for everything. That must have been why you dropped out of law school. It was my fault for expecting more from a failure like you."

"He's just trying to get in your head," Alistair told her.

"I know." Alexandra gripped her daggers harder, which Alistair didn't think was possible. Her blood boiled off her skin in a miasma of red steam. "That isn't my father. It's a monster wearing his skin."

They didn't need to share any more words. Alistair smoothly picked up Alexandra, letting her wrap her arms around him like a backpack. He activated **[Dash]**, taking her for a ride that exceeded the sound barrier with the extra Agility from "Good Samaritan."

It took less than a second to reach the ghost ship. Alistair jumped aboard with Alexandra in tow, landing on the spectral decks with a thud. And still, Admiral made no move to stop them. Indeed, he still had a supercilious smirk glued onto his face, as if anything they did was a complete joke.

Alistair activated **[Eyes of Truth]** again. He was down to 45 Karma, still a healthy amount, but he knew he needed to save some for the eventual confrontation with Dragonus. Was he getting ahead of himself? Perhaps, but as he flushed his body with his combat trance, such concerns felt trivial. The Fist Node was assurance of victory. *Fluid, then still. Soft, then hard. The Kiss of Death,* Alistair repeated to himself.

Whenever he drifted into the Mutra, he realized how many extraneous thoughts he had. Responsibilities. Emotions. Desires. All went to the wayside. Even his conviction that he needed to achieve the First Deepening to ameliorate the Blood Dragon's hunger faded, despite it being part of the reason why he dived into the Mutra in the first place.

He was left with pure martiality. Two fists and two elbows and two knees and two legs, plus a hard skull. The second stage of the Mutra held all secrets.

Alistair closed the gap to the Devil King in an instant and delivered a jab with his right hand. Crimson metal barely missed Admiral's cheek, as he swayed to the side just before contact.

That wasn't all; Alistair knew the reason he'd missed was that both of their bodies shifted slightly with the motion of the ghost ship. Now he understood the trade-off of Admiral's proto-Domain. Instead of oppressiveness and deadliness, the Devil King dealt with control and dominion.

Alexandra swooped in from the left, slashing with her poisonous dagger. The violet gas spread around her father, but tendrils of ectoplasm emerged from the buttons of his uniform and swatted it away.

The three of them danced with fist and sword. Alistair unleashed his full arsenal of moves. A backhanded fist to the face, followed up with a flying knee. Alistair didn't know the name to describe it, but his and Alexandra's Daos connected under the purview of War, synergizing and feeding off each other to form a gestalt energy greater than the sum of its parts. He would go for a left hook and Alexandra would be there with a swipe of her dagger.

Yet none of their moves landed. His Fist Node was in complete accordance with his actions, following the Daoist concept of wuwei. Well, Alistair doubted that it was even close to capturing true wuwei, but it worked for his level.

More Karma woefully rushed to his glowing eyes, but his vision couldn't help them achieve victory. His precognition struggled against the confines of the proto-Domain. In his seas, Admiral was sovereign.

Each time a blow would have landed, he shifted at the last second, or the ghost ship would heave in just the right direction. Admiral was clearly an amateur in martial arts, yet they couldn't touch him. His physical stats were high enough that he could evade them with the control of his seas.

Frustrated, Alexandra altered her strategy. Realizing that the environment was the problem, she gathered her newly formed Nature's Attendant Node and activated [Woodland Forest]. From the heels of her combat boots, plants rapidly grew in concentric circles. The ghost ship cracked beneath her as trees, shrubbery, and grass sprouted from nothing, emanating a soothing natural energy.

[Woodland Forest] expanded to a radius of twenty meters, ensnaring Admiral and the entire front deck of the ghost ship. Alistair felt his [Eyes of Truth] adjust, no longer tricked by the control of Fate the Devil King had over his proto-Domain. Alexandra rushed her father, focusing on the nature-aspected part of her Class. Alistair joined her, activating [Dash].

His body stopped short of Admiral, refusing to pass through the invisible barrier even with the power of his Ghost Node. Alexandra's territorial Skill counteracted Admiral's control, but not entirely. But Alistair had expected that, using his Agility of over 600 with the "Good Samaritan" buff to deliver a flurry of punches faster than the eye could see.

With his precise control of causality limited, the Devil King ate some punches to the face, black demon blood leaking from his nose. The **Devilsbane Gauntlets** were more effective against devils, as the name suggested.

The vial he always kept on his person hummed in the presence of its brethren, but Alistair couldn't focus on that. Time slowed down as he unleashed a [Force Fist]. At the same time, Alexandra swung down with [Nature's Revenge].

They were stopped in their tracks when Admiral unleashed all of his aura at once. Alistair saw it coming in his precognition, but the effects were much stronger than what he had seen. The explosion of liquid and mist affinity Mana physically exploded in a cloud of steam, nearly as strong as Dragonus's outburst. The watery aura felt hollow and defiling, reeking of misfortune, but the physical manifestation knocked them back several meters and destroyed the verdant forest.

Admiral drew a cutlass out of thin air, stabbing it into the ground. Ghostly chains shot out from the railings of the ship, wrapping around Alistair and Alexandra. He saw it coming with [Eyes of Truth], but he wasn't positioned to stop it.

Ectoplasmic gasses wafted from the blade, humming with death itself. The variegated spectral energy was hungry for a soul; Alistair could sense it with his ghost cultivation. The Devil King had a spiritual scythe that would sever their very souls. A ghost ship captain straight from the depths of Hell.

He charged at them with renewed fervor, his aura still steaming with unholy energy.

Alistair thrashed at the chains. The Skill was more of a temporary binding than a permanent bondage. Alexandra freed herself by ripping the chains out of the railings, while Alistair used **[Frozen Claw]** on both hands, freezing them so that he could more easily shatter the restraints.

Admiral reacted quickly, stabbing Alexandra in the abdomen. While Alistair's ability to see living souls was not as advanced as his sister's, it was obvious that the ghostly sword was attacking her spiritual network in a similar way to his **[Blood Hand]**. Her cry of pain stirred something deep inside of Alistair as he **[Dashed]** toward his fellow ghost cultivator.

The Devil King was prepared for Alistair's attack, hoisting his daughter up by the sword to give himself room to unveil a cannon of spectral energy from his chest. With his abundance of Mana, a torrent of ghostly water exploded from the cannon, blending the real and unreal.

Alistair didn't care. He was still submerged in the deepest stage of the Mutra despite the small interruption from seeing Alexandra's stabbing. There was something changing inside of him, something that moved his fist forward. His next attack was invoked from the infinite army of knives and confirmed through the red lips of his inner vision.

Fluid, then still. Soft, then hard. The Kiss of Death.

His fist streaked forth with a glowing coral outline. **[Force Fist]** refused to back down under any circumstances. Through the flowing Dao energy of his Fist Node, it took on an almost corporeal form, appearing as the luminescent fist of a real titanic humanoid.

An image formed in Alistair's mind. A colossal man, a World Titan who stood many times larger than the Earth itself. He was the same color as **[Force Fist]**, emanating pure and unblemished martial strength.

The World Titan's planet was being assaulted from the skies. Death rained down from the innumerable score of assault ships. They blotted out the sky, enormous technological abominations of shifting metal. Lasers, fire, gasses of death aura, and unadulterated killing intent came from the boundless satellites.

Trillions of souls cried out for their protector. And he answered.

Zenaitsu Morogoni's attack was so perfect that "punch" could not fully describe its majesty. Where his fist moved, the world crumbled. In one blow, the totality of the enemy's army was annihilated. Alistair felt utter awe as he witnessed the truest display of the Dao of the Fist he could possibly imagine. The fist of a guardian who would stop at nothing to defend those he cared about.

Achievement: Dao Node (I) (Dao of the Fist) — First Deepening.
Improves Kai'tazake Mutra. Reward: +55 Agility, +50 Strength, Upgrades {Assassin Fist} to third-level leaf {Psychopomp's Discipline}.

[Force Fist] tore apart the geyser of ghostly water and slammed into Admiral's body. The fajin felt stronger than ever before, launching the Devil King back like he was a football. When he hit the air above the railing of his ghost ship, he stopped as if by some invisible force, though Alistair could tell he took internal damage from the sudden deceleration.

The spiritual cutlass disappeared from Alexandra's stomach the moment Admiral lost contact with her, reappearing in his hand. Alistair used the short-lived moment to check on Alexandra. She coughed out some Mana and Dao energy in the form of a sparkling gas, but she was alive. The damage to her spiritual network was extensive, however.

Admiral jumped down from the railing, finally taking initiative. With the clench of his left fist, the ship tilted, sending them tumbling off the lowered side. At the same time, the Devil King's right hand grasped the air and pulled.

Alistair felt the world around him restrict. It would be folly to forget they were still in the Devil King's proto-Domain. His command was inviolable, especially since Alistair and Alexandra were off-balance from the sudden shift of the floor beneath them. The duo shot toward Alexandra's father as if pulled by gravity.

Another torrent of water shot out of the cannon from the Devil King's chest, larger than the previous version. The cresting fountain of energy widened into a fat cone, and out egressed a ghost whale, hungering for live prey.

Alistair anticipated this through his [Eyes of Truth], activating [Frozen Claw] in both hands. His Mana was down to 481, but he couldn't worry about that now. Alexandra was still recovering from the spiritual wound, meaning he had to cover for her as well as they zoomed toward Admiral.

The ghost whale grew as the water expanded until its head was over twenty-meters wide. Alistair took the icy tip from one glove of his **Devilsbane Gauntlets** and slammed it into the whale's rostrum. He infused the Dao of the Ghost into himself and Alexandra to partially avoid the force of the impact, but since the incoming object was also immaterial, it wasn't completely effective.

His Health dropped by 199 from the jarring impact, forcing him to cough up blood. But that didn't stop his ghostly ice from cutting into the whale, slicing it in half. While he sliced the cetacean in two with one clawed hand, he dedicated his other **[Frozen Claw]** to freezing the incoming water.

Because the liquid came from every direction, he couldn't crystallize it all, some spraying onto his face and body. The drops of Dao-made water seared him to the bone, frenziedly attacking him on a conceptual level. He was forced to cycle the Justice Node throughout his body in an extremely inefficient manner to guard against the drops of water.

All of that took less than a second, Alistair finding himself just a few meters away from his target. Yet despite not having Dev'rox to help him shoulder the cognitive load, his mental perception was far faster than ever before.

With the First Deepening of his Fist Node, everything about his martial arts had improved. The Mutra felt stronger, and {Psychopomp's Discipline} had a deeper moveset than {Assassin Fist}. Alistair renewed the flow of Karma to **[Eyes of Truth]**, dropping his total to below 30.

The First Deepening strengthened the connection between his Fist and Justice Node, using the idea of a martial guardian as a bridge. The trance, his technique, and Karma felt more merged than ever before.

Alexandra took her poisonous dagger and threw it at her father. The purple cloud mixed with the water as it traveled upstream to the source. Alistair took the chance to duck down, sliding underneath the cannon's stream.

Admiral cut off the surge of water as soon as he realized that the poison was spreading towards him. The dagger shrunk in the air without direct contact with Alexandra, but it was still large enough to deal serious damage while flying at such a high speed. The Devil King used his control of the proto-Domain to shift away from it, but that played right into Alistair's hand.

Alistair anticipated Admiral's destination with precision, sliding to align himself perfectly with that spot. With his right hand, he activated **[Hand of**

Karma], burning another 15 positive points. He balanced it with a [**Blood Hand**] on his left.

This time, Alistair wasn't cheap with his Karma. He allocated enough so that his Karmic Skill could properly fight against Admiral's control of his own proto-Domain.

Right as Alistair made it within a meter of the Devil King, the demon-blooded man pulled out his ultimate trump card. A spectral tower erupted from beneath the deck of the ghost ship. The green frigate crumbled into nonexistence.

Dozens of new spectral boats flew out of the ground and surrounded Admiral. Alistair swung his [**Blood Hand**] to counter the phantom energy, pumping his Ghost Node nearly dry. The Tier 2 Skill boiled with life force, synergizing with the **Devilsbane Gauntlets** that preferred blood affinity Mana. Indeed, every part of his current cultivation was suited for the absolute destruction of the Devil Kings. Admiral's aura stood out even more as a foul debasing of reality from the "Devil May Cry" Badge.

The rising navy battered Alexandra away and rushed through him as well, overwhelming his cycling Justice Node with excess energy. He partially mitigated the damage with his [**Blood Hand**], but he couldn't cover everything. The ghost ships slipped into the gaps in his crimson energy. His Health, Mana, and spiritual network all suffered greatly.

But that didn't stop him. Alistair cut through the final layer of protection, centimeters away from Admiral. The Devil King attempted to flee using his control of the proto-Domain, but Alistair countered with his [**Hand of Karma**].

Alistair thrust his [**Blood Hand**] forward. It was a culmination of everything—his **Devilsbane Gauntlets** wanting to fulfill their name's purpose, {Psychopomp's Discipline} guiding him to victory, and Karma cutting off inopportune threads of Fate.

Yet victory did not come without sacrifice. While Admiral could have taken less damage if he dodged, he instead thrust forward.

A pointed cutlass rammed into Alistair's torso as his [**Blood Hand**] dug into Admiral's shoulder. Purified blood essence and life force surged into Alistair's system as his own blood flowed forth in kind. Alistair knew that with the Devil King's immense aura and life force, along with his ridiculous stats, that there was no way his Skill would kill the man.

As he absorbed Admiral's memories and a tiny sliver of his ghostly power, Alistair used his talon hold on his opponent to keep him still. He slapped [Hand of Karma] onto Admiral's chest, further disrupting his spiritual network and Fate.

Two seconds. Two seconds of pain passed as Admiral increased the soul reap on his sword. Those two seconds were all he needed.

Through the threads of Fate and potential outcomes, Alistair had anticipated *his* return.

Richard clawed his way to the top of the ice walls from when Alexandra had parted the sea, which still held back the water of the proto-Domain. Half his face was chewed off, and his clothes were tattered and bloodied, but he was alive and angry.

Right after Alistair had grabbed onto Admiral, Richard activated his ultimate Skill. The world turned dark as a streak of red light shot through the Devil King's head, Alistair already having ducked down.

The second bullet flashed faster than last time. It contained an even more condensed truth of War and Star, blasting out from the Sniper's vantage point thirty meters away. The shooting star was like a new sun in the dead of night, blazing with actinic brilliance.

Admiral resisted with the force of a raging bull, but Alistair held on for dear life. It was just two seconds. [Blood Hand] and [Hand of Karma] worked to distract him as the supernova made its way to its destination.

Alistair held on even as his Health slipped to 148 from the drain of the spiritual cutlass. It was then that Holy Will of the "Devil May Cry" Badge kicked in. If he had to describe the second wind, it was like a divine energy drink that filled him to the brim with sacred fury. Nothing would break his hold.

The impact of Richard's special bullet took the form of a miniature supernova. Alistair was knocked back into Alexandra, who had fallen to the wayside from the myriad ships battering her. It looked like she had used [Healing Current] on herself, though from what he could tell, it wasn't as effective given the nature of her injuries.

The light of the supernova was still blinding his vision as the phantasmal boats vanished. They fell onto the sand below, unsure of where Admiral had ended up.

Alistair helped Alexandra to her feet. They both had taken serious damage, but hers was worse. She had more Constitution than him, but she lacked his ghost cultivation or Wisdom, both which made him more resistant to the soul reaping attack.

"He's still alive, but barely," Alistair told her, gathering his information from the distinct scent "Devil May Cry" gave all demonic entities.

Alexandra had an unreadable expression on her face. Alistair still wasn't sure how she was dealing with the revelation that her father was a Devil King. "Let's finish this," she replied.

Alistair located Admiral treading water on the reservoir opposite to Richard. The Sniper had collapsed after his last, gargantuan effort, his life force dwindling to a tiny point. The Devil King was slightly better off, though bleeding gallons of black blood from a hole in his forehead.

"Alex," he called out. "I'll see you on the outside. Our Fate shall be determined. So—"

Alistair cut him off with a Dao-empowered [**Lightning of Justice**]. The lightning smote from the skies on the sea of water, electrifying the dying Devil King and bringing his end.

As soon as Admiral died, the water evaporated, disappearing into thin air. The proto-Domain was gone, leaving them on the tropical island exactly where they started. Richard bled out during the collapse, leaving just the two of them.

Or just the four of them. Alistair had never been happier to see a flash of red light.

"Oi boss, you're looking knackered," Jesse said. "I did everything you asked. I'm sure you want an update of the situation."

"Let's get back to the base," Alistair said. "Alexandra needs healing."

A familiar presence perched on his shoulder. "Miss me?" Dev'rox smiled.

42 LUCIUS'S DEAL

PHARAOH DUSTED off soot from his burned chest. Jakk had gotten away.

It should have been an easy battle. The traitorous bastard was weaker than both of them. Yet with his newfound Devil King abilities, he had managed to evade death. Pharaoh's skill set lent itself to protracted victory, focusing on withering enemies down with entropy.

Everything had been going well until Dragonus had struck. From two kilometers away, a bolt of black fire had screeched through the air faster than sound. Not fast enough that they couldn't dodge, but Jakk had distracted them first with a blazing explosion of his own purple fire. Whimsy died on the spot.

When Pharaoh's new body emerged from the sand, he cursed. It had only cost him two of his fourteen lives, but Whimsy was gone. Despite her death not being permanent, it was painful to see his ally incinerated to dust. As her name indicated, her carefree attitude was a good complement to his own taciturn nature.

Jakk had used the opportunity to flee. With fire jets serving as propellant, he'd rocketed back toward the Devil Kings' base. It bore a resemblance to an old Gothic mansion, replete with pointed arches and flying buttresses that served no structural or defensive purpose.

Pharaoh noticed the way it seemed to absorb light. It was an attribute that all important Devil King structures seemed to possess. Costing an obscene amount of Mana, the property blocked all types of energy and communication, making the base a complete black box.

Pharaoh looked to his right. The watery proto-Domain had vanished, dropping off the three figures who'd been trapped inside. If they had killed Admiral, things were looking good for the humans. Behind the scenes, Alistair had organized a human alliance against the Devil Kings, involving himself, Pharaoh, and Brigid. And even though Carmen and Lucius weren't *directly* fighting the abominations, it looked like the Devil Kings had recruited the monsters and beasts to fight them.

But Pharaoh knew all that was subject to change. He didn't believe the Devil Kings would go down so easily. Whatever secret weapon they had, they would show it off soon enough.

———

Jesse used the ultimate version of **[Scarlet Flash]**: **[Scarlet Shift]**. He imbued the Dao of Imagination into the Skill. It had a cooldown of an hour, but it was necessary. If he was just a fraction of a second late, all three of them would be consumed in an inferno of black fire.

From the vantage point atop of his base, Dragonus used the most expensive condenser ring from the Yikayok Point Store to amplify his dragon breath. It had only three uses, so the leader of the Devil Kings was firing his shot early.

Just twenty-five minutes had passed since the beginning of the round. Dragonus had not realized that Jesse could teleport those that he wasn't touching. He had never used that particular Skill in public before for that exact purpose. Now the Devil Kings would wonder if he could use it all the time.

With the increased range of **[Scarlet Shift]**, they teleported directly into their own base. He could use one specific location as an anchor as long as he had personally been there.

"*Fasha!*" Alistair transmitted as soon as they landed. "*Alexandra needs your help.*"

The stone walls of the base shifted, opening a straight passage to the central chamber. Despite his injuries, Alistair picked up Alexandra, carrying her while ignoring her weak protests. The spiritual damage from the cutlass was serious. She was hemorrhaging pieces of her soul every second. Alistair didn't even know if Fasha could heal such a thing.

"Is there anything I can do with my ghost cultivation?" Alistair asked Dev'rox.

The imp shook his head. "You're much too weak to affect living souls."

Alistair left Jesse in the dust, rushing toward their headquarters. Caren opened a door for them. The central chamber had doubled in area, partially to accommodate the newcomers. A few people from the bottom seven teams sat inside, including President Ryder.

Fasha ran over to Alexandra. She placed her hands on Alexandra's chest, her fingers glowing with silver and clear energy redolent of Anthony's aura. It made sense since both of their abilities invoked an aspect of the Dao of Time. Fasha moved her hands down to Alexandra's stomach, where her father had stabbed her. A few seconds passed.

The woman shook her head. "I can't bring her back to full Health. She won't be able to use Dao energy for the rest of the round."

"It's fine," Alexandra wheezed. "We got my dad."

Caren gave Alistair an inquisitive look. Alistair responded with a glance that said, "I'll tell you later."

"You're beat up too," Fasha admonished, patting him on the head. "Come here."

Alistair complied, letting the healer work her magic. He swallowed a Tier 2 Mana pill, bringing his Mana up to 840. It didn't feel so bad at level 47. His improved body could more easily handle pills.

Fasha's entropic healing combined with taking a Tier 2 Health pill restored him to 500 Health. However, he still suffered from the same spiritual effects as Alexandra. Not to the same degree, but his Dao energy usage would be extremely limited going forward.

At least it wasn't like he had a lot left. All three of his Dao Nodes were at around 25% capacity. That part pissed Alistair off. It was a three versus one, and yet he had been forced to use so many resources and still had almost died. And that was against only the fourth most powerful Devil King. Alistair shuddered at the thought of how powerful George was.

But he didn't lose hope. Just the opposite, in fact. He had sworn to himself that he would grow stronger and surpass anyone who would do harm to others. He would live up to the promise. No matter what it cost him, no matter how hard he had to train.

First, he had to deal with an unspoken issue.

William stood in a corner, looking innocent as a dove. Alistair knew better. He had let the betrayal go on in order to trick the man on the other end, but it had gone on long enough.

Alistair walked up to William, who was chatting with a woman from one of the teams that Jesse had shuttled to their base. He swiftly grabbed the man's ear, pinching the small metal object he had been tapping since the beginning of the trial.

"When did Alfred first contact you?" Alistair asked with a stoic expression.

"Before this Quest even started," William said without skipping a beat. "FavorWood heard about my talents and wanted to recruit me."

"And you said yes?" he asked.

The room had realized what was going on. The newcomers all slithered away, leaving only Alistair's teammates watching the confrontation.

"Of course. My potential was languishing where I was. I would have been a fool not to," William said. "But I think you're misunderstanding what happened. I didn't betray you. I betrayed Lucius."

What? Alistair thought. He had seen William tapping his ear way too many times in earlier rounds. At first, it had passed by his attention as a random tic, but it seemed familiar. That was when he'd had his eureka moment. The other person he knew who tapped his ear like that was Alfred.

Alistair wasn't sure exactly how Alfred's Skill operated, so he wasn't expecting anything when he playfully slapped William's face to touch the bug. Yet it had worked. The moment he touched the piece of metallic spyware, he could talk to Alfred directly. From working with Alfred, he knew it only functioned within a certain range and had to be renewed with every new conversation. He and Alfred had exchanged only a few words in the brief time after Alistair grazed the bug.

"You think I'm so dumb that I wouldn't notice you using the Dao of the Ghost again? Of course I knew that you caught on to me and spoke to Alfred. I *let* you do that." William stood up, stretching out his arms. "I've been leading Lucius on since the beginning of this trial. Or at least since the moment I decided to help you over him."

Alistair scratched his head. Dev'rox unhelpfully laughed at his custodian's predicament. Alistair used the minimum amount of positive Karma for an **[Eyes of Truth]**, not willing to go any lower with the threat of the remaining Devil Kings. His Skill said that William was telling the truth. Considering the man's abilities, he didn't know if that was enough to guarantee a lack of falsehood.

"Let's say I believed you. Why?"

"A rising tide lifts all boats," William replied. "I've seen both of you first-hand, you and Lucius. The Brit, he's impressive, for sure. But you have something he doesn't. Something I can't put into words. If Earth is going to survive the Devil Kings and whatever other threats lurk in the future, I want you leading us."

"That doesn't inspire much confidence," Alistair said. "You make it sound like if a better opportunity popped up, you'd jump ship."

"If I lost confidence in your capacity to lead Earth to the promised land, I'd tell you that much." William grinned. "Maybe this will help you believe me. When I gave you the schematics for the base, I added a certain mechanism. The laser cannon and the mirror. Did you ever wonder what would happen if the bolt got sent straight down and into the Heart-Render Engine?"

Alistair looked at Caren, who was silently observing their conversation with his own analytical bent.

"I believe… it would cause our base to explode," Caren realized. "If the energies contained within the Heart-Render Engine were to be violently released by an outside source, it wouldn't fare well for anyone inside." He looked miffed that he hadn't realized that before.

"Precisely. If I intended to betray you, I would have already blown up our base. Lucius believes—arrogantly or correctly, your choice—that even without our team, he can defeat the Devil Kings. Alfred told you about his father's clandestine meeting with the Devil Kings, did he not?"

It was the first thing Alfred had mentioned in the short moment that he'd been able to communicate with Alistair in the last round. While it was unfortunate news, it wasn't completely out of left field.

"I received a message from Alfred shortly after Jesse brought everyone in," Caren said. "What he said would align with William's statements."

"Because I'm telling you the truth," William said. "I bet I could tell you exactly what they're saying in their lofty mansion right now." He affected a posh British accent. "'Daddy, I know you—

———

"—met with the Devil Kings."

Alfred had ordered everyone out except for family. That included his cousin, Allegra the Beast Tamer. Their tacit understanding was that by "family," he meant only his father and brother.

Lucius had constructed the inside of their base to look similar to the family manor back in Surrey. Alfred thought it was a gauche attempt by his father to appear blue-blooded. The Wood patriarch had always been insecure about his lack of pedigree. His own father had been an immigrant who managed to build a multi-million-pound fortune; Lucius turned those millions into billions.

Their meeting room had a marble floor and gold leaf balustrades. The center table was carved out of the finest mahogany wood. All were part of Lucius's unparalleled Skill, [**Audentes Fortuna Iuvat**]—Fortune favors the bold. His rank on the leaderboards being in the 60s was a complete mirage, a total smoke show.

Lucius Wood had a net worth of over *fifty million* Gold drachma. It was so high that his status screen registered it as 500 Platinum drachma instead. With his Skill, powered by the Dao of Money, he could copy the powers of others by burning money, even amplifying their power depending on how much he spent. And with [**Audentes Fortuna Iuvat**], he could freely shape his territory to match his image of wealth.

Alfred's heart rate accelerated. His knees felt wobbly. He had never openly defied his father in such a manner. After a few seconds, Lucius still hadn't responded, so he dared speak again.

"You can't hide that from me. I know you think you're above everyone and everything, but you're not. How could you? The Devil Kings killed Uncle Monty! Have you no decency? Are your wits gone? If Alistair and the rest of the human elite die, there's no way that we could defeat the Devil Kings on our own."

"Are you done?" Lucius's cold words cut deep. "I know I didn't raise my son to be an idiot. Of course I don't want the Devil Kings to be victorious. My plans aren't so simple. Take a look at the current situation."

Lucius snapped his fingers, summoning a spatial visualization of the battlefield. There was a red X over Ramesh's team, Beast Team 1, and the Monster Team.

"While there were a few unforeseen events, like Alistair harboring the six lowest rank teams, the trajectory is quite clear. The Devil Kings are losing ground. Brigid killed Gideon and Alistair and his allies defeated Admiral and two others. The monsters were obliterated by Carmen without suffering any losses, while we finished the mammalian Beast team and did significant damage to the reptilian team."

Lucius took out an **Annalist's Aid** from his inventory. The frosted glass marble started spinning in the palm of his hand, projecting mysterious symbols. After a short surge of speed, the marble settled on a holographic video feed from Lucius's perspective.

It showed his memory of a meeting with Dragonus and Admiral. The Greek shipping magnate had a permanently arrogant expression fixed onto his face, while Dragonus kept darting his eyes back and forth like he was a shifty fence looking out for the cops. Based on visuals alone, Admiral looked like the leader, with his imposing stature and haughty demeanor, commanding the room far more than the short and unassuming Dragonus. That estimation would be a fatal mistake. Alfred could tell that Dragonus's fiery aura surpassed Admiral's through the memory.

"You're a bold human to meet us alone," Admiral stated, his look of superiority extending to even the richest man on Earth.

"And you're late."

"We were dealing with another matter," Dragonus said in a surprisingly conciliatory tone. "What is it that you want?"

"A mutually beneficial deal," Lucius stated.

"We have no need for any deal," Admiral said.

Lucius went on, ignoring Admiral. "George Moulin, the leader of the Devil Kings—there is no doubt that he is the most powerful cultivator native to Earth. He was in the top 10 before being injected with demon blood. I barely noticed Nikolaos Lykaios on the leaderboard before, and now he's clearly one of the highest ranked Devil Kings. If his strength more than tripled, then there's no telling just how strong George is, who must have been the most naturally attuned to the procedure.

"There are a number of paradoxes that seem impossible to solve at first, yet after careful consideration, collapse into an obvious truth. The first paradox is the existence of the Devil Kings themselves. Even to our ignorant eyes, it is obvious you are unholy existences abhorred by the multiverse itself. It is a wonder that Heaven isn't striking you down where you stand. My sponsor mentioned something about 'breaking the Pact,' but was unable to divulge more than that. That leads to the second paradox. With your strength, why haven't you already run over the human settlements? There is something greater at play here."

Through the memory, Alfred could sense his father's anxiety and antici-pation, and how his confidence started to rise after he was allowed to speak uninterrupted. It was a strange feeling to be directly in his father's shoes.

"By the fact that you haven't already killed me, I know you have your own suspicions. I wonder how much George has deigned to tell you. Here's my speculation."

The Lucius from the memory let out a breath of air, ready to drop the bomb. "You're all one giant experiment. A test for the Prime Initiates of this world. That's why you can't be allowed to run rampant too soon. Before we match you in strength. Even if you defeat us, will you really be freed? This is the frontier, but I can't imagine the Emperor wants abominations under Heaven to be public news."

"What do you suggest?" Dragonus asked. Alfred could tell via his father's vision that his words rang true for the Devil King.

"The Satharvon Clan is one of the Eighty-Eight Progenitors. I've already discussed this with them. There's a potential deal on the table. Let us work together. We shed the weaker Devil Kings, the rest of humanity, and the Satharvons would be looking for potential recruits. As Fatewatchers, they excel at hiding inconvenient truths."

"Why should we believe any of this?" For the first time, Admiral lost his proud countenance.

"Do you think I'm stupid enough to lie to a family of cultivators strong enough to erase my bloodline from existence?" Lucius questioned.

Dragonus and Admiral took a minute to talk amongst themselves about Lucius's offer. When they came back, Dragonus sang a more amicable tune.

"We are willing to entertain a deal," he said. "But if you lied to us, you're a dead man."

"Perfect," Lucius said, tossing them a **Crystal Caller**. "This will allow us to talk over great distances. Only you can start the call, however."

The feed of Lucius's memory vanished, and he stored the **Annalist's Aid** back inside his inventory.

"I don't understand," Alfred said, his mind trying to keep up with all the revelations.

"Dream a little bigger, Son. I never dared speak to Lady Mishra about harboring Devil Kings. It's called a bluff. When the Devil Kings called me a few rounds ago, I told them to recruit the monsters and beasts, using the same premise that the Empire is clearly favoring humans. That's why the beasts attacked us almost immediately—they were under their control from the start."

"While I'm inclined to accept that you haven't sold your soul to the devil, none of what you're saying is actually good for us," Alfred said. "Us being humanity."

"Everything I do is for the good of the family, Alfred. Everything," Lucius said. "Blood must be paid in blood. Those two arrogant bastards will pay for killing my brother. You have my word."

Lucius tossed an entire Platinum drachma into the air. Like its gold counterpart, it was half the size of a two pence, but heavier and better crafted too. It too had an engraved ouroboros design, with an inscription reading, "Ad astra per aspera." Struggle leads to the stars. It disappeared midair, burning and melting at the same time into nothingness. Alfred could feel tens of drachma vanish with each second. Lucius was using his money-burning Skills for something big.

"I've already laid the trap for them. It's just a matter of time."

43 THE MAGIC DATE

SEVERAL HOURS PASSED after the initial conflict. Everyone remained holed up their bases, unwilling to risk venturing out with most of the teams still chugging along. Only three teams had been eliminated entirely. Alistair had a feeling that the others were mad at him for harboring those from the bottom seven teams. Since places 9 through 16 had already been eliminated, from their perspective, it was unfair that the weaker teams got a free lunch.

Alistair knew that it wasn't an entirely free lunch, but he couldn't just go out and say it. And it wasn't like they would accept it, anyway. If not for the pressing issue of the Devil Kings, the stronger teams probably would've teamed up against him instead. Though he wouldn't have needed to gather all the United Polities' allies if the Devil Kings didn't exist.

William's loyalties were still suspect, though Alistair believed in his teammate for some arcane reason. He still didn't want to risk any exposure from an actual betrayal, though. It was difficult enough to plan before, but with William as a potential leak, he was at his wit's end. If Caren also had a hidden secret, he was going to break something.

Using William's information and his own reasoning, Alistair had called Lucius to discuss a strategy. According to William, it was a legitimate 50/50 chance as to whether Lucius was working with the Devil Kings in good faith or whether he planned on betraying them. His prediction was that the wealthy Englishman was playing both sides, so he always came out on top, his true allegiance subject to change depending on the situation.

William believed that by his persuading of Alfred to rebel against his father, they'd forced Lucius's hand early, confirming his betrayal before he wanted to commit. Family was paramount to Lucius Wood. Alfred was the disfavored son, but his opinion still mattered.

Alistair was less confident in that assessment. Still, when he contacted Lucius with the **Crystal Caller**, the plan they concocted to defeat the Devil Kings felt secure on both sides.

Natural healing brought his Mana and Health back to full. Even with **[Carmela's Happy Pies]**, his spiritual network wasn't close to fully operational. His focused meditation barely moved the needle on the Dao energy reserves of his three Nodes. Unlike the previous demiplanes that felt disconnected from the Dao, the tropical island battlefield provided a normal connection to the truths of the multiverse—it was just that Alistair couldn't make good use of it at the moment.

"He's moving."

Caren's careful voice interrupted his deep meditation. Despite not being able to replenish his Dao energy, Alistair still focused as he unraveled the First Deepening of his Fist Node.

Dao Elements: Heaven on Earth, System Breaker, Ghost Drive, Samsaric Balancing, Punishment of Evil, Warrior Fist, Deathblow, Untouchable Speed, Kai'tazake Mutra

Since the last time he'd looked at his Dao Elements, there were a few changes. Indefatigable Drive changed to Ghost Drive, while One Against the World vanished. Unlike Heaven on Earth and Kai'tazake Mutra which were tied to his deepenings, those alterations didn't seem to have any effect on his stats.

The Dao Elements were a list of terms that were an attempt to encompass the totality of his Dao Path. Alistair assumed it was Kai'tazake Mutra that he deepened, forming a potential connection with Punishment of Evil and Heaven on Earth. He still couldn't understand how the concept of an unstoppable guardian fist was associated with assassination or a psychopomp—a mythical shepherd that guided souls into the afterlife.

"Where?" Alistair asked, opening his eyes.

"To the palm tree at the center. He's not alone either. There's a young woman with him."

"Intel on the woman?"

"Nil. Nothing in my vast archives. William has no idea either. She's the one the Devil Kings kept in their base while they goaded us with the other seven. Must be important to let her out."

Alistair climbed to the roof of their base, using the hole that William had built in as a secret self-destruction mechanism. William was, of course, no longer allowed to operate the laser cannon.

Sure enough, when Alistair squinted, he could make out Dragonus and a woman wearing a white dress. The Devil Kings' captain was carrying her like a stolen maiden, using massive wings of black fire to fly to the central tree at a leisurely pace.

"Contact the other bases," Alistair told Caren. "I'll get Jesse."

With Josiah and Delilah occupied, Alistair gathered Fasha, Jesse, William, and Alexandra. This time, he couldn't afford to spare anyone but Caren to defend their base. It was less important now that the Devil Kings were down to just four members.

Jesse had to save his remaining Dao energy for **[Scarlet Shift]**, so he took them one-by-one. It didn't matter, since Dragonus was taking his sweet time flying toward the tree, seemingly uninterested in attacking the various arrivals.

That didn't stop Alistair from playing it extremely carefully. Losing one of his teammates to a stray hypersonic fire missile was something he wanted to avoid at all costs. He spotted Pharaoh, Carmen, Brigid, Lucius, and their various teammates heading to the island's center as well. They were slower than Jesse's teleportation, but far faster than Dragonus.

The two other Devil Kings made their presence known. Unlike his and Lucius's teams, who sent out almost everyone, Pharaoh and Carmen had to deal with attacks from Jakk and Naima on their bases, respectively. Alistair also wondered how much of them not bringing more allies was a lack of trust. He had promised to have Jesse teleport them back to their base if Vritra attacked, but they would have to take him on his word for that. The Reptile Emperor was licking his wounds back in his base, one of three survivors from his team, along with the dinosaur fossil and alligator beasts.

Despite his presumed anger at the Mutated Pyromancer for killing Whimsy, Pharaoh forwent his grudge to join the other humans in facing

Dragonus, letting his subordinates and base defenses deal with the replacement Devil King.

When Dragonus got within a hundred meters of the tree, he roared, unleashing his immense draconic aura.

Alistair thought it was sad. While he had never met Long Junkai before his transformation, it was obvious that his black dragon bloodline was both pure and vigorous. After his initial shock at its overwhelming pressure, the draconic aura felt hollow and restrained, lacking the authentic, wild fury of a dragon.

Alistair couldn't imagine how painful that was. To have your Fate subverted, to have your Dao Path irrevocably altered.

While most of the humans flinched from the overwhelming aura, Alistair paid attention to the woman that Dragonus carried. [Eyes of Truth] revealed her to be Selene, a level 40 Mage. Yet despite her mundane readout, he sensed something strange emanating from her. To his aura sense, it looked like she was feeding Mana to Dragonus. While the volume was low—to his best estimate, around three per second—it was a continuous stream. Even with his prodigious Mana pool, he could only keep up such a drain for eight minutes. Had she only started giving her captain Mana now, or was she really the fountain of energy that she appeared to be?

"Stay on your toes," Alistair told his teammates.

"What do you think he's doing?" Fasha asked.

"Do none of you play video games?" William asked. "They must have called it a battle royale for a reason."

"You think there's an item in the tree?" Alistair raised an eyebrow. "Why didn't you say something earlier?"

"It wasn't obvious. If Dragonus hadn't realized it before, then it makes sense that I wouldn't realize it, either. I think he's going to get serious now."

As if responding to William's words, Dragonus raised a palm to the heavens, gathering an immense amount of fire affinity Mana in his palm. A secondary affinity, most likely destruction, joined with the fire, and perhaps a third, though Alistair couldn't tell.

A ball of black flames formed, first the size of a giant beach ball, but it quickly condensed, shrinking down to smaller than a basketball. The dark inferno had the same light-sucking property as the Devil King's base, which had vanished from the stronghold after Selene and Dragonus departed.

With a snap of his fingers, Dragonus set the world ablaze. From his condensed fireball, hundreds of streaks of flame rained down on the forces below.

Alistair jumped in front of his teammates and activated [**Frozen Claw**]. His opponent's strike was purely Mana-based, so Alistair had an easier time enforcing his freezing will with a trickle of the Ghost Node. With his injuries, a trickle was all he could manage.

He jumped into the air, grasping the first incendiary projectile with a frosted **Devilsbane Gauntlet**. The Skill was quick to crystallize the fire, cascading out behind him as it froze the surrounding attacks. The final missile came within half a meter of Fasha, the ice encasing it right in front of her face. Alexandra was there to defend her if his Skill had been too slow.

Many of those from the other teams weren't as lucky. There had been a debate between the other captains about bringing their weaker members. They could be liabilities in combat, but also could offer great benefits in supporting roles. William and Fasha were useless in physical combat, yet keeping them in the base meant leaving a ton of auxiliary capability on the table.

Brigid's team took heavy damage as the Combat Chef couldn't protect her teammates as well as Alistair. The others got to see firsthand the destructive energy of the black fire, which exploded on contact with anything it touched. Brigid pulled out a portobello mushroom from her chef's hat, tossing it in the air. The mushroom expanded in the air, growing to the size of a compact tent. It fell down on the sandy beach and covered most of her teammates under the cap.

Unfortunately, there were three near the periphery who weren't covered by the mushroom. Those who were under the cap weathered the storm. Instead of exploding like before, when the bolts of fire struck the mushroom, they dispersed across its surface.

Those with long-ranged abilities struck back. Carmen created a circle of crosses above her, firing them at the Devil King like a machine gun. Brigid opened her mushroom, taking out a vast array of ingredients. She threw them in the air and chopped them into pieces—mushrooms, onions, tomatoes, beef, and more.

Alistair felt her imbue Dao energy into her attack as a giant metal grater emerged from the sand beneath her. After she finished chopping the produce, she used her cleaver to slap them into the grater, which turned the ingredients into particulates that flew toward Dragonus. The entire process took less than a second and looked mouthwateringly delicious.

Dragonus didn't seem worried at all. He once again conjured an obscene amount of Mana, this time in the palms of his hands. In a twisted mirror of [Frozen Claw], every object he touched incinerated into dust, spreading a flaming web across the barrage of projectiles. After that was done, he kept on flying to the tree without a care in the world.

Alistair wasn't sure what to do. He had obviously seen Dragonus fly in from his base, but he had expected him to land at some point. It hadn't occurred to him that the Devil King could just *keep* flying. That was problematic, since Alistair didn't have any good long-range options.

[Lightning of Justice] had around a fifty-meter range, which wouldn't be enough. Alistair looked at his team.

"Already ahead of you," William said. "Jesse can make Fasha sticky and then you can carry her on your back. You go on ahead; Jesse will take the rest of us."

Fasha grabbed Alistair by the arm. "You better protect me," she whispered into his ear. "My healing is first class."

"Yes, ma'am," Alistair said.

When he had politely asked for his teammates to explain their abilities at the start of the trial, Jesse's Skills seemed almost random. The Australian could teleport, throw explosive energy balls, turn himself two-dimensional, and make other people extremely sticky. It sounded like a fictional character who'd given himself a set of useful abilities.

Alistair wasn't complaining, however, taking the healer woman on his back. With Jesse's adhesion Skill, she was firmly locked on. It would take an immense force for her to become detached—a force that would probably kill her first.

He activated [Dash], bringing the two of them to the foot of the palm tree. The diameter of the date palm tree was over fifteen meters, making it far thicker than any back on Earth. Alistair climbed the tree with ease, using the rectangular chunks of bark as handholds.

Alistair wasn't the only one with that idea—he saw Pharaoh and Brigid doing the same. Carmen and Lucius flew up, the latter using his older son as a lift. The Thaumaturge hovered around the climbers, keeping an eye out for Dragonus.

"You owe me for this one," Carmen grumbled to Alistair.

Dragonus was uninterested in them for the moment. The trunk naturally protected the group of climbing humans. He could have swerved around and tried to assault them. But instead, he leisurely continued forward with his unknown mission. By the time he touched down on the outermost leaf of the palm tree, Alistair had made it halfway up the trunk.

Alistair picked up the pace, climbing as fast as he could. It took another twenty seconds to reach the top. He jumped from leaf to leaf, getting to the top layer.

Just don't look down, Alistair told himself. He hated heights almost as much as he hated spiders and driving over bridges.

Dragonus hopped from leaf to leaf, Selene still in his arms. Unlike a typical date tree, where the fruits congregated in bunches close to the trunk, the fruits hung off the fronds at various intervals. Dragonus seemed to be checking them for something.

The others weren't letting him roam freely. Carmen fired her crosses in fast succession, pumping more Mana into them than usual. Bartholomew Wood sprayed bullets from a futuristic-looking machine gun, and Brigid sent razor-sharp onion slices at their enemy. There were more attackers, too, but Alistair couldn't even see them all with how much Mana flooded the sky.

It left him with another predicament. With all these ranged fighters unleashing their abilities, Alistair had a hard time chipping in. He did his best to move closer to Dragonus while avoiding the ocean of attacks above him. Fasha hopped off his back, the danger growing too high for the healer even with Jesse's sticky Skill.

Dragonus shook off the attacks like they were mere annoyances. A pillar of black fire descended from the sky, giving off an aura of Heavenly heat. It was certainly a false Heaven, as there was no way the thoroughly demonic being could conjure true Heavenly fire down on his enemies. It lacked the punch of Carmen's replica Heavenly tribulation.

The pillar of the false Heavens still possessed genuine power. Attached to his fist, it stretched over ten meters long. Dragonus wielded it with practiced ease, swatting away onions, bullets, sand, and more. If an attack was too big to deflect with the width of the pillar, he would spin it rapidly, forming a false divine mirror that reflected all blows.

All the while, he never stopped checking on the fruits underneath the trees.

Just what is he doing? Alistair thought to himself.

"Wait a second," Dev'rox murmured. "I've seen this before."

"What?"

"Back when I was doing tribulations for the Pathfinder AI, they occasionally had this type of setup. It took me a while to remember since it's been thousands of years. The Pathfinder is a quite lazy bastard, you know, reusing assets like that. One of the fruits on the tree is special."

"Special how?" Alistair asked.

"It's a **Supercharge Drakefruit Date**." Dev'rox shook his head. "It gives a five times Mana boost for a single attack."

Alistair cursed under his breath and relayed the information to his teammates and as many of his human allies as he could. However, the humans had spread out a fair amount as to attack Dragonus from all angles, making it hard to inform everyone. At least Lucius was easy to contact with the **Crystal Caller.**

Alistair made up his mind, activating **[Dash]** and using Dev'rox's space affinity Mana to bridge the distance to Dragonus. Besides spamming **[Lightning of Justice]**, he couldn't do much from afar. As for the incoming attacks from his own allies, he trusted that the Devil King would deal with those. It would force Dragonus to choose between two difficult options. On one hand, he could risk letting his enemies' ranged attacks through and hit them both, or he could waste time and energy blocking them while Alistair attacked him.

It looked like Pharaoh had the same idea. The clothing around the man's torso burned away as he emerged out of a cloud of sand behind Dragonus. The #1 ranker wasn't pulling any punches, immediately releasing his proto-Domain.

A wave of Dao energy passed over everything within a fifteen-meter-radius of Pharaoh. Open air and green leaves turned into a desert—the Dao of Lost Sands. Under the primordial sun's scorching rays, the ancient winds spoke of decay and old curses. Pharaoh's proto-Domain was larger and even stronger than Alistair remembered. He still had more total Dao energy with his single Dao Node, a testament to the purity of Pharaoh's will. He had likely already completed his Second Deepening before their match back in Saturn's château.

The difference was that this time, Pharaoh's enmity was directed at another. Alistair was a foreign element within his Dao, but a tolerated one.

Since he already had difficulty accessing his Dao, the proto-Domain didn't matter as much. Summoning a **[Frozen Claw]** and a **[Blood Hand]**, he charged at Dragonus.

Fire churned underneath Dragonus's skin. In an instant, a layer of black fire as dark as a rural night sky covered his entire body and the woman he carried. It was so dark that it almost looked like an absolute void—the only feature that distinguished it as fire was the flickering of the flames.

Alistair could feel a new Dao coming from the man, different from his previous fire of destructive rage. Like its appearance suggested, it was void. Nothingness and fire combined. It was a more complete version of the void-fire that the Pride Lord had used. Dragonus now wielded twin pillars of fire; one of fire mixed with void and the other mixed with destruction.

Jets of condensed sand and swarms of locusts headed straight for the cloaked Devil King, while Alistair rushed in with his Skills. All disappeared into the void. Alistair brought together his two upgraded Skills, channeling them through his **Devilsbane Gauntlets.**

Perhaps it was the crimson gloves' natural counter to demonic beings, but his attack cut into the voidfire veil, if just barely. Ice affinity Mana and blood affinity Mana worked in tandem as he tried to penetrate the infinite void.

Using Alistair as an anchor, Pharaoh geared up his offensive. The sand surrounding Dragonus suddenly took on an even stronger aura of decay than the rest of the proto-Domain, glowing black and purple. Pharaoh, too, could make his own fire, directing his entropic grit into the small cuts Alistair made.

A pang of alarm from **[Fighter's Instinct]** sent Alistair backpedaling from the Devil King. Without any other warning, the voidfire exploded, washing over Pharaoh's proto-Domain.

Alistair's Karma had recovered to 35, so he felt it safe to expunge 5 points into a **[Hand of Karma]**. At the same time, he activated **[Force Fist]** and punched the sand below him. He didn't want any business with the voidfire.

The **[Hand of Karma]** weakened the proto-Domain's grip on reality, while **[Force Fist]** broke through the sand firmament.

In a stroke of bad fortune, that left Alistair stranded in the air.

The portion of the lost sands he broke through was several meters offset from the leaf he stood on before. He gulped as he prepared for the 2.5-kilometer drop. With his Constitution and Ghost Node, he would be fine, but it would be a huge inconvenience.

"Jesse!" Alistair called out through their mental link. *"I need a little help!"*

As he fell, he looked up at Dragonus, who was rummaging through a cluster of fruits. Pharaoh was nowhere to be seen. A pit of unease formed in his stomach. The wrinkly brown fruit Dragonus held in his hands felt more substantial than the others.

Alistair activated **[Eyes of Truth]** on the date.

Item Name: Supercharge Drakefruit Date

Description: The Supercharge Drakefruit Date is a Legendary rarity item originating from the belly of a once living Profound realm drake-date tree. The Pathfinder AI purified this date to the utmost of its potential. Perfect for a one-time explosion of Mana, the fruit allows for a temporary surge of 5x the user's max Mana, or 5,000 Mana, whichever is lower.

Jesse wrapped his hand around Alistair's arm and teleported him back up to the tree, but it was too late. Dragonus, who'd freely used his Mana thanks to Selene juicing him up like a battery, consumed the date.

44 FAMILY CHAINS

THE EFFECT WAS IMMEDIATE. A surge of excess aura washed over the entire tropical island, making Alistair's hair stand on end.

All who witnessed the power fell silent. Alistair had felt the aura of cultivators who he believed were Visionaries, but they had always been cloaked. This was in the flesh.

Carmen, Bartholomew, Brigid, and their teammates did their best to attack the arising superpower, but to no avail. The power was too much for even Dragonus to fully control. His soulcore struggled to convert all the Mana within the **Supercharge Drakefruit Date** to his affinities, letting it run rampant throughout his meridians.

The pools of black fire that had taken the place of his eyes erupted. The red-and-black lines traveling from his eyes down his back sparked, also emitting an infernal blaze. Dragonfire flew out of his mouth, while the scales around his eyes and hands grew with the influx of energy.

Even if someone unleashed their ultimate Skill, expending all their life force and entire reserves of their Dao Nodes, Alistair doubted it would make it past the inferno. The concentrated Mana burned the very fabric of the physical demiplane. He could see spatial cracks and anomalous optical illusions form at the edges of the fire.

A few seconds after Dragonus finished consuming the Legendary rarity item, he stopped emitting fire. But his flames didn't disappear. Instead, all the excess Mana he'd spat out assembled above his head, forming a hundred-meter-long black dragon. It was the complete manifestation of his powerful bloodline. The majestic beast felt like more than simply a fiery apparition, carrying Dragonus's Dao Truths. Its appearance flickered between flames and real flesh and blood.

Alistair couldn't help but feel jealous upon seeing his face.

It was a look of pure, childlike joy. A giddy smile that reached his eyes, not of a madman but of an artist. The black dragon he'd created was an embodiment of his Dao Path. The ultimate culmination of his hopes, desires, and dreams. And most of all, there was barely any mark of a Devil King within its power—no hollowed and profane aura.

Not for the first time, Alistair wondered at how free the Devil Kings truly were. Who were the ones defying Fate, and who were the ones following the laid plans of Heaven?

That didn't mean he wouldn't kill them. Dragonus regained his composure, looking down on the humans below. He lifted his arms, ready to sunder his opponents.

Jesse was a hair's breadth away from expending his remaining Dao energy and using **[Scarlet Shift]** to evacuate everyone. He stopped himself at the last second after realizing that Dragonus wasn't directing the black dragon at those below—he was shooting it into the air.

Alistair watched in both terror and awe as the enormous creature of fire split in three. The congealed draconic form diverged at the neck, forming three smaller dragons made of flame, though they were still dozens of meters long.

Each constellation of fire affinity Mana resonated with a Dao of burning destruction. A lesser cultivator would have had his Dao Path shaken from the lamentation and rage. The unholy screech of the dragons was sung to the deepest circle of Hell—the black dragon's sorrowful cry before it was dragged into the infernal blaze of nothingness.

With the addition of the **Supercharge Drakefruit Date**, there was nothing that they could do but watch. The Dao Truths and absurd quantity of Mana were such that even if they all banded together for a counterattack, it still wouldn't have been enough.

The three black dragons spread out from the center, flying in wide arcs toward the edge of the island. It became obvious they were heading for the bases, but it was hard to tell which ones until they descended.

In a deafening explosion, they landed on three bases—those belonging to Pharaoh, Carmen, and Brigid. Alistair felt the heat even from the center of the island. The fire spread out with gasses stretching for hundreds of meters, a mushroom cloud emerging at the top. The shockwave emanated for kilometers, washing over Alistair like a strong breeze.

It made sense to Alistair. The attack was relatively slow. If Dragonus had directed it down on them, Jesse could have teleported them away, and the fastest among them would have escaped. By pointing his flames toward the bases, he had stationary targets. But that still left the question of what Dragonus hoped to achieve. Did he have information that enough devastating energy would destroy the beacons, eliminating the teams? Based on the fact that no one had disappeared, that couldn't be the case.

The plumes slowly dissipated. The blasts were so powerful that there was barely even a heap of charred rubble left. Alistair looked up at Dragonus. His aura lacked the killing intent it had before when they fought over the **Supercharge Drakefruit Date.** Alistair wondered what the Devil King's next move would be when it hit him like a ton of bricks.

They were too far away. He would never be able to make it in time. Alistair cursed the fact he and Jesse had gotten separated in the commotion. He messaged the teleporter mentally, telling him to come over, but by the time Jesse arrived, it was too late.

Like flickers on an old television, people started vanishing. Pharaoh and Carmen fizzled out, disappearing into thin air along with the rest of their teams.

The presence of Naima and Jakk attacking their bases finally made sense. They were powerful, but the bases were impossible to penetrate without overwhelming force. But if the bases didn't exist anymore? If they found a beacon in the ashes, they would bring it back to their base.

Alistair spared a thought for the awkward situation back on Earth. Whoever won the trial stood to win their seized subregions. He couldn't imagine they would be happy about the predicament. But first, he had to try saving Brigid's team from losing on the spot.

"Jesse, take William and deal with Brigid's situation," he ordered. Brigid's base was in between Pharaoh's and the Devil Kings', ripe for Jakk to steal her beacon. Jesse took William and ran over to the woman, grabbing her arm and teleporting her before she even knew what had happened.

While Alistair's fighting spirit hadn't declined in the slightest, the tension in the air was almost palpable as people wondered what would happen next. Victory was more realistic when it had been five teams against one. After seeing Dragonus display his immense power, the math was looking grim.

Lucius Wood was the intrepid defier who stood up first. "You'll never win. As long as I—"

Dragonus emptied the area of oxygen with a stream of fire from above, using the last of the energy from the **Supercharge Drakefruit Date**. Alistair felt bad for those trapped in the flames, but the Devil King releasing the power right away relieved him. If he kept it in reserve, it would never be safe to attack, knowing Dragonus could output enough energy to incinerate a city block.

Five streams of black fire billowed down from the sky, so hot they scorched the air itself. They formed a burning cage around Lucius and his team. Bartholomew did his best to help his family and other teammates, who were struggling from the lack of oxygen. Alistair wondered if thermobaric attacks were common to the fire cultivators of the multiverse, remembering his encounter with the Komodo dragon from the Beast team.

Metal skin over Bartholomew's chest and stomach grew forward, stretching like it was made of elastic. The Supersoldier pulled, shaping the metal into two RPGs. They were twice as large as those that Alistair remembered from Felons vs. Fellows. He fired them at the bounds of the cage where they exploded futilely against the fiery bars.

The fire shifted, morphing from chaotic torrents into literal chains. The interlinked flames shrunk and solidified their prison.

Alistair [Dashed] toward the flames as soon as he saw them. He activated [Frozen Claw] at the same time as he allocated his remaining 8 Upgrade Points to bringing the Skill to Tier 2. The ice affinity Mana felt more condensed around his palm and fingertips—colder and more solid, sizzling and steaming against the warm tropical air. Like [Blood Hand], it still required 40 Mana, but he could feel it had improved in Mana efficiency, making it stronger.

Dragonus glanced down at Alistair, seeing him run to rescue his prey. The Devil King brought down his hand, launching spears of condensed flame the size of fighter jets. Alistair stopped his [Dash] after predicting that the spears would collide with his trajectory. It was the right move, but it opened him up to a new volley of pointed polearms, all targeted at his position. They didn't blot out the heavens as much as Vritra's metal arsenal, but each contained many times more Mana.

All the while, Dragonus's cage continued to shrink. He formed the last spike of his Skill, sending it off as he flew toward Lucius. The spears rained down at set intervals in groups of ten, homing in on Alistair's location. Alistair became one with the wind as he dodged the blazing assault. He used all of his 600 plus Agility, darting from side to side to avoid the spears. He relied on pure instinct, lacking the time for higher thought.

Meanwhile, Bartholomew and his cousin, Allegra, worked to break through Dragonus's cage. Allegra, who could somehow still breathe, summoned an immense fulmar. The seabird was hundreds of times its natural size, with an evolved appearance marked by feathered armor and runic markings. The leviathan fulmar spat out a mass of orange stomach oil, much like its original species. However, at its current size, the oil gushed out like a waterfall, steaming against the chains.

Bartholomew removed the metallic casing that covered his hands, siphoning the malleable substance into a rectangular gray bar the size of a sword hilt. A glowing green blade over three-meters-long emerged from the top. An outside observer might have called it a lightsaber, but it had a flat edge and a pointed trapezoidal tip. Bartholomew's primary Dao Node was a hybrid of technology and war, while the aura his new blade emitted was easily identifiable as belonging to the Dao of the Sword.

Alistair's current situation was too distracting for him to notice much. The last wave of spears was about to rain down, and it had fifty flaming weapons instead of the usual ten.

Alistair took a deep breath and willed himself to channel {Psychopomp's Discipline}. It felt strange going through the storied movements of the ancient martial art without the Dao as his guide, but the physical motions were seared into his brain. {Assassin Fist} was an art dedicated to using speed and lethality to win at any cost, and {Psychopomp's Discipline} was a continuation of that.

His body's physical limits didn't change, but he became ever-so-slightly faster as {Psychopomp's Discipline} brought out his full potential. Minor inefficiencies fell to the wayside as Alistair danced around the spears. He swayed to the side, heat passing a centimeter above his shoulder. More and more of the black polearms fell in an unreadable pattern. Alistair bent back, touching his fingers on the ground, and propelled himself into a backward handspring, barely evading ten more spears.

Death's door awaited him at every corner, yet it only invigorated him. The spiritual damage he'd received from Admiral's soul reap had weakened his connection to the Dao, but it couldn't stop the thrill of combat from overtaking his mind. As he completed his handspring, he stretched out his arms, catching the last two spears with a [Frozen Claw] in each hand.

The Tier 2 Skill was twice as fast at freezing the energetic flames. Alistair skidded backward from the momentum, then shifted and turned his torso, throwing the spears back to their creator in one large swing.

In the infernal cage, Bartholomew focused the Dao of the Sword in his lightsaber-esque blade, slicing at the weakened part of the chain where the fulmar had spat its oil. His strikes conveyed an otherworldly level of sharpness, and he was close to breaking them free. But Dragonus had other plans.

Opening his mouth wide and revealing a pair of fangs, Dragonus bellowed at the top of his lungs. The ensuing shockwave deflected Alistair's frozen spears. Then the Devil King pivoted to the cage and, with the snap of a finger, broke most of the chains himself, freeing Bartholomew, Allegra and the rest of Lucius's team, who had passed out.

The breaking of the chains threw the weaker members to the ground. Lucius wasn't one of the spared.

Bartholomew was the only one strong and agile enough to hang on, dodging the dragonfire and activating the secondary boosters on his feet. The primary boosters on his back exploded with blue fire, carrying him to his father.

"Dad!" Bartholomew screamed, despair in his voice.

Before Bartholomew could rescue his father, the chains returned, coalescing around a single point. That point was Lucius Wood. With much less volume to cover, they formed a dense mass of black fire. Bartholomew raised his sword to cut down the chains, but he realized that if his attack was too strong, it would harm his father.

An apparition of a black dragon appeared behind Dragonus. Alistair felt the primal fury of the trapped beast, inciting the blood dragon locked within his own spiritual DNA. His ghost blood dragon bloodline was weaker than normal due to his spiritual injury. But even if he was fully healed, Alistair imagined the First Deepening of his Fist Node and {Psychopomp's Discipline} would help him control any unwanted emotions from it.

Dragonus moved swifter than Alistair would have imagined from the ranged magic wielder, diving at Bartholomew. One stomp to the chest sent the Supersoldier cratering into the ground. The Devil King grabbed Lucius and flew back into the sky, Selene still in his other arm and pumping him full of Mana.

"You should not have betrayed me," Dragonus admonished, holding Lucius's cage in the palm of his hand. "Nothing a bit of torture can't fix. I'll have your secrets before you croak."

Bartholomew emerged from the sand, though something was different. His eyes were pools of blue light, while his metallic skin had slid off entirely. The liquid alloy went through several iterations before settling on the shape of a giant sword hilt.

Alfred, who had woken back up, was screaming in his brother's ear, but Bartholomew was too far gone to listen. A surge of Mana from his soulcore strained his meridians, which bulged and glowed blue as the energy struggled its way to the sword hilt. Upon finally arriving at its destination, the Mana turned green, forming a sword similar to the previous weapon.

Predictably, his current weapon that used the metal of his entire body was stronger. Exactly how much stronger was what shocked Alistair. The blade must have been over a hundred meters long. It was just as thin as its smaller counterpart, humming with the Dao of the Sword. Bartholomew swung his plasma sword in one smooth motion, maneuvering the hundred-meter sword as easily as he would a chopstick.

The attack came too late. Dragonus was already flying back to his base by the time Bartholomew drew his sword, and he was flying fast. He'd already traveled a few hundred meters as the tip of the green energy blade came crashing down.

From Alistair's position, it was as if the Supersoldier had cleaved the world in twain—that was how sharp his sword was. A sword with less than a millimeter in breadth had sliced through reality. The force from the cut was propelled forward, heading straight for Dragonus.

While an outside observer would have found it strange that the Devil King didn't simply dodge to the left or right, Alistair understood right away. It was impossible. Bartholomew had likely exhausted everything for his slash. The will and intent were too strong to blithely ignore.

Dragonus picked up his speed, trying to outrun the reality-rending slash. Beneath him, the island divided down to its very core. Clouds of sand sprung free in the wake of the attack. He made it halfway back to his base when the slash caught up.

Once again, he flashed an apparition of a black dragon. The wave of sharpened air met phantasmal flesh. It tore it apart like there was nothing there.

For a moment, Alistair held out hope that Bartholomew's desperate attack had won them the round. Sadly, when the dust cleared, he saw it wasn't the case.

Two halves of Selene, the white dress-wearing Devil Princess, fell to the ground. She was bisected at the waist in Dragonus's arms. At the last second, upon realizing the danger of the incoming attack, he had spun around, letting his subordinate take the brunt of the blow. A nasty gash had still torn across the front of his body, stretching from head to toe and bleeding iniquitous blood.

They were enemies, but Alistair still felt weird seeing the lifeless body of the mage. From the continuous and steady amount of Mana she'd provided her captain, Alistair ascertained she had some kind of Mana regeneration Skill. Most likely a percentage-based regeneration based on her max Mana, rather than the flat amounts based on Intelligence that everyone else had. She alone had allowed Dragonus to be so profligate with his Skill usage. And when it was convenient, the man had discarded her. Of course, her death would not be permanent, but it was the principle of the thing.

With no further attacks coming his way, Dragonus returned to his base, the chained cocoon containing Lucius in tow.

Alistair let himself collapse on the warm beach in exhaustion. The false sunlight teased his eyes with its yellow glow. Even if it were real, at this point, he wasn't worried about going blind.

While he hadn't expected Carmen and Pharaoh to get eliminated, the rest was still going *relatively* according to plan. The next few hours would determine everything.

45 CAPTURE THE BEACON
FINALE

"JUST END IT," Lucius spat out.

"Not until you reveal all your secrets."

Dragonus had his prisoner wrapped in chains and hanging above a boiling lake of black liquid. The cavern they were in had no identifying features. The only light came from the ultraviolet radiation of the chains and the fire in the Devil King's eyes.

Every aspect of the room felt like it belonged in the underworld. The walls and floor sucked in the light, giving off an eerie black-and-white glow. The light-sucking appearance of their base was a side effect of the total seal on all Mana, both incoming and outgoing. It was impossible for any information to go in or out. Without Selene, Dragonus had to use his own Mana to power it, but he was at full capacity.

It would only be an hour more at the most, he estimated. Soon, the rest would fall like dominoes despite Admiral's blunder.

That idiot, he thought. Admiral had been far too cocky in challenging so many at once. There'd been too many instances of the rich bastard challenging his authority. But in a situation like this, he could have used the older man's advice. Truth be told, Dragonus had never been suited for leadership.

"Y-you'll... have to try... harder than that," Lucius managed through gritted teeth as Dragonus squeezed the chains tighter.

They had lost Selene as well. It was unfortunate—her spiritual detection had found the **Supercharge Drakefruit Date** in the first place, and her **[Fount of Mana]** was the only reason he could be so cavalier with his Mana.

But even if leadership didn't suit him, he would step up to fill the role. That was what George had entrusted him to do. Sure, they had lost Admiral and Selene, but it was inconsequential in the end. He was still alive and kicking, and that's all they needed. There was a reason that he was #3 and not Admiral. The gap between them was a quantum leap of strength.

"You're going to tell me the location of all your safehouses, the secrets to your real-life territories, all your abilities, and those of your closest allies. And when you do, I will give you the sweet release of death."

———

Even with three healers between both of their teams, there was nothing that could be done.

Bartholomew had expended every last drop of Dao energy in his desperate attempt to rescue his father. Alfred admonished him for his lack of planning.

"What on earth were you thinking?" he yelled, grabbing his brother's shoulder. "You're our second-best fighter after Alistair! And with his injuries, you were the most important! You wasted everything. It was supposed to be a believable struggle, not an all-out attack. What the hell happened?"

"I'm sorry," Bartholomew said, his head drooped down. His metallic skin hadn't yet recovered, making him look more vulnerable. "My emotions have been coming in peaks and troughs ever since I integrated the Natural Inheritance. My behavior was completely unacceptable."

Alfred shook his head. "It is what it is. Brigid and Jesse are our only main fighters now. Do you think that's enough, Alistair?"

"Hold up," Alistair said. "We might not be able to use Dao energy, but we can still fight. I'm not out of the count just yet."

"Be that as it may," Alfred countered, "Dragonus is strong enough to take on you, Brigid, my brother, and Jesse all at once. You know it, too. Not to mention the three remaining beasts, Jakk, and Naima. We're outgunned."

"It'll be fine. We don't need to worry about firepower. All that matters is stealing their beacon."

Alfred paced around the stone tiles of Alistair's base. They had agreed to retreat to his base to regroup after losing Lucius, though Brigid and her two remaining teammates couldn't join since they had to defend their base. Only Phoebe—whom Alistair knew as Medea from the first game—remained as the last defense. Alistair raised an eyebrow at their confidence in their base, but it was their prerogative.

"It would have been nice for you to give us a heads-up on your *extremely* expensive idea," Alfred said.

"It would be nice to know how your father plans to steal the Devil King's beacon, but we're both working on a trust basis, aren't we?" Alistair shot back. "At this point, my team is at the disadvantage. Plus, you poached my teammate and tried to turn him into a traitor."

"Oh, spare me the righteous indignation. We're both doing what's in our best interest. It's not as if we ever would have eliminated you before dealing with the Devil Kings. That would be poor judgment. And can you seriously tell me you're not plotting in the back of your mind right now?"

Alfred met Alistair eye-to-eye defiantly with a knowing grin. They held each other's gaze for a moment as they tried to assess the other's words. That was where Alistair thought he had the advantage with his Karmic sight, though he didn't know the full extent of Alfred's Spymaster powers. At the very least, he could read Alistair's body heat and heart rate, though such things were trivial to control at this point.

"You'll forgive me for being a bit paranoid," Alistair said. "But I apologize for any insinuation. You're right. You have to do what you have to do in a situation like this."

A knock came from outside the room, a circular chamber on the west wing of the base.

"*Secretary Ryder,*" Caren informed him from afar. "*It's time.*"

"Are you ready to sign away your future?" Alistair said to Alfred, stretching out his arms. "Well, 20% of it?"

———

Alexandra was being left behind, and she knew it.

The number had only been going up. She was #29 in the world now. Since she specialized in combat and combat alone, her true martial prowess was higher than that.

Yet despite that, the gap between her and Alistair was becoming unfathomable. Their battle against her father had proved that. What had she done that entire fight—thrown her knife?

It felt like every time she saw him, he had grown again in a new way. He was limitless potential, infinite growth made incarnate. And she couldn't compete.

Of course, Alistair never made her feel bad about it. He was ever the gracious winner, and that only made it worse. Why couldn't she get a personal ghost tutor? Alexandra didn't even have a sponsor. What would her future be after the end of the Quests?

She pushed those thoughts to the side. They were a team, she and Alistair. They met on the first day of the initiation. Those kinds of bonds would never break.

Alexandra snapped out of her thoughts, focusing on the plan. An hour had passed since Dragonus captured Lucius. It was time for a reckoning.

Brigid and her two remaining teammates ventured out to attack the Devil King base. Dragonus emerged from his light-swallowing fortress, soaring with dragon wings of flame.

Without the Mana from the date, he couldn't outright destroy them, but he could still slowly roast them alive. Literally. Dragonus floated outside, exuding a field of pure heat. Alexandra could feel the temperature rise even across the island. You could barely make out Brigid's form because of the air warping from the scalding aura.

"It's time," Alistair said. In the distance, Alexandra made out a titanic golden figure emerging from the heat shimmer. Brigid was making her move. "You ready?"

Alistair walked over from the open portcullis with the rest of the group, grabbing her hand. "We'll win, I promise."

Alexandra snorted. "Save it for the others. I'm fine."

Jesse came over with Marzhan, the #8 ranker and the strongest member in the United Polities divisions after Richard. She was an archer who could shoot and manipulate bone. She was also the only one in her group strong enough to hold her own as an individual.

"See you on the other side," Alistair said as he [Dashed] away, leaving a cloud of sand in his wake. Bartholomew joined him with his internal jet pack.

Jesse offered a hand to each of the women by his side. "Ladies, if you don't mind."

Alexandra took the Australian's arm, disappearing in a flash of red light. Space flew by in a dizzying moment, and then she was a hundred meters away from the Devil King.

Dragonus's terrifying power had no rival, not even her father's might coming close. Fiery dark aura flowed in living waves from his body, beating to the rhythm of his soulcore's breath. It was evil, darkness and fire all in one, so congealed that the innermost layer formed an inadvertent cloak of black flame around his skin. Another ten-meter radius around him was enveloped in a blackened haze of Mana, while the air distorted and writhed in all directions, encroaching farther than two city blocks.

The golden avatar of a woman clashed with the draconic man. Brigid's huge form radiated a homely aura that reminded Alexandra of her happiest Thanksgivings as a child. Brigid brought down a meat cleaver with two hands, aiming directly for Dragonus. On her shoulder, two figures shot waves of shiny blue runes that danced in the air on their way toward their target.

Dragonus countered by calling down a pseudo-Heavenly pillar of fire, once again attaching it to his fist. The spectral meat cleaver struck the pillar with immense force, sending out a wave of equal parts flame and golden aura. The runic script burned to ashes before even reaching the Devil King's cloak of fire, unable to withstand the extreme heat.

Alistair and Bartholomew arrived a few seconds after. Jesse saluted them, teleporting back to the base, leaving the four of them at the event horizon of Dragonus's mirage-like field.

Marzhan notched a bone arrow into her bow. It was matte black and unornamented, a direct contrast to the white of the arrow. The weapon was enormous, at least one-and-a-half times bigger than any compound bow Alexandra had seen before. Its size was exaggerated even more in the hands of the short and slim woman. Marzhan barely came up to Alexandra's chin, who had grown to the height of an average man from before the initiation.

The archer pulled back the bowstring, carefully aiming the arrow. Alexandra could see the immense draw weight and the tension in her arms. After a second of calibration, she loosed the projectile.

The bone arrow rocketed through the warped air, growing as it tore through the aura. By the time it reached Dragonus, it was the size of a cruise missile. Even the viscous aura surrounding the Devil King barely slowed it down.

While still holding up a pillar against the weight of Brigid's avatar, Dragonus turned and covered his arm in voidfire. The bone arrow exploded on impact, growing like an organic mass. It clashed against an equal and opposite explosion of voidfire. The blacker than black flames flickered with occasional impurities of orange fire beneath. Marzhan's bones ossified into a web-like crest that remained even after the fire vanished. Alexandra was impressed her single arrow was capable of even partially disjoining the fire and void Mana.

Void Mana isn't one of the Mana affinities I know, but it's also not Dao energy, Alexandra thought. Perhaps it was a combination of every single affinity all at once, she mused, though that seemed antithetical to the concept of the void.

Marzhan notched four arrows at once, this time aiming them at a higher angle. They soared through the air together, landing in a spacious square around Dragonus. Each arrow carried a bone thread that arched for hundreds of meters. However, that was the least interesting part about her Skill. A hair-thin thread of collagen descended from each arch, forming a makeshift harness around Alistair, Alexandra, Jesse, and Marzhan herself.

"Brace yourself," Marzhan said.

Suddenly, Alexandra felt herself accelerate forward, the harness pulling her along the bone arches like a rollercoaster. The bridge disintegrated as the party passed over it, its boney shards sprinkling onto the ground in a way reminiscent of falling acorns. Wherever the seeds fell, bone trees emerged. They were small at first, about as tall as grass, but the further they ziplined across the battlefield, the taller the trees grew. By the time Alexandra reached the apex of the arch, the trees were as big as centennial oaks, forming a thick skeletal canopy.

A sickening feeling of death clung to the forest. Its twisted growths looked like deciduous trees in the deep of winter, except made entirely of bone. Alexandra compared it to Oliver's pure death aura. Marzhan included chthonic, anti-life elements, twisting the venerable vitality of flora into putrefaction.

Dragonus wasn't about to let them terraform the terrain for free. He activated his fireball Skill from before, condensing Mana into a small sphere before unleashing it in streaks faster than the mortal eye could track. The battery of streaks rushed out in waves targeting each of their destination points.

Jakk reared his ugly head out of the Devil King base, along with the remaining beasts. The replacement Devil King soared through the air toward the incoming party while the beasts ran toward the battlefield.

Brigid used the opportunity to toss two golden apples into the air. With a sideways smack of her cleaver, she obliterated the fruits, spraying the golden juice all over. Because they were proportional to her avatar, that took the form of a waterfall of glittering apple juice.

The juice canceled out Dragonus's fire streaks in the most chaotic way possible, transmuting the flames into a half-gold, half-black serpentine plant. The newly formed plants ineffectually dropped onto the sand.

At that point, the four of them were just about to land. They brought the forest of bone behind them, growing in power and height every second. Even Alexandra—with her raging life force second to only Alistair—shivered in the presence of bones. Marzhan grew paler by the second as her skeletal creations seemingly fed on a combination of her life force, Dao energy, and Mana.

Alistair raised his right hand in the air, activating [Force Fist]. That was the signal.

Alexandra activated all of her requisite combat Skills at once. It was a miracle she could fight with the injury her father had given her, but Fasha and Ginko had done their best. She gritted her teeth and fought through the pain, slashing a [Partition Vitae] at Dragonus.

Bartholomew used a weaker and smaller version of the laser sword from before. Brigid pumped more of the golden energy into her cleaver, elongating it by nearly a dozen meters, and brought it down from a great height. Meanwhile, Alistair fearlessly [Dashed] behind Dragonus with a [Force Fist] in each hand.

The Skill had grown in size and opacity since Alexandra had first seen it. When he'd first used the Skill, the spectral fists were the size of large boxing gloves and mostly transparent, but now they were the hands of a coral-skinned giant. You could barely make out the crimson **Devilsbane Gauntlets** beneath the force-attuned Mana, though the metal still glowed brightly.

Their attacks all met at the same time.

Dragonus closed his eyes. In one moment, there was nothing, and in the next, there was a black sun.

It appeared out of nowhere above his head. Richard's bullets had covered the island in darkness, but this was different. The sphere of unholy destruction sucked the light out of reality. It absorbed everything—Mana, Dao energy, *nue*—even Alexandra's internal energy wanted to join the black sun.

The physical demiplane's sun disappeared. Why would it have reason to exist with a more perfect, more destructive counterpart right there? It only had a radius of ten meters, yet the concentrated ball of flames felt like the hottest thing Alexandra had ever seen. She could feel a black dragon's raging fire and burning destruction within the dark orb. She noticed that the light absorbing effect came from a dilution of voidfire.

Like a pulsing heart, the black sun released a wave of every kind of energy. *Nue,* Dao energy and Mana from the elemental affinities of fire and destruction. The wave consumed their attacks, eradicating them in an instant. Even Jakk, who had jetted in just behind his master, got blown away.

Alexandra couldn't help but worry for Alistair, who was the closest to the epicenter of the wave. She couldn't see him because Dragonus's Skill had absorbed so much light that it felt like the dead of night.

Dragonus suddenly stopped, withdrawing the sun in an instant. "Impossible! How—"

Whatever the Devil King was reacting to, he didn't have much time. The moment after the sun disappeared, a new light emerged above them.

A column of red light flashed into existence, completely surrounding Dragonus. Alexandra initially hoped that this newcomer's ability had delivered a deadly blow, before remembering that it was Jesse's teleportation Skill.

Even so, she knew it was foolish to underestimate the #7 ranker. Offensively, he offered less direct power than most of his peers, yet he was the linchpin of their team. As the light faded, dozens of people fell from the sky.

The skydivers were the members of the teams that they had jettisoned to their base at the beginning of the round. Jesse, Fasha—as well as Ginko, and Sword and Spear from Lucius's team—were at the top, while everyone else held hands in a massive circle.

Wispy blue mist interlaced between the hands of those in the circle. Unbreakable bonds formed, connecting everyone at a fundamental level. The aura of the group felt stronger than the sum of its parts, exuding the Dao. Alexandra's heart stirred at the display of perfect teamwork.

Individual bodies merged into the mist, which quickly grew opaque. By the time they landed on the ground, the smoke converged into a singular form. The form of a woman.

She looked vaguely like Secretary Ryder, retaining her pixie cut, though her features seemed to be an aggregation of the dozens of people that went into her transformation.

Dragonus turned on the jets, literally. He ignored the falling people, blasting black fire out of his palms and the soles of his feet. He even passed by Jakk, who had stumbled to his feet and was currently engaging Bartholomew in battle. Fleeing to his base took up all his attention. Though it seemed he was more alarmed by something happening in his fortress rather than the gestalt woman.

The woman dashed at a speed even greater than Alistair, intercepting Dragonus with an august palm that echoed a powerful Dao. The Devil King bounced a hundred meters away, crashing into the sand.

Alexandra couldn't believe how powerful the fusion was. In raw aura strength, she might have even exceeded Dragonus. It was hard to tell, since the tainted energy of the Devil King made direct comparisons difficult, but it was close either way.

"You were hiding this?" she asked Alistair through the link. He had turned his face up from under the sand after tanking the black sun's energy wave.

"Secretary Ryder made me promise to tell no one else but Lucius and Alfred, sorry," he said, **[Dashing]** forward to help the fused warrior.

"What is it?" she asked, running toward the fight along with the others.

"The United Polities' ultimate trump card. A representation of the ideals of democracy, rejecting a cultivator's individual might and substituting it for the will of the people. Fitting, isn't it?"

"I can't deny the power, but…" she said.

"I don't believe in it either."

Behind them, Allegra, Sword and Spear, and Ginko engaged the three incoming beasts, including Vritra. The Beast Tamer had summoned her entire menagerie of avian leviathans. Alexandra didn't think the four of them had a shot at winning, but anything to slow down the beasts would help.

The gestalt woman and Dragonus exchanged blows. While her attacks didn't contain an absurd amount of Dao energy, there was something about each blow that felt mesmerizing. It was as if her technique and Dao Path were integrated at a higher level.

Dragonus kept trying to retreat, only to be intercepted by their attacks again and again. Frustrated, he roared with the tenacity of a dragon, slowing some of the incoming attackers, including Alexandra herself. It did not affect the woman in the slightest.

The Devil King tapped into his storied bloodline, a phantom black dragon appearing behind him. While his Skills used more Dao energy and Mana, the fused warrior countered with simple palm strikes. Dragonus would swipe with a fiery claw, while the woman would counter with a casual block. Alexandra became fixated on her every movement. Her style, her technique—watching it was like reading a treatise on democracy, as silly as that sounded.

The warrior's moves outshone even Alistair's psychopomp martial arts, who had joined the fray. It became a crowded mess as everyone attacked the Devil King at once. Yet the man seemed squarely uninterested in fighting back. He did the bare minimum, but his gaze held only one object—his own base.

Alistair and Lucius had clearly worked out something behind the scenes. Alexandra didn't care to think about such things. She trusted Alistair. Whatever had happened, Dragonus believed it was a priority to return to his base. Perhaps his beacon was being taken out from under his nose.

"Cockroaches," Dragonus spat, though lacked venom in his voice. "Begone."

Using the draconic apparition, he spun around, warding off his attackers with a wall of fire. At the same time, he expelled an undiluted stream of dragonfire from the maw of his ethereal dragon. Instead of the usual fire and destruction, the black flames were voidfire. Blacker than black, they flickered like two-dimensional objects because of how well they absorbed light.

The mass of fire was larger than multiple Olympic swimming pools. In the blink of an eye, the cloud converged into ten points, each a little smaller than a basketball. Alexandra wanted to strike, but Alistair told her to hold back, sensing danger. She wasn't fast enough.

The streak of voidfire pierced her chest in an instant, flying out in a massive wave of death. Her last thought before she died was regret that she wasn't stronger.

Anything. She'd do anything to catch up.

———

Alistair coughed up blood as he assessed his side's damages. If only he had the mental link to everyone, perhaps he could have saved some of them. But probably not. He had only just managed to defend himself with a [Frozen Claw], and even then, the voidfire had singed his soul. The single attack brought him down to 350 Health.

Sword and Spear, Ginko, Fasha, and Alexandra had perished from the streaks of voidfire, along with Jakk and all the beasts except Vritra. It looked like Brigid's teammates had died from the black sun, and she'd been struck by a streak right in the face. Even the fusion lady couldn't stop the entire barrage and had made a valiant effort to convert Dragonus's Dao Heart with her techniques.

She was in the best position to resist the flame bolts, her palm striking most of them into nonexistence. After the voidfire spheres faded, she followed up on the attack, but Alistair could tell her transformation was fading. It would last a minute longer at most. The unity of the constituents couldn't last forever.

Bartholomew got picked up by his cousin Allegra, who had her fulmar from before, plus a mutated peregrine falcon. The latter bird looked like a cyborg, with a red laser eye and a metal beak. They were running short on manpower.

Vritra chased after them like a mad lizard, throwing metal spears that barely missed their target. Alistair wished them luck as he focused on Dragonus, who steadily advanced towards his base with every step.

The fused woman desperately tried stopping him, but it felt like she performed better when on the offensive. On the back foot, she just looked hopeless. She had dealt more damage to the Devil King captain than anybody yet. Her palm strikes left deep grooves on his cheek and chest, but he was still far from death.

When Dragonus got within a hundred meters of his base, Alistair gave the signal.

Another red flash appeared above the Devil King. Jesse passed out immediately after using his ultimate Skill a second time, emptied of all Mana. He wasn't alone.

Three objects fell from the sky with him. The upgraded laser cannon, the Heart-Render Engine, and William.

William laughed maniacally, pressing the button that fired the laser. It was already aimed at the core of the Heart-Render Engine, so he didn't have to do much.

Alistair had already started running before the explosion started. Though not as large or powerful as Dragonus's date-enhanced dragons, it still engulfed a fifteen-meter radius. The orange explosion was blinding, vaporizing the surrounding sand instantaneously. All the latent energies contained within the futuristic nuclear engine escaped at once.

When the light faded, he saw that Dragonus still lived. However, it looked like he had lost the fire in his eyes. The bodies of the fused woman, William, and Jesse had vanished. Dragonus crumbled to his knees, staring into the distance.

Alistair turned to see what the Devil King was looking at. On the opposite side of the island, he could see Alfred waving his arms, holding up a flashing beacon. They had done it. They had stolen the Devil King beacon.

Yet Alfred wasn't stepping inside his base.

Dev'rox chuckled. "A man has to gloat, doesn't he?"

The chase happening a few dozen meters away ended with Vritra's untimely doom. Out of nowhere, a platinum hand plunged through the Beast Lord's chest, killing him instantly. The body slumped off the hand, revealing Lucius. Threads of Fate warped around him as golden coins burned and melted into embers within the aura surrounding his body.

With a single leap, he bridged the gap to Alistair and Dragonus, grabbing the disgraced Devil King by the neck. The explosion of the Heart-Render Engine had dealt serious damage to the Devil King, black blood seeping out of multiple wounds. But he was alive. Alive, and not so injured that he should have taken the Englishman's assault without recourse. It seemed he was shocked by his imminent loss in the trial.

Despite not even being the subject of Lucius's look of contempt, Alistair shuddered. The Wood patriarch bored into Dragonus's soul, if he still had such a thing.

"Look at me, you *cockroach*," Lucius said. "You are worth less than the dirt on my boots, Devil King slave. Nothing in this world will make me happier than killing you on the outside, and your disgusting master. You and your kind will never lay a finger on my family again."

With that, Dragonus vanished like the others who'd had their beacon stolen. It felt anti-climactic. They had struggled for so long, only for their enemy to go out without a fight to the death.

And then there were two. Lucius versus Alistair. He took a quick head-count of everyone still alive. Himself, Caren, Delilah, and Josiah for his team, and Lucius, Bartholomew, Allegra, Alfred, and presumably Phoebe for the other side.

"How did you do it?" Alistair asked.

It was the one thing he didn't understand. They had set up the plan perfectly. Lucius had let himself be captured, bringing him to the inner sanctum of the Devil King's base. According to William, it was the most likely scenario, though there were other possibilities they had planned for.

With their inside man, they needed a distraction. Secretary Ryder's fusion Skill provided them the requisite time for Lucius to break free of his restraints and find the beacon.

But there was a problem. Lucius needed to free himself, which would alert Dragonus. Their timing had to be precise, otherwise the Devil King would return right away and ruin their plans. Their base was completely insulated from any Mana passing through, so it seemed impossible at first glance.

However, Alistair had come up with a solution. The sponsors.

They could clearly bypass any Foundation-level security. Lucius hadn't taken his sponsor meeting for the Quest either, so his sponsor could inform him of the exact moment when he should escape. The Lazarene Minister hadn't been happy about being used as a messenger, but he was willing to talk to the Satharvon representative. Passing on information didn't violate the ban on material assistance.

Plus, he had to do it at some point, with the Quest about to end prematurely. Alistair had multitasked, asking a bunch of questions while he had fought Dragonus a few minutes prior.

The only question that remained was how Lucius had transported the beacon over to his base in so little time. It was the one secret that he wouldn't give up.

Alistair was so distracted by Dragonus and Lucius that he didn't notice the other members of the latter's team had disappeared. Even in his extended Karmic sight and aura sense, they were nowhere to be found.

A sinking feeling washed over Alistair. He tried to lift his foot, but it refused to obey.

"Not so fast, my friend," Lucius said. "It's time for our friendly game."

"Friendly game?" Alistair raised an eyebrow, straining against his restraints. A burst of his remaining Karma would likely grant him freedom, but he needed to choose the right moment.

"It's just us now," Lucius said. "I daresay our alliance against the Devil Kings was a strapping success. Now we have to determine who wins the grand prize. And I don't want there to be any hard feelings between us."

"Of course not," Alistair agreed. He couldn't exactly blame the man for acting in his own best interests. "No matter what the outcome of this game is, I don't want our partnership to suffer."

Lucius conjured a pair of chairs that looked carved directly from raw wood with little polishing or embellishment. Alistair wasn't sure if that was some posh trend or just the man's personal taste. Accompanying the chairs, he added a glass table, a teapot, and two cups.

"After you," Lucius said, waiting for Alistair to sit. For a moment, he found the restriction on his movement lifted, but somehow only in the direction of the chairs. The Wood patriarch carefully poured cups of tea, making sure to serve Alistair first.

"You're not worried I'm going to finish you off here?" Alistair said, sipping the tea.

Lucius let out a mirthful chuckle with more than a hint of smugness. "You think that you can defeat me in your condition? It's obvious you cannot use any Dao energy. I, on the other hand, have not engaged in a fight this entire trial. But even if you could defeat me, it wouldn't matter. It's already done."

A footstool appeared as Lucius lifted up his legs, and a fluffy white pillow grew out of the chair's back.

"I don't follow?"

"You, my friend," Lucius said, "are not sufficiently paranoid. You should never have accepted the **Crystal Caller**."

Alistair checked his inventory, finding the item missing.

"I've spent almost ten million drachma hiding this from your eyes. It's no easy feat when the person you're trying to swindle can read the tides of Fate and has instincts as keen as a fox."

Alistair put even more effort into moving. An all-encompassing invisible force pushed against him, locking him down in his chair. Even without his aura sense, he could see hundreds of Gold drachma burning into thin air around his body. Alistair's suspicions were correct. Instead of using Karma to affect Fate like himself, Lucius could *pay* for influence.

The Dao of Money permeated the man's entire body. Alistair had thought that Anthony and Pharaoh had a precocious understanding of their Daos—but Lucius was at another level entirely. His harmonization with the Dao of Money transcended someone of their level, like Sally Ryder's fusion from before. Alistair wouldn't have been surprised if he was at a Third Deepening, or an equivalent level.

So this is what it looks like when someone is born for their path, Alistair thought. The power he expressed was not that of someone ranked in the 60s on the leaderboard.

Lucius tapped his tea glass. "It's time I answered your original question."

———

Caren was the protector of the hearth. He had never wanted the responsibility, but when the team needed him, he stepped up.

The base was so quiet when it was empty.

"Warning. Anomalous presence detected in the left wing."

The sensors connected to his **[Paper Mind]** went off at the detection of three intruders. He had been expecting them. They didn't know how it was going to happen, but Alistair had warned him to stay on alert once it became a 1v1 against Lucius's team.

A video feed showed three intruders—Bartholomew, Alfred, and Allegra —but it didn't last for long. Alfred used his Spymaster powers along with his brother's access to technology to shut down their cameras. Caren tried fighting it, but it was futile. Not even his quick mind could fend off Alfred's hacking.

Caren took a deep breath.

His head pounded.

He was tired.

He hadn't eaten since the beginning of the first trial, which was over a week ago.

The time for hiding was over. Caren had one last moment of hesitation, right before he heard the banging coming from outside the central room. He didn't care what would happen to his reputation. As long as he trusted in his team, as long as he trusted in Alistair, everything would be fine.

He pressed the third stainless steel button. The first button activated the laser cannon. The second button swiveled and reformed the mirror. The third button shut off the lights.

Caren climbed on top of the stone altar he had Alistair purchase and knelt. Knowing that he would have little fighting to do in previous rounds, he had kept the liquid stored in [Paper Container]. He unleashed all of it.

At the same time, he stabbed his own heart with three metal spikes. When his heartbeat stilled, Caren was reborn. Reborn in the Dao of the Bloody Pages. Reborn as a vampire.

Gallons and gallons of blood poured out of him, gushing onto the altar, which directed it into the pipes of their base. They would soon spread his blood throughout the entire base, making it his dominion and only his. The rest of the blood, he consumed. Vitality returned to his trembling body. His headache and somnolence vanished, replaced with a ravenous hunger to feed. He had just enough to nurse himself back to health but wasn't even close to being satisfied.

Caren bared his fangs in a smile. He opened the door to the room, not waiting for the intruders to break through. Blood gathered on the floor, rising up to his ankles. He was home again. A piece of origami paper fluttered out from his palm, floating in the air, absorbing the drips of blood coming from the pipes on the ceiling.

After this, no one would *ever* intrude on his home again.

———

"A bridge across space?" Alistair thought out loud. It was the only thing that made sense. How else could he have snuck three people in under all of their security? But through the **Crystal Caller**?

"Correct. The ultimate Trojan horse. Hiding such an obvious capability took quite the sum."

Alistair put down his cup of tea, also taking a moment to relax. "I didn't see that coming. But I think you're also missing something."

"Oh?"

"I have an advantage over you," Alistair said calmly.

A shadow of doubt flickered over Lucius's face. "And what is that?"

"Let's see what you're doing here. You've locked me down here because I'm the last moving part. I'm the wild card that could mess things up. Occupy me, and that's everyone. Your plan is foolproof. You have your three relatives go inside, defeat the last member of my team, and steal my beacon. But you're missing one thing—I trust my teammates.

"I believe in them. That's why Caren is the only one defending our base. But you couldn't trust Phoebe, could you? You knew she was in my game in the previous round. That cast a seed of doubt on her. You haven't entrusted her with anything important during this entire trial. And for this last mission, your key to victory, you had her stay home. That completely eliminated any chance of her messing up the heist."

Alistair saw the realization dawn on Lucius's face. "What have you done?"

"Remember Josiah and Delilah?"

———

They had laid in wait for hours in their miniature forms. Their shrinking Skill had a one time Mana cost, so they could keep it up indefinitely. Alistair had entrusted them with an important mission—failure was not an option.

After they saw the inside of Lucius's base in the previous round, the team had brainstormed on how they were going to infiltrate. Of course, the current base was more heavily reinforced, but the basic security principles were the same.

There were three main components.

The first was the runic symbols inlaid on the palisade walls that prevented entry from unauthorized users. The second was the mystical materials that made up the inner citadel. The last component was Alfred's extensive, non-magical security system, consisting of a network of cameras, heat signature detection, tripwires, and more.

Phoebe, their inside woman, could take out the first layer. She could also provide them a small hole to get past the second. For the third, they would have to deal with it themselves.

Their infiltration could have been a whole movie on its own, but they eventually made it in.

"Wish Alistair good luck when you see him," Phoebe told the two of them, handing over the beacon, a glass, and crystal cylinder with a glowing diamond inside. "I have a feeling I'll need his protection soon."

———

Lucius burned more money, to the extent that Platinum drachma replaced Gold. If he stopped Alistair and recovered the beacon, he could salvage the round. In a flash of platinum coins, he teleported over a hundred meters closer to the Maine Brothers.

Alistair activated **[Hand of Karma]**, pouring all of his positive Karma into the Skill. The familiar crimson energy warped the air, bending threads of Fate. If Lucius thought himself outside of Alistair's range, he was mistaken.

Alistair pulled **Laser Gun (II)** from his inventory. Anyone who believed his longest-range attack was **[Lightning of Justice]** was in for a wakeup call. Alistair shot Lucius right as the tycoon was about to teleport again, a supersonic laser bolt exploding into his back.

Alistair had no expectation that would take the man out. That was where his other trump card came in.

There was a reason he had been saving Dev'rox's power during the trial. In his mind's eye, he imagined the imp putting a claw on his shoulder. A deluge of spatial Mana flooded his system. **[Hand of Karma]** annihilated Lucius's bonds holding him to his seat, while the Dev'rox-assisted **[Dash]** cut grooves into the fabric of space, warping him *inside* of Lucius.

It was only for a brief moment, but it gave Alistair all the time he needed to cut off Lucius's Fate and block his meridians. The crimson energy flooded Lucius from the soulcore outward, until Alistair decohered, unable to occupy the same spatial location as his foe.

Alistair didn't come out unscathed. Without the Ghost Node, he was more affected by Lucius's internal energies. But he was willing to put his body on the line—as long as he stopped Lucius.

Alistair collapsed on the sand in agonizing pain. All of his internals were messed up from occupying the same place as someone else. Lucius's soul and spiritual network impressed themselves on his own, causing serious damage. With all his strength, he looked up.

His heart dropped.

Lucius stood tall. His short, golden hair glinted in the sun, sweat falling on his brow, but he would not fall. Alistair felt relieved looking into his aura sense, as he had indeed severed his meridians.

Yet the man did not give up. He should have been in excruciating pain like Alistair. His spiritual network had been sent into disarray. The threads of Fate resulting in victory had vanished. But he still put one foot in front of the other.

In the distance, Josiah and Delilah shifted into their giant forms to get back to the base faster. Lucius refused to quit. He was a man struggling against destiny itself, pouring his entire will into victory.

Alistair could only bring himself up to his knees, toiling against his faulty body as he crawled after Lucius. The man shone brilliant in the sun, casting a long shadow behind him. Alistair could see the pain in his face, the furious resolve to never give up.

What am I doing? Alistair asked himself. They had already won. He was just putting himself through more pain than was necessary. Yet seeing Lucius ignited a fire within him. *I'm not going to lose to anyone.*

Defying the will of the flesh, Alistair toiled to his feet. His body cried out in unimaginable pain for him to stop. Why not lie down and wait a few more seconds for victory?

By the time the two giants had returned to their base, Lucius had made it two meters forward. Alistair grasped his shoulder from behind. "Made it."

Then, the world turned dark.

Congratulations on placing 1st in [The Game of Life]!

46 FINISHING MOVE

"Fuck, fuck, fuck, fuck!" Oliver shouted.

As a last resort, he punched the walking eel with a fist imbued with his Dao of Death. He was no pugilist, but Alistair had given him some pointers.

The eel died instantly, unable to handle the power of death. An undistilled Dao Node was rare at his level, as far as Oliver understood. Not many could tap into pure Death.

But he could. His soulcore was already almost entirely attuned to Death affinity Mana. At only level 42, there were a few people higher leveled than him in the Northeast Order Freehold. However, they didn't have his foundations. The Necromancer build manual was a godsend in that regard.

"Watch your language," John said. Butterflies of flame soared into another three eels, combusting on contact. "That should be the last of them."

"I'm an adult, old man," Oliver said, popping a Health pill. "And they destroyed ten of my zombies!"

"You'll replace them with better ones."

"Yeah, I guess. Besides the generals and prince, those were the last of my orcs, though."

Oliver collapsed onto the ground. He was exhausted, even with the boost of energy from the pill. They had been fighting nonstop for almost twenty-four hours. An army of mutated electric eels had emerged out of the sewers in former New York City.

Alistair's capital had millions of drachma and tens of thousands of Land Credits worth of defenses, but their leader had disappeared before providing major defenses to the other cities. Paying back Anthony's debt had also slowed down the building of defenses outside of the core region.

The eels had killed thousands before they arrived to clear them out, and more had slithered out of the waterworks. It had taken reinforcements totaling in the hundreds to finish them all off. Even John, the temporary leader in Alistair's stead, came along.

Besides their defenses, part of the reason they could afford to personally intervene was the sudden moratorium.

For those not sent away, [The Game of Life] was different. The vast majority of humanity was not taking part in the series of games but rather a protracted war against unending waves of monsters.

As such, there was a temporary ban on capturing subregions by force. Even with the warnings, greedy people still tried, though the penalties of lost levels and even Badges (in egregious cases) stopped that almost as soon as it started.

It created an awkward situation where violence against someone inside their autochthonous subregion was prohibited, but elsewhere, it was the Wild West. Citizens could still choose to join a new freehold democratically. Which, with John's expert diplomacy and the backing of Alistair's renown, had been quite successful.

In terms of the Quest, each day brought a new monster wave. An endless bloodshed, though the Pathfinder AI said that it was just a morsel of the true [Armageddon] to come. Oliver shivered when he read those words.

"Is that the last of them?" Oliver asked.

"Appears so," John said, checking his status screen. Almost two days ago, there'd been a sudden alteration to Quest 5, reducing the time remaining from nearly two weeks to just two days. Something had happened in whatever magical world Alistair and their allies had been whisked off to. "Three hours left."

"We make a good squad, don't we?"

John reached out a hand to pull him up. "I've had as good a time as I could ask for, considering we've been fighting non-stop for the last two weeks."

Oliver accepted his hand. "But we're both glad Alistair's back."

"A ship can't stay adrift for too long without its captain."

———

Alistair came to in a pool of black goop, gasping for air. Then he remembered he could convert Mana to oxygen and coughed out the gunk.

A barrage of notifications assaulted him.

Congratulations on placing first in the Capture the Beacon trial of [The Game of Life]!

Payout for 1st place:
63,814 subregions (Current Total: 65,666), +4 levels, +100 Upgrade Points

Quest Complete: [The Game of Life]. Rewards: 200 Upgrade Points, 1,000,000 Gold drachma, 50,000 Land Store Credits, 1 Skill scroll.

Level up! *You are now level 51.* +12 Agility, +12 Intelligence, +12 Charisma, +12 free Attribute points, +92 Upgrade Points.

Badge Acquired: "1" (Untiered Legendary Badge): *Achieve number one on your homeworld's leaderboard at one point during the initiation.* All Attributes +20, All Attributes +10%. **Warning: You have exceeded the number of Badge slots you possess. Swap out Badges or buy another Badge slot.**

Alistair's eyes widened as he felt just how much stronger he had become. He allocated his free points, putting them into Constitution and Endurance. His total Attribute pool went up by almost 33% from the new Badge and levels. It felt unfair to double dip on the victory in trial two and the overall victory in the Quest, but hey, he wasn't going to complain about the Pathfinder AI deciding to change it up at the last second.

The wording of "1" made him happy—after stealing "World Leader" from Pharaoh, he didn't want to cause the man any more pain. But, he had to grin seeing that Badge. #1. It had been his unspoken goal for a while, and now he'd achieved it.

More worrisome than stealing a Badge was the subregion situation.

His current subregion readout was frankly absurd. 65,666 subregions? That was 40% of the total in the world. The *entire* world.

Alistair blinked three times, trying to comprehend the gravity of what he was seeing. At the end of the Quest 4, he had just over a thousand subregions, and he felt stretched thin protecting that. 65 times more territory felt like a dream. He had a mountain of money and credits, but would that be enough? Surely Pharaoh, Carmen, the monsters and beasts would be agitating for the return of their subregions, not to mention all the smaller rulers they had stolen from in turn.

Another notification answered those concerns, but also added new ones.

[Armageddon]: *Welcome to the final Quest of FX-14752's initiation. After this Quest, your planet, ruled by the newly appointed Global Mayor, will be inducted as a Basic world under Baron Zilvesky Aportamus of the Harmonious Note System, who answers to Countess Palava Roshin of the fifteenth province of the Disputed Shard, fief of House Lieverwacht. FX-14752 will be awarded a seat in the System Senate, and all privileges and responsibilities of a full citizen-state of the Final Frontier Empire.*

[Armageddon] consists of six waves of adversity that will test FX-14752 to the limit. Each wave will get successively more catastrophic and difficult, culminating in the final "Armageddon."

The Devil Kings, led by George Moulin, have been deemed as the "Harbingers" of [Armageddon]. They can achieve an early victory by killing the top ten rankers on the current leaderboard or controlling over 50% of the world's territory.

The position of Global Mayor, given the Devil Kings' failure to complete their task, will be the individual with the highest Contribution Score. Contribution Score is calculated via a combination of personal cultivation, territorial achievement and land improvement, and effectiveness in dealing with the incoming waves.

The name of the first wave is Earth Asunder and begins in a week's time. During the next week, violence between humans is prohibited as the current freeholds will be given a chance to shore up their defenses.

Task: Survive and prosper. Reward: Global Mayor. Time Limit: 6 months. Penalty: None.

Alistair gave a silent word of thanks to the Pathfinder AI for the week-long ban on violence. His drachma and Land Credits were piling up at a ridiculous rate. He would reach the two million cap in no time. Hopefully, he would get a chance to review everything in greater detail now. In the Quest, he couldn't access that information, or any information from the "outside," except for the raw subregion count.

The information about [Armageddon] was less detailed than he would have liked. Earth Asunder was an extremely vague name, and it wasn't clear what the Devil Kings being the "Harbingers" entailed. Were the Devil Kings the leaders of a wave of monsters? Or would they just benefit from the chaos?

The final prompt was for another Quest.

Quest Available: [Ultimate Skill]: *Every fighter needs their finishing move. Find requisite insight while killing powerful foes.*

Task: Variable. Reward: Expert Foundation Skill, Arcana (II) Achievement.

Accept (Y/N)?

It was unhelpfully vague, and Alistair wondered how the mechanics of the Quest worked. For his current batch of combat Skills, they came as the result of complicated upgrades. But he had developed the concepts behind them over time—they didn't come out of nowhere. Perhaps, like how people's initial Skills developed from their habits and experiences, he would have to develop the theory behind his finisher on his own, and the Pathfinder AI would fill in the details.

He pressed yes, of course. No way was Alistair about to turn down a finishing move.

Whatever the case, he needed to get back as soon as possible. Alistair jumped out of the pool, rushing to the cave's exit. Eavol awaited on the other side.

"Apologies, young master," the homunculus said. "The Pathfinder AI preferred this method over a complete bodily reconstruction since you were intact."

Alistair sped by him, shouting back as he ran. "How long?"

"Perhaps six hours. It's such a shame that those who died proper had an instant return in comparison, how terribly unfair—"

Alistair didn't hear the end of Eavol's sentence, jumping through the portal at the end of the long white corridor.

When the light faded, he found himself in the same place as when he'd started [The Game of Life]—the meeting room of his headquarters.

The twelve others in the room jumped back at the unexpected appearance of their leader. The room was busy, with most of the high-ranking members of the Northeast Order Freehold present.

"Alistair! Holy shit, where have you been?" Alexandra asked, one of the few who hadn't jumped back at his sudden arrival.

"Stupid Pathfinder made me heal in this black gunk instead of remaking my body like those who died," Alistair complained, taking his seat at the head of the table. "What's going on?"

"You arrived just in time," John said. "They're coming."

Alistair would have asked who "they" referred to, but he had a pretty good guess. He looked to Linda, the former architect in charge of their infrastructure.

"Linda, I'm going to give you a ton of Land Store Credits and drachma. You are going to improve all of our defenses, ASAP. Get as many of your subordinates working on bolstering our protection. You have my permission to hire as many people as you need. Lauren, you're going to give Linda and Felix and Carter as much money as they need from our bank. This is our number one priority. DEFCON 1."

"Already on it, boss," Linda said. "Keeping you in the loop on recent developments, there's been a significant geographic shift. As far as we know, the continents have collapsed into one supercontinent. The moment that people started returning, the geography of our subregions changed. We're in the mountains now, somehow."

Alistair remembered the text of The Commons of War and Peace explaining their subregions would be rearranged for anonymity.

He opened his status screen, navigating to the Land Store section. He could control various aspects of the freehold from that menu, including things like taxation level, gifting subregions to others, and overseeing his subordinates.

There was a list of over one hundred names listed as having fifty subregions in his freehold that he didn't recognize. Alistair had been curious about that before. If you were one of the losers, how did your subregions get reallocated?

His list held the answers. Everyone who personally possessed over fifty subregions got taken down to just fifty, the rest going to Alistair's personal horde. Based on his ownership level, it looked like those with under fifty simply had their territory confiscated.

The individual freeholders had certain rights and powers, like a real public company. It hadn't mattered so far, but technically, if 51% of the ownership decided to vote him out, they could. Because of the eight-way distribution of the subregions earned from the previous Quest, his current ownership was 8,001.

That was just 12.2% of the total freehold. The supermajority of the rest was spread between the other seven members of his team. He had signed William St. James, Jesse Waterfall, and Fasha binti Iksandar to contracts, folding them into his freehold.

It sounded like something the Final Frontier Empire would do. If he couldn't provide value for the shareholders and still wanted to maintain control, he'd have to keep them in line with force. Alistair was confident it wouldn't come to that.

"How are they getting here?" Alistair asked. "Shouldn't we have control of the entire territory of America? Not even just America—I mean, we should have a gigantic land mass."

John floated over a scroll. "It's a **Global Map**."

Alistair unfurled it, checking out the item. It opened a similar two-dimensional circular map like his old **Regional Map** except this one showed the entire globe. The landmass of the planet looked like one amorphous blob. It had been a long time since Alistair studied geography, but it looked similar to Pangea.

The Northeast Order Freehold was a shade of purple on the map, and it covered a huge portion of the landmass. Their capital was a red dot near the center of their territory.

"Our old 1,000-subregion territory that we had a solid hold of is contiguous, yes," John explained. "Technically, we could have our people shut off all **Teleportation Circles** in and out of the freehold. There are two problems with that. First, as you know, it's impossible to remove a destination that exists. We have nine foreign destination **Teleportation Circles**, each at the 100k drachma cost for the improved version. That's a ton of money to replace all of them. Second, it doesn't matter since they can easily find circles close to us that we don't control yet. We just increased our freehold's size sixty-five-times over. That's a vulnerability we can't fix."

"Plus," Alexandra said, "Alfred told me they already teleported here."

Alistair turned his head to her. "What?"

"He DMed me on the Soulnet Message Board. Not surprising, considering their information network is the best in the world. I'm sure they have basically infinite points to spend. But yeah, he said they would arrive in twenty minutes, thirty minutes ago."

"What a remarkably devious situation," Dev'rox commented. "I love it. How many angry protesters are you going to get, mad that you 'stole' their subregions? And you can't even kill them because of the ban on violence."

"I wouldn't kill them anyway," Alistair responded.

"Give them a good roughing up, then."

"I'm pretty sure that's banned, too."

Everyone in the room looked at him strangely, likely wondering why Alistair was silent for so long. He realized with some embarrassment that only Alexandra and Oliver knew about Dev'rox. He had only told them a couple of weeks after getting the ghost in the first place. Alistair didn't like sharing secrets that he didn't have to.

"Ahem, excuse me," Alistair began. "John, here's the list of all the new preferred shareholders. I'm sure some of them are coming now, but for the rest, contact them and let them know that we'll be integrating them within the freehold. Full suite of services with our academy, protection with public safety, food from our agricultural division, et cetera. But also, don't be coy about letting them know their place, if you know what I mean. We're the ones in control."

Alistair scanned the room, realizing there were two faces that he hadn't seen before. "Who are these people?"

John, who was sandwiched in the middle, wrapped his arms around the two of them. "This woman to my right is Celeste Mendoza. Thanks to her long-distance communication Skill, she's been smoothing everything over with coordination. To my left is Angelica DeForest, her assistant."

"Nice to meet you," Alistair said. "How did John find you?"

"I migrated from a surrounding subregion at the start of the last Quest," Celeste said.

Carter Delacroix, who was in charge of public safety, interrupted the conversation. "The first of them are dribbling in now. What should we do, boss?"

Alistair stood up from his seat. "I'll deal with it. Alexandra, Carter, with me. Everyone else, get to work."

———

New Boston had changed, even in the almost two weeks that Alistair had been gone. It was coming up on four months since the initiation, but it felt like years. With Linda's help, they were constructing twenty-story buildings of glass and metal that looked taken out of a sci-fi story.

She also had started to install a public transportation system. Unfortunately, they didn't have enough money to finish it while he was gone, but it connected half of the city. They had prioritized reconstructing the areas destroyed by Atavius's attack instead.

The public transportation took the form of hybrid lines powered by space and air Mana. Transparent and light-green energy flowed above the street. You could call it down by focusing your willpower. The lines of Mana would descend and bring you into the stream, and then a screen would ask for your destination.

From what Carter said, the incoming group was at the southern part of the city wall. "Wall" was somewhat of a misnomer—instead of a physical barrier, New Boston was protected by a diffuse energy field. Realistically, it wouldn't stop any miscreant above level 30, but it fed information to a system that registered the entry of any non-citizens.

The three of them entered the stream, shooting off at almost three hundred kilometers per hour. Since the g-forces of sharp turns would shred any ordinary person, the Mana stream consisted of mostly straight sections with some gentle curves.

It only took three minutes to arrive, the line ending at a reinforced region of the border. A three-story metal prism served as a sentry for the outlying area, with a laser eye that scanned several kilometers out for threats. The area it scanned was still their territory, but an ounce of prevention was worth a pound of cure.

A guard at the base of the prism rushed over to them. "I'm sorry, sir. I told them you were coming. They wouldn't take no for an answer."

"It's alright, Jeff. Let me take it from here," Alistair replied, patting the guard on the shoulder.

The group standing inside the energy wall impressed Alistair with their resourcefulness. It had only been six hours since the end of the Quest, yet there were over thirty people at his door.

It was almost amusing, Alistair thought. Like a class-action lawsuit, Carmen had scrounged together a bunch of shareholders who had lost everything. And now they were here to harass him.

Alistair put up his hands. "I'm not giving it back, sorry."

47 PROTEST

THE ONLY PEOPLE Alistair recognized were Carmen, Richard, Pharaoh, and a man named Carlos Garcia who was #18 in the world. For the rest of them, their uncloaked auras put them in the top 100, with levels estimated to be in the low 40s.

A tall and muscular man stepped forward. "I'm sure you can agree how unfair this process is, Alistair. Losing all our subregions because of the results of an arbitrary game?"

A woman by his side spoke up. "We're not asking for everything back, just half. We lost everything. What are we supposed to do?"

Carmen said nothing but gave him a murderous glare. He imagined she wasn't happy about the four weak teams that she'd placed behind. Which, to be fair, was entirely his doing. They would have certainly been eliminated first if Jesse hadn't rescued them all, and if Dev'rox hadn't secured their beacons.

But he wasn't going to apologize for that. Plus, he had paid a lot himself. He and Lucius had agreed to give 20% of their subregion prize to the United Polities in exchange for help from President Ryder's fusion. Alistair probably could have gotten a better deal, but he was already anxious to win, so he'd just wanted things to work out.

Now, he would stand his ground.

"I share your sympathies about the Final Frontier Empire, but I can't do that," Alistair said, shaking his head. "If you join the Northeast Order, I can guarantee your safety and a fair amount of cultivation resources along with opportunities to advance. But I can't give you back your subregions outright."

Alistair felt queasy being so harsh, but it had to be done. When he watched TV, he could always stomach blood and guts, but seeing betrayal was a different story. Not giving these people back their subregions he'd won in a sanctioned contest wasn't betrayal, but it didn't feel good, either. Maybe he needed to channel more of Alexandra's flippancy.

He met Pharaoh's gaze for a moment, the former #1 looking down sheepishly right after. Alistair couldn't get a good read of the man. Was he mad that Alistair had stolen his spot at the top? Pharaoh was so peculiar that it was hard to tell. It wouldn't surprise Alistair to hear that in a hundred years' time, he would become a cultivator archaeologist, diving for treasure in ancient ruins.

"Do you want to test us?" Carmen asked, her magical aura flaring with green sparks. "Not even you can stand up to all of us."

"On that note," Pharaoh said, "I'm afraid I can't agree. Whimsy and I are perfectly fine being unattached cultivators. I came here only to bring Elaine."

Alistair assumed that Elaine was the blond woman next to Pharaoh. She radiated a sunny aura and felt like one of the stronger ones there—around level 44, by his estimate.

"She was the one who ran everything for us. I'm sure she'll be a great help." After Pharaoh finished his sentence, he collapsed into a plume of sand.

Classic Pharaoh, Alistair thought. *Well, this isn't so bad now. We could use the extra help.*

Richard the Sniper scratched his head, looking at Carmen, then Alistair, and then back again to his partner. "Ma'am, I cannot say in words how in debt I am to you. I appreciate everything that you've done for me. However, in this, I cannot support you. The United Polities were very clear. I tried to tell you before, but it's hard to get in a word with you sometimes."

Carmen's left eye looked like it was going to pop out of its socket. Alistair could literally feel the rage dripping off her. At first, he thought she would snap at the Navy SEAL. That would have been interesting, if only to see how the Pathfinder's restriction on violence worked. But she didn't go on a tirade.

"My allies flee faster than birds in winter," Carmen muttered.

With her two most powerful backers dropping out, Alistair had a feeling that she wouldn't press any harder. But that assumption turned out to be wrong.

"You're going to regret this, Alistair, I promise." Carmen turned around, green embers still flying off her body. Her aura exploded, green electricity zapping the ground around them.

"If you want them back so badly, come and try us," Alexandra shouted back, though it was possible Carmen didn't hear her. When the aura vanished, she was gone. "That's right! I didn't think so!"

"Brave words to say when she actually *can't* try us at the moment," Alistair wryly commented.

Alexandra shrugged. "She's not going to come after us if her head's screwed on right. You're way too powerful now. Plus, wouldn't Lucius help us? You're real buddy-buddy with him now, aren't you?"

"I don't know about that," Alistair said. "We did what we had to do."

Most of the group left after Carmen, but a few stayed behind, including Pharaoh, who re-emerged from his cloud of sand. Alistair gave him a funny look.

"Can you blame me?" Pharaoh said. "I prefer not talking to Carmen any more than I have to. Talk to the others, I can wait."

Alistair gave everyone else a once over. "I assume you're still here because you're going to take up my offer?"

"It's a consideration," said the man whom Alistair assumed to be the leader of the five that remained. "Can we get more details about the arrangement?"

"Talk to Carter about that," Alistair said, motioning to his public safety head. "Okay, bye, thank you for coming."

Alistair got them moving along with haste.

"What are you going to do?" Alexandra asked once they were alone.

"What I have to," Alistair replied. "I'm still too weak. The battle against your father and Dragonus proved that. I can get people to install defenses for the Northeast Freehold—but those are meaningless if I can't defeat the Devil Kings in a fight."

He regretted mentioning Admiral right away, seeing the pain on Alexandra's face.

"Do you want to talk about it?" Alistair asked.

"It's fine," she said, flipping **Withering Promise**. "Fuck it. It's not fine at all, but what can I do about it? I'm gonna have to kill my own dad."

"It's not going to come down to that," Alistair promised.

"Oh, yeah? Are you going to do it for it me? Great, that's so much better."

"I didn't mean it like that."

"I know, I know." Alexandra sighed, returning her dagger to its scabbard. "I've been on edge since I found out."

"Well, if I'm being honest, what I said before was bullshit. I don't know what it will come down to. I'm pretending just as much as anybody else. It's a realistic possibility that you'll have to fight your dad."

"You really know how to talk to a woman, don't you, Alistair?" Alexandra joked. "I like it better when you don't bullshit me, though."

Pharaoh let out a loud coughing sound from a few meters away. Truth be told, Alistair had forgotten that the man had stuck around. With his aura cloaked, he blended right into the background, despite his unusual frame.

"I hate to interrupt a touching moment, but I did come here for a reason," he said. "Alistair, may we talk?"

Alistair turned back to Alexandra to ask for permission, but she was already leaving.

"I have to go talk to Oliver, anyway," she called out. "Good luck!"

Then it was just the two of them. It was difficult to get a read on the mysterious cultivator. Sometimes, Alistair thought the man aloof, looking down on the world. But other times, he seemed more like a jester.

"It's about Saturn," the man said.

"Saturn?" Alistair asked. "Didn't Jakk kill him before Quest 5 even started?"

"That's just it," Pharaoh said. "Why would a Devil Prince kill a Devil King? Why would the other Devil Kings even accept that?"

"Because might makes right?" Alistair offered.

"It's a possibility, but I think they're hiding something. The most logical explanation is that Saturn had something they didn't want getting out."

"Like a weakness?"

Pharaoh scratched his chin. "A Devil King weakness, the location of their hideout, or their future plans. We would have no way of knowing."

Alistair felt like he could guess where Pharaoh was going next. "The mansion?"

"Yes. I have been thinking about it for a while now. Whatever secrets he might have had, they're in that dungeon."

"Does it even still exist?" Alistair asked. "Wouldn't the Devil Kings have recovered it by now?"

"Not necessarily," Pharaoh said. "The system was the one that created the châteaus we entered. We have no idea where the original mansion is, if it still exists at all. If Saturn actually had kompromat on the Devil Kings, he would have been in hiding. I'm guessing he didn't expect the Pathfinder AI to issue a Quest for him."

"I see."

"Do you want to help me search for it? We can comb over the northeast next week while killing monsters and beasts."

Alistair mulled over his options. He had already given his money and instructions out. John was his right-hand man for a reason. There was a strong temptation to oversee and micromanage every aspect of his empire, but sometimes he had to let things go.

"That sounds like a great idea."

———

Alistair did some housekeeping before leaving.

Caren turned up in the capital. Alistair had been expecting that. He found the Chronicler in the inherited Hall of Mathematics tower. Alistair and his allies had turned Anthony's treasured secret into a public center of knowledge. That didn't mean the flying monkeys inside set their prices any lower, but at least the people could theoretically purchase the information they needed.

The breadth and depth of the information at their local Hall of Math was subpar compared to the thousand-meter-tall skyscraper on Faxor. Just fifty meters tall, the crystalline structure still amazed Alistair with its unbelievably ancient and awe-inspiring aura. The iridescent shine of the transparent and pearly crystals danced in the sunlight.

Alistair passed through the plasma energy field, stepping inside the Hall of Math. Like its larger counterpart, the inside was larger than the outside, though not to the same degree. If the diameter of the tower was perhaps ten meters, the inside had a diameter of thirty.

There was still enough space for dozens of scrolls, jade slips, books, and other artifacts arranged in circular patterns spiraling up the tower.

A flock of flying monkeys ferried a variety of strange items. Alistair spotted a white-fur variant with a marble that looked suspiciously similar to the one Nenna Spindoller had given him during Felons vs. Fellows. This one was blue, with a turbulent ocean inside instead of his black sphere containing a lightning storm.

He had never been able to crack the mystery of the Cabal or the marble. All [Eyes of Truth] said was that it was a Divine rarity item, the second-highest rarity possible, two levels higher than his Mythical rarity Badges. An information missive on the item would cost a tenth of a Palladium drachma —way, *way* out of his price range.

Alistair sensed Caren's aura on the first floor. He wasn't hiding the blood aspect anymore, his affinity out for the world to see. His blood Mana had a slightly different flavor than Alistair's, more thirsty and vital.

It didn't take long for Alistair to find his friend. Caren was stooped over in a chair, his face buried in a book.

"It's okay, I'm awake. Or, I am now." Caren removed the book from his face, sitting up straight in the blocky crystal chair. Red paper fluttered around him, glowing with illegible runes. "Are you here to discuss the elephant in the room? I'm ready for my execution."

That got a laugh out of Alistair. And Dev'rox, who for some reason had a particular liking for the man. "You're not in trouble. Unless you've been secretly killing and feeding on innocent civilians?"

Caren let out an indignant grunt. "Of course not."

"How did you survive the initiation?" Alistair asked. "I haven't really asked anyone. Because honestly, a little part of me is afraid to know the answer."

"Survive?" Caren let out a sad laugh. "I'm from a podunk town in the middle of nowhere. I was born there, I went to school there, I got married there, and I was going to die there. I was the local librarian, you see, and my wife was a teacher at the high school. She died in the initiation. My parents died while on a road trip from Atavius's initial attack. Just retired too. And then my brother died from bandits, my aunts and uncles died from monsters. Everyone I knew from before is dead."

"Oh," Alistair said. That reminded him that he still hadn't found his mother, despite his power and influence.

"I was the lucky one; got my first kill slamming down a book on a giant beetle. I became the strongest in my subregion. But it wasn't enough."

Alistair read between the lines. "So that was how you became a…"

"Vampire? I don't know what I am exactly. My main Class is Chronicler and my Subclass is Blood Hierocrat. Though I gained a Shaded One ancestry as well."

Alistair remembered the Shaded One criminal from Felons vs. Fellows, the Bleeder. Based on how the others treated him, he guessed that Shaded Ones were a pretty powerful species, corresponding with the Earth conception of a vampire.

Caren continued. "Sorry, I didn't mean to burden you with my whole life story. The lack of sleep has made me cranky. Unlike the rest of your blessed folk, I still need my six hours. The Pathfinder AI didn't seem to heal my mental fatigue."

"I didn't come here to reprimand you or anything," Alistair replied. "I was just genuinely curious about your abilities. I could feel you were holding something back, which is why I entrusted you to defend the base alone in the first place. But I didn't expect that. Maybe we can share pointers. My blood affinity has some similarities with yours."

"I've noticed," Caren said. "You absorb blood essence through your Skill, same as I. But instead of cultivating from it or improving your understanding of the Dao, it seems to boost your life force."

Alistair nodded. "Yep. My absorption is probably inferior to your natural techniques."

"It's to be expected. I have a whole Subclass and species dedicated to drinking blood. So talking to me is the *only* reason you dropped by the Hall of Math?"

"I'm going to pick up a map of the area," Alistair admitted. "But I was going to see you, regardless."

"In that case, I'm going to get some more beauty sleep," Caren said. "Can you tell the monkeys to wake me up in a day?"

———

With the automatic transfer from Alistair's contract with the United Polities, the current subregion count for the Northeast Freehold was 52,538. That came with certain advantages.

Alistair previously had to spend Upgrade Points to improve the cap on drachma taxation from one million to two million a month. But obviously having fifty thousand subregions contributed to a higher cap. Instead of two million a month, he had a base limit of 6.95 million, plus the extra million from before. A total cap of nearly eight million Gold drachma.

There was still an option to increase the cap by two million that cost 100 Upgrade Points, but Alistair didn't think it was worth it. He was already spending all of his wealth on other people; his Upgrade Points could go to his own improvement.

Alistair increased the taxation percentage to 5%, at least for now. He wasn't happy about it. It felt like a shitty thing to do, but he did it anyway. He wasn't pocketing any of that himself. And as much as people might hate the tax, they would hate getting killed by an endless horde of demon-blooded beasts even more.

The freehold's economy was really booming. While in the past, their primary income was from taxes, that had completely changed. As Alistair's appointed steward, John had opened up an official shop for their freehold.

You could access it on the same page as the System Store by swiping to the right. Any citizen of the freehold could access it, along with non-citizens within their borders, though they paid a 15% surcharge.

They sold a variety of goods in their storefront—crafted and dropped weapons, items, pills, and more. Felix Mujinga, their weapons crafter, was pulling huge numbers with his constructs.

Any citizen could sell their wares in the store, though they got hit with a 2.5% platform fee. That created another stream of revenue.

For Land Credit generation, their passive numbers grew every day as the land became more attuned to the Dao. Additionally, they had sacrificed some drachma in the System Store to buy a kilometer-long harvester.

The cylindrical machine churned the land underneath, producing credits. As far as Alistair understood it, tendrils from the rotating metal shaft mined the ground for raw materials and Chaos-touched Mana. Materials were sold directly to the Pathfinder AI directly, who bequeathed Land Store Credits in return.

Overall, they were raking in 400k drachma and 1k credits a day.

Alistair's next debt payment in a week and a half would be a piece of cake. The only problem now was the time crunch.

Land Store items actually increased in power over time, as a way to offset their relatively steep costs. If only he'd been able to start building those defenses a few weeks ago, before the last Quest. If they were already here, they could have served as a great foundation for further buttressing.

Ah, Anthony, Alistair thought. Messing him up from beyond the grave with his Ricci Empire debt.

He hadn't forgotten about the last—but certainly not least important—money-making method: Lauren Yoon. The treasurer of the Northeast Freehold had matured since the last time Alistair had been involved with her.

With her newest Class Skill, Alistair could deposit and withdraw money at a distance. It was the perfect addition now that Alistair was going hunting with Pharaoh.

With the final touches on his preparations almost complete, he turned to his 392 Upgrade Points. First, he had to spend 300 to open an eighth Badge slot for "1." A ninth Badge slot would cost him 400 Upgrade Points, much to his major chagrin.

The final 92 points had a variety of options to pick between. A bunch of his Skills were very close to a Tier upgrade, so he finished them off for just 23 points between four Skills. **[Hand of Karma]**, **[Ghost Whispers]** and **[Spectral Summoning]** all increased to Tier 3, and Alistair upgraded **[Carmela's Happy Pies]** to Tier 2.

Dev'rox fluttered about after the upgrade, landing on the ground. With a stubby arm, he picked up a rock and threw it. "I'm free!"

"Dev'rox, you could already affect the physical world. Didn't you stab Anthony in the heart with your tail?" Alistair questioned. "And you just carried the beacons in the last Quest a few hours ago?"

"Yes, but I had to expend energy to do that. Now, I can be as solid as a living being when I want! Well, as solid as a Foundation."

Alistair felt the imp's Mana pool increase by a sizable amount, going from around 400 to 600. It condensed even more, becoming increasingly attuned to the Dao of Space. Or more accurately, by allowing Dev'rox to be more real, his Dao naturally seeped into his Mana.

That left 69 Upgrade Points. Alistair was tempted between two choices.

Continuing down the Blood of the Devil Tree was the obvious answer, but the fourth-level leaf cost 100 points. Unlike most other trees, you could only pick one leaf per level.

First-level leaves of other trees and branches were cheap, but had lower impact. It was always more efficient to go down a path already trodden. But a first-level leaf in the Divine Law Branch of the Lawful Magistrate Tree caught his eye.

Alistair felt he had never had a good opportunity to invest in his Subclass's Talent Trees. There had always been something more pressing going on. That was except for Justice Quest, wherein he had a second-level leaf also entitled Justice Quest.

That leaf made it easier for him to find and save people in danger. Back then, Alistair had thought he was a genius, seeing the perfect synergy with "Deliverance of Justice." In practice, it hadn't done him much good so far. But he wasn't giving up yet. The use case was there, but he needed to be patient.

Lesser Vipassanā was one of the three base leaves in the Divine Law Branch. For only 15 Upgrade Points, it would improve his natural Karmic sight's detection of falsehoods. For 30 Upgrade Points, Lesser Samatha improved [Eyes of Truth] to reveal inner truths not even spoken aloud.

As expected, Lesser Vipassanā and Lesser Samatha didn't have a huge impact, given that the combined cost was only 45 Upgrade Points. But information was priceless.

Alistair had to choose between that or improving "Devil May Cry." After a minute of deliberation, he went with the Divine Law leaves. "Devil May Cry" only offered him a combat benefit when he was on his last legs, while the two leaves would help him suss out enemies from the get-go.

"And now, you're finally ready?" Dev'rox complained. "Pharaoh probably left you behind by now."

Alistair had been so preoccupied tidying up all the loose ends that he had almost forgotten that he was supposed to go with Pharaoh.

Dev'rox picked up more rocks and threw them as far as he could. Which was not very far at all. They plopped into a nearby stream. Alistair had visited Donna before he left, and she was situated near the river as a volunteer fisher. Her daughter Tamia was at the city daycare, one of the most protected regions of the entire freehold.

"Yes, I'm ready now. Let's go."

48 FIREWORM

"Mind if I tag along?" Alexandra jumped down from the roof of a fifteen-story building onto the pavement below. Even with magical reinforcement, it partially cracked from her impact, making Alistair groan internally.

"How did you even find me?" Alistair asked, pretending to be shocked to see her, even though he had sensed her coming through four different methods.

"Are you kidding?" Alexandra raised an eyebrow. "When you're not cloaking your aura, I can feel it from over a mile away."

"Oh, yeah." Alistair started cycling his Mana internally, producing a cloak that trapped 99% of his aura. "I was thinking that those people demanding their subregions back would be more intimidated if I didn't cloak myself, and then I forgot to turn it back on."

"Fuck those guys," Alexandra said. "You think they're going to be a problem?"

"I don't know," Alistair answered truthfully. "It seems like it's just Carmen and a few of her buddies that she gathered. If Richard and Pharaoh won't join her, and I have all the little guys on my side with the United Polities, I doubt she can do much about it. But even if she does try some-thing, we have bigger fish to fry right now."

She nodded slowly. "The Devil Kings."

"Dragonus's title was the 'Third Devil King.' Besides George, that means there's another one stronger than him. And even with the stats I just gained, I don't think I could take on Dragonus in a one-on-one fight."

"You'll surpass them," Alexandra promised. "I don't doubt that for a second."

"I hope you're right. Right now, the only major upgrades I can get are my species and this Skill Quest. Though, 'only' is doing a lot of work there. I have a feeling they won't be anything to scoff at."

"If it all goes to shit—if you can't beat 'em, join 'em," Alexandra said, miming a drink from a thin container.

"You mean this?" Alistair produced the vial of demon blood from his pocket. "I don't even think I can do that. I'd probably lose all of my justice-related stuff."

"What even is that, anyway? You never told me that, even though you showed me your cute ghost buddy."

Dev'rox snorted. "I'll be the bigger imp and take that as a compliment."

Alistair opened his mouth to speak, but his words sputtered out. That was the one secret he hadn't told a soul, not even Dev'rox, though his ghost had probably come to his own conclusion. They shared thoughts, after all. He had reaffirmed that decision ever since Kyraxadon tried to sic Heaven on him.

"It's okay if you don't wanna say," Alexandra said. "I understand if there's a reason you're not telling me."

"I want to, but it's too dangerous," Alistair settled on. "We should get going now."

The fishers, who were currently in a tug-of-war against a twenty-meter-long carp leviathan, were on the other side of the city to where Alistair had left Pharaoh an hour ago. Alistair gave Alexandra a pointed look.

"Really?" she asked, hand on hip.

"You're the one who's tagging along. Hop on." He smiled and bent down.

Alexandra shook her head but jumped on his back, maybe with a little more force than was necessary. Once she was secure, he started running. Maybe a bit faster than he normally would have.

"That's... a... bit tight," Alistair wheezed as he jumped onto the roof of a ten-story building. He activated [Dash], using his airwalking to hop to another building.

"You're not going to drop me," Alexandra said, her voice caught in the wind. "Why do you still have the vial on you? I thought you gave it to people to analyze."

Alistair carefully landed on the cement below. **Fall of Fleet** really helped disperse the sound and impact of the crash. They didn't leave a single crack, even with their combined weight and the nearly thirty-meter fall.

"I did give it to some former scientists, but it's basically a treasure beyond their pay grade. Dev'rox said that if it was a proper item, it would be Mythical rarity. I thought I'd keep, just in case."

Alistair weighed his options, realizing his life was wrapped in Alexandra's strong arms. But who got ahead by being a coward? "I've noticed you've put on a ton of weight, is it all the Constitution or is it the—"

He didn't get to finish the sentence.

———

"She's coming along, too?" Pharaoh asked.

The former #1 had patiently waited for Alistair's return at the checkpoint by the wall. When Alistair and Alexandra arrived, he was chatting with the guard Jeff in the chrome building.

"If that's fine with you," Alistair said.

"No problem."

"Where's Whimsy?" Alexandra asked. "I need to pay her back for the ass-whooping she gave us last time."

"Dealing with administrative duties, among other things," Pharaoh said.

"Do you have any notion of where Saturn's mansion is?" Alistair asked. "Or is this a complete crapshoot?"

"It's just a hunch," Pharaoh said. "Based on construction of the mansion and the fact only people in America got access to it, the real version is most likely here as well. And where better to hide than in a deserted wasteland inhabited only by beasts and monsters?"

Alistair shrugged. "Better than nothing, I guess."

He morphed his red bracelets into the **Devilsbane Gauntlets**, clanking them together. Pharaoh guided them a few kilometers away to a recent addition to the Northeast Order.

"Is this how you and Carmen got here?" Alistair asked. They stood in a makeshift wooden shack on the outskirts of an abandoned town. He was surprised there was a working **Teleportation Circle** there in the first place.

"Just I," Pharaoh said. "You should search the territory within a ten-kilometer radius. I'm sure you'll find where she came from."

Alistair made a note of the location of the shack, sending it to John via the Soulnet. Surprisingly, there was a destination in the **Teleportation Circle** besides one across the sea. Though Alistair supposed there was no oceanic gap anymore, given the recent morphing of Earth's continents.

The other location would bring them almost four hundred kilometers away, to a large swath of burned land. One of Atavius's kilometer-long bolts of fire had landed in former Pennsylvania. It had eradicated all life within a two-hundred-kilometer radius. Only a blackened husk of earth remained.

However, in the ensuing months, the Pathfinder AI had brought an influx of Mana and the Dao into the lands of Earth. There were reports of twisted spirits of flame—disfigured creatures borne of fire and ash. That wasn't even including the monsters that had festered without humans to cull them.

They stepped onto the disk, Pharaoh choosing the destination on the pop-up menu. Alistair's vision filled with blue light. Unlike the wild sensation of rushing through space he felt when traveling with Jesse, the **Teleportation Circle** was like a cool summer breeze. After only a few seconds, the light faded, replaced by an open town square.

Unlike the last settlement, this one wasn't abandoned. The circle was in the center of a bustling intersection, guarded by two men in armor holding spears. It looked like a small suburban town, based on the colonial-style houses and well-maintained strip mall.

Alistair checked the freehold section of his status screen. This subregion had entered his domain after [The Game of Life].

When he looked at the tallest building in the vicinity, a thirty-meter-tall castle tower, he saw an official representative of his own freehold. The woman was helping the locals construct a defensive barrier, directing them from her elevated vantage point.

Alistair chuckled at the familiar uniform. For all the lower-ranked officials, they had issued a set of protective black robes. An official insignia of a tri-colored fist of gold, coral, and baby blue sat right over the heart. Unfortunately, since it wasn't as durable (or comfy) as his own **Mammothskin Raiment,** he hadn't personally made the switch.

Whispers in the crowd began the moment the three of them showed up. A family of three were the closest, and a little girl pointed at him.'

Alistair was about to ask how far away it was, but all he needed to do was turn around. The entire horizon was a Stygian nightmare. Even many kilometers away, he could feel the heat and see the embers rising out of fissures in the earth. It had been months since the initial attack, yet the land had not fully healed.

Pharaoh nodded toward the charred wasteland. As the three of them walked through the town, a crowd formed at their feet.

"Is that him?" someone whispered. "It is!" another exclaimed. Cries of gratitude and adulations spread like wildfire. In just a few minutes, hundreds of people had gathered.

Alistair smiled and waved to the crowd, though many of them wanted more than that. A couple of boys went up to him for signatures, while many couples requested blessings for their kids. As if he could imbue some special characteristic.

Alistair paused to consider. Maybe he *could*—Karma worked in mysterious ways. Speaking of Karma, Alistair had 27 overdue procs of "Deliverance of Justice." But he didn't expect to get a chance to earn them now.

Suddenly, his hair stood on end. Something was coming, and Alistair was first to sense it. Or more accurately, smell its blood. It wasn't like anything he had ever encountered before.

"Shit!" he exclaimed. "Guys, we need to evacuate them right now!"

"What's going on?" Alexandra asked with a frown.

"Big, big... thingy," Alistair blabbered, unable to find the right words. At that moment, the two others must have felt it coming too, since Pharaoh immediately burned away his clothing while Alexandra used [Empower Weapon II] on her daggers.

She flared her aura and waved her enlarged weapons in huge arcs. "Go, go, go!" she shouted to the crowd, who was beginning to catch the drift.

For a moment, nothing happened. There were only the screams of the fleeing townspeople. Alistair wondered if his olfaction had gone awry, but then he felt the creature with all his other senses.

Cracks formed on the pavement, spreading for dozens of meters. The ground churned and groaned from the emergence of a behemoth from the depths of the earth. Thousands of tons of dirt and bedrock and concrete collapsed as the largest being Alistair had ever seen shot out of the ground.

The first sensation Alistair felt after laying eyes on the creature was awe. Awe, and then fear. It was a worm. An enormous, molten worm.

Its mouth was concave, filled with layers on layers of teeth that spiraled inward. Its skin flaked and sparked embers as it clashed against the collapsing terrain. The blackened skin and burn marks suggested an origin from the wasteland, and its attunement to the Dao of Fire confirmed it. There was a burning fire inside its mouth that continued throughout the visible length of its body, creating an internal glow that illuminated its alien physiology. It was no animal born of a mother, but a creature borne from the Dao itself.

The worm, whose mouth had to be almost forty meters wide, kept shooting up into the sky. When Alistair used [Eyes of Truth], it was so powerful that it didn't even show a level, returning question marks in every category. At level 51, he felt strong enough to gauge that it definitely exceeded the Beast Lord category, sitting somewhere at the start of the Beast Ruler range, the equivalent of Adept.

"Holy shit!" Alexandra whistled.

"Let's help them evacuate." Alistair didn't wait for his allies' response, [Dashing] toward those fleeing civilians. Funnily enough, with the average townsfolk in the mid-twenties in level, they could all sprint faster than a cheetah.

Then, he stopped and [Dashed] back. Pharaoh zoomed by on a cloud of condensed sand. "I'll deal with the evacuation."

Alistair gave him a sheepish grin. He had forgotten for a moment that he was a Magical Pugilist. If he wanted to help, he would need to ferry people one-by-one. He was better suited to warding off the worm.

At that point, the Beast Ruler had crested to its full height of over two hundred meters. There was no way it was fully out of the ground yet, but even a Dao-wrought firewyrm had to obey the laws of physics to some degree. It was going to come crashing down in a kilometer-long arc that would destroy large parts of the town and kill many of its inhabitants.

"No way," Alexandra said. "That's just plain stupid."

"This is my way," Alistair said. "If I can't risk my life for these people, then I don't deserve what I've got."

With that, he jumped.

It wasn't an ordinary jump—Dev'rox lent him spatial Mana to decrease the distance between him and the worm. Because of the wind turbulence, he ended up a few meters from the worm's head.

Alistair activated **[Blood Hand]**, throwing the bubbling hot liquid with a flick of his wrist. With his other hand, he used **[Frozen Claw]**. The latter Skill washed over the blood spatter, which had reached the body of the worm. It crystallized his blood into a sharp icicle, stabbing the worm's side like a gigantic toothpick.

He grabbed onto the crimson icicle, swinging across it like he was climbing the monkey bars. At the apex of his jump, Alistair reached the top of the worm's head.

Without **Mammothskin Raiment,** which insulated him against extreme heat and cold, he would surely have been burned despite his 227 Constitution. Embers scratched Alistair's face and fire erupted out of the small wound he'd carved with his two Skills.

Despair entered his heart as he took in the gravity of the situation. His stomach dropped upon seeing the two-hundred-meter drop beneath him. Everything looked so small. The worm projected a primal and unrefined fire that threatened to burn him to a crisp.

It would be so easy to jump off and run away. But that wasn't Alistair.

He condensed a full twenty points of positive Karma into his right hand. The Skill **[Hand of Karma]** felt even heavier now, its conceptual heft weighing heavily on the reality of the world. The beast's crimson energy expelled the Dao, and Alistair slapped his hand against the worm's hide.

Karmic energy dispersed in radiant lines through the worm's trunk. It passed under its skin and flooded its strange biology with parasitic Fate. Alistair knew he wasn't powerful enough to disrupt the entire worm, but at least it was something.

Crawling to the edge with unusual dexterity, he used another **[Frozen Claw]** to give himself an anchor. He clawed a small wound into the worm with his sharp fingertips and used that point to hang on. From there, he could grab the frozen blood spear he'd made before and slammed it in with more force.

Once he shoved in the full length of the crystallized weapon, he activated **[Blood Hand]**. The Ghost Node flowed through the Skill, adding a copious amount of Dao energy.

Alistair plunged his hand inside, the molten flesh burning unlike anything he had ever felt before. The pain was excruciating—it felt like his arm was going to melt off his skeleton. But he held on. He let go of his frozen anchor, only hanging on to the worm by dangling from his other arm.

[Blood Hand] struggled to handle the immense life force of the mysterious creature. Alistair doubled up, producing another [Blood Hand] with his right arm and grabbing his left shoulder, pumping in more blood affinity Mana.

For the purposes of his talent, apparently the worm counted as a beast since he gained a whopping 4 points of Endurance from his Skill.

The dark-red blood that poured into the worm was a combination of Alistair's own blood essence and life force, aspected Mana from his soulcore, and Dao energy. It spread out of him immediately through the beast's weakened spiritual network. The flesh nearby dulled out, losing its fiery sheen.

Alistair couldn't celebrate his success for too long. The Beast Ruler had finally felt Alistair's attack, and it was full of animal rage. The incandescent organs within burned brighter, emitting so much heat that even his **Mammothskin Raiment** couldn't keep up. His Health, which was over 1,000, dropped by 50 points a second from the scorching temperature.

The dead zone of spiritually destroyed flesh continued to spread the length of a city block in either direction before its growth almost halted to a dead stop.

Alistair knew he had to use the worm's anger to draw its attention away from the bystanders. He thought about his family and his missing mother. He thought about his Quest, and what he needed to do. Maybe it would be possible one day, but at the present he couldn't be some arhat that achieved enlightenment in seclusion. Alistair found inspiration in the crucible of danger, where steel sharpens steel, and where the lives of others depended on his actions.

The Kai'tazake Mutra embraced him like an old friend. The vision of Zenaitsu Morogoni weighed heavily on his mind. He cursed how impotent and fleeting human memory was. If only Alistair could see the World Titan's movements again, he would unlock all the secrets he needed. In lieu of that, he did his best to imitate what he remembered.

But he added his own spin. Was it perhaps arrogance to think himself more qualified than the being that had attained earth-shattering power? Perhaps. But one didn't grow stronger by merely copying.

Alistair brought his hand to the sky, activating [Force Fist].

Skill Upgraded: [Force Fist] (Tier 2 Expert Skill): *Force Fist.* Mana Cost: 60. Upgradeable (0/200).

At Tier 2, **[Force Fist]** had increased in Mana cost, unlike his two other new Skills, and with that came a boost of power. Alistair made the decision to open up his hand; instead of a fist, he brought down a knifehand strike. Or, as most people would call it—a karate chop.

The solid coral-colored hand descended with the full power of Fist Node. The Dao energy felt heavy—like his Karma—carrying Alistair's truths of pugilism and judgment. Like before with **[Frozen Claw]**, Alistair added another Dao to his attack—the Justice Node. Not only was it an act of martial prowess, but he was the executioner of divine judgment on this wretched beast.

The strike came down at a sideways angle on the worm's open wound. Alistair intended to knock the beast off course so that it wouldn't fall on the people below.

A rush of air temporarily blinded Alistair. The shockwave of his "Force Chop" sent him flying off the worm. As he soared down to earth and his vision returned, he caught a glimpse of the aftermath of his blow.

With his Dao energy and the newly upgraded **[Force Fist]**, the fajin effect was stronger than ever. Alistair imagined the worm was more injured from the sudden crumpling and warping of its body from the fajin rather than the actual force of the attack.

He watched in amazement. Something of his size could actually affect a creature that was kilometers long.

Gravel and concrete scratched his back as Alistair fell onto a road. With his weight, he cracked open the street and left a meter-deep crater. Alistair got up and dusted his singed coat. His danger sense didn't even go off. He was out here falling from two-hundred-meter heights and could barely give a damn.

The worm crashed onto the ground in the direction of Alistair's chop, safely away from the town and into a nearby forest. He held out hope that such a fall would be injurious for a beast of that size. However, as it fell, it righted its head and dove back into the ground, though not without a large explosion of trees and dirt. That sound echoed across the desolate landscape in every direction.

Alistair waited in apprehension about where the worm would go.

Luckily, it became clear right away that it was speeding away just as quickly as it had arrived, leaving a trail of burning forest where it came close to the surface.

After that, his body's tension disappeared and a giddy smile crept across Alistair's face. Yes, he had barely damaged the Beast Ruler worm, mostly owing his victory to the animal's natural instinct to avoid danger and a helpful fajin effect—but who cared? It was still over level 100, and he had warded it off.

"Deliverance of Justice": +24 free Attribute points.

Because of "Jack of All Trades," Alistair had a strong suspicion that there was a level 60 version of that Badge. That suspicion was proved correct when he allocated 12 points to Constitution, 9 to Endurance, and the 3 to Charisma. Those recent additions brought his Constitution and Endurance to exactly 250.

Badge Upgraded: "Jack of All Trades II" (Untiered Legendary Badge): *Achieve 2,500 total points of stats with at least 250 in every attribute before level 60.* All Attributes +21%.

A 6% increase in all Attributes from his previous "Jack of All Trades" Badge brought his total stats from 2,666 to 2,754. At first, Alistair thought the math was wrong, since that was a mere 3.3% increase in Attributes. He quickly realized he was being stupid. It was a percentage point increase, not a straight percentage increase. The 6% percentage points was an addition to his 71% increase to all Attributes, making the actual percent increase equal to comparing 77% to 71%. That math was slightly off since most of his stats had other bonuses.

"You're an idiot sometimes, Alistair," Alexandra called out, trucking him with a playful push.

"What's that for?"

"I thought you were going to die for a second. Do you realize what you look like right now? Your face is literally black with soot."

"What about the people?" Alistair asked, wiping off his face. "Are they all right?"

As if he knew the timing of their conversation, Pharaoh flew in on a cloud of sand. "Your magistrate is taking them to the safety of New Boston. No one died."

"I helped a couple of kids who fell down in the cracks," Alexandra said. "No biggie."

Alistair chuckled. "And you're lecturing me about trying to be too much of a hero."

"Well, I'm not a monster. What did you think—I was going to see a cute little girl with her leg crushed by a two-ton rock and say, 'Oh, sorry. Can't be bothered.'" Alexandra scrunched her nose. "And be very, very careful what your next words are."

"I'm surprised you didn't crush her with your iron grip. Not everyone can handle your *enthusiasm*."

"I hate to break this up," Pharaoh interrupted, "but I think you'll want to hear this. I believe this worm has given us the key to finding Saturn's mansion."

49 FIREBIRD

"I CAUGHT a whiff of Saturn off of the worm," Pharaoh explained. "He must've been experimenting with the creatures of this land."

Alistair didn't notice anything with his sense of smell, but then again, he had been a little preoccupied. Pharaoh must have seen the doubt on his face since he added, "I have a special penchant for Devil Kings. It's why I was able to turn Whimsy. The Pharaoh's Gift."

Shattered windows and cracks dotted many of the buildings in the town. Thankfully, Pharaoh and Alexandra had evacuated everyone safely. Alistair guessed they would probably not return with the threat of the fire beasts looming over their heads.

Whatever scouting method Pharaoh employed, he explained little. Alistair and Alexandra first followed him into the forest that the worm had burrowed into. The eccentric man would take out a vitreous rod, lick it, and then raise it high in the air as if detecting changes in the wind.

In the meantime, Alistair checked on his bloodline progress. After absorbing the blood essence of the worm, he was at 440/500 toward unlocking his bloodline. He could feel the ghostly blood dragon within him now, but it wasn't real yet. It was like a dream, imprisoned behind the humanity of his cells.

Alistair had a feeling that simple blood essence wouldn't be enough. His bloodline was more than just a set of special characteristics. It felt *alive*. And when it had encountered Dragonus's black dragon bloodline, the initial rage Alistair had felt was unlike anything else. The only way he could complete his bloodline would be by using **[Blood Hand]** on Dragonus.

He and Alexandra played with an erratic spinning top while Pharaoh did his dowsing. The top flew in the air, giving off cerulean sparks as the object of the game was to catch the flighty toy. Alistair checked his Contribution Score for [Armageddon] as they played, happily finding himself in first place.

It took the better part of an hour for Pharaoh to finally nod his head and say it was time to enter the barren land.

The demarcation between the bombarded section and the surrounding region was a literal black line. Where they stood, everything was salubrious and verdant. But not even a few meters away, the ground was charcoal black and simmered with intense heat.

The packed earth radiated heat like a convection oven, warping the air into squiggly lines. The bolt of Atavius's fire had eradicated the relief of the terrain, rendering everything flat and lifeless. A couple of hills and troughs here and there might once have been cloud-scraping mountains and deep valleys.

Flames occasionally lit up the horizon but with no obvious source. Alistair compared the Dao diffusing from the scorched earth to his experience in the facsimile Dao Heart beneath Saturn's château. It was harder to access his own Dao Nodes with the encroaching power of fire all around him. Though still easier than when inside a foreign proto-Domain, the lingering aspect of fire came from a source greater than a Foundation realm.

Alexandra kicked the desolate soil, digging up a chalky powder that crumbled in the wind and doubled back into her face. "Blargh," she let out, coughing up the disgusting specks. "This shit is gross."

At least by now Pharaoh seemed to know where he was going, jogging straight ahead with some actual expediency. Distance was hard to measure when everything was simply dark. After walking for a few kilometers, it all looked the same since an atmospheric fog covered their origin.

The only thing that changed was the temperature. It was a gradual change and difficult to notice. Only after they had been running for an hour did Alexandra speak up.

"Is it just me or is it getting hot?" she asked.

It had always been hot, at least by mortal standards. Alistair's superior body and **Mammothskin Raiment** messed up his barometer for temperature, but he would have said it was around 150 degrees Fahrenheit upon entering the zone. As he wiped the sweat away from his brow, it clearly had gone up to at least 300 degrees, if not higher.

"It's dry heat," Pharaoh remarked, ditching his regal garb. "Even a pre-initiation human could survive 200 degrees Celsius, if it was dry."

"That's 400 Fahrenheit, something like that?" Alexandra asked. "Are you sure that's right? Aren't ovens 400 degrees?"

"He's right," Alistair said. "I've been in a sauna close to that temperature before. Dry air carries heat really poorly and your sweat can evaporate."

"Hmph, okay." Alexandra resumed kicking the dirt, though the wind had stopped so she didn't get any ashes in her face. "It is getting hotter, though."

"We're only a fourth of the way to the center," Pharaoh said. "So far, the temperature has doubled. If that holds up, then it will be over a thousand degrees by the time we reach the center, Fahrenheit or Celsius."

"It's at the center, then?" Alistair asked. Pharaoh had been reticent with whatever findings he had made with his glass rod.

"All paths lead to the center," Pharaoh said mysteriously.

And so they trekked on. Another hour in and they were halfway there, according to Pharaoh. It was starting to feel actually hot for Alistair, like a warm summer day. They saw fires far more frequently now, blazes popping up every few minutes. And not little patches of flame, but full-on infernos that covered acres and acres of land.

At one point, they had to take an extremely circuitous route around a kilometer-long wall of fire. Alistair felt sick when saw it. The thick flames reminded him of that first day. They had burned here for months and months, and yet Atavius's Dao still wouldn't fully extinguish.

It became clear the fires weren't only physical either. They carried a spiritual presence that weighed heavily on his internal systems, regardless of how insulated he was from the heat. Alexandra was sweltering as well. Only Pharaoh seemed relatively unaffected, though Alistair chalked that up to his Sovereignty of Osiris bloodline. That man had tanked an entire [**Lightning of Justice**] without flinching. When he asked Pharaoh, the Egyptian cultivator explained that his bloodline reduced the power of magical attacks at a conceptual level.

Some time later, they were three-fourths of the way through.

They weren't telling time via the sun anymore. The surrounding flames grew until they were as tall as trees, marking the landscape in deadly groves. Scarlet, amber, and golden-orange burning gasses formed fractal shapes in the air. You couldn't make out exactly what they were supposed to be, but something weird was happening the closer they got to the center.

The Dao had become stifling, like an all-encompassing pressure on reality. Alistair felt it strain against his skin. It desired to subsume his entire body. All he could do was let his own spiritual weight stand against it. Meditating on his Dao Nodes helped alleviate the oppression, but every time he did so, he could feel their energies dwindle by a fraction.

Alistair wondered if this was what the Dao was like in the Imperial Heartlands. If he was a fire cultivator, he imagined it would have been an enlightening experience. For him, it was a test of will. He would not bend to the fire's remnant desires.

There was one upside—the environment was insane for growth. The ambient Mana that filled the atmosphere was fire-attuned, but their soul-cores had grown enough that they could filter it themselves. In what felt like just a few hours of travel, he had saturated his cells with enough Mana to advance to level 52. Pharaoh reached level 49, while Alexandra skipped two levels to 48.

Contrary to what he initially thought, it was also a fruitful experience for his personal Dao as well. Maybe it was a case of iron sharpening iron. Withstanding the foreign Dao seemed to create a stronger connection to his own Daos. It forced him to dig deeper and find hidden connections just to feel the presence of his Nodes.

While it couldn't compare to being in a comparable environment of Ghost, Fist, or Justice, it was far better than normal.

But something stopped Alistair in his tracks. For how long had they walked? Days? At their speed, they should have reached the center in half a day.

Alistair activated [Eyes of Truth], focusing with extreme precision on the cryptic flame formations. They were real, as he expected. An illusion couldn't replicate the effects they had experienced unless it was replacing all of reality. And there was no way something that powerful could slip under his nose. It would take a cultivator much mightier than anyone on Earth to do that.

Like he often did in scenarios when he needed advice, Alistair reached out to Dev'rox.

"I was beginning to wonder when you would ask," the imp said, flickering into existence in front of his face. As a purely spiritual being, the Dao affected him more, the heat warping his burgundy figure.

"Why didn't you say anything?"

"I *couldn't*, brat," Dev'rox said. "There was something preventing me. A machination of Fate, I suspect."

"How many days has it been?" Alistair asked.

"Four? I think?" Dev'rox answered. "It's hard to say since I can't see your star in the sky."

Pharaoh and Alexandra turned back when they saw Alistair had fallen behind.

"What are you doing, Alistair? Come on!" Alexandra waved for him to get moving.

"Guys, there's something seriously wrong. I think we've been walking for four days."

Alistair tried checking the Soulnet, but there was somehow too much interference. He had never seen a warning like that before. At least he could see, based on his freehold overview, that construction was going as planned. That there were already less than three days left before the start of [Armageddon] and the Earth Asunder wave sent shivers down his spine.

"That's impossible, Alistair," Pharaoh said. "We've been walking for less than eight hours. At our speed, we would have already been at the center by then."

"Yes! That's my point!" Alistair exclaimed. "We should be in the center since it's been four days. This place is messing with our heads."

"Can you provide evidence for this assertion?" Pharaoh asked. "I am not one to take your proclamations lightly."

Alistair activated **[Hand of Karma]**, draining his Karma down to 25 points. He went up to Pharaoh and Alexandra and touched their faces. Tiny green strands glinted in the orange light for a moment, before snapping back in place.

Whatever they were, they were obviously the work of a master. Alistair knew that Pharaoh had over 500 Intelligence and Wisdom, as well as a bloodline with anti-magical properties.

But that was what confused Alistair. Karmic control of Fate was a fickle game. Alistair himself was highly sensitive to Karmic abilities. In actuality, they had been walking forward. There was no doubt about that. It didn't seem possible for such thin green threads to have held them in place, trapping them in an illusion.

Alistair suspected they were merely there to alter their perception of time. In which case, something else had caused them to not reach their target.

"The green witch bitch," Pharaoh growled. "I have been misled."

"Carmen? I knew it," Alexandra declared smugly.

"No, no, not Carmen. Oracle. The second Devil King," Pharaoh said.

It all clicked into place. Alistair had gotten the rundown from Whimsy on each of the Devil Kings a while ago. Though at the time, Oracle was number three, not two.

Like Alistair, Oracle was a Karmic cultivator, though it was her main focus rather than a subspecialty. Considering her ranking, the fact that she'd sneaked Karmic threads under all their noses made perfect sense.

Alistair flared his [Eyes of Truth] once more, just to be safe. "We're really here, though. Fifty kilometers from the center, as you said."

The temperature was over 1,000 degrees Fahrenheit. Without any special gear or extra Constitution, Alexandra suffered the worst. The fire was all around them now, spontaneously forming in the air, on the ground, and everywhere one could imagine. Flickering in and out of existence, ephemeral yet at one with the Dao of Fire. The transient flames were accompanied by more permanent fixtures, though those were the weirdest parts of the wasteland.

Alistair could see scenes acted out with infernal actors, fire taking on different forms. The colors changed though always between warm hues— gold, maroon, vermilion, orange. The fire was plasma, but also wispy, and at times took on the form of a gaseous explosion.

The expression of fire was absolute. It was a burning passion that wiped away all regret and despair. An infinite growth that would cover the universe in its beauty until it collapsed in on itself. Alistair wondered if this was how Atavius saw his flames.

The three of them ducked as a towering golem of yellow fire swiped its elongated arms over them. Incidents like that had ticked up since passing the halfway mark. Based on the concentration ahead, things would only get worse the closer they came.

"You okay, Alexandra?" Alistair asked.

"Never better," she huffed.

"It should have only been twelve hours, but it's been four days. I can understand if you're starting to feel the heat."

"I said, I'm fine," she told him. "These flames could never match the passion of my rage." She winced, outwardly cringing. "Eesh, that was a little too much."

Alistair let out a muffled laugh. "Can't argue with that."

Now that he knew for sure something was up, Alistair focused all his senses on detecting the anomaly. That meant *all* of them. He had been working on juggling them at the same time for a while now. After they walked for a few more minutes, he came to a realization.

"It's the space," he said. "That's what's going on. It's being elongated. Instead of having to go two hundred kilometers, it's six thousand."

"How is that possible?" Alexandra asked.

"The Dao is the Dao," Pharaoh said. "It is as mysterious as it is deep."

Alistair paced around, thinking out loud. "The only reason I could tell is because I was carefully looking at our feet and the environment. I don't think it's something the Devil Kings could do. It's too advanced. It's probably the natural distortion caused by the radiation."

"So we're back to square one, then," Alexandra said.

"One foot in front of the other, that's the only way to go," Alistair said. "At least we've made progress and know it's not all an illusion."

She wiped sweat from her forehead with her tank top, revealing a toned stomach. "If we get to the center and there's nothing there, I'm going to wring Pharaoh alive."

The final push of the journey took half a day. With the end goal in sight, it gave them the extra push to start running. They had to pace themselves for Alexandra. While she actually had higher Agility than Pharaoh, the latter could use his sand cloud to travel.

Part of the way through the final stretch, Dev'rox spoke for the first time in a while.

"I'm bored out of my mind. I can't even take a form here or I'll burn alive. Or should I say... burn ghostly? Not sure how that should be phrased."

The heat was affecting them all now, even Pharaoh. Alistair was the embodiment of sweat, his **Mammothskin Raiment** soaked to the point it looked soggy, even though it was a thick fur coat. Just thinking took a lot of effort. His brain was frying in its skull, all of his mental power devoted to meditating on his Dao Nodes to stave off the imperious fire.

"Not a good time," he thought back.

"I wanted to ask you about your family, actually," Dev'rox replied.

"My family?"

"You're burning, not stupid. Yes, your family. Family is what you call your mother and father?"

"And my sister. I had extended relatives too, but they're all dead."

"I've seen your father and sister. What about your mother?"

Alistair strained as they ascended one of the few topological deviations, a massive hill that went up for nearly a kilometer at a forty-five-degree incline. They would have gone around it if it wasn't ten times wider than it was tall.

"I haven't seen her since before the initiation. She's a smart woman. She and my dad used to run a restaurant. She does all the books."

"That sounds like Zalarik the Wise. That's how he got his epithet. Never the strongest, he used his wits to rise to the top, primarily his ability to make money out of nothing."

"They have money in the Asura Hell?" Alistair asked incredulously.

Dev'rox snorted. "Are you kidding? Some say the Dao of Money is the greatest of them all, but don't say that within earshot of a Buddhist. Money is everywhere. Money could buy you a ticket out of the Asura Hell, if you had enough of it. You could get passage into the involved on the Physical Plane, or a deeper Hell. I was thinking Arbuda or Hahava."

"The involved? What's that?"

"I've only heard stories. There's the frontier, where we are, and then the core, situated around the Heart of All Creation and its leylines. The involved is in the middle. Too weak to be more than vassals of the core, and too strong to concern themselves much with the frontier."

"Those are the stories I want to hear about," Alistair said. "That's where I'll be one day. The core."

"You tell tall tales, my friend. Very tall tales," Dev'rox said. "What will you do when your mother withers to dust? When your sister's child's child dies of old age, as you remain a young man?"

"That won't happen. My sister will get to Adept on her own, and beyond.

That's a fact. That's what, like 5,000 years of lifespan? I'll get powerful enough to make my parents Adept too, providing them with all the resources they'll need. By the time they're aging, I'll have reached the peak."

"I hate quixotic idiots like you. Have you no shame?" Dev'rox chastised, half in jest. "Do you need Red to beat you up again to remind you what the elite of some backwater frontier universe looks like, let alone the core? Being so greedy makes me look like a bad teacher."

They went back and forth for some time. The distraction took out some of the sting of the fire. Though Alistair's screaming meridians were impossible to ignore.

The condensed Mana gave all three of them an additional level, though with a caveat. The fire affinity Mana was becoming way too concentrated, and when he tried to absorb the energy closest to the center, even Alistair's multiple-reinforced spiritual network couldn't resist the burns fully, forcing him to shut off all ambient absorption.

At last, they arrived.

At what, Alistair wasn't so sure. The last five hundred meters, he had to start using [Frozen Claw] to cool the temperature. The air became thick and oppressive, as if Alistair was swimming through a scorching plasma soup, the shifting currents making it feel like the very air was aflame.

The ice crystals from [Frozen Claw] carved a straight tunnel through the dense atmosphere while holding back the lingering Dao with his Ghost Node. Now that he had 1,751 max Mana, spamming a few 40 Mana Skills was inconsequential. Finally, through his tunnel of rapidly melting ice, he saw their destination.

A magnificent firebird crested over an enormous black-and-red mansion. Alistair recognized the creature as a figure from Slavic folklore. A symbol of luck but also a harbinger of doom.

Its wingspan was large enough to cover the whole château. The firebird spread its wings, displaying its radiant and majestic plumage, which bore the same hues as the flames. But it was not merely a being of fire—it *was* the fire. It was one with the Dao, unblemished in every aspect.

In pure strength, it couldn't compare to the Visionaries that Alistair had encountered, but he doubted they could match its unity. They stood at the feet of a true beast born from the Dao of Fire.

Upon seeing the trio arrive, the firebird cried out. All the fire in the vicinity froze in place upon hearing the bird's siren, sparkling like prisms in the light.

They cautiously approached, not wanting to disturb the beast. The firebird's cry had turned down the heat, so they could take their time.

"I never thought I'd see one in the flesh," Dev'rox said. "Count yourself lucky, brat."

"You carry the mark of my creator," the firebird crooned. Alistair jumped back, not expecting it to speak. Its voice was deep and ancient, feeling like the primordial fires of the early universe.

"I'm sorry?" Alistair asked, feeling the heat of the creature's gaze.

"My creator. Your Fates have intertwined. You must have met him before."

Alistair performed the bao quan li, or fist wrapping rite, bowing his head to the magical beast. "I have, great one. He is a criminal, a genocidal wastrel that attacked this planet unprovoked. He has received his trial and judgment, and I believe he is currently incarcerated on the prison planet Breon."

The firebird flapped its wings, the frozen flames flickering with its moves. **"There is no need to flatter me so. You are not as much of a junior as you think. I have not yet reached the title of Beast Ruler."**

"But you're far more powerful than that worm?"

"I am a firebird, a species derived from the fabric of the multiverse itself. A mere worm could not hope to hold a candle to me."

"I was wondering about that, Mr. Bird," Alexandra interjected, stepping fearlessly in front of Alistair. "How did you come to be?"

"Within the spiritual ether of the pure Dao of the Elements, patterns emerge. From man or beast or the interminable Heaven and Earth, a will exists. When this will condenses, it takes on the pinnacle form that represents its unadulterated self. For fire, it is the firebird. For time, it is the chronoweaver."

"I would expect that of a Visionary cultivator's Dao, but wasn't Atavius a mere Adept?" Alistair asked. "How could he create life itself?"

"An unusual circumstance," the bird said. Alistair couldn't help but stare at its glorious plumage, its feathers reflecting all the colors of flame. **"Haven't you wondered how he was able to wipe out your nations with a single blow? He was just 100 levels higher than you are now."**

"You know, I have been wondering that," Alistair mused.

"Your planet had essentially zero concentration of the Dao and Mana.

There were no extraneous substances in the way of Atavius's power. For such wicked desires as destroying a planet, the absence of the Dao was particularly important."

The firebird flapped its wings, conjuring images in the aerial flames depicting the events of that fateful day.

"With no competing forces, the Dao of Fire implanted itself everywhere. Following the initiation and the uplifting of your planet from the Pathfinder AI, the already existing regions of fire received a boost of energy. The entire planet will eventually become fire-attuned if nothing changes. I'm sure you've noticed the excess of fire cultivators by now."

It wasn't something at the forefront of his mind, but Alistair had noticed it—he chalked it up to fire being the stereotypical "coolest" superpower. Johnny from Anthony's empire, Jakk, Dragonus, and John all primarily used fire.

"What does that mean for us non-fire cultivators?" Pharaoh wondered.

"You shall be fine, children," the firebird said. "It is subject to change, though that would come at an additional price. Once the [Armageddon] is completed, FX-14752 will improve to a Basic planet. And then Journeyman, Expert, Master, and so forth. It is only at the Expert level that the inherent emanations of the planetary core would become unbearable to those not on the path of fire. At that point, most Planetary Lords and Ladies would have already quelled the fire. A paltry cost to a Visionary, especially for a lesser world.

"But may I shut my beak. You have already received enough information from me, yet you wish for another boon." The firebird used its wings to gesture to the mansion it perched on.

So there is something of Saturn's inside, Alistair thought to himself. He turned toward his companions. It sounded like the firebird wanted something from them in return for whatever was inside. While he was no folklorist, he knew that the mythological creature signified the beginning of a long and troubled journey. But Alistair was already on one of those.

Pharaoh and Alexandra looked at him to lead. "You require something?" he asked.

"Hmm," the firebird purred, a comely vibration that made the flames of the world flicker. "*Hmmm.* Tell me more of my creator. I only have the leftover knowledge of a Pathfinder AI instantiation. Impersonal information. I have never seen him in the flesh, like you have."

"The first feeling I had when I saw him was fear. But it was followed shortly by awe."

Alistair dug deep into his heart, saying things he had never dared to speak aloud. "No one knew what he was. Some thought he was a god or a demon. Some religions claimed he was punishment for our sins. The scientists said an alien, which I guess was the most correct.

"The fear you get when death is certain is unlike anything else. The sinking feeling of despair. The acknowledgment of your own mortality, of finality, of the end. That's what we all saw in the air. When our militaries failed to contain him with nukes, that was when most people broke."

"And you? What did you think?"

Alistair took a deep breath in, remembering the sounds, sights, smells of that day. The soft skin of his then-girlfriend, Katelyn, and her citrus perfume. Tommy and Nathan's laughter, and the silence as they all watched the television. "I wanted it. I wanted it more than I've ever wanted anything in my life. Not to harm others like Atavius, but to save them.

"Yet when I saw him in chains, his power reduced to level 30, he was pathetic. A hollow version of himself. Do I hate him? Yes. He's a wretch of a man. But if I believed that no one could be redeemed, it would go against what I believe in. I've killed monsters and humans. I'm not a pacifist by any means, but I do think that people deserve second chances."

"Even a man who killed billions of people? The fire that burns within me disagrees," said the beast.

"You seem like a good, uh, beast. Yet you were wrought out of Atavius's Dao. What that tells me is that the ideal he cultivates is not an evil fire. I've met fire cultivators who are only about consumption, who want to cause pain and rage with their wanton destruction. But I don't feel that from this fire. There's a passion here. I sense a cleansing fire, one that washes away the ills of the mind and the desires of the flesh. Perhaps Atavius knows his own iniquity and seeks to cultivate a higher, more noble end."

"Do you truly believe this, young one? What if you are wrong, and it is a mere means to an end for young Atavius."

"It's a theory. I don't know if it's true or not. Maybe one day I'll find out."

"Yet you would have killed him when he attacked your home world, if you had the power at the time." The firebird furled its wing to its beak, imitating the pose of a human in thought.

"Yes, I would have. But there's no contradiction there. The innocent lives are more important."

"You have given me much to think about, Alistair Tan," said the firebird. **"I accept this payment."**

In an instant, the huge frame of the firebird vanished, its feathers disintegrating into gold and red embers that danced in the plasmic air. In its place was the most beautiful woman Alistair had ever seen.

Glorious red hair went down to her knees, morphing from moment to moment like a liquid made of glittering fire. She wore a form-fitting red dress that hugged a shapely body, her skin pale but tinted orange. Her face was born from the Dao itself, her eyes red beacons of warmth.

She jumped down from the mansion. The flames in the air carried her gently, placing her right next to the trio.

"Don't be so shocked," she said, her voice the very nature of passionate flames. "All the beast species that count themselves among the Immemorial Races can attain human form after the formation of their Beast Cores. The lesser beasts must wait until the Half-Step Immortal stage."

She held out a dainty hand, though looks could be deceiving. Alistair felt an implacable strength from her. "This is what you seek, no?"

In her hand, she held an emerald-colored needle. At a first glance, it felt entirely ordinary.

Alistair gingerly picked up the needle by pinching it with his pointer finger and this thumb, carefully holding it up so Pharaoh and Alexandra could see.

"That's it?" Alexandra asked.

The woman who was also a firebird smiled, but it did not reach her eyes. "The young one known as Saturn was a lonely soul, though he brought great evil to my home. I am sworn to not lay a finger on any human cultivator, including the Devil Kings. A contradiction at its core. The young man whom I engaged with in dialectics on the natural sciences, philosophy, and aesthetics also tortured, experimented, and killed innocent souls in his basement. *My* basement.

"Before he died, he gave me this needle. He told me to give it to anyone who came looking for it that wasn't a Devil King. I think he knew he was going to die."

[Eyes of Truth] couldn't penetrate the purpose of the needle, declaring it to be **Experimental Cursed Needle #7.**

"And you don't know what it does?" Alistair asked, storing the needle in his inventory.

"I do not," she said. "All I know is that it is important. The Devil King, Oracle, came by looking for it. I evidently did not acquiesce to her demands. She blanketed my lands in Karmic threads that I could not see. I felt the alterations of Fate, but I was unable to interfere. For that, I am sorry."

"It's fine," Alistair said, though his thoughts were turning elsewhere. He had originally thought that Oracle had placed her illusions on the mansion itself when they were still fully allied with Saturn as a defensive mechanism. But from what the firebird said, it happened after his death.

That meant...

"Oh, no," Alistair let out. "Can you tell us what's on the outside?" he asked, turning to the firebird.

"I have already given away too much. I apologize, but I cannot."

"What is it?" Alexandra asked, though right as she said it, Alistair saw the realization dawn in her eyes. If Oracle had booby-trapped the flaming wasteland, then she would almost certainly know when someone set off her trap. And if this needle really was the weakness of the Devil Kings, it stood to reason that they would send a force to collect their prize.

"You're in a deep pickle," Dev'rox said. "And I can't even help you because of this infernal blaze."

"What do you think we should do?" he asked his ghostly mentor.

"I haven't the faintest idea, Alistair, though I'm flattered that you think of me as such a genius. If George, Oracle, Dragonus, and Admiral are really standing outside this area waiting for you, you're truly fucked."

"You're right."

Even with his 33% Attribute increase, would he be able to take on Dragonus, let alone George Moulin? He wracked his brain for a solution. They couldn't contact anyone with the Soulnet, Dev'rox couldn't fly away, and they couldn't fight their way out.

Pharaoh raised a finger. "If it comes down to it, I should be the first one out. I have all fourteen of my lives. Even if all of them attack me at once, there's no way they could kill me fourteen times before I was able to flee."

"That's a good idea," Alexandra said. "You go out first, take the heat. Alistair can carry me on his back and then do his **[Dash]** thing and maybe add a little spa—"

She stopped herself from exposing Dev'rox or Alistair's extra powers, continuing with, "spice, and hopefully we won't get bombarded by ice arrows or dragon breath."

"Sounds like a plan," Alistair said. "Firebird, I am eternally grateful to you for your help. Once I'm the Global Mayor and this planet is fully initiated, I'm sure there is a place for you on this world."

"So confident. I like it," she said. "My name is Selephita, by the way."

With that, she jumped into the air, warping the surroundings as she transformed back into her firebird form. The château's roof got back its majestic tenant.

Alistair turned to his partners. The way back was going to be quicker than the way in.

50 A TALE OF FATES

IT HAD TAKEN them sixteen hours to reach the center after they picked up the speed. If they kept the same speed on the way back, it would take them nearly three days to return. That was completely unacceptable, since Alistair needed to get back before the start of [Armageddon].

That left them with only one option—advanced piggybacking.

Alistair sighed as he let Pharaoh and Alexandra climb on. Alexandra went on last since she could use her immense strength to squeeze Pharaoh in place. This was not going to be fun.

If he needed to, Alistair could maintain a jogging pace of 400 kilometers per hour. It would slowly drain his Stamina, but it was their best option. According to his calculations, they would make it back with almost two full days before the final Quest.

It took all his willpower to brave the first fourth of the journey. His calculations went awry as it took far more Stamina than expected thanks to the oppressive heat. The playful creations of fire also took him off course several times, and he wasn't used to the weight distribution of Pharaoh plus Alexandra. They felt as light as a feather with his 340 Strength, but that didn't affect the physics of carrying two people.

The rest of the distance went smoothly, though as they neared the end, Alistair wanted to puke. His entire body strained from heat exhaustion and his muscles cried out for mercy.

As they grew closer to the divide between Selephita's preserve and the outside world, they cautiously slowed down. A quick glance at the Quest screen showed they still had one day and fifteen hours before the first wave would begin. But they first had to survive the next few minutes.

Alistair activated [Eyes of Truth], peering at the innumerable threads of Fate, trying to see if the Devil Kings were going to ambush them. He saw nothing. He expected the demonic aura detection granted by "Devil May Cry" and his fiftyfold improved sense of smell for demon blood to be even better on that front. Yet still nothing.

"I'm not getting anything," he told Alexandra and Pharaoh. "You?"

"I defer to you on matters of detection of demons, but I also have nothing," Pharaoh said.

Alexandra shook her head.

"Wouldn't they attack us here?" she wondered. "It's not like there's a protective barrier over these lands."

"They wouldn't risk it," Alistair said. "I have a feeling they're not entirely clear on what Selephita's restrictions are. These lands are the manifestation of fire on Earth. If there's anywhere they don't want to fight, it's here."

"I'll do my duty." Pharaoh slid out of Alexandra's grasp. As he walked away, he held up a hand and waved goodbye from behind, racing away on his cloud of sand.

"So dramatic," Dev'rox complained.

Alistair held his breath in anticipation. He prepared himself to [Dash] immediately, touching the friable soil with his fingertips like a sprinter.

Everything pointed to no one being there, but he didn't trust his senses. Surely the moment Pharaoh crossed the border, he was going to be assaulted by a flurry of Devil Kings.

It felt like Alistair's vision went in slow motion as Pharaoh's sand cloud hovered over green grass. The moment he breached the dividing line, he disintegrated into a pile of sand. Alistair had figured out that the range of his teleportation was around a hundred meters, and in quick succession, he chained his Skill over and over.

"Hold on tight."

Alistair activated [Dash], adding Dev'rox's space affinity Mana to shrink the distance in front of him.

Nearly 200 meters passed by in under half a second. Alistair was moving so fast he would have caused a sonic boom if it wasn't using the power of **[Dash]**. To an outside onlooker, he appeared to teleport because of the flicker aspect, though to Alistair it felt like one giant step.

While he lost momentum as he touched the ground, he pressed on right away. At Tier 3, **[Dash]**'s cooldown was an almost imperceptible 0.1 seconds. Alistair chained five more **[Dashes]** in a row. He moved over a kilometer, making it all the way to the village center and its **Teleportation Circle**.

Then he stopped.

"That's awkward," he said, letting Alexandra get off. "It looks like we were running for nothing."

"You don't sense anything?" she asked.

"Nil."

Pharaoh reappeared in front of them, forming out of a gust of sand. "And I wasn't attacked in the slightest."

"So… I guess they weren't waiting for us," Alistair said. "Now I feel stupid."

Pharaoh looked up at the sky, then back down at him. Alistair realized that they hadn't really had a discussion about who was going to keep the needle. He'd just taken it for himself without asking.

"The needle is yours," Pharaoh said, avoiding an uncomfortable situation. "I do not care for the responsibility. It is time to part ways."

"Are you sure you don't want to join our freehold?" Alistair asked. "You would be a great help. And you'd get a lot of benefits."

"I work best alone. I never wanted a freehold to begin with. The benefits were pretty good, though." Pharaoh reformed his ancient Egyptian clothing. "Elaine has everything you need."

"You're with the Corlyon Company, right? Would their symbol happen to be a blue crescent moon with a golden fist on top?" He was referring to the company that enslaved the Einzat Demon, Marizel, forcing her to work collecting Herax Turtle juices.

"No?"

"Ah, worth a shot," Alistair said. "Good luck to you."

Pharaoh waved goodbye, for real this time, and stepped onto the **Teleportation Circle**.

Alistair took out the needle, admiring its strange iridescent shine. "What do you think it does?"

"Sucks out all their demon blood?" Alexandra ventured.

"If only it were that easy," Alistair said. "Let's get home."

———

The moment he left the domain of fire, messages inundated his inbox. Alistair groaned internally.

When they returned to New Boston, the level of change in just five days shocked him. The city had grown seven large obelisks imbued with magic wards that would shock any intruder with bolts of lightning. In the sky, tiny electronic orbs cast a wide laser net, their purpose to detect Devil Kings and their ilk from kilometers away.

The first thing Alistair did was visit John. Their headquarters had increased in size substantially. What once was a temporary, makeshift fortress had turned into a sprawling palatial complex. It was easily the largest building in the city by volume, taking up acres and acres of land.

While once it was the workplace of a few people, it had blossomed into a busy center for all. Over one thousand people worked overtime, with twenty-two **Teleportation Circles** housed in the building alone.

There was an incessant revolving door of people coming and going. Especially through the circles. The uniformed officials going back and forth with resources for their border territories were one of the biggest contributors to the raucous environment.

Wherever he went, Alistair aimed for a benevolent, irenic approach. So far, it was a major success, but he felt it had more to do with people's fear of the #1 on the leaderboard rather than the goodness of their hearts.

If he was worried his reputation would cause people to take advantage of him, the United Polities were helpful on that front. They were publicly backing him for Global Mayor and their propaganda network was the best in the world.

Alistair knocked on the door to John's office, a titanic reinforced oak block that was over ten centimeters thick.

"You know you can come in," a deep voice called out.

"Just being polite," Alistair answered with a smile. He walked in to see his sister speaking to the official vice president of the Northeast Freehold. He acted surprised to see her, though obviously he'd detected her much earlier, even through the wards on the walls and door.

"Hey, Angie," Alistair said. "How's Baba doing?"

"Good. He misses Mama, though," she said, giving him a hug.

"We all do. Am I interrupting?"

"No, she was just leaving," John said. "But now that you're here, maybe she'll stay for a bit. We were talking about an issue that you will care about. The Devil Kings."

"Oh?" Alistair turned to his sister. "What about them?"

"It's a theory I've been concocting," she said. "I believe the Devil Kings are under George's direct control. Or something like a cascading network. Imagine that man and dog you found when hunting the Devil Kings as the lowest rung. Then someone like the serpent king would be above that. And then above that, a Devil King, and then above that, George himself.

"I've been in the lab, studying our subjects for hours on end. The conclusion I've come to is that the influence of demon blood is not on psychology nor is it mind control."

"Huh," Alistair said. "I was told the opposite. Though what I'm saying is third-hand knowledge, Whimsy said that a shadowy man told her that the Final Frontier Empire messed with the brains of 1% of the population to give them murderous impulses."

"Was that her exact wording?" Evangeline questioned. "She mentioned messing with brains?"

"Yes, if I recall correctly."

"I think we're talking about different things. The 1% were most likely turned via a different mechanism. My findings are only on demon blood and its effects. For that, it is Fate itself that is subverted."

She used her Spiritualist powers to conjure motes of Dao energy. To Alistair's senses, they felt unattuned and incomplete. The soul itself, made physical by the soulcore, consisted of this kind of original Dao energy. It was the pure spiritual ether, not of unbound truths but of human nature—the infinite transcendence of being.

As such, it was not meant to be free in the Physical Plane. In Alistair's vision, the Dao energy shifted and blurred. Most often, it settled upon the form of either a milky white plasma or a rainbow-colored gas.

Evangeline bent the Dao energy to her will. Of course it obeyed. This was the natural material of her own soul—she was one with it in every respect.

"Between your **Chord of Desire** and other mind control Skills and items that I've tested, I've found that the beguilement of the mind has a certain flavor to it," she explained. "It's not all the same, obviously, but it is the same category. With my [Soul Sight], you can see the changes plain as day when conducting a close examination. But none of the Devil Kings had that change.

"Changing psychology is another possible answer. But we have Doctors and people who argue strongly that they don't see changes to the brain that could answer this question of why they obey and why they seek to kill. The only explanation left is Fate. I've tested this hypothesis exhaustively. All the evidence points to it being true."

The Dao energy morphed into threads that looked awfully similar to the ones that Alistair saw in his Karmic vision. What exactly Fate was, he wasn't qualified to answer. It wasn't made of Dao energy, that was for sure, though Evangeline's mimicry looked decently accurate.

"The presence of demon blood warps Fate itself. Have you noticed this, Alistair?" Evangeline asked.

"I haven't really been focusing on it," Alistair admitted. "Their mark is distinct, for sure, but I haven't noticed it affecting Fate in particular."

He took out the vial of demon blood from his pocket. This time, he focused his Karmic sight directly on the vial of blood. It took a while, but he slowly began to notice slight perturbations in the fine threads of Fate surrounding the container.

"What does that mean?" he asked.

"It's hard to explain," she said, "but here's an example—there are two people in real life. One is a billionaire who has a loving wife and two kids, and the other is a drug addict who can't hold down a job and is constantly in and out of trouble with the law. They each made their own decisions to get there, but no one would be surprised to hear that the billionaire came from an upper middle-class family while the drug addict came from a lower-class family. The milieu you are born into and grow up in has a significant impact on your outcome—no one would deny that.

"I believe the demon blood is creating a milieu of—I guess, evil?—for those who have it in their system. While it is still technically possible for them not to do harm, the byproduct of their warped Fate is pulling them down negative paths."

"That sounds straight-up dystopian," Alistair said. "I wonder what it feels like for them. Do they recognize that it's happening? Or are they just going through the motions?"

"With no way to cure it, we aren't going to know," Evangeline said. "But that's not all. The second piece of the puzzle is control. I mentioned the cascading network of control before. Our best guess is that you have direct control over the Fate of anyone you donated blood to. The exception being George—maybe he is special because he was the first Devil King, so he can control the others despite not being the donor."

"Have we tested this?" Alistair rocked his vial, watching the tiny threads undulate around it.

She shook her head. "That's the problem. Any attempts at transferring demon blood have been utter failures. What did your scientists tell you before?"

"Uh…" Alistair looked up at the ceiling, struggling to remember. "It was a couple of weeks ago, but they told me it was above their pay grade."

"Before I came along, that was more or less the case. Without a Spiritualist or someone who can see souls, they weren't going to succeed. But I digress. The blood dissipates into thin air when we attempt a transfusion. That's the basic rundown. If you have any more questions, let me know. I'm headed back to the lab now." Evangeline nodded to him and John before taking her leave.

"What do you think?" John asked. He'd been listening to their conversation, silently taking in everything Evangeline had shared. "It's an intriguing theory. All I know is that I'm glad I didn't get selected to be a Devil King."

"Same," Alistair said, though their words didn't carry the gravity of the situation. "Anyway, I came here to catch up on everything."

The two of them talked for several minutes. While things looked good in the capital, John said that there were delays on the frontier. They at least had the requisite funds for defenses, in great part due to Lauren's [Cash Flow] Skill.

Her abilities had become public knowledge as people wondered where their money was going. They had worked out an agreement where she returned people's money with a certain amount of interest and kept the rest, essentially operating like a real bank. Once people leveled up and better contracts could be formed, they could have a properly functioning economy.

But they didn't have enough time nor manpower. They had to train people, equip them, and supervise them. The battlements and ramparts and weapons took time to install, and time was what they didn't have.

Still, it was impressive that they had equipped more than 40% of the border territory. At the moment, they only allowed people to join their freehold under the condition that they were still responsible for defending their territory. The Northeast Order Freehold couldn't keep expanding the protective zone, but they could shelter refugees. There were less and less of those, though—most people had found a side.

"Don't blame yourself," John said. "There's nothing you could have done to speed up the process. It's just a math equation."

"I know." Alistair clenched his fists. The start of [Armageddon] felt like a guillotine over his neck. "Our population is over 300 million. Can the core areas sustain a temporary refugee crisis? If Earth Asunder is anything like its name, people are going to flee to areas of relative safety. Do we have a large enough surplus of food and clean water?"

"It's... unlikely we could weather that for more than a few weeks," John admitted. "The main problem is a lack of shelter and food. The crop yields from cultivation-aided farmers are only at 50% of what we could do before the initiation using technology."

"Budget wise? Can we do anything about that? Like change the sliders a bit?"

John checked some scrolls on his desk, putting his forehead in his palms. "We could decrease educational spending for a bit. That would hurt our newly formed military but help us now."

"Do it," Alistair said. No one was going to starve to death on his watch. If they needed more martial prowess, he would deal with that. "Alright, catch you later."

Right before pressing the heavy door open, Alistair stopped and turned back. "I couldn't help but notice. You and Donna?"

John sighed, his glance darting away from his leader. "Can't keep anything from your eyes—"

Or my nose, Alistair thought.

"—can I? Now that's just absurd. How the hell did you figure that one out? Has my Fate entangled with that fine woman?"

"Have to keep some secrets, John," Alistair said with a wry smile. "Thanks for everything."

———

For the next day and a half, Alistair did not find a single second of rest.

Except if you included his secluded meditation. It was *restful*, but it definitely wasn't rest. Alistair focused on his variations of **[Force Fist]**, creating a chamber full of force affinity Mana and treasures involved in fisticuffs. He had decided to use **[Force Fist]** as the base for his finishing Skill.

Alistair felt the twelve major meridians of his body. Each had a different attunement, based on what kind of Mana flowed through it most often. While it wasn't like he was making a Skill on his own without the help of the Pathfinder AI, it would be helpful to understand the logic of how his meridians operated.

Developing the Skill itself was a dead end. No matter how good of a chamber he made, the Fist was not a Dao that you could reach the pinnacle of through meditation. He needed to gain insights through combat.

That left him with three hopes for surpassing Dragonus. He wasn't even considering George at this point. The Pathfinder AI wouldn't make things too unfair and have that monster show up yet, he hoped.

The first hope was his bloodline upgrade, the second was a First Deepening for the Justice Node, and the third was creating the finisher Skill.

After finishing his meditation, he swooped by Evangeline's lab, talked to Donna and his friends, and hunted some stray monsters. He tried not to focus on what was coming.

At last, the start of the sixth and final Quest, [Armageddon], was about to begin.

51 EARTH ASUNDER

ALISTAIR STARED AT A LIVE, three-dimensional projection of the planet. The supercontinent took up most of a single hemisphere, so you could take it all in from one angle.

The map displayed a political overview of the world. Perhaps 20% of the territory was taken up by an assortment of groups, the largest of which was Brigid Mwangi's freehold. The other 80% came down to four groups—the Northeast Order, FavorWood Manor, the Devil Kings, and the United Polities.

The Northeast Order took up the top section of the map. The Devil Kings were at the bottom with Lucius in the middle, and the other areas spread out in between. Alistair couldn't help but feel bad for Lucius. FavorWood's border with the Devil King territory took up half its southern length.

"It's all set up?" Alistair turned to Robert Oakland, who was in charge of the smaller tasks around the HQ.

"Yes, sir. This map is a truly amazing creation. It's a crafted item combining aspects of several Classes of the top brass here, on top of the Beast Core of a Komodo dragon."

Alistair reminisced about his fight with the beast during Capture the Beacon. It had reached level 75 in the intervening week. In fact, it was Oliver and Blaise who had slain the beast. He was impressed with the young man and the one-eyed archer, not necessarily expecting them capable of taking on something that he himself had struggled against. Though, he heard that they got lucky when a building fell on top of it.

Serves that thing right, Alistair grumbled.

Robert continued with his explanation, pointing to tiny red spots that blinked all across the projection. "These represent conflict areas. I've given you control over the projection, so if you focus on one, a more detailed readout will appear displaying all the information we have about that incident. In addition, there should be a real-time readout for subregion ownership changes. We can track that on an individual level, so we will know right away if we're getting attacked."

"That's amazing," Alistair said. "You guys make my life so much easier."

"It's nothing. We're just doing our part."

Unlike last time, it was only him, Robert, and Celeste (their communications head) inside the war room. The nature of **[Armageddon]** sounded so ominous, especially with Earth Asunder being the first wave, that he had his people spread out. Alistair's strategy was to minimize damage wherever it struck first.

That didn't mean he wasn't aware of how the enemy could take advantage of that. He specifically issued a **Teleportation Circle** for each high-ranking official. Alistair gave them some of the circles from inside the headquarters, but they had so many extra that it didn't affect their transportation capabilities, unless there was a flood of refugees. At any point, with Celeste's help, they could call back anyone they needed.

Alistair jangled his crimson bracelets, transforming them into **Devilsbane Gauntlets.** His inventory was at its hard limit, having hit ten items. It included things actually on his body, like the **Mammothskin Raiment** and **Fall of Fleet**. It didn't make much sense to him, but he wasn't the one making the rules.

The Quest readout said there was less than a minute left. Alistair breathed in and out, practicing the meditative techniques Zenaitsu Morogoni had left him. He imagined the enormous World Titan who defended his people against technological terrors from the sky.

The contradiction between a reaper and a guardian swirled in his mind like a raging tornado. The simple punch he saw in the vision had no traces of the formless, fluid style that portended certain death.

Was the World Titan just hiding his deathly attributes? Was he a mythological psychopomp, who had put down his scythe to become a guardian later in life? It was all so mysterious, and Alistair was certain he wouldn't get any solid answers for a long time. The level of power he saw in his vision far exceeded anything in the frontier.

A message from the Pathfinder AI interrupted his distracted thoughts.

Wave 1: Earth Asunder

The time of true Armageddon begins. Only you, the native inhabitants of FX-14752, can stop the end of your world.

FX-14752 is currently a Beginner grade planet, subject to the normal natural disasters and climatological currents of a planet of that grade. For Earth Asunder, those elements will be upgraded to those of a Journeyman planet.

The next month will be a continuous assault of hurricanes, tornadoes, earthquakes, volcanic eruptions, tsunamis, landslides, and more fantastical disasters. During this period, the rules for achieving Global Mayor for the Devil Kings still stand, and the methods to acquire subregions by domination, democratic approval, and purchase shall not be abrogated.

In addition to the normal ways you can earn Contribution Points as delineated in the text of [Armageddon], in Earth Asunder, you can earn them by stopping disasters. Any actions that involve saving civilians and imposing one's will over nature shall be rewarded.

Let Earth Asunder begin!

The moment he finished reading the screen, the floor beneath him rumbled. The building swayed. Then, it collapsed.

Like a mother rushing to protect her child, Robert's first reaction was to go for the map. He managed to reach the projection and grab the spinning metal globe at its core right as the ceiling crumpled.

While Alistair felt no danger, he was shocked. The Northeast Order headquarters was made of valyrik and reinforced with hundreds of scripts.

They had gone to great lengths to make it impregnable by any means, and it had been destroyed in seconds.

Alistair [Dashed] forward, grabbing Robert by the scruff of his collar. With a swift leap, he activated [Force Fist], imbuing it with his Fist Node.

The fist construct blew open the cracking wall. With Robert in tow, Alistair jumped out of the second story right as the headquarters fell into a massive sinkhole. A huge plume of debris washed over the two of them, forcing Alistair to [Dash] again to make it to safer ground.

"Safer" might have been an overstatement.

The entire earth rumbled like an angry god. Mountains and hills in the distance shuddered from the immense earthquake. Alistair had never seen anything like it. Planet Earth itself had never seen anything like it. An impossibly powerful earthquake rocked the ground with unrelenting abandon.

Luckily, it appeared that the headquarters was at the epicenter of the quake. Other buildings caved in, but most were unprotected. From what Alistair could see, over half of the skyline fell in an instant.

The death toll was staggering. Despite that, it could have been much worse. Most buildings took longer to fall than their HQ, so many people escaped. Alistair shuddered to think of what would have happened if such an earthquake hit before the initiation. Now, people could run three times as fast, easily lift fallen rocks, and withstand minor injuries much better.

It didn't settle the feelings within Alistair's heart.

Since the last time he had encountered mass death, his [Ghost Whispers] had gone up a tier, and he'd deepened his Ghost Node. The cries of the dead called out to the heavens. Alistair could almost see the bloody souls haunting him. He had promised them safety in his freehold, and he had reneged on that promise.

The surge of spiritual power from the disembodied souls gave him a jaw-dropping boost. There wasn't much in terms of new combat instincts, but who needed that when you had overwhelming strength?

He felt a pang of guilt in using the thousands of deceased ghosts for power, but he quelled that idea right away. They had died. There was nothing he could do about it. If he could use their fear, pain, and resentment to help others, that was his duty.

A crack emerged in the street, expanding block by block in seconds. It zipped under Alistair's feet, forcing him to jump back and separate from Robert. More concerning than the fissure itself was what came out of it.

A geyser of lava exploded from out of the crack. Several more followed the first, all in a line starting from the origin of the chasm and spreading out. The spray of bubbling liquid reached as high as ten meters, parting in the air and crashing into the ground. After the initial spurt, it kept pumping sluggish lava all over the streets, which promptly oozed into the buildings.

Besides the inherent destruction of the lava, creatures crawled out of the molten rock, too. Ugly, misshapen golems made of spindly, pyroclastic columns of rock that dripped magma. They reminded him of the firebird, Selephita, to some extent—but without even an iota of her pedigree. They were certainly no Immemorial Race or pure beast of an elemental Dao. Rather, Alistair felt they were streamlined representations of lava, created with little care for details.

Despite only being around level 40 beasts, there were hundreds, if not thousands, and they surpassed the average strength of his freehold's citizens.

Celeste was behind him when their headquarters fell, managing to escape the collapse through the hole Alistair had created. She tapped his shoulder.

"Similar reports everywhere. Each area comprising a thousand subregions is experiencing a different disaster. Alexandra's area has a Category 8 hurricane, if something like that existed. Lucius's capital is dealing with floods from every body of water."

Alistair shook his head. "Anything on Devil King activity?"

"Not yet," she said. "I'll keep my ear posted."

"Thanks."

"Wait." Celeste looked around nervously. Her hand trembled as she grabbed Alistair's arm. "There's something I have to tell you. I might not have another chance with this disaster."

"You'll be fine, I promise. What's that urgent?" Alistair asked, feeling the weight of the world on his soul as people died around him.

"It's all my fault. It's all my fault and mine alone." Celeste fell to her knees and pleaded at his feet, tears streaming down her cheeks. "I found this footage a couple days ago. I... I should have told someone, b-but you have to understand, it's... it's—"

Alistair took a knee, caressing her back to calm her down. "It's okay. Speak your mind."

Celeste composed herself quickly. She brushed off her sleeves and procured a flash drive. "I've been searching through tens of thousands of hours of archival footage. One of my Class Skills allows me to access the internals of dead technology. A few weeks ago, I got a description of your mother from your sister and father. I've been crawling through the video archive in my spare time."

Alistair waited with bated breath as Celeste plugged the flash drive into the back of her hand, a small recess opening to accept the item. The woman's eyes began to glow. Two beams shot out of her pupils, a small picture forming at the intersection of the two shafts of light.

A video began playing on her eye-screen. It was shaky, clearly taken from the phone of a panicked person.

A man's voice came from behind the camera. Alistair understood his speech as Mandarin even without the help of the soul translator.

"It's over," he said. "It's over. It's over. It's over."

The man kept repeating the phrase. He didn't even sound scared, just resigned.

It was easy to imagine why. The video showed a city somewhere in China. Alistair could tell right away it was at the start of the initiation. The people moved with such ugly inefficiency, showing a complete lack of strength and agility. No one was fighting, just running.

The crowd ran from a mob of zombies straight out of a horror movie. And not the slow ones, but the fast ones like in World War Z. Even in the small field of view of the phone's camera, Alistair could see hundreds of people in the background getting their faces chewed off.

One woman was the first to fight back. She was close to the man taking the video. Picking up a dead man's cane, she smacked a zombie in the head. Despite their unusual ferocity, the blow was enough to bring down the monster, which she followed up with ten more bludgeoning strikes until it stopped moving altogether.

That was the turning point. Seeing a small woman beat up a zombie ignited a fervor among the crowd. No longer enthralled by fear, a feverous spirit of violence took over. The crowd armed themselves with whatever makeshift weapons they could find.

If only the woman had lived to see the fruits of her effort.

A zombie, far faster than its brethren, rushed at her from behind. The man with the camera ran toward the woman, but he was too late. By the time the others dragged the zombie off and stomped it to death, the woman had bled out. Her upper body was a mangled mess, almost unrecognizable.

But Alistair already knew who she was. Li Wang, his mother.

The ground cracked beneath him. Aura spilled out of his body, forming a semi-transparent cloak infused with the colors of his Mana affinities. Pressure radiated from his body in every direction, as his unconstrained power came loose.

The only thing that stopped him from crying out in pain and unleashing his pent-up emotions in a roar was the trembling figure beneath him. Celeste held up her hand, pleading for him to stop with fearful eyes.

Alistair immediately restrained himself. His aura expression was so powerful it would have killed her if he continued. He never wanted to see those desperate eyes again. The eyes of those who should have looked at him with confidence and hope, now filled with fear.

Anger melted into sadness. Sadness melted into despair. For a moment, Alistair clung on to the hope that the video was fake, that she still lived. But in his heart of hearts, he knew. He just *knew.*

He clenched his fist so hard that he thought his bones would break. Even the raw gratification of slamming his fist into the pavement was denied to him, lest he kill everyone in the vicinity.

All he could do was offer up a tear while he stared at the ground, impotent in his rage and grief.

"Ow! What the fuck?" Alistair shouted. When he looked up, he saw that Dev'rox had stabbed the back of his neck with a barbed tail.

Celeste looked taken aback by the sudden appearance of the imp, backpedaling clumsily and stumbling to the ground.

"You have a job," Dev'rox said, not a hint of the usual sarcasm in his voice. "It's not a job I would've ever taken on, but I know you. Your mother is dead. You can't change the past. It's done. But you've accepted a great responsibility. Even if I don't give a damn, you're going to hate yourself if you stay here wallowing in your grief. I can barely stand you as is. If you go mopey on me, I may have to kill you myself before the multiverse does me a favor."

Alistair wiped fresh blood off the back of his neck. When he looked at the collapsing city around him, he knew what he had to do. Dev'rox nudged him again with his tail.

"Fuck off," Alistair said. "I'm up."

"Starting to curse, are we? That might liven things up a little."

With new vigor, Alistair stared into the cavern of lava and beasts before him. On the other side of the divide, Robert jumped up and down, waving to him. "Do you want me to throw you the map?" he shouted. "I can do that!"

"It's fine." Though he spoke with a conversational tone, Alistair's voice echoed like a megaphone. "Let me deal with the problem first."

The crack had grown to a width of ten meters, splitting the street in two. The ground beneath the buildings on either side protruded into the air, causing the structures to collapse inward. While most people escaped before the crack had widened, Alistair could still feel the departing souls of dozens of people.

Those who'd survived had to deal with the lava golems. The creatures were slow and lashed out at anything that moved. The problem was that they grew. Every solid object they came across was added to their molten body. The oldest lava golems had expanded to the size of bears, even if they'd initially only been the size of cats.

Alistair laid waste to them with a biblical vengeance. [Frozen Claw] was his method of divine retribution, and the molten beasts were the unrepentant sinners.

[Frozen Claw] had served Alistair more as a defensive Skill in the past, but now he used it to its full potential. With 307 Wisdom, it destroyed whatever so-called soul resided within the golems.

Alistair was a blur of motion. All an onlooker could see was a streak of cold, blue energy that zigzagged from beast to beast faster than the eye could follow. When that streak passed by a golem, it cooled into solid rock instantaneously, ice crystals encasing it in eternal slumber.

Alistair killed a hundred of them in seconds. He didn't give a damn about the lava bubbling to the surface, running across it like a pool of water. His Skill's freezing energy spread to the lava unintentionally, turning it into obsidian.

But his slaughter wasn't satisfying. He barely paid attention to "Deliverance of Justice" activating, which granted him 6 points of free Attributes that he allocated to Wisdom.

The more he killed, the more others took their place. Alistair activated **[Frozen Claw]** in his other hand as well, letting both drain his Mana at the same time. With his regeneration of nearly 3 points a minute, along with a max pool of 1,765, he wasn't concerned with his Mana situation.

In total, the chasm spread out in a straight line for almost five kilometers. Alistair covered that entire distance, sprinting from enemy to enemy in under a minute. He was a whirlwind of icy death. There was no need to invoke {Psychopomp's Discipline}, but he did so anyway, channeling his anger into his martial arts.

It was like his limbs were actually water, flowing in smooth and flexible movements that didn't seem physically possible. Alistair karate chopped his enemies' necks and sliced open their faces with elbows. When he finally reached the end, a presence stirred deep in the lava of the fissure.

"No thank you," Alistair said.

Alistair gathered Dao energy from the Fist Node, striking the lava with a massive open-palmed **[Force Fist]**.

The lava cavorted around him, fueled by the fajin effect of his Skill. It was so powerful that it cleared out all the lava to the very bottom of the chasm, revealing the monstrosity beneath. It had the same cracked molten skin and lava-like appearance as the rest of the golems, except it was the size of an elephant and radiated an aura signifying a beast that had formed a Beast Core.

Alistair couldn't let the lava come down and harm anyone, so he had to move fast. He maneuvered into a diving position in the air.

The boss golem raised a hand faster than should have been possible for a being of its size. Alistair would have received a hot slap across the face if he wasn't so in tune with Dev'rox.

While he dove for the golem, Dev'rox solidified himself underneath Alistair's feet. They had tested this technique once before, and it had worked, but now was the first real trial.

Dev'rox fulfilled the requirement of solid ground for **[Dash]**, serving as a springboard for Alistair to more than double in speed. A dash of spatially-attuned Mana shrunk the distance even further.

At the same time, Alistair activated **[Blood Hand]**. The thick blood Mana shone even brighter than normal despite its rich, crimson hue. Fueled by Alistair's rage, the laments of the ghosts, and the raw power of the Ghost Node, his hand pierced straight through the golem.

Alistair ripped the beast apart from head to toe in one fell swoop. Starting from the head, the sharpened fingertip of a **Devilsbane Gauntlet** pierced straight through the craggy skin. His momentum carried him through, **Mammothskin Raiment** protecting him from the beast's internal heat until he plopped out behind it.

He crashed into the ground hand-first, though the destructive descent slowed his approach. The columns of lava he'd splashed into the air disappeared with the death of the final beast. It seemed like clearing out the local instance of the disaster would erase its physical presence. That was good to know, but earthquakes still rocked the other parts of the city.

As he turned inward for a moment, he realized the ghostly power felt *intoxicating*. Anything was good to get his mind off his painful discovery, but **[Ghost Whispers]** wouldn't stop filling him with energy. Since he refused to let himself become despondent, it made him feel like a god.

Alistair ran over the golem, draining its remaining life force and incorporating it into his body. {Letting of the Beast} gave him a single point of Endurance, while the absorbed energy brought his bloodline to 499/500.

"We found him," a familiar voice called out from above.

"So we did," said another voice that Alistair recognized.

He looked up, but he didn't need to see them to feel their auras. Standing above him were Dragonus and Admiral.

52 BLOODLINE'S BOON

ALISTAIR ACTIVATED [EYES OF TRUTH], finding the Devil King's appearance to be genuine. His demonic detection from "Devil May Cry" didn't lie, either.

The corners of his mouth turned upward. The multiverse had answered his request for an enemy. Alistair wouldn't waste it.

His next [Dash] was by far the fastest he had ever used. Muscles contracted in unison, fueled by Mana. "Good Samaritan" added an extra 25% Agility, on top of the energy gathered from [Ghost Whispers]. In one instant, he was at the bottom of an enormous pit, and in the next, he was right on top of Dragonus.

To their credit, the Devil Kings reacted right away. Admiral issued his Dao field to lock Alistair down, while Dragonus activated his voidfire armor.

But they were too slow. Alistair pressed a [Blood Hand] into Dragonus's scaly face before voidfire could protect it. His claws impaled the Devil King's cheeks, drawing blood in floating streams that his gloves greedily inhaled.

Before he was trapped by Admiral's Dao pressure, Alistair [Dashed] back, all in less than the blink of an eye.

Pain came next. Blood essence and life force coursed into his body, finishing off the last point needed for his species evolution.

Bloodline Formed: (Ghost) Blood Dragon [Peon]. *Choice of two charac-teristics.*

{Bloodline Evolution} (Ghost) Blood Dragon [Peon] — *Draconic Physique, Emperor Will, Blood Affinity, Endless Mana, LOCKED, LOCKED, LOCKED, LOCKED.* (Upgradeable 500/500 – Only accepts blood essence) — COMPLETE.

Alistair's consciousness exited his body, traveling beyond the bounds of reality. Or at least that's what it felt like: excruciating pain, followed by his soul flying for what appeared to be thousands if not millions of light-years.

It seemed too absurd to be true—even as a Foundation realm cultivator, the expense for such a trip couldn't be cheap. But whether an illusion or not, Alistair suddenly stood before an impossibly enormous dragon.

Alistair struggled to comprehend the scale of everything he'd experienced. On his instantaneous journey, he had passed by flat worlds that felt larger than the entire Solar System. Megastructures of pristine beauty surrounding gigantic black holes, incomprehensibly complex in design. Titanic beings with skin of the starry night sky and rainbow-colored squids on their backs, moving with reality-shattering weight.

He finally arrived in the middle of a sector of blood. There was no other way for Alistair to describe it. The planets nearest to him were decimated, torn apart. An unimaginable amount of blood flowed through the remains, forming a massive web. Columns and columns of the sanguine material streamed toward one source. The dragon.

As you might expect, the creature was blood red. The color that blood took on after it was outside the body for several minutes—a deep hue veering on black.

It was shaped as a western dragon, with a capacious wingspan as wide as it was long, with spikes up and down its spine. The only reference for its size was Alistair's tiny spiritual body and the destroyed planets, and he couldn't wrap his mind around the scale.

"What's this?" the dragon spoke. Even though it wasn't even trying to convey authority, Alistair humbled himself before this being. It was obvious the dragon was the most powerful cultivator he had ever witnessed. While he wasn't there in person, the spiritual strength was indescribable.

When Alistair took a closer look, he realized the blood dragon wasn't solid. The light of a distant sun passed through its skin, revealing a translucent body. A ghostly body. This blood dragon had to be the ghost blood dragon that Alistair was taking his bloodline from.

"**Messy technologists invoking my power,**" the dragon roared with a decidedly male voice. "**How dare they intercede for the bloodline of a Foundation?**" His eyes glowed brightly for a moment, and Alistair found himself staring right into the reptilian eye of the beast. It was the same color as the dead of space, with an amber pupil. The eye stretched on endlessly, so long Alistair couldn't even begin to guess at its size.

Alistair was too scared to speak. Did the Final Frontier Empire really authorize this sort of meeting? You weren't supposed to die from a bloodline evolution, as far as Alistair knew. Surely they wouldn't allow that. Surely not.

He floated there silently for a few more seconds as he felt the omniscient gaze of the blood dragon penetrate his soul. This was no true meeting, Alistair understood. The system was protecting him in some way, otherwise he would have collapsed in on himself from the pressure the creature exerted.

"**Perhaps I judged rashly. You have the Sage's mark. Your Fate is uncertain, on the edge of Chaos. How intriguing.**"

Alistair couldn't hold back his curiosity. He had been searching for information on that for so long. "Who is the Sage? And what has he done to me?"

The dragon laughed. "**A bastard is what he is.**" Alistair got the sense he respected him more for daring to speak. "**The Sage of Eternal Mercy was the third fastest to reach Truthseeker in this aeon, just behind his peers Barimaeus and Lady Nightshade. He is the founder of the Eternal Mercy Sect. Among his titles are the Accursed of Heaven, the Bane of All Evil, and the Lost Rose of the Earthly Dao. His left palm inexorably faces upward, the largest obscuration of Heaven's eye on the Physical Plane.**

"**Every thousand years, he sends out a million Karmic envoys to candidates in the multiverse he believes show promise. Promise in accordance with his Dao Path of forgiveness, mercy, and justice. The goodness of the heart above all else. Even in the multiversal core, such blessings are not taken for granted. Is that enough for you, greedy Foundation?**"

"If he's so good, why does he have Heaven's enmity?" Alistair asked.

The dragon snorted. "**Insolence will only get you so far. You will find that out one day. Take the smallest piece of my flesh and begone. You may** have this token of advice—Heaven's gaze is more obscured than you believe. Kyraxadon, the parochial demon you encountered during your soulcore tribulation, had no authority to summon any of the divine progeny. It is indeed true that the Sage is a great enemy of those on high, but you are nowhere close to strong enough to warrant individual concern. His invocational prayer would not have succeeded, though you would have died in his wroth once he discovered this. You have less to fear from those beyond and more to fear from those near."

Alistair floated toward the surface of the dragon's eye, which looked like a flat plane of black, vitreous liquid. An unknown force raised his hand for him, specifically his pointer finger. For an amount of time so small it could not be named, Alistair touched the cornea.

That touch was all he needed. Any more would have killed him, in fact.

Alistair had so many more questions for the ghost blood dragon, who he guessed was a Truthseeker, but they would have to remain unanswered. In the same bound that took him through a nearly infinite amount of space, Alistair returned to Earth.

He had a few choices before him, but first, he had to deal with the incoming attacks.

While his vision of the almighty dragon had only taken an instant, Alistair was discombobulated by his sudden return. A pressurized jet of water came from straight ahead, while spears of black fire rained from the skies. They came close to piercing him, though Alistair managed to activate [Dash], using the omnidirectionality of the flicker aspect to go backward while still facing his enemies.

Bloodline Characteristic – Choose Two:
Draconic Physique, Emperor Will, Blood Affinity, Endless Mana.

Alistair didn't have time to think it over. Out of pure instinct, he selected Endless Mana and Draconic Physique.

Characteristic – Endless Mana: +25% Mana. +50% Mana regeneration.

Characteristic – Draconic Physique: Lifespan increased by 2,000 years. Life force bolstered with the bodily vigor of a dragon.

The two Devil Kings looked at each other. Alistair could smell their fear in the air like a shark sensing blood. The dragon's will inside of him roared with its full fury. Even he couldn't, or more accurately, wouldn't contain it. It became a physical roar that carried all of his pain and sorrow—the anger of the dead, his new dragon's vengeance, and even Dev'rox's hidden emotions. A cathartic dragon's cry, ironically stolen from Dragonus when he'd used [Blood Hand].

His roar was so powerful that it sent visible currents through the air, uprooting trees and shattering any window still intact. Streaks of red blood filled the air, carrying killing intent straight from Alistair's psyche.

Dragonus resisted the wave easier with his own black dragon bloodline, but Admiral temporarily froze from the sheer power of the roar.

Alistair moved with the majesty of a dragon, activating [Dash] and preparing a [Blood Hand]. While the final round of Capture the Beacon was only a week ago, the difference in his power was night and day. His overall physical prowess had nearly doubled, and he showed that to Alexandra's father.

Admiral called up a legion of ghost ships as a shield, but Alistair was too fast. At the last sea-green barrier, he used Dev'rox's Mana to shorten the distance further, crashing through the spectral wood with a Dao energy infused [Blood Hand].

Every aspect of his Dao was better integrated with the addition of his bloodline. Despite his Dao Nodes not growing, he could tell they became at least 25% more efficient and embodied within his Skills.

Dragonus tried to help his partner, but he had to be careful not to hit Admiral when attacking Alistair. He conjured two spheres of destructive black fire, sending focused flame streaks at him.

Alistair used [Frozen Claw] with his offhand, freezing the Devil King's attack. The streaks almost became another level of protection, blocking Dragonus's path after they fully crystallized.

As his [Blood Hand] shattered the ectoplasmic barrier, Admiral backpedaled, trying to open his proto-Domain, but Alistair's talons reached his face first. He grabbed the Devil King by the face, hoisting him into the air while compressing his claws to draw as much blood as possible.

Dragonus meant business now, calling down a flaming pillar of the false Heavens. It was even larger than the one he'd used before, stretching nearly fifteen meters end-to-end. Twirling it in his hands like a massive baton, it reminded Alistair of the Monkey King's infamous iron pillar from Chinese mythology. The Devil King condensed it to the size of a quarterstaff, thrusting it at Alistair. The black fire burst out with his thrust, soaring for Alistair's head.

Still holding onto Admiral's face, Alistair threw the man with all his strength. Admiral flew for several hundred meters, barreling through several empty buildings. The pseudo-Heavenly pillar grazed Alistair's thigh as he ducked out of the way. The burns hurt, but with his new bloodline and the high-octane boost of [Ghost Whispers], his flesh sealed off any foreign energy.

With Admiral briefly distracted, Alistair launched an all-out assault on Dragonus. Diving into the third stage of the Mutra, he finally let go of all his compulsions. The weight of his emotions vanished. Alistair activated [Eyes of Truth], accessing his precognitive vision.

It was hard to get a handle on Dragonus. The Devil King's Fate resisted prognostication, his force of will too strong for Alistair to form a fully accurate picture. But it was good enough.

Alistair refused to let Dragonus get any distance, [Dashing] in close. He swatted away more flaming streaks with [Frozen Claw], letting them clang to the ground. Alistair extended a [Force Fist] jab, narrowly missing Dragonus's head.

The Devil King dodged to the side, opening his mouth and exhaling a plume of dragonfire full of Dao energy. Alistair activated [Force Fist] in both hands, crossing his arms over each other with his palms facing outward. The giant coral-colored hands overlapped, forming a perfect protective barrier with the help of two of his Dao Nodes.

Alistair didn't wait for the fire to finish, pushing forward even as the flames wrapped around him and licked his sides and back with destructive heat. **Mammothskin Raiment** took the brunt of the torrid flames, but his Health still dropped below 1,000.

The next thrust of the pillar Alistair saw in advance. His body swerved to the right without thinking as the tip of the pillar flew forward, hidden beneath the flames. It passed by his face, missing by just a few centimeters.

He could feel that Admiral was rushing back to the fight, smelling the man's demonic aura. There would only be a few more seconds of their 1v1.

Thoughts without thinking, movement without motion. Alistair embodied the words of Zenaitsu Morogoni. *Fluid, then still. Soft, then hard. The Kiss of Death.*

No matter how well Dragonus wielded his fake pillar, he would never touch Alistair. They had similar bloodlines, but Alistair was in full communion with his Dao.

Dragonus had clearly trained with the quarterstaff. Even though it was a new capability, he had complete control over his thrusts. He twirled the weapon in grand arcs, carving out the ground below with destruction and fire Mana. Each momentous blow shattered the earth.

Alistair held no fear in his heart. Where the staff was, he was not. Simple movements, all strung together in harmony with the Dao of the Fist. It was made easier by the fact that he heavily outmatched Dragonus in Agility.

The next moment was crucial. Admiral's presence stank to the heavens, his demonic foulness encroaching as he rapidly scaled a pile of rubble. Alistair was in striking distance from Dragonus, having found the perfect opportunity after weathering his attacks.

The threads of Fate were murky. Either Dragonus would cast his draconic apparition, or he would use the black sun.

Alistair didn't believe Dragonus would use his finishing move so early. That would contradict his arrogance.

Dev'rox swooped in from behind, cutting out an arc of spatially-attuned Mana with his tail. At the last second, Dragonus realized there was a presence behind him. That short gap let Alistair move in.

In a testament to his perspicacity, Dragonus had already started growing his voidfire armor. But like last time, it was a moment too late. The draconic phantasm materialized, taking on the form of a huge black dragon behind him.

Dev'rox's lash harmlessly dissolved into the spectral dragon, which radiated terrifying energy. Alistair wasn't worried, his own blood dragon bloodline bleeding into his body even through the calmness of the Mutra. If he had been fully conscious, the fury of his bloodline might have triggered a fugue state.

Alistair rained two [Force Fists] from above as knifehand strikes, but he didn't stop there. As the two giant Mana outlines soared down, he used his ridiculous Agility to chop with both hands again, syncopating the blows for greater efficiency. Then he did it again, and again, and then three more times —all in the span of a tenth of a second.

The [Force Fist] Mana hands were slower than his real arms, so it looked like he had just cast his Skill twelve times at once. Inside each Skill, he imbued the Daos of Fist and Justice. Alistair felt reminded of the Thousand-Armed Avalokiteśvara, the bodhisattva of compassion. There was insight there for his finishing Skill, but his inspiration was still incomplete.

Each coral hand slammed Dragonus deeper and deeper into the ground. They were like turrets, continuously blasting the Devil King without respite. The blows rang with golden and coral light that shone with righteous fury and judgment, echoing like an eastern gong for kilometers.

The shockwave was no ordinary air pressure. Instead, it passed over the vicinity harmlessly. Only when it washed over Admiral did it have an effect, the successive twelve rings pushing him back over a hundred meters.

As for Dragonus, the cumulative weight of judgment also pushed him, but down deep into the earth.

Alistair stopped to catch his breath, leaving the Kai'takaze Mutra. Without the upgrade to his Mana pool, he wouldn't have felt comfortable spending 720 Mana on the sequence. He still had 892 Mana left, along with a Tier 2 Mana pill at his disposal.

He could tell that Dragonus was still alive, but now he had to deal with Admiral. The Fourth Devil King's face was bloodied, cut up in five distinct marks around his cheeks and forehead where Alistair grabbed him. His naval uniform dripped with blood, tattered from the shockwaves of his previous barrage. The look on his face was unmistakable. Pure anger.

Spiritual water exploded out of his robes. Alistair was prepared, [Dashing] backward. Unable to trap him within the theoretical confines of his proto-Domain, Admiral pulled back the torrent of water.

That was his current strategy. As long as he stayed far enough away from the Fourth Devil King, he could never be trapped inside his proto-Domain. Then, he could deal with Dragonus while he dodged all of Admiral's attacks, which weren't fast and relied more on area denial and terrain control.

Admiral could just use his proto-Domain anyway and trap his leader inside, but it seemed unlikely. Dragonus couldn't use his full power there as it risked opening a tear in the false reality.

A scaly hand emerged from the smoking crater Alistair had made. He was very happy that his own transformation hadn't seemed to change anything, except for perhaps his eyes, but he couldn't see those yet. No scales for him, thank you very much.

Dragonus climbed out of the hole. A huge gash went from his left shoulder down to his navel, dripping black blood.

The moment he emerged, he took out an object from his pocket. Alistair focused back on the fight, activating [Eyes of Truth] again. Monitoring his Karma, he was at 46, but he poured a substantial amount to discern what Dragonus was doing.

The object appeared to be some kind of sea bomb, with the little pegs spread around its surface. Whatever it was, it had hidden itself from his view until Dragonus presented it openly. It was covered with so many green threads of Fate that it felt sacred, or, conversely, cursed.

When he locked eyes with it, the threads unfurled, zooming at him with unprecedented speed. Even with all of his Agility, Alistair only evaded the first few, his leg getting entangled with a thread and causing him to trip.

It felt cool to the touch. The direct influence of Fate shuddered him to the core. Was this how his opponents felt when he used [Hand of Karma] on them?

The other threads latched on as well, binding him to the ground. The bomb came along for the ride, knocking him in the head.

Alistair struggled with all his might, to no avail. If he didn't free himself, this would spell his end. A flaming streak or ghost ship would come any second and extinguish his life. He would have let down everyone he ever cared about. His dreams of reaching the peak of the multiverse would be dashed. Never learning of the secrets and mysteries, never instantiating his true Heaven on Earth. With a final heave, Alistair released a combination of Karma and Dao energy, weakening the threads to the point that he could break them.

When he stood up, he didn't see Dragonus and Admiral about to finish him off.

Alexandra and Oliver were fighting the Devil Kings. The former jumped from a nearby building, plummeting down on an [Armageddon Slash]. The latter jumped off her back, opening his portals from above and raining down a barrage of laser beams from within.

Admiral met his daughter's attack with an arcing ghost ship that knocked her off course toward Alistair, while Dragonus recast his fire staff and twirled it around to make a reflective shield.

His two friends landed by his side.

"Miss me?" Alexandra teased.

53 DEV'ROX'S NEW POWERS

ALISTAIR WANTED to ask how they'd arrived, but there wasn't enough time for that. It was three against two now, though with Oliver's army, it was closer to a hundred against two.

The Necromancer opened dozens of portals behind the trio, his zombies walking out armed to the teeth.

The two most prominent members of his dead army were the Orc Prince Kalgur, and a skeleton Alistair had never seen before. It lacked any vitality whatsoever and was held together by Oliver's power. Despite its weak appearance, it was nearly as strong as Kalgur, Oliver's long-standing champion.

The new undead gave off a feeling of timelessness that was reminiscent of someone else. Alistair quickly realized that the skeleton had to be the bones of Anthony. However, he didn't have time to dwell on the revelation for long, as the Devil Kings struck.

With the hundred-odd members of the zombie army on the battlefield, Admiral let loose his waters again.

"We'll handle my father," Alexandra said to Alistair. "Go for the big shot."

He nodded, [Dashing] toward Dragonus, who was flying into the sky on concentrated fire jetting from his feet. As he ran, he caught the beginning of Alexandra and Oliver's battle.

Oliver surprised him the most. It had been weeks since they last fought side-by-side, and the teenager had a few new tricks up his sleeve.

Working in tandem with Kalgur, a Dimensionalist, he strung together a series of blue-ringed portals. Oliver set the initial location beneath the ground, while Kalgur set his portals in the sky. Except for a handful of elites, the army dropped through the ground and into the air above Admiral.

At the same time, the water crashed over the remaining troops, locking them in Admiral's proto-Domain. The speed of his Domain release had increased, the water washing over Alexandra and Oliver before they could react.

Alistair finally had a chance to see a proto-Domain from the outside. After the water spread out and trapped his companions, it instantly collapsed into a sphere no larger than the size of a classroom. The proto-Domain appeared to partially exist in the physical world while also being connected to the recesses of Admiral's soul.

Dragonus used his foot burners to ascend over the buildings. Alistair climbed after him like a madman. He dug his metallic claws into the concrete to create holds, scaling the height in less than a second.

Dragonus kept retreating. Only when he touched down on a wheat field several kilometers from their starting position did he stop. Alistair would have engaged earlier, but his instincts told him it was a trap.

The crops around the Devil King erupted in flames from the presence of his aura. The quiet wind spread the fire across the field, growing in overlapping concentric circles that petered out at Alistair's feet.

It was just another sign of Dragonus's callousness. He certainly knew that the crops were one of their primary food sources. The flames kept spreading, burning acres and acres of farmland. The moment the fire destroyed it all, Dragonus quenched it.

Alistair stared at the former human from across a divide of charred dirt. "I will have no mercy on you."

Dragonus said nothing. He conjured full body voidfire armor, leaving only his eyes unguarded. Raising both of his hands into the air, he called down two black flame pillars of the false Heavens. The profane nature of the Devil Kings coursed through them, intensifying to a level even greater than before. Alistair swore he could see black blood dripping from Dragonus's hidden palms, offering fuel to the fire. The Devil King gripped his two pillars as hard as he could, compressing them down to the size of batons.

It would be a lie to say that Alistair had nothing to lose. At that moment, he wanted to abandon caution and obliterate Dragonus at any cost. But he had greater responsibilities. He slipped into the Kai'tazake Mutra, finding refuge in the Kiss of Death.

Alistair held his arm out and beckoned for Dragonus to come to him. He did.

Boosted by his voidfire armor, Dragonus charged at a blinding speed. He dragged a baton along the scorched ground, melting the earth and leaving a void-like scar.

His first attack was an upward jab from the grounded pillar. Alistair cast **[Force Fist]** with both hands, not afraid to spend Mana because of the new Endless Mana boost from his bloodline.

He grabbed the pseudo-Heavenly pillar with the force projection of the Skill. Dragonus swung his other flaming baton at Alistair's midsection, which Alistair caught with his other spectral hand.

Fist and Justice met Void and Fire as both Daos and their related Mana affinities clashed against one another. With his ghost blood dragon blood-line, everything felt *easier*. Alistair had the same amount of Dao energy, but it flowed through his spiritual network and into his Skills effortlessly.

The coral hands of Zenaitsu Morogoni warped and melted against the profane pillars. Alistair pumped Mana into his Skill to repair the damage.

Dragonus's eyes of black fire stood out against the voidfire that covered the rest of his body. While his eyes were dark, they didn't suck in the light. Alistair met his opponent's gaze directly, their faces almost close enough to feel each other's breath. They both pushed against the other with their respective Skills, trying to impose their strength and will.

Alistair felt he had a small advantage in Strength. From their previous encounters, he had surmised that Dragonus was an all-rounder like himself, but with a focus on Intelligence, Wisdom, and Constitution. He pushed that advantage, pouring all his bodily might into forcing Dragonus down while activating **[Eyes of Karma]**.

When Dragonus was about to fall to his knees, he suddenly dropped both batons, leaving them in Alistair's gripped hands. He transitioned straight into a jabbing strike at Alistair's throat.

Alistair saw it coming. He also dropped the batons, letting them sink halfway into the charred ground. Using two **[Force Fists]**, he deflected the strike with his palms, and then prepared a knee, targeting the Devil King's abdomen with another strike that carried the full weight of his Dao energy.

Using the mysterious martial art found in {Psychopomp's Discipline}, his death blow found a miniscule weakness in the voidfire armor. But that wasn't the most important part of his attack. Alistair also combined [**Hand of Karma**] and [**Force Fist**] together.

It was something he had never tried before. There was no need to, just like how you didn't have to try flapping your arms to know you couldn't fly. But after upgrading his Karmic Skill to Tier 3, that had changed. He could feel something in the Skill shift, without even using it yet.

The coral outline of a giant knee erupted in a veil of crimson Karma. The air warped around the weight of the combined Skills, slicing threads of Fate.

Dragonus reacted quickly, redirecting the flames protecting his face to his stomach. The extra fire cushioned Alistair's blow, but he had foreseen that outcome.

At the same time as he brought up his knee, Alistair had already begun a hidden spearhand with his arm. The **Devilsbane Gauntlet** reflected a dark red hue underneath a snowstorm of ice aspected Mana. The crystalline fingertips glinted with razor-sharp edges as he directed his attack right for Dragonus's uncovered face.

Alistair's knee hit its target, a copious mixture of Karma, force Mana, and Dao energy striking Dragonus's armor with a deafening boom. For just one brief moment in time—longer than should've been possible by the laws of physics—the Devil King stood still.

The fajin effect of Alistair's [**Force Fist**] had become stronger at Tier 2, and even more so when counting the efficiency granted by his peon blood-line. The icy fingertips of [**Frozen Claw**] broke his opponent's draconic skin, creating four puncture wounds from the bottom of Dragonus's nose to the middle of his forehead.

Then time resumed and reality hit. Dragonus flew backward, crying out in a very human reaction from the broken blood vessels in his nose. His light-sucking armor had done its job of protecting him from Alistair's fusion knee strike, but he hadn't anticipated the explosive force of the attack.

Dragonus had a tough, draconic body. But it wasn't ready to go from zero to over a thousand kilometers an hour in a fraction of a second, all while under the mediation of the Fist Node.

Alistair couldn't even see where Dragonus landed, the stalks of unburnt wheat on the horizon covering the crash. What he did know was that besides sending the Devil King flying, **[Frozen Claw]** had spread its chilling tendrils into Dragonus's soul. While he didn't expect it to end the fight by any means, it was a foothold.

He had already **[Dashed]** once to chase after his prey, but Alistair's danger sense and Karmic sight warned him not to get too close. Dragonus reared his ugly head, smearing black blood over his scaly face. Twenty spheres of black flame flew into the air above them.

The fireballs contained three parts—raging destruction, eternal fire, and the void. The latter was more of a cherry on top, though, tempering the unruly black flames that wanted to devour the world.

Hundreds—no, thousands—of thin streaks of flame flew out in a panoply from the inferno. Dragonus was inventive with his assault—half came head-on, while a fourth shot up at a 45-degree angle, and then the final fourth flew at an even higher incline. Many arced around the bulk of the flurry, all homing in on one target.

"I'm on it," Dev'rox said.

The near-corporeal imp flew to confront the multitudinous bombard-ment. As a mass artillery Skill, none of the streaks carried a significant amount of Dao energy. However, it was still enough that Dev'rox couldn't stop it all by himself. Tracing a tiny claw in cryptic patterns, he manipulated space on a level that Alistair had never seen from his companion.

Great magical circles of transparent Mana flashed in a makeshift dome around Alistair. The circles gave off an recondite air, completely saturated with Dev'rox's particular brand of space affinity Mana. Unknown symbols and mysterious patterns shifted in clear, humming symbols. It was a system of power foreign to the present universe, yet it still carved reality as it pleased.

Alistair dealt with the streaks that flew at him directly, which made up the majority of the darkened sky. Still in the deepest stage of the Mutra, he moved without conscious thought. He swayed with the wind, with the Dao.

He took advantage of every gap and space in the hundreds of lines of fire. Alistair contorted his body like no human could, owing to his almost 900 Agility after the boost from "Good Samaritan."

There were some attacks that he could not avoid. **[Frozen Claw]** came in handy there. He poured the Ghost Node into his Skill, etherealizing the incoming fire with the "Permanent Haunt" division. Intangible ice passed through his body like a cold shower. Uncomfortable, but not harmful.

Meanwhile, Dev'rox's grand arcana changed the laws of space. Where the secondary waves of fire fell, they did not fall. The magical arrays spatially connected to one another, with the left array sending its incoming fire to the right, and the right to the left. The portal above Alistair's head was one-sided, throwing the streaks back up into the sky and into the incoming flames.

Explosions blotted out most of his natural vision.

The streaks collided with themselves, blooming in an enormous incendiary explosion that Alistair couldn't see the end of. With his aura sense, he knew that the Devil King's Mana was running out. Dragonus would only spend so much on his Skill.

Alistair caught and froze what he thought was the final wave. Another all-encompassing wave of fire proved him wrong.

While he pushed forward through the sea of streaks, he looked into the future, feeling for his opponent with his senses. The black sun grabbed his attention.

Dragonus had never finished his ultimate Skill in the last Quest. He had let forth just one wave of fire. Alistair had a feeling that multiple were possible.

While Dev'rox diverted the flames of destruction, Alistair focused on the black sun. It was already absorbing the light of the world along with any matter nearby. The threads of Fate bent to its absolute gravitational pull, clouding his sight of the future. And that was all Dragonus needed.

Alistair froze ten lines of fire in midair, [Frozen Claw] chaining multiple times. The hoarfrost grew into solid ice crystals almost instantly.

A wave of void-tinted dragonfire overwhelmed him before he could react. Later reflection would reveal that Dragonus had used his black sun as distraction to unleash dragonfire from the maw of his draconic apparition. Alistair didn't have time to think, bringing [Frozen Claw] in front of his body as he suffused the Ghost Node within himself.

Dev'rox, despite the danger he was in himself, redirected a circle toward the billowing flames. Their connection cut off as fire enveloped the Profound imp. Alistair had no way of knowing if the imp had died or was hidden in the dense flames.

In the face of the dragonfire, Alistair had no other option but to push forward. He activated [Dash], though the thick flames hampered his movement. It was a leap of faith on his part. There was no way to see the end of the fire. It was possible that he would kill himself by going into the deepest part of Dragonus's inferno. But Alistair had learned to trust his instincts.

Alistair burst forth from the flames. His skin had serious burns and his hair was on fire, but he was alive and kicking. He landed right in front of Dragonus, who glared at him with the arrogance and odium only a Devil King could muster.

54 THE DUEL OF DESTINY

ALISTAIR SAW that Dragonus breathed heavily, the man's fist resting in the dirt. A small drop of black blood trickled down his chin. The liquid oozed onto his loose-fitting dark robes, where it blended in with the cloth. While Dragonus hadn't exerted himself physically, using that much Mana and Dao energy in such a short period must have tired his body.

But Alistair wasn't in the best condition himself. Third-degree burns riddled his face, extremities, and anywhere else his **Mammothskin Raiment** couldn't protect. His vital organs were mostly unharmed, but the spiritual nature of the flames made his injuries more destructive than a purely physical fire.

Dragonus took advantage of the momentary lapse in Alistair's **[Eyes of Truth]**. He had turned it off to conserve Karma, which had dropped to 24 points. The Devil King opened his mouth and let out a fearsome dragon's roar. *Nue* and force affinity Mana combined, along with a draconic authority that grazed upon the Dao.

Time stood still. Alistair felt the build-up of energy within Dragonus's body. Looking deep inside himself, he focused on the effervescent blood essence he had stolen. While the Blood of the Devil base leaf purified the noxious elements of the demon blood, it still transferred its abilities.

Because of the similarity of their bloodlines, Alistair was able to hijack an entire Skill—**[Draconic Roar]**. All his practice with *nue* had led to this moment. He opened his mouth and let forth all of his suppressed emotions with a deafening cry.

Alistair's soulcore was more in tune with force Mana than Dragonus's. Specks of coral particles shimmered in the cone of condensed air and invisible *nue*, while the opposing **[Draconic Roar]** lacked any color. However, Dragonus had far more practice with the Skill than Alistair. Their roars canceled each other out, the air currents exploding upward as they collided in between the two men.

The force of their roars pushed them further apart. Dragonus almost skidded out of the wheat field and into a lake, taken aback by the superior physical power of Alistair's roar.

Catching his balance, Dragonus turned to see Alistair right in front of him, having **[Dashed]** in upon seeing the opportunity. He barely dodged a series of **[Force Fist]** punches and elbows. Alistair was methodical in his attacks, leaving almost zero room for error. He wrapped a hand around his opposite wrist, slicing with an elbow that cut into the Devil King's robes.

Dragonus opened his mouth, and a plume of black fire enveloped Alistair's vision. The propulsive force rocketed the Devil King over the surface of the lake as his dragon breath expanded in volume and heat. Boiling steam exploded from the water, covering the burnt field in a fine mist.

Alistair's danger sense buzzed before he saw the fireball. He ducked, escaping the initial salvo. The water was his haven, and he dove into the lake as the dragonfire expanded. From his underwater position, he could see the cone of flames widen and cover the surface of the water.

Alistair lost his focus and fell out of the Mutra, swimming forward in the limpid waters as he waited for the flames above to disappear. Perplexingly, even after a few seconds, the flames remained. Alistair raised an eyebrow. The Mana required to sustain that volume of fire after its initial blooming would have bankrupted even Dragonus, who still had a larger Mana pool than Alistair even after having acquired his bloodline.

Beyond simply persisting, the fire grew. Alistair dove deeper into the lake, and since the water was pristine, he could see from edge to edge. The black inferno grew to cover the entire lake, a hundred meters across.

The temperature continued to rise. Even as deep as he was, he began sweating as the waters grew scalding hot. The surface boiled first, sending steam out from the edges of the flames.

Alistair's [Eyes of Truth] hadn't seen this outcome. Either he hadn't teased out all of Dragonus's abilities in Capture the Beacon, or the Devil King had obtained something new. His Karmic sight performed worse against unknown threats, but Alistair had another speculation—it wasn't a Skill at all, but some kind of tinder stored in a Fate-warded container.

It reminded him of the everlasting fire in Selephita's dominion but on a smaller scale. The Dao made manifest, a physical reification of Dragonus's destruction and fire. Alistair knew that even with the Dao of the Ghost and his **Mammothskin Raiment**, he wouldn't survive for long if he emerged.

The problem was that the fires were only increasing in intensity. Every second, the lake shrunk as the surface turned to vapor. Every second, the remaining water got a little hotter.

Out of nowhere, a spear of fire shot down into the water. Then another. A whole arsenal of black spears shot through the inferno and into the lake.

They fell indiscriminately, so Alistair didn't have to dodge most of them. But the assault felt endless. He couldn't move as deftly in the water, and several spears almost hit their mark. Alistair was forced to activate [Frozen Claw]. He still tried dodging the ones he could, but with every passing second, more and more spears came down. Those that he couldn't evade he grabbed with his Skill, selectively crystallizing them and throwing them to the wayside.

After a minute, the temperature rose to the point where he was taking continual damage. [Frozen Claw] worked against the heat, but it was like an ant trying to take down a giant. His Health was dropping by a point every second, and it was only getting worse. The rain of spears didn't stop. Eventually, a spear made it through his defenses as his muscles tired, impaling his foot.

Alistair grunted in pain, causing a lapse in concentration. A second spear skewered his thigh.

In a fit of anger, Alistair poured Dao energy and a chunk of Mana into a new [Frozen Claw], summoning a barrier of ice around him with a wide swipe. The huge frozen crescent protected him from the next few spears, but it would only hold for so long. In the meantime, he had to think.

The situation had derailed ever since Alistair failed to anticipate Dragonus's hidden ability. Whatever the Skill or item was, he was now stuck. Had he relied too much on his readings of Fate?

Alistair refused to let doubt take over his mind. Did Zenaitsu Morgoni accede to fear when he destroyed the legion of technological horrors that threatened his planet? Did the Sage of Eternal Mercy fall to a mere underling on his home planet? The galaxy-devouring blood dragon he'd encountered refused to give up on his revenge even after passing through the gates of Death.

But that wasn't what was most important. This was Alistair's life. He would write his own destiny. One day, his story would be told in every corner of the multiverse. That meant it couldn't—*wouldn't*—end here.

Alistair swallowed a Tier 2 Mana pill, bringing him up to 715. Since he was at basically zero before, it was good enough.

Spears continued to rain down on his arch of ice, cracking it in many places. It would hold for a few more seconds.

He still had a fifth of the Fist Node, a fourth of the Justice Node, and perhaps half of the Ghost Node left. While he couldn't feel Dev'rox's presence through the thick flames, Alistair was confident the imp was out there.

At this point, it felt like they had been partners for a lifetime. They were completely in sync with one another. He would know exactly what to do when Alistair emerged.

The scalding water seared his extremities. The extreme pain should have made it more difficult for him to enter his trance, but it almost helped. Every cell in his body should have screamed for respite as the reservoir's scalding temperature overwhelmed his Constitution and overcoat. Maybe they did. The mortification of his flesh only let his mind find deeper refuge in the Dao of the Fist.

In reality, his body was shutting down. The water had become a supercritical fluid. It was so hot that it should have vaporized, but the physical boundary of the flames kept it grounded in the basin. Organ failure was imminent.

But why do I feel better than ever? As he embodied the concept in his martial arts, Alistair felt in tune with death. The Kiss of Death was the final stage of the Kai'tazake Mutra. Instead of the grim reaper, Alistair imagined the Black and White Impermanence. The psychopomps of Chinese mythology, they escorted spirits to the underworld. They felt as close as they'd ever been, eager to embrace him.

At his lowest point, which was also his highest, he opened the Justice Node. Not in a deepening, like he expected, but in a First Widening.

Achievement: Dao Node (I) (Dao of Justice) — First Widening. *Bridge of the Last Word added to Dao Elements.* Reward: +40 Endurance, +25 Charisma, +10% Endurance, +5% Charisma.

Bridge of the Last Word. Alistair felt the concept resonate within his soul. Unlike a deepening, which improved the understanding of an existing idea, a widening added a new aspect to his Dao. If a deepening made him stronger, a widening made him more versatile.

Bridge of the Last Word centered on returning souls to their rightful place, on becoming the reaper of the poetic home of lost souls. Alistair's hands were scythes and his feet were swords, all centered around bringing death. Not to invoke fear in his enemies but as an innate aspect of reality.

At first glance, it seemed weird, since the idea almost verged on the Kai'tazake Mutra. But that was the whole point. The widening was a bridge from Justice to Fist, but also between Justice and Ghost. He was righting souls, an idea that touched on both the Fist and Ghost. The stat benefits weren't as strong as his previous deepenings, but in exchange, he now felt a deeper synergy between his Dao Nodes that would make them greater than the sum of their parts.

Right before he was about to pass out, he activated **[Force Fist]**.

Not just any **[Force Fist]**. He poured everything into his Skill. This would be the finest creation he ever made.

Crouching down, he wrapped his left hand around his right wrist. As the coral outline appeared around his right hand, he tried something new. He activated **[Frozen Claw]**, not around his **Devilsbane Gauntlets**, but around the Mana projection. It took all his concentration and expertise that he had accrued from weeks of using the Skill, but it worked.

The attack's final layer was easier. **[Hand of Karma]** flowed over the **[Frozen Claw]** projection, as Alistair imbued all his remaining Karma into the hybrid Skill. Fist and Justice Dao energy intertwined through the fabric of the Mana, solidifying the energy construct and lending it conceptual weight.

Alistair turned sideways, coiling his arm like a snake. He turned his shoulder down and inward, like a disc golf player going for a long hole, except more vertical.

He unleashed the Skill in an upward arc with all his might. It bankrupted his newly refreshed Fist and Justice Nodes as he attacked with the singular goal of returning Dragonus to his rightful place.

A superhuman coral hand cut into the bottom of the lake and zoomed up. It was almost solid, covered with a brumal layer of ice-attuned Mana that crystallized the surrounding water. On top of that was the blazing aura of crimson Karma. All three strata harmonized with one another, the chop carving through everything in its path.

Alistair dimly saw that he got an achievement. His consciousness slipped away as he fell to the empty ground of the former lake. The heat stopped, so he knew something had worked, but he struggled to stay awake. He had truly put his soul into that attack. If it failed, so be it.

"You're giving up that easy?" a scathing voice called out.

Dev'rox, Alistair thought. The imp merged into Alistair's body, jolting him to full awareness. It wasn't healing, per se; it was more like a second wave of mental fortitude. Dev'rox, having a mind of his own, helped Alistair's willpower supersede his body's exhaustion.

Alistair came to at the bottom of the lake. The remaining water had been formed into two huge frozen waves at opposite ends, leaving the middle third of the lake empty. But more important was what had happened above him.

The impressive atmosphere of black fire had completely vanished. There was a deep split in the earth where Alistair had swung his hand. It went on so far into the distance that he could not even see the end.

"That's more like it," Dev'rox said. Alistair could tell the imp was hurt from the earlier voidfire. Alistair was in too much pain to respond, even mentally. Hoisting himself up on the lake's bank, he gulped down a Tier 2 Health pill.

Purifying fire healed his system from the inside as he made it to flat land. His Health, which had come dangerously close to 0, shot back to 250. That still put him closer to death than he would have liked.

On the other side of the lake was a field of barley. The moment Alistair's line of sight breached the waterline, he saw Dragonus.

The Third Devil King was on all fours, coughing up blood. A vertical gash went from his chest to his stomach and bled profusely. Alistair hoped that Dragonus would have died from his attack, but this was good enough.

The notification he received was not for completing [Ultimate Skill], like he'd expected. Instead, it was for Arcana II for doing something new with a Skill. Since it didn't require any manual upgrades, he ignored it.

Alistair [Dashed] toward his opponent, going for a [Force Fist]-laden jab. Dragonus moved far faster than he anticipated, catching the blow with a palm full of fire. From the orange-red glow in the Devil King's blood vessels, it became clear that he had taken a Health pill while he was prostrate.

After their previous terrain-altering attacks, their next exchange stuck to the basics.

They fought with their fists. Alistair conjured two plain [Force Fists] the size of boxing gloves, while Dragonus surrounded one hand in a cloak of voidfire and the other with his standard destructive flames.

With Alistair's lack of Karma and empty Fist Node, it was as level playing field as Dragonus could hope for. Alistair relied on only his innate skill at hand-to-hand combat, which was still much higher than the Devil King's.

Alistair took the initiative, stringing together elegant combos while Dragonus flailed around, relying on his Mana and sturdy Constitution. Alistair started with boxing techniques, throwing a jab and then a left hook, following it up with an uppercut.

The Devil King parried the blows with his flaming fists, ducking under a flying roundhouse kick. But he was unable to attack in return. For every five blows Alistair threw, Dragonus only managed one. He was able to divert most of the attacks, but Alistair consistently pushed back.

The longer Dragonus's flames burned, the hotter they became. Because of the added aspect of destruction, they flared wildly, cutting into Alistair's arms. The small lacerations didn't even cauterize because of the Dao the flames imparted, and blood stained the inside of his **Mammothskin Raiment.**

On the flip side, Dragonus's Constitution had to be over 600. Alistair felt like he was slamming into concrete with bare hands. He performed a hand-spring into a capoeira-style kick, grazing his opponent's shoulder enough to send him off-kilter.

Dragonus used a hand to catch his balance, casting his warped copy of [Frozen Claw]. A jagged line of ash spread in a fractal pattern and headed straight for Alistair. The Magical Pugilist batted it away with his [Force Fist], though the ash incinerated the protective layer of Mana. He barely managed to reform the Skill in time as the top layer of his skin peeled off.

Alistair glided through the rest of the disintegrating cinders by infusing himself with the Dao of Ghost. As his last remaining source of Dao energy, he used the minimum amount. His Health dropped to 101, but he kept over 40% of his Dao Node.

Dragonus swiped wildly with the fury of a dragon. His features turned even more reptilian, his skin darkening, scales forming not only near the corners of his eyes but all over his face. The phantasmal dragon that some-times appeared behind and over his body flashed in and out of existence.

But those aspects fought against what Dragonus had been reborn as. The red and black lines that signified a Devil King flickered. It was as if his bloodline and Devil Kingship were fighting one another.

Alistair used that momentary confusion to attack. A naked elbow struck Dragonus in the chin. He quickly turned that into a backfist, slamming the man's jaw with [Force Fist]-strengthened knuckles.

Dragonus tumbled into the dirt. However, when Alistair felt a sharp prick of pain, he glanced down and discovered a needle of dragonfire stuck in his belly.

Dev'rox pulled it out with his stubby arms before Alistair had a chance to react. It must have happened when he elbowed Dragonus, somehow bypassing his danger sense. Warm blood flowed from the wound. Normally, he wouldn't have taken out the piercing weapon, but the fire was too dangerous to keep inside his body.

Alistair ignored the wound and turned to follow Dragonus. His oppo-nent was recovering from the punch. It was the perfect time to strike, but Alistair was struck by a haunting feeling. Even without Karma, he had inured himself to the workings of Fate long enough to recognize looming catastrophe.

He had no other choice but to mortgage his Fate. He dropped to -10 Karma, activating a powerful [Eyes of Karma].

In his shadowy vision of the future, he saw Dragonus coalesce all his remaining energy into a black sun, disabling Alistair in an instant. The wave of dark quintessence traveled faster than a [Dash] and spread out in a radius of a hundred meters. The next wave was even larger and finished him off. And that wasn't the last one—Alistair was sure of it. Therefore, the only option was forward.

Alistair [Dashed] toward Dragonus as the man closed his eyes. Even with Alistair's unlucky Karmic state, the Devil King could not bypass his physical limitations. Because of his dwindling Dao energy and his injuries, it took him longer to summon the black sun.

While Alistair had barely used **[Blood Hand]** this fight, he had not forgotten about the Skill. A **Devilsbane Gauntlet** bubbled with sanguine aura, synergizing with the Mana affinity it loved best. Dev'rox compressed the space in between them, floating out of his body at the same time.

Suddenly, Dragonus opened his eyes, violating Alistair's Karmic sight. From his robes, he drew a golden gourd ornamented with a spiraling Chinese dragon. A smoky trail of burning incense rose out of the gourd. The moment the smell hit Alistair's nose, he knew it was what had fueled the Dao flames earlier. The incense felt like a sacred piece of the Heavens, stolen by the Devil Kings.

Yet this was all within Alistair's predictions. The existence of the Fate-warded gourd didn't throw him off, and he stopped his **[Dash]** a meter short.

Dragonus breathed fire, the incense serving as fuel. The moment the flames touched the smoke, it shifted, becoming a spiritual fire as much as a physical one. The flames expanded rapidly with the help of the incense.

Dev'rox waved at Alistair from above the fire. *That cheeky bastard.* With **[Spectral Summoning]** at Tier 3, you couldn't tell that he was a ghost anymore. The Ghost Node coursed through his newly draconic body, synchronizing with the imp. Then the imp snapped his stubby fingers.

Alistair swapped places with Dev'rox. With the ghost's solid form, he could act on reality more than ever before. Like the arcane arrays, he was regaining his old tricks.

Unlike Dev'rox, Alistair was subject to the laws of gravity. He dove into Dragonus, who hadn't expected the sudden shift.

[Blood Hand] latched onto the Devil King's shoulder. Alistair struggled against the man's toughened muscles and skin, channeling the lamentations of the dead with **[Ghost Whispers]** and imbuing almost all of his remaining Dao energy.

Dragonus howled in pain. He writhed like a madman, wild flames erupting out of his orifices in an attempt to shake Alistair off.

Alistair hung on for dear life. Sitting on the Devil King's shoulders, he plunged his hand as deep into Dragonus's shoulder as he could. Abundant life force flowed out of the gash in red streams, gathering in his gauntlets.

His Health dropped below 100 as Dragonus's skin set ablaze. The Devil

King tried to activate Skills with his hands, but Alistair locked down the man's free arm by holding his entire upper body in a bear hug.

Holy Will of the "Devil May Cry" Badge kicked in, giving the second wind that the description promised. Alistair dug deeper, refusing to let go. Life force and blood essence flowed out of his enemy's body in massive chunks. It would only take a few more seconds to drain him dry.

Dragonus knew it too. He gathered himself and closed his eyes. A black sun was about to appear.

Alistair saw this in the last vestiges of his **[Eyes of Karma]**. Before Dragonus's eyelids were halfway down, he withdrew **[Blood Hand]** from the shoulder, grabbing the man's neck instead.

Wielding the last embers of Holy Will, Alistair threw the man as far as he could. He aimed at the city where they'd started.

Halfway through Dragonus's flight, a black sun the size of a beach ball appeared over his head. Even from Alistair's location over a kilometer away, he could see the color drain out of the world. The gravitational field of the sun drew out a small trickle of Dao energy and Mana from his body, though he was already just about out of the former and had only 153 of the latter.

A brilliant wave of light-sucking flames erupted from the black sun. Dragonus was still flying through the air as it happened, the star-like sphere stationary at the position it initially appeared.

The real sun disappeared, an aeon of darkness taking hold. For a moment, it was as if the world stood still.

In spite of being so far away, Alistair ran like the wind in the opposite direction. The sun spewed out its mass in a solar flare.

The black wave traveled faster than the speed of sound, emanating from its source in every direction. Nothing was spared from the wrath of the dragon star. The crops, the ground, even the air itself—all vanished in the blink of an eye.

Alistair's saving grace was that by the time it reached him, it had diluted significantly. When the wave passed over the barley, it was only set on fire rather than obliterating it outright.

He **[Dashed]** away, though his body failed him when he tried to activate the Skill again. He had used up too much Stamina, something that had never happened before. There wasn't even a Stamina pill in his inventory.

The wave of fire passed over him, barely more than a warm breeze. Not for the first time, he thanked his thick wooly coat. He was nearly two kilometers away from the sun, so if it had killed him from that distance, he would have been pissed off.

For a moment, Alistair feared a second or even third wave, but when he looked to the sky, Earth's yellow sun had returned. Dragonus's false star had vanished. Most likely, he'd lacked the Dao energy to fuel any successive waves.

Wait a second, Alistair thought. *Where's Dev'rox?*

For a moment, he feared the worst, that the wave had annihilated his companion. But when he listened to [Ghost Whispers], he could sense Dev'rox far away and still moving. Moving in the direction where Alistair had thrown Dragonus.

Wha—

Alistair's thoughts were interrupted by a sudden change in scenery. One moment he was on his hands and knees in a field of barley, and in the next, he was on top of a building back in New Boston.

Dev'rox must have followed Dragonus's flying body and swapped places with Alistair again. He looked down, taking in the situation.

His aim was better than expected. The Third Devil King had flown through several buildings along his journey, landing in and cracking a marble fountain in the middle of a circular walkway.

The walkway was a renovation of a former hotel, refitted to become one of the three academies in the city. The academy building, a cosmopolitan-style hotel with two stone towers built into the sides, had serious structural damage. There were shattered windows, broken beams, and collapsed floors. Hopefully, the Warrior trainees had already escaped.

Besides Dragonus, Alistair also saw Alexandra and Oliver in battle against Admiral. It was two blocks down, though rapidly moving toward his location.

Admiral's naval uniform was in tatters, and he was bleeding from his bare chest. His friends were running from a flood of water and a series of green ghost ships while the Fourth Devil King cackled.

Alexandra and Oliver looked even worse than their opponent. Alexandra's entire left arm was missing, and Oliver was being carried by his skeleton as Kalgur stood steadfast against the flood.

The Orc Prince gave off a solemn presence befitting of his royalty. Somehow, he conveyed far deeper emotions with his black orbs of eyes than he had ever done while alive. He held up a palm to the incoming Devil King, chanting in a mystical language.

A mangled distortion of reality appeared, blue portal lines intersecting each other in dense fractals. The destinations of the portals were all within the boundary line of the distortion itself—mixing and extending inward like a cancerous spatial tumor—until it took on a recognizable form.

Kalgur visibly strained but kept his palm up. Alistair could see that whatever spell he was casting would be his last. The orc was putting his "life force" behind it, though as an undead creation, it was more of a mutation of the being's original life force.

Alistair hoisted himself over the railing of the building and jumped down. While he descended, he could've sworn he saw the orc wink at his master.

A beautiful azure woman formed out of the tears in space. Standing five meters tall, she held back the ocean's assault with her bare hands. She grabbed onto Admiral's water, forcibly pushing it away, forming an extra set of arms to arrest the momentum of the ghost ships.

At that point, Alexandra saw Dragonus's slumped over form and looked up to see Alistair fall off the building. They were so close to one another, yet still so far.

Dragonus stood up. Despite flying through tons of brick and metal, as well as the missing chunk of flesh in his shoulder, he was alive.

He self-detonated.

Realizing that he was not long for this world, Dragonus plunged a hand into his heart. His body should have been too tough for that, but he did it anyway. With Dragonus equidistant from him and Alexandra, Alistair [Dashed] forward instead of away, grabbing Alexandra. He had recovered just enough Stamina for one use of the Skill.

He pushed her to the side, landing on top of her as he shielded her from the explosion. She had a higher Constitution than him, but even with his 102 Health, he was healthier than her. The skeleton instinctively did the same for Oliver, warding him with a barrier of frozen time.

The world grew hot and Alistair dug in with all he had. His negative Karma weighed heavily in his mind, an onerous burden that revealed his weakness. If he was stronger, he wouldn't have had to take out a loan on his future.

Finally, the flames subsided, and he looked up.

Dragonus was no more.

Achievement Upgraded: True Origin (Arcana II) — *Create something new of your own design.* Reward: +100 Upgrade Points OR Receive synthesized attack as an official Skill, reducing activation time to 0.25 seconds, with Mana Cost of 400 and cooldown of 24 hours.

Level up! *You are now level 54.* +3 Agility, +3 Intelligence, +3 Charisma, +3 free Attribute points, +23 Upgrade Points.

Quest Update: Task Completion: Kill 2/12 Devil Kings. Bonus Reward: 40 Upgrade Points.

"Deliverance of Justice": +1 free Attribute point.

Alistair cursed his own decisions. After allocating the points from "Deliverance of Justice," he had 495 Charisma. If only he had five more points, he could have doubled his base Karma.

He ignored the achievement, since neither reward would help him at the moment. He couldn't spare time to think about what to use his Upgrade Points for, as Admiral had broken through Kalgur's portal woman.

The Orc Prince collapsed into dust, having fulfilled his purpose. Admiral came charging through, his tsunami growing to the height of the nearby apartment complexes. While injured, Alistair was nowhere near as close to death's door as the three of them.

Alistair emptied himself of all thoughts. While he couldn't invoke the Mutra with his Fist Node empty, he was still an expert in meditation.

He labored to stand. If this was it, he'd go out fighting.

A sharp prod sapped his attention. Dev'rox had poked his tail into Alistair's cheek.

"There's only one option."

55 VICTORY OR DEFEAT

"You're right," Alistair weakly thought. He was ready.

Dev'rox reached into the pocket of his robe, drawing out the vial of demon blood. Alistair could feel the noxious presence call out to him. It was ugly and malformed, full of dark promise.

Alistair closed his eyes and opened his mouth. If this was the price he had to pay to save his friends, he would do it.

Not like I planned on dying anyway, he chuckled to himself. His path would be inevitably altered, and he wasn't even sure how it would affect his Daos, anti-demon powers or bloodline—but there were no other options.

A second passed and Alistair still didn't feel the inky liquid on his tongue. He opened his eyes.

Of course. That was the only thing that made sense.

Dev'rox pressed the vial against Alexandra's lips, pouring the demon blood down her throat. Alistair weakly reached out a hand in protest, but he didn't mean it. He put his hand on Alexandra's back, supporting her half-conscious body.

"Do you accept?" Dev'rox asked.

"I do," Alexandra made out, barely louder than a whisper.

Alistair remembered Dev'rox's words from a long time ago. "*While both parties still breathe, the blood of a demon replaces the blood of a human. Untold power at an untold price.*"

Dev'rox was no living demon, but he had certainly grown opaque and solid, capable of altering causality. Alistair had no idea how the details of the Pact worked, but he hoped this was a loophole.

Alexandra finished imbibing the black liquid. Alistair's heart skipped a beat as for a second but nothing happened. Then, there was an explosion of aura.

Alexandra, who was one cut away from death, saw her body revitalized. Wounds stitched back together and her left arm regrew, fueled by the unholy substance. She used a combination of regrowth and pure life affinity Mana, her vitality tinged with the Path of Nature. The outburst of Mana was not sunny and verdant. It was vibrant with the natural fury of life, but dark and full of decay.

A mutated version of [Woodland Forest] spread out from her feet, black and white ashen trees blooming like wildfire. They carried the demonic aura of the Devil Kings, combined with a hollow version of her Dao of the Nature's Attendant.

Alexandra looked unconscious as she spasmed, the nascent energies within her ricocheting throughout her meridians. It was up to her willpower and skill to control it. If she failed, her spiritual network would collapse from the inside out, killing her.

Oliver bought them a few seconds. His face was bloodied beyond recognition, but he raised his hand and used the last trickle of Mana he had to open a portal above the incoming Devil King.

A sword soared down from the opened rift. A sword that Alistair hadn't expected to see: Anthony's former weapon, **Sun's End Vanquishment Sword**.

Even now, twenty-one levels ahead of when he fought the time-based cultivator, the katana still stood out with its unparalleled quality. The half-glass, half-obsidian sword exuded an aura that explained its name perfectly, heralding the end of all life.

While it wasn't as powerful without a wielder, the sword was still dangerous. The force of gravity brought it straight down on Admiral.

Meanwhile, Alexandra was reining in the demon blood. Her aura was still expanding, yet her control over it improved by the second. She tamed the chaotic energy, making it hers. Her Class and Daos were uniquely suited to mastering the infusion.

With one last pulse of black Mana, Alexandra opened her eyes. Her brown irises were gone, replaced with pools of fire. Like Dragonus, she had her own color—a vivacious green, bordering on lime. Red and black lines traveled up from her eyes, weaving through her hair and down her neck.

Admiral halted his forward march to let the katana fall to the ground, which pierced the street with a chaotic explosion that warped the surroundings. Oliver purposefully dropped the sword several meters in front of the Devil King, forcing the man to come to a halt to avoid it.

Alexandra activated [Barbarian's Fury], a cloak of evaporating blood mixing nicely with her pulsing aura. She looked up at her father with a mixture of disgust and rage. Enlarging her whitesteel dagger, she let the man come to her.

In the meantime, the [Woodland Forest] kept expanding. While unrefined, Alistair felt hints of a proto-Domain within the forest's boundary. The Dao field expressed Alexandra's understanding of nature and war, combined with the corruption of a newborn Devil King.

Three types of trees emerged in her woodlands. Some had white trunks and black leaves, others had black trunks and white leaves, while the rest retained their natural colors. The normal trees carried the weight of nature, while the other two held the inverse of pristine nature, perverted by the essence of a Devil King. Pale red embers flickered off the leaves, carrying her barbaric Dao.

The trees met Admiral's spiritual ocean, the two spiritual domains clashing against one another. Alexandra's was not as developed as her father's, but she put more of her heart and soul into it, forcing back the ships.

Admiral, seeing that he wouldn't succeed with brute force, jumped off his ghost ship and into the chaotic hole created by Sun's End Vanquishment Sword. The humming air didn't bother him at all as he drew a ghostly cutlass from thin air.

Stabbing it into the ground, spectral chains shot out of the sword and at the three of them. The skeleton picked up Oliver and retreated. Alistair supposed that was for the best. Oliver was completely out of Mana and Dao energy and so injured a slight breeze might kill him.

Alistair was too tired to dodge, but Alexandra covered for him. She sliced the chains before they could reach them.

[Woodland Forest] grew to its greatest possible extent, taking up the entire block of the ruined city. Alexandra must have designated him as friendly, otherwise the foreign Dao would have invaded his system. Admiral sliced the trees apart with his cutlass like a rainforest explorer, cackling as he made his way to his daughter.

Alexandra took a deep breath. Alistair could only imagine the emotions she was going through. Grabbing her dagger with both hands, she rushed Admiral with more speed than she had ever shown before.

She went for a stabbing blow, thrusting with immense force. Admiral sidestepped the stab, which destroyed the wall of an apartment building. He slashed down with his spiritual weapon, but Alexandra intercepted his biceps with her forearm, stopping the slice before it got close.

Seeing an opening, she delivered a palm strike to his chest, sending him back several meters. The two of them went at each other relentlessly— Alistair would have called their technique sloppy, but there was a certain evolutionary merit to their styles.

While the haymakers and giant sword arcs seemed inefficient, Alistair felt a stirring of the Dao of War. If the Sword represented the height of sterile mastery, and the Fist living martiality, Alexandra's Barbaric Fury was even further down the spectrum of control. Technique became the lack of technique, and the lack of technique became technique.

She swung her dagger with singular purpose, yet full of infinite possibilities. Admiral couldn't keep up. He blocked and blocked, but was forced back by his daughter's relentless assault.

Alexandra arced her sword with one hand, aiming for the face. Admiral reinforced his forearm with a layer of spectral energy to block. He took the blow well, his armor cracking. They both skidded back from the impact, throwing up concrete as they tore across the street.

Admiral reached out with his other hand, making a pulling motion. Chunks of collapsed buildings flew toward his location, threatening to smash Alexandra into pulp.

Trees bent down to block the incoming debris. She used her terrain advantage, harassing the Devil King with her control over the forest. When he turned to cut down a tree, she would swoop in, bringing down an [Armageddon Slash] that quintupled the weight of her weapon.

Alexandra only got five charges of the Skill every twenty-four hours, so Alistair thought she would have used them already, but it seemed that the demon blood transfusion replenished her cooldown.

The weight of the Skill carved out a crater that took up most of the street.

She retreated and let her forest take over again, forcing Admiral to pour resources into defending against the Dao-wrought trees.

Once he focused his attention on the trees, she soared right back, using the canopy of trees to hide her next attack. Another **[Armageddon Slash]** forced Admiral to summon a vertical ghost frigate, deflecting the Skill with a mass of ghostly energy.

While their battle raged, Alistair brought himself to his feet. His Ghost Node had less than 1% of its total reserve, and he had 111 Mana and 103 Health. However, because of internal damage, he couldn't use any of his Skills.

"Dev'rox?" Alistair called out with a weak voice.

"You're not the only one that's injured," the imp said aloud, materializing a meter away. "It took a lot out of me pouring the vial, believe it or not."

"How much juice you got left?"

"Enough for one more swap," Dev'rox said.

Alistair smiled. "Go on, then."

"Your fell Karma stinks like an eterra's excrement," Dev'rox said. "If I die because of your maladjusted Fate, I'll kill you."

"I'm not forcing you—" Alistair began, but the imp had already flown away. Perhaps as much as Alistair had grown from Dev'rox, Dev'rox had changed just as much.

Alexandra's heavy **Withering Promise** pressed against the ghost frigate, forcing Admiral deeper into the ground. The crater grew to over five meters in depth, widening to the size of a merry-go-round. Her trees encroached on the ground, following their guardian.

But Alistair knew that it was an illusory advantage. The huge jolt of energy Alexandra had received from the demon blood was wearing off. Her movements were growing slower and more tired. It was obvious her injuries were affecting her, her Mana beginning to falter. Even her regeneration couldn't keep up with the internal damage. Green sparks of healing energy worked tirelessly to knit together wounds and suffuse exhausted cells, but it was a losing effort.

By Alistair's estimate, with both in peak condition, her overall aura was slightly weaker than her father's. But Admiral was the least injured of all of them. If Alexandra didn't end the fight soon, she would lose.

The frigate, which looked comical standing vertically in front of Admiral, began to crack. Alexandra knew this was her moment and put everything behind her attack.

She activated **[Armageddon Slash]** again, overlapping with the previous iteration of the Skill. Her muscles bulged and strained under the weight of the dagger. It wasn't only a matter of physical weight, which she could handle, as most of the mass was held up by Admiral's body, not her arms. But it had a conceptual weight, too. Multiplying **[Armageddon Slash]** touched on the concept of weight in the Dao. It barely fit into the purview of her Barbaric Rage Node, making the Skill difficult to handle.

Alexandra screamed in pain as the gravity of her whitesteel dirk warped space and shattered the spectral boat. Admiral looked shocked for a moment but quickly shifted into gear. He spread his arms, a jet of pressurized water shooting out of his chest.

The Dao energy-infused water split against **Withering Promise**. The weapon didn't redirect the jet entirely, both streams of noxious water glancing Alexandra's shoulders and stomach.

It was an ugly sight. Blood and flesh tinged the color of the water. Pressurized water could cut diamonds, making quick work of even Alexandra's high Constitution. The grip around her dagger wavered, and as the water cannon ended, she landed on top of her father.

Her dagger sliced into the older man's shoulder, but without her full force behind it, the wound was minor. Alexandra's weight knocked him over, sending them tumbling into the bottom of the crater.

[Woodland Forest] was unique for a dominion Skill, as even after Alexandra lost focus, it still remained present. Her Dao fueled the rapid, unnatural growth, but in the end, the organic material of the trees was physical.

As such, the infant forest came down on Admiral with nature's wrath, intent on protecting its mother.

The normal trees collapsed inward, great oak and maple trees the height of city buildings crashing down. The black trees with white leaves emitted a gaseous poison, a purple mist that reminded Alistair of her **Tang Clan Dirk**. Finally, the white trees with black leaves summoned shadowy gnomes. The black leaves morphed into thousands upon thousands of little creatures, who ran down the trunks with brutish anger.

When he first saw the trees fall, Alistair grew nervous for Dev'rox, but

[Woodland Forest] appeared to be imprinted with Alexandra's own consciousness. It noted her allies and planned accordingly.

Dev'rox snapped his fingers, and Alexandra appeared in his place.

With an enormous boom, the thousands of tons of arboreal matter collapsed on top of Admiral. The purple mist seeped in anywhere not covered by the trees, and the gnomes passed over the fallen trunks, attacking everything that moved with squat knives.

Alistair ran over to Alexandra, who swayed unsteadily. Now it was his turn to help her. His adept sense for life force told him that she was about to die. Her lifeline was running out, and it was all his fault.

He didn't know that for a fact, but he felt it was true in his bones. Every time he had gone into negative Karma before, something bad had happened. And because of his lack of strength, Alexandra was going to truly perish, never to enter the cycle of reincarnation. A true souldeath.

"Stay with me!" Alistair shouted, though he didn't know if she could hear him. *Bum. Bum.* The pulse of both her heart and her life force dwindled by the second.

Alistair was no healer. He had never tried using his power over blood essence for that purpose. But there was a first for everything.

He activated [Blood Hand] and pressed it against Alexandra's chest, right over her heart. [Blood Hand] was no healing Skill, but he used its power over blood to pump life essence into her. If he could stabilize her condition, she could hopefully handle a Tier 2 Health pill.

Alistair fed her the red orb, tilting her head up as she swallowed it. His heart skipped a beat as he waited for the pill to kick in. Thankfully, the purifying flames of the Health worked in no time, stitching together wounds and revitalizing her overworked body.

The demon blood had done a number on her system, so she wouldn't be in fighting condition anytime soon, but at least she wouldn't die. Alistair noticed that his Karma had returned to a neutral state. Like he suspected, Fate was his creditor and had chosen this timeline as payment. While he would never know for sure if Alexandra would have had to become a Devil King without his fell Karma, the guilt would be with him forever.

Alistair gingerly rested Alexandra on the ground, turning his attention to the tomb of trees containing the Devil King.

The shadowy gnomes dissipated into thin air, while the poison settled into the bark of the fallen trees, tinging them purple. Alistair could smell

Admiral's demonic scent from underneath the rubble. The man was alive but barely clinging onto this world.

Dev'rox floated out of the crater. Alistair had never seen him so beat up before. The imp was bleeding, black ectoplasm evaporating from dozens of scratches.

"I'm fine," Dev'rox said, though Alistair knew that was a lie. The ghost fluttered to him with a meager spirit, joining his body for refuge.

Alistair, all alone, started digging. His body strained as he heaved the trees out of the way. He was careful not to let any unexposed part of his body touch the poison-saturated bark, grasping everything with his **Devilsbane Gauntlets**.

At last, he reached the final layer that covered the Devil King. Alistair hunched over with his hands on his knees, panting. Admiral's foul scent nearly overpowered his weakened body. Alistair felt the Devil King's life force dwindling, but he was prepared for a fight.

After one last exertion of effort, Alistair picked up the last tree covering the body and pushed it to the side, where it fell over with a thud.

The entire time, he stayed focused on where he expected Admiral to be, anticipating an attack. But it turned out to be inconsequential. That man was in no condition to fight.

Alexandra's father moaned, his cries muffled beneath a misshapen face. There were more parts of his body covered in wounds than not, smoke and shadow leaking from minor cuts. Poison suffused his cells, lending his tan skin a sickly purple hue.

"I have not had my fill," Admiral croaked. In a testament to an unbroken will, he flipped over and began crawling toward Alistair. The agony looked unimaginable, as his bare muscles and fat rubbed against the rough dirt.

Alistair considered punching the Devil King and putting him out of his misery. But after a few seconds, he realized that Admiral was not writhing toward him. He was trying to climb out of the crater.

Seeing as he was not a threat, Alistair let him try. Admiral mirrored Sisyphus pushing a boulder up a hill, spending every last drop of his vanishing life force to make it to the top. It was almost admirable.

Alistair walked up the crater and watched Admiral drag himself toward his true target—Alexandra. His ungraceful crawl grew slower, a long streak of blood staining the ground he trod over.

"Aaargh!" Admiral let out a cry of pain. He was so close now, just a few body lengths away from his daughter.

Alistair put his foot down on the Devil King's back, arresting his momentum. "I can't let you get any closer. You're too dangerous."

Admiral glanced up at him, his flaming eyes pools of fury. "So cruel," he whispered. "It's my daughter."

"You can say your goodbyes from here."

A memory flashed through Alistair's head, from all the way back when he'd used **[Blood Hand]** on Admiral during their battle in [The Game of Life].

Admiral—no, Nikolaos—held his daughter over the bow of a small yacht. The young Alexandra giggled and kicked her stubby legs. Nikolaos wore a warm smile, nothing like the austere and arrogant figure that Alistair knew.

They had the same eyes, he realized. When he didn't have pools of fire, his irises were light brown, the same as his daughter's.

A woman in her thirties came barging out of the cabin, shouting in Greek. She and Nikolaos argued for a few seconds, but he ended up putting down Alexandra back on the deck. The toddler protested, batting her tiny fists on her father's shins.

Alistair somehow knew that the woman was Alexandra's mother, Elena. This was the vacation where she had died in a boating accident. The last time they were all together as a family.

The memory passed. Alistair remained firm in his resolve. It was too dangerous to let him any closer, even in his ruined state.

Alistair took out **Experimental Cursed Needle #7** from his inventory, placing it at Admiral's jugular. In his investigation of the item, it had proved to not have any special characteristics. It was barely tougher and sharper than a normal needle, making it unsuitable as a weapon, which was why he hadn't used it against Dragonus.

Even now, as he pressed it into Admiral's neck, it took a few seconds of extreme pressure to puncture the skin, and that was with the man bleeding out and dying.

Eventually, he pierced through and drew blood. Alistair didn't notice any changes, unable to read the threads of Fate with his zero Karma. But relief washed over Admiral's face.

"Thank you," Admiral said.

"What does it do?" Alistair asked.

"It severs our connection to George. It doesn't reverse the effects of being a Devil King."

Alistair crouched to get on Admiral's level, who had stopped crawling after accepting his fate. "Are you telling me that without George's Fate control, you wouldn't be following him?"

The Devil King laughed and coughed at the same time, dark blood spurting out of his mouth and onto the ground. "Who can say? He's a charismatic man. I'm not looking for penance. I alone wanted power at any cost."

"Why did he send you two here?" Alistair asked. "Where are the others?"

"I'm no traitor," Admiral said. His voice grew weaker—it would only be a few more seconds until he passed on. "Now let me die while I can still see my Alexandra."

Alexandra was in no condition to speak. It would take several days for her to wake up. Her unconscious body lay prone on the cracked pavement several meters away. Despite the grime and blood blemishing her skin, she gave off an otherworldly serenity, owing to her Daos that still lingered in the air.

Admiral stretched out his hand as far as Alistair let him, a rare smile creasing his bloodstained lips. There was a silence in the air, anyone else having fled the scene. But even in the silence, Alistair still heard all the phantasmal cries of his city.

Nikolaos Lykaios died. In one moment, his life force still pulsed, and in the next, it was still. As with all Devil Kings and Princes, his soulcore crumbled before his ethereal soul exited and plunged into the recesses of the earth.

Alistair said the verse that Dev'rox had recited for Sessen Esshei, optimistically hoping for clemency on Nikolaos's soul. It quickly passed beyond Alistair's perception. Finally, it was over.

Alistair fell to his knees. A notification alerted him he had reached level 55. The three points of Charisma brought him above 500, increasing his max Karma to 90 and restoring 30 points. Not that it would help now.

He had willed his body to go beyond its limits. His limbs felt like they were weighed down with titanium cuffs. But it wasn't good enough. Oliver was who-knows-where with only a skeleton to protect him, and Alexandra was helpless in her current state. With lava cracks and aftershocks still happening across the city, they weren't safe.

Checking his inventory, he took out a red Health pill. He twirled it in his fingers, pressing it against his lips. Of course, he knew the dangers of taking two pills in quick succession, even after putting them through **Zanibar's Purification Ring**. It wouldn't kill him, but it could permanently harm his cultivation.

Thankfully, he never had to make that decision. Before he swallowed the pill, he felt a warm, familiar presence. The aura of a Flamesmith—John Desmond.

He wasn't alone. Dozens of soldiers above the soulcore stage, adorned with the tri-colored fist insignia, followed him. Blaise stood at his side, firing electric arrows at any straggling lava golems. A group of fifty civilians followed. Alistair smiled when he saw Donna and Tamia among them.

"We've got it from here," John said.

Angelic sprites carried stretchers of fire into the sky, picking up Oliver, Alexandra, and Alistair. The solid flame constructs felt nostalgic to Alistair, imbued with a Dao of Fire that was so unlike Dragonus's flames. Full of protection and love, John's creations were of a path that eschewed violence, dedicated to beauty and creativity.

With a burden lifted from his shoulders, Alistair passed out.

56 ONE LAST PROMISE

Blaire Fractal checked her Attowatch. Five more minutes left, and her shift would be over. She looked out her window, still not used to the majesty of the city.

Blaire had grown up on a feeder planet in the multiversal core. Migrants from the involved—the intermediate space between the frontier and the core —thought that anyone who grew up in the core were spoiled brats, but that wasn't true. Her planet's ruler was a mere Exalted, and they only produced an Ascendant realm every ten thousand years. A Divine cultivator was such a rarity that the last time a native reached it—over fifty million years ago— they threw a party that lasted a decade.

Since she was a young girl, she had always wanted to see those enormous worlds of the multiversal core, worlds larger than entire galaxies on the frontier. Now that she was here, it was a tad underwhelming.

Not that the cybernetic habitat lacked in anything—the quality of the Dao, Mana, and wealth was mind-blowing. The only issue was that it was simply too large for Blaire to comprehend in its entirety. She could only view planet-sized chunks of Ergodicity Prime-2 at a time, each superior to her homeworld, but never seeing the whole picture.

Still, looking out at the endless horizon, she felt so small. In her small section of the city-planet, there were trillions upon trillions of souls. Mostly transhumans with some other species mixed in. Blaire had relatively few cyber-upgrades compared to her peers.

"How are you liking your first week?"

Blaire looked up. It was her boss, an android named ACT-09. The artificial lifeform was a pure white humanoid with no facial features, its entire body completely smooth. She could never get used to how its voice appeared out of nowhere, with no mouth to speak of.

"It's good," she replied, "but I thought there would be more, uh, hands-on action."

"All in time, all in time," ACT-09 said. "You graduated from Thought-Warrior academy only a few months ago. We are searching for a suitable position."

Blaire sighed. It's what she got for choosing a non-AI world. 80% of the Sublimed Machine Faction was run by their immortal, nigh-omniscient, deified artificial intelligence, the Prime Thinker, and its subsystems. However, as a democratic polity, 20% of the biological-primary population of the Sublimed Machine refused to be governed by a purely silicon being. It was a testament to the unity of the polity that they were still together after the split occurred over a hundred billion years ago.

On Ergodicity Prime-2, actual people ran administrative roles. She had thought that the primacy of living beings would mean more opportunities for advancement, but it was looking like she had miscalculated.

A beep came on her virtual screen. There was an anomaly on the frontier. Or rather, an immensely powerful being was complaining about something on the frontier.

Blaire mentally controlled the picture, narrowing down the message. Her eyes widened when she saw the origin—Damoklas the Destroyer. A notorious criminal, the ghost of a Truthseeker blood dragon, whose species had been hunted to extinction by the Draconic Coalition. Every young child knew the story—the blood dragons were vicious tyrants that sucked worlds dry, insatiable in their eternal quest for sanguine essence.

As a ghost, Damoklas only wielded power in the Divine realm. He had fled civilized space, seeking refuge in the Uncharted Tempest, where he slaughtered innocents and regained strength. And, as was the policy of the Sublimed Machine, they didn't give a damn about that.

Blaire read the message. Damoklas claimed that their Pathfinder AI system had connected him to a Foundation realm from a distant frontier universe.

Impossible, she thought. Frontier Pathfinders didn't have that kind of authorization. She used her recent training to navigate through millions of streams of data, finding the aberrant Pathfinder's universe.

Their official records named it FUNV-159123X, though locals knew it as the Final Frontier Empire. ACT-09 instantly gave her permission to root the Pathfinder AI, allowing her unparalleled access to the internals of the program, bypassing privacy protocols.

It was true. The Grade-4 Pathfinder AI had requested and been instantly granted spiritual interdimensional transportation for one Alistair Tan. But it made no sense.

"Sir, the readout is saying that a Foundation realm from an outer frontier universe accessed Damoklas's bloodline."

"Don't be asinine," ACT-09 admonished. "That cannot be."

ACT-09 commandeered the system from her and checked for himself.

"ERROR! ERROR! ERROR!" her station repeated as ACT-09 tried to access information about the cultivator. "Access denied—insufficient authority."

"Insufficient authority?" The android scoffed. "I am a Grade-4C Thought-Warrior with jurisdiction over an entire division!"

"It's sealed from a higher authority," Blaire realized, pointing at the error message. "Someone with at least Grade-2 authorization closed this up."

ACT-09 composed himself. It was funny that the metallic being was so emotional, proving just how inaccurate some stereotypes could be. "You're correct, Blaire. I forget myself. This situation doesn't call for that level of concern. There are prodigies on the frontier all the time that the Pathfinder notices. Most likely, the Pathfinder saw potential and asked for a favor from a higher-up. My problem is that it bypassed us. We're supposed to be in charge of that. I'll submit a formal complaint."

"Do you think this will hamper our relationship with Damoklas, sir?" Blaire asked.

"That foul dragon would have killed the Foundation if he displeased him. I'm more worried about how easily High Command is bypassing us. They've talked about cuts in our program for centuries." ACT-09 shook his head—such a human-like gesture. "Redouble your efforts. We have to prove to them that we're not useless. Forget about this Foundation—I'll deal with the fallout."

Blaire nodded and started shifting through hundreds of streams of data, all stemming from satellite polities on the frontier. She figured that if she got on the android's good side, she might get an active duty assignment once her internship was over. As a Visionary realm under the age of fifty, she was impressive even by core standards. Her bored mind itched for battle.

She looked over the warnings once more. ACT-09 dismissed it out of hand, but something inside her stirred. To access a Truthseeker's bloodline on the Akashic Records, four months after initiation on a formerly mortal world? She would be keeping an eye out for this Alistair Tan.

―――――

Earth, FavorWood Manor

Floods, Lucius Wood thought. *Why did it have to be floods?*

He was prepared for just about every other type of natural disaster. He had gambled on floods, reasoning that since they were so hard to deal with, he could ignore them.

The Pathfinder AI was never that generous.

A conservative estimate was that over two hundred thousand had died in the capital within the first hour. All they had was an underground shelter, repurposed from his familial manor against tornadoes and hurricanes. It only held fifty thousand, so his construction workers had to work against the clock. The floods came and went at periodic intervals, bringing malicious water nymphs that were almost impossible to kill when in their element.

Waterproofing the tunnels was only possible through his Skill, [Audentes Fortuna Iuvat]. He burned drachma by the thousands, altering physical reality to his will. He poured cement into every crack in the ceiling and walls. When he'd expanded the shelter against potential tornadoes, he hadn't expected to have to make it waterproof.

[Audentes Fortuna Iuvat's] material manifestations only lasted a few hours unless he continued burning drachma. He hoped it would be good enough while his sons went off to find the source of the flood.

Information from the rest of the world inundated his mind. Like his youngest son, his Quaestor Class was partially information based. He could connect directly into the Soulnet without fully diving in, capable of looking at any local source.

Humanity's fate wasn't looking good. But what else did they expect given an ultimate Quest named [Armageddon]?

The largest freeholds suffered the worst, the natural disaster proportionate to their ability to deal with it. Millions died in the first few hours.

Lucius grew alarmed when he saw the reports of Devil King activity. There were credible sources claiming that almost every major freehold had been attacked—except for theirs.

He scanned the bulletins, checking in on Alistair. While he was still miffed about losing in Capture the Beacon, Lucius had to admit he had a soft spot for the man. He reminded him of a younger and squarer version of himself.

There were reports of a draconic man wielding black fire and a man in a naval uniform attacking Alistair's territory. Lucius snorted. Alistair had a lot on his plate.

Other reports carried darker tidings. Several messages corroborated the deaths of Carmen and Richard. Lucius scarcely believed it, remembering their impressive showing on the tropical island. Yet news was reported from numerous independent authors.

A single woman was responsible. Oracle, the Second Devil King. Information about her was scarce, even to Lucius. All that was known about her was that she was a Karmic cultivator with great command of Fate, far stronger than Alistair in that regard.

A chilling cold snapped Lucius out of his mental sphere. He jumped down from the scaffolding, falling into a puddle. Small leaks here and there caused pools of water to form in the tunnel, but nothing devastating.

The rest of his people were far deeper in the shelter in a more protected area. Lucius had only Sword and Spear and a few other guards with him, who defended the front area where the shelter connected to the inner yard of his manor.

The walls of the tunnel stretched almost twenty meters high and were made of steel-reinforced stone. Fluorescent lights created an eerie, artificial atmosphere.

Lucius looked down at his fingertips. Hoarfrost was forming over his knuckles. He wiped more of the stuff off his eyebrows. Looking at his men, they were experiencing the same effects.

Oh no, Lucius thought. *Oh no.*

"Did you think I would forget your betrayal?" a voice called out from behind him. "I thought you would have known better than to cross me, Lucius."

———

EARTH, NEW BOSTON

Alistair dreams. He sees murky visions, bizarre creatures that shift and transform when he looks at them closely.

Instead of the five dreams he had during his recovery from his fight against Anthony Ricci, he has one. In this dream, he sees a clan of creatures, hunted to the ends of the world. They are reviled, despised, misunderstood. The rulers of the age wish to rid creation of them, for they are the only beings not under their purview.

The creatures call them oppressors, adversaries—creation calls them gods. The annals of history debate the truth of those propositions.

In the end, there can only be one ruler in Heaven. The clan must go, never to be seen again. A fierce debate rises among the leaders of the creatures.

The young prince, bright as the morning star, tells his brethren they must not give in to the demands. They belong as much as anyone else, he argues. They should fight to the last.

The astute philosopher, the first wizened one, says they must not fight, but not give in. The middle way. She tells them they will forever be hunted, but it is better to die free than live as a slave. To hide in the recesses of creation, beyond the sight of watchful eyes.

The greedy king, who holds the most sway of all, declares his compatriots foolish. How could they stand up to the wrath of Heaven? It is a folly, he tells everyone. Their only salvation is to listen and obey.

And so the great nation is split in three. Alistair feels the pain of these people deep in his bones, the ineffable sorrow of their divide. In his temporary wisdom, he sees the tragic future this split entails. He screams for them to stop, for them to change course. It is impossible. This is aeons past, long etched into the Akashic Records.

Tears stream down Alistair's face. And then he wakes.

———

Alistair wiped warm liquid from under his eyes. *Are those tears?* He didn't remember having a sad dream.

The first thing he felt was terrible, aching pain. It was like he had been in a coma for weeks and was just waking up, his muscles going unused for too long. But that actually might have been the case.

He was in a white hospital bed, IVs hooked up to his arm. His room was spacious and spare, with no windows and plain, modern-looking furniture. A machine to his right tracked his vitals.

Alistair hopped out of bed, overshooting his step by a long shot. It was like his brain's signals were getting jumbled by his out of practice body. He crashed into the floor, making a small dent in the white tiling.

"Sir! Sir, you're still recovering. Please be careful," said a woman to his right. She wore nurse's scrubs and looked shocked to see him awake. Alistair had no idea who she was, but she gave off a pleasant therapeutic aura.

"How long have I been here?" Alistair asked the nurse. "What's your name?"

"Cecilia," she answered. "And you've been here for five days."

"Five days..." Alistair felt an ominous feeling overcome him, but he couldn't figure out why. Missing that much time was bad, but there was another reason he wasn't thinking of.

Fuck, Alistair thought, scrambling to take out the hardened business card of Farsa Strongbite, the Visionary cultivator that had delivered his debt. The card had a single word on both faces—"LATE."

Alistair groaned. Why did he cut it so closely with the payments? He had been way too greedy with the interest and paid the price. When he focused on the slip and paid off his debt, it took away 5.2 million Gold drachma and 32,373 Land Credits. New text ran over the card, saying that because of a late installment, his future payments had doubled.

Alistair was so mad he wanted to punch the wall. Why didn't it automatically collect from him while he was unconscious? He had the amount, after all.

He supposed he was lucky that Lauren had survived. Since he could still withdraw money from her storage, he knew that was the case. After paying off the debts, he only had 500k drachma and 50k Land Credits, as most of his fortune went toward building defenses.

Not that they've done much, Alistair thought. Despite the natural disaster and Devil King attacks, he was making 300k Gold drachma and 700 Land Store Credits a day.

Alistair grabbed a piece of the wall, turning it into an apple pie. Cecilia looked shocked.

"Tell them I'm up," he said while he gobbled down the dessert. "I need a few minutes before I do anything."

It turned out that his room wasn't in a hospital at all, but a heavily guarded underground bunker. It was hermetically sealed from the inside out, Fate-warded with mystical sutras and reinforced with dozens of meters of valyrik. His people weren't taking any chances with his safety.

Of course, he knew that they probably had information streams alerting them to the slightest changes in his condition. They certainly were aware he was awake. But this would buy him time.

Alistair ran out the door and through the dimly lit hallway of the shelter. There were two other rooms. He checked on them, but they didn't have anyone inside. He detected traces of Alexandra's aura in one of them.

That was curious. Alexandra had been far more injured than him, yet she had already recovered. Now that he thought about it, five days was an unusually long time for him to recover. His Endurance was over 300 now and he kept himself saturated with [Carmela's Happy Pies].

Searching inward, he found the answer in his unruly bloodline. The infinitesimally small portion of the blood dragon's ghost he had obtained still ravaged inside him. His body adjusting to the foreign spiritual DNA continued to hamper his physical healing. The acclimation of a dragon's spirit to his human makeup was not easygoing.

The compound was relatively compact, and he found the exit at the end of the hallway. A huge steel slab with a door locking wheel blocked his path. Alistair turned the wheel to unseal the exit.

Midday light blazed down, giving Alistair a temporary shock as his eyes adjusted to the brightness. The compound unexpectedly led out into a meadow on the outskirts of town.

The skyline of his city stood in the distance. His people must have stopped the earthquake, as he saw rebuilt skyscrapers and sprawling edifices. It had only been five days, but he knew how resourceful Northeast Freeholders were.

Earth Asunder promised a continuous assault of Journeyman-level natural disasters, so they couldn't grow complacent; that said, Alistair needed a moment's rest. From his perspective, he had gone instantaneously from passing out after Nikolaos's death to waking up in the hospital bed.

The moment Alistair left the compound, he felt a familiar presence above him. The exit of the reinforced structure was set into the shadow of a large hill. He looked back, seeing an endless expanse of daisies and dandelions dotting the grass that seemed to reach the horizon. There were minor cracks all around from the earthquakes, though they were naturally healing as the bucolic aura of the soil and flora regenerated the terrain. The meadow was one of the few preserves centered on a Natural Inheritance—a magical object found in the physical world that was a focal point and source of a particular type of Mana. It was similar to a universal Dao Heart, except concentrated on one particular affinity.

Alistair jumped to the top of the hill with ease. It felt nice to stretch his legs. Sometimes all the fighting made him forget how good it was to be able to leap tall buildings in a single bound.

Alexandra was sitting cross-legged at the top of the hill, her eyes closed. Life-attuned Mana saturated her being in the form of sparks and streams of sprightly green energy. Her Devil King aura had settled down, and she no longer reeked to his demonic olfaction. The black and red lines running down her scalp weren't visible under her thick hair, and the pools of fire that had replaced her eyes were more muted.

"Looks like you're finally up," Alexandra said, opening her eyes and smiling. "I've had to hold down the fort for you. How is it that my body was nearly destroyed from the inside out from drinking that demon blood and I woke up before you?"

Alistair sat down next to her. "Hey—I had to incorporate a distinguished dragon bloodline. At least, I think it was distinguished. He was pretty big."

There was a moment of silence. Alexandra broke it with a question. "How are you doing?"

"Okay," Alistair said. "I was going to ask you the same thing."

"I'm fine, I guess. I already knew that this was an inevitability as soon as we learned that my dad was a Devil King." Alexandra stretched her arms, yawning.

"And you now? Are you a Devil King?"

Alexandra shook her head. "I don't think so. But I'm not just a Devil Prince either. In my species section, it says I'm a Stage 0 Devil King. I think it has to do with Dev'rox. The Devil Princes get their blood from the Devil Kings, which weakens it since it's not directly from the source. With Dev'rox giving the blood to me, I'm in-between a true Devil King and a Devil Prince."

"I see," Alistair said, taking a deep breath. The next words rested on his tongue for a while until he gathered the courage to speak. "My mother died."

Alexandra gave him a crestfallen look. "I'm sorry. What happened?"

"It was at the start of the initiation. I selfishly had some people with electronic Classes crawling through terabytes of data, looking for even the slightest clue to where she was. Turns out, she died in the first few hours from a monster wave. She went out like a hero, though. She lit the fire under everyone, getting them to fight back."

"Hah. Opposite of my dad, going out as a Devil King. What a piece of shit."

"Maybe," Alistair said. "Or maybe it was because of the demon blood? Or when the Final Frontier Empire initially messed with people's minds to create chaos?"

"Who knows? Doesn't feel so bad to me." Alexandra shrugged with her hands up. "Your sister was right about the Fate stuff, I think. It's not as though I've become a stark raving murderer."

Alexandra flipped **Withering Promise**, letting the blade sink into the dirt when it fell. She reached into the air as if to grab something, sighing. "There is a difference, though. It's like everything that exists is a drab version of itself. A muddy, darkened counterpart. Even this beautiful meadow sucks."

"Let me try something."

Alistair focused his Karmic sight on Alexandra, peering into the connections that formed the web of reality. Besides her sticking out to his sense of smell, when he looked closely, he could see the aberrations in her Fate. Her internal threads were slightly off-kilter, possessing a warped characteristic that was hard to put into words.

Alistair let a small amount of Karmic energy trickle into her, soothing those distortions and smoothing out her Karmic web.

"What was that?" she said, sitting to attention. "Everything's... normal again."

"I messed with your Karma," Alistair said. "It will only last a few minutes at best, and I typically can't afford to spend Karma so freely, but I thought it might help."

Alexandra's smile reached her eyes as she looked around at the world with a child's curiosity. "Thanks."

"Did my dad say anything to you?" she asked after looking around for a bit. "Like any last words?"

"He said he wanted to see you," Alistair said truthfully.

"Oh."

"I'm tired of this," Alistair said. "All this death and despair. They want us to accept it as normal, but I can't do that.

"You know how they tell you that there are some things that you have to accept? Acceptance—the last of the five stages of grief. Maybe that's pseudo-science. I don't know. But that's what everyone says, right? Well, I can't bow down to that. I'll never bow down to that. There is something better—there *has* to be—for everyone. Where no one has to lose a loved one ever again. I'll carve up the multiverse if I have to. If Heavenly tribulations try to stop me, I'll storm the gates of Heaven myself. That's my one last promise."

Alistair had gotten so animated, he had stood up with a clenched fist. Naked aura reverberated out of his body, glowing softly with the different shades of his four affinities.

"One last promise?" Alexandra asked. "You made more promises before? Do I need to keep an eye out for an angry mob of people you betrayed?"

Alistair gave her a pointed look. They both laughed, but he still meant what he said. It was his last promise because every other kind of covenant fell under that idea. It was his Dao made real.

"Sorry," he said. "I've been ignoring the messages, but I really have to go now. They've been spamming me ever since I woke up. A lot of shit has gone down."

"Don't let me hold you up," she replied. "Good luck with that, by the way."

Alistair grinned and made a series of **[Dashes]** toward the city, flickering from point to point.

"How do you like the idea of hunting some Devil Kings?" Alistair asked his ghostly mentor.

"I think that's a great idea," Dev'rox said. "Those abominations need to be wiped off the face of the earth. Except for Alexandra, of course."

Alistair nodded. "Let's do this."

ABOUT THE AUTHOR

Strungbound enjoyed reading Fantasy and Science Fiction from a young age, including such authors as David Gemmell, Ursula K. Le Guin, Robert Jordan, Arthur C. Clarke, and Iain Banks. Discovering LitRPG and cultivation stories was a more recent evolution, stemming from finally deciding to read Cradle after seeing it constantly recommended. He loved it right away and became an instant fan of the genre, which eventually led to a desire to write.

Author website:

www.ingramcontent.com/pod-product-compliance
Lightning Source LLC
Chambersburg PA
CBHW030537020726
47494CB00005B/1407